The Novelette
Before 1900

Edited by

Ronald Paulson

Rice University,   Houston, Texas

Prentice-Hall, Inc.,   *Englewood Cliffs, New Jersey*

PRENTICE-HALL INTERNATIONAL, INC., *London*
PRENTICE-HALL OF AUSTRALIA, PTY., LTD., *Sydney*
PRENTICE-HALL OF CANADA, LTD., *Toronto*
PRENTICE-HALL OF INDIA (PRIVATE), LTD., *New Delhi*
PRENTICE-HALL OF JAPAN, INC., *Tokyo*

Prentice-Hall English Literature Series
MAYNARD MACK, *Editor*

LIBRARY OF CONGRESS CATALOG CARD NUMBER: 65-13174

PRINTED IN THE UNITED STATES OF AMERICA   62533-C

Table of Contents

Introduction

Novelette is a term that designates a distinctive, yet certainly vague, genre: a narrative in prose that is longer than a short story and shorter than a novel. But definition cannot be only a matter of length; the novelette's formal qualities distinguish it from a merely short novel. It lacks the diffuseness as well as the length of a novel, and it covers more ground as well as more space than its modern offspring, the short story.

Historically, the novelette—or rather its continental equivalents, the *nouvelle*, the *novella*, the *novelle*—represented a first break with the dominant literary form of the Middle Ages, the romance. Boccaccio and the Italians, followed by the Spaniards and the French, sought a more realistic form for portraying everyday life; and so they reduced the inordinate length of the romance (the novel in France is still called a *roman*), stripped away some of its idealized conventions, turned love into seduction and adultery, and moved their subject from past to present (thus the name *novella*, "new"), locating it in the contemporary world, often in an urban setting among middle- and upper-class Italians. As late as the mid-eighteenth century in England the word *novel* itself still designated what we think of as a novelette: "A small tale, generally of love," as Samuel Johnson defined it in his *Dictionary* (1755). The novel we know today that developed in eighteenth-century France and England, in particular through Pierre de Marivaux and Samuel Richardson, is in one sense an expanded or "dilated" novelette.[1]

Novella. Boccaccio's *novelle* in his *Decameron* (1353) establish characteristics of the genre that have persisted to the present. Although Boccaccio's tales are the length of what we would now call a short story, they delineate a complete action, usually a courtship or a love affair, whereas a modern short story presents only a fragment which implies the rest of a completed action. In many of the most famous of Boccaccio's *novelle* the story is built around a symbolic object, such as the heart sent to Sigismunda (first tale of the fourth day), the head of her lover that Elizabeth sets in a pot of basil (fifth tale, fourth day), and—the example in this collection—the falcon that represents Federigo's love for his lady (ninth tale, fifth day). This characteristic, though by no means uncommon in modern novelettes, points less to the invariable presence of a symbol than to a close structural unity around a single point.[2]

Another characteristic of the Boccaccio *novella* is the frame action of a storyteller and listeners. From this frame follows the novelette's tendency toward using first-person narrators to tell the story; the point of view is very seldom omniscient. But at the same time perspective is achieved by the device of an editor, a listener, or even the third-person narrator who maintains a single point of view but varies his distance. The novelette tends to circle its narrow subject, moving away for better perspective.

A sophisticated speaker-audience relationship follows: a cultivated audience and so a stylishly told tale. In the *Decameron* the reader is always aware of a contrast between the order, social and aesthetic, of the group of fugitives from the plague who have gathered in safety in the country and the chaos of plague-ridden Florence. However low or gross the action itself, the tale-teller's tone is always suitably detached and

---

[1] See George Sherburn, *The Restoration and Eighteenth Century*, in *A Literary History of England*, ed. Baugh (New York, 1948), p. 803. See also Ian Watt, *The Rise of the English Novel* (Berkeley and Los Angeles, 1957), p. 164.

[2] One of the German theorists of the *novelle*, Paul Heyse, argues that the *novelle's* substances must be reducible to five lines, as in the notices at the head of Boccaccio's tales; that a concrete symbol must be at the center of the story (the so-called *Falkentheorie*); and that the story must convey the impression of strangeness ("new" in that sense). See Heyse's *Jugenderinnerungen und Bekenntnisse*, 5th ed. (Stuttgart and Berlin, 1912), II, 68.

stylized. Artistry, style, a fine polish—these are characteristics of the novelette that set it off from the novel and, to a lesser degree, from the short story. The novel, it has been said, requires careless, sloppy writing to suggest a close, sweaty hold on reality. The particularities of time, place, and custom—the local color so dear to the novel—are never introduced in the *Decameron* for their own sake but only insofar as they affect or advance the action. This last may suggest one reason why the genre never became as popular in England as in France.

The Picaresque Tale. Boccaccio's enormously popular *novelle* led to the imitations of Boiardo, Bandello, and others, who tended to produce shortened versions of the old romance against which the *novella* originally rebelled.[3] The picaresque tale arose in Spain as a separate reaction against the romance, one which went to an extreme of contentual realism (as the gross) and formal realism (as the chaotic, the sensuously particular) far beyond the intention of Boccaccio and his followers. *Lazarillo de Tormes* (1554), the first of these, is the length of a *novella* but differs from the form in certain important ways: its episodes are not sufficiently unified and its brevity is in fact due to its fragmentary—perhaps unfinished—state. It could—as its successors did—carry on indefinitely, adding one episode to another, connected only by the central figure of the rootless rogue. The action is not the single, neat event of the *novella* but an untailored lifetime, truncated by a stint in prison or the galleys, and so not even rounded off by death. Moreover, the progression, an enumeration of examples and a survey of social classes and types, is of the simplest.

The picaresque tale becomes a true novelette when one of two things happens. First, as in some of Cervantes' *Exemplary Novels* (1613, especially *Rinconete and Cortadillo*), the roguish lifetime is boiled down to an epitome of one or two episodes; or second, as in Voltaire's *Candide* (1759), the episodic structure is domesticated and ordered around a single situation and its progression becomes, in Kenneth Burke's terminology, repetitive, a continuous "restatement of the same thing in different ways."[4] *Candide* at first glance appears another picaresque tale: a youth undergoes a series of experiences and ends as unheroically, tending his garden, as Lazarillo did tending the local priest's mistress. But between *Lazarillo* and *Candide* are a new picaresque model, *The Arabian Nights* (translated into French at the beginning of the eighteenth century) and the French temperament itself. The overwhelming sense of life in *Lazarillo* has been distanced by an elegant style, if not boiled away as dross; reality as presentation is replaced by reality as analysis. *Candide* is not a survey of society, of professions, and of servant-master relationships, but a single shapely anecdote concerning a youth's education, structured by a graduated series of ascents and plunges as he rises to peaks of Panglossian optimism and falls to depths of uncomfortable realism. Voltaire called this a *conte philosophique*, and although it is more precisely a satire, it is unlike most non-French satires in its unity of effect.

French Nouvelle. The form and length of the *nouvelle,* the French equivalent of Boccaccio's *novella,* has been so congenial to the French that it has remained a characteristic mode of their fiction ever since—explaining why there are more French examples of the genre in this collection than any other nationality. The most famous French *nouvelles* were Madame de Lafayette's *Princess of Clèves* (1678), the Abbé Prévost's *Manon Lescaut* (the last volume of his *Memoirs of a Gentleman of Quality,* 1731), and Benjamin Constant's *Adolphe* (1816). These *nouvelles* have in common the action of a romantic affair and an analytic concern with the psychology of passion. Once past the *Princess of Clèves,* they slip into the form of the *récit personnel* or the memoir—the hero intensely reliving one part of his life; and in many cases the narrative has an autobiographical origin. (One can point to modern equivalents, for example, Gide's *Immoralist.*) But, significantly, the hero looks back on an affair that is over; and the event is often further distanced by the mediation of a friend or an editor who has found the manuscript.

The *nouvelle* had absolutely no counterpart in English fiction until the late nine-

---

[3] See Charles Sorel, *La Bibliothèque française* (1664) and *De la Connaissance des bons Livres* (1672).

[4] *Counterstatement* (New York, 1931; 1957 ed.), p. 125.

teenth century. Although novelists like Richardson did indeed *present* psychological reality, and often the emotion of love, they showed no interest in analyzing it. Richardson's aim, in fact, was to immerse his reader in the tense moment; analysis, and the distancing that it requires, would have destroyed this effect. The more analytic novel of Henry Fielding turned its tools of analysis on moral rather than psychological states. In France the long novels as well, from Marivaux's to Stendahl's and Flaubert's, preferred analysis and criticism to presentation, the detection of form to the reveling in life. The great exception to this rule—and therefore frequently condemned by French critics [5]—was Honoré de Balzac, who was closer in many ways to the English tradition of Richardson and even of Smollett (and later Dickens) than to the French.

Conte Moral. A typically French offshoot of the *nouvelle,* the *conte moral,* was the direct progenitor of the novelette in England. The *conte moral* differs from the *conte philosophique* in its use of a single exemplum; in a test case of some sort contrasting sets of behavior are brought together and resolved into contrasting, and appropriate, sets of consequences. The French master of this form was Voltaire's disciple, Jean François Marmontel (1723-1799), whose *Contes Moraux* (1770) exerted a direct influence on Maria Edgeworth's early *Parent's Assistant* (1796). Edgeworth abandoned the exotic, often Oriental settings of Marmontel and placed her exemplum solidly in contemporary Ireland, but she retained the educational and moralistic (as opposed to satiric) tone. In *Waste Not, Want Not,* a provident and an improvident boy are contrasted, beginning with one's carelessly cutting the cord around a package he is given, through a series of succeeding catastrophes for him (and triumphs for his opposite number).[6] In *Castle Rackrent* (1800) the English realism of presentation subdues but does not altogether obliterate the morality play, and we have the first genuinely English novelette. The *récit personnel* is employed not to analyze but to convey the physical presence of Thady and his masters and their estates. The combination of moral exemplum and local color attracted Ivan Turgenev in Russia and, perhaps through him, Henry James, the American who resided most of his life in England and wove elaborate and subtle moralities about the relationships between the old world and the new.

German Novelle. Because of the German need to classify and the great upsurge of literary criticism in Germany in the eighteenth century, the *novelle* is a more copiously written-about, and to some extent more rigid, form than any of the others that we have mentioned. It is also more Romantic, since it served as one manifestation of that movement in Germany. It seems to have followed directly from the Italian *novella* of Boccaccio without the interference of the French, and so psychology is less important than symbolism. Goethe, whose tale called *Novelle* is very close, even in length, to one like *The Falcon,* distinguished between drama, which deals with events that are the outcome of character, and the novel, which deals with events that are external to the character, that merely *happen* to him. Thus the hero of the German *novelle* is usually passive and is, so to speak, struck by lightning. As E. K. Bennett has shown, the form "presupposes an irrationalist view of life. It is a presentation not of character as fate as in the drama, but of chance as fate." [7] It is also, accordingly, concerned to a large extent with events rather than actions and is fatalistic in the sense that it emphasizes "the one event which, in order to be worth narrating, produces a great change in the life and fortunes of the hero" (p. 5). "By its very nature it relates not the natural course of events, but the exception to that course of events" (p. 42). Inevitably a large quotient of fantasy entered the German

---

5 See, e.g., Martin Turnell, *The Novel in France* (London, 1950), pp. 211ff.; Turnell's admiration for Balzac's *nouvelle, Le Curé de Tours,* however, is generous and deserved (pp. 238-41).

6 For an account of these, see P. H. Newby, *Maria Edgeworth* (London, 1950), pp. 27-29.

7 Goethe, *Wilhelm Meisters Lehrjahr,* Bk. V, Chap. 7; Bennett, *A History of the German Novelle* (Cambridge, 1934), p. 8. Throughout this section on the German *novelle* I am indebted to Bennett's excellent study. See also Arnold Hirsch, *Der Gattungsbegriff 'Novelle'* (Berlin, 1928).

novelle, and it counts among its practitioners E. T. A. Hoffmann and, in the twentieth century, Franz Kafka, who combine scrupulous realism with the fantastic—and purely fatalistic—event, such as a man's finding himself turned into a beetle. Paul Ernst has noted that the *novelle* tends "to represent the improbable in such a manner as to give the impression of the purest probability." [8]

Even the most realistic *novelle* gives this impression of strangeness, of something unique and unaccountable but perfectly true, because of its emphasis on the one deciding event. Kleist's best *novellen, The Marquise of O——* and *Michael Kohlhaas,* illustrate all these characteristics. Kleist's tales are, as he called them, *"moralische Erzählungen"* not in the Edgeworthian sense but as works that pose moral problems—dilemmas or enigmas—that have to be dealt with by the characters. The whole nature of things for Kleist is irrational, and in this difficult world his characters are forced to operate.

Novelette. The English novelette and its Russian equivalent are not as clearly defined as their Italian, French, and German counterparts. The vague word did not become at all frequent in England until well into the nineteenth century, when it meant anything from a short novel to a long short story. The full-fledged novel was now the dominant prose form in Europe, while the short story was finding a lucrative market in periodicals. In England the only writer who took the form seriously was Henry James, whose love of the *nouvelle* (as he preferred to call it) prevented him from placing many of his fictions in periodicals that held to "the hard-and-fast rule of the 'from six to eight thousand words'" of the short story. In Russia only Turgenev wrote naturally in the shorter form, and even his novels tend to be long novelettes; but Dostoyevsky embedded novelettes within his novels and published a few on the side, and Tolstoy turned late in life from the novel to a form more appropriate to parabolic fictions. Only with the rise of the *symboliste* movement and the end of the century did the novelette take a new lease on life.

From this brief survey we can draw some general conclusions about the novelette. (1) Its scope is narrow. James carefully distinguished between *nouvelle* and novel: the *nouvelle,* he said, remains an "anecdote," "something that has oddly happened to someone," with the single focus on that person.[9] When the anecdote is enlarged into a dramatic action in which "something that has oddly happened" happens to other characters as well, and the focal points multiply, it has become a short novel. Length finally makes little difference. A short story, on the other hand, does not have this potential for expanding into a novel. (2) But at the same time, as James liked to remark (p. 220), the "shapely *nouvelle*" has and maintains "a form proper to itself," by which I take him to mean that the writer need not pointlessly expand his material into a novel once it has fully expressed itself (become what James calls "the idea happily *developed*"). (3) There is no space in the novelette for the novel's preoccupation with time. Whereas the novel shows characters developing and changing in time, the novelette brings together characters who are already fully developed and (as in a play) has them reveal themselves in one characteristic action. This single event may, of course, produce a change in the character, although often it only brings out something that is already latent in him. (4) It follows that the novelette is chiefly characterized by its unity of effect. It usually says something as large and important as a novel (as contrasted with a short story), but because of its length, it says it with a much greater economy of means. Its "main merit and sign," says James, "is the effort to do the complicated thing with a strong brevity and lucidity—to arrive, on behalf of the multiplicity, at a certain science of control" (p. 231). (5) Finally, as these points suggest, the novelette customarily employs an artistry of presentation unique in the usually helter-skelter world of long prose fiction. For a wide grasp or great depth a reader turns to the novel, but for a perfect artifact, and the different aesthetic experience that goes with it, he may turn to the novelette.

---

8 *Der Weg zur Form* (Berlin, 1928), p. 288.
9 R. P. Blackmur, *The Art of the Novel: Critical Prefaces by Henry James* (New York, 1948), p. 181.

The Falcon

The Ninth Story of the Fifth Day of the *Decameron* (1353)

Giovanni Boccaccio

J. M. Rigg, translator

Giovanni Boccaccio (1313–1375) was the son of a Florentine merchant, who sent him out as a commercial traveler; finding him a failure, his father tried to make him a lawyer, with as little success. By 1341 Boccaccio was producing poems inspired by his love for Maria d'Aquino, whom he called Fiammetta: *Il Filocolo, Il Filostrato, La Teseide, Ameto, L'Amorosa Visione,* and *L'Amorosa Fiammetta.* In 1348 the Black Death struck Florence, taking one out of every five lives. This plague which, in a sense, marked the end of the Middle Ages in Europe provided Boccaccio with a frame action for a group of prose tales that disregarded the romantic conventions of his earlier work and presented contemporary middle- and upper-class life. Finished by 1353 (though not printed until 1471), the *Decameron* consists of one hundred *novelle* told on ten successive days by a group of ten young Florentines who have fled their plague-ravaged city for a safe retreat in the country. Boccaccio's career was rounded out with a savage satire, *Il Corbaccio,* written immediately after he finished the *Decameron,* and a *Vita di Dante.*

There are useful discussions of Boccaccio and the *Decameron* in Francesco de Sanctis, *History of Italian Literature,* trans. Joan Redfern (New York, 1959), I, 333–59; Erich Auerbach, *Mimesis,* trans. Willard Trask (Princeton, N. J., 1953), pp. 203–31; and T. C. Chubb, *The Life of Giovanni Boccaccio* (New York, 1930). The J. M. Rigg translation, the first complete translation into English, was published in New York in 1903.

Federigo degli Alberighi loves and is not loved in return: he wastes his substance by lavishness until nought is left but a single falcon, which, his lady being come to see him at his house, he gives her to eat: she, knowing his case, changes her mind, takes him to husband and makes him rich.

So ended Filomena; and the queen, being ware that besides herself only Dioneo (by virtue of his privilege) was left to speak, said with gladsome mien:—'Tis now for me to take up my parable; which, dearest ladies, I will do with a story like in some degree to the foregoing, and that, not only that you may know how potent are your charms to sway the gentle heart, but that you may also learn how upon

1

fitting occasions to make bestowal of your guerdons of your own accord, instead of always waiting for the guidance of Fortune, which most times, not wisely, but without rule or measure, scatters her gifts.

You are then to know, that Coppo di Borghese Domenichi, a man that in our day was, and perchance still is, had in respect and great reverence in our city, being not only by reason of his noble lineage, but, and yet more, for manners and merit most illustrious and worthy of eternal renown, was in his old age not seldom wont to amuse himself by discoursing of things past with his neighbours and other folk; wherein he had not his match for accuracy and compass of memory and concinnity of speech. Among other good stories, he would tell, how that there was of yore in Florence a gallant named Federigo di Messer Filippo Alberighi, who for feats of arms and courtesy had not his peer in Tuscany; who, as is the common lot of gentlemen, became enamoured of a lady named Monna Giovanna, who in her day held rank among the fairest and most elegant ladies of Florence; to gain whose love he jousted, tilted, gave entertainments, scattered largess, and in short set no bounds to his expenditure. However the lady, no less virtuous than fair, cared not a jot for what he did for her sake, nor yet for him.

Spending thus greatly beyond his means, and making nothing, Federigo could hardly fail to come to lack, and was at length reduced to such poverty that he had nothing left but a little estate, on the rents of which he lived very straitly, and a single falcon, the best in the world. The estate was at Campi, and thither, deeming it no longer possible for him to live in the city as he desired, he repaired, more in love than ever before; and there, in complete seclusion, diverting himself with hawking, he bore his poverty as patiently as he might.

Now, Federigo being thus reduced to extreme poverty, it so happened that one day Monna Giovanna's husband, who was very rich, fell ill, and, seeing that he was nearing his end, made his will, whereby he left his estate to his son, who was now growing up, and in the event of his death without lawful heir named Monna Giovanna, whom he dearly loved, heir in his stead; and having made these dispositions he died.

Monna Giovanna, being thus left a widow, did as our ladies are wont, and repaired in the summer to one of her estates in the country which lay very near to that of Federigo. And so it befell that the urchin began to make friends with Federigo, and to shew a fondness for hawks and dogs, and having seen Federigo's falcon fly not a few times, took a singular fancy to him, and greatly longed to have him for his own, but still did not dare to ask him of Federigo, knowing that Federigo prized him so much. So the matter stood when by chance the boy fell sick; whereby the mother was sore distressed, for he was her only son, and she loved him as much as might be, insomuch that all day long she was beside him, and ceased not to comfort him, and again and again asked him if there were aught that he wished for, imploring him to say the word, and, if it might by any means be had, she would assuredly do her utmost to procure it for him. Thus repeatedly exhorted, the boy said:—"Mother mine, do but get me Federigo's falcon, and I doubt not I shall soon be well." Whereupon the lady was silent a while, bethinking her what she should do. She knew that Federigo had long loved her, and had

never had so much as a single kind look from her: wherefore she said to herself:—
How can I send or go to beg of him this falcon, which by what I hear is the best
that ever flew, and moreover is his sole comfort? And how could I be so unfeeling
as to seek to deprive a gentleman of the one solace that is now left him? And so,
albeit she very well knew that she might have the falcon for the asking, she was
perplexed, and knew not what to say, and gave her son no answer. At length,
however, the love she bore the boy carried the day, and she made up her mind,
for his contentment, come what might, not to send, but to go herself and fetch
him the falcon. So:—"Be of good cheer, my son," she said, "and doubt not thou
wilt soon be well; for I promise thee that the very first thing that I shall do
tomorrow morning will be to go and fetch thee the falcon." Whereat the child was
so pleased that he began to mend that very day.

On the morrow the lady, as if for pleasure, hied her with another lady to
Federigo's little house, and asked to see him. 'Twas still, as for some days past, no
weather for hawking, and Federigo was in his garden, busy about some small
matters which needed to be set right there. When he heard that Monna Giovanna
was at the door, asking to see him, he was not a little surprised and pleased, and
hied him to her with all speed. As soon as she saw him, she came forward to meet
him with womanly grace, and having received his respectful salutation, said to
him:—"Good morrow, Federigo," and continued:—"I am come to requite thee
for what thou hast lost by loving me more than thou shouldst: which compensation is this, that I and this lady that accompanies me will breakfast with thee
without ceremony this morning." "Madam," Federigo replied with all humility,
"I mind not ever to have lost aught by loving you, but rather to have been so much
profited that, if I ever deserved well in aught, 'twas to your merit that I owed it,
and to the love that I bore you. And of a surety had I still as much to spend as I
have spent in the past, I should not prize it so much as this visit you so frankly
pay me, come as you are to one who can afford you but a sorry sort of hospitality."
Which said, with some confusion, he bade her welcome to his house, and then led
her into his garden, where, having none else to present to her by way of companion, he said:—"Madam, as there is none other here, this good woman, wife of
this husbandman, will bear you company, while I go to have the table set." Now,
albeit his poverty was extreme, yet he had not known as yet how sore was the
need to which his extravagance had reduced him; but this morning 'twas brought
home to him, for that he could find nought wherewith to do honour to the lady,
for love of whom he had done the honours of his house to men without number:
wherefore, distressed beyond measure, and inwardly cursing his evil fortune, he
sped hither and thither like one beside himself, but never a coin found he, nor
yet aught to pledge. Meanwhile it grew late, and sorely he longed that the lady
might not leave his house altogether unhonoured, and yet to crave help of his own
husbandman was more than his pride could brook. In these desperate straits his
glance happened to fall on his brave falcon on his perch in his little parlour. And
so, as a last resource, he took him, and finding him plump, deemed that he would
make a dish meet for such a lady. Wherefore, without thinking twice about it, he
wrung the bird's neck, and caused his maid forthwith pluck him and set him on

a spit, and roast him carefully; and having still some spotless table-linen, he had the table laid therewith, and with a cheerful countenance hied him back to his lady in the garden, and told her that such breakfast as he could give her was ready. So the lady and her companion rose and came to table, and there, with Federigo, who waited on them most faithfully, ate the brave falcon, knowing not what they ate.

When they were risen from table, and had dallied a while in gay converse with him, the lady deemed it time to tell the reason of her visit: wherefore, graciously addressing Federigo, thus began she:—"Federigo, by what thou rememberest of thy past life and my virtue, which, perchance, thou hast deemed harshness and cruelty, I doubt not thou must marvel at my presumption, when thou hearest the main purpose of my visit; but if thou hadst sons, or hadst had them, so that thou mightest know the full force of the love that is borne them, I should make no doubt that thou wouldst hold me in part excused. Nor, having a son, may I, for that thou hast none, claim exemption from the laws to which all other mothers are subject, and, being thus bound to own their sway, I must, though fain were I not, and though 'tis neither meet nor right, crave of thee that which I know thou dost of all things and with justice prize most highly, seeing that this extremity of thy adverse fortune has left thee nought else wherewith to delight, divert and console thee; which gift is no other than thy falcon, on which my boy has so set his heart that, if I bring him it not, I fear lest he grow so much worse of the malady that he has, that thereby it may come to pass that I lose him. And so, not for the love which thou dost bear me, and which may nowise bind thee, but for that nobleness of temper, whereof in courtesy more conspicuously than in aught else thou hast given proof, I implore thee that thou be pleased to give me the bird, that thereby I may say that I have kept my son alive, and thus made him for aye thy debtor."

No sooner had Federigo apprehended what the lady wanted, than, for grief that 'twas not in his power to serve her, because he had given her the falcon to eat, he fell a weeping in her presence, before he could so much as utter a word. At first the lady supposed that 'twas only because he was loath to part with the brave falcon that he wept, and as good as made up her mind that he would refuse her: however, she awaited with patience Federigo's answer, which was on this wise:—"Madam, since it pleased God that I should set my affections upon you there have been matters not a few, in which to my sorrow I have deemed Fortune adverse to me; but they have all been trifles in comparison of the trick that she now plays me: the which I shall never forgive her, seeing that you are come here to my poor house, where, while I was rich, you deigned not to come, and ask a trifling favour of me, which she has put it out of my power to grant: how 'tis so, I will briefly tell you. When I learned that you, of your grace, were minded to breakfast with me, having respect to your high dignity and desert, I deemed it due and seemly that in your honour I should regale you, to the best of my power, with fare of a more excellent quality than is commonly set before others; and, calling to mind the falcon which you now ask of me, and his excellence, I judged him meet food for you, and so you have had him roasted on the trencher this morning;

and well indeed I thought I had bestowed him; but, as now I see that you would fain have had him in another guise, so mortified am I that I am not able to serve you, that I doubt I shall never know peace of mind more." In witness whereof he had the feathers and feet and beak of the bird brought in and laid before her.

The first thing the lady did, when she had heard Federigo's story, and seen the relics of the bird, was to chide him that he had killed so fine a falcon to furnish a woman with a breakfast; after which the magnanimity of her host, which poverty had been and was powerless to impair, elicited no small share of inward commendation. Then, frustrate of her hope of possessing the falcon, and doubting of her son's recovery, she took her leave with the heaviest of hearts, and hied her back to the boy: who, whether for fretting, that he might not have the falcon, or by the unaided energy of his disorder, departed this life not many days after, to the exceeding great grief of his mother. For a while she would do nought but weep and bitterly bewail herself; but being still young, and left very wealthy, she was often urged by her brothers to marry again, and though she would rather have not done so, yet being importuned, and remembering Federigo's high desert, and the magnificent generosity with which he had finally killed his falcon to do her honour, she said to her brothers:—"Gladly, with your consent, would I remain a widow, but if you will not be satisfied except I take a husband, rest assured that none other will I ever take save Federigo degli Alberighi." Whereupon her brothers derided her, saying:—"Foolish woman, what is't thou sayst? How shouldst thou want Federigo, who has not a thing in the world?" To whom she answered:—"My brothers, well wot I that 'tis as you say; but I had rather have a man without wealth than wealth without a man." The brothers, perceiving that her mind was made up, and knowing Federigo for a good man and true, poor though he was, gave her to him with all her wealth. And so Federigo, being mated with such a wife, and one that he had so much loved, and being very wealthy to boot, lived happily, keeping more exact accounts, to the end of his days.

Candide

or The Optimist (1759)

Voltaire

Tobias Smollett and others, translators

François Marie Arouet, known as Voltaire (1694–1778), was a dramatist, historian, *philosophe,* satirist, polemicist, poet, and much more. Though destined for the legal profession, he determined after the success of his first tragedy, *Oedipe* (1718), to become a man of letters. It was also about this time that he adopted the name Voltaire, probably as an anagram of Arouet l. j. (*le jeune*). In and out of the Bastille for writing lampoons and committing other indiscretions, Voltaire withdrew from France and spent the years 1726 to 1729 in England, acquainting himself with the works of the English freethinkers Shaftesbury, Toland, and Tindal on the one hand, and the satires of Swift and Pope on the other. His subsequent writing reflects both influences.

Voltaire was again in France, making money through speculation, until 1749, after which he lived on and off with Frederick the Great of Prussia. After his final break with Frederick in 1753 he returned to France, and in 1755 he settled in Geneva, Switzerland, living the remainder of his long life strategically near the French-Swiss border. His output in all literary genres was immense, but his most popular and enduring works were the *contes philosophiques* to which he devoted himself after 1749: *Zadig, Candide, The Princess of Babylon, The White Bull, The Huron* (*L'Ingénu*), and *Micromégas.* They are all witty attacks on various forms of authority: clerical, political, and literary. For information on the *conte philosophique* as practiced by Voltaire, see Ira O. Wade, *Voltaire's Micromégas* (Princeton, 1950), and *Voltaire's Candide* (Princeton, 1959). André Maurois' biography (New York, 1932) is readable and informative.

Candide, published in 1759, was Voltaire's reaction to two stimuli: Leibnitz's optimistic philosophy that this is "the best of all possible worlds" and the catastrophic Lisbon earthquake of 1755. Voltaire simply tested the first by letting it collide with the second. The translation is that of Tobias Smollett and others, who also translated a spurious continuation (1762), revised by William F. Fleming (New York, 1901). The notes are based on Smollett's.

6

Chapter I

*How Candide Was Brought Up in a Magnificent Castle
and How He Was Driven Thence*

In the country of Westphalia, in the castle of the most noble baron of Thunder-ten-tronckh, lived a youth whom nature had endowed with a most sweet disposition. His face was the true index of his mind. He had a solid judgment joined to the most unaffected simplicity; and hence, I presume, he had his name of Candide. The old servants of the house suspected him to have been the son of the baron's sister, by a very good sort of a gentleman of the neighborhood, whom that young lady refused to marry, because he could produce no more than threescore and eleven quarterings in his arms; the rest of the genealogical tree belonging to the family having been lost through the injuries of time.

The baron was one of the most powerful lords in Westphalia; for his castle had not only a gate, but even windows; and his great hall was hung with tapestry. He used to hunt with his mastiffs and spaniels instead of greyhounds; his groom served him for huntsman; and the parson of the parish officiated as his grand almoner. He was called My Lord by all his people, and he never told a story but every one laughed at it.

My lady baroness weighed three hundred and fifty pounds, consequently was a person of no small consideration; and then she did the honors of the house with a dignity that commanded universal respect. Her daughter was about seventeen years of age, fresh colored, comely, plump, and desirable. The baron's son seemed to be a youth in every respect worthy of the father he sprung from. Pangloss, the preceptor, was the oracle of the family, and little Candide listened to his instructions with all the simplicity natural to his age and disposition.

Master Pangloss taught the metaphysico-theologo-cosmolo-nigology. He could prove to admiration that there is no effect without a cause; and, that in this best of all possible worlds, the baron's castle was the most magnificent of all castles, and my lady the best of all possible baronesses.

It is demonstrable, said he, that things cannot be otherwise than as they are; for as all things have been created for some end, they must necessarily be created for the best end. Observe, for instance, the nose is formed for spectacles, therefore we wear spectacles. The legs are visibly designed for stockings, accordingly we wear stockings. Stones were made to be hewn, and to construct castles, therefore My Lord has a magnificent castle; for the greatest baron in the province ought to be the best lodged. Swine were intended to be eaten, therefore we eat pork all the year round: and they, who assert that everything is *right,* do not express themselves correctly; they should say that everything is *best.*

Candide listened attentively, and believed implicitly, for he thought Miss Cunegund excessively handsome, though he never had the courage to tell her so. He concluded that next to the happiness of being baron of Thunder-ten-tronckh, the next was that of being Miss Cunegund, the next that of seeing her every day, and the last that of hearing the doctrine of Master Pangloss, the greatest philosopher of the whole province, and consequently of the whole world.

One day when Miss Cunegund went to take a walk in a little neighboring wood which was called a park, she saw, through the bushes, the sage Doctor Pangloss giving a lecture in experimental philosophy to her mother's chambermaid, a little brown wench, very pretty, and very tractable. As Miss Cunegund had a great disposition for the sciences, she observed with the utmost attention the experiments, which were repeated before her eyes; she perfectly well understood the force of the doctor's reasoning upon causes and effects. She retired greatly flurried, quite pensive and filled with the desire of knowledge, imagining that she might be a *sufficing reason* for young Candide, and he for her.

On her way back she happened to meet the young man; she blushed, he blushed also; she wished him a good morning in a flattering tone, he returned the salute, without knowing what he said. The next day, as they were rising from dinner, Cunegund and Candide slipped behind the screen. The miss dropped her handkerchief, the young man picked it up. She innocently took hold of his hand, and he as innocently kissed hers with a warmth, a sensibility, a grace—all very particular; their lips met; their eyes sparkled; their knees trembled; their hands strayed. The baron chanced to come by; he beheld the cause and effect, and, without hesitation, saluted Candide with some notable kicks on the breech, and drove him out of doors. The lovely Miss Cunegund fainted away, and, as soon as she came to herself, the baroness boxed her ears. Thus a general consternation was spread over this most magnificent and most agreeable of all possible castles.

Chapter II

What Befell Candide Among the Bulgarians

Candide, thus driven out of this terrestrial paradise, rambled a long time without knowing where he went; sometimes he raised his eyes, all bedewed with tears, towards heaven, and sometimes he cast a melancholy look towards the magnificent castle, where dwelt the fairest of young baronesses. He laid himself down to sleep in a furrow, heartbroken, and supperless. The snow fell in great flakes, and, in the morning when he awoke, he was almost frozen to death; however, he made shift to crawl to the next town, which was called Wald-berghoff-trarbk-dikdorff, without a penny in his pocket, and half dead with hunger and fatigue. He took up his stand at the door of an inn. He had not been long there, before two men dressed in blue, fixed their eyes steadfastly upon him. "Faith, comrade," said one of them to the other, "yonder is a well-made young fellow, and of the right size." Upon which they made up to Candide, and with the greatest civility and politeness invited him to dine with them. "Gentlemen," replied Candide, with a most engaging modesty, "you do me much honor, but upon my word I have no money." "Money, sir!" said one of the blues to him, "young persons of your appearance and merit never pay anything; why, are not you five feet five inches high?" "Yes, gentlemen, that is really my size," replied he, with a low bow. "Come then, sir, sit down along with us; we will not only pay your reckoning, but will never suffer such a clever young fellow as you to want money. Men were born to assist one another." "You are perfectly right, gentlemen," said Candide, "this is precisely the doctrine of Master Pangloss; and I am convinced that everything is for the best." His generous companions next entreated him to accept of a few crowns, which he readily complied with, at the same time offering them his note for the payment, which they refused, and sat down to table. "Have you not a great affection for—" "O yes! I have a great affection for the lovely Miss Cunegund." "May be so," replied one of the blues, "but that is not the question! We ask you whether you have not a great affection for the king of the Bulgarians?" "For the king of the Bulgarians?" said Candide, "oh Lord! not at all, why I never saw him in my life." "Is it possible! oh, he is a most charming king! Come, we must drink his health." "With all my heart, gentlemen," says Candide, and off he tossed his glass. "Bravo!" cry the blues; "you are now the support, the defender, the hero of the Bulgarians; your fortune is made; you are in the high road to glory." So saying, they handcuffed him, and carried him away to the regiment. There he was made to wheel about to the right, to the left, to draw his rammer, to return his rammer, to present, to fire, to march, and they gave him thirty blows with a cane; the next day he performed his exercise a little better, and they gave him but twenty; the day following he came off with ten, and was looked upon as a young fellow of surprising genius by all his comrades.

Candide was struck with amazement, and could not for the soul of him conceive how he came to be a hero. One fine spring morning, he took it into his head to take a walk, and he marched straight forward, conceiving it to be a privilege of the human species, as well as of the brute creation, to make use of their legs how and when they pleased. He had not gone above two leagues when he was overtaken by four other heroes, six feet high, who bound him neck and heels, and carried him to a dungeon. A courtmartial sat upon him, and he was asked which he liked better, to run the gauntlet six and thirty times through the whole regiment, or to have his brains blown out with a dozen musket-balls? In vain did he remonstrate to them that the human will is free, and that he chose neither; they obliged him to make a choice, and he determined, in virtue of that divine gift called free will, to run the gauntlet six and thirty times. He had gone through his discipline twice, and the regiment being composed of 2,000 men, they composed for him exactly 4,000 strokes, which laid bare all his muscles and nerves from the nape of his neck to his stern. As they were preparing to make him set out the third time our young hero, unable to support it any longer, begged as a favor that they would be so obliging as to shoot him through the head; the favor being granted, a bandage was tied over his eyes, and he was made to kneel down. At that very instant, his Bulgarian majesty happening to pass by made a stop, and inquired into the delinquent's crime, and being a prince of great penetration, he found, from what he heard of Candide, that he was a young metaphysician, entirely ignorant of the world; and therefore, out of his great clemency, he condescended to pardon him, for which his name will be celebrated in every journal, and in every age. A skilful surgeon made a cure of the flagellated Candide in three weeks by means of emollient unguents prescribed by Dioscorides. His sores were now skinned over and he was able to march, when the king of the Bulgarians gave battle to the king of the Abares.

Chapter III

How Candide Escaped from the Bulgarians, and What Befell Him Afterwards

Never was anything so gallant, so well accoutred, so brilliant, and so finely disposed as the two armies. The trumpets, fifes, hautboys, drums, and cannon made such harmony as never was heard in hell itself. The entertainment began by a discharge of cannon, which, in the twinkling of an eye, laid flat about 6,000 men on each side. The musket bullets swept away, out of the best of all possible worlds, nine or ten thousand scoundrels that infested its surface. The bayonet was next the sufficient reason of the deaths of several thousands. The whole might amount to thirty thousand souls. Candide trembled like a philosopher, and concealed himself as well as he could during this heroic butchery.

At length, while the two kings were causing *Te Deums* to be sung in their camps, Candide took a resolution to go and reason somewhere else upon causes and effects. After passing over heaps of dead or dying men, the first place he came to was a neighboring village, in the Abarian territories, which had been burned to the ground by the Bulgarians, agreeably to the laws of war. Here lay a number of old men covered with wounds, who beheld their wives dying with their throats cut, and hugging their children to their breasts, all stained with blood. There several young virgins, whose bodies had been ripped open, after they had satisfied the natural necessities of the Bulgarian heroes, breathed their last; while others, half burned in the flames, begged to be despatched out of the world. The ground about them was covered with the brains, arms, and legs of dead men.

Candide made all the haste he could to another village, which belonged to the Bulgarians, and there he found the heroic Abares had enacted the same tragedy. Thence continuing to walk over palpitating limbs, or through ruined buildings, at length he arrived beyond the theatre of war, with a little provision in his budget, and Miss Cunegund's image in his heart. When he arrived in Holland his provision failed him; but having heard that the inhabitants of that country were all rich and Christians, he made himself sure of being treated by them in the same manner as at the baron's castle, before he had been driven thence through the power of Miss Cunegund's bright eyes.

He asked charity of several grave-looking people, who one and all answered him, that if he continued to follow this trade they would have him sent to the house of correction, where he should be taught to get his bread.

He next addressed himself to a person who had just come from haranguing a numerous assembly for a whole hour on the subject of charity. The orator, squinting at him under his broad-brimmed hat, asked him sternly, what brought him thither and whether he was for the good old cause? "Sir," said Candide, in a submissive manner, "I conceive there can be no effect without a cause; everything is necessarily concatenated and arranged for the best. It was necessary that I should be banished from the presence of Miss Cunegund; that I should afterwards run the gauntlet; and it is necessary I should beg my bread, till I am able to get it: all this could not have been otherwise." "Hark ye, friend," said the orator, "do you hold the pope to be Antichrist?" "Truly, I never heard anything about it," said Candide, "but whether he is or not, I am in want of something to eat." "Thou deservest not to eat or to drink," replied the orator, "wretch, monster, that thou art! hence! avoid my sight, nor ever come near me again while thou livest." The orator's wife happened to put her head out of the window at that instant, when, seeing a man who doubted whether the pope was Antichrist, she discharged upon his head a utensil full of water. Good heavens, to what excess does religious zeal transport womankind!

A man who had never been christened, an honest anabaptist named James, was witness to the cruel and ignominious treatment showed to one of his brethren, to a rational, two-footed, unfledged being. Moved with pity he carried him to his own house, caused him to be cleaned, gave him meat and drink, and made him a present of two florins, at the same time proposing to instruct him in his own trade of weaving Persian silks, which are fabricated in Holland. Candide, penetrated with so much goodness, threw himself at his feet, crying, "Now I am convinced that my Master Pangloss told me truth when he said that everything was for the best in this world; for I am infinitely more affected with your extraordinary generosity than with the inhumanity of that gentleman in the black cloak, and his wife." The next day, as Candide was walking out, he met a beggar all covered with scabs, his eyes sunk in his head, the end of his nose eaten off, his mouth drawn on one side, his teeth as black as a cloak, snuffling and coughing most violently, and every time he attempted to spit out dropped a tooth.

Chapter IV

How Candide Found His Old Master Pangloss Again
and What Happened to Him

Candide, divided between compassion and horror, but giving way to the former, bestowed on this shocking figure the two florins which the honest anabaptist, James, had just before given to him. The spectre looked at him very earnestly, shed tears and threw his arms about his neck. Candide started back aghast. "Alas!" said the one wretch to the other, "don't you know your dear Pangloss?" "What do I hear? Is it you, my dear master! you I behold in this piteous plight? What dreadful misfortune has befallen you? What has made you leave the most magnificent and delightful of all castles? What has become of Miss Cunegund, the mirror of young ladies, and nature's masterpiece?" "Oh Lord!" cried Pangloss, "I am so weak I cannot stand," upon which Candide instantly led him to the anabaptist's stable, and procured him something to eat. As soon as Pangloss had a little refreshed himself, Candide began to repeat his inquiries concerning Miss Cunegund. "She is dead," replied the other. "Dead!" cried Candide, and immediately fainted away; his friend restored him by the help of a little bad vinegar, which he found by chance in the stable. Candide opened his eyes, and again repeated: "Dead! is Miss Cunegund dead? Ah, where is the best of worlds now? But of what illness did she die? Was it of grief on seeing her father kick me out of his magnificent castle?" "No," replied Pangloss, "her body was ripped open by the Bulgarian soldiers, after they had subjected her to as much cruelty as a damsel could survive; they knocked the baron, her father, on the head for attempting to defend her; my lady, her mother, was cut in pieces; my poor pupil was served in just the same manner as his sister, and as for the castle, they have not left one stone upon another; they have destroyed all the ducks, and the sheep, the barns, and the trees; but we have had our revenge, for the Abares have done the very same thing in a neighboring barony, which belonged to a Bulgarian lord."

At hearing this, Candide fainted away a second time, but, having come to himself again, he said all that it became him to say; he inquired into the cause and effect, as well as into the sufficing reason that had reduced Pangloss to so miserable a condition. "Alas," replied the preceptor, "it was love; love, the comfort of the human species; love, the preserver of the universe; the soul of all sensible beings; love! tender love!" "Alas," cried Candide, "I have had some knowledge of love myself, this sovereign of hearts, this soul of souls; yet it never cost me more than a kiss and twenty kicks on the backside. But how could this beautiful cause produce in you so hideous an effect?"

Pangloss made answer in these terms: "O my dear Candide, you must remember Pacquette, that pretty wench, who waited on our noble baroness; in her arms I tasted the pleasures of paradise, which produced these hell-torments with which you see me devoured. She was infected with an ailment, and perhaps has since died of it; she received this present of a learned cordelier, who derived it from the fountain head; he was indebted for it to an old countess, who had it of a captain of horse, who had it of a marchioness, who had it of a page, the page had it of a Jesuit, who, during his novitiate, had it in a direct line from one of the fellow-adventurers of Christopher Columbus; for my part I shall give it to nobody, I am a dying man."

"O sage Pangloss," cried Candide, "what a strange genealogy is this! Is not the devil the root of it?" "Not at all," replied the great man, "it was a thing unavoidable, a necessary ingredient in the best of worlds; for if Columbus had not caught in an island in America this disease, which contaminates the source of generation, and frequently impedes propagation itself, and is evidently opposed to the great end of nature, we should have had neither chocolate nor cochineal. It is also to be observed, that, even to the present time, in this continent of ours, this malady, like our religious controversies, is peculiar to ourselves. The Turks, the Indians, the Persians, the Chinese, the Siamese, and the Japanese are entirely unacquainted with it; but there is a sufficing reason for them to know it in a few centuries. In the meantime, it is making prodigious havoc among us, especially in those armies composed of well-disciplined hirelings, who determine the fate of nations; for we may safely affirm, that, when an army of thirty thousand men engages another equal in size, there are about twenty thousand infected with syphilis on each side."

"Very surprising, indeed," said Candide, "but you must get cured." "Lord help me, how can I?" said Pangloss; "my dear friend, I have not a penny in the world; and you know one cannot be bled or have a clyster without money."

This last speech had its effect on Candide; he flew to the charitable anabaptist, James; he flung himself at his feet, and gave him so striking a picture of the miserable condition of his friend that the good man without any further hesitation agreed to take Doctor Pangloss into his house, and to pay for his cure. The cure was effected with only the loss of one eye and an ear. As he wrote a good hand, and understood accounts tolerably well, the anabaptist made him his bookkeeper. At the expiration of two months, being obliged by some mercantile affairs to go to Lisbon he took the two philosophers with him in the same ship; Pangloss, during the course of the voyage, explained to him how everything was so constituted that it could not be better. James did not quite agree with him on this point: "Men," said he "must, in some things, have deviated from their original innocence; for they were not born wolves, and yet they worry one another like those beasts of prey. God never gave them twenty-four pounders nor bayonets, and yet they have made cannon and bayonets to destroy one another. To this account I might add not only bankruptcies, but the law which seizes on the effects of bankrupts, only to cheat the creditors." "All this was indispensably necessary," replied the one-eyed doctor, "for private misfortunes are public benefits; so that the more private misfortunes there are, the greater is the general good." While he was arguing in this manner, the sky was overcast, the winds blew from the four quarters of the compass, and the ship was assailed by a most terrible tempest, within sight of the port of Lisbon.

Chapter V

A Tempest a Shipwreck, an Earthquake; and What Else Befell
Dr. Pangloss, Candide, and James the Anabaptist

One-half of the passengers, weakened and half-dead with the inconceivable anxiety and sickness which the rolling of a vessel at sea occasions through the whole human frame, were lost to all sense of the danger that surrounded them. The others made loud outcries, or betook themselves to their prayers; the sails were blown into shreds, and the masts were brought by the board. The vessel was a total wreck. Every one was busily employed, but nobody could be either heard or obeyed. The anabaptist, being upon deck, lent a helping hand as well as the rest, when a brutish sailor gave him a blow and laid him speechless; but, with the violence of the blow the tar himself tumbled headforemost overboard, and fell upon a piece of the broken mast, which he immediately grasped. Honest James, forgetting the injury he had so lately received from him, flew to his assistance, and, with great difficulty, hauled him in again, but, in the attempt, was, by a sudden jerk of the ship, thrown overboard himself, in sight of the very fellow whom he had risked his life to save, and who took not the least notice of him in this distress. Candide, who beheld all that passed and saw his benefactor one moment rising above water, and the next swallowed up by the merciless waves, was preparing to jump after him, but was prevented by the philosopher

Pangloss, who demonstrated to him that the roadstead of Lisbon had been made on purpose for the anabaptist to be drowned there. While he was proving his argument *a priori,* the ship foundered, and the whole crew perished, except Pangloss, Candide, and the sailor who had been the means of drowning the good anabaptist. The villain swam ashore; but Pangloss and Candide reached the land upon a plank.

As soon as they had recovered from their surprise and fatigue they walked towards Lisbon; with what little money they had left they thought to save themselves from starving after having escaped drowning.

Scarcely had they ceased to lament the loss of their benefactor and set foot in the city, when they perceived that the earth trembled under their feet, and the sea, swelling and foaming in the harbor, was dashing in pieces the vessels that were riding at anchor. Large sheets of flames and cinders covered the streets and public places; the houses tottered, and were tumbled topsy-turvy even to their foundations, which were themselves destroyed, and thirty thousand inhabitants of both sexes, young and old, were buried beneath the ruins. The sailor, whistling and swearing, cried, "Damn it, there's something to be got here." "What can be the *sufficing reason* of this phenomenon?" said Pangloss. "It is certainly the day of judgment," said Candide. The sailor, defying death in the pursuit of plunder, rushed into the midst of the ruin, where he found some money, with which he got drunk, and, after he had slept himself sober he purchased the favors of the first good-natured wench that came in his way, amidst the ruins of demolished houses and the groans of half-buried and expiring persons. Pangloss pulled him by the sleeve; "Friend," said he, "this is not right, you trespass against the *universal reason,* and have mistaken your time." "Death and zounds!" answered the other, "I am a sailor and was born at Batavia, and have trampled[1] four times upon the crucifix in as many voyages to Japan; you have come to a good hand with your *universal reason."*

In the meantime, Candide, who had been wounded by some pieces of stone that fell from the houses, lay stretched in the street, almost covered with rubbish. "For God's sake," said he to Pangloss, "get me a little wine and oil! I am dying." "This concussion of the earth is no new thing," said Pangloss, "the city of Lima in South America, experienced the same last year; the same cause, the same effects; there is certainly a train of sulphur all the way underground from Lima to Lisbon. "Nothing is more probable," said Candide; "but for the love of God a little oil and wine." "Probable!" replied the philosopher, "I maintain that the thing is demonstrable." Candide fainted away, and Pangloss fetched him some water from a neighboring spring.

The next day, in searching among the ruins, they found some eatables with which they repaired their exhausted strength. After this they assisted the inhabitants in relieving the distressed and wounded. Some, whom they had humanely assisted, gave them as good a dinner as could be expected under such terrible circumstances. The repast, indeed, was mournful, and the company moistened

---

[1] The Dutch traders to Japan were actually obliged to trample upon a crucifix, in token of their aversion to the Christian religion, which the Japanese abhorred.

their bread with their tears; but Pangloss endeavored to comfort them under this affliction by affirming that things could not be otherwise than they were: "For," said he, "all this is for the very best end, for if there is a volcano at Lisbon it could be in no other spot; and it is impossible but things should be as they are, for everything is for the best."

By the side of the preceptor sat a little man dressed in black, who was one of the *familiars* of the Inquisition. This person, taking him up with great complaisance, said, "Possibly, my good sir, you do not believe in original sin; for, if everything is best, there could have been no such thing as the fall or punishment of man."

"I humbly ask your excellency's pardon," answered Pangloss, still more politely; "for the fall of man and the curse consequent thereupon necessarily entered into the system of the best of worlds." "That is as much as to say, sir," rejoined the *familiar,* "you do not believe in free will." "Your excellency will be so good as to excuse me," said Pangloss, "free will is consistent with absolute necessity; for it was necessary we should be free, for in that the will—"

Pangloss was in the midst of his proposition, when the inquisitor beckoned to his attendant to help him to a glass of port wine.

Chapter VI

How the Portuguese Made a Superb Auto-da-fé to Prevent any Future Earthquakes,
and How Candide Underwent Public Flagellation

After the earthquake, which had destroyed three-fourths of the city of Lisbon, the sages of that country could think of no means more effectual to preserve the kingdom from utter ruin than to entertain the people with an *auto-da-fé,*[2] it having been decided by the University of Coimbra that the burning of a few people alive by a slow fire, and with great ceremony, is an infallible preventive of earthquakes.

In consequence thereof they had seized on a Biscayan for marrying his godmother, and on two Portuguese for taking out the bacon of a larded pullet they were eating; after dinner they came and secured Doctor Pangloss, and his pupil Candide, the one for speaking his mind, and the other for seeming to approve what he had said. They were conducted to separate apartments, extremely cool, where they were never incommoded with the sun. Eight days afterwards they were each dressed in a *sanbenito,* and their heads were adorned with paper mitres. The mitre and *sanbenito* worn by Candide were painted with flames reversed and with devils that had neither tails nor claws; but Doctor Pangloss's devils had both tails and claws, and his flames were upright. In these habits they marched in procession, and heard a very pathetic sermon, which was followed by an anthem, accompanied by bagpipes. Candide was flogged to some tune,

---

2 An *auto-da-fé* was actually to have been celebrated the very day on which the earthquake destroyed Lisbon. Everybody knows that an *auto-da-fé* is a general jail delivery from the prisons of the Inquisition, when the wretches condemned by that tribunal are brought to the stake, or otherwise stigmatized in public.

while the anthem was being sung; the Biscayan and the two men who would not eat bacon were burned, and Pangloss was hanged, which is not a common custom at these solemnities. The same day there was another earthquake, which made most dreadful havoc.

Candide, amazed, terrified, confounded, astonished, all bloody, and trembling from head to foot, said to himself, "If this is the best of all possible worlds, what are the others? If I had only been whipped, I could have put up with it, as I did among the Bulgarians; but, oh my dear Pangloss! my beloved master! thou greatest of philosophers! that ever I should live to see thee hanged, without knowing for what! O my dear anabaptist, thou best of men, that it should be thy fate to be drowned in the very harbor! O Miss Cunegund, you mirror of young ladies! that it should be your fate to have your body ripped open!"

He was making the best of his way from the place where he had been preached to, whipped, absolved and blessed, when he was accosted by an old woman, who said to him: "Take courage, child, and follow me."

Chapter VII

How the Old Woman Took Care of Candide, and How He Found the Object of His Love

Candide followed the old woman, though without taking courage, to a decayed house, where she gave him a pot of pomatum to anoint his sores, showed him a very neat bed, with a suit of clothes hanging by it; and set victuals and drink before him. "There," said she, "eat, drink, and sleep, and may our blessed lady of Atocha, and the great St. Anthony of Padua, and the illustrious St. James of Compostella, take you under their protection. I shall be back to-morrow." Candide struck with amazement at what he had seen, at what he had suffered, and still more with the charity of the old woman, would have shown his acknowledgment by kissing her hand. "It is not my hand you ought to kiss," said the old woman; "I shall be back to-morrow. Anoint your back, eat, and take your rest."

Candide, notwithstanding so many disasters, ate and slept. The next morning, the old woman brought him his breakfast; examined his back, and rubbed it herself with another ointment. She returned at the proper time, and brought him his dinner; and at night, she visited him again with his supper. The next day she observed the same ceremonies. "Who are you?" said Candide to her. "Who has inspired you with so much goodness? What return can I make you for this charitable assistance?" The good old beldame kept a profound silence. In the evening she returned, but without his supper; "Come along with me," said she, "but do not speak a word." She took him by the arm, and walked with him about a quarter of a mile into the country, till they came to a lonely house surrounded with moats and gardens. The old conductress knocked at a little door, which was immediately opened, and she showed him up a pair of back stairs, into a small, but richly furnished apartment. There she made him sit down on a brocaded sofa, shut the door upon him, and left him. Candide thought himself in a trance;

he looked upon his whole life, hitherto, as a frightful dream, and the present moment as a very agreeable one.

The old woman soon returned, supporting, with great difficulty, a young lady, who appeared scarce able to stand. She was of a majestic mien and stature, her dress was rich, and glittering with diamonds, and her face was covered with a veil. "Take off that veil," said the old woman to Candide. The young man approached, and, with a trembling hand, took off her veil. What a happy moment! What surprise! He thought he beheld Miss Cunegund; he did behold her—it was she herself. His strength failed him, he could not utter a word, he fell at her feet. Cunegund fainted upon the sofa. The old woman bedewed them with spirits; they recovered—they began to speak. At first they could express themselves only in broken accents; their questions and answers were alternately interrupted with sighs, tears, and exclamations. The old woman desired them to make less noise, and after this prudent admonition left them together. "Good heavens!" cried Candide, "is it you? Is it Miss Cunegund I behold, and alive? Do I find you again in Portugal? then you have not been ravished? they did not rip open your body, as the philosopher Pangloss informed me?" "Indeed but they did," replied Miss Cunegund; "but these two accidents do not always prove mortal." "But were your father and mother killed?" "Alas!" answered she, "it is but too true!" and she wept. "And your brother?" "And my brother also." "And how came you into Portugal? And how did you know of my being here? And by what strange adventure did you contrive to have me brought into this house? And how—" "I will tell you all," replied the lady, "but first you must acquaint me with all that has befallen you since the innocent kiss you gave me, and the rude kicking you received in consequence of it."

Candide, with the greatest submission, prepared to obey the commands of his fair mistress; and though he was still filled with amazement, though his voice was low and tremulous, though his back pained him, yet he gave her a most ingenuous account of everything that had befallen him, since the moment of their separation. Cunegund, with her eyes uplifted to heaven, shed tears when he related the death of the good anabaptist James, and of Pangloss; after which she thus related her adventures to Candide, who lost not one syllable she uttered, and seemed to devour her with his eyes all the time she was speaking.

Chapter VIII

Cunegund's Story

"I was in bed, and fast asleep, when it pleased heaven to send the Bulgarians to our delightful castle of Thunder-ten-tronckh, where they murdered my father and brother, and cut my mother in pieces. A tall Bulgarian soldier, six feet high, perceiving that I had fainted away at this sight, attempted to ravish me; the operation brought me to my senses. I cried, I struggled, I bit, I scratched, I would have torn the tall Bulgarian's eyes out, not knowing that what had happened at my father's castle was a customary thing. The brutal soldier, enraged at my resistance, gave me a wound in my left leg with his hanger, the mark of which I still carry." "Methinks I long to see it," said Candide, with all imaginable simplicity. "You shall," said Cunegund, "but let me proceed." "Pray do," replied Candide.

She continued. "A Bulgarian captain came in, and saw me weltering in my blood, and the soldier still as busy as if no one had been present. The officer, enraged at the fellow's want of respect to him, killed him with one stroke of his sabre as he lay upon me. This captain took care of me, had me cured, and carried me as a prisoner of war to his quarters. I washed what little linen he possessed, and cooked his victuals: he was very fond of me, that was certain; neither can I deny that he was well made, and had a soft, white skin, but he was very stupid, and knew nothing of philosophy: it might plainly be perceived that he had not been educated under Doctor Pangloss. In three months, having gambled away all his money, and having grown tired of me, he sold me to a Jew, named Don Issachar, who traded in Holland and Portugal, and was passionately fond of women. This Jew showed me great kindness, in hope of gaining my favors; but he never could prevail on me to yield. A modest woman may be once ravished; but her virtue is greatly strengthened thereby. In order to make sure of me, he brought me to this country-house you now see. I had hitherto believed that nothing could equal the beauty of the castle of Thunder-ten-tronckh; but I found I was mistaken.

"The grand inquisitor saw me one day at mass, ogled me all the time of service, and when it was over, sent to let me know he wanted to speak with me about some private business. I was conducted to his palace, where I told him all my story; he represented to me how much it was beneath a person of my birth to belong to a circumcised Israelite. He caused a proposal to be made to Don Issachar, that he should resign me to his lordship. Don Issachar, being the court banker, and a man of credit, was not easy to be prevailed upon. His lordship threatened him with an *auto-da-fé;* in short, my Jew was frightened into a compromise, and it was agreed between them, that the house and myself should belong to both in common; that the Jew should have Monday, Wednesday, and the Sabbath to himself; and the inquisitor the other four days of the week. This agreement has subsisted almost six months; but not without several contests, whether the space from Saturday night to Sunday morning belonged to the old or the new law. For my part, I have hitherto withstood them both, and truly I believe this is the very reason why they are both so fond of me.

"At length to turn aside the scourge of earthquakes, and to intimidate Don Issachar, my lord inquisitor was pleased to celebrate an *auto-da-fé*. He did me the honor to invite me to the ceremony. I had a very good seat; and refreshments of all kinds were offered the ladies between mass and the execution. I was dreadfully shocked at the burning of the two Jews, and the honest Biscayan who married his godmother; but how great was my surprise, my consternation, and concern, when I beheld a figure so like Pangloss, dressed in a *sanbenito* and mitre! I rubbed my eyes, I looked at him attentively. I saw him hanged, and I fainted away: scarce had I recovered my senses, when I saw you stripped of clothing;

this was the height of horror, grief, and despair. I must confess to you for a truth, that your skin is whiter and more blooming than that of the Bulgarian captain.This spectacle worked me up to a pitch of distraction. I screamed out, and would have said, 'hold, barbarians!' but my voice failed me; and indeed my cries would have signified nothing. After you had been severely whipped, how is it possible, I said to myself, that the lovely Candide and the sage Pangloss should be at Lisbon, the one to receive a hundred lashes, and the other to be hanged by order of my lord inquisitor, of whom I am so great a favorite? Pangloss deceived me most cruelly, in saving that everything is for the best.

"Thus agitated and perplexed, now distracted and lost, now half dead with grief, I revolved in my mind the murder of my father, mother, and brother, committed before my eyes; the insolence of the rascally Bulgarian soldier; the wound he gave me in the groin; my servitude; my being a cook-wench to my Bulgarian captain; my subjection to the hateful Jew, and my cruel inquisitor; the hanging of Doctor Pangloss; the *Miserere* sung while you were being whipped; and particularly the kiss I gave you behind the screen, the last day I ever beheld you. I returned thanks to God for having brought you to the place where I was, after so many trials. I charged the old woman who attends me to bring you hither as soon as was convenient. She has punctually executed my orders, and I now enjoy the inexpressible satisfaction of seeing you, hearing you, and speaking to you. But you must certainly be half-dead with hunger; I myself have a great inclination to eat, and so let us sit down to supper."

Upon this the two lovers immediately placed themselves at table, and, after having supped, they returned to seat themselves again on the magnificent sofa already mentioned, where they were in amorous dalliance, when Señor Don Issachar, one of the masters of the house, entered unexpectedly; it was the Sabbath day, and he came to enjoy his privilege, and sigh forth his passion at the feet of the fair Cunegund.

Chapter IX

What Happened to Cunegund, Candide, the Grand Inquisitor, and the Jew

This same Issachar was the most choleric little Hebrew that had ever been in Israel since the captivity of Babylon. "What," said he, "thou Galilean slut? the inquisitor was not enough for thee, but this rascal must come in for a share with me?" In uttering these words, he drew out a long poniard, which he always carried about him, and never dreaming that his adversary had any arms, he attacked him most furiously; but our honest Westphalian had received from the old woman a handsome sword with the suit of clothes. Candide drew his rapier, and though he was very gentle and sweet-tempered, he laid the Israelite dead on the floor at the fair Cunegund's feet.

"Holy Virgin!" cried she, "what will become of us? A man killed in my apartment! If the peace-officers come, we are undone." "Had not Pangloss been hanged," replied Candide, "he would have given us most excellent advice, in this emergency; for he was a profound philosopher. But, since he is not here, let us consult the old woman." She was very sensible, and was beginning to give her advice, when another door opened on a sudden. It was now one o'clock in the morning, and of course the beginning of Sunday, which, by agreement, fell to the lot of my lord inquisitor. Entering he discovers the flagellated Candide with his drawn sword in his hand, a dead body stretched on the floor, Cunegund frightened out of her wits, and the old woman giving advice.

At that very moment, a sudden thought came into Candide's head. If this holy man, thought he, should call assistance, I shall most undoubtedly be consigned to the flames, and Miss Cunegund may perhaps meet with no better treatment: besides, he was the cause of my being so cruelly whipped; he is my rival; and as I have now begun to dip my hands in blood, I will kill away, for there is no time to hesitate. This whole train of reasoning was clear and instantaneous; so that, without giving time to the inquisitor to recover from his surprise, he ran him through the body, and laid him by the side of the Jew. "Here's another fine piece of work!" cried Cunegund. "Now there can be no mercy for us, we are excommunicated; our last hour is come. But how could you, who are of so mild a temper, despatch a Jew and an inquisitor in two minutes' time?" "Beautiful maiden," answered Candide, "when a man is in love, is jealous, and has been flogged by the Inquisition, he becomes lost to all reflection."

The old woman then put in her word: "There are three Andalusian horses in the stable, with as many bridles and saddles; let the brave Candide get them ready: madam has a parcel of moidores and jewels, let us mount immediately, though I have lost one of nature's cushions; let us set out for Cadiz; it is the finest weather in the world, and there is great pleasure in travelling in the cool of the night."

Candide, without any further hesitation, saddled the three horses; and Miss Cunegund, the old woman, and he, set out, and travelled thirty miles without once halting. While they were making the best of their way, the Holy Brotherhood entered the house. My lord, the inquisitor, was interred in a magnificent manner, and master Issachar's body was thrown upon a dunghill.

Candide, Cunegund, and the old woman, had by this time reached the little town of Avacena, in the midst of the mountains of Sierra Morena, and were engaged in the following conversation in an inn, where they had taken up their quarters.

Chapter X

*In What Distress Candide, Cunegund, and the Old Woman Arrive at Cadiz;
and of Their Embarkation*

"Who could it be that has robbed me of my moidores and jewels?" exclaimed Miss Cunegund, all bathed in tears. "How shall we live? What shall we do? Where shall I find inquisitors and Jews who can give me more?" "Alas!" said the old woman, "I have a shrewd suspicion of a reverend father cordelier, who lay last night in the same inn with us at Badajoz; God forbid I should condemn any one wrongfully, but he came into our room twice, and he set off in the morning long before us." "Alas!" said Candide, "Pangloss has often demonstrated to me that the goods of this world are common to all men, and that everyone has an equal right to the enjoyment of them; but, according to these principles, the cordelier ought to have left us enough to carry us to the end of our journey. Have you nothing at all left, my dear Miss Cunegund?" "Not a maravedi," replied she. "What is to be done then?" said Candide. "Sell one of the horses," replied the old woman, "I will get up behind Miss Cunegund, though I have only one cushion to ride on, and we shall reach Cadiz."

In the same inn there was a Benedictine friar, who bought the horse very cheap. Candide, Cunegund, and the old woman, after passing through Lucina, Chellas, and Letrixa, arrived at length at Cadiz. A fleet was then getting ready, and troops were assembling in order to induce the reverend fathers, Jesuits of Paraguay, who were accused of having excited one of the Indian tribes in the neighborhood of the town of the Holy Sacrament, to revolt against the kings of Spain and Portugal. Candide, having been in the Bulgarian service, performed the military exercise of that nation before the general of this little army with so intrepid an air, and with such agility and expedition, that he received the command of a company of foot. Being now made a captain, he embarked with Miss Cunegund, the old woman, two valets, and the two Andalusian horses, which had belonged to the grand inquisitor of Portugal.

During their voyage they amused themselves with many profound reasonings on poor Pangloss's philosophy. "We are now going into another world, and surely it must be there that everything is for the best; for I must confess that we have had some little reason to complain of what passes in ours, both as to the physical and moral part. Though I have a sincere love for you," said Miss Cunegund, "yet I still shudder at the reflection of what I have seen and experienced." "All will be well," replied Candide, "the sea of this new world is already better than our European seas: it is smoother, and the winds blow more regularly." "God grant it," said Cunegund, "but I have met with such terrible treatment in this world that I have almost lost all hopes of a better one." "What murmuring and complaining is here indeed!" cried the old woman: "If you had suffered half what I have, there might be some reason for it." Miss Cunegund could scarce refrain from laughing at the good old woman, and thought it droll enough to pretend to a greater share of misfortunes than her own. "Alas! my good dame," said she, "unless you had been ravished by two Bulgarians, had received two deep wounds in your belly, had seen two of your own castles demolished, had lost two fathers, and two mothers, and seen both of them barbarously murdered before your eyes, and to sum up all, had two lovers whipped at an *auto-da-fé,* I cannot see how you could be more unfortunate than I. Add to this, though born a baroness, and bearing seventy-two quarterings, I have been reduced to the station of a cookwench." "Miss," replied the old woman, "you do not know my family as yet;

but if I were to show you my posteriors, you would not talk in this manner, but suspend your judgment." This speech raised a high curiosity in Candide and Cunegund; and the old woman continued as follows:

Chapter XI

The History of the Old Woman

"I have not always been blear-eyed. My nose did not always touch my chin; nor was I always a servant. You must know that I am the daughter of Pope Urban X,[3] and of the princess of Palestrina. To the age of fourteen I was brought up in a castle, compared with which all the castles of the German barons would not have been fit for stabling, and one of my robes would have bought half the province of Westphalia. I grew up, and improved in beauty, wit, and every graceful accomplishment; and in the midst of pleasures, homage, and the highest expectations. I already began to inspire the men with love. My breast began to take its right form, and such a breast! white, firm, and formed like that of Venus of Medici; my eyebrows were as black as jet, and as for my eyes, they darted flames and eclipsed the lustre of the stars, as I was told by the poets of our part of the world. My maids, when they dressed and undressed me, used to fall into an ecstasy in viewing me before and behind: and all the men longed to be in their places.

"I was contracted in marriage to a sovereign prince of Massa Carara. Such a prince! as handsome as myself, sweet-tempered, agreeable, witty, and in love with me over head and ears. I loved him, too, as our sex generally do for the first time, with rapture, transport, and idolatry. The nuptials were prepared with surprising pomp and magnificence; the ceremony was attended with feasts, carousals, and burlettas: all Italy composed sonnets in my praise, though not one of them was tolerable. I was on the point of reaching the summit of bliss, when an old marchioness, who had been mistress to the prince, my husband, invited him to drink chocolate. In less than two hours after he returned from the visit, he died of most terrible convulsions. But this is a mere trifle. My mother, distracted to the highest degree. and yet less afflicted than I, determined to absent herself for some time from so fatal a place. As she had a very fine estate in the neighborhood of Gaeta, we embarked on board a galley, which was gilded like the high altar of St. Peter's, at Rome. In our passage we were boarded by a Sallee rover. Our men defended themselves like true pope's soldiers; they flung themselves upon their knees, laid down their arms, and begged the corsair to give them absolution *in articulo mortis.*

"The Moors presently stripped us as bare as ever we were born. My mother, my maids of honor, and myself, were served all in the same manner. It is amazing how quick these gentry are at undressing people. But what surprised me most was, that they made a rude sort of surgical examination of parts of the body which are sacred to the functions of nature. I thought it a very strange kind of ceremony; for thus we are generally apt to judge of things when we have not

---

[3] There never was a tenth pope of that name; so that this number is mentioned to avoid scandal.

seen the world. I afterwards learned that it was to discover if we had any diamonds concealed. This practice has been established since time immemorial among those civilized nations that scour the seas. I was informed that the religious knights of Malta never fail to make this search whenever any Moors of either sex fall into their hands. It is a part of the law of nations, from which they never deviate.

"I need not tell you how great a hardship it was for a young princess and her mother to be made slaves and carried to Morocco. You may easily imagine what we must have suffered on board a corsair. My mother was still extremely handsome, our maids of honor, and even our common waiting-women, had more charms than were to be found in all Africa. As to myself, I was enchanting; I was beauty itself, and then I had my virginity. But, alas! I did not retain it long; this precious flower, which had been reserved for the lovely prince of Massa Carara, was cropped by the captain of the Moorish vessel, who was a hideous negro, and thought he did me infinite honor. Indeed, both the princess of Palestrina and myself must have had very strong constitutions to undergo all the hardships and violences we suffered before our arrival at Morocco. But I will not detain you any longer with such common things; they are hardly worth mentioning.

"Upon our arrival at Morocco we found that kingdom deluged with blood. Fifty sons of the emperor Muley Ishmael were each at the head of a party. This produced fifty civil wars of blacks against blacks, of tawnies against tawnies, and of mulattoes against mulattoes. In short, the whole empire was one continued scene of carnage.

"No sooner were we landed than a party of blacks, of a contrary faction to that of my captain, came to rob him of his booty. Next to the money and jewels, we were the most valuable things he had. I witnessed on this occasion such a battle as you never beheld in your cold European climates. The northern nations have not that fermentation in their blood, nor that raging lust for women that is so common in Africa. The natives of Europe seem to have their veins filled with milk only; but fire and vitriol circulate in those of the inhabitants of Mount Atlas and the neighboring provinces. They fought with the fury of the lions, tigers, and serpents of their country, to decide who should have us. A Moor seized my mother by the right arm, while my captain's lieutenant held her by the left; another Moor laid hold of her by the right leg, and one of our corsairs held her by the other. In this manner almost all of our women were dragged by four soldiers. My captain kept me concealed behind him, and with his drawn scimitar cut down everyone who opposed him; at length I saw all our Italian women and my mother mangled and torn in pieces by the monsters who contended for them. The captives, my companions, the Moors who took us, the soldiers, the sailors, the blacks, the whites, the mulattoes, and lastly, my captain himself, were all slain, and I remained alone expiring upon a heap of dead bodies. Similar barbarous scenes were transacted every day over the whole country, which is of three hundred leagues in extent, and yet they never missed the five stated times of prayer enjoined by their prophet Mahomet.

"I disengaged myself with great difficulty from such a heap of corpses, and made a shift to crawl to a large orange-tree that stood on the bank of a neighboring rivulet, where I fell down exhausted with fatigue, and overwhelmed with horror, despair, and hunger. My senses being overpowered, I fell asleep, or rather seemed to be in a trance. Thus I lay in a state of weakness and insensibility between life and death, when I felt myself pressed by something that moved up and down upon my body. This brought me to myself. I opened my eyes, and saw a pretty fair-faced man, who sighed and muttered these words between his teeth, *O che sciagura d'essere senza coglioni!*

Chapter XII

The Adventures of the Old Woman Continued

"Astonished and delighted to hear my native language, and no less surprised at the young man's words, I told him that there were far greater misfortunes in the world than what he complained of. And to convince him of it, I gave him a short history of the horrible disasters that had befallen me; and as soon as I had finished, fell into a swoon again. He carried me in his arms to a neighboring cottage, where he had me put to bed, procured me something to eat, waited on me with the greatest attention, comforted me, caressed me, told me that he had never seen anything so perfectly beautiful as myself, and that he had never so much regretted the loss of what no one could restore to him. 'I was born at Naples,' said he, 'where they make eunuchs of thousands of children every year; some die of the operation; some acquire voices far beyond the most tuneful of your ladies; and others are sent to govern states and empires. I underwent this operation very successfully, and was one of the singers in the princess of Palestrina's chapel.' 'How,' cried I, 'in my mother's chapel!' 'The princess of Palestrina, your mother!' cried he, bursting into a flood of tears. 'Is it possible you should be the beautiful young princess whom I had the care of bringing up till she was six years old, and who at that tender age promised to be as fair as I now behold you?' 'I am the same,' I replied. 'My mother lies about a hundred yards from here cut in pieces and buried under a heap of dead bodies.'

"I then related to him all that had befallen me, and he in return acquainted me with all his adventures, and how he had been sent to the court of the king of Morocco by a Christian prince to conclude a treaty with that monarch; in consequence of which he was to be furnished with military stores, and ships to enable him to destroy the commerce of other Christian governments.[4] 'I have executed my commission,' said the eunuch; 'I am going to take ship at Ceuta, and I'll take you along with me to Italy. *Ma che sciagura d'essere senza coglioni!*'

"I thanked him with tears of joy, but, instead of taking me with him into Italy, he carried me to Algiers, and sold me to the dey of that province. I had not been long a slave when the plague, which had made the tour of Africa, Asia,

---

[4] This is too just a reproach upon those Christian powers, who, for the thirst of lucre, shamefully patronize, and supply the barbarians of Africa with the means of gratifying their rapacity, and of exercising cruelties which are a disgrace to human nature.

and Europe, broke out at Algiers with redoubled fury. You have seen an earthquake; but tell me, Miss, have you ever had the plague?"

"Never," answered the young baroness.

"If you had ever had it," continued the old woman, "you would own an earthquake was a trifle to it. It is very common in Africa; I was seized with it. Figure to yourself the distressed condition of the daughter of a pope, only fifteen years old, and who in less than three months had felt the miseries of poverty and slavery; had been debauched almost every day; had beheld her mother cut into four quarters; had experienced the scourges of famine and war; and was now dying of the plague at Algiers. I did not, however, die of it; but my eunuch, and the dey, and almost the whole seraglio of Algiers, were swept off.

"As soon as the first fury of this dreadful pestilence was over, a sale was made of the dey's slaves. I was purchased by a merchant who carried me to Tunis. This man sold me to another merchant, who sold me again to another at Tripoli; from Tripoli I was sold to Alexandria, from Alexandria to Smyrna, and from Smyrna to Constantinople. After many changes, I at length became the property of an aga of the janissaries, who, soon after I came into his possession, was ordered away to the defence of Azoff, then besieged by the Russians.

"The aga, being very fond of women, took his whole seraglio with him, and lodged us in a small fort, with two black eunuchs and twenty soldiers for our guard. Our army made a great slaughter among the Russians; but they soon returned us the compliment. Azoff was taken by storm, and the enemy spared neither age, sex, nor condition, but put all to the sword, and laid the city in ashes. Our little fort alone held out; they resolved to reduce us by famine. The twenty janissaries, who were left to defend it, had bound themselves by an oath never to surrender the place. Being reduced to the extremity of famine, they found themselves obliged to kill our two eunuchs, and eat them rather than violate their oath. But this horrible repast soon failing them, they next determined to devour the women.

"We had a very pious and humane man, who gave them a most excellent sermon on this occasion, exhorting them not to kill us all at once; 'Cut off only one of the steaks of each of those ladies,' said he, 'and you will fare extremely well; if you are under the necessity of having recourse to the same expedient again, you will find the like supply a few days hence. Heaven will approve of so charitable an action, and work your deliverance.'

"By the force of this eloquence he easily persuaded them, and all of us underwent the operation. The man applied the same balsam as they do to children after circumcision. We were all ready to give up the ghost.

"The janissaries had scarcely time to finish the repast with which we had supplied them, when the Russians attacked the place by means of flat-bottomed boats, and not a single janissary escaped. The Russians paid no regard to the condition we were in; but there are French surgeons in all parts of the world, and one of them took us under his care, and cured us. I shall never forget, while I live, that as soon as my wounds were perfectly healed he made me certain proposals. In general, he desired us all to be of a good cheer, assuring us that the like had happened in many sieges; and that it was perfectly agreeable to the laws of war.

"As soon as my companions were in a condition to walk, they were sent to Moscow. As for me, I fell to the lot of a boyard, who put me to work in his garden, and gave me twenty lashes a day. But this nobleman having about two years afterwards been broken alive upon the wheel, with about thirty others, for some court intrigues, I took advantage of the event, and made my escape. I travelled over a great part of Russia. I was a long time an innkeeper's servant at Riga, then at Rostock, Wismar, Leipsic, Cassel, Utrecht, Leyden, The Hague, and Rotterdam: I have grown old in misery and disgrace, living with only one buttock, and having in perpetual remembrance that I am a pope's daughter. I have been a hundred times upon the point of killing myself, but still I was fond of life. This ridiculous weakness is, perhaps, one of the dangerous principles implanted in our nature. For what can be more absurd than to persist in carrying a burden of which we wish to be eased? to detest, and yet to strive to preserve our existence? In a word, to caress the serpent that devours us, and hug him close to our bosoms till he has gnawed into our hearts?

"In the different countries which it has been my fate to traverse, and at the many inns where I have been a servant, I have observed a prodigious number of people who held their existence in abhorrence, and yet I never knew more than twelve who voluntarily put an end to their misery; namely, three negroes, four Englishmen, as many Genevese, and a German professor, named Robek. My last place was with the Jew, Don Issachar, who placed me near your person, my fair lady; to whose fortunes I have attached myself, and have been more concerned with your adventures than with my own. I should never have even mentioned the latter to you, had you not a little piqued me on the head of sufferings; and if it were not customary to tell stories on board a ship in order to pass away the time. In short, my dear Miss, I have a great deal of knowledge and experience in the world, therefore take my advice: divert yourself, and prevail upon each passenger to tell his story, and if there is one of them all that has not cursed his existence many times, and said to himself over and over again that he was the most wretched of mortals, I give you leave to throw me head-foremost into the sea."

Chapter XIII

How Candide Was Obliged to Leave the Fair Cunegund and the Old Woman

The fair Cunegund, being thus made acquainted with the history of the old woman's life and adventures, paid her all the respect and civility due to a person of her rank and merit. She very readily acceded to her proposal of engaging the passengers to relate their adventures in their turns, and was at length, as well as Candide, compelled to acknowledge that the old woman was in the right. "It is a thousand pities," said Candide, "that the sage Pangloss should have been hanged contrary to the custom of an *auto-da-fé*, for he would have given us a most admirable lecture on the moral and physical evil which overspreads the earth and sea; and I think I should have courage enough to presume to offer (with all due respect) some few objections."

While everyone was reciting his adventures, the ship continued her way, and at length arrived at Buenos Ayres, where Cunegund, Captain Candide, and the old woman, landed and went to wait upon the governor Don Fernando d'Ibaraa y Figueora y Mascarenes y Lampourdos y Souza. This nobleman carried himself with a haughtiness suitable to a person who bore so many names. He spoke with the most noble disdain to everyone, carried his nose so high, strained his voice to such a pitch, assumed so imperious an air, and stalked with so much loftiness and pride, that everyone who had the honor of conversing with him was violently tempted to bastinade his excellency. He was immoderately fond of women, and Miss Cunegund appeared in his eyes a paragon of beauty. The first thing he did was to ask her if she was not the captain's wife. The air with which he made this demand alarmed Candide, who did not dare to say he was married to her, because indeed he was not; neither did he venture to say she was his sister, because she was not: and though a lie of this nature proved of great service to one of the ancients, and might possibly be useful to some of the moderns, yet the purity of his heart would not permit him to violate the truth. "Miss Cunegund," replied he, "is to do me the honor to marry me, and we humbly beseech your excellency to condescend to grace the ceremony with your presence."

Don Fernando d'Ibaraa y Figueora y Mascarenes y Lampourdos y Souza, twirling his mustachio, and putting on a sarcastic smile, ordered Captain Candide to go and review his company. The gentle Candide obeyed, and the governor was left with Miss Cunegund. He made her a strong declaration of love, protesting that he was ready to give her his hand in the face of the church, or otherwise, as should appear most agreeable to a young lady of her prodigious beauty. Cunegund desired leave to retire a quarter of an hour to consult the old woman, and determine how she should proceed.

The old woman gave her the following counsel: "Miss, you have seventy-two quarterings in your arms, it is true, but you have not a penny to bless yourself with: it is your own fault if you do not become the wife of one of the greatest noblemen in South America, with an exceeding fine mustachio. What business have you to pride yourself upon an unshaken constancy? You have been outraged by a Bulgarian soldier; a Jew and an inquisitor have both tasted of your favors. People take advantage of misfortunes. I must confess, were I in your place, I should, without the least scruple, give my hand to the governor, and thereby make the fortune of the brave Captain Candide." While the old woman was thus haranguing, with all the prudence that old age and experience furnish, a small bark entered the harbor, in which was an alcayde and his alguazils. Matters had fallen out as follows:

The old woman rightly guessed that the cordelier with the long sleeves, was the person who had taken Miss Cunegund's money and jewels, while they and Candide were at Badajoz, in their flight from Lisbon. This same friar attempted to sell some of the diamonds to a jeweller, who presently knew them to have belonged to the grand inquisitor, and stopped them. The cordelier, before he was hanged, acknowledged that he had stolen them, and described the persons, and the road they had taken. The flight of Cunegund and Candide was already the town-talk. They sent in pursuit of them to Cadiz; and the vessel which had been sent to make the greater despatch, had now reached the port of Buenos Ayres. A report was spread that an alcayde was going to land, and that he was in pursuit of the murderers of my lord, the inquisitor. The sage old woman immediately saw what was to be done. "You cannot run away," said she to Cunegund, "but you have nothing to fear; it was not you who killed my lord inquisitor: besides, as the governor is in love with you, he will not suffer you to be ill-treated; therefore stand your ground." Then hurrying away to Candide, she said: "Be gone hence this instant, or you will be burned alive." Candide found there was no time to be lost; but how could he part from Cunegund, and whither must he fly for shelter?

Chapter XIV

The Reception Candide and Cacambo Met with Among the Jesuits in Paraguay

Candide had brought with him from Cadiz such a footman as one often meets with on the coasts of Spain and in the colonies. He was the fourth part of a Spaniard, of a mongrel breed, and born in Tucuman. He had successively gone through the profession of a singing boy, sexton, sailor, monk, peddler, soldier, and lackey. His name was Cacambo; he had a great affection for his master, because his master was a very good man. He immediately saddled the two Andalusian horses. "Come, my good master, let us follow the old woman's advice, and make all the haste we can from this place without staying to look behind us." Candide burst into a flood of tears: "O, my dear Cunegund, must I then be compelled to quit you just as the governor was going to honor us with his presence at our wedding! Cunegund, so long lost and found again, what will now become of you?" "Lord!" said Cacambo, "she must do as well as she can; women are never at a loss. God takes care of them, and so let us make the best of our way." "But whither wilt thou carry me? where can we go? what can we do without Cunegund?" cried the disconsolate Candide. "By St. James of Compostella," said Cacambo, "you were going to fight against the Jesuits of Paraguay; now let us go and fight for them; I know the road perfectly well; I'll conduct you to their kingdom; they will be delighted with a captain that understands the Bulgarian drill; you will certainly make a prodigious fortune. If we cannot succeed in this world we may in another. It is a great pleasure to see new objects and perform new exploits."

"Then you have been in Paraguay?" asked Candide. "Ay, marry, I have," replied Cacambo; "I was a scout in the college of the Assumption, and am as well acquainted with the new government of Los Padres as I am with the streets of Cadiz. Oh, it is an admirable government, that is most certain! The kingdom is at present upwards of three hundred leagues in diameter, and divided into thirty provinces; the fathers there are masters of everything, and the people have no money at all; this you must allow is the masterpiece of justice and reason. For my part, I see nothing so divine as the good fathers, who wage war in this part of the world against the troops of Spain and Portugal, at the same time that they hear the confessions of those very princes in Europe; who kill Spaniards in America and send them to heaven at Madrid. This pleases me exceedingly, but let us push forward; you are going to see the happiest and most fortunate of all mortals. How charmed will those fathers be to hear that a captain who understands the Bulgarian military drill is coming among them."

As soon as they reached the first barrier, Cacambo called to the advance guard, and told them that a captain wanted to speak to my lord, the general. Notice was given to the main guard, and immediately a Paraguayan officer ran to throw himself at the feet of the commandant to impart this news to him. Candide and Cacambo were immediately disarmed, and their two Andalusian horses were seized. The two strangers were conducted between two files of musketeers, the commandant was at the further end with a three-cornered cap on his head, his gown tucked up, a sword by his side, and a half-pike in his hand; he made a sign, and instantly four-and-twenty soldiers drew up round the newcomers. A sergeant told them that they must wait, the commandant could not speak to them; and that the reverend father provincial did not suffer any Spaniard to open his mouth but in his presence, or to stay above three hours in the province. "And where is the reverend father provincial?" said Cacambo. "He has just come from mass and is at the parade," replied the sergeant, "and in about three hours' time you may possibly have the honor to kiss his spurs." "But," said Cacambo, "the captain, who, as well as myself, is perishing of hunger, is no Spaniard, but a German; therefore, pray, might we not be permitted to break our fast till we can be introduced to his reverence?"

The sergeant immediately went and acquainted the commandant with what he heard. "God be praised," said the reverend commandant, "since he is a German I will hear what he has to say; let him be brought to my arbor."

Immediately they conducted Candide to a beautiful pavilion adorned with a colonade of green marble, spotted with yellow, and with an intertexture of vines, which served as a kind of cage for parrots, humming-birds, guinea-hens, and all other curious kinds of birds. An excellent breakfast was provided in vessels of gold; and while the Paraguayans were eating coarse Indian corn out of wooden dishes in the open air, and exposed to the burning heat of the sun, the reverend father commandant retired to his cool arbor.

He was a very handsome young man, round-faced, fair, and fresh-colored, his eyebrows were finely arched, he had a piercing eye, the tips of his ears were red, his lips vermilion, and he had a bold and commanding air; but such a boldness as neither resembled that of a Spaniard nor of a Jesuit. He ordered Candide and Cacambo to have their arms restored to them, together with their two Andalusian horses. Cacambo gave the poor beasts some oats to eat close by the arbor, keeping a strict eye upon them all the while for fear of surprise.

Candide having kissed the hem of the commandant's robe, they sat down to table. "It seems you are a German," said the Jesuit to him in that language. "Yes, reverend father," answered Candide. As they pronounced these words they looked at each other with great amazement and with an emotion that neither could conceal.

"From what part of Germany do you come?" said the Jesuit.

"From the dirty province of Westphalia," answered Candide. "I was born in the castle of Thunder-ten-tronckh."

"Oh heavens! is it possible?" said the commandant.

"What a miracle!" cried Candide.

"Can it be you?" said that commandant.

On this they both drew a few steps backwards, the running into each other's arms, embraced, and wept profusely. "Is it you then, reverend father? You are the brother of the fair Miss Cunegund? You that was slain by the Bulgarians! You the baron's son! You a Jesuit in Paraguay! I must confess this is a strange world we live in. O Pangloss! Pangloss! what joy would this have given you if you had not been hanged."

The commandant dismissed the negro slaves, and the Paraguayans who presented them with liquor in crystal goblets. He returned thanks to God and St. Ignatius a thousand times; he clasped Candide in his arms, and both their faces were bathed in tears. "You will be more surprised, more affected, more transported," said Candide, "when I tell you that Miss Cunegund, your sister, whose belly was supposed to have been ripped open, is in perfect health."

"Where?"

"In your neighborhood, with the governor of Buenos Ayres; and I myself was going to fight against you." Every word they uttered during this long conversation was productive of some new matter of astonishment. Their souls fluttered on their tongues, listened in their ears, and sparkled in their eyes. Like true Germans, they continued a long while at table, waiting for the reverend father; and the commandant spoke to his dear Candide as follows:

Chapter XV

How Candide Killed the Brother of His Dear Cunegund

"Never while I live shall I lose the remembrance of that horrible day on which I saw my father and mother barbarously butchered before my eyes, and my sister ravished. When the Bulgarians retired we searched in vain for my dear sister. She was nowhere to be found; but the bodies of my father, mother, and myself, with two servant maids and three little boys, all of whom had been murdered by the remorseless enemy, were thrown into a cart to be buried in a chapel belonging to the Jesuits, within two leagues of our family seat. A Jesuit sprinkled us with some holy water, which was confounded salty, and a few drops of it went into my eyes; the father perceived that my eyelids stirred a little; he put his hand upon my breast and felt my heart beat; upon which he gave me proper assistance, and at the end of three weeks I was perfectly recovered. You know, my dear Candide,

I was very handsome; I became still more so, and the reverend father Croust, superior of that house, took a great fancy to me; he gave me the habit of the order, and some years afterwards I was sent to Rome. Our general stood in need of new recruits of young German Jesuits. The sovereigns of Paraguay admit of as few Spanish Jesuits as possible; they prefer those of other nations, as being more obedient to command. The reverend father-general looked upon me as a proper person to work in that vineyard. I set out in company with a Polander and a Tyrolese. Upon my arrival I was honored with a subdeaconship and a lieutenancy. Now I am colonel and priest. We shall give a warm reception to the king of Spain's troops; I can assure you they will be well excommunicated and beaten. Providence has sent you hither to assist us. But is it true that my dear sister Cunegund is in the neighborhood with the governor of Buenos Ayres?"

Candide swore that nothing could be more true; and the tears began again to trickle down their cheeks. The baron knew no end of embracing Candide, he called him his brother, his deliverer.

"Perhaps," said he, "my dear Candide, we shall be fortunate enough to enter the town, sword in hand, and recover my sister Cunegund."

"Ah! that would crown my wishes," replied Candide; "for I intended to marry her; and I hope I shall still be able to effect it."

"Insolent fellow!" cried the baron. "You! you have the impudence to marry my sister, who bears seventy-two quarterings! really, I think you have an insufferable degree of assurance to dare so much as to mention such an audacious design to me."

Candide, thunderstruck at the oddness of this speech, answered: "Reverend father, all the quarterings in the world are of no signification. I have delivered your sister from a Jew and an inquisitor; she is under many obligations to me, and she is resolved to give me her hand. My master, Pangloss, always told me that mankind are by nature equal. Therefore, you may depend upon it that I will marry your sister."

"We shall see to that, villain!" said the Jesuit baron of Thunder-ten-tronckh, and struck him across the face with the flat side of his sword. Candide in an instant drew his rapier and plunged it up to the hilt in the Jesuit's body; but in pulling it out reeking hot, he burst into tears.

"Good God!" cried he, "I have killed my old master, my friend, my brother-in-law; I am the best man in the world, and yet I have already killed three men; and of these three two were priests."

Cacambo, who was standing sentry near the door of the arbor, instantly ran up.

"Nothing remains," said his master, "but to sell our lives as dearly as possible; they will undoubtedly look into the arbor; we must die sword in hand."

Cacambo, who had seen many of this kind of adventures, was not discouraged. He stripped the baron of his Jesuit's habit and put it upon Candide, then gave him the dead man's three-cornered cap and made him mount on horseback. And this was done as quick as thought.

"Gallop, master," cried Cacambo; "everybody will take you for a Jesuit going to give orders; and we shall have passed the frontiers before they will be able to overtake us." He flew as he spoke these words, crying out aloud in Spanish, "Make way; make way for the reverend father-colonel."

Chapter XVI

What Happened to Our Two Travellers with Two Girls, Two Monkeys, and the Savages, Called Oreillons

Candide and his valet had already passed the frontiers before it was known that the German Jesuit was dead. The wary Cacambo had taken care to fill his wallet with bread, chocolate, some ham, some fruit, and a few bottles of wine. They penetrated with their Andalusian horses into a strange country, where they could discover no beaten path. At length a beautiful meadow, intersected with purling rills, opened to their view. Cacambo proposed to his master to take some nourishment, and he set him an example.

"How can you desire me to feast upon ham, when I have killed the baron's son and am doomed never more to see the beautiful Cunegund? What will it avail me to prolong a wretched life that must be spent far from her in remorse and despair? And then what will the journal of Trévoux say?" was Candide's reply.

While he was making these reflections he still continued eating. The sun was now on the point of setting when the ears of our two wanderers were assailed with cries which seemed to be uttered by a female voice. They could not tell whether these were cries of grief or of joy; however, they instantly started up, full of that inquietude and apprehension which a strange place naturally inspires. The cries proceeded from two young women who were tripping disrobed along the mead, while two monkeys followed close at their heels biting at their limbs. Candide was touched with compassion; he had learned to shoot while he was among the Bulgarians, and he could hit a filbert in a hedge without touching a leaf. Accordingly he took up his double-barrelled Spanish gun, pulled the trigger, and laid the two monkeys lifeless on the ground.

"God be praised, my dear Cacambo, I have rescued two poor girls from a most perilous situation; if I have committed a sin in killing an inquisitor and a Jesuit, I have made ample amends by saving the lives of these two distressed damsels. Who knows but they may be young ladies of a good family, and that the assistance I have been so happy to give them may procure us great advantage in this country?"

He was about to continue when he felt himself struck speechless at seeing the two girls embracing the dead bodies of the monkeys in the tenderest manner, bathing their wounds with their tears, and rending the air with the most doleful lamentations.

"Really," said he to Cacambo, "I should not have expected to see such a prodigious share of good nature."

"Master," replied the knowing valet, "you have made a precious piece of work of it; do you know that you have killed the lovers of these two ladies?"

"Their lovers! Cacambo, you are jesting! It cannot be! I can never believe it."

"Dear sir," replied Cacambo, "you are surprised at everything; why should you think it so strange that there should be a country where monkeys insinuate themselves into the good graces of the ladies? They are the fourth part of a man as I am the fourth part of a Spaniard."

"Alas!" replied Candide, "I remember to have heard my master Pangloss say that such accidents as these frequently came to pass in former times, and that these commixtures are productive of centaurs, fauns, and satyrs; and that many of the ancients had seen such monsters; but I looked upon the whole as fabulous."

"Now you are convinced," said Cacambo, "that it is very true, and you see what use is made of those creatures by persons who have not had a proper education; all I am afraid of is that these same ladies may play us some ugly trick."

These judicious reflections operated so far on Candide as to make him quit the meadow and strike into a thicket. There he and Cacambo supped, and after heartily cursing the grand inquisitor, the governor of Buenos Ayres, and the baron, they fell asleep on the ground. When they awoke they were surprised to find that they could not move; the reason was that the Oreillons who inhabit that country, and to whom the ladies had given information of these two strangers, had bound them with cords made of the bark of trees. They saw themselves surrounded by fifty naked Oreillons armed with bows and arrows, clubs, and hatchets of flint; some were making a fire under a large cauldron; and others were preparing spits, crying out one and all, "A Jesuit! a Jesuit! we shall be revenged; we shall have excellent cheer; let us eat this Jesuit; let us eat him up."

"I told you, master," cried Cacambo, mournfully, "that these two wenches would play us some scurvy trick."

Candide, seeing the cauldron and the spits, cried out, "I suppose they are going either to boil or roast us. Ah! what would Pangloss say if he were to see how pure nature is formed? Everything is right; it may be so; but I must confess it is something hard to be bereft of dear Miss Cunegund, and to be spitted like a rabbit by these barbarous Oreillons."

Cacambo, who never lost his presence of mind in distress, said to the disconsolate Candide: "Do not despair; I understand a little of the jargon of these people; I will speak to them."

"Ay, pray do," said Candide, "and be sure you make them sensible of the horrid barbarity of boiling and roasting human creatures, and how little of Christianity there is in such practices."

"Gentlemen," said Cacambo, "you think perhaps you are going to feast upon a Jesuit; if so, it is mighty well; nothing can be more agreeable to justice than thus to treat your enemies. Indeed the law of nature teaches us to kill our neighbor, and accordingly we find this practised all over the world; and if we do not indulge ourselves in eating human flesh, it is because we have much better fare; but for your parts, who have not such resources as we, it is certainly much better judged to feast upon your enemies than to throw their bodies to the fowls of the air; and thus lose all the fruits of your victory. But surely, gentlemen, you would not choose to eat your friends. You imagine you are going to roast a Jesuit, whereas my master is your friend, your defender, and you are going to spit the very man who has been destroying your enemies; as to myself, I am your countryman; this gentleman is my master, and so far from being a Jesuit, give me leave to tell you he has very lately killed one of that order, whose spoils he now wears, and which have probably occasioned your mistake. To convince you of the truth of what I say, take the habit he has on and carry it to the first barrier of the Jesuits' kingdom, and inquire whether my master did not kill one of their officers. There will be little or no time lost by this, and you may still reserve our bodies in your power to feast on if you should find what we have told you to be false. But, on the contrary, if you find it to be true, I am persuaded you are too well acquainted with the principles of the laws of society, humanity, and justice, not to use us courteously, and suffer us to depart unhurt."

This speech appeared very reasonable to the Oreillons; they deputed two of their people with all expedition to inquire into the truth of this affair, who acquitted themselves of their commission like men of sense, and soon returned with good tidings for our distressed adventurers. Upon this they were loosed, and those who were so lately going to roast and boil them now showed them all sorts of civilities; offered them girls, gave them refreshments, and reconducted them to the confines of their country, crying before them all the way, in token of joy: "He is no Jesuit, he is no Jesuit."

Candide could not help admiring the cause of his deliverance. "What men! what manners!" cried he; "if I had not fortunately run my sword up to the hilt in the body of Miss Cunegund's brother, I should have certainly been eaten alive. But, after all, pure nature is an excellent thing; since these people, instead of eating me, showed me a thousand civilities as soon as they knew I was not a Jesuit."

Chapter XVII

Candide and His Valet Arrive in the Country of El Dorado —What They Saw There

When they got to the frontiers of the Oreillons, "You see," said Cacambo to Candide, "this hemisphere is not better than the other; now take my advice and let us return to Europe by the shortest way possible."

"But how can we get back?" said Candide; "and whither shall we go? To my own country? The Bulgarians and the Abares are laying that waste with fire and sword; or shall we go to Portugal? There I shall be burned; and if we abide here we are every moment in danger of being spitted. But how can I bring myself to quit that part of the world where my dear Miss Cunegund has her residence?"

"Let us return towards Cayenne," said Cacambo; "there we shall meet with some Frenchmen; for you know those gentry ramble all over the world; perhaps they will assist us, and God will look with pity on our distress."

It was not so easy to get to Cayenne. They knew pretty nearly whereabouts it lay; but the mountains, rivers, precipices, robbers, savages, were dreadful obstacles in the way. Their horses died with fatigue and their provisions were at an end.

They subsisted a whole month on wild fruit, till at length they came to a little river bordered with cocoa trees; the sight of which at once revived their drooping spirits and furnished nourishment for their enfeebled bodies.

Cacambo, who was always giving as good advice as the old woman herself, said to Candide: "You see there is no holding out any longer; we have travelled enough on foot. I spy an empty canoe near the river side; let us fill it with cocoanuts, get into it, and go down with the stream; a river always leads to some inhabited place. If we do not meet with agreeable things, we shall at least meet with something new."

"Agreed," replied Candide; "let us recommend ourselves to Providence."

They rowed a few leagues down the river, the banks of which were in some places covered with flowers; in others barren; in some parts smooth and level, and in others steep and rugged. The stream widened as they went further on, till at length it passed under one of the frightful rocks, whose summits seemed to reach the clouds. Here our two travellers had the courage to commit themselves to the stream, which, contracting in this part, hurried them along with a dreadful noise and rapidity. At the end of four-and-twenty hours they saw daylight again; but their canoe was dashed to pieces against the rocks. They were obliged to creep along, from rock to rock, for the space of a league, till at length a spacious plain presented itself to their sight. This place was bounded by a chain of inaccessible mountains. The country appeared cultivated equally for pleasure and to produce the necessaries of life. The useful and agreeable were here equally blended. The roads were covered, or rather adorned, with carriages formed of glittering materials, in which were men and women of a surprising beauty, drawn with great rapidity by red sheep of a very large size; which far surpassed the finest coursers of Andalusia, Tetuan, or Mecquinez.

"Here is a country, however," said Candide, "preferable to Westphalia."

He and Cacambo landed near the first village they saw, at the entrance of which they perceived some children covered with tattered garments of the richest brocade, playing at quoits. Our two inhabitants of the other hemisphere amused themselves greatly with what they saw. The quoits were large, round pieces, yellow, red, and green, which cast a most glorious lustre. Our travellers picked some of them up, and they proved to be gold, emeralds, rubies, and diamonds; the least of which would have been the greatest ornament to the superb throne of the Great Mogul.

"Without doubt," said Cacambo, "those children must be the king's sons that are playing at quoits." As he was uttering these words the schoolmaster of the village appeared, who came to call the children to school.

"There," said Candide, "is the preceptor of the royal family."

The little ragamuffins immediately quitted their diversion, leaving the quoits on the ground with all their other playthings. Candide gathered them up, ran to the schoolmaster, and, with a most respectful bow, presented them to him, giving him to understand by signs that their royal highnesses had forgot their gold and precious stones. The schoolmaster, with a smile, flung them upon the ground, then examining Candide from head to foot with an air of admiration, he turned his back and went on his way.

Our travellers took care, however, to gather up the gold, the rubies, and the emeralds.

"Where are we?" cried Candide. "The king's children in this country must have an excellent education, since they are taught to show such a contempt for gold and precious stones."

Cacambo was as much surprised as his master. They then drew near the first house in the village, which was built after the manner of a European palace. There was a crowd of people about the door, and a still greater number in the house. The sound of the most delightful instruments of music was heard, and the most agreeable smell came from the kitchen. Cacambo went up to the door and heard those within talking in the Peruvian language, which was his mother tongue; for every one knows that Cacambo was born in a village of Tucuman, where no other language is spoken.

"I will be your interpreter here," said he to Candide. "Let us go in; this is an eating-house."

Immediately two waiters and two servant-girls, dressed in cloth of gold, and their hair braided with ribbons of tissue, accosted the strangers and invited them to sit down to the ordinary. Their dinner consisted of four dishes of different soups, each garnished with two young paroquets, a large dish of bouillé that weighed two hundred weight, two roasted monkeys of a delicious flavor, three hundred humming-birds in one dish, and six hundred fly-birds in another; some excellent ragouts, delicate tarts, and the whole served up in dishes of rock-crystal. Several sorts of liquors extracted from the sugar-cane, were handed about by the servants who attended.

Most of the company were chapmen and wagoners, all extremely polite; they asked Cacambo a few questions with the utmost discretion and circumspection; and replied to his in a most obliging and satisfactory manner.

As soon as dinner was over, both Candide and Cacambo thought they should pay very handsomely for their entertainment by laying down two of those large gold pieces which they had picked off the ground; but the landlord and landlady burst into a fit of laughing and held their sides for some time. When the fit was over, "Gentlemen," said the landlord, "I plainly perceive you are strangers, and such we are not accustomed to charge; pardon us, therefore, for laughing when you offered us the common pebbles of our highways for payment of your reckoning. To be sure, you have none of the coin of this kingdom; but there is no necessity of having any money at all to dine in this house. All the inns, which are established for the convenience of those who carry on the trade of this nation, are maintained by the government. You have found but very indifferent entertainment here, because this is only a poor village; but in almost every other of these public houses you will meet with a reception worthy of persons of your merit." Cacambo explained the whole of this speech of the landlord to Candide, who listened to it with the same astonishment with which his friend communicated it.

"What sort of a country is this," said the one to the other, "that is unknown to all the world; and in which Nature has everywhere so different an appearance to what she has in ours? Possibly this is that part of the globe where everything is right, for there must certainly be some such place. And, for all that Master Pangloss could say, I often perceived that things went very ill in Westphalia."

Chapter XVIII

What They Saw in the Country of El Dorado

Cacambo vented all his curiosity upon his landlord by a thousand different questions; the honest man answered him thus: "I am very ignorant, sir, but I am contented with my ignorance; however, we have in this neighborhood an old man retired from court, who is the most learned and communicative person in the whole kingdom." He then conducted Cacambo to the old man; Candide acted now only a second character, and attended his valet. They entered a very plain house, for the door was nothing but silver, and the ceiling was only of beaten gold, but wrought in such elegant taste as to vie with the richest. The antechamber, indeed, was only incrusted with rubies and emeralds; but the order in which everything was disposed made amends for this great simplicity.

The old man received the strangers on his sofa, which was stuffed with humming-birds' feathers; and ordered his servants to present them with liquors in golden goblets, after which he satisfied their curiosity in the following terms:

"I am now one hundred and seventy-two years old, and I learned of my late father, who was equerry to the king, the amazing revolutions of Peru, to which he had been an eye-witness. This kingdom is the ancient patrimony of the Incas, who very imprudently quitted it to conquer another part of the world, and were at length conquered and destroyed themselves by the Spaniards.

"Those princes of their family who remained in their native country acted more wisely. They ordained, with the consent of their whole nation, that none of the inhabitants of our little kingdom should ever quit it; and to this wise ordinance we owe the preservation of our innocence and happiness. The Spaniards had some confused notion of this country, to which they gave the name of *El Dorado;* and Sir Walter Raleigh, an Englishman, actually came very near it about three hundred years ago; but the inaccessible rocks and precipices with which our country is surrounded on all sides, have hitherto secured us from the rapacious fury of the people of Europe, who have an unaccountable fondness for the pebbles and dirt of our land, for the sake of which they would murder us all to the very last man."

The conversation lasted some time and turned chiefly on the form of government, their manners, their women, their public diversions, and the arts. At length, Candide, who had always had a taste for metaphysics, asked whether the people of that country had any religion.

The old man reddened a little at this question.

"Can you doubt it?" said he; "do you take us for wretches lost to all sense of gratitude?"

Cacambo asked in a respectful manner what was the established religion of El Dorado. The old man blushed again, and said: "Can there be two religions, then? Ours, I apprehend, is the religion of the whole world; we worship God from morning till night."

"Do you worship but one God?" said Cacambo, who still acted as the interpreter of Candide's doubts.

"Certainly," said the old man; "there are not two, not three, nor four Gods. I must confess the people of your world ask very extraordinary questions."

However, Candide could not refrain from making many more inquiries of the old man; he wanted to know in what manner they prayed to God in El Dorado.

"We do not pray to him at all," said the reverend sage; "we have nothing to ask of Him, He has given us all we want, and we give Him thanks incessantly." Candide had a curiosity to see some of their priests, and desired Cacambo to ask the old man where they were. At which he smiling said:

"My friends, we are all of us priests; the king and all the heads of families sing solemn hymns of thanksgiving every morning, accompanied by five or six thousand musicians."

"What!" said Cacambo, "have you no monks among you to dispute, to govern, to intrigue, and to burn people who are not of the same opinion with themselves?"

"Do you take us for fools?" said the old man. "Here we are all of one opinion, and know not what you mean by your monks."

During the whole of this discourse Candide was in raptures, and he said to himself, "What a prodigious difference is there between this place and Westphalia; and this house and the baron's castle. Ah, Master Pangloss! had you ever seen El Dorado, you would no longer have maintained that the castle of Thunder-ten-tronckh was the finest of all possible edifices; there is nothing like seeing the world, that's certain."

This long conversation being ended, the old man ordered six sheep to be harnessed and put to the coach,[5] and sent twelve of his servants to escort the travellers to court.

"Excuse me," said he, "for not waiting on you in person, my age deprives me of that honor. The king will receive you in such a manner that you will have no reason to complain; and doubtless you will make a proper allowance for the customs of the country if they should not happen altogether to please you."

Candide and Cacambo got into the coach, the six sheep flew, and, in less than a quarter of an hour, they arrived at the king's palace, which was situated at the further end of the capital. At the entrance was a portal two hundred and twenty feet high and one hundred wide; but it is impossible for words to express the materials of which it was built. The reader, however, will readily conceive that they must have a prodigious superiority over the pebbles and sand, which we call gold and precious stones.

Twenty beautiful young virgins in waiting received Candide and Cacambo on their alighting from the coach, conducted them to the bath and clad them in robes woven of the down of humming-birds; after which they were introduced by the great officers of the crown of both sexes to the king's apartment, between two files of musicians, each file consisting of a thousand, agreeable to the custom of

---

[5] Meaning Peruvian sheep, a kind of beast of burden, native of Peru, very different from the sheep of Europe.

the country. When they drew near to the presence-chamber, Cacambo asked one of the officers in what manner they were to pay their obeisance to his majesty; whether it was the custom to fall upon their knees, or to prostrate themselves upon the ground; whether they were to put their hands upon their heads, or behind their backs; whether they were to lick the dust off the floor; in short, what was the ceremony usual on such occasions.

"The custom," said the great officer, "is to embrace the king and kiss him on each cheek."

Candide and Cacambo accordingly threw their arms round his majesty's neck, who received them in the most gracious manner imaginable, and very politely asked them to sup with him.

While supper was preparing orders were given to show them the city, where they saw public structures that reared their lofty heads to the clouds; the market-places decorated with a thousand columns; fountains of spring water, besides others of rose water, and of liquors drawn from the sugar-cane, incessantly flowing in the great squares; which were paved with a kind of precious stones that emitted an odor like that of cloves and cinnamon. Candide asked to see the high court of justice, the parliament; but was answered that they had none in that country, being utter strangers to lawsuits. He then inquired if they had any prisons; they replied none. But what gave him at once the greatest surprise and pleasure was the palace of sciences, where he saw a gallery two thousand feet long, filled with the various apparatus in mathematics and natural philosophy.

After having spent the whole afternoon in seeing only about the thousandth part of the city, they were brought back to the king's palace. Candide sat down at the table with his majesty, his valet Cacambo, and several ladies of the court. Never was entertainment more elegant, nor could any one possibly show more wit than his majesty displayed while they were at supper. Cacambo explained all the king's *bons mots* to Candide, and, although they were translated, they still appeared to be *bons mots*. Of all the things that surprised Candide, this was not the least. They spent a whole month in this hospitable place, during which time Candide was continually saying to Cacambo:

"I own, my friend, once more, that the castle where I was born is a mere nothing in comparison to the place where we now are; but still Miss Cunegund is not here, and you yourself have doubtless some fair one in Europe for whom you sigh. If we remain here we shall only be as others are; whereas, if we return to our own world with only a dozen of El Dorado sheep, loaded with the pebbles of this country, we shall be richer than all the kings in Europe; we shall no longer need to stand in awe of the inquisitors; and we may easily recover Miss Cunegund."

This speech was perfectly agreeable to Cacambo. A fondness for roving, for making a figure in their own country, and for boasting of what they had seen in their travels, was so powerful in our two wanderers that they resolved to be no longer happy; and demanded permission of the king to quit the country.

"You are about to do a rash and silly action," said the king. "I am sensible my kingdom is an inconsiderable spot; but when people are tolerably at their ease in any place, I should think it would be to their interest to remain there. Most assuredly, I have no right to detain you, or any strangers, against your wills; this is an act of tyranny to which our manners and our laws are equally repugnant; all men are by nature free; you have therefore an undoubted liberty to depart whenever you please, but you will have many and great difficulties to encounter in passing the frontiers. It is impossible to ascend that rapid river which runs under high and vaulted rocks, and by which you were conveyed hither by a kind of miracle. The mountains by which my kingdom are hemmed in on all sides, are ten thousand feet high, and perfectly perpendicular; they are above ten leagues across, and the descent from them is one continued precipice. However, since you are determined to leave us, I will immediately give orders to the superintendent of my carriages to cause one to be made that will convey you very safely. When they have conducted you to the back of the mountains, nobody can attend you farther; for my subjects have made a vow never to quit the kingdom, and they are too prudent to break it. Ask me whatever else you please."

"All we shall ask of your majesty," said Cacambo, "is only a few sheep laden with provisions, pebbles, and the clay of your country."

The king smiled at the request, and said: "I cannot imagine what pleasure you Europeans find in our yellow clay; but take away as much of it as you will, and much good may it do you."

He immediately gave orders to his engineers to make a machine to hoist these two extraordinary men out of the kingdom. Three thousand good machinists went to work and finished it in about fifteen days, and it did not cost more than twenty millions sterling of that country's money. Candide and Cacambo were placed on this machine, and they took with them two large red sheep, bridled and saddled, to ride upon, when they got on the other side of the mountains; twenty others to serve as sumpters for carrying provisions; thirty laden with presents of whatever was most curious in the country, and fifty with gold, diamonds, and other precious stones. The king, at parting with our two adventurers, embraced them with the greatest cordiality.

It was a curious sight to behold the manner of their setting off, and the ingenious method by which they and their sheep were hoisted to the top of the mountains. The machinists and engineers took leave of them as soon as they had conveyed them to a place of safety, and Candide was wholly occupied with the thoughts of presenting his sheep to Miss Cunegund.

"Now," cried he, "thanks to heaven, we have more than sufficient to pay the governor of Buenos Ayres for Miss Cunegund, if she is redeemable. Let us make the best of our way to Cayenne, where we will take shipping and then we may at leisure think of what kingdom we shall purchase with our riches.

Chapter XIX

What Happened to Them at Surinam, and How Candide Became Acquainted with Martin

Our travellers' first day's journey was very pleasant; they were elated with the prospect of possessing more riches than were to be found in Europe, Asia, and Africa together. Candide, in amorous transports, cut the name of Miss Cunegund on almost every tree he came to. The second day two of their sheep sunk in a morass, and were swallowed up with their lading; two more died of fatigue; some few days afterwards seven or eight perished with hunger in a desert, and others, at different times, tumbled down precipices, or were otherwise lost, so that, after travelling about a hundred days they had only two sheep left of the hundred and two they brought with them from El Dorado. Said Candide to Cacambo:

"You see, my dear friend, how perishable the riches of this world are; there is nothing solid but virtue."

"Very true," said Cacambo, "but we have still two sheep remaining, with more treasure than ever the king of Spain will be possessed of; and I espy a town at a distance, which I take to be Surinam, a town belonging to the Dutch. We are now at the end of our troubles, and at the beginning of happiness."

As they drew near the town they saw a negro stretched on the ground with only one half of his habit, which was a kind of linen frock; for the poor man had lost his left leg and his right hand.

"Good God," said Candide in Dutch, "what dost thou here, friend, in this deplorable condition?"

"I am waiting for my master, Mynheer Vanderdendur, the famous trader," answered the negro.

"Was it Mynheer Vanderdendur that used you in this cruel manner?

"Yes, sir," said the negro; "it is the custom here. They give a linen garment twice a year, and that is all our covering. When we labor in the sugar works, and the mill happens to snatch hold of a finger, they instantly chop off our hand; and when we attempt to run away, they cut off a leg. Both these cases have happened to me, and it is at this expense that you eat sugar in Europe; and yet when my mother sold me for ten patacoons on the coast of Guinea, she said to me, 'My dear child, bless our fetiches; adore them forever; they will make thee live happy; thou hast the honor to be a slave to our lords the whites, by which thou wilt make the fortune of us thy parents.' Alas! I know not whether I have made their fortunes; but they have not made mine: dogs, monkeys, and parrots are a thousand times less wretched than I. The Dutch fetiches who converted me tell me every Sunday that the blacks and whites are all children of one father, whom they call Adam. As for me, I do not understand anything of genealogies; but if what these preachers say is true, we are all second cousins; and you must allow that it is impossible to be worse treated by our relations than we are."

"O Pangloss!" cried out Candide, "such horrid doings never entered the imagination. Here is an end of the matter; I find myself, after all, obliged to renounce thy Optimism."

"Optimism," said Cacambo, "what is that?"

"Alas!" replied Candide, "it is the obstinacy of maintaining that everything is best when it is worst." And so saying he turned his eyes towards the poor negro, and shed a flood of tears; and in this weeping mood he entered the town of Surinam.

Immediately upon their arrival our travellers inquired if there was any vessel in the harbor which they might send to Buenos Ayres. The person they addressed themselves to happened to be the master of a Spanish bark, who offered to agree with them on moderate terms, and appointed them a meeting at a public house. Thither Candide and his faithful Cacambo went to wait for him, taking with them their two sheep.

Candide, who was all frankness and sincerity, made an ingenuous recital of his adventures to the Spaniard, declaring to him at the same time his resolution of carrying off Miss Cunegund from the governor of Buenos Ayres.

"O ho!" said the shipmaster, "if that is the case, get whom you please to carry you to Buenos Ayres; for my part, I wash my hands of the affair. It would prove a hanging matter to us all. The fair Cunegund is the governor's favorite mistress." These words were like a clap of thunder to Candide; he wept bitterly for a long time, and, taking Cacambo aside, he said to him, "I'll tell you, my dear friend, what you must do. We have each of us in our pockets to the value of five or six millions in diamonds; you are cleverer at these matters than I; you must go to Buenos Ayres and bring off Miss Cunegund. If the governor makes any difficulty give him a million; if he holds out, give him two; as you have not killed an inquisitor, they will have no suspicion of you. I'll fit out another ship and go to Venice, where I will wait for you. Venice is a free country, where we shall have nothing to fear from Bulgarians, Abares, Jews, or Inquisitors."

Cacambo greatly applauded this wise resolution. He was inconsolable at the thoughts of parting with so good a master, who treated him more like an intimate friend than a servant; but the pleasure of being able to do him a service soon got the better of his sorrow. They embraced each other with a flood of tears. Candide charged him not to forget the old woman. Cacambo set out the same day. This Cacambo was a very honest fellow.

Candide continued some days longer at Surinam, waiting for any captain to carry him and his two remaining sheep to Italy. He hired domestics, and purchased many things necessary for a long voyage; at length Mynheer Vanderdendur, skipper of a large Dutch vessel, came and offered his service.

"What will you have," said Candide, "to carry me, my servants, my baggage, and these two sheep you see here, directly to Venice?"

The skipper asked ten thousand piastres, and Candide agreed to his demand without hesitation.

"Ho, ho!" said the cunning Vanderdendur to himself, "this stranger must be very rich; he agrees to give me ten thousand piastres without hesitation." Returning a little while after he tells Candide that upon second consideration he could not undertake the voyage for less than twenty thousand. "Very well; you shall have them," said Candide.

"Zounds!" said the skipper to himself, "this man agrees to pay twenty thousand piastres with as much ease as ten." Accordingly he goes back again, and tells him roundly that he will not carry him to Venice for less than thirty thousand piastres.

"Then you shall have thirty thousand," said Candide.

"Odso!" said the Dutchman once more to himself, "thirty thousand piastres seem a trifle to this man. Those sheep must certainly be laden with an immense treasure. I'll e'en stop here and ask no more; but make him pay down the thirty thousand piastres, and then we may see what is to be done farther." Candide sold two small diamonds, the least of which was worth more than all the skipper asked.

He paid him beforehand, the two sheep were put on board, and Candide followed in a small boat to join the vessel in the road. The skipper took advantage of his opportunity, hoisted sail, and put out to sea with a favorable wind. Candide, confounded and amazed, soon lost sight of the ship. "Alas!" said he, "this is a trick like those in our old world!"

He returned back to the shore overwhelmed with grief; and, indeed, he had lost what would have made the fortune of twenty monarchs.

Straightway upon his landing he applied to the Dutch magistrate; being transported with passion he thundered at the door, which being opened, he went in, told his case, and talked a little louder than was necessary. The magistrate began with fining him ten thousand piastres for his petulance, and then listened very patiently to what he had to say, promised to examine into the affair on the skipper's return, and ordered him to pay ten thousand piastres more for the fees of the court.

This treatment put Candide out of all patience; it is true, he had suffered misfortunes a thousand times more grievous, but the cool insolence of the judge, and the villainy of the skipper raised his choler and threw him into a deep melancholy. The villainy of mankind presented itself to his mind in all its deformity, and his soul was a prey to the most gloomy ideas. After some time, hearing that the captain of a French ship was ready to set sail for Bordeaux, as he had no more sheep loaded with diamonds to put on board, he hired the cabin at the usual price; and made it known in the town that he would pay the passage and board of any honest man who would give him his company during the voyage; besides making him a present of ten thousand piastres, on condition that such person was the most dissatisfied with his condition, and the most unfortunate in the whole province.

Upon this there appeared such a crowd of candidates that a large fleet could not have contained them. Candide, willing to choose from among those who appeared most likely to answer his intention, selected twenty, who seemed to him the most sociable, and who all pretended to merit the preference. He invited them to his inn, and promised to treat them with a supper, on condition that every man should bind himself by an oath to relate his own history; declaring at the same time, that he would make choice of that person who should appear to him the most deserving of compassion, and the most justly dissatisfied with his condition in life; and that he would make a present to the rest.

This extraordinary assembly continued sitting till four in the morning. Candide, while he was listening to their adventures, called to mind what the old woman had said to him in their voyage to Buenos Ayres, and the wager she had laid that there was not a person on board the ship but had met with great misfortunes. Every story he heard put him in mind of Pangloss.

"My old master," said he, "would be confoundedly put to it to demonstrate his favorite system. Would he were here! Certainly if everything is for the best, it is in El Dorado, and not in the other parts of the world."

At length he determined in favor of a poor scholar, who had labored ten years for the booksellers at Amsterdam: being of opinion that no employment could be more detestable.

This scholar, who was in fact a very honest man, had been robbed by his wife, beaten by his son, and forsaken by his daughter, who had run away with a Portuguese. He had been likewise deprived of a small employment on which he subsisted, and he was persecuted by the clergy of Surinam, who took him for a Socinian. It must be acknowledged that the other competitors were, at least, as wretched as he; but Candide was in hopes that the company of a man of letters would relieve the tediousness of the voyage. All the other candidates complained that Candide had done them great injustice, but he stopped their mouths by a present of a hundred piastres to each.

Chapter XX

What Befell Candide and Martin on Their Passage

The old philosopher, whose name was Martin, took shipping with Candide for Bordeaux. Both had seen and suffered a great deal, and had the ship been going from Surinam to Japan round the Cape of Good Hope, they could have found sufficient entertainment for each other during the whole voyage, in discoursing upon moral and natural evil.

Candide, however, had one advantage over Martin: he lived in the pleasing hopes of seeing Miss Cunegund once more; whereas, the poor philosopher had nothing to hope for; besides, Candide had money and jewels, and, notwithstanding he had lost a hundred red sheep laden with the greatest treasure outside of El Dorado, and though he still smarted from the reflection of the Dutch skipper's knavery, yet when he considered what he had still left, and repeated the name of Cunegund, especially after meal times, he inclined to Pangloss' doctrine.

"And pray," said he to Martin, "what is your opinion of the whole of this system? what notion have you of moral and natural evil?"

"Sir," replied Martin, "our priest accused me of being a Socinian; but the real truth is, I am a Manichæan."

"Nay, now you are jesting," said Candide; "there are no Manichæans existing at present in the world."

"And yet I am one," said Martin; "but I cannot help it. I cannot for the soul of me think otherwise."

"Surely the devil must be in you," said Candide.

"He concerns himself so much," replied Martin, "in the affairs of this world that it is very probable he may be in me as well as everywhere else; but I must confess, when I cast my eye on this globe, or rather globule, I cannot help thinking that God has abandoned it to some malignant being. I always except El Dorado. I scarce ever knew a city that did not wish the destruction of its neighboring city; nor a family that did not desire to exterminate some other family. The poor in all parts of the world bear an inveterate hatred to the rich, even while they creep and cringe to them; and the rich treat the poor like sheep, whose wool and flesh they barter for money; a million of regimented assassins traverse Europe from one end to the other, to get their bread by regular depredation and murder, because it is the most gentlemanlike profession. Even in those cities which seem to enjoy the blessings of peace, and where the arts flourish, the inhabitants are devoured with envy, care, and inquietudes, which are greater plagues than any experienced in a town besieged. Private chagrins are still more dreadful than public calamities. In a word," concluded the philosopher, "I have seen and suffered so much that I am a Manichæan."

"And yet there is some good in the world," replied Candide.

"May be so," said Martin, "but it has escaped my knowledge."

While they were deeply engaged in this dispute they heard the report of cannon, which redoubled every moment. Each took out his glass, and they spied two ships warmly engaged at the distance of about three miles. The wind brought them both so near the French ship that those on board her had the pleasure of seeing the fight with great ease. After several smart broadsides the one gave the other a shot between wind and water which sunk her outright. Then could Candide and Martin plainly perceive a hundred men on the deck of the vessel which was sinking, who, with hands uplifted to heaven, sent forth piercing cries, and were in a moment swallowed up by the waves.

"Well," said Martin, "you now see in what manner mankind treat one another."

"It is certain," said Candide, "that there is something diabolical in this affair." As he was speaking thus he spied something of a shining red hue, which swam close to the vessel. The boat was hoisted out to see what it might be, when it proved to be one of his sheep. Candide felt more joy at the recovery of this one animal than he did grief when he lost the other hundred, though laden with the large diamonds of El Dorado.

The French captain quickly perceived that the victorious ship belonged to the crown of Spain; that the other was a Dutch pirate, and the very same captain who had robbed Candide. The immense riches which this villain had amassed, were buried with him in the deep, and only this one sheep saved out of the whole.

"You see," said Candide to Martin, "that vice is sometimes punished; this villain, the Dutch skipper, has met with the fate he deserved."

"Very true," said Martin, "but why should the passengers be doomed also to destruction? God has punished the knave, and the devil has drowned the rest."

The French and Spanish ships continued their cruise, and Candide and Martin their conversation. They disputed fourteen days successively, at the end of which they were just as far advanced as the first moment they began. However, they had the satisfaction of disputing, of communicating their ideas, and of mutually comforting each other. Candide embraced his sheep with transport.

"Since I have found thee again," said he, "I may possibly find my Cunegund once more."

Chapter XXI

Candide and Martin, while Thus Reasoning with Each Other,
Draw Near to the Coast of France

At length they descried the coast of France, when Candide said to Martin, "Pray Mr. Martin, were you ever in France?"

"Yes, sir," said Martin, "I have been in several provinces of that kingdom. In some, one-half of the people are fools and madmen; in some, they are too artful; in others, again, they are, in general, either very good-natured or very brutal;

while in others, they affect to be witty, and in all, their ruling passion is love, the next is slander, and the last is to talk nonsense."

"But, pray, Mr. Martin, were you ever in Paris?"

"Yes, sir, I have been in that city, and it is a place that contains the several species just described; it is a chaos, a confused multitude, where everyone seeks for pleasure without being able to find it; at least, as far as I have observed during my short stay in that city. At my arrival I was robbed of all I had in the world by pickpockets and sharpers, at the fair of St. Germain. I was taken up myself for a robber, and confined in prison a whole week; after which I hired myself as corrector to a press, in order to get a little money towards defraying my expenses back to Holland on foot. I knew the whole tribe of scribblers, malcontents, and fanatics. It is said the people of that city are very polite; I believe they may be."

"For my part, I have no curiosity to see France," said Candide; "you may easily conceive, my friend, that after spending a month in El Dorado, I can desire to behold nothing upon earth but Miss Cunegund; I am going to wait for her at Venice. I intend to pass through France, on my way to Italy. Will you not bear me company?" "With all my heart," said Martin; "they say Venice is agreeable to none but noble Venetians; but that, nevertheless, strangers are well received there when they have plenty of money; now I have none, but you have, therefore I will attend you wherever you please." "Now we are upon this subject," said Candide, "do you think that the earth was originally sea, as we read in that great book which belongs to the captain of the ship?" "I believe nothing of it," replied Martin, "any more than I do of the many other chimeras which have been related to us for some time past." "But then, to what end," said Candide, "was the world formed?" "To make us mad," said Martin. "Are you not surprised," continued Candide, "at the love which the two girls in the country of the Oreillons had for those two monkeys?—You know I have told you the story." "Surprised?" replied Martin, "not in the least; I see nothing strange in this passion. I have seen so many extraordinary things that there is nothing extraordinary to me now." "Do you think," said Candide, "that mankind always massacred one another as they do now? were they always guilty of lies, fraud, treachery, ingratitude, inconstancy, envy, ambition, and cruelty? were they always thieves, fools, cowards, gluttons, drunkards, misers, calumniators, debauchees, fanatics, and hypocrites?" "Do you believe," said Martin, "that hawks have always been accustomed to eat pigeons when they came in their way?" "Doubtless," said Candide. "Well then," replied Martin, "if hawks have always had the same nature, why should you pretend that mankind change theirs?" "Oh," said Candide, "there is a great deal of difference; for free will——" and reasoning thus they arrived at Bordeaux.

Chapter XXII

What Happened to Candide and Martin in France

Candide staid no longer at Bordeaux than was necessary to dispose of a few of the pebbles he had brought from El Dorado, and to provide himself with a post-chaise for two persons, for he could no longer stir a step without his philosopher

Martin. The only thing that gave him concern was the being obliged to leave his sheep behind him, which he intrusted to the care of the academy of sciences at Bordeaux, who proposed, as a prize subject for the year, to prove why the wool of this sheep was red; and the prize was adjusted to a northern sage, who demonstrated by A plus B, minus C, divided by Z, that the sheep must necessarily be red, and die of the mange.

In the meantime, all the travellers whom Candide met with in the inns, or on the road, told him to a man, that they were going to Paris. This general eagerness gave him likewise a great desire to see this capital; and it was not much out of his way to Venice.

He entered the city by the suburbs of St. Marceau, and thought himself in one of the vilest hamlets in all Westphalia.

Candide had not been long at his inn, before he was seized with a slight disorder, owing to the fatigue he had undergone. As he wore a diamond of an enormous size on his finger and had among the rest of his equipage a strong box that seemed very weighty, he soon found himself between two physicians, whom he had not sent for, a number of intimate friends whom he had never seen, and who would not quit his bedside, and two women devotees, who were very careful in providing him hot broths.

"I remember," said Martin to him, "that the first time I came to Paris I was likewise taken ill; I was very poor, and accordingly I had neither friends, nurses, nor physicians, and yet I did very well."

However, by dint of purging and bleeding, Candide's disorder became very serious. The priest of the parish came with all imaginable politeness to desire a note of him, payable to the bearer in the other world. Candide refused to comply with his request; but the two devotees assured him that it was a new fashion. Candide replied, that he was not one that followed the fashion. Martin was for throwing the priest out of the window. The clerk swore Candide should not have Christian burial. Martin swore in his turn that he would bury the clerk alive if he continued to plague them any longer. The dispute grew warm; Martin took him by the shoulders and turned him out of the room, which gave great scandal, and occasioned a *procès-verbal*.

Candide recovered, and till he was in a condition to go abroad had a great deal of good company to pass the evenings with him in his chamber. They played deep. Candide was surprised to find he could never turn a trick; and Martin was not at all surprised at the matter.

Among those who did him the honors of the place was a little spruce abbé of Périgord, one of those insinuating, busy, fawning, impudent, necessary fellows, that lay wait for strangers on their arrival, tell them all the scandal of the town, and offer to minister to their pleasures at various prices. This man conducted Candide and Martin to the playhouse; they were acting a new tragedy. Candide found himself placed near a cluster of wits: this, however, did not prevent him from shedding tears at some parts of the piece which were most affecting, and best acted. One of these talkers said to him between the acts. "You are greatly to blame to shed tears; that actress plays horribly, and the man that plays with her still worse, and the piece itself is still more execrable than the representation. The author does not understand a word of Arabic, and yet he has laid his scene in Arabia, and what is more, he is a fellow who does not believe in innate ideas. To-morrow I will bring you a score of pamphlets that have been written against him." "Pray, sir," said Candide to the abbé, "how many theatrical pieces have you in France?" "Five or six thousand," replied the abbé. "Indeed! that is a great number," said Candide, "but how many good ones may there be?" "About fifteen or sixteen." "Oh! that is a great number," said Martin.

Candide was greatly taken with an actress, who performed the part of Queen Elizabeth in a dull kind of tragedy that is played sometimes. "That actress," said he to Martin, "pleases me greatly; she has some sort of resemblance to Miss Cunegund. I should be very glad to pay my respects to her." The abbé of Perigord offered his service to introduce him to her at her own house. Candide, who was brought up in Germany, desired to know what might be the ceremonial used on those occasions, and how a queen of England was treated in France. "There is a necessary distinction to be observed in these matters," said the abbé. "In a country town we take them to a tavern; here in Paris, they are treated with great respect during their life time, provided they are handsome, and when they die we throw their bodies upon a dunghill." "How?" said Candide, "throw a queen's body upon a dunghill!" "The gentleman is quite right," said Martin, "he tells you nothing but the truth. I happened to be at Paris when Miss Monimia made her exit, as one may say, out of this world into another. She was refused what they call here the rites of sepulture; that is to say, she was denied the privilege of rotting in a churchyard by the side of all the beggars in the parish. They buried her at the corner of Burgundy street, which must certainly have shocked her extremely, as she had very exalted notions of things." "This is acting very impolitely," said Candide. "Lord!" said Martin, "what can be said to it? it is the way of these people. Figure to yourself all the contradictions, all the inconsistencies possible, and you may meet with them in the government, the courts of justice, the churches, and the public spectacles of this odd nation." "Is it true," said Candide, "that the people of Paris are always laughing?" "Yes," replied the abbé, "but it is with anger in their hearts; they express all their complaints by loud bursts of laughter, and commit the most detestable crimes with a smile on their faces."

"Who was that great overgrown beast," said Candide, "who spoke so ill to me of the piece with which I was so much affected, and of the players who gave me so much pleasure?" "A very good-for-nothing sort of a man I assure you," answered the abbé, "one who gets his livelihood by abusing every new book and play that is written or performed; he dislikes much to see any one meet with success, like eunuchs, who detest every one that possesses those powers they are deprived of; he is one of those vipers in literature who nourish themselves with their own venom; a pamphlet-monger." "A pamphlet-monger!" said Candide, "what is that?" "Why, a pamphlet-monger," replied the abbé, "is a writer of pamphlets—a fool."

Candide, Martin, and the abbé of Périgord argued thus on the staircase, while they stood to see the people go out of the playhouse. "Though I am very anxious to see Miss Cunegund again," said Candide, "yet I have a great inclination to sup with Miss Clairon, for I am really much taken with her."

The abbé was not a person to show his face at this lady's house, which was frequented by none but the best company. "She is engaged this evening," said he, "but I will do myself the honor to introduce you to a lady of quality of my acquaintance, at whose house you will see as much of the manners of Paris as if you had lived here for forty years."

Candide, who was naturally curious, suffered himself to be conducted to this lady's house, which was in the suburbs of St. Honoré. The company was engaged at basset; twelve melancholy punters held each in his hand a small pack of cards, the corners of which were doubled down, and were so many registers of their ill fortune. A profound silence reigned throughout the assembly, a pallid dread had taken possession of the countenances of the punters, and restless inquietude stretched every muscle of the face of him who kept the bank; and the lady of the house, who was seated next to him, observed with lynx's eyes every play made, and noted those who tallied, and made them undouble their cards with a severe exactness, though mixed with a politeness, which she thought necessary not to frighten away her customers. This lady assumed the title of marchioness of Parolignac. Her daughter, a girl of about fifteen years of age, was one of the punters, and took care to give her mamma a hint, by signs, when any one of the players attempted to repair the rigor of their ill fortune by a little innocent deception. The company were thus occupied when Candide, Martin, and the abbé made their entrance; not a creature rose to salute them, or indeed took the least notice of them, being wholly intent upon the business in hand. "Ah!" said Candide, "my lady baroness of Thunder-ten-tronckh would have behaved more civilly."

However, the abbé whispered in the ear of the marchioness, who half raising herself from her seat, honored Candide with a gracious smile, and gave Martin a nod of her head, with an air of inexpressible dignity. She then ordered a seat for Candide, and desired him to make one of their party at play; he did so, and in a few deals lost near a thousand pieces; after which they supped very elegantly, and every one was surprised at seeing Candide lose so much money without appearing to be the least disturbed at it. The servants in waiting said to each other, "This is certainly some English lord."

The supper was like most others of its kind in Paris. At first every one was silent; then followed a few confused murmurs, and afterwards several insipid jokes passed and repassed, with false reports, false reasonings, a little politics, and a great deal of scandal. The conversation then turned upon the new productions in literature. "Pray," said the abbé, "good folks, have you seen the romance written by the Sieur Gauchat, doctor of divinity?" "Yes," answered one of the company, "but I had not patience to go through it. The town is pestered with a swarm of impertinent productions, but this of Dr. Gauchat's outdoes them all. In short, I was so cursedly tired of reading this vile stuff that I even resolved to come here, and make a party at basset." "But what say you to the archdeacon T——'s miscellaneous collection," said the abbé. "Oh my God!" cried the marchioness of Parolignac, "never mention the tedious creature! only think what pains he is at to tell one things that all the world knows; and how he labors an argument that is hardly worth the slightest consideration! how absurdly he makes use of other people's wit! how miserably he mangles what he has pilfered from them! The man makes me quite sick! A few pages of the good archdeacon are enough in conscience to satisfy any one."

There was at the table a person of learning and taste, who supported what the marchioness had advanced. They next began to talk of tragedies. The lady desired to know how it came about that there were several tragedies, which still continued to be played, though they would not bear reading? The man of taste explained very clearly how a piece may be in some manner interesting without having a grain of merit. He showed, in a few words, that it is not sufficient to throw together a few incidents that are to be met with in every romance, and that to dazzle the spectator the thoughts should be new, without being far-fetched; frequently sublime, but always natural; the author should have a thorough knowledge of the human heart and make it speak properly; he should be a complete poet, without showing an affectation of it in any of the characters of his piece; he should be a perfect master of his language, speak it with all its purity, and with the utmost harmony, and yet so as not to make the sense a slave to the rhyme. "Whoever," added he, "neglects any one of these rules, though he may write two or three tragedies with tolerable success, will never be reckoned in the number of good authors. There are very few good tragedies; some are idyls, in very well-written and harmonious dialogue; and others a chain of political reasonings that set one asleep, or else pompous and high-flown amplifications, that disgust rather than please. Others again are the ravings of a madman, in an uncouth style, unmeaning flights, or long apostrophes to the deities, for want of knowing how to address mankind; in a word a collection of false maxims and dull commonplace."

Candide listened to this discourse with great attention, and conceived a high opinion of the person who delivered it; and as the marchioness had taken care to place him near her side, he took the liberty to whisper her softly in the ear and ask who this person was that spoke so well. "He is a man of letters," replied her ladyship, "who never plays, and whom the abbé brings with him to my house sometimes to spend an evening. He is a great judge of writing, especially in tragedy; he has composed one himself, which was damned, and has written a book that was never seen out of his bookseller's shop, excepting only one copy, which he sent me with a dedication, to which he had prefixed my name." "Oh the great man," cried Candide, "he is a second Pangloss."

Then turning towards him, "Sir," said he, "you are doubtless of opinion that everything is for the best in the physical and moral world, and that nothing could be otherwise than it is?" "I, sir!" replied the man of letters, "I think no such thing, I assure you; I find that all in this world is set the wrong end uppermost. No one knows what is his rank, his office, nor what he does, nor what he should do. With the exception of our evenings, which we generally pass tolerably merrily, the rest of our time is spent in idle disputes and quarrels, Jansenists against Molinists, the parliament against the Church, and one armed body of men against another; courtier against courtier, husband against wife, and relations against relations. In short, this world is nothing but one continued scene of civil war."

"Yes," said Candide, "and I have seen worse than all that; and yet a learned man, who had the misfortune to be hanged, taught me that everything was marvellously well, and that these evils you are speaking of were only so many shades in a beautiful picture." "Your hempen sage," said Martin, "laughed at you; these shades, as you call them, are most horrible blemishes." "The men make these blemishes," rejoined Candide, "and they cannot do otherwise." "Then it is not their fault," added Martin. The greatest part of the gamesters, who did not understand a syllable of this discourse, amused themselves with drinking, while Martin reasoned with the learned gentleman; and Candide entertained the lady of the house with a part of his adventures.

After supper the marchioness conducted Candide into her dressing-room, and made him sit down under a canopy. "Well," said she, "are you still so violently fond of Miss Cunegund of Thunder-ten-tronckh?" "Yes, madam," replied Candide. The marchioness said to him with a tender smile, "You answer me like a young man born in Westphalia; a Frenchman would have said, 'It is true, madam, I had a great passion for Miss Cunegund; but since I have seen you, I fear I can no longer love her as I did.' " "Alas! madam," replied Candide, "I will make you what answer you please." "You fell in love with her, I find, in stooping to pick up her handkerchief which she had dropped; you shall pick up my garter." "With all my heart, madam," said Candide, and he picked it up. "But you must tie it on again," said the lady. Candide tied it on again. "Look ye, young man," said the marchioness, "you are a stranger; I make some of my lovers here in Paris languish for me a whole fortnight; but I surrender to you at first sight, because I am willing to do the honors of my country to a young Westphalian." The fair one having cast her eye on two very large diamonds that were upon the young stranger's finger, praised them in so earnest a manner that they were in an instant transferred from his finger to hers.

As Candide was going home with the abbé he felt some qualms of conscience for having been guilty of infidelity to Miss Cunegund. The abbé took part with him in his uneasiness; he had but an inconsiderable share in the thousand pieces Candide had lost at play, and the two diamonds which had been in a manner extorted from him; and therefore very prudently designed to make the most he could of his new acquaintance, which chance had thrown in his way. He talked much of Miss Cunegund, and Candide assured him that he would heartily ask pardon of that fair one for his infidelity to her, when he saw her at Venice.

The abbé redoubled his civilities and seemed to interest himself warmly in everything that Candide said, did, or seemed inclined to do.

"And so, sir, you have an engagement at Venice?" "Yes, Monsieur l'Abbé," answered Candide, "I must absolutely wait upon Miss Cunegund;" and then the pleasure he took in talking about the object he loved, led him insensibly to relate, according to custom, part of his adventures with that illustrious Westphalian beauty.

"I fancy," said the abbé, "Miss Cunegund has a great deal of wit, and that her letters must be very entertaining." "I never received any from her," said Candide; "for you are to consider that, being expelled from the castle upon her account, I could not write to her, especially as soon after my departure I heard she was dead; but thank God I found afterwards she was living. I left her again after this, and now I have sent a messenger to her near two thousand leagues from here, and wait here for his return with an answer from her."

The artful abbé let not a word of all this escape him, though he seemed to be musing upon something else. He soon took his leave of the two adventurers, after having embraced them with the greatest cordiality. The next morning, almost as soon as his eyes were open, Candide received the following billet:

"My Dearest Lover—I have been ill in this city these eight days. I have heard of your arrival, and should fly to your arms were I able to stir. I was informed of your being on the way hither at Bordeaux, where I left the faithful Cacambo, and the old woman, who will soon follow me. The governor of Buenos Ayres has taken everything from me but your heart, which I still retain. Come to me immediately on the receipt of this. Your presence will either give me new life, or kill me with the pleasure."

At the receipt of this charming, this unexpected letter, Candide felt the utmost transports of joy; though, on the other hand, the indisposition of his beloved Miss Cunegund overwhelmed him with grief. Distracted between these two passions he took his gold and his diamonds, and procured a person to conduct him and Martin to the house where Miss Cunegund lodged. Upon entering the room he felt his limbs tremble, his heart flutter, his tongue falter; he attempted to undraw the curtain, and called for a light to the bedside. "Lord, sir," cried a maid servant, who was waiting in the room, "take care what you do, Miss cannot bear the least light," and so saying she pulled the curtain close again. "Cunegund! my dear Cunegund!" cried Candide, bathed in tears, "how do you do? If you cannot bear the light, speak to me at least." "Alas! she cannot speak," said the maid. The sick lady then put a plump hand out of the bed and Candide first bathed it with tears, then filled it with diamonds, leaving a purse of gold upon the easy chair.

In the midst of his transports came an officer into the room, followed by the abbé, and a file of musketeers. "There," said he, "are the two suspected foreigners"; at the same time he ordered them to be seized and carried to prison. "Travellers are not treated in this manner in the country of El Dorado," said Candide. "I am more of a Manichæan now than ever," said Martin. "But pray, good sir, where are you going to carry us?" said Candide. "To a dungeon, my dear sir," replied the officer.

When Martin had a little recovered himself, so as to form a cool judgment of what had passed, he plainly perceived that the person who had acted the part of Miss Cunegund was a cheat; that the abbé of Périgord was a sharper who had imposed upon the honest simplicity of Candide, and that the officer was a knave, whom they might easily get rid of.

Candide following the advice of his friend Martin, and burning with impatience to see the real Miss Cunegund, rather than be obliged to appear at a court of justice, proposed to the officer to make him a present of three small diamonds, each of them worth three thousand pistoles. "Ah, sir," said this understrapper of justice, "had you committed ever so much villainy, this would render you the honestest man living, in my eyes. Three diamonds worth three thousand pistoles! why, my dear sir, so far from carrying you to jail, I would lose my life to serve you. There are orders for stopping all strangers; but leave it to me, I have a brother at Dieppe, in Normandy; I myself will conduct you thither, and if you have a diamond left to give him he will take as much care of you as I myself should."

"But why," said Candide, "do they stop all strangers?" The abbé of Périgord made answer that it was because a poor devil of the country of Atrebata heard somebody tell foolish stories, and this induced him to commit a parricide; not such a one as that in the month of May, 1610, but such as that in the month of December, in the year 1594, and such as many that have been perpetrated in other months and years, by other poor devils who had heard foolish stories.

The officer then explained to them what the abbé meant. "Horrid monsters," exclaimed Candide, "is it possible that such scenes should pass among a people who are perpetually singing and dancing? Is there no flying this abominable country immediately, this execrable kingdom where monkeys provoke tigers? I have seen bears in my country, but men I have beheld nowhere but in El Dorado. In the name of God, sir," said he to the officer, "do me the kindness to conduct me to Venice, where I am to wait for Miss Cunegund." "Really, sir," replied the officer, "I cannot possibly wait on you farther than Lower Normandy." So saying, he ordered Candide's irons to be struck off, acknowledged himself mistaken, and sent his followers about their business, after which he conducted Candide and Martin to Dieppe, and left them to the care of his brother. There happened just then to be a small Dutch ship in the harbor. The Norman, whom the other three diamonds had converted into the most obliging, serviceable being that ever breathed, took care to see Candide and his attendants safe on board this vessel, that was just ready to sail for Portsmouth in England. This was not the nearest way to Venice, indeed, but Candide thought himself escaped out of hell, and did not, in the least, doubt but he should quickly find an opportunity of resuming his voyage to Venice.

Chapter XXIII

*Candide and Martin Touch Upon the English Coast
—What They See There*

"Ah Pangloss! Pangloss! ah Martin! Martin! ah my dear Miss Cunegund! what sort of a world is this?" Thus exclaimed Candide as soon as he got on board the Dutch ship. "Why something very foolish, and very abominable," said Martin. "You are acquainted with England," said Candide; "are they as great fools in that country as in France?" "Yes, but in a different manner," answered Martin. "You know that these two nations are at war about a few acres of barren land in the neighborhood of Canada, and that they have expended much greater sums in the contest than all Canada is worth. To say exactly whether there are a greater number fit to be inhabitants of a madhouse in the one country than the other, exceeds the limits of my imperfect capacity; I know in general that the people we are going to visit are of a very dark and gloomy disposition."

As they were chatting thus together they arrived at Portsmouth. The shore on each side of the harbor was lined with a multitude of people, whose eyes were steadfastly fixed on a lusty man who was kneeling down on the deck of one of the men-of-war, with something tied before his eyes. Opposite to this personage stood four soldiers, each of whom shot three bullets into his skull, with all the composure imaginable; and when it was done, the whole company went away perfectly well satisfied. "What the devil is all this for?" said Candide, "and what demon, or foe of mankind, lords it thus tyrannically over the world?" He then asked who was that lusty man who had been sent out of the world with so much ceremony. When he received for answer, that it was an admiral. "And pray why do you put your admiral to death?" "Because he did not put a sufficient number of his fellow-creatures to death. You must know, he had an engagement with a French admiral, and it has been proved against him that he was not near enough to his antagonist." "But," replied Candide, "the French admiral must have been as far from him." "There is no doubt of that; but in this country it is found requisite, now and then, to put an admiral to death, in order to encourage the others to fight."

Candide was so shocked at what he saw and heard, that he would not set foot on shore, but made a bargain with the Dutch skipper (were he even to rob him like the captain of Surinam) to carry him directly to Venice.

The skipper was ready in two days. They sailed along the coast of France, and passed within sight of Lisbon, at which Candide trembled. From thence they proceeded to the Straits, entered the Mediterranean, and at length arrived at Venice. "God be praised," said Candide, embracing Martin, "this is the place where I am to behold my beloved Cunegund once again. I can confide in Cacambo, like another self. All is well, all very well, all as well as possible."

Chapter XXIV

Of Pacquette and Friar Giroflée

Upon their arrival at Venice Candide went in search of Cacambo at every inn and coffee-house, and among all the ladies of pleasure, but could hear nothing of him. He sent every day to inquire what ships were in, still no news of Cacambo. "It is strange," said he to Martin, "very strange that I should have had time to sail from Surinam to Bordeaux; to travel thence to Paris, to Dieppe, to Portsmouth; to sail along the coast of Portugal and Spain, and up the Mediterranean to spend some months at Venice; and that my lovely Cunegund should not have arrived. Instead of her, I only met with a Parisian impostor, and a rascally abbé of Périgord. Cunegund is actually dead, and I have nothing to do but follow her. Alas! how much better would it have been for me to have remained in the paradise of El Dorado than to have returned to this cursed Europe! You are in the right, my dear Martin; you are certainly in the right; all is misery and deceit."

He fell into a deep melancholy, and neither went to the opera then in vogue, nor partook of any of the diversions of the carnival; nay, he even slighted the fair sex. Martin said to him, "Upon my word, I think you are very simple to imagine that a rascally valet, with five or six millions in his pocket, would go in search of your mistress to the further end of the world, and bring her to Venice to meet you. If he finds her he will take her for himself; if he does not, he will take another. Let me advise you to forget your valet Cacambo, and your Mistress Cunegund." Martin's speech was not the most consolatory to the dejected Candide. His melancholy increased, and Martin never ceased trying to prove to him that there is very little virtue or happiness in this world; except, perhaps, in El Dorado, where hardly anybody can gain admittance.

While they were disputing on this important subject, and still expecting Miss Cunegund, Candide perceived a young Theatin friar in St. Mark's Place, with a girl under his arm. The Theatin looked fresh-colored, plump, and vigorous; his eyes sparkled; his air and gait were bold and lofty. The girl was pretty, and was singing a song; and every now and then gave her Theatin an amorous ogle and wantonly pinched his ruddy cheeks. "You will at least allow," said Candide to Martin, "that these two are happy. Hitherto I have met with none but unfortunate people in the whole habitable globe, except in El Dorado; but as to this couple, I would venture to lay a wager they are happy." "Done!" said Martin, "they are not what you imagine." "Well, we have only to ask them to dine with us," said Candide, "and you will see whether I am mistaken or not."

Thereupon he accosted them, and with great politeness invited them to his inn to eat some macaroni, with Lombard partridges and caviare, and to drink a bottle of Montepulciano, Lacryma Christi, Cyprus, and Samos wine. The girl blushed; the Theatin accepted the invitation and she followed him, eyeing Candide every now and then with a mixture of surprise and confusion, while the tears stole down her cheeks. No sooner did she enter his apartment than she cried out. "How, Mr. Candide, have you quite forgot your Pacquette? do you not know her again?" Candide had not regarded her with any degree of attention before, being wholly occupied with the thoughts of his dear Cunegund. "Ah! is it you, child? was it you that reduced Doctor Pangloss to that fine condition I saw him in?"

"Alas! sir," answered Pacquette, "it was I, indeed. I find you are acquainted with everything; and I have been informed of all the misfortunes that happened to the whole family of my lady baroness and the fair Cunegund. But I can safely swear to you that my lot was no less deplorable; I was innocence itself when you saw me last. A cordelier, who was my confessor, easily seduced me; the consequences proved terrible. I was obliged to leave the castle some time after the baron kicked you out from there; and if a famous surgeon had not taken compassion on me, I had been a dead woman. Gratitude obliged me to live with him some time as a mistress; his wife, who was a very devil for jealousy, beat me unmercifully every day. Oh! she was a perfect fury. The doctor himself was the most ugly of all mortals, and I the most wretched creature existing, to be continually beaten for a man whom I did not love. You are sensible, sir, how dangerous it was for an ill-natured woman to be married to a physician. Incensed at the behavior of his wife, he one day gave her so affectionate a remedy for a slight cold she had caught that she died in less than two hours in most dreadful convulsions. Her relations prosecuted the husband, who was obliged to fly, and I was sent to prison. My innocence would not have saved me, if I had not been tolerably handsome. The judge gave me my liberty on condition he should succeed the doctor. However, I was soon supplanted by a rival, turned off without a farthing, and obliged to continue the abominable trade which you men think so pleasing, but which to us unhappy creatures is the most dreadful of all sufferings. At length I came to follow the business at Venice. Ah! sir, did you but know what it is to be obliged to receive every visitor; old tradesmen, counsellors, monks, watermen, and abbés; to be exposed to all their insolence and abuse; to be often necessitated to borrow a petticoat, only that it may be taken up by some disagreeable wretch; to be robbed by one gallant of what we get from another; to be subject to the extortions of civil magistrates; and to have forever before one's eyes the prospect of old age, a hospital, or a dunghill, you would conclude that I am one of the most unhappy wretches breathing."

Thus did Pacquette unbosom herself to honest Candide in his closet, in the presence of Martin, who took occasion to say to him, "You see I have half won the wager already."

Friar Giroflée was all this time in the parlor refreshing himself with a glass or two of wine till dinner was ready. "But," said Candide to Pacquette, "you looked so gay and contented, when I met you, you sang and caressed the Theatin with so much fondness, that I absolutely thought you as happy as you say you are now miserable." "Ah! dear sir," said Pacquette, "this is one of the miseries of the trade; yesterday I was stripped and beaten by an officer; yet to-day I must appear good-humored and gay to please a friar."

Candide was convinced and acknowledged that Martin was in the right. They sat down to table with Pacquette and the Theatin; the entertainment was agreeable, and towards the end they began to converse together with some freedom. "Father," said Candide to the friar, "you seem to me to enjoy a state of happiness that even kings might envy; joy and health are painted in your countenance. You have a pretty wench to divert you; and you seem to be perfectly well contented with your condition as a Theatin."

"Faith, sir," said Friar Giroflée, "I wish with all my soul the Theatins were every one of them at the bottom of the sea. I have been tempted a thousand times to set fire to the convent and go and turn Turk. My parents obliged me, at the age of fifteen, to put on this detestable habit only to increase the fortune of an elder-brother of mine, whom God confound! Jealousy, discord, and fury, reside in our convent. It is true I have preached often paltry sermons, by which I have got a little money, part of which the prior robs me of, and the remainder helps to pay my girls; but, at night, when I go hence to my convent, I am ready to dash my brains against the walls of the dormitory; and this is the case with all the rest of our fraternity."

Martin, turning towards Candide, with his usual indifference, said, "Well, what think you now? have I won the wager entirely?" Candide gave two thousand piastres to Pacquette, and a thousand to Friar Giroflée, saying, "I will answer that this will make them happy." "I am not of your opinion," said Martin, "perhaps this money will only make them wretched." "Be that as it may," said

Candide, "one thing comforts me; I see that one often meets with those whom one never expected to see again; so that, perhaps, as I have found my red sheep and Pacquette, I may be lucky enough to find Miss Cunegund also." "I wish," said Martin, "she one day may make you happy; but I doubt it much." "You lack faith," said Candide. "It is because," said Martin, "I have seen the world."

"Observe those gondoliers," said Candide, "are they not perpetually singing?" You do not see them," answered Martin, "at home with their wives and brats. The doge has his chagrin, gondoliers theirs. Nevertheless, in the main, I look upon the gondolier's life as preferable to that of the doge; but the difference is so trifling that it is not worth the trouble of examining into."

"I have heard great talk," said Candide, "of the Senator Pococuranté, who lives in that fine house at the Brenta, where, they say, he entertains foreigners in the most polite manner." "They pretend this man is a perfect stranger to uneasiness. I should be glad to see so extraordinary a being," said Martin. Candide thereupon sent a messenger to Seignor Pococuranté, desiring permission to wait on him the next day.

Chapter XXV

Candide and Martin Pay a Visit to Seignor Pococuranté, a Noble Venetian

Candide and his friend Martin went in a gondola on the Brenta, and arrived at the palace of the noble Pococuranté. The gardens were laid out in elegant taste, and adorned with fine marble statues; his palace was built after the most approved rules of architecture. The master of the house, who was a man of affairs, and very rich, received our two travellers with great politeness, but without much ceremony, which somewhat disconcerted Candide, but was not at all displeasing to Martin.

As soon as they were seated, two very pretty girls, neatly dressed, brought in chocolate, which was extremely well prepared. Candide could not help making encomiums upon their beauty and graceful carriage. "The creatures are well enough," said the senator; "I amuse myself with them sometimes, for I am heartily tired of the women of the town, their coquetry, their jealousy, their quarrels, their humors, their meannesses, their pride, and their folly; I am weary of making sonnets, or of paying for sonnets to be made on them; but after all, these two girls begin to grow very indifferent to me."

After having refreshed himself, Candide walked into a large gallery, where he was struck with the sight of a fine collection of paintings. "Pray," said Candide, "by what master are the two first of these?" "They are by Raphael," answered the senator. "I gave a great deal of money for them seven years ago, purely out of curiosity, as they were said to be the finest pieces in Italy; but I cannot say they please me: the coloring is dark and heavy; the figures do not swell nor come out enough; and the drapery is bad. In short, notwithstanding the encomiums lavished upon them, they are not, in my opinion, a true representation of nature. I approve of no paintings save those wherein I think I behold nature herself; and there are few, if any, of that kind to be met with. I have what is called a fine collection, but I take no manner of delight in it."

While dinner was being prepared Pococuranté ordered a concert. Candide praised the music to the skies. "This noise," said the noble Venetian, "may amuse one for a little time, but if it were to last above half an hour, it would grow tiresome to everybody, though perhaps no one would care to own it. Music has become the art of executing what is difficult; now, whatever is difficult cannot be long pleasing.

"I believe I might take more pleasure in an opera, if they had not made such a monster of that species of dramatic entertainment as perfectly shocks me; and I am amazed how people can bear to see wretched tragedies set to music; where the scenes are contrived for no other purpose than to lug in, as it were by the ears, three or four ridiculous songs, to give a favorite actress an opportunity of exhibiting her pipe. Let who will die away in raptures at the trills of a eunuch quavering the majestic part of Cæsar or Cato, and strutting in a foolish manner upon the stage, but for my part I have long ago renounced these paltry enter- tainments, which constitute the glory of modern Italy, and are so dearly purchased by crowned heads." Candide opposed these sentiments; but he did it in a discreet manner; as for Martin, he was entirely of the old senator's opinion.

Dinner being served they sat down to table, and, after a hearty repast, returned to the library. Candide, observing Homer richly bound, commended the noble Venetian's taste. "This," said he, "is a book that was once the delight of the great Pangloss, the best philosopher in Germany." "Homer is no favorite of mine," answered Pococuranté, coolly; "I was made to believe once that I took a pleasure in reading him; but his continual repetitions of battles have all such a resemblance with each other; his gods that are forever in haste and bustle, without ever doing anything; his Helen, who is the cause of the war, and yet hardly acts in the whole performance; his Troy, that holds out so long, without being taken: in short, all these things together make the poem very insipid to me. I have asked some learned men, whether they are not in reality as much tired as myself with reading this poet: those who spoke ingenuously, assured me that he had made them fall asleep, and yet that they could not well avoid giving him a place in their libraries; but that it was merely as they would do an antique, or those rusty medals which are kept only for curiosity, and are of no manner of use in commerce."

"But your excellency does not surely form the same opinion of Virgil?" said Candide. "Why, I grant," replied Pococuranté, "that the second, third, fourth, and sixth books of his Æneid are excellent; but as for his pious Æneas, his strong Cloanthus, his friendly Achates, his boy Ascanius, his silly king Latinus, his ill-bred Amata, his insipid Lavinia, and some other characters much in the same strain, I think there cannot in nature be anything more flat and disagreeable. I must confess I prefer Tasso far beyond him; nay, even that sleepy taleteller Ariosto."

"May I take the liberty to ask if you do not experience great pleasure from reading Horace?" said Candide. "There are maxims in this writer," replied

Pococuranté, "whence a man of the world may reap some benefit; and the short measure of the verse makes them more easily to be retained in the memory. But I see nothing extraordinary in his journey to Brundusium, and his account of his bad dinner; nor in his dirty, low quarrel between one Rupillius, whose words, as he expresses it, were full of poisonous filth; and another, whose language was dipped in vinegar. His indelicate verses against old women and witches have frequently given me great offence: nor can I discover the great merit of his telling his friend Mæcenas, that if he will but rank him in the class of lyric poets, his lofty head shall touch the stars. Ignorant readers are apt to judge a writer by his reputation. For my part, I read only to please myself. I like nothing but what makes for my purpose." Candide, who had been brought up with a notion of never making use of his own judgment, was astonished at what he heard; but Martin found there was a good deal of reason in the senator's remarks.

"O ! here is a Tully," said Candide; "this great man I fancy you are never tired of reading?" "Indeed I never read him at all," replied Pococuranté. "What is it to me whether he pleads for Rabirius or Cluentius? I try causes enough myself. I had once some liking for his philosophical works; but when I found he doubted everything, I thought I knew as much as himself, and had no need of a guide to learn ignorance."

"Ha!" cried Martin, "here are fourscore volumes of the memoirs of the Academy of Sciences; perhaps there may be something curious and valuable in this collection." "Yes," answered Pococuranté; "so there might if any one of these compilers of this rubbish had only invented the art of pin-making: but all these volumes are filled with mere chimerical systems, without one single article conducive to real utility."

"I see a prodigious number of plays," said Candide, "in Italian, Spanish, and French." "Yes," replied the Venetian; "there are I think three thousand, and not three dozen of them good for anything. As to those huge volumes of divinity, and those enormous collections of sermons, they are not all together worth one single page in Seneca; and I fancy you will readily believe that neither myself, nor anyone else, ever looks into them."

Martin, perceiving some shelves filled with English books, said to the senator: "I fancy that a republican must be highly delighted with those books, which are most of them written with a noble spirit of freedom." "It is noble to write as we think," said Pococuranté; "it is the privilege of humanity. Throughout Italy we write only what we do not think; and the present inhabitants of the country of the Cæsars and Antonines dare not acquire a single idea without the permission of a Dominican father. I should be enamored of the spirit of the English nation, did it not utterly frustrate the good effects it would produce by passion and the spirit of party."

Candide, seeing a Milton, asked the senator if he did not think that author a great man. "Who?" said Pococuranté sharply; "that barbarian who writes a tedious commentary in ten books of rumbling verse, on the first chapter of Genesis? that slovenly imitator of the Greeks, who disfigures the creation, by making the Messiah take a pair of compasses from heaven's armory to plan the world; whereas Moses represented the Deity as producing the whole universe by his *fiat?* Can I think you have any esteem for a writer who has spoiled Tasso's hell and the devil; who transforms Lucifer sometimes into a toad, and at others into a pygmy; who makes him say the same thing over again a hundred times; who metamorphoses him into a school-divine; and who, by an absurdly serious imitation of Ariosto's comic invention of firearms, represents the devils and angels cannonading each other in heaven? Neither I nor any other Italian can possibly take pleasure in such melancholy reveries; but the marriage of Sin and Death, and snakes issuing from the womb of the former, are enough to make any person sick that is not lost to all sense of delicacy. This obscene, whimsical, and disagreeable poem met with the neglect it deserved at its first publication; and I only treat the author now as he was treated in his own country by his contemporaries."

Candide was sensibly grieved at this speech, as he had a great respect for Homer, and was fond of Milton. "Alas!" said he softly to Martin, "I am afraid this man holds our German poets in great contempt." "There would be no such great harm in that," said Martin. "O what a surprising man!" said Candide, still to himself; "what a prodigious genius is this Pococuranté! nothing can please him."

After finishing their survey of the library, they went down into the garden, when Candide commended the several beauties that offered themselves to his view. "I know nothing upon earth laid out in such bad taste," said Pococuranté; "everything about it is childish and trifling; but I shall have another laid out to-morrow upon a nobler plan."

As soon as our two travellers had taken leave of his excellency, "Well," said Candide to Martin, "I hope you will own that this man is the happiest of all mortals, for he is above everything he possesses." "But do not you see," answered Martin, "that he likewise dislikes everything he possesses? It was an observation of Plato, long since, that those are not the best stomachs that reject, without distinction, all sorts of aliments." "True," said Candide, "but still there must certainly be a pleasure in criticising everything, and in perceiving faults where others think they see beauties." "That is," replied Martin, "there is a pleasure in having no pleasure." "Well, well," said Candide, "I find that I shall be the only happy man at last, when I am blessed with the sight of my dear Cunegund." "It is good to hope," said Martin.

In the meanwhile, days and weeks passed away, and no news of Cacambo. Candide was so overwhelmed with grief, that he did not reflect on the behavior of Pacquette and Friar Giroflée, who never stayed to return him thanks for the presents he had so generously made them.

Chapter XXVI

Candide and Martin Sup with Six Sharpers—Who They Were

One evening as Candide, with his attendant Martin, was going to sit down to supper with some foreigners who lodged in the same inn where they had taken up their quarters, a man with a face the color of soot came behind him, and taking him by the arm, said, "Hold yourself in readiness to go along with us; be sure you do not fail." Upon this, turning about to see from whom these words came, he beheld Cacambo. Nothing but the sight of Miss Cunegund could have given him greater joy and surprise. He was almost beside himself. After embracing this dear friend, "Cunegund!" said he, "Cunegund is come with you doubtless! Where, where is she? Carry me to her this instant, that I may die with joy in her presence." "Cunegund is not here," answered Cacambo; "she is in Constantinople." "Good heavens! in Constantinople! but no matter if she were in China, I would fly thither. Quick, quick, dear Cacambo, let us be gone." "Soft and fair," said Cacambo, "stay till you have supped. I cannot at present stay to say anything more to you; I am a slave, and my master waits for me; I must go and attend him at table: but mum! say not a word, only get your supper, and hold yourself in readiness."

Candide, divided between joy and grief, charmed to have thus met with his faithful agent again, and surprised to hear he was a slave, his heart palpitating, his senses confused, but full of the hopes of recovering his dear Cunegund, sat down to table with Martin, who beheld all these scenes with great unconcern, and with six strangers, who had come to spend the carnival at Venice.

Cacambo waited at table upon one of those strangers. When supper was nearly over, he drew near to his master, and whispered in his ear, "Sire, your majesty may go when you please; the ship is ready"; and so saying he left the room. The guests, surprised at what they had heard, looked at each other without speaking a word; when another servant drawing near to his master, in like manner said, "Sire, your majesty's post-chaise is at Padua, and the bark is ready." The master made him a sign, and he instantly withdrew. The company all stared at each other again, and the general astonishment was increased. A third servant then approached another of the strangers, and said, "Sire, if your majesty will be advised by me, you will not make any longer stay in this place; I will go and get everything ready"; and instantly disappeared.

Candide and Martin then took it for granted that this was some of the diversions of the carnival, and that these were characters in masquerade. Then a fourth domestic said to the fourth stranger, "Your majesty may set off when you please"; saying which, he went away like the rest. A fifth valet said the same to a fifth master. But the sixth domestic spoke in a different style to the person on whom he waited, and who sat near to Candide. "Troth, sir," said he, "they will trust your majesty no longer, nor myself neither; and we may both of us chance to be sent to jail this very night; and therefore I shall take care of myself, and so adieu." The servants being all gone, the six strangers, with Candide and Martin, remained in a profound silence. At length Candide broke it by saying, "Gentlemen, this is a very singular joke upon my word; how came you all to be kings? For my part I own frankly, that neither my friend Martin here, nor myself, have any claim to royalty."

Cacambo's master then began, with great gravity, to deliver himself thus in Italian. "I am not joking in the least, my name is Achmet III. I was grand seignor for many years; I dethroned my brother, my nephew dethroned me, my viziers lost their heads, and I am condemned to end my days in the old seraglio.

My nephew, the Grand Sultan Mahomet, gives me permission to travel sometimes for my health, and I am come to spend the carnival at Venice."

A young man who sat by Achmet, spoke next, and said: "My name is Ivan. I was once emperor of all the Russias, but was dethroned in my cradle. My parents were confined, and I was brought up in a prison, yet I am sometimes allowed to travel, though always with persons to keep a guard over me, and I am come to spend the carnival at Venice."

The third said: "I am Charles Edward, king of England; my father has renounced his right to the throne in my favor. I have fought in defence of my rights, and near a thousand of my friends have had their hearts taken out of their bodies alive and thrown in their faces. I have myself been confined in a prison. I am going to Rome to visit the king my father, who was dethroned as well as myself; and my grandfather and I have come to spend the carnival at Venice."

The fourth spoke thus: "I am the king of Poland; the fortune of war has stripped me of my hereditary dominions. My father experienced the same vicissitudes of fate. I resign myself to the will of Providence, in the same manner as Sultan Achmet, the Emperor Ivan, and King Charles Edward, whom God long preserve; and I have come to spend the carnival at Venice."

The fifth said: "I am king of Poland also. I have twice lost my kingdom; but Providence has given me other dominions, where I have done more good than all the Sarmatian kings put together were ever able to do on the banks of the Vistula; I resign myself likewise to Providence; and have come to spend the carnival at Venice."

It now came to the sixth monarch's turn to speak: "Gentlemen," said he, "I am not so great a prince as the rest of you, it is true, but I am, however, a crowned head. I am Theodore,[6] elected king of Corsica. I have had the title of majesty, and am now hardly treated with common civility. I have coined money, and am not now worth a single ducat. I have had two secretaries, and am now without a valet. I was once seated on a throne, and since that have lain upon a truss of straw, in a common jail in London, and I very much fear I shall meet with the same fate here in Venice, where I came, like your majesties, to divert myself at the carnival."

The other five kings listened to this speech with great attention; it excited their compassion; each of them made the unhappy Theodore a present of twenty sequins, and Candide gave him a diamond, worth just a hundred times that sum. "Who can this private person be," said the five princes to one another, "who is able to give, and has actually given, a hundred times as much as any of us?"

---

6 This remarkable personage, after having lain in the common prison of the king's bench, for a paltry debt, was cleared by an act of parliament, passed for the relief of insolvent debtors; and the schedule of his effects, delivered for the benefit of his creditors, contained his right and pretensions to the crown of Corsica. He died at London in extreme misery, to the reproach of the English nation, which had at one time acknowledged him as a sovereign prince, and their ally.

Just as they rose from table, in came four serene highnesses, who had also been stripped of their territories by the fortune of war, and had come to spend the remainder of the carnival at Venice. Candide took no manner of notice of them; for his thoughts were wholly employed on his voyage to Constantinople, where he intended to go in search of his lovely Miss Cunegund.

Chapter XXVII

Candide's Voyage to Constantinople

The trusty Cacambo had already engaged the captain of the Turkish ship that was to carry Sultan Achmet back to Constantinople, to take Candide and Martin on board. Accordingly they both embarked, after paying their obeisance to his miserable highness. As they were going on board, Candide said to Martin, "You see we supped in company with six dethroned kings, and to one of them I gave charity. Perhaps there may be a great many other princes still more unfortunate. For my part I have lost only a hundred sheep, and am now going to fly to the arms of my charming Miss Cunegund. My dear Martin, I must insist on it, that Pangloss was in the right. All is for the best." "I wish it may be," said Martin. "But this was an odd adventure we met with at Venice. I do not think there ever was an instance before of six dethroned monarchs supping together at a public inn." "This is not more extraordinary," said Martin, "than most of what has happened to us. It is a very common thing for kings to be dethroned; and as for our having the honor to sup with six of them, it is a mere accident, not deserving our attention."

As soon as Candide set his foot on board the vessel, he flew to his old friend and valet Cacambo; and throwing his arms about his neck, embraced him with transports of joy. "Well," said he, "what news of Miss Cunegund? Does she still continue the paragon of beauty? Does she love me still? How does she do? You have, doubtless, purchased a superb palace for her at Constantinople."

"My dear master," replied Cacambo, "Miss Cunegund washes dishes on the banks of the Propontis, in the house of a prince who has very few to wash. She is at present a slave in the family of an ancient sovereign named Ragotsky, whom the grand Turk allows three crowns a day to maintain him in his exile; but the most melancholy circumstance of all is, that she is turned horribly ugly." "Ugly or handsome," said Candide, "I am a man of honor; and, as such, am obliged to love her still. But how could she possibly have been reduced to so abject a condition, when I sent five or six millions to her by you?" "Lord bless me," said Cacambo, "was not I obliged to give two millions to Seignor Don Fernando d'Ibaraa y Fagueora y Mascarenes y Lampourdos y Souza, the governor of Buenos Ayres, for liberty to take Miss Cunegund away with me? and then did not a brave fellow of a pirate gallantly strip us of all the rest? And then did not this same pirate carry us with him to Cape Matapan, to Milo, to Nicaria, to Samos, to Petra, to the Dardanelles, to Marmora, to Scutari? Miss Cunegund and the old woman are now servants to the prince I have told you of; and I myself am slave to the dethroned sultan." "What a chain of shocking accidents!" exclaimed Candide. "But after all, I have still some diamonds left, with which I can easily procure Miss Cunegund's liberty. It is a pity though she is grown so ugly."

Then turning to Martin, "What think you, friend," said he, "whose condition is most to be pitied, the Emperor Achmet's, the Emperor Ivan's, King Charles Edward's, or mine?" "Faith, I cannot resolve your question," said Martin, "unless I had been in the breasts of you all." "Ah!" cried Candide, "was Pangloss here now, he would have known, and satisfied me at once." "I know not," said Martin, "in what balance your Pangloss could have weighed the misfortunes of mankind, and have set a just estimation on their sufferings. All that I pretend to know of the matter is that there are millions of men on the earth, whose conditions are a hundred times more pitiable than those of King Charles Edward, the Emperor Ivan, or Sultan Achmet." "Why, that may be," answered Candide.

In a few days they reached the Bosphorus; and the first thing Candide did was to pay a high ransom for Cacambo: then, without losing time, he and his companions went on board a galley, in order to search for his Cunegund on the banks of the Propontis, notwithstanding she was grown so ugly.

There were two slaves among the crew of the galley, who rowed very ill, and to whose bare backs the master of the vessel frequently applied a lash. Candide, from natural sympathy, looked at these two slaves more attentively than at any of the rest, and drew near them with an eye of pity. Their features, though greatly disfigured, appeared to him to bear a strong resemblance with those of Pangloss and the unhappy baron Jesuit, Miss Cunegund's brother. This idea affected him with grief and compassion: he examined them more attentively than before. "In troth," said he, turning to Martin, "if I had not seen my master Pangloss fairly hanged, and had not myself been unlucky enough to run the baron through the body, I should absolutely think those two rowers were the men."

No sooner had Candide uttered the names of the baron and Pangloss, than the two slaves gave a great cry, ceased rowing, and let fall their oars out of their hands. The master of the vessel, seeing this, ran up to them, and redoubled the discipline of the lash. "Hold, hold," cried Candide, "I will give you what money you shall ask for these two persons." "Good heavens! it is Candide," said one of the men. "Candide!" cried the other. "Do I dream," said Candide, "or am I awake? Am I actually on board this galley? Is this my lord baron, whom I killed? and that my master Pangloss, whom I saw hanged before my face?"

"It is I! it is I!" cried they both together. "What! is this your great philosopher?" said Martin. "My dear sir," said Candide to the master of the galley, "how much do you ask for the ransom of the baron of Thunder-ten-tronckh, who is one of the first barons of the empire, and of Mr. Pangloss, the most profound metaphysician in Germany?" "Why, then, Christian cur," replied the Turkish captain, "since these two dogs of Christian slaves are barons and metaphysicians, who no doubt are of high rank in their own country, thou shalt give me fifty thousand sequins." "You shall have them, sir; carry me back as quick as thought to Constantinople, and you shall receive the money immediately—No! carry me first to Miss Cunegund." The captain, upon Candide's first proposal, had already tacked about, and he made the crew ply their oars so effectually that the vessel flew through the water, quicker than a bird cleaves the air.

Candide bestowed a thousand embraces on the baron and Pangloss. "And so then, my dear baron, I did not kill you? and you, my dear Pangloss, are come to life again after your hanging? But how came you slaves on board a Turkish galley?" "And is it true that my dear sister is in this country?" said the baron. "Yes," said Cacambo. "And do I once again behold my dear Candide?" said Pangloss. Candide presented Martin and Cacambo to them; they embraced each other, and all spoke together. The galley flew like lightning, and soon they were got back to port. Candide instantly sent for a Jew, to whom he sold for fifty thousand sequins a diamond richly worth one hundred thousand, though the fellow swore to him all the time by Father Abraham that he gave him the most he could possibly afford. He no sooner got the money into his hands, than he paid it down for the ransom of the baron and Pangloss. The latter flung himself at the feet of his deliverer, and bathed him with his tears: the former thanked him with a gracious nod, and promised to return him the money the first opportunity. "But is it possible," said he, "that my sister should be in Turkey?" "Nothing is more possible," answered Cacambo, "for she scours the dishes in the house of a Transylvanian prince." Candide sent directly for two Jews, and sold more diamonds to them; and then he set out with his companions in another galley, to deliver Miss Cunegund from slavery.

Chapter XXVIII

What Befell Candide, Cunegund, Pangloss, Martin, Etc.

"Pardon," said Candide to the baron; "once more let me entreat your pardon, reverend father, for running you through the body." "Say no more about it," replied the baron; "I was a little too hasty I must own; but as you seem to be desirous to know by what accident I came to be a slave on board the galley where you saw me, I will inform you. After I had been cured of the wound you gave me, by the college apothecary, I was attacked and carried off by a party of Spanish troops, who clapped me in prison in Buenos Ayres, at the very time my sister was setting out from there. I asked leave to return to Rome, to the general of my order, who appointed me chaplain to the French ambassador at Constantinople. I had not been a week in my new office, when I happened to meet one evening with a young Icoglan, extremely handsome and well made. The weather was very hot; the young man had an inclination to bathe. I took the opportunity to bathe likewise. I did not know it was a crime for a Christian to be found naked in company with a young Turk. A cadi ordered me to receive a hundred blows on the soles of my feet, and sent me to the galleys. I do not believe that there was ever an act of more flagrant injustice. But I would fain know how my sister came to be a scullion to a Transylvanian prince, who has taken refuge among the Turks?"

"But how happens it that I behold you again, my dear Pangloss?" said

Candide. "It is true," answered Pangloss, "you saw me hanged, though I ought properly to have been burned; but you may remember, that it rained extremely hard when they were going to roast me. The storm was so violent that they found it impossible to light the fire; so they hanged me because they could do no better. A surgeon purchased my body, carried it home, and prepared to dissect me. He began by making a crucial incision from my navel to the clavicle. It is impossible for anyone to have been more lamely hanged than I had been. The executioner was a subdeacon, and knew how to burn people very well, but as for hanging, he was a novice at it, being quite out of practice; the cord being wet, and not slipping properly, the noose did not join. In short, I still continued to breathe; the crucial incision made me scream to such a degree, that my surgeon fell flat upon his back; and imagining it was the devil he was dissecting, ran away, and in his fright tumbled down stairs. His wife hearing the noise, flew from the next room, and seeing me stretched upon the table with my crucial incision, was still more terrified than her husband, and fell upon him. When they had a little recovered themselves, I heard her say to her husband, 'My dear, how could you think of dissecting a heretic? Don't you know that the devil is always in them? I'll run directly to a priest to come and drive the evil spirit out.' I trembled from head to foot at hearing her talk in this manner, and exerted what little strength I had left to cry out, 'Have mercy on me!' At length the Portuguese barber took courage, sewed up my wound, and his wife nursed me; and I was upon my legs in a fortnight's time. The barber got me a place to be lackey to a knight of Malta, who was going to Venice; but finding my master had no money to pay me my wages, I entered into the service of a Venetian merchant, and went with him to Constantinople.

"One day I happened to enter a mosque, where I saw no one but an old man and a very pretty young female devotee, who was telling her beads; her neck was quite bare, and in her bosom she had a beautiful nosegay of tulips, roses, anemones, ranunculuses, hyacinths, and auriculas; she let fall her nosegay. I ran immediately to take it up, and presented it to her with a most respectful bow. I was so long in delivering it that the imam began to be angry; and, perceiving I was a Christian, he cried out for help; they carried me before the cadi, who ordered me to receive one hundred bastinadoes, and sent me to the galleys. I was chained in the very galley and to the very same bench with the baron. On board this galley there were four young men belonging to Marseilles, five Neapolitan priests, and two monks of Corfu, who told us that the like adventures happened every day. The baron pretended that he had been worse used than myself; and I insisted that there was far less harm in taking up a nosegay, and putting it into a woman's bosom, than to be found stark naked with a young Icoglan. We were continually whipped, and received twenty lashes a day with a heavy thong, when the concatenation of sublunary events brought you on board our galley to ransom us from slavery."

"Well, my dear Pangloss," said Candide to him, "when you were hanged, dissected, whipped, and tugging at the oar, did you continue to think that everything in this world happens for the best?" "I have always abided by my first opinion," answered Pangloss; "for, after all, I am a philosopher, and it would not become me to retract my sentiments; especially as Leibnitz could not be in the wrong: and that pre-established harmony is the finest thing in the world, as well as a *plenum* and the *materia subtilis*."

Chapter XXIX

In What Manner Candide Found Miss Cunegund and the Old Woman Again

While Candide, the baron, Pangloss, Martin, and Cacambo, were relating their several adventures, and reasoning on the contingent or non-contingent events of this world; on causes and effects; on moral and physical evil; on free will and necessity; and on the consolation that may be felt by a person when a slave and chained to an oar in a Turkish galley; they arrived at the house of the Transylvanian prince on the coasts of the Propontis. The first objects they beheld there, were Miss Cunegund and the old woman, who were hanging some tablecloths on a line to dry.

The baron turned pale at the sight. Even the tender Candide, that affectionate lover, upon seeing his fair Cunegund all sunburnt, with blear eyes, a withered neck, wrinkled face and arms, all covered with a red scurf, started back with horror; but, recovering himself, he advanced towards her out of good manners. She embraced Candide and her brother; they embraced the old woman, and Candide ransomed them both.

There was a small farm in the neighborhood, which the old woman proposed to Candide to make shift with till the company should meet with a more favorable destiny. Cunegund, not knowing that she was grown ugly, as no one had informed her of it, reminded Candide of his promise in so peremptory a manner that the simple lad did not dare to refuse her; he then acquainted the baron that he was going to marry his sister. "I will never suffer," said the baron, "my sister to be guilty of an action so derogatory to her birth and family; nor will I bear this insolence on your part: no, I never will be reproached that my nephews are not qualified for the first ecclesiastical dignities in Germany; nor shall a sister of mine ever be the wife of any person below the rank of a baron of the empire." Cunegund flung herself at her brother's feet, and bedewed them with her tears; but he still continued inflexible. "Thou foolish fellow," said Candide, "have I not delivered thee from the galleys, paid thy ransom, and thy sister's, too, who was a scullion, and is very ugly, and yet condescend to marry her? and shalt thou pretend to oppose the match! If I were to listen only to the dictates of my anger, I should kill thee again." "Thou mayest kill me again," said the baron; "but thou shalt not marry my sister while I am living."

Chapter XXX

Conclusion

Candide had, in truth, no great inclination to marry Miss Cunegund; but the extreme impertinence of the baron determined him to conclude the match; and Cunegund pressed him so warmly, that he could not recant. He consulted

Pangloss, Martin, and the faithful Cacambo. Pangloss composed a fine memorial, by which he proved that the baron had no right over his sister; and that she might, according to all the laws of the empire, marry Candide with the left hand. Martin concluded to throw the baron into the sea; Cacambo decided that he must be delivered to the Turkish captain and sent to the galleys; after which he should be conveyed by the first ship to the father-general at Rome. This advice was found to be good; the old woman approved of it, and not a syllable was said to his sister; the business was executed for a little money; and they had the pleasure of tricking a Jesuit, and punishing the pride of a German baron.

It was altogether natural to imagine, that after undergoing so many disasters, Candide, married to his mistress and living with the philosopher Pangloss, the philosopher Martin, the prudent Cacambo, and the old woman, having besides brought home so many diamonds from the country of the ancient Incas, would lead the most agreeable life in the world. But he had been so robbed by the Jews, that he had nothing left but his little farm; his wife, every day growing more and more ugly, became headstrong and insupportable; the old woman was infirm, and more ill-natured yet than Cunegund. Cacambo, who worked in the garden, and carried the produce of it to sell at Constantinople, was above his labor, and cursed his fate. Pangloss despaired of making a figure in any of the German universities. And as to Martin, he was firmly persuaded that a person is equally ill-situated everywhere. He took things with patience. Candide, Martin, and Pangloss, disputed sometimes about metaphysics and morality. Boats were often seen passing under the windows of the farm laden with effendis, bashaws, and cadis, that were going into banishment to Lemnos, Mytilene and Erzerum. And other cadis, bashaws, and effendis, were seen coming back to succeed the place of the exiles, and were driven out in their turns. They saw several heads curiously stuck upon poles, and carried as presents to the sublime porte. Such sights gave occasion to frequent dissertations; and when no disputes were in progress, the irksomeness was so excessive that the old woman ventured one day to tell them, "I would be glad to know which is worst, to be ravished a hundred times by negro pirates, to have one buttock cut off, to run the gauntlet among the Bulgarians, to be whipped and hanged at an *auto-da-fé*, to be dissected, to be chained to an oar in a galley; and, in short, to experience all the miseries through which every one of us hath passed, or to remain here doing nothing?" "This," said Candide, "is a grand question."

This discourse gave birth to new reflections, and Martin especially concluded that man was born to live in the convulsions of disquiet, or in the lethargy of idleness. Though Candide did not absolutely agree to this, yet he did not determine anything on that head. Pangloss avowed that he had undergone dreadful sufferings; but having once maintained that everything went on as well as possible, he still maintained it, and at the same time believed nothing of it.

There was one thing which more than ever confirmed Martin in his detestable principles, made Candide hesitate, and embarrassed Pangloss, which was the arrival of Pacquette and Brother Giroflée one day at their farm. This couple had been in the utmost distress; they had very speedily made away with their three thousand piastres; they had parted, been reconciled; quarrelled again, been thrown into prison; had made their escape, and at last Brother Giroflée had turned Turk. Pacquette still continued to follow her trade; but she got little or nothing by it. "I foresaw very well," said Martin to Candide, "that your presents would soon be squandered, and only make them more miserable. You and Cacambo have spent millions of piastres, and yet you are not more happy than Brother Giroflée and Pacquette." "Ah!" said Pangloss to Pacquette, "it is heaven that has brought you here among us, my poor child! Do you know that you have cost me the tip of my nose, one eye, and one ear? What a handsome shape is here! and what is this world!" This new adventure engaged them more deeply than ever in philosophical disputations.

In the neighborhood lived a famous dervish who passed for the best philosopher in Turkey; they went to consult him: Pangloss, who was their spokesman, addressed him thus: "Master, we come to entreat you to tell us why so strange an animal as man has been formed?"

"Why do you trouble your head about it?" said the dervish; "is it any business of yours?" "But, my reverend father," said Candide, "there is a horrible deal of evil on the earth." "What signifies it," said the dervish, "whether there is evil or good? When his highness sends a ship to Egypt does he trouble his head whether the rats in the vessel are at their ease or not?" "What must then be done?" said Pangloss. "Be silent," answered the dervish. "I flattered myself," replied Pangloss, "to have reasoned a little with you on the causes and effects, on the best of possible worlds, the origin of evil, the nature of the soul, and a pre-established harmony." At these words the dervish shut the door in their faces.

During this conversation, news was spread abroad that two viziers of the bench and the mufti had just been strangled at Constantinople, and several of their friends empaled. This catastrophe made a great noise for some hours. Pangloss, Candide, and Martin, as they were returning to the little farm, met with a good-looking old man, who was taking the air at his door, under an alcove formed of the boughs of orange-trees. Pangloss, who was as inquisitive as he was disputative, asked him what was the name of the mufti who was lately strangled. "I cannot tell," answered the good old man; "I never knew the name of any mufti, or vizier breathing. I am entirely ignorant of the event you speak of; I presume that in general such as are concerned in public affairs sometimes come to a miserable end; and that they deserve it: but I never inquire what is doing at Constantinople; I am contented with sending thither the produce of my garden, which I cultivate with my own hands." After saying these words, he invited the strangers to come into his house. His two daughters and two sons presented them with divers sorts of sherbet of their own making; besides caymac, heightened with the peels of candied citrons, oranges, lemons, pineapples, pistachio nuts, and Mocha coffee unadulterated with the bad coffee of Batavia or the American islands. After which the two daughters of this good Mussulman perfumed the beards of Candide, Pangloss, and Martin.

"You must certainly have a vast estate," said Candide to the Turk; who replied, "I have no more than twenty acres of ground, the whole of which I cultivate myself with the help of my children; and our labor keeps off from us three great evils—idleness, vice, and want."

Candide, as he was returning home, made profound reflections on the Turk's discourse. "This good old man," said he to Pangloss and Martin, "appears to me to have chosen for himself a lot much preferable to that of the six kings with whom we had the honor to sup." "Human grandeur," said Pangloss, "is very dangerous, if we believe the testimonies of almost all philosophers; for we find Eglon, king of Moab, was assassinated by Aod; Absalom was hanged by the hair of his head, and run through with three darts; King Nadab, son of Jeroboam, was slain by Baaza; King Ela by Zimri; Okosias by Jehu; Athaliah by Jehoiada; the kings Jehooiakim, Jeconiah, and Zedekiah, were led into captivity: I need not tell you what was the fate of Crœsus, Astyages, Darius, Dionysius of Syracuse, Pyrrhus, Perseus, Hannibal, Jugurtha, Ariovistus, Cæsar, Pompey, Nero, Otho, Vitellius, Domitian, Richard II of England, Edward II, Henry VI, Richard III, Mary Stuart, Charles I, the three Henrys of France, and the emperor Henry IV." "Neither need you tell me," said Candide, "that we must take care of our garden." "You are in the right," said Pangloss; "for when man was put into the garden of Eden, it was with an intent to dress it: and this proves that man was not born to be idle." "Work then without disputing," said Martin; "it is the only way to render life supportable."

The little society, one and all, entered into this laudable design; and set themselves to exert their different talents. The little piece of ground yielded them a plentiful crop. Cunegund indeed was very ugly, but she became an excellent hand at pastry-work; Pacquette embroidered; the old woman had the care of the linen. There was none, down to Brother Giroflée, but did some service; he was a very good carpenter, and became an honest man. Pangloss used now and then to say to Candide, "There is a concatenation of all events in the best of possible worlds; for, in short, had you not been kicked out of a fine castle for the love of Miss Cunegund; had you not been put into the Inquisition; had you not travelled over America on foot; had you not run the baron through the body; and had you not lost all your sheep, which you brought from the good country of El Dorado, you would not have been here to eat preserved citrons and pistachio nuts." "Excellently observed," answered Candide; "but let us take care of our garden."

Castle Rackrent

(1800)

Maria Edgeworth

Maria Edgeworth (1767–1849) lived most of her life in Ireland and gained her first-hand knowledge of the Irish landowners and peasantry from assisting her father, Richard Lovell Edgeworth, in the management of his estate. The elder Edgeworth was one of the great nineteenth-century eccentrics, hatching numerous curious inventions and theories on everything from education to farming. With his stimulation—and his strongly didactic bent—Maria began to write educational tracts, including juvenile stories (*The Parent's Assistant,* 1796). *Castle Rackrent* was written in 1798, one of the few works that did not have her father's active supervision, and was published anonymously in 1800; its success was so great that her name appeared on the second edition. She continued to write in the tradition of Marmontel's *contes moraux,* crossed with Crabbe's realistic village tales-in-verse and her own Irish experiences, producing *Moral Tales for Young People* (5 vols.) and a novel, *Belinda,* in 1801; *Popular Tales* and *The Mock Griselda* in 1804; *Leonora* in 1806; and in 1809 the first series of *Tales of Fashionable Life,* and in 1812 the second (3 vols. each). The latter included *The Absentee,* one of her best novelettes. She remained single, supervised her father's estate after his death, and continued to publish until her death. See P. H. Newby, *Maria Edgeworth* (London, 1950); and Elizabeth Inglis-Jones, *The Great Maria* (London, 1959).

Castle Rackrent was written in the conventional form of the edited manuscript. The sophisticated "editor's" notes act as an ironic commentary on and extension of Thady's naïve text; and so I have retained as many as space permits. All the necessary explanatory notes remain.

Editor's Preface

The prevailing taste of the public for anecdote has been censured and ridiculed by critics who aspire to the character of superior wisdom; but if we consider it in a proper point of view, this taste is an incontestable proof of the good sense and profoundly philosophic temper of the present times. Of the members who study, or at least who read history, how few derive any advantage from their labours! The heroes of history are so decked out by the fine fancy of the professed historian; they talk in such measured prose, and act from such sublime or such diabolical motives, that few have sufficient taste, wickedness, or heroism, to sympathise in their fate. Besides, there is much uncertainty even in the best authenticated ancient or modern histories; and that love of truth, which in some minds is innate and immutable, necessarily leads to a love of secret memoirs and private anecdotes. We cannot judge either of the feelings or of the characters of men with perfect accuracy, from their actions or their appearance in public; it is from their careless conversations, their half-finished sentences, that we may hope with the greatest probability of success to discover their real characters. The life of a great or of a little man written by himself, the familiar letters, the diary of any individual published by his friends or by his enemies, after his decease, are esteemed important literary curiosities. We are surely justified, in this eager desire, to collect the most minute facts relative to the domestic lives, not only of the great and good, but even of the worthless and insignificant, since it is only by a comparison of their actual happiness or misery in the privacy of domestic life that we can form a just estimate of the real reward of virtue, or the real punishment of vice. That the great are not as happy as they seem, that the external circumstances of fortune and rank do not constitute felicity, is asserted by every moralist: the historian can seldom, consistently with his dignity, pause to illustrate this truth; it is therefore to the biographer we must have recourse. After we have beheld splendid characters playing their parts on the great theatre of the world, with all the advantages of stage effect and decoration, we anxiously beg to be admitted behind the scenes, that we may take a nearer view of the actors and actresses.

Some may perhaps imagine that the value of biography depends upon the judgment and taste of the biographer; but on the contrary it may be maintained, that the merits of a biographer are inversely as the extent of his intellectual powers and of his literary talents. A plain unvarnished tale is preferable to the most highly ornamented narrative. Where we see that a man has the power, we may naturally suspect that he has the will to deceive us; and those who are used to literary manufacture know how much is often sacrificed to the rounding of a period, or the pointing of an antithesis.

That the ignorant may have their prejudices as well as the learned cannot be disputed; but we see and despise vulgar errors: we never bow to the authority of him who has no great name to sanction his absurdities. The partiality which blinds a biographer to the defects of his hero, in proportion as it is gross, ceases to be dangerous; but if it be concealed by the appearance of candour, which men of great abilities best know how to assume, it endangers our judgment sometimes, and sometimes our morals. If her Grace the Duchess of Newcastle, instead of penning her lord's elaborate eulogium, had undertaken to write the life of Savage, we should not have been in any danger of mistaking an idle, ungrateful libertine for a man of genius and virtue. The talents of a biographer are often fatal to his reader. For these reasons the public often judiciously countenance those who, without sagacity to discriminate character, without elegance of style to relieve the tediousness of narrative, without enlargement of mind to draw any conclusions from the facts they relate, simply pour forth anecdotes, and retail conversations, with all the minute prolixity of a gossip in a country town.

The author of the following Memoirs has upon these grounds fair claims to the public favour and attention; he was an illiterate old steward, whose partiality to *the family,* in which he was bred and born, must be obvious to the reader. He tells the history of the Rackrent family in his vernacular idiom, and in the full confidence that Sir Patrick, Sir Murtagh, Sir Kit, and Sir Condy Rackrent's affairs will be as interesting to all the world as they were to himself. Those who were acquainted with the manners of a certain class of the gentry of Ireland some years ago, will want no evidence of the truth of honest Thady's narrative; to those who are totally unacquainted with Ireland, the following Memoirs will perhaps be scarcely intelligible, or probably they may appear perfectly incredible. For the information of the *ignorant* English reader, a few notes have been subjoined by the editor, and he had it once in contemplation to translate the language of Thady into plain English; but Thady's idiom is incapable of translation, and, besides, the authenticity of his story would have been more exposed to doubt if it were not told in his own characteristic manner. Several years ago he related to the editor the history of the Rackrent family, and it was with some difficulty that he was persuaded to have it committed to writing; however, his feelings for *'the honour of the family,'* as he expressed himself, prevailed over his habitual laziness, and he at length completed the narrative which is now laid before the public.

The editor hopes his readers will observe that these are 'tales of other times;' that the manners depicted in the following pages are not those of the present age; the race of the Rackrents has long since been extinct in Ireland; and the drunken Sir Patrick, the litigious Sir Murtagh, the fighting Sir Kit, and the slovenly Sir Condy, are characters which could no more be met with at present in Ireland, than Squire Western or Parson Trulliber in England. There is a time when individuals can bear to be rallied for their past follies and absurdities, after they have acquired new habits and a new consciousness. Nations, as well as individuals, gradually lose attachment to their identity, and the present generation is amused, rather than offended, by the ridicule that is thrown upon its ancestors.

Probably we shall soon have it in our power, in a hundred instances, to verify the truth of these observations.

When Ireland loses her identity by an union with Great Britain, she will look back, with a smile of good-humoured complacency, on the Sir Kits and Sir Condys of her former existence.

Monday Morning[1]

Having, out of friendship for the family, upon whose estate, praised be Heaven! I and mine have lived rent-free time out of mind, voluntarily undertaken to publish the MEMOIRS OF THE RACKRENT FAMILY, I think it my duty to say a few

---

[1] Thady begins his memoirs of the Rackrent Family by dating *Monday morning,* because no great undertaking can be auspiciously commenced in Ireland on any morning but *Monday morning.* 'Oh, please God we live till Monday morning, we'll set the slater to mend the roof of the house. On Monday morning we'll fall to, and cut the turf. On Monday morning we'll see and begin mowing. On Monday morning, please your honour, we'll begin and dig the potatoes,' etc.

All the intermediate days, between the making of such speeches and the ensuing Monday, are wasted: and when Monday morning comes, it is ten to one that the business is deferred to *the next* Monday morning. The Editor knew a gentleman, who, to counteract this prejudice, made his workmen and labourers begin all new pieces of work upon a Saturday.

words, in the first place, concerning myself. My real name is Thady Quirk, though in the family I have always been known by no other than 'Honest Thady,' afterward, in the time of Sir Murtagh, deceased, I remember to hear them calling me 'Old Thady,' and now I've come to 'Poor Thady'; for I wear a long greatcoat[2] winter and summer, which is very handy, as I never put my arms into the sleeves; they are as good as new, though come Holantide next I've had it these seven years: it holds on by a single button round my neck, cloak fashion. To look at me, you would hardly think 'Poor Thady' was the father of Attorney Quirk; he is a high gentleman, and never minds what poor Thady says, and having better than fifteen hundred a year, landed estate, looks down upon honest Thady; but I wash my hands of his doings, and as I have lived so will I die, true and loyal to the family. The family of the Rackrents is, I am proud to say, one of the most ancient in the kingdom. Everybody knows this is not the old family name, which was O'Shaughlin, related to the kings of Ireland—but that was before my time. My grandfather was driver to the great Sir Patrick O'Shaughlin, and I heard him, when I was a boy, telling how the Castle Rackrent estate came to Sir Patrick; Sir Tallyhoo Rackrent was cousin-german to him, and had a fine estate of his own, only never a gate upon it, it being his maxim that a car was the best gate. Poor gentleman! he lost a fine hunter and his life, at last, by it, all in one day's hunt. But I ought to bless that day, for the estate came straight into *the* family, upon one condition, which Sir Patrick O'Shaughlin at the time took sadly to heart, they say, but thought better of it afterwards, seeing how large a stake depended upon it: that he should, by Act of Parliament, take and bear the surname and arms of Rackrent.

Now it was that the world was to see what was *in* Sir Patrick. On coming into the estate he gave the finest entertainment ever was heard of in the country; not a man could stand after supper but Sir Patrick himself, who could sit out the best man in Ireland, let alone the three kingdoms itself.[3] He had his house, from one year's end to another, as full of company as ever it could hold, and fuller; for rather than be left out of the parties at Castle Rackrent, many gentlemen, and

---

2 The cloak, or mantle, as described by Thady, is of high antiquity. Spenser, in his *View of the State of Ireland,* proves that it is not, as some have imagined, peculiarly derived from the Scythians, but that 'most nations of the world anciently used the mantle; for the Jews used it, as you may read of Elias's mantle, etc.; the Chaldees also used it, as you may read in Diodorus; the Egyptians likewise used it, as you may read in Herodotus, and may be gathered by the description of Berenice in the Greek Commentary upon Callimachus; the Greeks also used it anciently, as appeared by Venus's mantle lined with stars, though afterward they changed the form thereof into their cloaks, called Pallai, as some of the Irish also use; and the ancient Latins and Romans used it, as you may read in Virgil, who was a great antiquary, that Evander, when Æneas came to him at his feast, did entertain and feast him sitting on the ground, and lying on mantles: insomuch that he useth the very word mantile for a mantle—

"Humi mantilia sternunt:"

so that it seemeth that the mantle was a general habit to most nations, and not proper to the Scythians only.'

3 *Let alone,* in this sentence, means *put out of consideration.* The phrase, *let alone,* which is now used as the imperative of a verb, may in time become a conjunction, and may exercise the ingenuity of some future etymologist. The celebrated Horne Tooke has proved most satisfactorily, that the conjunction *but* comes from the imperative of the Anglo-Saxon verb (*beoutan*) *to be out;* also, that *if* comes from *gif,* the imperative of the Anglo-Saxon verb which signifies *to give,* etc.

those men of the first consequence and landed estates in the country—such as the O'Neills of Ballynagrotty, and the Moneygawls of Mount Juliet's Town, and O'Shannons of New Town Tullyhog—made it their choice, often and often, when there was no room to be had for love nor money, in long winter nights, to sleep in the chicken-house, which Sir Patrick had fitted up for the purpose of accommodating his friends and the public in general, who honoured him with their company unexpectedly at Castle Rackrent; and this went on I can't tell you how long. The whole country rang with his praises!—Long life to him! I'm sure I love to look upon his picture, now opposite to me; though I never saw him, he must have been a portly gentleman—his neck something short, and remarkable for the largest pimple on his nose, which, by his particular desire, is still extant in his picture, said to be a striking likeness, though taken when young. He is said also to be the inventor of raspberry whisky, which is very likely, as nobody has ever appeared to dispute it with him, and as there still exists a broken punch-bowl at Castle Rackrent, in the garret, with an inscription to that effect—a great curiosity. A few days before his death he was very merry; it being his honour's birthday, he called my grandfather in—God bless him!—to drink the company's health, and filled a bumper himself, but could not carry it to his head, on account of the great shake in his hand; on this he cast his joke, saying, 'What would my poor father say to me if he was to pop out of the grave, and see me now? I remember when I was a little boy, the first bumper of claret he gave me after dinner, how he praised me for carrying it so steady to my mouth. Here's my thanks to him—a bumper toast.' Then he fell to singing the favourite song he learned from his father—for the last time, poor gentleman—he sung it that night as loud and as hearty as ever, with a chorus:

> He that goes to bed, and goes to bed sober,
> Falls as the leaves do, falls as the leaves do, and dies in October;
> But he that goes to bed, and goes to bed mellow,
> Lives as he ought to do, lives as he ought to do, and dies an honest fellow

Sir Patrick died that night: just as the company rose to drink his health with three cheers, he fell down in a sort of fit, and was carried off; they sat it out, and were surprised, on inquiry in the morning, to find that it was all over with poor Sir Patrick. Never did any gentleman live and die more beloved in the country by rich and poor. His funeral was such a one as was never known before or since in the county! All the gentlemen in the three counties were at it; far and near, how they flocked! my great-grandfather said, that to see all the women, even in their red cloaks, you would have taken them for the army drawn out. Then such a fine whillaluh![4] you might have heard it to the farthest end of the county, and happy the man who could get but a sight of the hearse! But who'd have thought

---

4 *Whillaluh.*—Ullaloo, Gol, or lamentation over the dead

Magnoque ululante tumultu.—Virgil.
Ululatibus omne
Implevere nemus.—Ovid.

A full account of the Irish Gol, or Ullaloo, and of the Caoinan or Irish funeral song, with its first semichorus, second semichorus, full chorus of sighs and groans, together with the Irish words and music, may be found in the fourth volume of the *Transactions of the Royal Irish Academy*.

it? Just as all was going on right, through his own town they were passing, when the body was seized for debt—a rescue was apprehended from the mob; but the heir, who attended the funeral, was against that, for fear of consequences, seeing that those villains who came to serve acted under the disguise of the law: so, to be sure, the law must take its course, and little gain had the creditors for their pains. First and foremost, they had the curses of the country: and Sir Murtagh Rackrent, the new heir, in the next place, on account of this affront to the body, refused to pay a shilling of the debts, in which he was countenanced by all the best gentlemen of property, and others of his acquaintance; Sir Murtagh alleging in all companies that he all along meant to pay his father's debts of honour, but the moment the law was taken of him, there was an end of honour to be sure. It was whispered (but none but the enemies of the family believe it) that this was all a sham seizure to get quit of the debts which he had bound himself to pay in honour.

It's a long time ago, there's no saying how it was, but this for certain, the new man did not take at all after the old gentleman; the cellars were never filled after his death, and no open house, or anything as it used to be; the tenants even were sent away without their whisky.[5] I was ashamed myself, and knew not what to say for the honour of the family; but I made the best of a bad case, and laid it all at my lady's door, for I did not like her anyhow, nor anybody else; she was of the family of the Skinflints, and a widow; it was a strange match for Sir Murtagh; the people in the country thought he demeaned himself greatly, but I said nothing: I knew how it was. Sir Murtagh was a great lawyer, and looked to the great Skinflint estate; there, however, he overshot himself; for though one of the co-heiresses, he was never the better for her, for she outlived him many's the long day—he could not see that to be sure when he married her. I must say for her, she made him the best of wives, being a very notable, stirring woman, and looking close to everything. But I always suspected she had Scotch blood in her veins; anything else I could have looked over in her, from a regard to the family. She was a strict observer, for self and servants, of Lent, and all fast-days, but not holidays. One of the maids having fainted three times the last day of Lent, to keep soul and body together, we put a morsel of roast beef into her mouth, which came from Sir Murtagh's dinner, who never fasted, not he; but somehow or other it unfortunately reached my lady's ears, and the priest of the parish had a complaint made of it the next day, and the poor girl was forced, as soon as she could walk, to do penance for it, before she could get any peace or absolution, in the

---

5 It is usual with some landlords to give their inferior tenants a glass of whisky when they pay their rents. Thady calls it *their* whisky; not that the whisky is actually the property of the tenants, but that it becomes their *right* after it has been often given to them. In this general mode of reasoning respecting *rights* the lower Irish are not singular, but they are peculiarly quick and tenacious in claiming these rights. 'Last year your honour gave me some straw for the roof of my house and I *expect* your honour will be after doing the same this year.' In this manner gifts are frequently turned into tributes. The high and low are not always dissimilar in their habits. It is said, that the Sublime Ottoman Porte is very apt to claim gifts as tributes: thus it is dangerous to send the Grand Seignor a fine horse on his birthday one year, lest on his next birthday he should expect a similar present, and should proceed to demonstrate the reasonableness of his expectations.

house or out of it. However, my lady was very charitable in her own way. She had a charity school for poor children, where they were taught to read and write gratis, and where they were kept well to spinning gratis for my lady in return; for she had always heaps of duty yarn from the tenants, and got all her household linen out of the estate from first to last; for after the spinning, the weavers on the estate took it in hand for nothing, because of the looms my lady's interest could get from the Linen Board to distribute gratis. Then there was a bleach-yard near us, and the tenant dare refuse my lady nothing, for fear of a lawsuit Sir Murtagh kept hanging over him about the water-course. With these ways of managing, 'tis surprising how cheap my lady got things done, and how proud she was of it. Her table the same way, kept for next to nothing;[6] duty fowls, and duty turkeys, and duty geese, came as fast as we could eat 'em, for my lady kept a sharp look-out, and knew to a tub of butter everything the tenants had, all round. They knew her way, and what with fear of driving for rent and Sir Murtagh's lawsuits, they were kept in such good order, they never thought of coming near Castle Rackrent without a present of something or other—nothing too much or too little for my lady— eggs, honey, butter, meal, fish, game, grouse, and herrings, fresh or salt, all went for something. As for their young pigs, we had them, and the best bacon and hams they could make up, with all young chickens in spring; but they were a set of poor wretches, and we had nothing but misfortunes with them, always breaking and running away. This, Sir Murtagh and my lady said, was all their former landlord Sir Patrick's fault, who let 'em all get the half-year's rent into arrear; there was something in that to be sure. But Sir Murtagh was as much the contrary way; for let alone making English tenants[7] of them, every soul, he was always driving and driving, and pounding and pounding, and canting[8] and canting, and replevying and replevying, and he made a good living of trespassing cattle; there was always some tenant's pig, or horse, or cow, or calf, or goose, trespassing, which was so great a gain to Sir Murtagh, that he did not like to hear me talk of repairing fences. Then his heriots and duty-work[9] brought him in something, his turf was cut, his potatoes set and dug, his hay brought home, and, in short, all the work

---

6 In many leases in Ireland, tenants were *formerly* bound to supply an inordinate quantity of poultry to their landlords. The Editor knew of thirty turkeys being reserved in one lease of a small farm.

7 An English tenant does not mean a tenant who is an Englishman, but a tenant who pays his rent the day that it is due. It is a common prejudice in Ireland, amongst the poorer classes of people, to believe that all tenants in England pay their rents on the very day when they become due. An Irishman, when he goes to take a farm, if he wants to prove to his landlord that he is a substantial man, offers to become an *English tenant*.

8 *Canting* does not mean talking or writing hypocritical nonsense, but selling substantially by auction.

9 It was formerly common in Ireland to insert clauses in leases, binding tenants to furnish their landlords with labourers and horses for several days in the year. Much petty tyranny and oppression have resulted from this feudal custom. Whenever a poor man disobliged his landlord, the agent sent to him for his duty work; and Thady does not exaggerate when he says, that the tenants were often called from their own work to do that of their landlord. Thus the very means of earning their rent were taken from them: whilst they were getting home their landlord's harvest, their own was often ruined, and yet their rents were expected to be paid as punctually as if their time had been at their own disposal. This appears the height of absurd injustice.

about his house done for nothing; for in all our leases there were strict clauses heavy with penalties, which Sir Murtagh knew well how to enforce; so many days' duty-work of man and horse, from every tenant, he was to have, and had, every year; and when a man vexed him, why, the finest day he could pitch on, when the cratur was getting in his own harvest, or thatching his cabin, Sir Murtagh made it a principle to call upon him and his horse; so he taught 'em all, as he said, to know the law of landlord and tenant. As for law, I believe no man, dead or alive, ever loved it so well as Sir Murtagh. He had once sixteen suits pending at a time, and I never saw him so much himself: roads, lanes, bogs, wells, ponds, eel-wires, orchards, trees, tithes, vagrants, gravelpits, sandpits, dunghills, and nuisances, everything upon the face of the earth furnished him good matter for a suit. He used to boast that he had a lawsuit for every letter in the alphabet. How I used to wonder to see Sir Murtagh in the midst of the papers in his office! Why, he could hardly turn about for them. I made bold to shrug my shoulders once in his presence, and thanked my stars I was not born a gentleman to so much toil and trouble; but Sir Murtagh took me up short with his old proverb, 'Learning is better than house or land.' Out of forty-nine suits which he had, he never lost one but seventeen;[10] the rest he gained with costs, double costs, treble costs sometimes; but even that did not pay. He was a very learned man in the law, and had the character of it; but how it was I can't tell, these suits that he carried cost him a power of money: in the end he sold some hundreds a year of the family estate; but he was a very learned man in the law, and I know nothing of the matter, except having a great regard for the family; and I could not help grieving when he sent me to post up notices of the sale of the fee simple of the lands and appurtenances of Timoleague.

'I know, honest Thady,' says he, to comfort me, 'what I'm about better than you do; I'm only selling to get the ready money wanting to carry on my suit with spirit with the Nugents of Carrickashaughlin.'

He was very sanguine about that suit with the Nugents of Carrickashaughlin. He could have gained it, they say, for certain, had it pleased Heaven to have spared him to us, and it would have been at the least a plump two thousand a year in his way; but things were ordered otherwise—for the best to be sure. He dug up a fairy-mount[11] against my advice, and had no luck afterwards. Though a learned man in the law, he was a little too incredulous in other matters. I warned him that

---

10 Thady's language in this instance is a specimen of a mode of rhetoric common in Ireland. An astonishing assertion is made in the beginning of a sentence, which ceases to be in the least surprising, when you hear the qualifying explanation that follows. Thus a man who is in the last stage of staggering drunkenness will, if he can articulate, swear to you— 'Upon his conscience now, and may he never stir from the spot alive if he is telling a lie, upon his conscience he has not tasted a drop of anything, good or bad, since morning at-all-at-all, but half a pint of whisky, please your honour.'

11 These fairy-mounts are called ant-hills in England. They are held in high reverence by the common people in Ireland. A gentleman, who in laying out his lawn had occasion to level one of these hillocks, could not prevail upon any of his labourers to begin the ominous work. He was obliged to take a *loy* from one of their reluctant hands, and began the attack himself. The labourers agreed that the vengeance of the fairies would fall upon the head of the presumptuous mortal who first disturbed them in their retreat.

I heard the very Banshee[12] that my grandfather heard under Sir Patrick's window a few days before his death. But Sir Murtagh thought nothing of the Banshee, nor of his cough, with a spitting of blood, brought on, I understand, by catching cold in attending the courts, and overstraining his chest with making himself heard in one of his favourite causes. He was a great speaker with a powerful voice; but his last speech was not in the courts at all. He and my lady, though both of the same way of thinking in some things, and though she was as good a wife and great economist as you could see, and he the best of husbands, as to looking into his affairs, and making money for his family; yet I don't know how it was, they had a great deal of sparring and jarring between them. My lady had her privy purse; and she had her weed ashes,[13] and her sealing money[14] upon the signing of all the leases, with something to buy gloves besides; and, besides, again often took money from the tenants, if offered properly, to speak for them to Sir Murtagh about abatements and renewals. Now the weed ashes and the glove money he allowed her clear perquisites; though once when he saw her in a new gown saved out of the weed ashes, he told her to my face (for he could say a sharp thing) that she should not put on her weeds before her husband's death. But in a dispute about an abatement my lady would have the last word, and Sir Murtagh grew mad;[15] I was within hearing of the door, and now I wish I had made bold to step in. He spoke so loud, the whole kitchen was out on the stairs.[16] All on a sudden he stopped, and my lady too. Something has surely happened, thought I; and so it was, for Sir Murtagh in his passion broke a blood-vessel, and all the law in the land could do nothing in that case. My lady sent for five physicians, but Sir Murtagh died, and was buried. She had a fine jointure settled upon her, and took herself away, to the great joy of the tenantry. I never said anything one way or the other whilst she was part of the family, but got up to see her go at three o'clock in the morning.

'It's a fine morning, honest Thady,' says she; 'good-bye to ye.' And into the carriage she stepped, without a word more, good or bad, or even half-a-crown; but I made my bow, and stood to see her safe out of sight for the sake of the family.

Then we were all bustle in the house, which made me keep out of the way, for I walk slow and hate a bustle; but the house was all hurry-skurry, preparing for

12 The Banshee is a species of aristocratic fairy, who, in the shape of a little hideous old woman, has been known to appear, and heard to sing in a mournful supernatural voice under the windows of great houses, to warn the family that some of them are soon to die. In the last century every great family in Ireland had a Banshee, who attended regularly; but latterly their visits and songs have been discontinued.

13 By ancient usage in Ireland, all the weeds on a farm belonged to the farmer's wife, or to the wife of the squire who holds the ground in his own hands. The great demand for alkaline salts in bleaching rendered these ashes no inconsiderable perquisite.

14 Formerly it was the custom in Ireland for tenants to give the squire's lady from two to fifty guineas as a perquisite upon the sealing of their leases. The Editor not very long since knew of a baronet's lady accepting fifty guineas as sealing money, upon closing a bargain for a considerable farm.

15 Sir Murtagh grew angry.

16 *The whole kitchen was out on the stairs*—means that all the inhabitants of the kitchen came out of the kitchen, and stood upon the stairs. These, and similar expressions, show how much the Irish are disposed to metaphor and amplification.

my new master. Sir Murtagh, I forgot to notice, had no childer;[17] so the Rackrent estate went to his younger brother, a young dashing officer, who came amongst us before I knew for the life of me whereabouts I was, in a gig or some of them things, with another spark along with him, and led horses, and servants, and dogs, and scarce a place to put any Christian of them into; for my late lady had sent all the feather-beds off before her, and blankets and household linen, down to the very knife-cloths, on the cars to Dublin, which were all her own, lawfully paid for out of her own money. So the house was quite bare, and my young master, the moment ever he set foot in it out of his gig, thought all those things must come of themselves, I believe, for he never looked after anything at all, but harum-scarum called for everything as if we were conjurors, or he in a public-house. For my part, I could not bestir myself anyhow; I had been so much used to my late master and mistress, all was upside down with me, and the new servants in the servants' hall were quite out of my way; I had nobody to talk to, and if it had not been for my pipe and tobacco, should, I verily believe, have broke my heart for poor Sir Murtagh.

But one morning my new master caught a glimpse of me as I was looking at his horse's heels, in hopes of a word from him. 'And is that old Thady?' says he, as he got into his gig: I loved him from that day to this, his voice was so like the family; and he threw me a guinea out of his waistcoat-pocket, as he drew up the reins with the other hand, his horse rearing too; I thought I never set my eyes on a finer figure of a man, quite another sort from Sir Murtagh, though withal, *to me,* a family likeness. A fine life we should have led, had he stayed amongst us, God bless him! He valued a guinea as little as any man: money to him was no more than dirt, and his gentleman and groom, and all belonging to him, the same; but the sporting season over, he grew tired of the place, and having got down a great architect for the house, and an improver for the grounds, and seen their plans and elevations, he fixed a day for settling with the tenants, but went off in a whirlwind to town, just as some of them came into the yard in the morning. A circular letter came next post from the new agent, with news that the master was sailed for England, and he must remit £500 to Bath for his use before a fortnight was at an end; bad news still for the poor tenants, no change still for the better with them. Sir Kit Rackrent, my young master, left all to the agent; and though he had the spirit of a prince, and lived away to the honour of his country abroad, which I was proud to hear of, what were we the better for that at home? The agent was one of your middlemen,[18] who grind the face of the poor, and can never

---

17 This is the manner in which many of Thady's rank, and others in Ireland, formerly pronounced the word *children.*

18 There was a class of men, termed middlemen, in Ireland, who took large farms on long leases from gentlemen of landed property, and let the land again in small portions to the poor, as under-tenants, at exorbitant rents. The *head landlord,* as he was called, seldom saw his *under-tenants;* but if he could not get the *middleman* to pay him his rent punctually, he *went to his land, and drove the land for his rent;* that is to say, he sent his steward, or bailiff, or driver, to the land to seize the cattle, hay, corn, flax, oats, or potatoes, belonging to the under-tenants, and proceeded to sell these for his rents. It sometimes happened that these unfortunate tenants paid their rent twice over, once to the *middleman,* and once to the *head landlord.*

bear a man with a hat upon his head: he ferreted the tenants out of their lives; not a week without a call for money, drafts upon drafts from Sir Kit; but I laid it all to the fault of the agent; for, says I, what can Sir Kit do with so much cash, and he a single man? But still it went. Rents must be all paid up to the day, and afore; no allowance for improving tenants, no consideration for those who had built upon their farms; no sooner was a lease out, but the land was advertised to the highest bidder; all the old tenants turned out, when they spent their substance in the hope and trust of a renewal from the landlord. All was now let at the highest penny to a parcel of poor wretches, who meant to run away, and did so, after taking two crops out of the ground. Then fining down the year's rent came into fashion—anything for the ready penny; and with all this and presents to the agent and the driver,[19] there was no such thing as standing it. I said nothing, for I had a regard for the family; but I walked about thinking if his honour Sir Kit knew all this, it would go hard with him but he'd see us righted; not that I had anything for my own share to complain of, for the agent was always very civil to me when he came down into the country, and took a great deal of notice of my son Jason. Jason Quirk, though he be my son, I must say was a good scholar from his birth, and a very 'cute lad: I thought to make him a priest,[20] but he did better for himself; seeing how he was as good a clerk as any in the county, the agent gave him his rent accounts to copy, which he did first of all for the pleasure of obliging the gentleman, and would take nothing at all for his trouble, but was always proud to serve the family. By and by a good farm bounding us to the east fell into his honour's hands, and my son put in a proposal for it: why shouldn't he, as well as another? The proposals all went over to the master at the Bath, who knowing no more of the land than the child unborn, only having once been out a-grousing on it before he went to England; and the value of lands, as the agent informed him, falling every year in Ireland, his honour wrote over in all haste a bit of a letter, saying he left it all to the agent, and that he must let it as well as he could— to the best bidder, to be sure—and send him over £200 by return of post: with this the agent gave me a hint, and I spoke a good word for my son, and gave out in the country that nobody need bid against us. So his proposal was just the thing, and he a good tenant; and he got a promise of an abatement in the rent after the first year, for advancing the half-year's rent at signing the lease, which was wanting

---

The characteristics of a middleman were servility to his superiors and tyranny towards his inferiors: the poor detested this race of beings. In speaking to them, however, they always used the most abject language, and the most humble tone and posture—'*Please your honour; and please your honour's honour,*' they knew must be repeated as a charm at the beginning and end of every equivocating, exculpatory, or supplicatory sentence; and they were much more alert in doffing their caps to those new men than to those of what they call *good old families.* A witty carpenter once termed these middlemen *journeymen gentlemen.*

[19] A man who is employed to drive tenants for rent; that is, to drive the cattle belonging to tenants to pound. The office of driver is by no means a sinecure.

[20] It was customary amongst those of Thady's rank in Ireland, whenever they could get a little money, to send their sons abroad to St. Omer's, or to Spain, to be educated as priests. Now they are educated at Maynooth. The Editor has lately known a young lad, who began by being a post-boy, afterwards turn into a carpenter, then quit his plane and work-bench to study his *Humanities,* as he said, at the college of Maynooth; but after he had gone through his course of Humanities, he determined to be a soldier instead of a priest.

to complete the agent's £200 by the return of the post, with all which my master wrote back he was well satisfied. About this time we learnt from the agent, as a great secret, how the money went so fast, and the reason of the thick coming of the master's drafts: he was a little too fond of play; and Bath, they say, was no place for no young man of his fortune, where there were so many of his own countrymen, too, hunting him up and down, day and night, who had nothing to lose. At last, at Christmas, the agent wrote over to stop the drafts, for he could raise no more money on bond or mortgage, or from the tenants, or anyhow, nor had he any more to lend himself, and desired at the same time to decline the agency for the future, wishing Sir Kit his health and happiness, and the compliments of the season, for I saw the letter before ever it was sealed, when my son copied it. When the answer came there was a new turn in affairs, and the agent was turned out; and my son Jason, who had corresponded privately with his honour occasionally on business, was forthwith desired by his honour to take the accounts into his own hands, and look them over, till further orders. It was a very spirited letter to be sure: Sir Kit sent his service, and the compliments of the season, in return to the agent, and he would fight him with pleasure to-morrow, or any day, for sending him such a letter, if he was born a gentleman, which he was sorry (for both their sakes) to find (too late) he was not. Then, in a private postscript, he condescended to tell us that all would be speedily settled to his satisfaction, and we should turn over a new leaf, for he was going to be married in a fortnight to the grandest heiress in England, and had only immediate occasion at present for £200, as he would not choose to touch his lady's fortune for travelling expenses home to Castle Rackrent, where he intended to be, wind and weather permitting, early in the next month; and desired fires, and the house to be painted, and the new building to go on as fast as possible, for the reception of him and his lady before that time; with several words besides in the letter, which we could not make out because, God bless him! he wrote in such a flurry. My heart warmed to my new lady when I read this: I was almost afraid it was too good news to be true; but the girls fell to scouring, and it was well they did, for we soon saw his marriage in the paper, to a lady with I don't know how many tens of thousand pounds to her fortune: then I watched the postoffice for his landing; and the news came to my son of his and the bride being in Dublin, and on the way home to Castle Rackrent. We had bonfires all over the country, expecting him down the next day, and we had his coming of age still to celebrate, which he had not time to do properly before he left the country; therefore, a great ball was expected, and great doings upon his coming, as it were, fresh to take possession of his ancestors' estate. I never shall forget the day he came home; we had waited and waited all day long till eleven o'clock at night, and I was thinking of sending the boy to lock the gates, and giving them up for that night, when there came the carriages thundering up to the great hall door. I got the first sight of the bride; for when the carriage door opened, just as she had her foot on the steps, I held the flam[21] full in her face to light her, at which she shut her eyes, but I had a full view of the rest of her, and greatly shocked I was, for by that light she was little better

---

[21] Short for flambeau.

than a blackamoor, and seemed crippled; but that was only sitting so long in the chariot.

'You're kindly welcome to Castle Rackrent, my lady,' says I (recollecting who she was). 'Did your honour hear of the bonfires?'

His honour spoke never a word, nor so much as handed her up the steps—he looked to me no more like himself than nothing at all; I know I took him for the skeleton of his honour. I was not sure what to say next to one or t'other, but seeing she was a stranger in a foreign country, I thought it but right to speak cheerful to her; so I went back again to the bonfires.

'My lady,' says I, as she crossed the hall, 'there would have been fifty times as many; but for fear of the horses, and frightening your ladyship, Jason and I forbid them, please your honour.'

With that she looked at me a little bewildered.

'Will I have a fire lighted in the state-room to-night?' was the next question I put to her, but never a word she answered; so I concluded she could not speak a word of English, and was from foreign parts. The short and the long of it was, I couldn't tell what to make of her; so I left her to herself, and went straight down to the servants' hall to learn something for certain about her. Sir Kit's own man was tired, but the groom set him a-talking at last, and we had it all out before ever I closed my eyes that night. The bride might well be a great fortune—she was a *Jewish* by all accounts, who are famous for their great riches. I had never seen any of that tribe or nation before, and could only gather that she spoke a strange kind of English of her own, that she could not abide pork or sausages, and went neither to church or mass. Mercy upon his honour's poor soul, thought I; what will become of him and his, and all of us, with his heretic blackamoor at the head of the Castle Rackrent estate? I never slept a wink all night for thinking of it; but before the servants I put my pipe in my mouth, and kept my mind to myself, for I had a great regard for the family; and after this, when strange gentlemen's servants came to the house, and would begin to talk about the bride, I took care to put the best foot foremost, and passed her for a nabob in the kitchen, which accounted for her dark complexion and everything.

The very morning after they came home, however, I saw plain enough how things were between Sir Kit and my lady, though they were walking together arm in arm after breakfast, looking at the new building and the improvements.

'Old Thady,' said my master, just as he used to do, 'how do you do?'

'Very well, I thank your honour's honour,' said I; but I saw he was not well pleased, and my heart was in my mouth as I walked along after him.

'Is the large room damp, Thady?' said his honour.

'Oh damp, your honour! how should it be but as dry as a bone,' says I, 'after all the fires we have kept in it day and night? It's the barrack-room[22] your honour's talking on.'

'And what is a barrack-room, pray, my dear?' were the first words I ever heard out of my lady's lips.

---

[22] Formerly it was customary, in gentlemen's houses in Ireland, to fit up one large bed-chamber with a number of beds for the reception of occasional visitors. These rooms were called Barrack-rooms.

'No matter, my dear,' said he, and went on talking to me, ashamed-like I should witness her ignorance. To be sure, to hear her talk one might have taken her for an innocent, for it was, 'What's this, Sir Kit? and what's that, Sir Kit?' all the way we went. To be sure, Sir Kit had enough to do to answer her.

'And what do you call that, Sir Kit?' said she; 'that—that looks like a pile of black bricks, pray, Sir Kit?'

'My turf-stack, my dear,' said my master, and bit his lip.

Where have you lived, my lady, all your life, not to know a turf-stack when you see it? thought I; but I said nothing. Then by and by she takes out her glass, and begins spying over the country.

'And what's all that black swamp out yonder, Sir Kit?' says she.

'My bog, my dear,' says he, and went on whistling.

'It's a very ugly prospect, my dear,' says she.

'You don't see it, my dear,' says he, 'for we've planted it out; when the trees grow up in summer-time——' says he.

'Where are the trees,' said she, 'my dear?' still looking through her glass.

'You are blind, my dear,' says he; 'what are these under your eyes?'

'These shrubs?' said she.

'Trees,' said he.

'Maybe they are what you call trees in Ireland, my dear,' said she; 'but they are not a yard high, are they?'

'They were planted out but last year, my lady,' says I, to soften matters between them, for I saw she was going the way to make his honour mad with her: 'they are very well grown for their age, and you'll not see the bog of Allybally-carricko'shaughlin at-all-at-all through the skreen, when once the leaves come out. But, my lady, you must not quarrel with any part or parcel of Allyballycarrick-o'shaughlin, for you don't know how many hundred years that same bit of bog has been in the family; we would not part with the bog of Allyballycarricko'shaughlin upon no account at all; it cost the late Sir Murtagh two hundred good pounds to defend his title to it and boundaries against the O'Learys, who cut a road through it.'

Now one would have thought this would have been hint enough for my lady, but she fell to laughing like one out of their right mind, and made me say the name of the bog over, for her to get it by heart, a dozen times; then she must ask me how to spell it, and what was the meaning of it in English—Sir Kit standing by whistling all the while. I verily believed she laid the corner-stone of all her future misfortunes at that very instant; but I said no more, only looked at Sir Kit.

There were no balls, no dinners, no doings; the country was all disappointed— Sir Kit's gentleman said in a whisper to me, it was all my lady's own fault, because she was so obstinate about the cross.

'What cross?' says I; 'is it about her being a heretic?'

'Oh, no such matter,' says he; 'my master does not mind her heresies, but her diamond cross—it's worth I can't tell you how much, and she has thousands of English pounds concealed in diamonds about her, which she as good as promised to give up to my master before he married; but now she won't part with any of them, and she must take the consequences.'

Her honeymoon, at least her Irish honeymoon, was scarcely well over, when his honour one morning said to me, 'Thady, buy me a pig!' and then the sausages were ordered, and here was the first open breaking-out of my lady's troubles. My lady came down herself into the kitchen to speak to the cook about the sausages, and desired never to see them more at her table. Now my master had ordered them, and my lady knew that. The cook took my lady's part, because she never came down into the kitchen, and was young and innocent in housekeeping, which raised her pity; besides, said she, at her own table, surely my lady should order and disorder what she pleases. But the cook soon changed her note, for my master made it a principle to have the sausages, and swore at her for a Jew herself, till he drove her fairly out of the kitchen; then, for fear of her place, and because he threatened that my lady should give her no discharge without the sausages, she gave up, and from that day forward always sausages, or bacon, or pig-meat in some shape or other, went up to table; upon which my lady shut herself up in her own room, and my master said she might stay there, with an oath: and to make sure of her, he turned the key in the door, and kept it ever after in his pocket. We none of us ever saw or heard her speak for seven years after that:[23] he carried her dinner himself. Then his honour had a great deal of company to dine with him, and balls in the house, and was as gay and gallant, and as much himself as before he was married; and at dinner he always drank my Lady Rackrent's good health and so did the company, and he sent out always a servant with his compliments to my Lady Rackrent, and the company was drinking her ladyship's health, and begged to know if there was anything at table he might send her, and the

---

[23] This part of the history of the Rackrent family can scarcely be thought credible; but in justice to honest Thady, it is hoped the reader will recollect the history of the celebrated Lady Cathcart's conjugal imprisonment. The editor was acquainted with Colonel M'Guire, Lady Cathcart's husband: he has lately seen and questioned the maid-servant who lived with Colonel M'Guire during the time of Lady Cathcart's imprisonment. Her ladyship was locked up in her own house for many years, during which period her husband was visited by the neighbouring gentry, and it was his regular custom at dinner to send his compliments to Lady Cathcart, informing her that the company had the honour to drink her ladyship's health, and begging to know whether there was any thing at table that she would like to eat? The answer was always, 'Lady Cathcart's compliments, and she has everything she wants.' An instance of honesty in a poor Irishwoman deserves to be recorded. Lady Cathcart had some remarkably fine diamonds, which she had concealed from her husband, and which she was anxious to get out of the house, lest he should discover them. She had neither servant nor friend to whom she could entrust them, but she had observed a poor beggar woman, who used to come to the house; she spoke to her from the window of the room in which she was confined; the woman promised to do what she desired, and Lady Cathcart threw a parcel containing the jewels to her. The poor woman carried them to the person to whom they were directed, and several years afterwards, when Lady Cathcart recovered her liberty, she received her diamonds safely.

At Colonel M'Guire's death her ladyship was released. The editor, within this year, saw the gentleman who accompanied her to England after her husband's death. When she first was told of his death she imagined that the news was not true, and that it was told only with an intention of deceiving her. At his death she had scarcely clothes sufficient to cover her; she wore a red wig, looked scared, and her understanding seemed stupefied; she said that she scarcely knew one human creature from another; her imprisonment lasted above twenty years. These circumstances may appear strange to an English reader; but there is no danger in the present times that any individual should exercise such tyranny as Colonel M'Guire's with impunity, the power being now all in the hands of Government, and there being no possibility of obtaining from Parliament an Act of indemnity for any cruelties.

man came back, after the sham errand, with my Lady Rackrent's compliments, and she was very much obliged to Sir Kit—she did not wish for anything, but drank the company's health. The country, to be sure, talked and wondered at my lady's being shut up, but nobody chose to interfere or ask any impertinent questions, for they knew my master was a man very apt to give a short answer himself, and likely to call a man out for it afterwards: he was a famous shot, had killed his man before he came of age, and nobody scarce dared look at him whilst at Bath. Sir Kit's character was so well known in the country that he lived in peace and quietness ever after, and was a great favourite with the ladies, especially when in process of time, in the fifth year of her confinement, my Lady Rackrent fell ill and took entirely to her bed, and he gave out that she was now skin and bone, and could not last through the winter. In this he had two physicians' opinions to back him (for now he called in two physicians for her), and tried all his arts to get the diamond cross from her on her death-bed, and to get her to make a will in his favour of her separate possessions; but there she was too tough for him. He used to swear at her behind her back after kneeling to her face, and call her in the presence of his gentleman his stiff-necked Israelite, though before he married her that same gentleman told me he used to call her (how he could bring it out, I don't know) 'my pretty Jessica!' To be sure it must have been hard for her to guess what sort of a husband he reckoned to make her. When she was lying, to all expectation, on her death-bed of a broken heart, I could not but pity her, though she was a Jewish, and considering too it was no fault of hers to be taken with my master, so young as she was at the Bath, and so fine a gentleman as Sir Kit was when he courted her; and considering too, after all they had heard and seen of him as a husband, there were now no less than three ladies in our country talked of for his second wife, all at daggers drawn with each other, as his gentleman swore, at the balls, for Sir Kit for their partner—I could not but think them bewitched, but they all reasoned with themselves that Sir Kit would make a good husband to any Christian but a Jewish, I suppose, and especially as he was now a reformed rake; and it was not known how my lady's fortune was settled in her will, nor how the Castle Rackrent estate was all mortgaged, and bonds out against him, for he was never cured of his gaming tricks; but that was the only fault he had, God bless him!

My lady had a sort of fit, and it was given out that she was dead, by mistake: this brought things to a sad crisis for my poor master. One of the three ladies showed his letters to her brother, and claimed his promises, whilst another did the same. I don't mention names. Sir Kit, in his defence, said he would meet any man who dared to question his conduct; and as to the ladies, they must settle it amongst them who was to be his second, and his third, and his fourth, whilst his first was still alive, to his mortification and theirs. Upon this, as upon all former occasions, he had the voice of the country with him, on account of the great spirit and propriety he acted with. He met and shot the first lady's brother: the next day he called out the second, who had a wooden leg, and their place of meeting by appointment being in a new-ploughed field, the wooden-leg man stuck fast in it. Sir Kit, seeing his situation, with great candour fired his pistol over his head;

upon which the seconds interposed, and convinced the parties there had been a slight misunderstanding between them: thereupon they shook hands cordially, and went home to dinner together. This gentleman, to show the world how they stood together, and by the advice of the friends of both parties, to re-establish his sister's injured reputation, went out with Sir Kit as his second, and carried his message next day to the last of his adversaries: I never saw him in such fine spirits as that day he went out—sure enough he was within ames-ace of getting quit handsomely of all his enemies; but unluckily, after hitting the toothpick out of his adversary's finger and thumb, he received a ball in a vital part, and was brought home, in little better than an hour after the affair, speechless on a hand-barrow to my lady. We got the key out of his pocket the first thing we did, and my son Jason ran to unlock the barrack-room, where my lady had been shut up for seven years, to acquaint her with the fatal accident. The surprise bereaved her of her senses at first, nor would she believe but we were putting some new trick upon her, to entrap her out of her jewels, for a great while, till Jason bethought himself of taking her to the window, and showed her the men bringing Sir Kit up the avenue upon the hand-barrow, which had immediately the desired effect; for directly she burst into tears, and pulling her cross from her bosom, she kissed it with as great devotion as ever I witnessed, and lifting up her eyes to heaven, uttered some ejaculation, which none present heard; but I take the sense of it to be, she returned thanks for this unexpected interposition in her favour when she had least reason to expect it. My master was greatly lamented: there was no life in him when we lifted him off the barrow, so he was laid out immediately, and 'waked' the same night. The country was all in an uproar about him, and not a soul but cried shame upon his murderer, who would have been hanged surely, if he could have been brought to his trial, whilst the gentlemen in the country were up about it; but he very prudently withdrew himself to the Continent before the affair was made public. As for the young lady who was the immediate cause of the fatal accident, however innocently, she could never show her head after at the balls in the county or any place; and by the advice of her friends and physicians, she was ordered soon after to Bath, where it was expected, if anywhere on this side of the grave, she would meet with the recovery of her health and lost peace of mind. As a proof of his great popularity, I need only add that there was a song made upon my master's untimely death in the newspapers, which was in everybody's mouth, singing up and down through the country, even down to the mountains, only three days after his unhappy exit. He was also greatly bemoaned at the Curragh, where his cattle were well known; and all who had taken up his bets were particularly inconsolable for his loss to society. His stud sold at the cant[24] at the greatest price ever known in the county; his favourite horses were chiefly disposed of amongst his particular friends, who would give any price for them for his sake; but no ready money was required by the new heir, who wished not to displease any of the gentlemen of the neighbourhood just upon his coming to settle amongst them; so a long credit was given where requisite, and the cash has never been gathered in from that day to this.

[24] See note 8.

But to return to my lady. She got surprisingly well after my master's decease. No sooner was it known for certain that he was dead, than all the gentlemen within twenty miles of us came in a body, as it were, to set my lady at liberty, and to protest against her confinement, which they now for the first time understood was against her own consent. The ladies too were as attentive as possible, striving who should be foremost with their morning visits; and they that saw the diamonds spoke very handsomely of them, but thought it a pity they were not bestowed, if it had so pleased God, upon a lady who would have become them better. All these civilities wrought little with my lady, for she had taken an unaccountable prejudice against the country, and everything belonging to it, and was so partial to her native land, that after parting with the cook, which she did immediately upon my master's decease, I never knew her easy one instant, night or day, but when she was packing up to leave us. Had she meant to make any stay in Ireland, I stood a great chance of being a great favourite with her; for when she found I understood the weather-cock, she was always finding some pretence to be talking to me, and asking me which way the wind blew, and was it likely, did I think, to continue fair for England. But when I saw she had made up her mind to spend the rest of her days upon her own income and jewels in England, I considered her quite as a foreigner, and not at all any longer as part of the family. She gave no vails to the servants at Castle Rackrent at parting, notwithstanding the old proverb of 'as rich as a Jew,' which she, being a Jewish, they built upon with reason. But from first to last she brought nothing but misfortunes amongst us; and if it had not been all along with her, his honour, Sir Kit, would have been now alive in all appearance. Her diamond cross was, they say, at the bottom of it all; and it was a shame for her, being his wife, not to show more duty, and to have given it up when he condescended to ask so often for such a bit of a trifle in his distresses, especially when he all along made it no secret he married for money. But we will not bestow another thought upon her. This much I thought it lay upon my conscience to say, in justice to my poor master's memory.

'Tis an ill wind that blows nobody no good: the same wind that took the Jew Lady Rackrent over to England brought over the new heir to Castle Rackrent.

Here let me pause for breath in my story, for though I had a great regard for every member of the family, yet without compare Sir Conolly, commonly called, for short, amongst his friends, Sir Condy Rackrent, was ever my great favourite, and, indeed, the most universally beloved man I had ever seen or heard of, not excepting his great ancestor Sir Patrick, to whose memory he, amongst other instances of generosity, erected a handsome marble stone in the church of Castle Rackrent, setting forth in large letters his age, birth, parentage, and many other virtues, concluding with the compliment so justly due, that 'Sir Patrick Rackrent lived and died a monument of old Irish hospitality.'

Sir Condy Rackrent, by the grace of God heir-at-law to the Castle Rackrent estate, was a remote branch of the family. Born to little or no fortune of his own, he was bred to the bar, at which, having many friends to push him and no mean natural abilities of his own, he doubtless would in process of time, if he could have borne the drudgery of that study, have been rapidly made King's Counsel at the least; but things were disposed of otherwise, and he never went the circuit but twice, and then made no figure for want of a fee, and being unable to speak in public. He received his education chiefly in the college of Dublin, but before he came to years of discretion lived in the country, in a small but slated house within view of the end of the avenue. I remember him, bare footed and headed, running through the street of O'Shaughlin's Town, and playing at pitch-and-toss, ball, marbles, and what not, with the boys of the town, amongst whom my son Jason was a great favourite with him. As for me, he was ever my white-headed boy: often's the time, when I would call in at his father's, where I was always made welcome, he would slip down to me in the kitchen, and, love to sit on my knee whilst I told him stories of the family and the blood from which he was sprung, and how he might look forward, if the then present man should die without childer, to being at the head of the Castle Rackrent estate. This was then spoke quite and clear at random to please the child, but it pleased Heaven to accomplish my prophecy afterwards, which gave him a great opinion of my judgment in business. He went to a little grammar-school with many others, and my son amongst the rest, who was in his class, and not a little useful to him in his book-learning, which he acknowledged with gratitude ever after. These rudiments of his education thus completed, he got a-horseback, to which exercise he was ever addicted, and used to gallop over the country while yet but a slip of a boy, under the care of Sir Kit's huntsman, who was very fond of him, and often lent him his gun, and took him out a-shooting under his own eye. By these means he became well acquainted and popular amongst the poor in the neighbourhood early, for there was not a cabin at which he had not stopped some morning or other, along with the huntsman, to drink a glass of burnt whisky out of an eggshell, to do him good and warm his heart and drive the cold out of his stomach. The old people always told him he was a great likeness of Sir Patrick, which made him first have an ambition to take after him, as far as his fortune should allow. He left us when of an age to enter the college, and there completed his education and nineteenth year, for as he was not born to an estate, his friends thought it incumbent on them to give him the best education which could be had for love or money, and a great deal of money consequently was spent upon him at College and Temple. He was a very little altered for the worse by what he saw there of the great world, for when he came down into the country to pay us a visit, we thought him just the same man as ever—hand and glove with every one, and as far from high, though not without his own proper share of family pride, as any man ever you see. Latterly, seeing how Sir Kit and the Jewish lived together, and that there was no one between him and the Castle Rackrent estate, he neglected to apply to the law as much as was expected of him, and secretly many of the tenants and others advanced him cash upon his note of hand value received, promising bargains of leases and lawful interest, should he ever come into the estate. All this was kept a great secret for fear the present man, hearing of it, should take it into his head to take it ill of poor Condy, and so should cut him off for ever by levying a fine, and suffering a recovery to dock the entail.[25] Sir Murtagh would have been the man for that; but Sir Kit was too much taken up philandering to consider the law in this case, or any other. These practices I have mentioned to account for the state of his affairs—I mean Sir Condy's upon his coming into the Castle Rackrent estate. He could not command a penny of his first year's income, which, and keeping no accounts, and the great sight of company he did, with many other causes too numerous to mention, was the origin of his distresses. My son Jason, who was now established agent, and knew every-thing, explained matters out of the face to Sir Conolly, and made him sensible of his embarrassed situation. With a great nominal rent-roll, it was almost all paid away in interest; which being for convenience suffered to run on, soon doubled the principal, and Sir Condy was obliged to pass new bonds for the interest, now grown principal, and so on. Whilst this was going on, my son requiring to be paid for his trouble and many years' service in the family gratis, and Sir Condy not willing to take his affairs into his own hands, or to look them even in the face, he gave my son a bargain of some acres which fell out of lease at a reasonable rent. Jason set the land, as soon as his lease was sealed, to under-tenants, to make the rent, and got two hundred a year profit rent; which was little enough considering his long agency. He bought the land at twelve years' purchase two years after-wards, when Sir Condy was pushed for money on an execution, and was at the same time allowed for his improvements thereon. There was a sort of hunting-lodge upon the estate, convenient to my son Jason's land, which he had his eye upon about this time; and he was a little jealous of Sir Condy, who talked of setting it to a stranger who was just come into the country—Captain Moneygawl was the man. He was son and heir to the Moneygawls of Mount Juliet's Town, who had a great estate in the next county to ours; and my master was loth to disoblige the young gentleman, whose heart was set upon the Lodge; so he wrote him back that the Lodge was at his service, and if he would honour him with his company at Castle Rackrent, they could ride over together some morning and look at it before signing the lease. Accordingly, the captain came over to us, and he and Sir Condy grew the greatest friends ever you see, and were for ever out a-shooting or hunting together, and were very merry in the evenings; and Sir Condy was invited of course to Mount Juliet's Town; and the family intimacy that had been in Sir Patrick's time was now recollected, and nothing would serve Sir Condy but he must be three times a week at the least with his new friends, which grieved me, who knew, by the captain's groom and gentleman, how they talked of him at Mount

---

25 The English reader may perhaps be surprised at the extent of Thady's legal knowledge, and at the fluency with which he pours forth law-terms; but almost every poor man in Ireland, be he farmer, weaver, shopkeeper, or steward, is, besides his other occupations, occasionally a lawyer. The nature of processes, ejectments, custodiams, injunctions, replevins, etc., is perfectly known to them, and the terms as familiar to them as to any attorney. They all love law. It is a kind of lottery, in which every man, staking his own wit or cunning against his neighbour's property, feels that he has little to lose, and much to gain. 'I'll have the law of you, so I will!' is the saying of an Englishman who expects justice. 'I'll have you before his honour,' is the threat of an Irishman who hopes for partiality.

Juliet's Town, making him quite, as one may say, a laughing-stock and a butt for the whole company; but they were soon cured of that by an accident that surprised 'em not a little, as it did me. There was a bit of a scrawl found upon the waiting-maid of old Mr. Moneygawl's youngest daughter, Miss Isabella, that laid open the whole; and her father, they say, was like one out of his right mind, and swore it was the last thing he ever should have thought of, when he invited my master to his house, that his daughter should think of such a match. But their talk signified not a straw, for as Miss Isabella's maid reported, her young mistress was fallen over head and ears in love with Sir Condy from the first time that ever her brother brought him into the house to dinner. The servant who waited that day behind my master's chair was the first who knew it, as he says; though it's hard to believe him, for he did not tell it till a great while afterwards; but, however, it's likely enough, as the thing turned out, that he was not far out of the way, for towards the middle of dinner, as he says, they were talking of stage-plays, having a play-house, and being great play-actors at Mount Juliet's Town; and Miss Isabella turns short to my master, and says:

'Have you seen the play-bill, Sir Condy?'

'No, I have not,' said he.

'Then more shame for you,' said the captain her brother, 'not to know that my sister is to play Juliet to-night, who plays it better than any woman on or off the stage in all Ireland.'

'I am very happy to hear it,' said Sir Condy; and there the matter dropped for the present.

But Sir Condy all this time, and a great while afterwards, was at a terrible nonplus; for he had no liking, not he, to stage-plays, nor to Miss Isabella either—to his mind, as it came out over a bowl of whisky-punch at home, his little Judy M'Quirk, who was daughter to a sister's son of mine, was worth twenty of Miss Isabella. He had seen her often when he stopped at her father's cabin to drink whisky out of the eggshell, out hunting, before he came to the estate, and, as she gave out, was under something like a promise of marriage to her. Anyhow, I could not but pity my poor master, who was so bothered between them, and he an easy-hearted man, that could not disoblige nobody—God bless him! To be sure, it was not his place to behave ungenerous to Miss Isabella, who had disobliged all her relations for his sake, as he remarked; and then she was locked up in her chamber, and forbid to think of him any more, which raised his spirit, because his family was, as he observed, as good as theirs at any rate, and the Rackrents a suitable match for the Moneygawls any day in the year; all which was true enough. But it grieved me to see that, upon the strength of all this, Sir Condy was growing more in the mind to carry off Miss Isabella to Scotland, in spite of her relations, as she desired.

'It's all over with our poor Judy!' said I, with a heavy sigh, making bold to speak to him one night when he was a little cheerful, and standing in the servants' hall all alone with me, as was often his custom.

'Not at all,' said he; 'I never was fonder of Judy than at this present speaking; and to prove it to you,' said he—and he took from my hand a halfpenny change that I had just got along with my tobacco—'and to prove it to you, Thady,' says he, 'it's a toss-up with me which I should marry this minute, her or Mr. Moneygawl of Mount Juliet's Town's daughter—so it is.'

'Oh—boo! boo!' says I, making light of it, to see what he would go on to next; 'your honour's joking, to be sure; there's no compare between our poor Judy and Miss Isabella, who has a great fortune, they say.'

'I'm not a man to mind a fortune, nor never was,' said Sir Condy, proudly, 'whatever her friends may say; and to make short of it,' says he, 'I'm come to a determination upon the spot.' With that he swore such a terrible oath as made me cross myself. 'And by this book,' said he, snatching up my ballad-book, mistaking it for my prayer-book, which lay in the window,—'and by this book,' says he, 'and by all the books that ever were shut and opened, it's come to a toss-up with me, and I'll stand or fall by the toss; and so Thady, hand me over that *pin* out of the ink-horn;' and he makes a cross on the smooth side of the halfpenny; 'Judy M'Quirk,' says he, 'her mark.'

God bless him! his hand was a little unsteadied by all the whisky-punch he had taken, but it was plain to see his heart was for poor Judy. My heart was all as one as in my mouth when I saw the halfpenny up in the air, but I said nothing at all; and when it came down I was glad I had kept myself to myself, for to be sure now it was all over with poor Judy.

'Judy's out a luck,' said I, striving to laugh.

'I'm out a luck,' said he; and I never saw a man look so cast down: he took up the halfpenny off the flag, and walked away quite sober-like by the shock. Now, though as easy a man, you would think, as any in the wide world, there was no such thing as making him unsay one of these sort of vows,[26] which he had learned to reverence when young, as I well remember teaching him to toss up for bog-berries on my knee. So I saw the affair was as good as settled between him and Miss Isabella, and I had no more to say but to wish her joy, which I did the week afterwards, upon her return from Scotland with my poor master.

My new lady was young, as might be supposed of a lady that had been carried off by her own consent to Scotland; but I could see her at first through her veil, which, from bashfulness or fashion, she kept over her face.

'And am I to walk through all this crowd of people, my dearest love?' said she to Sir Condy, meaning us servants and tenants, who had gathered at the back gate.

'My dear,' said Sir Condy, 'there's nothing for it but to walk, or to let me carry you as far as the house, for you see the back road is too narrow for a carriage,

---

26 It has been maliciously and unjustly hinted that the lower classes of the people of Ireland pay but little regard to oaths; yet it is certain that some oaths or vows have great power over their minds. Sometimes they swear they will be revenged on some of their neighbours; this is an oath that they are never known to break. But, what is infinitely more extraordinary and unaccountable, they sometimes make and keep a vow against whisky; these vows are usually limited to a short time. A woman who has a drunken husband is most fortunate if she can prevail upon him to go to the priest, and make a vow against whisky for a year, or a month, or a week, or a day.

and the great piers have tumbled down across the front approach; so there's no driving the right way, by reason of the ruins.'

'Plato, thou reasonest well!' said she, or words to that effect, which I could noways understand; and again, when her foot stumbled against a broken bit of a car-wheel, she cried out, 'Angels and ministers of grace defend us!' Well, thought I, to be sure, if she's no Jewish, like the last, she is a mad woman for certain, which is as bad: it would have been as well for my poor master to have taken up with poor Judy, who is in her right mind anyhow.

She was dressed like a mad woman, moreover, more than like any one I ever saw afore or since, and I could not take my eyes off her, but still followed behind her; and her feathers on the top of her hat were broke going in at the low back door, and she pulled out her little bottle out of her pocket to smell when she found herself in the kitchen, and said, 'I shall faint with the heat of this odious, odious place.'

'My dear, it's only three steps across the kitchen, and there's a fine air if your veil was up,' said Sir Condy; and with that threw back her veil, so that I had then a full sight of her face. She had not at all the colour of one going to faint, but a fine complexion of her own, as I then took it to be, though her maid told me after it was all put on; but even, complexion and all taken in, she was no way, in point of good looks, to compare to poor Judy, and withal she had a quality toss with her; but maybe it was my over-partiality to Judy, into whose place I may say she stepped, that made me notice all this.

To do her justice, however, she was, when we came to know her better, very liberal in her housekeeping—nothing at all of the skinflint in her; she left everything to the housekeeper, and her own maid, Mrs. Jane, who went with her to Scotland, gave her the best of characters for generosity. She seldom or ever wore a thing twice the same way, Mrs. Jane told us, and was always pulling her things to pieces and giving them away, never being used, in her father's house, to think of expense in anything; and she reckoned to be sure to go on the same way at Castle Rackrent; but when I came to inquire, I learned that her father was so mad with her for running off, after his locking her up and forbidding her to think any more of Sir Condy, that he would not give her a farthing; and it was lucky for her she had a few thousands of her own, which had been left to her by a good grandmother, and these were very convenient to begin with. My master and my lady set out in great style; they had the finest coach and chariot, and horses and liveries, and cut the greatest dash in the county, returning their wedding visits; and it was immediately reported that her father had undertaken to pay all my master's debts, and of course all his tradesmen gave him a new credit, and everything went on smack smooth, and I could not but admire my lady's spirit, and was proud to see Castle Rackrent again in all its glory. My lady had a fine taste for building, and furniture, and playhouses, and she turned everything topsy-turvy, and made the barrack-room into a theatre, as she called it, and she went on as if she had a mint of money at her elbow; and to be sure I thought she knew best, especially as Sir Condy said nothing to it one way or the other. All he asked—

God bless him!—was to live in peace and quietness, and have his bottle or his whisky-punch at night to himself. Now this was little enough, to be sure, for any gentleman; but my lady couldn't abide the smell of the whisky-punch.

'My dear,' says he, 'you liked it well enough before we were married, and why not now?'

'My dear,' said she, 'I never smelt it, or I assure you I should never have prevailed upon myself to marry you.'

'My dear, I am sorry you did not smell it, but we can't help that now,' returned my master, without putting himself in a passion, or going out of his way, but just fair and easy helped himself to another glass, and drank it off to her good health.

All this the butler told me, who was going backwards and forwards unnoticed with the jug, and hot water, and sugar, and all he thought wanting. Upon my master's swallowing the last glass of whisky-punch my lady burst into tears, calling him an ungrateful, base, barbarous wretch; and went off into a fit of hysterics, as I think Mrs. Jane called it, and my poor master was greatly frightened, this being the first thing of the kind he had seen; and he fell straight on his knees before her, and, like a good-hearted cratur as he was, ordered the whisky-punch out of the room, and bid 'em throw open all the windows, and cursed himself: and then my lady came to herself again, and when she saw him kneeling there, bid him get up, and not forswear himself any more, for that she was sure he did not love her, and never had. This we learned from Mrs. Jane, who was the only person left present at all this.

'My dear,' returns my master, thinking, to be sure, of Judy, as well he might, 'whoever told you so is an incendiary, and I'll have 'em turned out of the house this minute, if you'll only let me know which of them it was.'

'Told me what?' said my lady, starting upright in her chair.

'Nothing at all, nothing at all,' said my master, seeing he had overshot himself, and that my lady spoke at random; 'but what you said just now, that I did not love you, Bella; who told you that?'

'My own sense,' she said, and she put her handkerchief to her face, and leant back upon Mrs. Jane, and fell to sobbing as if her heart would break.

'Why now, Bella, this is very strange of you,' said my poor master; 'if nobody has told you nothing, what is it you are taking on for at this rate, and exposing yourself and me for this way?'

'Oh, say no more, say no more; every word you say kills me,' cried my lady; and she ran on like one, as Mrs. Jane says, raving, 'Oh, Sir Condy, Sir Condy! I that had hoped to find in you——'

'Why now, faith, this is a little too much; do, Bella, try to recollect yourself, my dear; am not I your husband, and of your own choosing, and is not that enough?'

'Oh, too much! too much!' cried my lady, wringing her hands.

'Why, my dear, come to your right senses, for the love of heaven. See, is not the whisky-punch, jug and bowl and all, gone out of the room long ago? What is it, in the wide world, you have to complain of?'

But still my lady sobbed and sobbed, and called herself the most wretched of women; and among other out-of-the-way provoking things, asked my master, was he fit company for her, and he drinking all night? This nettling him, which it was hard to do, he replied, that as to drinking all night, he was then as sober as she was herself, and that it was no matter how much a man drank, provided it did noways affect or stagger him: that as to being fit company for her, he thought himself of a family to be fit company for any lord or lady in the land; but that he never prevented her from seeing and keeping what company she pleased, and that he had done his best to make Castle Rackrent pleasing to her since her marriage, having always had the house full of visitors, and if her own relations were not amongst them, he said that was their own fault, and their pride's fault, of which he was sorry to find her ladyship had so unbecoming a share. So concluding, he took his candle and walked off to his room, and my lady was in her tantarums for three days after; and would have been so much longer, no doubt, but some of her friends, young ladies, and cousins, and second cousins, came to Castle Rackrent, by my poor master's express invitation, to see her, and she was in a hurry to get up, as Mrs. Jane called it, a play for them, and so got well, and was as finely dressed, and as happy to look at, as ever; and all the young ladies, who used to be in her room dressing of her, said in Mrs. Jane's hearing that my lady was the happiest bride ever they had seen, and that to be sure a love-match was the only thing for happiness, where the parties could any way afford it.

As to affording it, God knows it was little they knew of the matter; my lady's few thousands could not last for ever, especially the way she went on with them; and letters from tradefolk came every post thick and threefold, with bills as long as my arm, of years' and years' standing. My son Jason had 'em all handed over to him, and the pressing letters were all unread by Sir Condy, who hated trouble, and could never be brought to hear talk of business, but still put it off and put it off, saying, 'Settle it anyhow,' or, 'Bid 'em call again to-morrow,' or, 'Speak to me about it some other time.' Now it was hard to find the right time to speak, for in the mornings he was a-bed, and in the evenings over his bottle, where no gentleman chooses to be disturbed. Things in a twelvemonth or so came to such a pass there was no making a shift to go on any longer, though we were all of us well enough used to live from hand to mouth at Castle Rackrent. One day, I remember, when there was a power of company, all sitting after dinner in the dusk, not to say dark, in the drawing-room, my lady having rung five times for candles, and none to go up, the housekeeper sent up the footman, who went to my mistress, and whispered behind her chair how it was.

'My lady,' says he, 'there are no candles in the house.'

'Bless me,' says she; 'then take a horse and gallop off as fast as you can to Carrick O'Fungus, and get some.'

'And in the meantime tell them to step into the playhouse, and try if there are not some bits left,' added Sir Condy, who happened to be within hearing. The man was sent up again to my lady, to let her know there was no horse to go, but one that wanted a shoe.

'Go to Sir Condy then; I know nothing at all about the horses,' said my lady; 'why do you plague me with these things?' How it was settled I really forget, but to the best of my remembrance, the boy was sent down to my son Jason's to borrow candles for the night. Another time, in the winter, and on a desperate cold day, there was no turf in for the parlour and above stairs, and scarce enough for the cook in the kitchen. The little *gossoon*[27] was sent off to the neighbours, to see and beg or borrow some, but none could he bring back with him for love or money; so, as needs must, we were forced to trouble Sir Condy—'Well, and if there's no turf to be had in the town or country, why, what signifies talking any more about it; can't ye go and cut down a tree?'

'Which tree, please your honour?' I made bold to say.

'Any tree at all that's good to burn,' said Sir Condy; 'send off smart and get one down, and the fires lighted, before my lady gets up to breakfast, or the house will be too hot to hold us.'

He was always very considerate in all things about my lady, and she wanted for nothing whilst he had it to give. Well, when things were tight with them about this time, my son Jason put in a word again about the Lodge, and made a genteel offer to lay down the purchase-money, to relieve Sir Condy's distresses. Now Sir Condy had it from the best authority that there were two writs come down to the sheriff against his person, and the sheriff, as ill-luck would have it, was no friend of his, and talked how he must do his duty, and how he would do it, if it was against the first man in the country, or even his own brother, let alone one who had voted against him at the last election, as Sir Condy had done. So Sir Condy was fain to take the purchase-money of the Lodge from my son Jason to settle matters; and sure enough it was a good bargain for both parties, for my son bought the fee-simple of a good house for him and his heirs for ever, for little or nothing, and by selling of it for that same my master saved himself from a gaol. Every way it turned out fortunate for Sir Condy, for before the money was all gone there came a general election, and he being so well beloved in the county, and one of the oldest families, no one had a better right to stand candidate for the vacancy; and he was called upon by all his friends, and the whole county I may say, to declare himself against the old member, who had little thought of a contest. My master did not relish the thoughts of a troublesome canvass, and all the ill-will he might bring upon himself by disturbing the peace of the county, besides the expense, which was no trifle; but all his friends called upon one another to subscribe, and they formed themselves into a committee, and wrote all his circular letters for him, and engaged all his agents, and did all the business unknown to him; and he was well pleased that it should be so at last, and my lady herself was very sanguine about the election; and there was open house kept night and day at Castle Rackrent, and I thought I never saw my lady look so well in her life as she did at that time. There were grand dinners, and all the gentlemen

---

[27] A little boy—from the French word *garçon*. In most Irish families there used to be a barefooted gossoon, who was slave to the cook and the butler, and who, in fact, without wages, did all the hard work of the house. Gossoons were always employed as messengers. The Editor has known a gossoon to go on foot, without shoes or stockings, fifty-one English miles between sunrise and sunset.

drinking success to Sir Condy till they were carried off; and then dances and balls, and the ladies all finishing with a raking pot of tea in the morning.[28] Indeed, it was well the company made it their choice to sit up all nights, for there were not half beds enough for the sights of people that were in it, though there were shake-downs in the drawing-room always made up before sunrise for those that liked it. For my part, when I saw the doings that were going on, and the loads of claret that went down the throats of them that had no right to be asking for it, and the sights of meat that went up to table and never came down, besides what was carried off to one or t'other below stair, I couldn't but pity my poor master, who was to pay for all; but I said nothing, for fear of gaining myself ill-will. The day of election will come some time or other, says I to myself, and all will be over; and so it did, and a glorious day it was as any I ever had the happiness to see.

'Huzza! huzza! Sir Condy Rackrent for ever!' was the first thing I hears in the morning, and the same and nothing else all day, and not a soul sober only just when polling, enough to give their votes as became 'em, and to stand the brow-beating of the lawyers, who came tight enough upon us; and many of our free-holders were knocked off, having never a freehold that they could safely swear to, and Sir Condy was not willing to have any man perjure himself for his sake, as was done on the other side, God knows; but no matter for that. Some of our friends were dumbfounded by the lawyers asking them: Had they ever been upon the ground where their freeholds lay? Now, Sir Condy being tender of the consciences of them that had not been on the ground, and so could not swear to a freehold when cross-examined by them lawyers, sent out for a couple of cleaveseful of the sods of his farm of Gulteeshinnagh; and as soon as the sods came into town, he set each man upon his sod, and so then, ever after, you know, they could fairly swear they had been upon the ground. We gained the day by this piece of

---

[28] We should observe, this custom has long since been banished from the higher orders of Irish gentry. The mysteries of a raking pot of tea, like those of the Bona Dea, are supposed to be sacred to females; but now and then it has happened that some of the male species, who were either more audacious, or more highly favoured than the rest of their sex, have been admitted by stealth to these orgies. The time when the festive ceremony begins varies according to circumstances, but it is never earlier than twelve o'clock at night; the joys of a raking pot of tea depending on its being made in secret, and at an unseasonable hour. After a ball, when the more discreet part of the company has departed to rest, a few chosen female spirits, who have footed it till they can foot it no longer, and till the sleepy notes expire under the slurring hand of the musician, retire to a bedchamber, call the favourite maid, who alone is admitted, bid her *put down the kettle,* lock the door, and amidst as much giggling and scrambling as possible, they get round a tea-table, on which all manner of things are huddled together. Then begin mutual railleries and mutual confidences amongst the young ladies, and the faint scream and the loud laugh is heard, and the romping for letters and pocket-books begins, and gentlemen are called by their surnames, or by the general name of fellows! pleasant fellows! charming fellows! odious fellows! abominable fellows! and then all prudish decorums are forgotten, and then we might be convinced how much the satirical poet was mistaken when he said—

There is no woman where there's no reserve.

The merit of the original idea of a raking pot of tea evidently belongs to the washerwoman and the laundry-maid. But why should not we have *Low life above stairs* as well as *High life below stairs?*

honesty.[29] I thought I should have died in the streets for joy when I seed my poor master chaired, and he bareheaded, and it raining as hard as it could pour; but all the crowds following him up and down, and he bowing and shaking hands with the whole town.

'Is that Sir Condy Rackrent in the chair?' says a stranger man in the crowd.

'The same,' says I. 'Who else should it be? God bless him!'

'And I take it, then, you belong to him?' says he.

'Not at all,' says I; 'but I live under him, and have done so these two hundred years and upwards, me and mine.'

'It's lucky for you, then,' rejoins he, 'that he is where he is; for was he anywhere else but in the chair, this minute he'd be in a worse place; for I was sent down on purpose to put him up,[30] and here's my order for so doing in my pocket.'

It was a writ that villain the wine merchant had marked against my poor master for some hundreds of an old debt, which it was a shame to be talking of at such a time as this.

'Put it in your pocket again, and think no more of it anyways for seven years to come, my honest friend,' say I; 'he's a member of Parliament now, praised be God, and such as you can't touch him: and if you'll take a fool's advice, I'd have you keep out of the way this day, or you'll run a good chance of getting your deserts amongst my master's friends, unless you choose to drink his health like everybody else.'

'I've no objection to that in life,' said he. So we went into one of the public-houses kept open for my master; and we had a great deal of talk about this thing and that. 'And how is it,' says he, 'your master keeps on so well upon his legs? I heard say he was off Holantide twelvemonth past.'

'Never was better or heartier in his life,' said I.

'It's not that I'm after speaking of,' said he; 'but there was a great report of his being ruined.'

'No matter,' says I, 'the sheriffs two years running were his particular friends, and the sub-sheriffs were both of them gentlemen, and were properly spoken to;

---

[29] In a dispute which occurred some years ago in Ireland, between Mr. E. and Mr. M., about the boundaries of a farm, an old tenant of Mr. M's cut a *sod* from Mr. M.'s land, and inserted it in a spot prepared for its reception in Mr. E.'s land; so nicely was it inserted, that no eye could detect the junction of the grass. The old man, who was to give his evidence as to the property, stood upon the inserted sod when the *viewers* came, and swore that the ground he *then stood upon* belonged to his landlord, Mr. M.

The Editor had flattered himself that the ingenious contrivance which Thady records, and the similar subterfuge of this old Irishman, in the dispute concerning boundaries, were instances of 'cuteness unparalleled in all but Irish story: an English friend, however, has just mortified the Editor's national vanity by an account of the following custom, which prevails in part of Shropshire. It is discreditable for women to appear abroad after the birth of their children till they have been *churched*. To avoid this reproach, and at the same time to enjoy the pleasure of gadding, whenever a woman goes abroad before she has been to church, she takes a tile from the roof of her house, and puts it upon her head: wearing this panoply all the time she pays her visits, her conscience is perfectly at ease; for she can afterwards safely declare to the clergyman, that she 'has never been from under her own roof till she came to be churched.'

[30] To put him in gaol.

and so the writs lay snug with them, and they, as I understand by my son Jason the custom in them cases is, returned the writs as they came to them to those that sent 'em—much good may it do them!—with a word in Latin, that no such person as Sir Condy Rackrent, Bart., was to be found in those parts.'

'Oh, I understand all those ways better—no offence—than you,' says he, laughing, and at the same time filling his glass to my master's good health, which convinced me he was a warm friend in his heart after all, though appearances were a little suspicious or so at first. 'To be sure,' says he, still cutting his joke, 'when a man's over head and shoulders in debt, he may live the faster for it, and the better if he goes the right way about it; or else how is it so many live on so well, as we see every day, after they are ruined?'

'How is it,' says I, being a little merry at the time—'how is it but just as you see the ducks in the chicken-yard, just after their heads are cut off by the cook, running round and round faster than when alive?'

At which conceit he fell a-laughing, and remarked he had never had the happiness yet to see the chicken-yard at Castle Rackrent.

'It won't be long so, I hope,' says I; 'you'll be kindly welcome there, as everybody is made by my master: there is not a freer-spoken gentleman, or a better beloved, high or low, in all Ireland.'

And of what passed after this I'm not sensible, for we drank Sir Condy's good health and the downfall of his enemies till we could stand no longer ourselves. And little did I think at the time, or till long after, how I was harbouring my poor master's greatest of enemies myself. This fellow had the impudence, after coming to see the chicken-yard, to get me to introduce him to my son Jason; little more than the man that never was born did I guess at his meaning by this visit: he gets him a correct list fairly drawn out from my son Jason of all my master's debts, and goes straight round to the creditors and buys them all up, which he did easy enough, seeing the half of them never expected to see their money out of Sir Condy's hands. Then, when this base-minded limb of the law, as I afterwards detected him in being, grew to be sole creditor over all, he takes him out a custodiam on all the denominations and sub-denominations, and even carton[31] and half-carton upon the estate; and not content with that, must have an execution against the master's goods and down to the furniture, though little worth, of Castle Rackrent itself. But this is a part of my story I'm not come to yet, and it's bad to be forestalling: ill news flies fast enough all the world over.

To go back to the day of the election, which I never think of but with pleasure and tears of gratitude for those good times: after the election was quite and clean over, there comes shoals of people from all parts, claiming to have obliged my master with their votes, and putting him in mind of promises which he could never remember himself to have made: one was to have a freehold for each of his four

---

31 Thady means cartron, and half-cartron. 'According to the old record in the black book of Dublin, a *cantred* is said to contain 30 *villatas terras,* which are also called *quarters* of land (quarterons, *cartrons*); every one of which quarters must contain so much ground as will pasture 400 cows, and 17 plough-lands. A knight's fee was composed of 8 hydes, which amount to 160 acres, and that is generally deemed about a *plough-land.*'

sons; another was to have a renewal of a lease; another an abatement; one came to be paid ten guineas for a pair of silver buckles sold my master on the hustings, which turned out to be no better than copper gilt; another had a long bill for oats, the half of which never went into the granary to my certain knowledge, and the other half was not fit for the cattle to touch; but the bargain was made the week before the election, and the coach and saddle-horses were got into order for the day, besides a vote fairly got by them oats; so no more reasoning on that head. But then there was no end to them that were telling Sir Condy he had engaged to make their sons excisemen, or high constables, or the like; and as for them that had bills to give in for liquor, and beds, and straw, and ribands, and horses, and post-chaises for the gentlemen freeholders that came from all parts and other countries to vote for my master, and were not, to be sure, to be at any charges, there was no standing against all these; and, worse than all, the gentlemen of my master's committee, who managed all for him, and talked how they'd bring him in without costing him a penny, and subscribed by hundreds very genteelly, forgot to pay their subscriptions, and had laid out in agents' and lawyers' fees and secret service money to the Lord knows how much; and my master could never ask one of them for their subscription you are sensible, nor for the price of a fine horse he had sold one of them; so it all was left at his door. He could never, God bless him again! I say, bring himself to ask a gentleman for money, despising such sort of conversation himself; but others, who were not gentlemen born, behaved very uncivil in pressing him at this very time, and all he could do to content 'em all was to take himself out of the way as fast as possible to Dublin, where my lady had taken a house fitting for him as a member of Parliament, to attend his duty in there all the winter. I was very lonely when the whole family was gone, and all the things they had ordered to go, and forgot, sent after them by the car. There was then a great silence in Castle Rackrent, and I went moping from room to room, hearing the doors clap for want of right locks, and the wind through the broken windows, that the glazier never would come to mend, and the rain coming through the roof and best ceilings all over the house for want of the slater, whose bill was not paid, besides our having no slates or shingles for that part of the old building which was shingled and burnt when the chimney took fire, and had been open to the weather ever since. I took myself to the servants' hall in the evening to smoke my pipe as usual, but missed the bit of talk we used to have there sadly, and ever after was content to stay in the kitchen and boil my little potatoes,[32] and put up my bed there, and every post-day I looked in the newspaper, but no news of my master in the House; he never spoke good or bad, but, as the butler wrote down word to my son Jason, was very ill-used by the Government about a place that was promised him and never given, after his supporting them against his conscience very honourably, and being greatly abused for it, which hurt him greatly, he having the name of a great patriot in the country before. The house and living in Dublin too were not to be had for nothing, and my son Jason said, 'Sir Condy

---

[32] Thady does not mean by this expression that his potatoes were less than other people's, or less than the usual size. *Little* is here used only as an Italian diminutive, expressive of fondness.

must soon be looking out for a new agent, for I've done my part, and can do no more. If my lady had the bank of Ireland to spend, it would go all in one winter, and Sir Condy would never gainsay her, though he does not care the rind of a lemon for her all the while.'

Now I could not bear to hear Jason giving out after this manner against the family, and twenty people standing by in the street. Ever since he had lived at the Lodge of his own he looked down, howsomever, upon poor old Thady, and was grown quite a great gentleman, and had none of his relations near him; no wonder he was no kinder to poor Sir Condy than to his own kith or kin. In the spring it was the villain that got the list of the debts from him brought down the custodiam, Sir Condy still attending his duty in Parliament; and I could scarcely believe my own old eyes, or the spectacles with which I read it, when I was shown my son Jason's name joined in the custodiam; but he told me it was only for form's sake, and to make things easier than if all the land was under the power of a total stranger. Well, I did not know what to think; it was hard to be talking ill of my own, and I could not but grieve for my poor master's fine estate, all torn by these vultures of the law; so I said nothing, but just looked on to see how it would all end.

It was not till the month of June that he and my lady came down to the country. My master was pleased to take me aside with him to the brewhouse that same evening, to complain to me of my son and other matters, in which he said he was confident I had neither art nor part; he said a great deal more to me, to whom he had been fond to talk ever since he was my white-headed boy before he came to the estate; and all that he said about poor Judy I can never forget, but scorn to repeat. He did not say an unkind word of my lady, but wondered, as well he might, her relations would do nothing for him or her, and they in all this great distress. He did not take anything long to heart, let it be as it would, and had no more malice or thought of the like in him than a child that can't speak; this night it was all out of his head before he went to his bed. He took his jug of whisky-punch—my lady was grown quite easy about the whisky-punch by this time, and so I did suppose all was going on right betwixt them, till I learnt the truth through Mrs. Jane, who talked over the affairs to the housekeeper, and I within hearing. The night my master came home, thinking of nothing at all but just making merry, he drank his bumper toast 'to the deserts of that old curmudgeon my father-in-law, and all enemies at Mount Juliet's Town.' Now my lady was no longer in the mind she formerly was, and did noways relish hearing her own friends abused in her presence, she said.

'Then why don't they show themselves your friends,' said my master, 'and oblige me with the loan of the money I condescended, by your advice, my dear, to ask? It's now three posts since I sent off my letter, desiring in the postscript a speedy answer by the return of the post, and no account at all from them yet.'

'I expect they'll write to *me* next post,' says my lady, and that was all that passed then; but it was easy from this to guess there was a coolness betwixt them, and with good cause.

The next morning, being post-day, I sent off the gossoon early to the post-office, to see was there any letter likely to set matters to rights, and he brought back one with the proper post-mark upon it, sure enough, and I had no time to examine or make any conjecture more about it, for into the servants' hall pops Mrs. Jane with a blue bandbox in her hand, quite entirely mad.

'Dear ma'am, and what's the matter?' says I.

'Matter enough,' says she; 'don't you see my bandbox is wet through, and my best bonnet here spoiled, besides my lady's, and all by the rain coming in through that gallery window that you might have got mended if you'd had any sense, Thady, all the time we were in town in the winter?'

'Sure, I could not get the glazier, ma'am,' says I.

'You might have stopped it up anyhow,' says she.

'So I did, ma'am, to the best of my ability; one of the panes with the old pillow-case, and the other with a piece of the old stage green curtain. Sure I was as careful as possible all the time you were away, and not a drop of rain came in at that window of all the windows in the house, all winter, ma'am, when under my care; and now the family's come home, and it's summer-time, I never thought no more about it, to be sure; but dear, it's a pity to think of your bonnet, ma'am. But here's what will please you, ma'am—a letter from Mount Juliet's Town for my lady.

With that she snatches it from me without a word more, and runs up the back stairs to my mistress; I follows with a slate to make up the window. This window was in the long passage, or gallery, as my lady gave out orders to have it called, in the gallery leading to my master's bedchamber and hers. And when I went up with the slate, the door having no lock, and the bolt spoilt, was ajar after Mrs. Jane, and, as I was busy with the window, I heard all that was saying within.

'Well, what's in your letter, Bella, my dear?' says he: 'you're a long time spelling it over.'

'Won't you shave this morning, Sir Condy?' says she, and put the letter into her pocket.

'I shaved the day before yesterday,' said he, 'my dear, and that's not what I'm thinking of now; but anything to oblige you, and to have peace and quietness, my dear'—and presently I had a glimpse of him at the cracked glass over the chimney-piece, standing up shaving himself to please my lady. But she took no notice, but went on reading her book, and Mrs. Jane doing her hair behind.

'What is it you're reading there, my dear?—phoo, I've cut myself with this razor; the man's a cheat that sold it me, but I have not paid him for it yet. What is it you're reading there? Did you hear me asking you, my dear?'

'*The Sorrows of Werter*,' replies my lady, as well as I could hear.

'I think more of the sorrows of Sir Condy,' says my master, joking like. 'What news from Mount Juliet's Town?'

'No news,' says she, 'but the old story over again; my friends all reproaching me still for what I can't help now.'

'Is it for marrying me?' said my master, still shaving. 'What signifies, as you say, talking of that, when it can't be help'd now?'

With that she heaved a great sigh that I heard plain enough in the passage.

'And did not you use me basely, Sir Condy,' says she, 'not to tell me you were ruined before I married you?'

'Tell you, my dear!' said he. 'Did you ever ask me one word about it? And had not you friends enough of your own, that were telling you nothing else from morning to night, if you'd have listened to them slanders?'

'No slanders, nor are my friends slanderers; and I can't bear to hear them treated with disrespect as I do,' says my lady, and took out her pocket-handkerchief; 'they are the best of friends, and if I had taken their advice——. But my father was wrong to lock me up, I own. That was the only unkind thing I can charge him with; for if he had not locked me up, I should never have had a serious thought of running away as I did.'

'Well, my dear,' said my master, 'don't cry and make yourself uneasy about it now, when it's all over, and you have the man of your own choice, in spite of 'em all.'

'I was too young, I know, to make a choice at the time you ran away with me, I'm sure,' says my lady, and another sigh, which made my master, half-shaved as he was, turn round upon her in surprise.

'Why, Bell,' says he, 'you can't deny what you know as well as I do, that it was at your own particular desire, and that twice under your own hand and seal expressed, that I should carry you off as I did to Scotland, and marry you there.'

'Well, say no more about it, Sir Condy,' said my lady, pettish-like; 'I was a child then, you know.'

'And as far as I know, you're little better now, my dear Bella, to be talking in this manner to your husband's face; but I won't take it ill of you, for I know it's something in that letter you put into your pocket just now that has set you against me all on a sudden, and imposed upon your understanding.'

'It's not so very easy as you think it, Sir Condy, to impose upon my understanding,' said my lady.

'My dear,' says he, 'I have, and with reason, the best opinion of your understanding of any man now breathing; and you know I have never set my own in competition with it till now, my dear Bella,' says he, taking her hand from her book as kind as could be—'till now, when I have the great advantage of being quite cool, and you not; so don't believe one word your friends say against your own Sir Condy, and lend me the letter out of your pocket, till I see what it is they can have to say.'

'Take it then,' says she; 'and as you are quite cool, I hope it is a proper time to request you'll allow me to comply with the wishes of all my own friends, and return to live with my father and family, during the remainder of my wretched existence, at Mount Juliet's Town.'

At this my poor master fell back a few paces, like one that had been shot.

'You're not serious, Bella,' says he; 'and could you find it in your heart to leave me this way in the very middle of my distresses, all alone?' But recollecting himself after his first surprise, and a moment's time for reflection, he said, with a great deal of consideration for my lady, 'Well, Bella, my dear, I believe you are right; for what could you do at Castle Rackrent, and an execution against the goods coming down, and the furniture to be canted, and an auction in the house all next week? So you have my full consent to go, since that is your desire; only you must not think of my accompanying you, which I could not in honour do upon the terms I always have been, since our marriage, with your friends. Besides, I have business to transact at home; so in the meantime, if we are to have any breakfast this morning, let us go down and have it for the last time in peace and comfort, Bella.'

Then as I heard my master coming to the passage door, I finished fastening up my slate against the broken pane; and when he came out I wiped down the window-seat with my wig,[33] and bade him a 'good-morrow' as kindly as I could, seeing he was in trouble, though he strove and thought to hide it from me.

'This window is all racked and tattered,' says I, 'and it's what I'm striving to mend.'

'It *is* all racked and tattered, plain enough,' says he, 'and never mind mending it, honest old Thady,' says he; 'it will do well enough for you and I, and that's all the company we shall have left in the house by and by.'

'I'm sorry to see your honour so low this morning,' says I; 'but you'll be better after taking your breakfast.'

'Step down to the servants' hall,' said he, 'and bring me up the pen and ink into the parlour, and get a sheet of paper from Mrs. Jane, for I have business that can't brook to be delayed; and come into the parlour with the pen and ink yourself, Thady, for I must have you to witness my signing a paper I have to execute in a hurry.'

Well, while I was getting of the pen and ink-horn, and the sheet of paper, I ransacked my brains to think what could be the papers my poor master could have to execute in such a hurry, he that never thought of such a thing as doing business afore breakfast in the whole course of his life, for any man living; but this was for my lady, as I afterwards found, and the more genteel of him after all her treatment.

I was just witnessing the paper that he had scrawled over, and was shaking the ink out of my pen upon the carpet, when my lady came in to breakfast, and she started as if it had been a ghost; as well she might, when she saw Sir Condy writing at this unseasonable hour.

'That will do very well, Thady,' says he to me, and took the paper I had signed to, without knowing what upon the earth it might be, out of my hands, and walked, folding it up, to my lady.

'You are concerned in this, my Lady Rackrent,' said he, putting it into her hands; 'and I beg you'll keep this memorandum safe, and show it to your friends the first thing you do when you get home; but put it in your pocket now, my dear, and let us eat our breakfast, in God's name.'

---

[33] Wigs were formerly used instead of brooms in Ireland for sweeping or dusting tables, stairs, etc. The Editor doubted the fact till he saw a labourer of the old school sweep down a flight of stairs with his wig; he afterwards put it on his head again with the utmost composure, and said, 'Oh, please your honour, it's never a bit the worse.'

It must be acknowledged that these men are not in any danger of catching cold by taking off their wigs occasionally, because they usually have fine crops of hair growing under their wigs. The wigs are often yellow, and the hair which appears from beneath them black; the wigs are usually too small, and are raised up by the hair beneath, or by the ears of the wearers.

'What is all this?' said my lady, opening the paper in great curiosity.

'It's only a bit of a memorandum of what I think becomes me to do whenever I am able,' says my master; 'you know my situation, tied hand and foot at the present time being, but that can't last always, and when I'm dead and gone the land will be to the good, Thady, you know; and take notice it's my intention your lady should have a clear five hundred a year jointure off the estate afore any of my debts are paid.'

'Oh, please your honour,' says I, 'I can't expect to live to see that time, being now upwards of fourscore years of age, and you a young man, and likely to continue so, by the help of God.'

I was vexed to see my lady so insensible too, for all she said was, 'This is very genteel of you, Sir Condy. You need not wait any longer, Thady.' So I just picked up the pen and ink that had tumbled on the floor, and heard my master finish with saying, 'You behaved very genteel to me, my dear, when you threw all the little you had in your power along with yourself into my hands; and as I don't deny but what you may have had some things to complain of,'—to be sure he was thinking then of Judy, or of the whisky-punch, one or t'other, or both,—'and as I don't deny but you may have had something to complain of, my dear, it is but fair you should have something in the form of compensation to look forward to agreeably in future; besides, it's an act of justice to myself, that none of your friends, my dear, may ever have it to say against me, I married for money, and not for love.'

'That is the last thing I should ever have thought of saying of you, Sir Condy,' said my lady, looking very gracious.

'Then, my dear,' said Sir Condy, 'we shall part as good friends as we met; so all's right.'

I was greatly rejoiced to hear this, and went out of the parlour to report it all to the kitchen. The next morning my lady and Mrs. Jane set out for Mount Juliet's Town in the jaunting-car. Many wondered at my lady's choosing to go away, considering all things, upon the jaunting-car, as if it was only a party of pleasure; but they did not know till I told them that the coach was all broke in the journey down, and no other vehicle but the car to be had. Besides, my lady's friends were to send their coach to meet her at the cross-roads; so it was all done very proper.

My poor master was in great trouble after my lady left us. The execution came down, and everything at Castle Rackrent was seized by the gripers, and my son Jason, to his shame be it spoken, amongst them. I wondered, for the life of me, how he could harden himself to do it; but then he had been studying the law, and had made himself Attorney Quirk; so he brought down at once a heap of accounts upon my master's head. To cash lent, and to ditto, and to ditto, and to ditto and oats, and bills paid at the milliner's and linen-draper's, and many dresses for the fancy balls in Dublin for my lady, and all the bills to the workmen and tradesmen for the scenery of the theatre, and the chandler's and grocer's bills, and tailor's, besides butcher's and baker's, and, worse than all, the old one of that base wine merchant's, that wanted to arrest my poor master for the amount on the election day, for which amount Sir Condy afterwards passed his note of hand, bearing lawful interest from the date thereof; and the interest and compound interest was now mounted to a terrible deal on many other notes and bonds for money borrowed, and there was, besides, hush-money to the sub-sheriffs, and sheets upon sheets of old and new attorneys' bills, with heavy balances, 'as per former account furnished,' brought forward with interest thereon; then there was a powerful deal due to the Crown for sixteen years' arrear of quit-rent of the town-lands of Carrickshaughlin, with driver's fees, and a compliment to the receiver every year for letting the quit-rent run on to oblige Sir Condy, and Sir Kit afore him. Then there were bills for spirits and ribands at the election time, and the gentlemen of the committee's accounts unsettled, and their subscription never gathered; and there were cows to be paid for, with the smith and farrier's bills to be set against the rent of the demesne, with calf and hay money; then there was all the servants' wages, since I don't know when, coming due to them, and sums advanced for them by my son Jason for clothes, and boots, and whips, and odd moneys for sundries expended by them in journeys to town and elsewhere, and pocket-money for the master continually, and messengers and postage before his being a Parliament man. I can't myself tell you what besides; but this I know, that when the evening came on the which Sir Condy had appointed to settle all with my son Jason, and when he comes into the parlour, and sees the sight of bills and load of papers all gathered on the great dining-table for him, he puts his hands before both his eyes, and cried out, 'Merciful Jasus! what is it I see before me?' Then I sets an arm-chair at the table for him, and with a deal of difficulty he sits him down, and my son Jason hands him over the pen and ink to sign to this man's bill and t'other man's bill, all which he did without making the least objections. Indeed, to give him his due, I never seen a man more fair and honest, and easy in all his dealings, from first to last, as Sir Condy, or more willing to pay every man his own as far as he was able, which is as much as any one can do.

'Well,' says he, joking like with Jason, 'I wish we could settle it all with a stroke of my grey goose quill. What signifies making me wade through all this ocean of papers here; can't you now, who understand drawing out an account, debtor and creditor, just sit down here at the corner of the table and get it done out for me, that I may have a clear view of the balance, which is all I need be talking about, you know?'

'Very true, Sir Condy; nobody understands business better than yourself,' says Jason.

'So I've a right to do, being born and bred to the bar,' says Sir Condy. 'Thady, do step out and see are they bringing in the things for the punch, for we've just done all we have to do for this evening.'

I goes out accordingly, and when I came back Jason was pointing to the balance, which was a terrible sight to my poor master.

'Pooh! pooh! pooh!' says he. 'Here's so many noughts they dazzle my eyes, so they do, and put me in mind of all I suffered larning of my numeration table, when I was a boy at the day-school along with you, Jason—units, tens, hundreds, tens of hundreds. Is the punch ready, Thady?' says he, seeing me.

'Immediately; the boy has the jug in his hand; it's coming upstairs, please your honour, as fast as possible,' says I, for I saw his honour was tired out of his life; but Jason, very short and cruel, cuts me off with—'Don't be talking of punch yet awhile; it's no time for punch yet a bit—units, tens, hundreds,' goes he on, counting over the master's shoulder, units, tens, hundreds, thousands.

'A-a-ah! hold your hand,' cries my master. 'Where in this wide world am I to find hundreds, or units itself, let alone thousands?'

'The balance has been running on too long,' says Jason, sticking to him as I could not have done at the time, if you'd have given both the Indies and Cork to boot; 'the balance has been running on too long, and I'm distressed myself on your account, Sir Condy, for money, and the thing must be settled now on the spot, and the balance cleared off,' says Jason.

'I'll thank you if you'll only show me how,' says Sir Condy.

'There's but one way,' says Jason, 'and that's ready enough. When there's no cash, what can a gentleman do but go to the land?'

'How can you go to the land, and it under custodiam to yourself already?' says Sir Condy; 'and another custodiam hanging over it? And no one at all can touch it, you know, but the custodees.'

'Sure, can't you sell, though at a loss? Sure you can sell, and I've a purchaser ready for you,' says Jason.

'Have you so?' says Sir Condy. 'That's a great point gained. But there's a thing now beyond all, that perhaps you don't know yet, barring Thady has let you into the secret.'

'Sarrah bit of a secret, or anything at all of the kind, has he learned from me these fifteen weeks come St. John's Eve,' says I, 'for we have scarce been upon speaking terms of late. But what is it your honour means of a secret?'

'Why, the secret of the little keepsake I gave my Lady Rackrent the morning she left us, that she might not go back empty-handed to her friends.'

'My Lady Rackrent, I'm sure, has baubles and keepsakes enough, as those bills on the table will show,' says Jason; 'but whatever it is,' says he, taking up his pen, 'we must add it to the balance, for to be sure it can't be paid for.'

'No, nor can't till after my decease,' says Sir Condy; 'that's one good thing.' Then colouring up a good deal, he tells Jason of the memorandum of the five hundred a year jointure he had settled upon my lady; at which Jason was indeed mad, and said a great deal in very high words, that it was using a gentleman who had the management of his affairs, and was, moreover, his principal creditor, extremely ill to do such a thing without consulting him, and against his knowledge and consent. To all which Sir Condy had nothing to reply, but that, upon his conscience, it was in a hurry and without a moment's thought on his part, and he was very sorry for it, but if it was to do over again he would do the same; and he appealed to me, and I was ready to give my evidence, if that would do, to the truth of all he said.

So Jason with much ado was brought to agree to a compromise.

'The purchaser that I have ready,' says he, 'will be much displeased, to be sure, at the encumbrance on the land, but I must see and manage him. Here's a deed ready drawn up; we have nothing to do but to put in the consideration money and our names to it.'

'And how much am I going to sell?—the lands of O'Shaughlin's Town, and the lands of Gruneaghoolaghan, and the lands of Crookagnawaturgh,' says he, just reading to himself. 'And—oh, murder, Jason! sure you won't put this in—the castle, stable, and appurtenances for Castle Rackrent?'

'Oh, murder!' says I, clapping my hands; 'this is too bad, Jason.'

'Why so?' said Jason. 'When it's all, and a great deal more to the back of it, lawfully mine, was I to push for it.'

'Look at him,' says I, pointing to Sir Condy, who was just leaning back in his arm-chair, with his arms falling beside him like one stupefied; 'is it you, Jason, that can stand in his presence, and recollect all he has been to us, and all we have been to him, and yet use him so at the last?'

'Who will you find to use him better, I ask you?' said Jason; 'if he can get a better purchaser, I'm content; I only offer to purchase, to make things easy, and oblige him; though I don't see what compliment I am under, if you come to that. I have never had, asked, or charged more than sixpence in the pound, receiver's fees, and where would he have got an agent for a penny less?'

'Oh, Jason! Jason! how will you stand to this in the face of the county, and all who know you?' says I; 'and what will people think and say when they see you living here in Castle Rackrent, and the lawful owner turned out of the seat of his ancestors, without a cabin to put his head into, or so much as a potato to eat?'

Jason, whilst I was saying this, and a great deal more, made me signs, and winks, and frowns; but I took no heed, for I was grieved and sick at heart for my poor master, and couldn't but speak.

'Here's the punch,' says Jason, for the door opened; 'here's the punch!'

Hearing that, my master starts up in his chair, and recollects himself, and Jason uncorks the whisky.

'Set down the jug here,' says he, making room for it beside the papers opposite to Sir Condy, but still not stirring the deed that was to make over all.

Well, I was in great hopes he had some touch of mercy about him when I saw him making the punch, and my master took a glass; but Jason put it back as he was going to fill again, saying: 'No, Sir Condy, it shan't be said of me I got your signature to this deed when you were half-seas over: you know your name and handwriting in that condition would not, if brought before the courts, benefit me a straw; wherefore, let us settle all before we go deeper into the punch-bowl.'

'Settle all as you will,' said Sir Condy, clapping his hands to his ears; 'but let me hear no more. I'm bothered to death this night.'

'You've only to sign,' said Jason, putting the pen to him.

'Take all, and be content,' said my master. So he signed; and the man who brought in the punch witnessed it, for I was not able, but crying like a child; and besides, Jason said, which I was glad of, that I was no fit witness, being so old and doting. It was so bad with me, I could not taste a drop of the punch itself, though my master himself, God bless him! in the midst of his trouble, poured out a glass for me, and brought it up to my lips.

'Not a drop; I thank your honour's honour as much as if I took it, though.' And

I just set down the glass as it was, and went out, and when I got to the street door the neighbours' childer, who were playing at marbles there, seeing me in great trouble left their play, and gathered about me to know what ailed me; and I told them all, for it was a great relief to me to speak to these poor childer, that seemed to have some natural feeling left in them; and when they were made sensible that Sir Condy was going to leave Castle Rackrent for good and all, they set up a whillaluh that could be heard to the farthest end of the street; and one—fine boy he was—that my master had given an apple to that morning, cried the loudest; but they all were the same sorry, for Sir Condy was greatly beloved amongst the childer, for letting them go a-nutting in the demesne, without saying a word to them, though my lady objected to them. The people in the town, who were the most of them standing at their doors, hearing the childer cry, would know the reason of it; and when the report was made known, the people one and all gathered in great anger against my son Jason, and terror at the notion of his coming to be landlord over them, and they cried, 'No Jason! no Jason! Sir Condy! Sir Condy! Sir Condy Rackrent for ever!' And the mob grew so great and so loud, I was frightened, and made my way back to the house to warn my son to make his escape, or hide himself for fear of the consequences. Jason would not believe me till they came all round the house, and to the windows with great shouts. Then he grew quite pale, and asked Sir Condy what had he best do?

'I'll tell you what you had best do,' said Sir Condy, who was laughing to see his fright; 'finish your glass first, then let's go to the window and show ourselves, and I'll tell 'em—or you shall, if you please—that I'm going to the Lodge for change of air for my health, and by my own desire, for the rest of my days.'

'Do so,' said Jason, who never meant it should have been so, but could not refuse him the Lodge at this unseasonable time. Accordingly, Sir Condy threw up the sash and explained matters, and thanked all his friends, and bid them look in at the punch-bowl, and observe that Jason and he had been sitting over it very good friends; so the mob was content, and he sent them out some whisky to drink his health, and that was the last time his honour's health was ever drunk at Castle Rackrent.

The very next day, being too proud, as he said to me, to stay an hour longer in a house that did not belong to him, he sets off to the Lodge, and I along with him not many hours after. And there was great bemoaning through all O'Shaughlin's Town, which I stayed to witness, and gave my poor master a full account of when I got to the Lodge. He was very low, and in his bed, when I got there, and complained of a great pain about his heart; but I guessed it was only trouble and all the business, let alone vexation, he had gone through of late; and knowing the nature of him from a boy, I took my pipe, and whilst smoking it by the chimney began telling him how he was beloved and regretted in the county, and it did him a deal of good to hear it.

"Your honour has a great many friends yet that you don't know of, rich and poor, in the county,' says I; 'for as I was coming along the road I met two gentlemen in their own carriages, who asked after you, knowing me, and wanted to know where you was and all about you, and even how old I was. Think of that.'

Then he wakened out of his doze, and began questioning me who the gentlemen were. And the next morning it came into my head to go, unknown to anybody, with my master's compliments, round to many of the gentlemen's houses, where he and my lady used to visit, and people that I knew were his great friends, and would go to Cork to serve him any day in the year, and I made bold to try to borrow a trifle of cash from them. They all treated me very civil for the most part, and asked a great many questions very kind about my lady and Sir Condy and all the family, and were greatly surprised to learn from me Castle Rackrent was sold, and my master at the Lodge for health; and they all pitied him greatly, and he had their good wishes, if that would do; but money was a thing they unfortunately had not any of them at this time to spare. I had my journey for my pains, and I, not used to walking, nor supple as formerly, was greatly tired, but had the satisfaction of telling my master, when I got to the Lodge, all the civil things said by high and low.

'Thady,' says he, 'all you've been telling me brings a strange thought into my head. I've a notion I shall not be long for this world anyhow, and I've a great fancy to see my own funeral afore I die.' I was greatly shocked, at the first speaking, to hear him speak so light about his funeral, and he to all appearance in good health; but recollecting myself, answered:

'To be sure it would be as fine a sight as one could see,' I dared to say, 'and one I should be proud to witness, and I did not doubt his honour's would be as great a funeral as ever Sir Patrick O'Shaughlin's was, and such a one as that had never been known in the county afore or since.' But I never thought he was in earnest about seeing his own funeral himself till the next day he returns to it again.

'Thady,' says he, 'as far as the wake[34] goes, sure I might without any great trouble have the satisfaction of seeing a bit of my own funeral.'

'Well, since your honour's honour's so bent upon it,' says I, not willing to cross him, and he in trouble, 'we must see what we can do.'

So he fell into a sort of sham disorder, which was easy done, as he kept his bed, and no one to see him; and I got my shister, who was an old woman very handy about the sick, and very skilful, to come up to the Lodge to nurse him; and we gave out, she knowing no better, that he was just at his latter end, and it answered beyond anything; and there was a great throng of people, men, women, and childer, and there being only two rooms at the Lodge, except what was locked up full of Jason's furniture and things, the house was soon as full and fuller than it could hold, and the heat, and smoke, and noise wonderful great; and standing amongst them that were near the bed, but not thinking at all of the dead, I was startled by the sound of my master's voice from under the greatcoats that had been thrown all at top, and I went close up, no one noticing.

'Thady,' says he, 'I've had enough of this; I'm smothering, and can't hear a word of all they're saying of the deceased.'

'God bless you, and lie still and quiet,' says I, 'a bit longer, for my shister's afraid of ghosts, and would die on the spot with fright was she to see you come to life all on a sudden this way without the least preparation.'

---

[34] A 'wake' in England is a meeting avowedly for merriment; in Ireland it is a nocturnal meeting avowedly for the purpose of watching and bewailing the dead, but in reality for gossiping and debauchery.

So he lays him still, though well nigh stifled, and I made all haste to tell the secret of the joke, whispering to one and t'other, and there was a great surprise, but not so great as we had laid out it would. 'And aren't we to have the pipes and tobacco, after coming so far to-night?' said some; but they were all well enough pleased when his honour got up to drink with them, and sent for more spirits from a shebeen-house,[35] where they very civilly let him have it upon credit. So the night passed off very merrily, but to my mind Sir Condy was rather upon the sad order in the midst of it all, not finding there had been such a great talk about himself after his death as he had always expected to hear.

The next morning, when the house was cleared of them, and none but my shister and myself left in the kitchen with Sir Condy, one opens the door and walks in, and who should it be but Judy M'Quirk herself! I forgot to notice that she had been married long since, whilst young Captain Moneygawl lived at the Lodge, to the captain's huntsman, who after a whilst 'listed and left her, and was killed in the wars. Poor Judy fell off greatly in her good looks after her being married a year or two; and being smoke-dried in the cabin, and neglecting herself like, it was hard for Sir Condy himself to know her again till she spoke; but when she says, 'It's Judy M'Quirk, please your honour; don't you remember her?'

'Oh, Judy, is it you?' says his honour. 'Yes, sure, I remember you very well; but you're greatly altered, Judy.'

'Sure it's time for me,' says she. 'And I think your honour, since I seen you last —but that's a great while ago—is altered too.'

'And with reason, Judy,' says Sir Condy, fetching a sort of a sigh. 'But how's this, Judy?' he goes on. 'I take it a little amiss of you that you were not at my wake last night.'

'Ah, don't be being jealous of that,' says she; 'I didn't hear a sentence of your honour's wake till it was all over, or it would have gone hard with me but I would have been at it, sure; but I was forced to go ten miles up the country three days ago to a wedding of a relation of my own's, and didn't get home till after the wake was over. But,' says she, 'it won't be so, I hope, the next time,[36] please your honour.'

'That we shall see, Judy,' says his honour, 'and maybe sooner than you think for, for I've been very unwell this while past, and don't reckon anyway I'm long for this world.'

At this Judy takes up the corner of her apron, and puts it first to one eye and then to t'other, being to all appearance in great trouble; and my shister put in her word, and bid his honour have a good heart, for she was sure it was only the gout that Sir Patrick used to have flying about him, and he ought to drink a glass or a bottle extraordinary to keep it out of his stomach; and he promised to take her advice, and sent out for more spirits immediately; and Judy made a sign to me, and I went over to the door to her, and she said, 'I wonder to see Sir Condy so low: has he heard the news?'

---

[35] A hedge alehouse. Shebeen properly means weak, small-beer, taplash.

[36] At the coronation of one of our monarchs the King complained of the confusion which happened in the procession. The great officer who presided told his Majesty that 'it should not be so next time.'

'What news?' says I.

'Didn't ye hear it, then?' says she; 'my Lady Rackrent that was is kilt[37] and lying for dead, and I don't doubt but it's all over with her by this time.'

'Mercy on us all,' says I; 'how was it?'

'The jaunting-car it was that ran away with her,' says Judy. 'I was coming home that same time from Biddy M'Guggin's marriage, and a great crowd of people too upon the road, coming from the fair of Crookaghnawaturgh, and I sees a jaunting-car standing in the middle of the road, and with the two wheels off and all tattered. "What's this?" says I. "Didn't ye hear of it?" says they that were looking on; "it's my Lady Rackrent's car, that was running away from her husband, and the horse took fright at a carrion that lay across the road, and so ran away with the jaunting-car, and my Lady Rackrent and her maid screaming, and the horse ran with them against a car that was coming from the fair with the boy asleep on it, and the lady's petticoat hanging out of the jaunting-car caught, and she was dragged I can't tell you how far upon the road, and it all broken up with the stones just going to be pounded, and one of the road-makers, with his sledge-hammer in his hand, stops the horse at the last; but my Lady Rackrent was all kilt and smashed, and they lifted her into a cabin hard by, and the maid was found after where she had been thrown in the gripe of a ditch, her cap and bonnet all full of bog water, and they say my lady can't live anyway." Thady, pray now is it true what I'm told for sartain, that Sir Condy has made over all to your son Jason?'

'All,' says I.

'All entirely?' says she again.

'All entirely,' says I.

'Then,' says she, 'that's a great shame; but don't be telling Jason what I say.'

'And what is it you say?' cries Sir Condy, leaning over betwixt us, which made Judy start greatly. 'I know the time when Judy M'Quirk would never have stayed so long talking at the door and I in the house.'

'Oh!' says Judy, 'for shame, Sir Condy; times are altered since then, and it's my Lady Rackrent you ought to be thinking of.'

'And why should I be thinking of her, that's not thinking of me now?' says Sir Condy.

'No matter for that,' says Judy, very properly; 'it's time you should be thinking of her, if ever you mean to do it at all, for don't you know she's lying for death?'

'My Lady Rackrent!' says Sir Condy, in a surprise; 'why it's but two days since we parted, as you very well know, Thady, in her full health and spirits, and she, and her maid along with her, going to Mount Juliet's Town on her jaunting-car.'

'She'll never ride no more on her jaunting-car,' said Judy, 'for it has been the death of her, sure enough.'

'And is she dead then?' says his honour.

'As good as dead, I hear,' says Judy; 'but there's Thady here as just learnt the

---

[37] This word frequently occurs in the preceding pages, where it means not *killed,* but much *hurt.* In Ireland, not only cowards, but the brave 'die many times before their death.' —There *killing is no murder.*

whole truth of the story as I had it, and it's fitter he or anybody else should be telling it you than I, Sir Condy: I must be going home to the childer.'

But he stops her, but rather from civility in him, as I could see very plainly, than anything else, for Judy was, as his honour remarked at her first coming in, greatly changed, and little likely, as far as I could see—though she did not seem to be clear of it herself—little likely to be my Lady Rackrent now, should there be a second toss-up to be made. But I told him the whole story out of the face, just as Judy had told it to me, and he sent off a messenger with his compliments to Mount Juliet's Town that evening, to learn the truth of the report, and Judy bid the boy that was going call in at Tim M'Enerney's shop in O'Shaughlin's Town and buy her a new shawl.

'Do so,' said Sir Condy, 'and tell Tim to take no money from you, for I must pay him for the shawl myself.' At this my shister throws me over a look, and I says nothing, but turned the tobacco in my mouth, whilst Judy began making a many words about it, and saying how she could not be beholden for shawls to any gentleman. I left her there to consult with my shister, did she think there was anything in it, and my shister thought I was blind to be asking her the question, and I thought my shister must see more into it than I did, and recollecting all past times and everything, I changed my mind, and came over to her way of thinking, and we settled it that Judy was very like to be my Lady Rackrent after all, if a vacancy should have happened.

The next day, before his honour was up, somebody comes with a double knock at the door, and I was greatly surprised to see it was my son Jason.

'Jason, is it you?' said I; 'what brings you to the Lodge?' says I. 'Is it my Lady Rackrent? We know that already since yesterday.'

'Maybe so,' says he; 'but I must see Sir Condy about it.'

'You can't see him yet,' says I; 'sure he is not awake.'

'What then,' says he, 'can't he be wakened, and I standing at the door?'

'I'll not be disturbing his honour for you, Jason,' says I; 'many's the hour you've waited in your time, and been proud to do it, till his honour was at leisure to speak to you. His honour,' says I, raising my voice, at which his honour wakens of his own accord, and calls to me from the room to know who it was I was speaking to. Jason made no more ceremony, but follows me into the room.

'How are you, Sir Condy?' says he; 'I'm happy to see you looking so well; I came up to know how you did to-day, and to see did you want for anything at the Lodge.'

'Nothing at all, Mr. Jason, I thank you,' says he; for his honour had his own share of pride, and did not choose, after all that had passed, to be beholden, I suppose, to my son; 'but pray take a chair and be seated, Mr. Jason.'

Jason sat him down upon the chest, for chair there was none, and after he had set there some time, and a silence on all sides,

'What news is there stirring in the country, Mr. Jason M'Quirk?' says Sir Condy, very easy, yet high like.

'None that's news to you, Sir Condy, I hear,' says Jason. 'I am sorry to hear of my Lady Rackrent's accident.'

'I'm much obliged to you, and so is her ladyship, I'm sure,' answered Sir Condy, still stiff; and there was another sort of a silence, which seemed to lie the heaviest on my son Jason.

'Sir Condy,' says he at last, seeing Sir Condy disposing himself to go to sleep again, 'Sir Condy, I daresay you recollect mentioning to me the little memorandum you gave to Lady Rackrent about the £500 a year jointure.'

'Very true,' said Sir Condy; 'it is all in my recollection.'

'But if my Lady Rackrent dies, there's an end of all jointure,' says Jason.

'Of course,' says Sir Condy.

'But it's not a matter of certainty that my Lady Rackrent won't recover,' says Jason.

'Very true, sir,' says my master.

'It's fair speculation, then, for you to consider what the chance of the jointure of those lands, when out of custodiam, will be to you.'

'Just five hundred a year, I take it, without any speculation at all,' said Sir Condy.

'That's supposing the life dropt, and the custodiam off, you know; begging your pardon, Sir Condy, who understands business, that is a wrong calculation.'

'Very likely so,' said Sir Condy; 'but, Mr. Jason, if you have anything to say to me this morning about it, I'd be obliged to you to say it, for I had an indifferent night's rest last night, and wouldn't be sorry to sleep a little this morning.'

'I have only three words to say, and those more of consequence to you, Sir Condy, than me. You are a little cool, I observe; but I hope you will not be offended at what I have brought here in my pocket,' and he pulls out two long rolls, and showers down golden guineas upon the bed.

'What's this?' said Sir Condy; 'it's long since'—but his pride stops him.

'All these are your lawful property this minute, Sir Condy, if you please,' said Jason.

'Not for nothing, I'm sure,' said Sir Condy, and laughs a little. 'Nothing for nothing, or I'm under a mistake with you, Jason.'

'Oh, Sir Condy, we'll not be indulging ourselves in any unpleasant retrospects,' says Jason; 'it's my present intention to behave, as I'm sure you will, like a gentle-man in this affair. Here's two hundred guineas, and a third I mean to add if you should think proper to make over to me all your right and title to those lands that you know of.'

'I'll consider of it,' said my master; and a great deal more, that I was tired listening to, was said by Jason, and all that, and the sight of the ready cash upon the bed, worked with his honour; and the short and the long of it was, Sir Condy gathered up the golden guineas, and tied them up in a handkerchief, and signed some paper Jason brought with him as usual, and there was an end of the business: Jason took himself away, and my master turned himself round and fell asleep again.

I soon found what had put Jason in such a hurry to conclude this business. The little gossoon we had sent off the day before with my master's compliments to Mount Juliet's Town, and to know how my lady did after her accident, was stopped early this morning, coming back with his answer through O'Shaughlin's Town, at Castle Rackrent, by my son Jason, and questioned of all he knew of my lady from the servant at Mount Juliet's Town; and the gossoon told him my Lady Rackrent was not expected to live over night; so Jason thought it high time to be moving to the Lodge, to make his bargain with my master about the jointure afore it should be too late, and afore the little gossoon should reach us with the news. My master was greatly vexed—that is, I may say, as much as ever I seen him—when he found how he had been taken in; but it was some comfort to have the ready cash for immediate consumption in the house, anyway.

And when Judy came up that evening, and brought the childer to see his honour, he unties the handkerchief, and—God bless him! whether it was little or much he had, 'twas all the same with him—he gives 'em all round guineas apiece.

'Hold up your head,' says my shister to Judy, as Sir Condy was busy filling out a glass of punch for her eldest boy—'Hold up your head, Judy; for who knows but we may live to see you yet at the head of the Castle Rackrent estate?'

'Maybe so,' says she, 'but not the way you are thinking of.'

I did not rightly understand which way Judy was looking when she made this speech till a while after.

'Why, Thady, you were telling me yesterday that Sir Condy had sold all entirely to Jason, and where then does all them guineas in the handkerchief come from?'

'They are the purchase-money of my lady's jointure,' says I.

Judy looks a little bit puzzled at this. 'A penny for your thoughts, Judy,' says my shister; 'hark, sure Sir Condy is drinking her health.'

He was at the table in the room,[38] drinking with the exciseman and the gauger, who came up to see his honour, and we were standing over the fire in the kitchen.

'I don't much care is he drinking my health or not,' says Judy; 'and it is not Sir Condy I'm thinking of, with all your jokes, whatever he is of me.'

'Sure you wouldn't refuse to be my Lady Rackrent, Judy, if you had the offer?' says I.

'But if I could do better!' says she.

'How better?' says I and my shister both at once.

'How better?' says she. 'Why, what signifies it to be my Lady Rackrent and no castle? Sure what good is the car, and no horse to draw it?'

'And where will ye get the horse, Judy?' says I.

'Never mind that,' says she; 'maybe it is your own son Jason might find that.'

'Jason!' says I; 'don't be trusting to him, Judy. Sir Condy, as I have good reason to know, spoke well of you when Jason spoke very indifferently of you, Judy.'

'No matter,' says Judy; 'it's often men speak the contrary just to what they think of us.'

'And you the same way of them, no doubt,' answered I. 'Nay, don't be denying it, Judy, for I think the better of ye for it, and shouldn't be proud to call ye the daughter of a shister's son of mine, if I was to hear ye talk ungrateful, and anyway disrespectful of his honour.'

---

38 The principal room in the house.

'What disrespect,' says she, 'to say I'd rather, if it was my luck, be the wife of another man?'

'You'll have no luck, mind my words, Judy,' says I; and all I remembered about my poor master's goodness in tossing up for her afore he married at all came across me, and I had a choking in my throat that hindered me to say more.

'Better luck, anyhow, Thady,' says she, 'than to be like some folk, following the fortunes of them that have none left.'

'Oh! King of Glory!' says I, 'hear the pride and ungratitude of her, and he giving his last guineas but a minute ago to her childer, and she with the fine shawl on her he made her a present of but yesterday!'

'Oh, troth, Judy, you're wrong now,' says my shister, looking at the shawl.

'And was not he wrong yesterday, then,' says she, 'to be telling me I was greatly altered, to affront me?'

'But, Judy,' says I, 'what is it brings you here then at all in the mind you are in; is it to make Jason think the better of you?'

'I'll tell you no more of my secrets, Thady,' says she, 'nor would have told you this much, had I taken you for such an unnatural fader as I find you are, not to wish your own son preferred to another.'

'Oh, troth, you are wrong now, Thady,' says my shister.

Well, I was never so put to it in my life: between these womens, and my son and my master, and all I felt and thought just now, I could not, upon my conscience, tell which was the wrong from the right. So I said not a word more, but was only glad his honour had not the luck to hear all Judy had been saying of him, for I reckoned it would have gone nigh to break his heart; not that I was of opinion he cared for her as much as she and my shister fancied, but the ungratitude of the whole from Judy might not plase him; and he could never stand the notion of not being well spoken of or beloved like behind his back. Fortunately for all parties concerned, he was so much elevated at this time, there was no danger of his understanding anything, even if it had reached his ears. There was a great horn at the Lodge, ever since my master and Captain Moneygawl was in together, that used to belong originaily to the celebrated Sir Patrick, his ancestor; and his honour was often fond of telling the story that he learned from me when a child, how Sir Patrick drank the full of this horn without stopping, and this was what no other man afore or since could without drawing breath. Now Sir Condy challenged the gauger, who seemed to think little of the horn, to swallow the contents, and had it filled to the brim with punch; and the gauger said it was what he could not do for nothing, but he'd hold Sir Condy a hundred guineas he'd do it.

'Done,' says my master; 'I'll lay you a hundred golden guineas to a tester[39] you don't.'

'Done,' says the gauger; and done and done's enough between two gentlemen. The gauger was cast, and my master won the bet, and thought he'd won a hundred

---

[39] Sixpence; from the French word *tête*, a head—a piece of silver stamped with a head, which in old French was called *un testion*, and which was about the value of an old English sixpence. 'Tester' is used in Shakspeare.

guineas, but by the wording it was adjudged to be only a tester that was his due by the exciseman. It was all one to him; he was as well pleased, and I was glad to see him in such spirits again.

The gauger—bad luck to him!—was the man that next proposed to my master to try himself, could he take at a draught the contents of the great horn.

'Sir Patrick's horn!' said his honour; 'hand it to me: I'll hold you your own bet over again I'll swallow it.'

'Done,' says the gauger; 'I'll lay ye anything at all you do no such thing.'

'A hundred guineas to sixpence I do,' says he; 'bring me the handkerchief.' I was loth, knowing he meant the handkerchief with the gold in it, to bring it out in such company, and his honour not very able to reckon it. 'Bring me the handkerchief, then, Thady,' says he, and stamps with his foot; so with that I pulls it out my greatcoat pocket, where I had put it for safety. Oh, how it grieved me to see the guineas counting upon the table, and they the last my master had! Says Sir Condy to me, 'Your hand is steadier than mine to-night, old Thady, and that's a wonder; fill you the horn for me.' And so, wishing his honour success, I did; but I filled it, little thinking of what would befall him. He swallows it down, and drops like one shot. We lifts him up, and he was speechless, and quite black in the face. We put him to bed, and in a short time he wakened, raving with a fever on his brain. He was shocking either to see or hear.

'Judy! Judy! have you no touch of feeling? Won't you stay to help us nurse him?' says I to her, and she putting on her shawl to go out of the house.

'Im frightened to see him,' says she, 'and wouldn't nor couldn't stay in it; and what use? He can't last till the morning.' With that she ran off. There was none but my shister and myself left near him of all the many friends he had.

The fever came and went, and came and went, and lasted five days, and the sixth he was sensible for a few minutes, and said to me, knowing me very well, 'I'm in a burning pain all withinside of me, Thady.' I could not speak, but my shister asked him would he have this thing or t'other to do him good? 'No,' says he, 'nothing will do me good no more,' and he gave a terrible screech with the torture he was in; then again a minute's ease—'brought to this by drink,' says he. 'Where are all the friends?—where's Judy? Gone, hey? Ay, Sir Condy has been a fool all his days,' said he; and there was the last word he spoke, and died. He had but a very poor funeral after all.

If you want to know any more, I'm not very well able to tell you; but my Lady Rackrent did not die, as was expected of her, but was only disfigured in the face ever after by the fall and bruises she got; and she and Jason, immediately after my poor master's death, set about going to law about that jointure; the memorandum not being on stamped paper, some say it is worth nothing, others again it may do; others say Jason won't have the lands at any rate; many wishes it so. For my part, I'm tired wishing for anything in this world, after all I've seen in it; but I'll say nothing—it would be a folly to be getting myself ill-will in my old age. Jason did not marry, nor think of marrying Judy, as I prophesied, and I am not sorry for it: who is? As for all I have here set down from memory and hearsay of the family, there's nothing but truth in it from beginning to end. That you may depend upon, for where's the use of telling lies about the things which everybody knows as well as I do?

The Editor could have readily made the catastrophe of Sir Condy's history more dramatic and more pathetic, if he thought it allowable to varnish the plain round tale of faithful Thady. He lays it before the English reader as a specimen of manners and characters which are perhaps unknown in England. Indeed, the domestic habits of no nation in Europe were less known to the English than those of their sister country, till within these few years.

Mr. Young's picture of Ireland,[40] in his tour through that country, was the first faithful portrait of its inhabitants. All the features in the foregoing sketch were taken from the life, and they are characteristic of that mixture of quickness, simplicity, cunning, carelessness, dissipation, disinterestedness, shrewdness, and blunder, which, in different forms and with various success, has been brought upon the stage or delineated in novels.

It is a problem of difficult solution to determine whether a union will hasten or retard the amelioration of this country. The few gentlemen of education who now reside in this country will resort to England. They are few, but they are in nothing inferior to men of the same rank in Great Britain. The best that can happen will be the introduction of British manufacturers in their places.

Did the Warwickshire militia, who were chiefly artisans, teach the Irish to drink beer? or did they learn from the Irish to drink whisky?

---

[40] Arthur Young, *A Tour in Ireland, made between the Years 1776 and 1779* [Ed.].

The Marquise of O——

(1810)

Heinrich von Kleist

Martin Greenberg, translator

During a short tormented life, Bernd Heinrich Wilhelm von Kleist (1777–1811) produced eight *novellen* and eight plays, as well as essays, anecdotes, topical journalism, and a novel (lost). Son of a retired army officer in Frankfort on the Oder, Kleist followed his father's example and served in the Prussian army, retiring as a lieutenant at twenty-two. Thereafter he studied philosophy and law, and in 1800 worked for a short time as a functionary in the Prussian Ministry of Finance; he then traveled in France and Switzerland, turning from one occupation and location to another. He was arrested by the French as a spy in 1807, and from 1808 until his death, in a suicide pact with a friend's incurably ill wife, he worked on various periodicals.

His reading of Kant proved to him the impossibility of man's achieving truth and perfection, and this discrepancy between the Categorical Imperative and the human creature amid the humanly possible informs all his work. Though *Michael Kohlhaas* is the masterpiece among his *novellen*, *The Marquise of O——*, the first, is the most typical and best shows the characteristics and potentials of the genre. It was written in 1805 and published with the other seven *novellen* in 1810. Its reputation, needless to say, was scandalous.

The translation by Martin Greenberg is copyright 1960 by Criterion Books, Inc., reprinted by permission of the publisher from *The Marquise of O——* by Heinrich von Kleist (New York, 1960). For further reading, see Thomas Mann's introduction to Greenberg's translation and E. K. Bennett's *History of the German Novelle* (Cambridge, 1934), pp. 37–46.

In M——, a large town in northern Italy, the widowed Marquise of O——, a lady of unblemished reputation and the mother of several well-bred children, published the following notice in the newspapers: that, without her knowing how, she was in the family way; that she would like the father of the child she was going to bear to report himself; and that her mind was made up, out of consideration for her people, to marry him. The lady whom unalterable circumstances forced to take this unusual step, which she did so bravely in the face of the derision it was bound to excite in the world, was the daughter of Colonel

119

G——, Commandant of the citadel of M——. Three years or so previously, her husband, the Marquis of O——, to whom she had been devoted heart and soul, had died during a trip to Paris on family business. After his death, yielding to the wishes of Madam G——, her worthy mother, she left the estate near V—— where she had lived until then and returned to the Commandant's house with her two children. There she spent the following years in strict seclusion, occupying her time with painting, reading, educating her children, and caring for her parents: until the —— War suddenly filled the neighborhood with troops of nearly all the powers, including those of Russia. Colonel G——, who was under orders to defend the fortress, urged his wife and daughter to retire to the latter's estate near V—— or to his son's place. But before the ladies could make up their minds as between the hardships of a siege or the horrors they might be exposed to in the open country, the citadel was invested by Russian troops and commanded to surrender. Announcing to his family that he would carry on as if they were not there, the Colonel retorted with shot and shell. The enemy in turn bombarded the fortress. He set the magazines ablaze, captured an outworks, and, when the Colonel delayed to answer a second summons to surrender, ordered a night assault and carried the fort by storm.

Just as the Russian troops, supported by a violent cannonade, were breaking into the citadel, the left wing of the Commandant's residence caught fire and the women were forced to flee. The Colonel's wife panted after her daughter, who was flying down the stairs with her children, and shouted for them all to keep together and take refuge in the cellars; but a shell exploding in the house at that very moment made the confusion there complete. The Marquise, flinging open a door, found herself in the citadel square, where the flashing of the cannon in violent action lit up the night and drove her, helpless to know where she should turn, back inside the burning building. Here, unluckily, just as she was about to escape by the back door, she ran into a troop of enemy sharpshooters who fell silent the instant they laid eyes on her, slung their muskets, and, gesturing obscenely, marched her off with them. In vain the Marquise screamed for help to her terror-stricken women fleeing through the back gate as she was flung back and forth among the horrible gang of quarreling soldiers. They dragged her to the rear castle yard, where she was on the point of collapsing to the ground under the filthy abuse inflicted on her when a Russian officer, hearing her screams, came running up and began to lay about him with furious strokes, scattering the dogs panting after their prey. To the Marquise he seemed a very angel from heaven. He smashed the last of the murderous brutes, whose arms were wound about her slender figure, in the face with the hilt of his sword and made him reel back with the blood gushing from his mouth; then, saluting her courteously in French, he offered her his arm and led her, speechless from all she had gone through, to the other wing of the residence, which had not caught fire yet, where she fainted dead away. A little while after, when her terrified women appeared, he told them to call a doctor; promised them, as he put his hat on, that she would soon recover; and returned to the fray.

In a short time the square was entirely in the hands of the Russians, and the

Commandant, who kept up a resistance only because no quarter was offered him, was just falling back with his dwindling force on the entrance door to the residence when the Russian officer, with a heated face, came out of that very door and called on him to surrender. The Commandant answered that that was just what he had been waiting for, handed him his sword, and asked permission to go into the castle and look for his family. The Russian officer who, judging by his actions, was one of the leaders of the assault, granted his request on condition that he was accompanied by a guard; he placed himself hurriedly at the head of a detachment, threw his force into the fighting wherever it was still in doubt, and posted men as fast as possible at all the strong points of the fort. No sooner was this done than he ran back to the drill square and ordered his men to battle the roaring flames which were threatening to spread in every direction, himself performing prodigies of exertion when his orders were not carried out with the necessary zeal. One minute he was scrambling among the burning gables, hose in hand, aiming the stream of water at the flames, the next minute he had darted into the magazines and, striking terror to the souls of his fellow Asiatics, was rolling out powder kegs and live grenades. Meanwhile the Commandant had passed inside the house and was horrified to learn about the misfortune that had befallen his daughter. The Marquise, however, who had entirely recovered without the help of any doctor, just as the Russian officer said she would, and who was overjoyed to find all her people safe and sound and stayed in bed only to allay their extreme anxiety about her, assured him that her one wish was to get up and tell her rescuer how grateful she was to him. She already knew that he was Count F——, Lieutenant-Colonel of the T——th Rifle Corps and Knight of the Order of Merit and of several others. She asked her father to beg him not to leave the citadel before he had made an appearance, if only for a minute or so, at the residence. The Commandant, who respected his daughter's feeling, returned without delay to the fort, where he found the Count on the ramparts, going up and down among his battered troops and issuing an uninterrupted stream of orders; and, no better opportunity offering, he then and there conveyed his grateful daughter's wish to him. The Count promised him that he was only waiting to snatch a moment from his duties to pay her his respects. He had been anxious all along to hear how the Marquise was, but the reports of some of his officers had drawn him back into the thick of the fighting.

At daybreak the Commanding General of the Russian forces arrived to inspect the fort. He paid his respects to the Commandant, regretted that his bravery had not been helped by better luck, and gave him leave to go wherever he liked on his parole. The Commandant thanked him earnestly and said how much this day had put him in debt to the Russians in general and to the young Count F——, Lieutenant-Colonel of the T——th Rifle Corps, in particular. The General asked what had happened; when he was told the story of the criminal attack on the Commandant's daughter, he became furious. Calling the Count forward by name, he praised his noble-spirited conduct in a short speech, which caused the officer to blush furiously, and ended his words by ordering the villains who had dis-honored the Czar's name to be shot; would he tell him who they were? Count

F—— gave a confused reply, in which he said that he could not give the General their names because it had been impossible to recognize their faces by the feeble glimmer of the castle-yard lamps. The General, who had heard that the castle was already in flames at the time of the episode, looked surprised; it was possible, he remarked, to recognize people one knew well by their voices in the dark; and ordered him, when the Count shrugged his shoulders with an embarrassed air, to investigate the matter at once. But just then somebody pressed forward from the back of the circle and reported that one of the villains whom the Count had wounded had fallen in the corridor and that the Commandant's people had lugged him into a closet where he still was. The General sent a guard to fetch the man; questioned him briefly; and, when he had revealed the names of the others, had the whole crew, five all told, shot. When this was done, the General posted a small garrison in the fort and issued marching orders to the rest of his troops; the officers scattered on the double to their different corps; the Count made his way through the crowd of hurrying soldiers to the Commandant and said how very sorry he was, but under the circumstances he could only send his warmest regards to the Marquise; and in less than an hour the entire fort was clear of Russians again.

The family now began to think how they might find some occasion in the future to tell the Count how grateful they felt toward him; imagine their horror, then, when they learned that he had been killed in a skirmish on the very same day that he had marched away from the fort. The messenger who brought this news to M—— had with his own eyes seen him carried off, mortally wounded in the chest, toward P——, where he had died, according to a reliable report, at the very moment when the bearers were lifting him from their shoulders. The Commandant went in person to the posthouse to see if he could learn anything more about the Russian's death. He discovered that when the Count was hit on the battlefield he had cried out, "Julietta, with this shot you are avenged!" and after that had never opened his lips again. The Marquise was inconsolable for having let the chance slip to throw herself at his feet. She made the most violent accusations against herself for not having gone to him in the fort when he declined (probably, as she thought, from modesty) to come to her in the castle; pitied the unfortunate lady, with the same name as her own, whom he had been thinking about even as he was dying; tried in vain to learn her whereabouts so as to tell her the unhappy news; and could not get the thought of him out of her own mind until several months had passed.

At this time the family were obliged to move out of the Commandant's residence to make room for the Russian commander. At first they thought of going to Colonel G——'s estate, which was very much the Marquise's inclination; but as the Colonel had no liking for country life, they ended by taking a house in town and fixing it up to live there permanently. Their life now flowed back into its accustomed channels. The Marquise had resumed the long-interrupted education of her children, and in her leisure hours turned to her easel and her books, when, quite unaccountably for someone who had always been a paragon of good heath, she found herself troubled by a persistent indisposition that made it impossible for her to see anyone for weeks on end. She suffered from nausea, dizziness, and fainting spells, and was at a loss to explain her strange condition. One morning, as the family sat at tea and her father had gone out of the room for a moment, the Marquise, rousing herself from a lengthy fit of abstraction, said to her mother, "If a woman were to tell me that she felt the way I did just now when I picked up the cup, I should certainly think to myself that she was pregnant." Madam G—— said she didn't know what her daughter meant. The Marquise explained that she had just felt the same sort of twinge she had had when she was carrying her second child. Madam G—— said it was perhaps the spirit of fantasy that her daughter was going to be delivered of, and laughed. Yes, the Marquise replied in the same humorous spirit, and Morpheus was the father or one of his attendant dreams. But then the Colonel came back, the conversation was interrupted, and when the Marquise recovered a few days later the whole thing was forgotten.

Not long after this, just when the Commandant's son, who was Forest Warden, happened to be at home, the family were frightened out of their wits to hear a servant enter the room and announce that Count F—— was there. "Count F——!" gasped father and daughter together, and they all fell speechless. The servant swore that his eyes and ears had not deceived him and that the visitor was already waiting in the anteroom. The Commandant immediately jumped up to open the door himself, and the Count entered, handsome as a young god, even if his face was rather pale. After they had gotten over their surprise and the Count had assured the parents—who said no, it couldn't be, he must be dead—that he was very much alive, he turned, with an expression of great tenderness on his face, to the daughter; and the very first thing he asked her was, how did she feel? Very well, the Marquise said, she only wanted to know how he had come back from the dead. But he would not let his question drop and said she was not telling him the truth; her face showed signs of unusual fatigue; unless he was much mistaken, she was feeling ill. The Marquise, softened by the warmth with which he spoke, replied: very well, her fatigue, since he would have it so, was perhaps the last trace of an indisposition that had troubled her several weeks ago; she did not think that anything more would come of it. To which he replied, with an outburst of delight: nor did he!—and he asked her if she would marry him. The Marquise did not know what to make of such behavior. Blushing deeply, she looked at her mother who, in turn, was staring in embarrassment at her husband and son; whereupon the Count went up to the Marquise and, taking her hand as if to kiss it, asked her if she had understood him. The Commandant inquired if he would not like to sit down; and with elaborate courtesy, touched nevertheless with some solemnity, he drew a chair up for the Count.

"Indeed," said the Colonel's wife, "we shall go on thinking you are a ghost until you've told us how you rose up out of the grave in which they buried you at P——." Letting go the lady's hand, the Count sat down and said that he was forced to be very brief: he had been wounded mortally in the breast and carried to P——; for months there he had despaired of his life; during this time his only thoughts had been for the Marquise; he could not describe the pleasure and the pain that coupled together in his image of her; after his recovery, he had returned to the army, where he had felt a terrible restlessness; more than once he had reached for a pen to pour his heart out to the Colonel and the Marquise; but unexpectedly he was sent to Naples with dispatches; he could not be sure that he wouldn't be sent from there to Constantinople—he might even have to go to St. Petersburg; meanwhile it was impossible for him to go on living any longer without a clear understanding about something that was absolutely necessary for his soul's peace; he had not been able to resist taking a few steps in that direction while passing through M——; in short, he cherished the hope of obtaining the Marquise's hand, and he implored them as earnestly as he knew how to give his suit an immediate answer.

After a long pause, the Commandant replied that the offer, if seriously intended, as he did not doubt it was, was a very flattering one. But his daughter had made up her mind, after the death of her husband, the Marquis of O——, never to marry again. However, as the Count had recently laid so great an obligation on her, it was not impossible that this should sway her from her resolution; he asked him to allow her a little time to think the matter over quietly. The Count assured him that his friendly answer was a great encouragement to his hopes; that in other circumstances it would have made him perfectly content; that he appreciated fully how boorish it seemed for him to ask for more; but that compelling reasons, into which it was impossible for him to go, made a definite answer extremely desirable; that the horses which were to take him to Naples were already hitched to his carriage; and that he implored them with all his heart and soul, if there was anybody in that house to take his part—here he shot a look at the Marquise— not to let him ride away without a more favorable reply. The Colonel, rather taken aback by such insistence, said that although the gratitude his daughter felt for him justified his assuming a great deal, it did not justify his assuming so much; she could not take a step on which the happiness of her life depended without giving it prudent consideration beforehand. It was absolutely necessary for his daughter to enjoy the pleasure of his closer acquaintance before declaring herself. He invited him to return to M—— after his trip was done and be their guest for a while. If after that—but not before—the Marquise thought that she could find her happiness with him, he would be only too happy to hear that she had given him the answer he wanted. The Count blushed and said that during the whole trip he had foreseen that his impatient desires would meet with this fate; that he looked forward to being utterly miserable during the interim period; that although he could hardly like the unhappy part he was now compelled to play, he would not deny that a closer acquaintance was all to the good; that he believed he could answer for his reputation, although it was a question whether any consideration should be given to that most deceptive of all things; that the only dishonorable act he had ever committed was a secret from the world and he was already on the way to making it good—in short, that he was an honorable man, and he begged the Commandant to accept his assurance of the truthfulness of all he said. The Commandant smiled faintly, though without a trace of irony, and said that he quite agreed with everything the Count had said. He had never come across a young man who in so short a time had revealed so many superior traits of character. He was pretty well convinced that a brief period of reflection would overcome all present hesitation; but before he talked things over with his own family as well as with the Count's, no other course was possible. At this, the Count announced that his parents were dead and he was his own master. His uncle was General K——, on whose assent to the marriage he could rely. He added that he possessed considerable means and would be able to make Italy his home.

The Commandant bowed politely, explained his wishes once again, and requested him not to press his suit any further until he returned from his trip. The Count, after a short pause in which he showed every sign of extreme uneasiness, turned to the Marquise's mother and said that he had done everything possible to get out of having to make the trip; that he had gone as far as he dared in importuning the Commanding General and General K——, his uncle, to be relieved of the mission, but that they hoped that the journey would rouse him out of the melancholy still weighing on him from his illness; and that, for this reason, he was now completely miserable.

The family did not know what to say to this. The Count rubbed his forehead and went on, saying that if there were any hope of his coming nearer the goal he sought, he would put off his departure for a day or even more. And he looked in turn at the Commandant, the Marquise, and her mother. The Commandant stared at the floor with an expression of displeasure and did not speak. His wife said, "Go along, why don't you, and make your trip to Naples; then come back to M—— and give us the pleasure of your company for a while; we'll see about everything else after that."

The Count sat where he was for a minute and seemed to be trying to decide what he should do. Then, getting up and putting his chair aside, he said that since he was forced to recognize that the hopes with which he had entered their house were premature, and since the family insisted on a closer acquaintance, which he was far from blaming them for, he would send his dispatches back to the headquarters at Z——, for them to be forwarded by some other means, and accept their kind invitation to be a guest in their house for a few weeks. Then he paused for a moment, standing by the wall with his hand on the chair, and gazed at the Commandant. The latter replied that he would feel extremely sorry if the passion that the Count seemed to cherish for his daughter should get him into serious trouble; right now the Count must know what he absolutely had to do and what he didn't, and whether he could send the dispatches back and occupy the room they had for him. At these words they saw the Count change color; he kissed Madam G——'s hand, bowed to the others, and withdrew.

The family did not know what to make of such behavior. The mother said that surely it was not possible that he should think of sending the dispatches he was carrying to Naples back to Z—— simply because he had not been able, on his way through M——, during a five minutes' conversation, to persuade a lady whom he did not know at all to consent to his proposal of marriage. The Forest Warden exclaimed that such reckless behavior would certainly be punished by nothing less than imprisonment in a fortress! And such a man would be dismissed into the bargain, added the Commandant. However, the latter continued, there was not danger of that. The Count had only been talking wildly; he would think twice before returning the dispatches. But the mother, when she learned about this danger, was extremely apprehensive that he would send them back. His headstrong, single-minded nature, she thought, was capable of just such a deed. She begged her son to run after him and dissuade him from a step that promised nothing but disaster. The Forest Warden replied that his interfering in that way would have the opposite effect and only encourage the Count to hope that he could gain his purpose by this stratagem. The Marquise thought the same thing, although she was convinced that, unless her brother did something, the Count would certainly send the dispatches back; he would rather bring disaster on himself than show himself up for an empty talker. All were agreed that his behavior was extraordinary and that he seemed accustomed to capturing ladies' hearts, like fortresses, by storm.

At this moment the Commandant noticed that the Count's coach was standing ready before the door. He called his family to the window and asked a servant, who came into the room just then, whether the Count was still in the house. The servant said that he was below in the servants' hall, in the company of an adjutant, writing letters and sealing packets. The Commandant, repressing his dismay, hurried downstairs with his son and asked the Count, whom he found conducting his business at a most unsuitable table, if he didn't care to step into his own room, and if there was not anything else he might do for him. The Count's pen continued to dash across the paper as he said no, thank you, his business was already done; he asked the Commandant what the time was as he sealed the letter, and, after giving the adjutant the whole portfolio, wished the latter, a pleasant journey. The Commandant, who could not believe his eyes, said to the Count, as the adjutant left the house, "Sir, unless you have very weighty reasons——"

"The most compelling reasons," the Count interrupted, and walked with the adjutant to the carriage and opened the door for him.

"In that case," the Commandant continued, "I would at least send along the dispatches——"

"Impossible," the Count retorted as he helped the adjutant to his seat. "The dispatches wouldn't do any good in Naples without me. I thought of that too. Drive on!"

"And your uncle's letters?" called the adjutant, leaning out of the coach door.

"They can reach me," replied the Count, "at M——."

"Drive on!" the adjutant called, and away went the carriage.

Count F—— now turned to the Commandant and asked him if he would be good enough to have somebody show him to his room. He would have the honor of doing that himself, the disconcerted Colonel replied; he called to the Count's servants and his own to look after the luggage, and conducted him to the guest room; after which he stiffly said good day. The Count dressed; left the house to report to the military governor of the place; and for the rest of the day was nowhere to be seen, only returning to the house just before dinner.

Meanwhile the family were feeling extremely upset. The Forest Warden described how peremptorily the Count had answered the Commandant's questions;

said his returning the dispatches looked to him quite deliberately done; and asked what on earth could be the reason for wooing at a post-horse gallop. The Commandant said that he could not make head or tail of the business and ordered his family not to mention it again in his presence. The mother kept peering out of the window from one minute to the next to see if the Count had not come back regretting his hasty decision and wanting to undo it. Finally when it got dark she sat down next to the Marquise, who was working busily at a table and seemed to shun conversation, and asked her in an undertone, while the father was pacing up and down the room, what she made of the whole thing. Looking hesitantly toward the Commandant, the Marquise said that if her father had prevailed on him to go to Naples, everything would have been all right. "To Naples!" exclaimed the Commandant, who had overheard what she said. "Should I have had the priest sent for? Or should I have had him locked up and sent to Naples under guard?"

"No, no," the Marquise said. "But a real effort to remonstrate with him would have had an effect." And she bent down, a trifle unwillingly, over her work again.

At last, toward evening, the Count appeared. They were only waiting for the matter to come up again, after the first greetings were over, so as to attack him with their combined force and get him to retrieve what he had done, if that was still possible. But they waited in vain. During the entire dinner he carefully skirted everything that might have touched on the subject and talked instead to the Commandant about tht war and to the Forest Warden about hunting. When he happened to mention the skirmish at P—— in which he had been wounded, the mother drew him into an account of his illness, asking him how it had been in the little town and if he had had everything he needed there. In the course of this conversation he told them a number of things that were interesting for what they revealed about his passion for the Marquise: how she had seemed always to be at his bedside during his illness; how in his feverish delirium he kept confusing her image with that of a swan that he had seen as a boy on his uncle's estate; how he was especially moved by the recollection of a time when he had spattered the swan with mud and it had dived silently under the water to rise up pure and shining again; how the Marquise, in the shape of the swan, was always swimming about on a flaming flood and he had called out Thinka, which was the name of the swan from his boyhood, but had not been able to make her come to him, for all her pleasure lay in gliding up and down and haughtily puffing out her breast—suddenly he said, with a deep blush, that he was terribly in love with her; looked down at his plate again, and was silent. As last it was time to get up from the table; the Count, after a few words with the mother, bowed to the company and retired to his room, leaving them standing there in complete perplexity again. The Commandant thought that they should let matters take their course. In doing what he did, the Count was probably counting on the influence of his relatives, for otherwise he would be ignominiously dismissed. Madam G—— asked her daughter what she thought of him after all this, and whether she could find it in her to say something to him that would avert a catastrophe. "Mother dear," replied the Marquise, "I am afraid I can't. I am sorry that my gratitude should be put to such a hard test. But I had made up my mind not to remarry; I really shouldn't want to put my happiness at stake a second time, and certainly not without giving the whole matter a lot of thought." The Forest Warden said that if that was her firm resolve, it would be a help to the Count, even so, to know it; it seemed evident to him that he needed to be given some sort of definite answer. The Colonel's wife replied that since this young man, who was the possessor of so many unusual qualities, had said that he was willing to live in Italy, she thought it was only fair to give his offer some consideration and to test the Marquise's determination not to remarry. The Forest Warden dropped into a chair next to his sister and asked her if she liked the way the Count looked. The Marquise answered with some embarrassment, "I like him and I don't like him," and appealed to the way the others felt.

"Supposing," said Madam G——, "that nothing that we are able to learn about him while he is away in Naples contradicts the general impression you have of him now, and supposing he renews his offer on his return, what answer would you give him then?"

"In that case," replied the Marquise, "since in fact his desire to marry me seems so strong—" she hesitated at this point and her eyes glistened—"in that case I would be ready to satisfy it for the sake of what I owe him."

Her mother, who had always wished her daughter to remarry, was hard put to it to conceal the joy this declaration gave her, and wondered what it would lead to. The Forest Warden got up restlessly from his chair and said that if the Marquise thought there was any possibility of her favoring the Count with her hand, then something ought to be said to him right away which would make it possible to avert the consequences of the crazy thing he had done. His mother thought so too. After all, she said, with a man like that there was no great risk, since one need hardly fear that the rest of his life would not be in keeping with all those superior qualities he had demonstrated on the night the Russians stormed the fortress. The Marquise looked down at the ground with a tense and nervous expression. "Perhaps he might be told," her mother went on, as she took her hand, "something to the effect that until he returns from Naples, you won't enter into any other engagement."

"I can promise him that," the Marquise said. "Only I am afraid that it won't be enough for him and will get us all embroiled."

"Let me worry about that!" her mother said with elation, and turned her head to look for the Commandant. "Lorenzo," she asked, "what do you think?" and she began to rise from her chair. The Commandant, who had heard everything, continued standing at the window and looking out into the street without saying anything. The Forest Warden promised them that with this harmless assurance he would guarantee to get the Count out of the house.

"Well, go ahead and do it! Do it right now" his father explained, turning away from the window. "Here I am, surrendering to this Russian a second time!"

His wife jumped up at these words, kissed him and her daughter, and, while her husband smiled at her bustling energy, wanted to know how they could tell the Count about it right away. It was decided, at the Forest Warden's suggestion, to ask him if he would not care to join the family for a moment if he were still dressed. The Count sent back the answer that he would be honored to join them at once, and hardly had the valet returned with this message than he himself burst into the room, with great strides of joy, and threw himself down at the Marquise's feet in a state of intense emotion. The Commandant was about to speak when the Count, springing to his feet, said that he knew everything that he needed to know, kissed his hand and that of his wife, hugged the Marquise's brother, and asked them if they would do him the favor of helping him to find a traveling coach. The Marquise, though her feelings had been stirred by this scene, said, "I really am afraid, Count F——, lest your impetuous hopes——"

"Not at all! Not at all!" replied the Count. "You've agreed to nothing, if the reports you get about me should clash with the feeling that moved you to call me back this room." On hearing this, the Commandant gave him a hearty hug, the Forest Warden offered him his own carriage on the spot, a soldier was sent running to the posthouse to hire horses, and, all in all, his leaving occasioned more rejoicing than ever they had known at anybody's coming. He hoped, said the Count, to overtake the adjutant with the dispatches at B——, from where he would go on to Naples by a shorter way than through M——; in Naples he would do everything possible to get out of having to make the trip to Constantinople; and since his mind was made up, if the worst came to worst, to sham illness, he promised them that, unless he ran into unavoidable delays, he would be back in M—— without fail in about four to six weeks. Just then his orderly reported that the horses were harnessed and everything was ready for his departure. The Count picked up his hat, went up to the Marquise, and took her hand. "Well, Julietta," he said, "I feel a great deal easier now,"—and he put his hand in hers—"although it was my dearest wish to marry you before I left."

"Marry her!" they all exclaimed.

"Marry her," the Count reiterated, kissed the Marquise's hand, and assured her, when she asked him if he had taken leave of his senses, that a day would come when she would understand his meaning. The family were ready to get angry; but he immediately bade goodbye to them all very warmly, begged them not to bother their heads about what he had just said, and took his departure.

Several weeks passed, during which the family anxiously awaited, with very different feelings, the outcome of this strange affair. The Commandant received a polite letter from General K——, the Count's uncle; the Count himself wrote from Naples; the answers the family received to their inquiries spoke quite well of him; in short, the engagement seemed as good as concluded when the Marquise's indisposition came back again stronger than ever. And for the first time she noticed an inexplicable change in her figure. She spoke frankly to her mother about her condition and said she did not know what to make of it. Her mother, who felt very anxious about her daughter's health because of these strange attacks, wanted her to call a doctor in for consultation. But the Marquise was against the idea and hoped that her natural vigor would prevail; she suffered the sharpest pains for several days without following her mother's advice, until recurrent sensations of so unusual a kind filled her with such alarm that she had the doctor called; he was a man who enjoyed her father's fullest confidence. Inviting him to sit down on the divan—her mother was away just then—after a brief introduction she told him jokingly what her condition looked like to her. The doctor gave her a searching look; deliberated a while after he had finished his careful examination; and then said, with an expression of great earnestness, that the Marquise's diagnosis was perfectly correct. When she asked him what he meant and he had explained himself quite clearly, observing with a smile he was unable to repress that she was in perfect health and needed no physician, the Marquise tugged the bell cord while she looked at him very hard from the side, and asked him to leave. Speaking under her breath as if he were not worth bothering about, she muttered that it was no pleasure for her to joke with him about such things. The doctor testily replied that he wished she had always been as little inclined to joking as she was now, took his hat and stick, and got up to go. The Marquise promised him that she would report his insults to her father. The physician retorted that he would swear to his opinion in a court of law, opened the door, bowed, and began to leave the room. As he stooped to pick up a glove that he had dropped, the Marquise asked, "But how is it possible, Doctor?" The doctor said he didn't really see any need for him to tell her about the ultimate causes of things, bowed once more and left.

The Marquise stood there as if thunderstruck. Then she pulled herself together and was about to run to her father when she recalled the intensely serious manner of the man who she thought had insulted her, and her limbs were paralyzed. She threw herself down on the couch in a state of violent agitation. Mistrusting herself, she reviewed every minute of the past year, and decided she had gone mad when she thought about what had just happened. At last her mother came in; when she asked her in alarm why she was so upset, her daughter told her what the physician had said. Madam G—— unhesitatingly called him a shameless, frivolous quack and encouraged her daughter in her determination to tell her father how the doctor had insulted her. The Marquise assured her that the doctor had spoken in deadly earnest and that he seemed perfectly prepared to repeat his mad opinion to her father's face. Madam G——, now more than a little frightened, wanted to know if she thought there was any possibility of her being in such a condition.

"Graves would start to teem first," the Marquise said, "and the womb of a corpse give birth!"

"You are a strange child," her mother said, giving her a tight hug. "Why are you so upset then? If you *know* that it isn't so, why should a doctor's opinion, even the opinion of a whole panel of doctors, bother you? He either made a mistake or he was being malicious, but what difference does it make to you? I think, however, that the right thing for us to do is to tell your father."

"Oh my God!" exclaimed the Marquise, with a convulsive start. "How can I feel calm about it? Don't my own internal sensations, which I am only too familiar with, argue against me? If I knew that somebody else had these symptoms, wouldn't I myself think that she was pregnant?"

"Oh, how awful!" the Colonel's wife replied.

"Malice or mistake!" the Marquise continued. "Why should a man who seemed to deserve our respect until today try to hurt me in such a mean and wanton way? Me, who never once offended him? Who received him with absolute confidence, anticipating in advance the gratitude I would feel toward him? And whose own wish, as his first words showed, seemed an honest and straightforward one to help, not to cause me greater pain than I have ever felt before? But if, since a choice has to be made," she went on, while her mother steadily regarded her, "I conclude that he made a mistake, how is it possible for me to believe that a physician, even a mediocre one, could err in such a matter?"

Her mother said, with a touch of sharpness, "And yet it has to be one or the other."

"Yes indeed, Mother dear," the Marquise replied, her face reddening with an expression of injured innocence as she kissed her hand, "so it does. Although my condition is such an enigma that you must allow me to have my doubts. I swear, for such an assurance is needed, that I am as innocent as my own children; your own conscience cannot be clearer, more honorable. Nevertheless, I must ask you to send for a midwife; I need to convince myself about the way things really are with me and, whatever the result, find some peace of mind."

"A midwife!" Madam G—— cried in a shocked voice. "A clear conscience and a midwife!" And she was unable to speak.

"A midwife, Mother dear," the Marquise repeated, falling on her knees before her, "and this very instant, or I'll go mad."

"Very well," the Colonel's wife replied. "But please make sure you don't have the confinement under my roof." And she got up to leave the room. The Marquise, following her with outstretched arms, prostrated herself on the ground and embraced her knees. "If a life against which it was impossible to level one reproach," she cried with the eloquence of grief, "a life that followed your example, gives me a right to your respect, if any maternal feeling still pleads for me in your heart as long as my guilt is still not absolutely clear, please don't forsake me at this terrible time!"

"Please tell me why you are so upset," her mother said. "Is it just because of what the doctor said? Just because of these internal sensations you have?"

"Yes, Mother," the Marquise said, with her hand on her heart. "There is no other reason."

"No other, Julietta?" her mother asked. "Think a moment. A misstep, as unspeakably painful as it would be to me, does, well, sometimes happen, and in the end I should have to forgive you; but if you went and invented some fairy tale about a revolution in nature in order to escape your mother's censure, and piled one blasphemous oath on another so as to impose on a heart that is only too ready to believe everything you say, that would be more shameful than I know how to say; I could never love you again."

"May the kingdom of heaven lie as open to me some day as my heart is open to you now," cried the Marquise. "I have concealed nothing from you, Mother."

This exclamation, which was uttered with so much pathos, shook her mother deeply. "Oh heavens!" she cried. "My darling child, how sorry I am for you!" And she raised her daughter up, kissed her, and held her in her arms. "What in the world are you afraid of, then? Come, you look quite ill to me." And she wanted to take her to her bed. But the Marquise, whose tears were flowing copious and fast, protested that she was very well and that there was nothing wrong with her except for that strange and inexplicable condition.

"Condition!" her mother burst out again. "What condition? If you are so sure about your memory, isn't it madness to be so terribly afraid? Can't these vague internal sensations of yours have deceived you?"

"No, no!" the Marquise said. "I haven't deceived myself! If you'll just call the midwife in, you will see that this dreadful thing which is destroying me is true."

"Come, my darling," said Madam G——, who was beginning to fear for her reason. "Come along with me and lie down. Whatever was it that you think the doctor told you? How flushed your face is! All your limbs are trembling! What could the doctor have told you?"—and now completely skeptical of what the Marquise said had passed between her and the doctor, she drew her daughter away with her.

"Dear, best Mother!" the Marquise said, smiling through her tears. "I've not gone out of my mind. The doctor told me that I was pregnant. Send for the midwife and, the instant she says it isn't so, I'll feel easy again."

"Good, fine," the Colonel's wife said, stifling her fear. "She'll come right away; since you are absolutely set on having her laugh in your face, I'll get her in right away so she can tell you what a dreamer you are, and not quite right in the head." And she pulled the bell cord and immediately sent one of her people to fetch the midwife.

The Marquise was still lying in her mother's arms, her breast heaving apprehensively, when the woman appeared and heard Madam G——'s explanation of the strange idea that was making her daughter ill: the Marquise swore that her behavior had always been virtuous and yet, deluded by some kind of mysterious sensations, she insisted on being examined by an experienced woman. The midwife, as she probed the Marquise, gabbled about young blood and the cunning of the world; when she finished, she said she had had to do with similar cases in the past; all the young widows who found themselves in her predicament would absolutely have it that they had been living on a desert island; at the same time she spoke soothingly to the Marquise and promised her that the lighthearted buccaneer who had landed in the night would soon come back to her. When the Marquise heard this, she fainted dead away. The Colonel's wife could not subdue her motherly feelings and, with the help of the midwife, labored to revive her; but her anger got the better of her when her daughter came to. "Julietta!" she cried, in accents of intense suffering, "Won't you please, please tell me the truth and say who the father is?" She still seemed ready to forgive her. But when the Marquise said she would lose her mind, her mother got up from the couch and shouted, "Go on, then! You are a contemptible creature! I curse the hour I bore you!" and she ran out of the room.

The Marquise, who was about to swoon again, drew the midwife down to her and laid her violently trembling head on her breast. In a faltering voice she asked her how inflexible the laws of nature were: was it possible to conceive without one's knowing it? The midwife smiled, undid the Marquise's dress, and said that that was not the present case. No, no, of course not, the Marquise hastened to say, she had known when she conceived, she only wanted to know in general whether such an occurrence was possible in nature. The midwife answered that, with the exception of the Holy Virgin, no such thing had ever happened to any woman on this earth. The Marquise trembled more and more violently. Fearing that she was going to give birth any minute, she clutched the midwife in terror and begged her not to leave her. The woman tried to reassure her, telling her that her confinement was still a long way off, advising her how in such cases one could escape the cackling of the world, and promising her that everything would turn out all right. But as these words, which were meant to comfort her, only pierced her bosom like so many knife thrusts, the Marquise managed to get a grip on herself, announced that she was feeling better, and asked her companion to leave.

Hardly was the midwife out of the room when the Marquise received a note from her mother that read as follows: "It is Colonel G——'s wish that in view of the existing circumstances the Marquise should leave his house. He sends her herewith all the papers concerning her property, and trusts that God will spare him the misery of ever seeing her again."

The letter, however, was wet with tears and in one corner a word—"dictated" —had been erased. The Marquise burst into tears. Weeping over her parents' mistake and the injustice into which these good people were led, she stumbled to her mother's apartment. Madam G— was with her father, she was told; she tottered to her father's apartment. When she found the door shut against her, she sank to the ground in front of it and in a pitiable voice called all the saints to witness that she was innocent. She must have been there for several minutes or so before the Forest Warden came out and, with an inflamed face, said that the Commandant refused to see her. The Marquise, sobbing brokenly, exclaimed, "Dear brother!" pushed against him into the room, cried, "My beloved father!" and stretched her arms out to the Commandant. He turned his back on her and hurried into his bedroom. When she followed him there he shouted, "Go away!" and tried to slam the door; but she wailed and pleaded and would not let him do it, until he suddenly gave up and retreated, pursued by the Marquise, to the far wall of the room, where he stood with his back to her. Just as she threw herself at his feet and hugged his knees in her trembling arms, a pistol that he had snatched from the wall went off and the shot crashed into the ceiling.

"Dear God!" cried the Marquise, got up from her knees as white as a corpse, and ran from her father's apartment. "Order the carriage for me," she shouted as she came into her apartment; dropped into a chair deathly tired; dressed her children as fast as possible; and had her things packed. Just as she was holding her younger child between her knees and wrapping a last shawl around him before getting into the coach, the Forest Warden entered and said that her father had ordered her to leave the children behind in his care.

"My children!" she exclaimed, and stood up. "Go and tell that unnatural father of yours that he can come and put a pistol bullet through me, but that he won't take my children away from me!" And with all the pride of innocence she picked her two children up in her arms, carried them into the coach without her brother's daring to stop her, and drove away.

Having learned how strong she was through this courageous effort, she was suddenly able to raise herself, as if by her own bootstraps, out of the depths into which fate had cast her. The turmoil in her breast quieted as soon as she was on the open road, she kissed her children, the precious spoils of her struggle, over and over again, and felt quite pleased with herself when she thought about the victory she had won over her brother, thanks to the strength of her unspotted conscience. Her reason, which had been strong enough not to crack under the strain of her uncanny situation, now bowed before the great, holy and inscrutable scheme of things. She saw the impossibility of persuading her family of her innocence, understood that she must accept that fact if she did not want to be destroyed, and in a matter of days after her arrival at V—— her grief had given way to a heroic resolution to arm herself with pride against the onslaughts of the world. She decided to withdraw into herself entirely, to concentrate all her energies on the education of the two children she already possessed, and to lavish all her mother love on the third that God had made her a gift of. She made plans for restoring her beautiful estate, which, owing to her long absence, had fallen a little into disrepair, once she was over her confinement; sat in the summer-house and knitted little caps and stockings for little limbs, while she thought about a comfortable arrangement of the rooms; and also which one she would fill with books and which would be best to put her easel in. And so, before the date of Count F——'s return from Naples arrived, she had become quite reconciled to living a life of ever greater seclusion. The porter was given orders to let nobody into the house. One thought only she could not endure, that the young being whom she had conceived in the purest innocence and whose origin seemed more divine to her than other people's just because it was more mysterious, should bear a stigma in society. An unusual means to discover its father occurred to her, a means that, when she first thought of it, made her start in pure terror and drop her knitting. Tossing restlessly through long sleepless nights, she kept turning the idea, which wounded her in her most sensitive feelings, over in her mind so as to accustom herself to it. Meanwhile she tried repeatedly to get in touch with the man who had deceived her so, even though she had made up her mind that he must belong beyond all redemption to the scum of his sex, and could only have sprung from the blackest and filthiest mire, whatever one might think of the place he now occupied in the world. But as her own feelings of independence grew stronger and stronger, and as she reflected that a gem keeps its value regardless of how it is mounted, she plucked up her courage, one morning when the new life stirred inside her, and had inserted in the newspapers of M—— that extraordinary appeal of which the reader was apprised at the beginning of this story.

Count F——, whom unavoidable business detained in Naples, had meanwhile written to the Marquise a second time to say that other circumstances might arise which would make it desirable for her to keep the tacit promise she had given him. As soon as he could get excused from making the trip to Constantinople, and his other obligations permitted, he left Naples and came right to M——, arriving only a few days after the time he had said he would. The Commandant received him with an embarrassed expression, said that urgent business called him away from the house, and asked the Forest Warden to entertain the guest in the meantime. The Forest Warden led him to his room and, after a brief exchange of greetings, inquired if he knew anything about what had occurred in the Commandant's house during his absence. The Count paled and answered, "No." Whereupon the Forest Warden told him about the shame that the Marquise had brought upon the family, recounting the whole story that our readers have just heard. The Count struck his forehead. "Why were so many obstacles put in my way!" he cried, forgetting himself. "If the marriage had taken place, we should have been spared all this shame and suffering!" The Forest Warden gaped at him and asked whether he was crazy enough to want to marry someone so contemptible. The Count retorted that she was worth more than the whole world that condemned her; that he had absolute confidence in her innocence, and that he would go to V—— today and renew his marriage proposal. At once he picked up his hat, said goodbye to the Forest Warden, who thought he had taken leave of his senses, and left.

Jumping on a horse, he galloped off to V——. When he dismounted at the gate and tried to enter the hall, the porter told him that the Marquise would not see anyone. The Count asked him whether this ban applied to a friend of the house as well as to strangers, to which the porter replied that there were no exceptions he knew of, and right after inquired with a doubtful air if he were not Count F——. "No," replied the Count, after looking at him sharply, and, turning to his servant and speaking loud enough for the porter to hear, he said that in that case they would stop at an inn and he would announce himself to the Marquise in writing. As soon as he was out of the porter's sight, he turned a corner and slipped along the wall of a great garden that stretched behind the house. Entering the garden through an open gate that he discovered, he walked up a path and was just about to climb the slope at the rear of the house when he caught sight, in a summerhouse off to one side, of the charming and mysterious figure of the Marquise, who was busily working at a small table. He walked silently toward her and stood in the entrance to the summerhouse before she noticed him, three short steps away from her.

"Count F——!" exclaimed the Marquise, looking up in surprise and blushing. The Count smiled, stood for a moment in the entrance without moving, then sat down next to her with such modest importunity that it was impossible for her to take alarm, and slipped his arm around her waist before she could think what to do. "Where did you come from, Count, how is it possible——?" the Marquise asked, and looked shyly at the ground.

"From M——," the Count replied, pressing her gently to him, "through a back gate that I found standing open. I was sure you would forgive me if I came in."

"Didn't they say anything to you in M—— about——?" she said, without moving in his arms, and stopped.

"They told me everything, dear Lady," replied the Count. "But as I am absolutely convinced of your innocence——"

"What!" exclaimed the Marquise, standing up and trying to free herself from his embrace. "In spite of that you are willing to come here——!"

"In spite of the world," he said, holding her fast, "in spite of your family, even in spite of your own lovely self," and he kissed her fervently on the breast.

"Please go away!" the Marquise cried.

"As convinced," he said, "my darling Julietta, as if I were ommiscient, as if my own soul lived in your bosom."

"Let me go!" she cried.

"I've come here," he said—and he would not let her go—"to repeat my proposal and to receive my happiness from your hand if you will hear my suit."

"Let me go this instant! I order you to!" And she wrenched herself from his arms and started from the summerhouse.

"Darling! Paragon!" he whispered, getting up and reaching out to hold her.

"Did you hear me!" the Marquise panted, turning and eluding his grasp.

"Only let me whisper one secret to you!" begged the Count as he grabbed clumsily at the smooth arm slipping through his hands.

"I won't hear a word," the Marquise retorted, gave him a push against his chest, fled up the slope, and disappeared.

He was halfway up the slope in pursuit, determined to make her listen to him at whatever cost, when the door banged shut in front of him and he heard the bolt shoot home in rattling haste. He stopped short, not knowing what to do and wondering if he should climb through an open window at the side of the house and keep on until he reached his goal; but as hard as it was for him in every way to give up, he saw no help for it now. Angry with himself for letting her get away from him, he stole down the slope and left the garden to look for his horses. He felt that his attempt to explain himself to her directly had irretrievably failed, and, going at a slow walk back toward M——, he revolved in his mind the letter he now saw himself condemned to write. But in the evening, when he was in the blackest mood possible, whom should he run into at the common table of an inn but the Forest Warden, who immediately wanted to know if his suit had succeeded at V——. The Count answered with a short "No" and was tempted to say something nasty and snubbing; but for the sake of courtesy, he added after a while that he had decided to write to her and would shortly have the whole thing cleared up. The Forest Warden said that he was sorry that the Count's passion for the Marquise had robbed him of his senses. He had to tell him, however, that she was already getting ready to make another choice, he rang for the latest papers and handed the Count the sheet that contained her appeal to the father of her child. The blood rushed to his face as the Count read it through. His mood changed abruptly. The Forest Warden asked him whether he thought the man the Marquise was looking for would appear? "Without a doubt!" the Count retorted as he bent over the paper and greedily devoured what it said. Then, after going to the window for a moment while folding up the paper, he said, "Now everything is all right! Now I know what I have to do!" He turned around and courteously asked the Forest Warden if he would see him again soon; said goodbye, and went away fully reconciled to his fate.

Meanwhile some lively scenes had taken place at the Commandant's house. The Colonel's wife was very angry at her husband's violent rage and at her own weakness in tamely submitting to the tyrannical expulsion of her daughter from her home. When the shot had sounded in the Commandant's bedroom and her daughter had come rushing out, she had fainted away; true, she had recovered at once, but all the Commandant had said when she awoke was that he was sorry she had been frightened for nothing, and he had tossed the discharged pistol on a table. Later, when they were talking about demanding the children from the Marquise, she had timidly remarked that they had no right to take such a step; she pleaded, in a voice still weak and pathetic from the fainting fit, that there should be no more violent scenes in the house; but the Commandant had only turned to the Forest Warden and, livid with rage, had said, "Go and bring them here!" When Count F——'s second letter arrived, the Commandant ordered it sent to the Marquise at V——; she, as they learned later from the messenger, merely laid it aside and said thank you. The Colonel's wife, who was in the dark about so many things in the whole affair, and especially about her daughter's intention to enter into a new marriage for which she had not the slightest desire, vainly tried to bring the subject of the Count's proposal up again. But the Colonel always asked her, in a way that resembled an order more than a request, not to speak to him about it; on one such occasion, when he happened to be taking down a portrait of his daughter that still hung on the wall, he told his wife that he wanted to wipe the Marquise out of his memory completely, and that he no longer had a daughter. It was at this point that the Marquise's extraordinary appeal appeared in the newspapers. Madam G——, absolutely dazed by it, went holding the newspaper, which her husband had given her, into his room, where she found him working at a table, and asked him what in the world he thought about it all? The Commandant, without looking up from his writing, said, "Oh, of course, she's innocent."

"What!" Madam G—— burst out in complete astonishment; "Innocent?"

"She did it in her sleep," the Commandant said, without looking up.

"In her sleep!" Madam G—— replied; "Such a terrible thing could——?"

"Idiot!" shouted the Commandant, pushed his papers into a heap, and left the room.

The next time the newspapers appeared, the Colonel's wife read the following reply, the ink of which was still wet, in one of them, as she and her husband were sitting at breakfast: "If the Marquise of O—— will come to the house of her father, Colonel G——, at eleven o'clock in the morning on the 3rd of——, the person whom she is looking for will appear there to throw himself at her feet."

Before she had read halfway through the announcement, the Colonel's wife was struck speechless; hastily glancing at the end, she handed the paper to the Commandant. The Colonel read it through three times, as if he could not believe his eyes. "Now for heaven's sake, Lorenzo," exclaimed his wife, "tell me what you think about it!"

"The vile creature" replied the Commandant and stood up. "The cunning impostor! Ten times the shamelessness of a bitch joined to ten times the slyness of a fox would not equal hers? What a face! Did you ever see two such eyes? A cherub's look is no truer!" And he went on in this vein and could not calm himself.

"But if it is a trick," his wife asked, "what in the world can she hope to gain by it?"

"What does she hope to gain by it? She wants to carry her contemptible pretense to the bitter end," the Colonel replied. "She has already learned by heart the story that the two of them, he and she, intend to tell us here at eleven o'clock in the morning of the third. 'My dear little daughter,' I am supposed to say, 'I didn't realize that, who could have believed it, I beg your pardon, receive my blessing, all is forgiven.' But there is a bullet here for the man who crosses my threshold on the morning of the third! I think, therefore, that it would be better to have the servants put him out of the house."

After reading the newspaper notice over again, Madam G—— said that, if it were a choice between two incredibilities, she would rather believe in some mysterious action of fate than in the infamy of a daughter otherwise so excellent. But before she had a chance to finish what she was saying, the Commandant shouted, "Do me the favor of keeping still! I can't stand hearing one more word about it!" and he left the room.

A few days later the Commandant received a letter from the Marquise in which she asked him, with the most touching respect, to have the goodness to send on to her at V——, since she was denied the favor of being allowed to enter her father's house, the man who would appear on the morning of the third. The Colonel's wife happened to be there when he received the letter; and, noticing the confusion of feelings plainly reflected in his face—for if the whole thing were a deception, what motive could he impute to his daughter now that she did not seem to be asking for his forgiveness—she was emboldened to propose a plan to him that she had been nursing for some time in her troubled breast. While the Colonel continued to stare vacuously at the newspaper, she said that a notion had occurred to her: would he allow her to visit V—— for a day or so? If the Marquise really knew the man who had published the reply to her appeal and he was only pretending to be a stranger to her, she knew how to put her in a position where she would have to betray herself even though she were the most cunning dissembler in the world. The Commandant answered her by tearing the letter to bits with sudden violence: she knew very well that he wanted to have nothing to do with the Marquise, and he forbade her to communicate with her in any way. He sealed the torn pieces in an envelope, addressed it to the Marquise, and gave it back to the messenger; that was his answer. Hiding the exasperation she felt at his crazy obstinacy, which destroyed any possibility of getting to the bottom of the business, his wife decided to carry out her plan in spite of him. The following morning, taking one of the Commandant's soldiers with her, she rode over to V—— while her husband was still in bed. When her carriage drew up before the gates of the estate, the porter told her that nobody was allowed to see the Marquise. Madam G—— said that she had been told that that was so, but asked him nevertheless to go in and announce that Madam G—— was there. He said it would not do any good, since there was not a person in the world that the Marquise would speak to. Madam G—— replied that the Marquise must certainly have mentioned her, as she was her mother, and that he was not to dawdle any longer but to do his duty. It was hardly a moment between the porter's going into the house on what he considered to be a useless errand and the Marquise's bursting out of the door, running toward the gate, and falling on her knees before the coach. Madam G—— got out of the carriage with the help of the soldier and, more than a little moved, lifted her daughter from the ground. Overcome with emotion, the Marquise bent over her mother's hand and, while the tears streamed down her face, she led her, with great deference, into the house.

"Dear, dear Mother," she said, after showing her to the couch but remaining standing herself and drying her eyes, "what happy chance must I thank for your coming to visit me?" Madam G—— gave her daughter an affectionate hug and said she simply had to come to see her to beg her pardon for the brutal way in which she had been turned out of her father's house.

"Pardon!" the Marquise broke in, and wanted to kiss her hands. But her mother would not let her and went on, "Not only did the answer that just appeared in the newspapers to your advertisement convince me as well as your father that you are innocent; I also have to tell you that the man himself appeared in person at the house, to our great and pleasant surpise."

"Who appeared——?" the Marquise exclaimed, sitting down beside her mother; "which man appeared in person?"—and her face was tense with expectation.

"The one who wrote that answer," Madam G—— replied, "the very man you addressed your appeal to, he himself in person."

"Then for goodness' sake," the Marquise said, her breast heaving violently, "who is he?" And again, "Who is he?"

"That," Madam G—— replied, "I would rather let you guess. Just imagine it —yesterday when we were having tea, right in the middle of our reading the answer in the newspaper, a man whom all of us know very well rushed into the room in wild despair and fell at your father's feet and, a moment after, at mine. We didn't know what to make of it all and asked him to explain himself. His conscience, he said, left him no peace, he was the scoundrel who had deceived the Marquise; he must know how his crime was judged and, if vengeance on him was demanded, he came himself to satisfy that demand."

"But who is he? Who? Who?" the Marquise cried.

"As I have said," continued Madam G——, "a young and otherwise well-bred man whom we should never have thought capable of such a despicable act. But I hope, my daughter, that you won't be horrified to learn that he is of humble station and lacks all those qualities which we should otherwise require of a husband for you."

"Just the same, Mother dear," the Marquise said, "he can't be entirely unworthy, since he threw himself at your feet before mine. But who is he, won't you please tell me who he is?"

"Well," her mother replied, "he is Leopardo, the chasseur, whom your father had come from the Tyrol not long ago and whom I have brought along with me, as you may have noticed, to introduce to you as your bridegroom."

"Leopardo, the chasseur!" cried the Marquise, clapping her hand to her forehead in despair.

"What are you afraid of?" the Colonel's wife asked. "Have you any reason to doubt he is the one?"

"How? Where? When?" the Marquise asked in bewilderment.

"He will only tell you that," she said. "Shame and love, he says, make it impossible for him to talk to anyone else but you. But, if you like, we can open the door to the anteroom where he is waiting with a beating heart, and while I go off somewhere you can see if you can get him to tell his secret."

"Oh, my God!" the Marquise exclaimed. "I once dozed off on the couch in the midday heat and when I woke up I saw him slinking away!" And she hid her shame-reddened face in her small hands.

Her mother dropped on her knees in front of her. "Oh my daughter!" she cried. "Oh my wonderful daughter!" and she threw her arms around her. "And oh your contemptible mother!" she said, burying her face in her daughter's lap.

"What's the matter, Mother?" the Marquise asked in dismay.

"I want you to know," her mother continued, "you who are purer than the angels, that there is not a word of truth in anything I said; that my soul is so corrupt that I could not believe in such radiant innocence as yours; and that I needed to play this shameful trick in order to convince myself."

"My darling mother," said the Marquise, and full of joy she bent down to lift her up.

"No," she said, "I won't budge from here, you marvelous, saintly girl, until you say you can forgive my vicious behavior."

"I forgive you, Mother, oh I do! Stand up," cried the Marquise. "Oh please do!"

"First tell me," said Madam G——, "if you can ever love and respect me as you used to."

"My adored mother!" the Marquise said, and also went down on her knees. "I never lost the reverence and love I feel for you. How could anybody have believed me when the circumstances were so queer? I am so happy that you don't blame me."

"From now on," Madam G—— said, getting to her feet with the help of her daughter, "I will wait upon you hand and foot, my darling child. You shall have your confinement in my house; if the circumstances were different and I were expecting you to present me with a young prince, I shouldn't take care of you with greater tenderness and consideration. I'll not budge from your side again the rest of my days. I defy the whole world; from now on your shame is the only glory I wish, if only you will think well of me again and forget the cruel way in which I repudiated you." The Marquise tried to comfort her with endless caresses and reassurances, but the evening came, and then midnight, before she succeeded. The following day, when the old lady's excitement, which gave her a fever during the night, had somewhat abated, mother, daughter, and grandchildren drove back to M——. The journey was like a triumph. They were as jolly as they could be and joked about Leopardo, the chasseur, who was sitting up front in the coachman's box; her mother said to the Marquise that she saw her blush every time she looked at his broad back. The Marquise responded to this with something between a sigh and a smile. "Who knows," she said, "who will finally show up at eleven o'clock on the morning of the third!"

Thereafter, the closer they drew to M——, the more serious they became, in anticipation of the fateful scene that was about to take place. When they alighted in front of the house, Madam G——, saying not a word about her plans, took her daughter to her old rooms, told her to make herself at home, and, declaring that she would be back shortly, slipped away. An hour later she returned, her face quite flushed. "Did you ever see such a fellow?" she said, secretly pleased nevertheless. "Such a doubting Thomas! It took me a whole hour to convince him, and now of course he is sitting there and crying!"

"Who?" the Marquise asked.

"Who else but the one who has the most reason to cry."

"You don't mean Father?" the Marquise said.

"Like a baby!" her mother said. "If I hadn't had to wipe the tears out of my own eyes, I would have burst out laughing as soon as I was out of the room."

"And all because of me?" the Marquise asked, getting up. "And I sit here——?"

"Don't you budge!" Madam G—— exclaimed. "Why did he dictate that letter to me? Let him come looking for you here if he ever wants to see me again."

"Mother dear!" begged the Marquise.

"I won't relent!" her mother interrupted. "Why did he reach for that pistol!"

"I implore you!"

"No, you won't," Madam G—— replied, pushing her daughter back into her chair. "And if he doesn't come here by this evening, you and I will go away tomorrow." The Marquise said it would be cruel and unjust to do that. But her mother said: "Be quiet"—for just then she heard a sound of sobbing drawing near: "Here he is now!"

"Where?" the Marquise asked, and listened. "Can that be someone at the door, that terrible——?"

"Of course," Madam G—— replied. "He wants us to let him in."

"Let me go!" cried the Marquise and jumped out of her chair.

"If you love me, Julietta," replied the Colonel's wife, "then stay where you are." And at that very instant the Commandant entered, holding his handkerchief to his eyes. Madam G—— took up a position in front of her daughter, as if to protect her, and turned her back to the Colonel.

"Dear, dear Father," cried the Marquise and stretched her arms out to him.

"Don't you budge!" commanded her mother. "Do you hear?" The Commandant stood in the middle of the room and wept. "Let him apologize to you," continued Madam G——. "Why must he be so violent! And why must he be so obstinate! I love him, but I love you too; I honor him, but you too. And if I must make a choice, then I'll stay with you because you are the better one." The Commandant bent down until he was almost doubled over and roared so loudly that the walls rang.

"Oh my God!" exclaimed the Marquise, gave in to her mother all at once, reached for her handkerchief, and let her own tears flow.

Madam G—— said, "He can't even speak," and moved a little to one side. At which her daughter got up, put her arms around the Commandant, and begged him to calm himself. She herself was weeping furiously. She asked him if he would not sit down; she tried to persuade him to sit down; she pushed a chair toward him for him to sit on; but he would not say one word; there was no budging him from where he was, and yet he would not take a seat, just stood there in the center of the room, his head bowed to the ground, and cried. The Marquise turned halfway toward her mother as she held him up and said that he would get ill; even her mother seemed to waver in her firmness when she saw how convulsed he was. But when the Commandant yielded to the incessant pleadings of his daughter and finally sat down, and she crouched at his feet and caressed and comforted him incessantly, the mother started talking again, said that it served him right and that perhaps he would now come back to his senses, walked out of the room and left them alone.

Once outside, she wiped her own tears away, and wondered if the violent agitation of feeling to which she had exposed him might not be a danger to his health and if it were perhaps advisable to send for a doctor. For the evening meal, she prepared everything that she could think of that had a fortifying and soothing effect, turned back the coverlets of his bed and warmed the sheets so that she could tuck him in as soon as he appeared on his daughter's arm, and, when he still did not come and the table was already laid, tiptoed to the Marquise's room to hear what was going on. As she listened with her ear against the door, she heard a soft whisper that subsided into silence at that very moment; it seemed to have come from the Marquise; and as she was able to see through the keyhole, her daughter was sitting on the Commandant's lap, something he never in his life had allowed her to do. Finally she opened the door and peered in—and her heart leaped for joy: her daughter lay motionless in her father's arms, her head thrown back and her eyes closed, while he sat in the armchair, with tear-choked, glistening eyes, and pressed long, warm and avid kisses on her mouth: just as if he were her lover! Her daughter did not speak, her husband did not speak; he hung over her as if she were his first love and held her mouth and kissed it. The mother's delight was indescribable; standing unobserved behind the chair, she hesitated to disturb the joy of reconciliation that had come to her home. At last she moved nearer and, peering around one side of the chair, she saw her husband again take his daughter's face between his hands and with unspeakable delight bend down and press his lips against her mouth. On catching sight of her, the Commandant looked away with a frown and was about to say something; but calling out, "Oh, what a face!" she kissed him in her turn so that his frown went away, and with a joke dispelled the intense emotion filling the hushed room. She invited them both to supper, and they followed her to the table like a pair of newlyweds; the Commandant, to be sure, seemed quite cheerful during the meal, but he ate and spoke little, from time to time a sob escaped him, and he stared down at his plate and played with his daughter's hand.

Next day the great question was, who would appear at eleven o'clock of the following morning, for it was now the eve of the dreaded third. Father and mother, and the brother as well—for he too had made it up with his sister—were all agreed that, if the man were at all passable, the Marquise should marry him; everything that could possibly make the Marquise's position a happy one should be done. But if his circumstances were such that even with their help a marked discrepancy would still exist between his position and the Marquise's, then her parents were against the marriage; the Marquise could stay with them as before and they would adopt the child. She, however, seemed inclined to stick to her promise, providing the man was not an out-and-out scoundrel, and to give her child a father at whatever cost to herself. In the evening the mother asked how they should receive the visitor. The Commandant thought the best thing would be to leave the Marquise alone around eleven o'clock. But the Marquise insisted that she wanted her two parents present, and her brother too, since she had no wish to share any kind of secrets with the person. Also she thought that their visitor's answer to her advertisement, in which he proposed the Commandant's house as the meeting place, suggested that he too wished to have her family present—a fact about the reply, she had to confess, that had won her good opinion. Madam G—— pointed out that her father and her brother would have very awkward parts indeed to play in the proceeding, and asked her daughter to excuse the men; but she was perfectly agreeable to being present herself. After a moment's reflection her daughter accepted this suggestion.

And finally, after a night of the most anxious suspense, the morning of the dreaded third arrived. As the clock struck eleven, the two women were sitting in the reception room, dressed as if for a betrothal; you could have heard the pounding of their hearts if the clatter of the morning had been hushed. The eleventh stroke was still shivering in the air when the door opened to admit Leopardo, the chasseur, whom their father had sent to the Tyrol for. The women paled when they saw him. "Count F——'s carriage," he announced, "is at the door and he begs to be received."

"Count F——!" the two exclaimed together, in utter consternation. The Marquise shouted, "Bolt the door! We are not at home to him," jumped up and was about to push the chasseur, who was standing in her way, out of the room and bar the door herself when the Count entered, wearing the same uniform, plus his decorations and sword, that he had worn during the capture of the fortress. The Marquise felt like sinking into the ground with confusion; she snatched up a handkerchief she had left on the chair and meant to fly into a neighboring room; but Madam G—— caught hold of her hand, cried, "Julietta!"—and as if choking on her own thoughts, her voice failed her. Riveting her eyes on the Count, Madam G—— repeated, "Julietta, please!" and tried to pull her daughter back. "After all, whom were we waiting for——?"

"Oh no, surely not for him!" she cried, suddenly turning around and shooting the Count a look that crackled like lightning while a deathlike pallor spread across her face. The Count went down on one knee to her; his right hand was pressed against his heart, his head hung down on his breast, and he stared with burning intensity in front of him, saying nothing.

"Whom else!" gasped the Colonel's wife. "We are such idiots—whom else but him——?"

The Marquise stood stiffly erect over him and said, "I am going out of my mind, Mother."

"You goose!" her mother retorted, pulled her to her and whispered something in her ear. The Marquise turned away and, hiding her face in her hands, went and fell on the sofa. "What's the matter with you!" her mother cried. "What has happened that you weren't expecting?" The Count did not move from the mother's side; still kneeling, he caught up the hem of her dress and kissed it. "Dear, kind, gracious lady!" he whispered and a tear rolled down his cheek.

"Get up, Count, please get up!" the Colonel's wife said. "Go over there and make her feel better; that way we shall all be reconciled and everything will be forgiven and forgotten." The Count stood up, crying. Getting down again before the Marquise, he took her hand as delicately as if it were made of gold that his slightest touch would tarnish. But she stood erect, crying, "Go away! Go away! Go away! I was ready for some villain of a fellow, but not—not—not the devil!" and, walking around him as if he had the plague, she opened the door and said, "Call the Colonel!"

"Julietta!" her mother panted. The Marquise looked with murderous fierceness first at the Count and then at her mother; her breast heaved, her eyes blazed; one of the Furies could not have looked more terrible. The Colonel and the Forest Warden entered. "Father," she called out before he had even come through the doorway, "I can't marry this man!" thrust her hand into a vessel of holy water fastened behind the door, with a sweep of her arm sprinkled her father, mother and brother with the water, and disappeared.

The Commandant looked surprised and asked what had happened; his face went white when he saw Count F—— in the room. The mother took the Count's hand and said, "Don't ask any questions. This young man is sincerely sorry for what he has done; give him your blessing, come, give it to him, and all will end well." The Count looked completely crushed. The Commandant laid his hand on him; his eyelids twitched, his lips were as white as chalk. "May God's curse avoid this head!" he cried. "When do you mean to get married?"

"Tomorrow," the mother answered for him, for he was absolutely speechless. "Tomorrow or today. Whatever you wish; the Count, who has shown such praiseworthy eagerness to redeem his offense, will certainly prefer the earliest possible date."

"Then I shall have the pleasure of meeting you tomorrow morning at eleven at St. Augustine's Church," the Commandant said, bowed to him, asked his wife and son to accompany him to the Marquise's room, and left the Count standing there.

They tried in vain to get the Marquise to explain her strange behavior; she was in a violent fever, would not hear of the marriage, and begged them to leave her alone. When they asked her why she had suddenly changed her mind and what made the Count more obnoxious to her than somebody else, she stared blankly at her father and did not answer. Madam G—— asked her if she had forgotten that she was going to be a mother; she said that in this case she had to think of herself more than of her child and, calling on all the angels and saints as witnesses, she swore again that she would never marry. Her father, seeing that she was extremely overwrought, said that she must keep her word, left the room, and, after duly exchanging notes with the Count, gave all the necessary orders for the wedding. He also submitted a marriage contract to the Count in which the latter renounced all his rights as a husband, at the same time that he agreed to do anything and everything that might be required of him. The Count signed the paper and sent it back moistened with his tears. The next morning, when the Commandant brought the contract to the Marquise, he found her somewhat more composed. Sitting up in bed, she read it over several times, folded it up reflectively, unfolded it, and read it over again; and then announced that she would be at St. Augustine's Church at eleven o'clock.

She got up, dressed herself without a word, got into the coach with all her family when the hour sounded, and drove to the church.

The Count was not allowed to join them until they were at the church door. During the entire ceremony the Marquise stared straight ahead at the altar painting; she did not even vouchsafe the man with whom she exchanged rings a passing glance. After the service the Count gave her his arm; but as soon as they were out of the church the Countess bowed to him; the Commandant asked him if he might have the honor of seeing him occasionally in his daughter's apartment, to which the Count stammered something in reply that nobody could understand, pulled his hat off to the company, and went away. He took a place in M—— and several months went by without his so much as setting foot in the Commandant's house, where the Countess continued to stay.

Thanks only to the delicate, honorable, and exemplary way he behaved whenever he encountered the family, he was invited, after the Countess was duly delivered of a son, to the latter's baptism. The Countess, sitting up in bed with rugs around her shoulders, saw him only for a moment as he stood in the doorway and bowed respectfully to her from the distance. Into the cradle among the gifts with which the guests welcomed the newborn child he tossed two papers, one of which, as it turned out when he departed, was a gift of 20,000 rubles to the boy, the other a will making the mother, in case he died, the heiress of everything he owned. From that day on, thanks to Madam G——'s management, he was invited to the house more often; he was free to come and go, and soon no evening passed in which he did not appear there. When his feelings told him that everybody, seeing what an imperfect place the world in general was, had pardoned him, he began to court his wife the Countess anew. After a year she consented for the second time, and a second marriage was celebrated, happier than the first, after which the whole family moved to V——. A whole line of young Russians now followed the first; and when the Count once asked his wife, in a happy moment, why on that terrible third of the month, when she seemed ready to accept any villain of a fellow that came along, she had fled from him as if from the Devil, she threw her arms around his neck and said: he wouldn't have looked like a devil to her then if he had not seemed like an angel to her at his first appearance.

Adolphe:
an Anecdote

Found Among the Papers of an Unknown Person, and Published (1816) by

Benjamin Constant

Alexander Walker, translator

During a busy life as a liberal politician and an able parliamentarian, Henri Benjamin Constant de Rebecque (1767–1830) published a single *nouvelle, Adolphe*. Born in Lausanne, Switzerland, he lost his mother a few days after his birth, and the upbringing given him by his father, a colonel in the French army, is suggested in the early pages of *Adolphe*. Constant, a precocious youth who could read Greek when he was five, was shuttled from Lausanne to Paris to Oxford to the German University of Erlangen and thence to the University of Edinburgh. A long and checkered political career, in which he changed sides more than once, ended with his appointment as president of the French council of state in the year of his death.

Autobiographical in origin, *Adolphe* is built upon Constant's liaison with Madame de Staël (1766–1817), whom he met in Lausanne in 1794 and followed to Paris; by 1796 she was his mistress, and the relationship lasted, despite quarrels, for ten years. The reference to an earlier liaison (Chap. I) may refer to a more or less platonic relationship he established with a much older woman, Madame de Charrière, which lasted from 1787 until he met Madame de Staël. Constant wrote one version of *Adolphe* in 1806, immediately after his final break with Madame de Staël; he rewrote it in 1807, read it often in public, made a final draft in 1810, and finally published it in 1816. His *Cahier rouge*, not published until 1907, contains his autobiography for the years 1767 to 1787; he also left two other sketches of novels, now lost. His major work of nonfiction was *The History of Religion* (5 vols., 1825–1831).

The translation is by Alexander Walker (London, 1816; Philadelphia, 1817), revised by the editor with the addition of the passages Constant suppressed from the 1716 edition and returned to the 1724 edition (see pp. 183–85). For additional reading, see Martin Turnell's useful essay on *Adolphe* in *The Novel in France* (London, 1950), pp. 79–122.

Advertisement By The Editor

I travelled through Italy, many years ago. I was delayed at an inn of Cerenza, a little village of Calabria, by an overflowing of the Neto. There was, at the same inn, a stranger who was detained by the same cause. He was very silent, and seemed sad. He showed no impatience. I complained sometimes to him, as the only man to whom, in that place, I could speak of the delay which our journey experienced. It is the same to me, he replied, whether I am here or elsewhere. Our landlord, who had been talking with a Neapolitan domestic, who served that stranger without knowing his name, informed me he did not travel from curiosity; for he visited neither ruins, nor scenes, nor monuments, nor men. He read much; but never in a connected manner. He walked at night, always alone; and often passed whole days, seated, immoveable, his head reclining on both his hands.

At the moment when the re-establishment of the communications permitted us to depart, the stranger fell very ill. Humanity made it my duty to prolong my abode near him, that I might take care of him. There was, at Cerenza, only a village surgeon. I wished to send to Cozenza to procure some more efficacious assistance. It is not worth while, said the stranger: the man who is here is precisely such a one as I stand in need of. He was right: more so perhaps than he imagined; for that man cured him. I did not believe you were so skilful, said he to him, fretfully, on discharging him; he then thanked me for my care, and departed.

Several months after, I received, at Naples, a letter from the landlord at Cerenza, with a casket found on the road which leads to Strongoli—the road which the stranger and I had taken; though separately. The innkeeper, who had sent it to me, thought himself certain that it belonged to one of us. It enclosed many very old letters, without any addresses, or of which the addresses and the signatures were effaced, a portrait of a lady, and a bundle of papers containing the anecdote or history which we are about to read. The stranger, who was the proprietor of these effects, had not, on quitting me, left any means of writing to him. I preserved them nearly ten years, uncertain what use I ought to make of them; when having, by chance, spoken of them to some persons in a city of Germany, one of them earnestly solicited that I would entrust him with the manuscript of which I was the depository. At the expiration of eight days, the manuscript was returned to me, with a letter which I have placed at the end of this history, because it will be unintelligible, if read before the history itself.

This letter determined me as to the actual publication, by assuring me that it could neither offend nor compromise any one. I have not altered one word from the original. Even the suppression of proper names does not originate with me. They were designated, only as they are now, by initial letters.

Chapter I

At twenty-two years of age, I completed my studies in the university of Göttingen.—The intention of my father, minister of the Elector of ——, was, that I should travel over the most remarkable countries of Europe. He meant afterwards to recall me to him, to introduce me into the department of which the direction was confided to him, and to prepare me, one day, to fill his situation. I had obtained, by study tolerably persevering, in the midst of a very dissipated life, successes which had distinguished me above my fellow students, and which had made my father conceive of me hopes, perhaps greatly exaggerated.

These hopes had rendered him very indulgent as to many errors which I had committed. He had never permitted me to suffer from the effects of these errors: he had always granted, sometimes anticipated, my desires in that respect.

Unfortunately his conduct was rather noble and generous than affectionate. I deeply felt all his claims to my gratitude and my respect. But no confidence had ever existed between us. He had in mind somewhat of an ironical turn, which ill accorded with my disposition. I then wished only to abandon myself to those primitive and wild impressions which throw the soul out of the common sphere, and inspire it with disdain for all surrounding objects. I found in my father, not a censor, but a cold and sarcastic observer, who at first smiled with pity, and who soon after broke off the conversation with impatience. I do not recollect having had a conference of an hour with him during the first eighteen years of my life. His letters were affectionate, and full of rational and sensible advice. But no sooner were we together than there appeared in him somewhat of constraint which I could not explain, and which affected me in a painful manner. I knew not then what timidity was, that inward anxiety which pursues us even to the latest period of life, which throws back upon the heart our deepest impressions, which freezes our words, which disfigures, while yet in the mouth, all that we attempt to say, and which permits us not to express ourselves except by vague words, or by an irony more or less bitter, as if we wished to revenge ourselves on our very senti-ments for the misery we experience in not being able to make them known. I did not know that, even with his son, my father was timid; and that often, after having long expected from me some testimonies of affection which his seeming coolness appeared to interdict, he left me with tears in his eyes, and lamented to others that I had no regard for him.

My constraint with him had great influence on my disposition. As timid as himself, but more agitated, because I was younger, I accustomed myself to shut up within my own mind all that I felt, to form none but solitary plans, to depend on none but myself for their execution, and to consider the advice, the interest, the assistance, and even the mere appearance of others as a constraint and an obstacle. I contracted the habit of never speaking of what I was engaged in, of yielding to conversation only as to an irksome necessity, and of then animating it by a perpetual pleasantry, which rendered it less fatiguing to me, and which assisted me to conceal my real thoughts. Thence arose a certain reserve with which my friends, even to this day, reproach me, and a difficulty of conversing seriously, which it always requires an effort from me to surmount. Thence proceeded, at the same time, an ardent desire of independence, a great impatience of the ties by which I was surrounded, and an invincible terror at the formation of new ones. I found not myself at ease but when alone, and such even at present is the effect of that disposition of mind, that when, under the least important circumstances, I ought to form any determination, the human figure distracts me, and my natural tendency is to fly from it in order to deliberate in peace. I had not, however, the excessive egotism which such a disposition seemed to indicate. While I myself was the sole object of my interest, I was feebly interested even about myself. I had, at the bottom of my heart, a need of sensibility, which I did not perceive; but which, finding nothing to satisfy itself, successively detached me from all the objects that, in their turn, attracted my curiosity. That indifference was further strengthened by the idea of death, an idea which had struck me when very young, and of which I have never conceived how men should so easily shake off the thought. I had, when seventeen years of age, seen an aged person die, whose mind, of a remarkable and peculiar turn, had begun to unfold mine. That person, like so many others, had, at the beginning of her career, encountered the world of which she was ignorant, with the feeling of great energy of mind and of faculties truly powerful. Like so many others also, in consequence of not having yielded to factitious but necessary rules of society, she had seen her hopes disappointed—her youth pass without pleasure, and old age had, at length, reached her without subduing her. She lived in a castle adjoining one of our estates, discontented and retired, having her mind alone for a resource, and with that mind analyzing every thing.—During nearly a year, in our inexhaustible conversations, we had viewed life in all its forms, and death always as the end of all. And after having familiarly conversed with her so much about death, I had seen death strike her before my eyes.

This event had filled me with a sentiment of uncertainty respecting destiny, and with a vague reverie which did not abandon me. I preferred reading in the poets whatever reminded me of the brevity of human life. I found that no object was worth the trouble of any effort. It is singular enough that this impression should have grown weaker, precisely as years have accumulated over me. Is it because there is in hope something doubtful, and because when it retires from the career of man, that career assumes a character more severe but more definite? Is it because life appears so much the more real when all its illusions evanish, as the ridge of the mountain is better designated in the horizon when the clouds are dispersed?

I repaired, on quitting Göttingen, to the little town of D——. That town was the residence of a prince, who, like most of those in Germany, governed with mildness a country of small extent, protected enlightened men who came to reside there, and granted to all a perfect liberty of opinion; but who, confined by ancient usage to the society of his courtiers, collected consequently, even around himself, only men in a great measure of insignificant or of inferior abilities. I was received, at this court, with the curiosity which is naturally inspired by every stranger who is about to break the circle of monotony and etiquette. During some months, I observed nothing that could attract my attention. I was grateful for the kindness shewn to me. But sometimes my timidity prevented me from profiting by it: sometimes the fatigue of an agitation without object made me prefer solitude to the insipid pleasures in which they invited me to participate. I bore no hatred to any one; but few persons inspired me with interest. Now, men are hurt at indifference. They ascribe it to malevolence or to affectation. They are unwilling to believe that we naturally get tired with them. Sometimes I endeavoured to constrain my weariness: I took refuge in a profound taciturnity:—they took that taciturnity for disdain. At other times, wearied of my silence, I permitted myself to indulge in some pleasantries, and my mind being put in motion, carried me beyond all bounds. I revealed, in one day, all the absurdities which I had observed in the course of a month. The confidants of my sudden and involuntary effusions did not thank me for it; and they were right: for it was the necessity for speaking, and not confidence which actuated me. I had contracted, in my conversations with the person who had first developed my ideas, an insurmountable aversion for all common maxims and all dogmatic rules. When then I heard mediocrity discourse with complacency on principles well established and sufficiently incontestable in morals, in customs, or in religion, matters which it willingly enough puts on the same level, I felt myself urged to contradict it; not because I had adopted opposite opinions, but because I was impatient of a conviction so firm and so obstinate. I know not what instinct warned me besides to mistrust those general axioms so exempt from all restriction, so pure from every shade. Fools make of their morality a compact and indivisible mass, in order that it may mix as little as possible with their actions, and may leave them free as to all the details.

I soon gained, by such behaviour, a great reputation of levity, derision and wickedness. My bitter expressions were considered as proofs of a malevolent mind, my pleasantries as out-rages against whatever was most respectable. Those whom I had been to blame in ridiculing, found it convenient to make a common cause with the principles which they accused me of calling in question. Because, without wishing it, I had made them laugh at the expence of each other, all united against me. They seemed to say, that in exposing their foibles, I betrayed a confidence which they had reposed in me. They seemed to say, that in exhibiting themselves to my view, such as they were, they had obtained, on my part, a promise of silence. I was not conscious of having accepted that too burthensome agreement. They had found pleasure in giving themselves full scope. I found it in observing them, and in describing them; and that which they called an act of perfidy appeared to me a satisfaction quite innocent and altogether allowable.

I wish not here to justify myself. I have long since renounced that frivolous and facile employment of a mind without experience. I will only say, and that for others as well as myself, who am now sheltered from the world, that it requires time to accustom ourselves to mankind, such as interest, affectation, vanity, and fear have rendered it to us. The astonishment of our early youth, at the aspect of a society so factitious and so laboured, announces rather a natural heart than a bad mind. That society, besides, has nothing to fear from it. It weighs so heavily upon us—its dull influence is so powerful, that it is not long of fashioning us after the universal model. We are then no longer surprised but at our former surprise, and we find ourselves at ease under our new form, as we at last breathe freely in a crowded theatre, though in entering we breathe only with effort.

If any escape from that general destiny, they shut up in themselves their secret dissent. They perceive, in most frivolities, the germ of vices. They no longer jest, because contempt succeeds mockery, and contempt is silent.

There was then formed, in the little society which surrounded me, a vague inquietude respecting my character. They could not ascribe to me any blamable action. They could not even deny me some which seemed to announce generosity or devotedness; but they said that I was an immoral man, a man little to be trusted—epithets ingeniously contrived to insinuate facts which men are ignorant of, and to leave that to be guessed which they know not.

Chapter II

Absent, inattentive, tired, I did not perceive the impression which I produced, and I divided my time between studies which I often interrupted, projects which I did not execute, and pleasures which interested me but little, when a circumstance very frivolous in appearance produced, in my disposition, an important revolution.

A young man with whom I was tolerably intimate endeavoured, for some months, to render himself agreeable to one of the women who were the least insipid in the society in which we lived. I was the disinterested confidant of his enterprize. After long continued efforts, he succeeded in gaining her love; and as he had not concealed from me his reverses and his troubles, he thought himself obliged to communicate to me his success. Nothing equalled his transports and the excess of his joy. The sight of such happiness made me regret that I had not yet made a trial of it. I had not hitherto had any female intimacy which could flatter my self-love. A new futurity appeared to unveil itself to my eyes. A new want made itself felt at the bottom of my heart. There was, in that want, much vanity no doubt, but there was not in it vanity alone. There was perhaps in it even less of this than I myself imagined. The sentiments of man are mixed and confused; they are composed of a multitude of varied impressions which escape observation; and language, always too coarse and too general, may well serve to designate them, but it never serves to define them.

I had, in my father's house, adopted, with regard to women, a system sufficiently immoral. My father, strictly attentive as he might be to exterior proprieties, allowed himself frequently enough to hold light discourse on the ties of love. He looked upon them as amusements, if not permitted, at least excusable, and considered marriage alone in any serious respect. It was a principle of his, that a young man ought with care to avoid the commission of what may be called a folly; that is, contracting a durable engagement with a person who may not be perfectly his equal in fortune, birth, and exterior advantages. Moreover, all women, so long as there was no intention of marriage, might in his opinion, without inconvenience, be taken, and then abandoned; and I have seen him smile with a kind of approbation at that parody of a well known sentiment:—this gives them so little pain and us so much of pleasure.

It is not sufficiently understood how deep an impression words of that kind make in early youth, and how much at an age when all the opinions are still doubtful and wavering, children are astonished to see contradicted, by pleasantries which every one applauds, the direct rules which have been given them. These rules are, in their eyes, only common forms which their parents have agreed to repeat to them for the acquittal of their conscience; and those pleasantries seem to them to include the true secret of life.

Tormented by a vague emotion, I will be loved, said I, and I looked around me: I saw no person who could inspire me with love—no person who seemed to me susceptible of feeling it. I interrogated my heart and my inclinations: I did not feel any tendency to preference. I was thus inwardly agitated when I became acquainted with Count de P——, a man of forty years of age, whose family was allied to mine. He proposed to me to visit him. Unfortunate visit! He had with him his mistress, a native of Poland, celebrated for her beauty, though she was not very young. This lady, in spite of her disadvantageous situation, had evinced, on several occasions, a distinguished character. Her family, considerably illustrious in Poland, had been ruined during the troubles of that country. Her father had been proscribed. Her mother had sought an asylum in France, and had carried thither her daughter, whom she had left, at her death, completely deserted. Count de P—— became enamoured of her. I have always been ignorant how an acquaintance was formed, which, when I first saw Ellenor, had long been established, and, if I may say so, consecrated. Had the fatality of her situation, or the inexperience of her age, plunged her into a career which was equally repugnant to her education, to her habits, and to the pride which constituted a very remarkable portion of her character? That which I know, and which all the world has known, is that the fortune of Count de P—— having been almost entirely exhausted, and his liberty threatened, Ellenor had given him such proofs of devotedness, had rejected with such contempt the most brilliant offers, had shared his perils and his poverty with so much zeal and even joy, that the most scrupulous severity could not hesitate to render justice to the purity of her motives and the disinterestedness of her conduct. It was to her activity, to her courage, to her judgment, and to sacrifices of every kind which she had supported without complaint, that her lover owed the recovery of part of his property. They had come to reside at D——, to prosecute a suit which might restore, in its integrity, to Count de P—— his ancient opulence, and they reckoned on residing there about two years.

Ellenor had but an ordinary mind: yet her ideas were just; and her expressions, always simple, were sometimes striking by the nobleness and the elevation of her sentiments. She had many prejudices, but all her prejudices were in the inverse sense of her interest. She attached the greatest value to regularity of conduct, precisely because hers was not regular according to received notions. She was very religious, because religion rigorously condemned her mode of life. She severely repelled, in conversation, whatever would have appeared to other women only innocent pleasantries, because she always feared that some might think themselves authorized by her condition to address to her improper language. She would have wished to receive the visits of men only of the most elevated rank, and of irreproachable manners, because those women with whom she shuddered to be compared, ordinarily form for themselves a mixed society, and, resigning themselves to the loss of consideration, seek, in their associations, only amusement. Ellenor, in a word, was engaged in a constant struggle with her destiny. She protested, if I may say so, by each of her actions and her words, against the class of society in which she found herself placed: and as she felt that reality was more powerful than her, and that her efforts made no change in her situation, she was very wretched. She brought up two children whom she had had by Count de P——with an excessive austerity. One would have said that a secret revolt blended itself with the attachment, rather passionate than tender, which she showed them, and rendered them, in some measure, distressing to her. When, with good intention, there was made to her some remark on the growth of her children, on the talents which they promised to possess, on the career which they would have to follow, she was seen to turn pale with the idea that it would one day be necessary she should avow to them their birth. But the slightest danger, an hour of absence, brought her back to them with an anxiety in which was discerned a kind of remorse, and a desire to confer on them, by her caresses, the happiness which she herself did not experience. This opposition between her sentiments and the place which she occupied in the world had rendered her temper very unequal. Often she was pensive and silent: sometimes she spoke with impetuosity. As she was tormented with a particular idea, in the midst of the most general conversation, she never remained perfectly calm. But even in consequence of that circumstance there was, in her manner, something impetuous and unexpected, which rendered her more striking than she naturally would have been. The oddness of her position supplied in her the place of novelty of ideas. She was examined with interest and curiosity, as we examine a beautiful storm.

Presented to my view, at a moment when my heart had need of love, my vanity of success, Ellenor appeared a conquest worthy of myself. On her part she found pleasure in the society of a man different from those she had hitherto seen. Her circle was composed of some friends or relations of her lover and of their wives, whom the ascendancy of Count de P—— had obliged to receive his mistress. The husbands were destitute of sentiments as well as of ideas; the wives differed not from their husbands but by a mediocrity more restless and more agitated because they had not, like them, that tranquillity of mind which results from occupation and the regularity of duties. A pleasantry more light, a conversation more varied, a particular mixture of melancholy and of gaiety, of depression and of interest, of enthusiasm and of irony, surprised and attached Ellenor. She herself spoke several languages, imperfectly it is true, but always with vivacity, sometimes with grace. Her ideas seemed to burst through obstacles, and to spring from that struggle more agreeable, more ingenuous, and more new: for foreign idioms again give youth to thoughts, and disembarrass them of those turns which make them appear alternately common and affected. We read together the English poets: we walked together. I often went to see her in the morning: I returned in the evening: I conversed with her upon a thousand subjects.

I thought to make, as a cold and impartial observer, an examination of her character and of her mind. But each word she uttered seemed to me invested with an inexplicable grace. The wish to please her, introducing into my life a new interest, animated my existence in an unusual manner. I attributed to her charms this almost magical effect. I should have enjoyed it still more completely without the engagement which I had made towards my self-love. This self-love formed a sort of intermediate being between Ellenor and me. I thought myself obliged to advance in the quickest manner towards the object which I had proposed. I did not then give myself up without reserve to my impressions. I longed to have spoken; for it seemed to me that I had only to speak in order to succeed. I did not think that I loved Ellenor; but, even then I could not have been contented not to please her. She occupied me incessantly. I formed a thousand projects; I invented a thousand means of conquest, with that experienced foppery which believes itself sure of success, because it has attempted nothing.

Still, however, an invincible timidity arrested me. All my addresses expired on my lips, or terminated quite otherwise than I had projected. I struggled internally: I was indignant against myself.

I sought, at last, a mode of reasoning which might extricate me from that struggle with honour in my own eyes. I said to myself, that it was necessary I should precipitate nothing, that Ellenor was too little prepared for the avowal which I meditated, and that it was better to wait yet awhile. To live in quietness with ourselves, we almost always disguise, in calculations and in systems, our impotencies and our weakness. This satisfies that portion of us which is, if I may say so, the spectator of the other.

This situation prolonged itself. Each day, I fixed the following as the invariable epoch of a positive declaration; and each following day passed away like the former. My timidity left me as soon as I withdrew from Ellenor. I then resumed my skilful plans and my profound combinations. But scarcely did I again approach her, when anew I found myself trembling and troubled. Whoever had read my heart in her absence, would have taken me for a cold and unfeeling seducer. Whoever had seen me at her side, would have believed he discovered in me a lover inexperienced, interdicted, and impassioned. They would have been equally deceived in these two opinions. There is no complete unity in man; and scarce any one is entirely sincere, or entirely deceitful.

Convinced by these reiterated experiments, that I should never have the courage to speak to Ellenor, I determined to write to her. Count de P—— was absent. The combats which I had long waged with my proper character, the impatience which I experienced in not being able to surmount it, and my uncertainty respecting the success of my attempt, threw into my letter an agitation which greatly resembled love. Heated, besides, as I was by my own language, I felt, in concluding my letter, a little of the passion which I had sought to express with all the force that was possible.

Ellenor saw, in my letter, what it was natural to see there, the fleeting transport of a man who was ten years younger than her, whose heart opened to sentiments which were yet unknown to him, and who merited more of pity than of anger. She answered me with kindness, gave me affectionate advice, offered me sincere friendship, but declared to me that, until the return of Count de P——, she could not receive me.

This answer overwhelmed me. My imagination, irritated by the obstacle, took possession of my whole being. The love, which an hour before I applauded myself for feigning, I seemed all at once to experience with fury. I ran to Ellenor: I was informed that she had gone out. I wrote to her; I supplicated her to grant me a last interview; I painted to her, in heartrending terms, my despair, and the fatal projects which her cruel determination had inspired me with. During a great part of the day, I vainly expected an answer. I did not succeed in calming my inexpressible suffering except by repeating to myself, that the next day I should brave every difficulty to penetrate to the presence of Ellenor, and to speak with her. They brought me, in the evening, some lines from her: they were mild. I thought I remarked in them an impression of regret and of sadness. But she persisted in her resolution, which she announced to me as incapable of being shaken. I went again to her the following day. She had gone to a country seat, of which her servants were ignorant of the name. They had not even any means of forwarding to her a letter.

I remained long immovable at her door, no more imagining that there was any chance of finding her again. I was myself amazed at what I suffered. My memory retraced the moments when I had said that I aspired only to success, and that this was a mere attempt which I should renounce without reluctance. I had no conception of the violent, the insuperable grief which tore my heart. In this way, passed several days. I was equally incapable of amusement and of study. I wandered incessantly before the door of Ellenor. I walked in the town as if, at the turning of every street, I might hope to meet her. One morning, during one of those rambles without object, which served to replace my agitation by fatigue, I perceived the carriage of Count de P——, who returned from his journey. He knew me, and alighted. After some common expressions, disguising my trouble, I spoke to him of the sudden departure of Ellenor. Yes, said he, one of her friends, some leagues hence, has experienced I know not what disagreeable event, which has made Ellenor believe that her consolations would be useful. She has gone without consulting me. She is one over whom all her sentiments dominate, and whose mind, always active, finds almost repose in devotedness. But her presence here is to me extremely necessary. I am going to write to her. She will certainly return in a few days.

This assurance calmed me. I found my grief allayed. For the first time, since the departure of Ellenor, I could breathe without difficulty. Her return was less speedy than Count de P—— expected. I had, however, resumed my habitual mode of life, and the anguish which I had experienced began to be dissipated, when, at the expiration of a month, M. de P—— informed me that Ellenor would arrive that night. As he attached great value to the maintenance, in society, of the place which her character merited, and from which her situation seemed to exclude her, he had invited to sup with him several ladies from among his relations and friends who had consented to see Ellenor.

My recollections returned, at first confusedly, and soon after more vividly. My self-love blended with them. I was embarrassed, humiliated, to meet a woman who had treated me like a child. I thought I saw her smiling on my approach at the circumstance of a short absence having calmed the effervescence of a young head; and I discerned, in that smile, a sort of contempt for myself. By degrees my sentiments awoke. I had risen that very day, thinking no longer of Ellenor: an hour after receiving the news of her arrival, her image wandered before my eyes, reigned in my heart, and I had a fever of fear lest I should not behold her.

I remained at home all the day: I kept myself hid, if I may say so: I trembled lest the slightest movement should prevent our meeting. Nothing, however, was more simple, more certain: but I desired it with so much ardour, that it appeared to me impossible. Impatience devoured me. Every instant, I looked at my watch. I was obliged to open my window to breathe. My blood burned me, while circulating through my veins.

At last, I heard the hour strike at which I was to repair to the Count's. All at once, my impatience was changed into timidity. I dressed myself slowly. I no longer felt that I was urged to arrive. I had such dread lest my hope should be deceived, a sentiment so lively of the anguish which I ran the risk of experiencing, that I would have willingly consented to adjourn all.

It was tolerably late when I entered M. de P——'s. I perceived Ellenor seated at the bottom of the room. I dared not advance: It seemed to me as if every body had their eyes fixed on me: I went to conceal myself in a corner of the drawing-room, behind a group of gentlemen who were talking together. Thence I contemplated Ellenor. She seemed to me slightly changed. She was more pale than usual. The Count discovered me in the kind of retreat in which I had sheltered myself. He came to me, took me by the hand, and conducted me toward Ellenor. I present to you, said he, laughing, the gentleman whom your unexpected departure has most astonished. Ellenor was speaking with a lady who was seated beside her. When she saw me, her words were suspended upon her lips. She remained quite disconcerted. I was greatly so myself.

They might possibly understand us. I addressed to Ellenor indifferent questions. We both resumed an appearance of calmness. Supper was announced. I offered to Ellenor my arm, which she could not refuse. If you do not promise, said I, while conducting her, to receive me to-morrow at eleven, I depart this instant; I abandon my country, and my family, and my father; I break all my connexions; I abjure all my duties; and I go, no matter where, to finish, as soon as possible, a life which you take pleasure in embittering. Adolphe, she replied, and she hesitated. I made a movement to retire. I know not what my features expressed; but I had never experienced a contraction so violent.

Ellenor looked at me. Terror, blended with affection, was depicted in her countenance. I will receive you to-morrow, said she; but I conjure you.... Many persons followed us. She could not finish what she meant to say. I pressed her hand with my arm. We seated ourselves at table.

I could have wished to seat myself by the side of Ellenor, but the master of the house had otherwise decided. I was placed nearly opposite to her. At the beginning of supper, she was pensive. When spoken to, she replied with sweetness: but she soon fell again into a distraction of mind. One of her friends, struck by her silence and lowness of spirits, asked her if she were ill. I have not been well lately, she replied, and even at present I am greatly shaken. I aimed at producing, in the mind of Ellenor, an agreeable impression. I wished, by shewing myself amiable and sprightly, to dispose her in my favour, and prepare her for the interview which she had granted me. I tried then a thousand ways to fix her attention. I turned the conversation to subjects which I knew interested her. Those seated near to us mixed in it. I was inspired by her presence: I succeeded in getting her to listen to me. I soon saw her smile: I felt at this such joy, my looks expressed so much of gratitude, that she could not avoid being affected. Her sadness and distraction were dispelled. She no longer resisted the secret charm which the sight of the happiness I owed to her diffused through her soul, and when we retired from table our hearts were in intelligence, as if we had never been separated. You see, said I, in giving her my hand to re-enter the drawing-room, that you dispose of my whole existence: what have I done that you find pleasure in rendering it wretched?

Chapter III

I passed the night without sleep. There was no longer in my mind any question either of calculations or of projects. I found myself truly enamoured. It was no longer the hope of success which excited me to act. The need of seeing her whom I loved—of enjoying her presence, governed me exclusively. It was now eleven. I repaired to Ellenor. She awaited me. She wished to speak. I begged her to hear me. I seated myself near her, for I could scarcely support myself, and I proceeded in these terms, not without being obliged to interrupt myself often.

I come not to appeal against the sentence which you have pronounced. I come not to retract an avowal which may have offended you. I should wish to do so in vain. This love which you repel is indestructible. The effort even, which at this moment I make to speak to you with a little calmness, is a proof of the violence of the sentiment which offends you. But it is no longer to speak to you on that subject that I have solicited an audience. It is, on the contrary, to ask you to forget it, to receive me as heretofore, to banish the remembrance of an instant of delirium, to punish me not for your knowledge of a secret which I ought to have shut up in the recesses of my mind. You know my situation; that character which they call whimsical and wild; that heart estranged from all the interests of the world, solitary in the midst of men, and which suffers nevertheless from the loneliness to which it is condemned. Your friendship sustained me. Without that friendship, I cannot live. I have become habituated to you. You have permitted that sweet habitude to grow and form itself. What have I done to lose that only consolation of an existence so sad and so gloomy? I am dreadfully wretched. I have no longer the courage to support so lengthened an affliction. I hope for nothing; I ask for nothing; I wish only to see you; but I must see you, if I am to live.

Ellenor remained silent. What fear you, I resumed? What is it that I require? That which you grant to every indifferent person. Is it the world which you dread?

That world, absorbed in its solemn frivolities, will not read any thing in a heart such as mine. How should I not be prudent? Does it not affect my life? Ellenor, yield to my prayer. You will find in it some pleasure. It will have for you some charm to be thus beloved, to see me near you, occupied about you alone, existing only for you, owing to you every feeling of happiness of which I am yet susceptible, snatched by your presence from suffering and despair.

I continued long in the same strain, raising every objection, reiterating in a thousand ways every argument which plead in my favour. I was so submissive, so resigned, I asked so little, I should have been rendered so wretched by a refusal!

Ellenor was affected. She imposed on me several conditions. She consented not to receive me except it were seldom, in the midst of a numerous society, under a stipulation that I should never speak to her of love. I promised what she wished. We were both content, I to have re-acquired the treasure with the loss of which I had been threatened; Ellenor to find herself at once generous, compassionate, and prudent.

I availed myself next day of the permission which I had obtained. I continued to do so, also, on the following days. Ellenor no longer thought it necessary that my visits should be less frequent. Soon nothing appeared to her more simple than to see me every day. Ten years of fidelity had inspired M. de P—— with entire confidence. He allowed to Ellenor the greatest liberty. As he had to struggle against public opinion which wished to exclude his mistress from the circle in which he was called on to live, he desired to see the society of Ellenor increase. His house filled was, as he thought, an undeniable proof of his triumph over opinion.

When I arrived, I perceived in the countenance of Ellenor an expression of pleasure. When she was engaged in conversation, her eyes naturally turned towards me. There was nothing of interest related to which she did not call my attention. But she was never alone. Whole evenings passed away without my being able to say any thing else to her than a few insignificant or interrupted words. It was not long ere I grew irritated at so much constraint. I became gloomy, silent, unequal in my temper, bitter in my discourse. I could scarcely restrain myself when any other person conversed aside with Ellenor; I abruptly interrupted these conversations. It little signified to me that any one might be offended by it; and I was not always checked by the fear of compromising her. She complained to me of this change. What wish you? I said to her with impatience. You believe without doubt that you have done much for me. I am compelled to tell you that you deceive yourself. I do not understand your new manner of conduct. Formerly you lived retired. You shunned a tiresome society. You avoided those eternal conversations which are prolonged, precisely because they ought never to have commenced. Now, your door is open to all the world. It might be said, that in asking you to receive me, I have obtained for the whole universe the same favour as for myself. I confess to you, in seeing you formerly so prudent, I did not expect to find you so frivolous.

I discerned, in the features of Ellenor, an impression of dissatisfaction and of sadness. Dear Ellenor, said I, suddenly softening my language, do I not then deserve to be distinguished from the thousand troublesome persons who beset you? Has not friendship its secrets? Is it not mistrustful and timid, in the midst of noise and of the crowd?

Ellenor feared, that by shewing herself inflexible, she should see renewed those imprudencies which alarmed her for herself and for me. The idea of a rupture with me no longer had access to her heart. She consented to receive me sometimes alone.

Then, were quickly modified the severe regulations which she had prescribed to me. She permitted me to depict to her my love. She familiarized herself by degrees to this language. Soon she confessed to me that she loved.

I passed some hours at her feet, proclaiming myself the happiest of men, lavishing on her a thousand assurances of tenderness, of devotion, and of eternal respect. She related to me what she had suffered in endeavouring to withdraw herself from me; that at times she had hoped I would discover this in spite of her efforts; how the slightest noise which struck her ear seemed to announce my arrival; what trouble, what joy, what fear she had felt on seeing me again; by what distrust of herself, to reconcile the bias of her heart with prudence, she had abandoned herself to the distractions of the world, and had sought the crowd which she shunned before. I made her repeat the minutest details; and the history of some weeks seemed to us that of a whole life. Love supplies the want of long recollections, by a species of magic. All other affections have need of the past. Love creates, as by enchantment, a past with which it surrounds us. It gives us, if I may say so, the consciousness of having lived for years, with a being who but lately was to us almost a stranger. Love is but a luminous point, and yet it seems to take possession of time. A few days ago, and it did not exist. Soon, it will exist no longer. But while it does exist, it sheds its splendour on the period which has preceded, as well as upon that which is to follow it.

This calm, however, lasted but a short while. Ellenor was so much the more on her guard against her weakness, that she was pursued by the remembrance of her errors; and my imagination, my desires, a system of foppery, which I did not myself perceive, revolted against an attachment but partially successful: always timid, often irritated, I complained, I raved, I loaded Ellenor with reproaches. More than once she formed the project to break a connexion which diffused through her life only inquietude and trouble. More than once I appeased her by my supplications, my disavowals, and my tears.

Ellenor, I wrote to her one day, you know not all that I suffer. Near you, at a distance from you, I am equally wretched. During the hours which separate us, I wander at random, bent under the load of an existence which I know not how to support. Society distresses me: solitude overwhelms me. Those indifferent persons who observe me, who know nothing of what engages me, who regard me with a curiosity without interest, with an astonishment without pity, those men who dare to speak to me of other objects than you, carry into my breast a mortal grief. I shun them; but alone, I seek in vain that air which may penetrate into my oppressed bosom. I throw myself upon that ground which should open to swallow me up for ever. I lay my head upon the cold stone which should calm the burning fever which devours me. I drag myself towards that hill whence your house is observed. I remain there, my eyes fixed on that retreat which I shall never inhabit with you:—and if I had sooner met you, you might have been mine. I should have clasped in my arms the only being whom nature has formed for my heart, for that heart which has suffered so much because it sought you, and found you not till it was too late! When at last these hours of delirium are passed, when the moment arrives when I may see you, I trembling take the road to your abode. I fear lest all those whom I meet should suspect the sentiments which I feel. I stop, I walk slowly, I delay the instant of happiness, of that happiness which every thing menaces, which I believe myself always on the point of losing—a happiness imperfect and troubled, against which conspire, perhaps, every moment, both fatal events and jealous looks, and tyrannical caprices, and your own will. When I touch the threshold of your door, when I am opening it, a new terror seizes me. I advance as one guilty, asking favour of all the objects which strike my view, as if all were enemies, as if all envied me the hour of felicity, which I am once more about to enjoy. The slightest sound alarms me; the slightest movement around me dismays me. The noise even of my footstep makes me draw back. Even near you, I yet fear lest some obstacle should suddenly place itself between you and me. At length, I see you, I see you and I respire, and I contemplate you and I pause, like the fugitive who touches the protecting soil which is to save him from death. But even then, when all my being rushes as it were forward to you, when I should have such need to repose myself from so much anguish, to lay my head on your knees, to give free course to my tears, it is necessary that I, with violence, constrain myself, that even near you, I yet live a life of effort. Not one instant for the effusion of the heart! Not one instant for unreserve! Your looks are upon me. You are embarrassed, almost offended at my trouble. I know not what constraint has succeeded those delicious hours, when you at least confessed to me your love. Time flies away; new interests call you; you never forget them; you never delay the instant which removes me. Strangers come; it is no longer permitted me to look upon you; I feel that I must fly to conceal myself from the suspicions which surround me. I leave you more agitated, more lacerated, more mad than before: I quit you and I again fall into that frightful loneliness, where I struggle without meeting a single being on whom I can support myself, on whom I can repose for a moment.

Ellenor had never thus been loved. M. de P—— had for her an affection very sincere, much gratitude for her devotedness, much respect for her character. But there was always, in his manner, a seeming superiority over a woman who had resigned herself publicly to him, without his having espoused her. He might have contracted ties more honorable, according to the common opinion: he did not represent this to her: he did not, perhaps, represent it to himself: but that which we do not represent does not exist the less, and whatever exists is guessed at. Ellenor had not hitherto had any notion of that impassioned sentiment, of that existence lost in her own, of which even my phrensy, my injustice, and my reproaches were only proofs the more irrefragable. Her resistance had exalted all my sensations, all my ideas. I passed from passions which alarmed her to submission, to tenderness, to idolatrous veneration. I considered her as a celestial being. My love approached to adoration, and it had for her so much the more of charm since she feared incessantly lest she should be humbled in an opposite way. She at last resigned herself to me entirely.

Woe to the man who, in the first moments of a connexion of love, believes not that that connexion must be eternal! Woe to him who, in the arms of the mistress he has just obtained, preserves a fatal forethought, and foresees that he shall be able to detach himself from her! A woman whom her heart hurries away, has at that instant, something affecting and sacred. It is not pleasure, it is not nature, it is not the senses which are corruptors: it is the calculations to which society accustoms us, and the reflections which experience produces. I loved, I respected Ellenor a thousand times more after she had become mine. I walked with pride in the midst of men: I carried above them a commanding look. The air which I breathed was in itself alone an enjoyment. I threw myself before nature to thank her for the unexpected boon, the immense boon which she had deigned to bestow upon me.

Chapter IV

Charm of love, who can portray you? That persuasion that we have found the being whom nature had destined for us, that sudden day shed over life, and which seems to us to explain its mystery, that unknown value attached to the minutest circumstances, those rapid hours all whose details escape remembrance even by their sweetness, and which leave in our souls only one long impression of happiness, that playful gaiety which blends itself sometimes without cause to an habitual soft emotion, so much of pleasure in presence, and in absence so much of hope, that detachment from all vulgar cares, that superiority over all that surrounds us, that certainty that henceforth the world cannot affect us where we live, that mutual intelligence which divines each thought, and which answers to each emotion! Charm of love, he who has experienced you, knows not how to describe you.

M. de P—— was obliged, on urgent business, to absent himself during six weeks. I passed this time with Ellenor, almost without interruption. Her attachment seemed to have increased from the sacrifice which she had made me. She never permitted me to leave her without endeavouring to retain me. When I departed, she enquired of me when I should return. Two hours of separation were, to her insupportable. She fixed, with anxious precision, the instant of my return. I consented to it with joy; I was grateful, I was happy in the sentiment which she testified for me. The interests of common life, however, do not permit themselves to bend arbitrarily to all our desires. It was sometimes inconvenient for me to have all my steps preindicated, and all my moments thus calculated. I was obliged to precipitate all my measures, to break with most of my relations. I knew not what to reply to my acquaintances, when they proposed to me some party, which, in a natural situation, I should not have had a motive for refusing. I did not regret, when with Ellenor, these pleasures of social life, in which I had never taken much interest. But I could have wished that she had permitted me to renounce them more freely. I should have experienced more pleasure in returning to her of my own accord, without being told that the hour had arrived, that she waited for me with anxiety, and without the idea of her pain mixing with that of the happiness which I was about to taste on finding her again. Ellenor constituted, without doubt, a vivid pleasure of my existence; but she was no longer an object; she had become a tie. I feared, besides, to compromise her. My continual presence could not but surprise her servants, her children who might observe me. I trembled at the idea of deranging her existence. I felt that we could not be united for ever, and that it was my sacred duty to respect her repose. I gave her then councils of prudence, while throughout I assured her of my love. But the more I gave her of advice of this kind, the less was she disposed to listen to me. At the same time, I feared terribly to afflict her. As soon as I saw, on her countenance, an expression of grief, her will became mine. I was not at my ease except when she was pleased with me. When by insisting on the necessity of withdrawing for a few moments, I had been able to leave her, the image of the grief which I had caused her followed me everywhere. I was seized by a fever of remorse which redoubled every moment, and which at last became irresistible. I flew to her: it was my delight to console her, to appease her. But in proportion as I drew near her abode, a sentiment of discontent with that singular empire mixed itself with my other sentiments. Ellenor herself was violent. She felt, I believe, for me what she had never felt for any one. In her former intimacy her heart had been hurt by a painful dependance. She was with me at perfect ease, because we were in a state of perfect equality. She was raised again in her own eyes, by a love pure from all calculation, from all interest. She knew that I was well assured she loved me only for myself. But it resulted from her complete abandonment with me, that she disguised from me none of her emotions, and when I re-entered her chamber, impatient at re-entering there sooner than I should have wished, I found her sad or irritated. I had suffered for two hours, at a distance from her, from the idea that she suffered at a distance from me. I suffered for two hours when with her, before being able to appease her.

Still, however, I was not unhappy. I said to myself it was sweet to be loved, even with exigence. I felt that I was a benefit to her. Her happiness was necessary to me, and I knew myself necessary to her happiness.

Besides, the indistinct idea that, by the mere nature of things that intimacy could not last, a melancholy idea in many respects, served nevertheless to calm me in my fits of fatigue or of impatience. The connexion of Ellenor with Count de P——, the disproportion of our ages, the difference of our situations, my departure, which various circumstances had already retarded, but of which the period was near—all these considerations engaged me still to give and to receive the most of happiness that was possible. I believed myself certain of years: I did not dispute about days.

The Count de P—— returned. It was not long ere he suspected my relations with Ellenor. He received me every day with an air more cold and more gloomy. I spoke earnestly to Ellenor of the dangers which she ran. I entreated her to permit me to interrupt for some days my visits. I represented to her the interests of her reputation, of her fortune, of her children. She listened to me a long time in silence. She was pale as death. One way or other, she at last said, you will depart soon. Let us not anticipate that moment: do not distress yourself about me. Let us gain days, let us gain hours: days, hours, are all I want. I know not what presentiment tells me, Adolphe, that I shall die in your arms.

We continued then to live as before: I always uneasy, Ellenor always sad, Count de P—— reserved and gloomy. At last, the letter which I expected arrived. My father directed me to repair to him. I took that letter to Ellenor. Already! she said, after having read it: I did not think it would have been so soon. Then, bursting into tears, she took my hand and she said: Adolphe, you see I cannot live without you: I know not what will become of me hereafter: but I conjure you to depart not yet: find pretexts to remain. Ask of your father to permit you prolong your abode six months more. Six months! is that then so long? I wished to oppose her resolution, but she wept so bitterly, she was so agitated, her features bore the impression of a suffering so acute, that I could not continue. I threw myself at her feet. I clasped her in my arms. I assured her of my love; and I departed in order to write to my father. I wrote indeed under the agitation which the grief of Ellenor had inspired. I alleged a thousand causes of delay; I held up the utility of continuing at D—— some courses which I had not been able to follow at Göttingen; and when I sent my letter to the post, it was with ardour that I desired to obtain the consent which I asked.

I returned in the evening to Ellenor. She was seated on a sopha. Count de P—— was near the chimney, and far enough from her. The two children were at the bottom of the chamber, not playing, and bearing on their countenances that amazement of childhood when it remarks an agitation of which it does not suspect the cause. I apprised Ellenor by a gesture that I had done what she wished. A ray of joy sparkled in her eyes, but quickly disappeared. We said nothing. The silence became embarrassing to all of us. I am assured, sir, said the Count to me at last, that you are just about to depart. I answered that I was uncertain of it. It appears to me, he replied, that at your age one ought not to delay entering on some career: however, added he, looking at Ellenor, every one here does not perhaps think as I do.

The answer of my father was not long waited for. I trembled on opening his letter for the grief which a refusal would cause to Ellenor. It seemed to me even that I should have shared that grief with equal bitterness. But on reading the consent which he granted me, all the inconveniences of a prolongation of abode suddenly presented themselves to my mind. Still six months more of uneasiness and constraint, cried I!—Six months during which I offend a man who has testified friendship for me, expose a woman who loves me, run the risk of depriving her of the only situation where she might live tranquil and esteemed, deceive my father, and why?—in order not to brave, for an instant, a grief which soon or late is inevitable! Do we not experience that grief every day in detail, and drop by drop? I do only harm to Ellenor. My sentiment, such as it is, cannot satisfy her. I sacrifice myself for her without advantage to her happiness, and I myself live here without utility, without independence, having not an instant's freedom, unable to respire an hour in peace. I went to Ellenor, altogether occupied with these reflections. I found her alone. I remain yet six months, said I to her.—You announce to me that news very dryly.—It is because I fear much, I acknowledge, the consequences of that delay to both of us.—It seems to me that to you, at least, they could not well be very troublesome.—You know very well, Ellenor, that it is never with myself that I am occupied most.—It is scarely either with the happiness of others.—The conversation had taken a stormy direction. Ellenor was hurt at my regrets, in a case where she thought I ought to share her joy: I was so at the triumph she had obtained over my former resolutions. The scene became violent. We broke out into mutual reproaches. Ellenor accused me of having deceived her, of having had for her only a transitory inclination, of having alienated from her the affection of the Count, of having placed her again, in the eyes of the public, in the equivocal situation from which she had endeavoured all her life to escape. I was irritated to see that she turned against me what I had done only in obedience to her and through fear of afflicting her. I complained of my constrained life, of my youth consumed in inaction, of the despotism which she exercised over all my proceedings. While speaking thus, I saw her face suddenly covered with tears: I stopped, I retraced my steps, I disavowed, I explained. We embraced: but a first blow was struck—a first barrier was overcome. We had both pronounced irreparable words. We might conceal, but not forget them. There are things which we are long of saying, but when once they are said, we never cease to repeat them.

We lived thus four months, in forced relations, sometimes mild, never completely free, finding still pleasure in this, but no longer discovering in it any charm. Ellenor, however, did not detach herself from me. After our most violent quarrels, she was as eager to see me again, she fixed as carefully the hour of our interviews, as if our union had been the most peaceful and the most tender. I have often thought that my conduct even contributed to retain Ellenor in this disposition. If I had loved her as she loved me, she would have been more calm: she would, on her part, have reflected on the dangers which she braved. But all prudence was odious to her, because prudence came from me. She did not calculate her sacrifices, because she was entirely occupied in making me accept them. She had not time to become cool with regard to me, because all her time and all her energies were employed to preserve me. The period again fixed for my departure approached; and I experienced, in thinking of it, a mixture of pleasure and regret, like to that which a man feels who must purchase a certain cure by a painful operation.

One morning, Ellenor wrote me to repair to her immediately. The Count, said she, forbids my receiving you again. I will not obey that tyrannical order. I have followed that man in proscription, I have saved his fortune, I have promoted all his interests. He may leave me now. I cannot leave you. It is easy to imagine what were my entreaties to divert her from a project which I did not understand.—I spoke to her of the opinion of the public. That opinion, she answered, has never been just towards me. I have fulfilled, during ten years, my duties better than any other woman, and that opinion has not the less repelled me from the rank which I merited.—I recalled to her mind her children. My children are those of M. de P——. He has acknowledged them: he will take care of them. They will be but too happy to forget a mother, of whom they have to share only the shame.—I redoubled my entreaties. Hear me, she said: if I break with the Count, will you refuse to see me? Will you refuse it? she resumed, seizing my arm with a violence which made me tremble. No, assuredly, I answered, and the more you may be unhappy, the more shall I be devoted to you. But consider.... All is considered, she interrupted. He is coming in: do you retire now: come not here again.

I passed the remainder of the day in inexpressible agony. Two days elapsed without my hearing of Ellenor. I suffered from being ignorant of her fate; I suffered even from not seeing her: and I was astonished at the misery which that privation caused me. I sincerely wished, however, that she had renounced the resolution which I dreaded so much on her account, and I began to flatter myself with this, when a woman presented to me a note in which Ellenor entreated me to come to her in a particular street, and at a particular house, on the third floor. I ran thither, hoping yet that, not being able to receive me at M. de P——'s, she had wished for the last time to converse with me elsewhere. I found her, making the arrangements of a permanent establishment. She approached me with an air at once content and timid, endeavouring to read in my eyes the impression I received. The rupture is complete, said she, I am perfectly free. I have, as my own fortune, seventy-five louis of yearly income: that is enough for me. You remain here yet six weeks. When you go, I shall perhaps be able to be near you. You perhaps will again come to see me:—and, as if she had dreaded an answer, she entered into a multiplicity of details relative to her plans. She endeavoured, in a thousand ways, to persuade me that she should be happy, that she had sacrificed nothing for me, that the step she had taken suited her, independently of me. It was visible that she made a great effort, and that she but half-believed what she said to me. She deafened herself by her words, for fear of hearing mine: she prolonged her discourse with activity to retard the moment when my objections might plunge her again into despair. I could not find in my heart to advance any objection. I accepted her sacrifice; I thanked her for it; I told her that I was glad of it; I told her much more: I assured her that I had always desired that an irrevocable determination should render it my duty never to quit her. I ascribed my indecision to a sentiment of delicacy, which forbade me to consent to that which should subvert her situation. I had not, in a word, any other thought than to drive far from her all pain, all fear, all regret, all doubt respecting my sentiments. Whilst I spoke to her, I looked at nothing beyond that object, and I was sincere in my promises.

Chapter V

The separation of Ellenor and Count de P—— produced in public an effect which it was not difficult to foresee. Ellenor lost, in one instant, the fruit of ten years of devotedness and of constancy. She was confounded with all the women of her class who, without scruple, deliver themselves up to a thousand successive inclinations. The abandonment of her children made her be regarded as an unnatural mother; and the women of an irreproachable reputation repeated with satisfaction that the neglect of the virtue the most essential to their sex extended itself soon to every other. At the same time they expressed their pity for her, in order not to lose the pleasure of blaming me. They saw in my conduct that of a seducer, of an ungrateful man, who had violated hospitality, and, to gratify a momentary whim, had sacrificed the repose of two persons, of whom I ought to have respected the one, and have spared the other. Some friends of my father addressed to me serious representations. Others, less open with me, made me feel their disapprobation by indirect insinuations. The young men, on the contrary, expressed their delight at the addresses with which I had supplanted the Count, and by a thousand pleasantries which I wished in vain to repress, they congratulated me on my conquest, and promised to imitate me. I cannot describe what I had to suffer both from that severe censure and from these shameful encomiums. I am convinced that if I had loved Ellenor, I should have recovered public opinion for her and for myself. Such is the force of true passion, that, when it speaks, false interpretations and factitious rules are silent. But I was only a weak man, grateful and over-ruled. I was not sustained by any impulse which sprung from the heart. I expressed myself, therefore, with embarrassment: I endeavoured to end the conversation; and if it were prolonged, I finished it by some harsh words, which shewed to others that I was ready to seek a quarrel with them. In effect, I had much rather fought them than answered them.

Ellenor was not long in perceiving that public opinion was against her. Two relations of M. de P——, whom he had compelled by his ascendancy to be intimate with her, gave the greatest publicity to their rupture, happy to indulge their long restrained malevolence under shelter of the austere principles of morality. The men continued to see Ellenor; but it introduced into their manners somewhat of familiarity which indicated that she was no longer supported by a powerful protector, nor justified by an union almost consecrated. Some visited her, because, said they, they had always known her; others because she was yet beautiful, and because recent levity had given them pretensions which they did not seek to disguise from her. Each assigned a reason for his intimacy with her: that is to say, each thought that that intimacy had need of excuse. Thus the unfortunate Ellenor saw herself fallen for ever into the state from which, all her life, she had wished to emerge. Every thing contributed to crush her mind, and to wound her pride. She considered the abandonment of some as a proof of contempt, the assiduity of others as the indication of some insulting hope. She suffered in solitude, she blushed in society. Ah! without doubt, I ought to have consoled her, I ought to have pressed her to my heart, and to have said to her: Let us live for each other; let us forget the men who neglect us; let us be happy in our own esteem, and in our own love. I even attempted this. But what can a resolution taken by duty do to revive a sentiment which is extinguishing?

Ellenor and I dissembled with each other. She ventured not to confide to me her troubles—the results of a sacrifice which she well knew I had not demanded of her. I had accepted this sacrifice:—I dared not complain of a misfortune which I had foreseen, and which I had not had the resolution to prevent. We were, therefore, silent as to the only thought which occupied us constantly. We lavished caresses on each other, we spoke of love; but we spoke of love for fear of speaking of any thing else.

From the moment in which there exists a secret between two hearts which love, from the moment in which one of the two has been able to resolve to hide from the other a single idea, the charm is broken, the happiness destroyed. Passion, injustice, distraction even revive it. But dissimulation throws into love a foreign element which perverts and tarnishes it in the eyes even of those who love.

By a strange contradiction, whilst I repelled with the most violent indignation the slightest insinuation against Ellenor, I myself contributed to wrong her in my general conversations. I submitted to her wishes, but I had taken a horror to the empire of woman. I never ceased to inveigh against their weakness, their exigence, the despotism of their grief. I proclaimed the harshest principles; and the same man, who resisted not a tear, who yielded to mute sadness, who was pursued in absence by the image of the suffering which he had caused, showed himself, in all his discourse, scornful and unpitying. All my direct eulogies of Ellenor destroyed not the impression which such discourses produced. They hated me, they pitied her, but they esteemed her not. They blamed her for not having inspired in her lover more consideration for her sex and more respect for the ties of the heart.

A gentleman who was in the habit of visiting Ellenor, and who, since her rupture with the Count de P——, had testified for her the most ardent passion, having, by his indiscreet persecutions, forced her no longer to receive him, indulged in abusive railleries against her, which it appeared to me impossible to suffer. We fought. I wounded him dangerously. I was wounded myself. I cannot describe the mixture of trouble, of terror, of gratitude, and of love, which were depicted on the features of Ellenor when she again saw me after that event. She took up her abode with me, in spite of my entreaties. She did not leave me a single instant, until my recovery. She read to me during the day; she watched over me during the greater part of the night: she observed my slightest movements: she anticipated all my desires: her ingenious goodness multiplied her faculties and doubled her strength. She assured me incessantly she would not have survived me. I was penetrated with affection: I was torn with remorse. I could have wished to find in myself the means of recompensing an attachment so constant and so tender. I called to my aid remembrance, imagination, reason even, the sentiment of duty. Useless efforts! the difficulty of the situation, the certainty of a futurity which must separate us, and perhaps somewhat of revolt against a tie which it was impossible for me to break, devoured me inwardly. I reproached myself within the ingratitude which I strove to hide from her. I was afflicted when she seemed to doubt of a love which was so necessary to her. I did not less afflict myself when she seemed to believe it. I felt her to be better than myself. I despised myself for being unworthy of her. It is a frightful misfortune not to be loved when we love. But it is a very great one to be passionately loved, when we love no longer. That life which I had just exposed for Ellenor, I would have given a thousand times that she might be happy without me.

The six months which my father had granted me, were expired: it was necessary to think of departing. Ellenor did not oppose my departure. She tried not even to retard it. But she made me promise, that, two months after, I would again return to her, or that I would permit her to rejoin me. I swore this to her solemnly. What engagement would I not have taken at a moment in which I saw her struggle against herself, and restrain her grief! She might have exacted of me not to leave her. At the bottom of my heart, I felt that her tears would not be disobeyed. I was grateful that she did not exercise her power. It seemed to me that I loved her the better for it. I myself, besides, did not separate without deep regret from a being who was so entirely devoted to me. There is in intimacies which are prolonged something so profound! They become without our knowledge so intimate a part of our existence! We form at a distance, with serenity, the resolution to break them; we imagine that we wait with impatience the time of executing it: but when that moment does arrive, it fills us with terror; and such is the waywardness of our miserable heart, that we quit with dreadful anguish, those near whom we dwell without pleasure.

During my absence, I wrote regularly to Ellenor. I was divided between the fear that my letters gave her pain, and the desire of describing to her only the sentiment which I experienced. I could have wished that she had divined my thoughts; but, that she had divined them without being afflicted. I congratulated myself, when I had been able to substitute the words of affection, of friendship, of devotedness, for those of love. But suddenly, I represented to myself the poor Ellenor, sad and solitary, having my letters alone for a consolation; and, at the end of two cold and measured pages, I rapidly added some ardent or tender expressions, calculated to deceive her anew. So that, without ever saying in them enough to satisfy her, I said always enough to deceive her. Strange species of duplicity, of which even the success turned against myself, prolonged my agony, and was insupportable to me!

I reckoned, with inquietude, the days, the hours which elapsed. I sought by my vows to render more slow the progress of time. I trembled on seeing approach the period of executing my promise. I could conceive no means of departing. I discovered none by which Ellenor might settle in the same town with myself. Perhaps, for I must be sincere, perhaps, I desired it not. I compared my independent and tranquil life with the life of precipitation, of trouble and of torment to which her passion condemned me. I found myself so well in being free, in going, in coming, in walking out, and in returning without any one interfering in it! I reposed myself, if I may say so, in the indifference of others, from the fatigue of her love.

I dared not, however, leave Ellenor to suspect that I wished to renounce our projects. She had understood, by my letters, that it would be difficult for me to quit my father. She wrote me that she was, in consequence, commencing preparations for her departure. It was long ere I opposed her resolution. I gave her no definite reply on the subject. I signified to her vaguely that I should always be delighted to know her; then I added—to render her happy. Sad equivocations, embarrassed language, which I lamented to see so obscure, and which I trembled to render more clear! I determined at last to speak to her with frankness. I said to myself that I owed it to her. I raised up my conscience against my weakness. I fortified myself with the idea of her repose against the image of her grief. I walked hastily in my chamber, reciting aloud what I proposed to say to her. But scarcely had I traced some lines when my disposition changed. I no longer looked at my words according to the sense which they should contain, but according to the effect which they could not fail to produce: and a supernatural power directing, as if in spite of me, my subject hand, I confined myself to the recommending to her a delay of some months. I had not said what I thought. My letter bore no character of sincerity. The reasons which I assigned were weak, because they were not the true ones.

The answer of Ellenor was impetuous. She was indignant at my desire not to see her. What did she ask of me? To live unknown beside me. What could I dread from her presence, in an unknown retreat, in the middle of a great town where no one knew her? She had sacrificed all for me—fortune, children, reputation. She required no other reward for these sacrifices than to attend me as a humble slave, to spend with me some minutes every day, to enjoy the moments which I could devote to her. She had resigned herself to two months of absence: not because that absence appeared to her necessary, but because I seemed to wish it: and when she had, in adding painfully days to days, attained the time which I myself had fixed, I proposed to her to renew this lengthened punishment! She might have deceived herself: she might have given up her days to a man obdurate and unfeeling: I was the master of my actions; but I was not able to compel her to suffer, abandoned as she was by him for whom she had sacrificed all.

Ellenor immediately followed that letter. She informed me of her arrival. I repaired to her with the firm resolution of testifying to her great joy. I was impatient to re-assure her heart and to procure for her, momentarily at least, some happiness or serenity. But she had been hurt. She examined me with distrust. She soon discerned the efforts which I made. She irritated my pride by her reproaches. She reviled my character. She pourtrayed me so miserable in my weakness, that she revolted me against her yet more than against myself. An extravagant fury seized us. All respect was renounced, all delicacy forgot. It might have been said, that we were urged one against another by the furies. All that hatred the most implacable had invented against us, we mutually applied to each other: and those two unhappy beings, who alone knew each other on the earth, who alone could render themselves justice, could understand and console each other, seemed two irreconcilable enemies, bent on tearing each other to pieces.

We quitted each other, after a scene of three hours; and for the first time in our lives, we quitted each other without explanation, without reparation. Scarcely was I at a distance from Ellenor when profound grief succeeded my anger. I found myself in a kind of stupor, quite stunned with what had passed. I repeated my words with astonishment: I did not comprehend my conduct: I sought in myself what could have misled me.

It was very late: I dared not return to Ellenor. I promised to myself to see her early the next day; and I returned to my father's. There was much company there: it was easy for me, in a numerous assembly, to remain aside, and to disguise my distress. When we were alone, my father said: I am assured that the former mistress of Count de P—— is in this town. I have always left you much liberty, and I have never wished to know any thing of your connexions; but it is not becoming, at your age, to have an avowed mistress: and I now acquaint you, that I have taken measures that she may be removed hence. On uttering these words, he left me. I followed him even into his chamber. He made me a sign to retire. My father, said I, God is my witness that I have not brought Ellenor hither. God is my witness that I wish she were happy, and I would consent at that price never to see her again. But take care what you do. In thinking to separate me from her, you may easily attach me to her for ever.

I called immediately to me a valet who had accompanied me in my travels, and who knew my intimacy with Ellenor. I directed him to discover instantly, if possible, what were the measures of which my father had spoken to me. He returned in two hours. The secretary of my father had confided to him, under the seal of secrecy, that Ellenor would on the following day receive the order to depart. Ellenor driven away, cried I, driven away with opprobrium! She who has come here only on my account, she whose heart I have torn, she whom I have seen, without pity, bathed in tears! Where then will she lay her head, unfortunate, wandering and solitary, in a world whose esteem I have wrested from her? To whom will she tell her griefs? My resolution was soon taken. I gained to my interests the man who served me: I lavished on him money and promises. I ordered a post chaise by six in the morning at the gate of the town. I formed a thousand projects for my eternal reunion with Ellenor. I loved her more than I had ever loved her. All my heart had returned to her. I was proud of protecting her. I was eager to hold her in my arms. Love had re-entered entirely into my soul. I experienced a fever of the head, of the heart, of the senses, which overwhelmed my existence. If, at this moment, Ellenor had wished to detach herself from me, I would have died at her feet to have retained her.

The day appeared. I ran to Ellenor. She was in bed, having passed the night in crying. Her eyes were yet moist, and her hair was dishevelled. She saw me enter with surprise. Come, said I, let us depart. She wished to answer. Let us depart, I resumed: hast thou, on the earth, another protector, another friend but me? Are not my arms thine only asylum? She resisted. I have important reasons, added I, and which are personal to me. In the name of heaven, follow me. I forced her away. During the journey, I overwhelmed her with caresses, I pressed her to my heart, I answered her questions only by embraces. I told her at last, that having perceived in my father the intention to separate us, I had felt that I could not be happy without her, that I wished to consecrate to her my life, and to be united to her by every species of tie. Her gratitude was at first extreme: but she soon discovered contradictions in my recital. By dint of urging, she extorted from me the truth. Her joy disappeared. Her features were covered with a darker shade. Adolphe, said she, you are deceived respecting yourself. You are generous; you devote yourself to me because I am persecuted. You think you feel love, and you feel only pity.

Why did she pronounce these fatal words? Why did she reveal to me a secret which I wished to be ignorant of? I strove to re-assure her. I attained it perhaps;

but the truth had crossed my mind: its movement was destroyed. I was determined in my sacrifice; but I was not the more happy on that account: and already there existed in me a thought which again I was reduced to the necessity of concealing.

Chapter VI

When we had arrived on the frontier, I wrote to my father. My letter was respectful; but there was in it much bitterness. I took it ill of him that he had drawn closer my ties in pretending to break them. I informed him that I would not leave Ellenor till, being properly situated, she should have no further need of me. I entreated him not to force me, by being exasperated against her, to remain for ever attached to her. I waited for his answer in order to form a determination respecting our establishment. "You are twenty-four years of age, he replied: I shall not exert over you an authority which draws to an end, and of which I have never made use. I shall even conceal, as much as I may be able, your strange proceeding. I shall spread the report that you are gone by my order, and on my business. I shall contribute liberally to your expences. You will yourself soon feel that the life which you lead is not one which is suitable to you. Your birth, your talents, your fortune have assigned to you in the world another rank than that of companion to a woman without country and without avowal. Your letter proves to me already that you are not satisfied with yourself. Reflect that there is nothing gained by prolonging a situation at which we blush. You consume uselessly the finest years of your youth, and that loss is irreparable.

The letter of my father pierced me to the heart. I had a hundred times said to myself that which he said to me. I had been a hundred times ashamed of my life, gliding away in obscurity and in inaction. I should have preferred reproaches, menaces. I should have had some glory in resisting, and I should have felt the necessity of summoning up my strength, to defend Ellenor against the perils which might have assailed her. But there were no perils. I was left perfectly free; and that liberty served me only to bear more impatiently the yoke which I had the appearance of choosing.

We settled at Caden, a little town of Bohemia. I repeated to myself, that since I had assumed responsibility for the fate of Ellenor, she must not be made to suffer. I succeeded in constraining myself. I shut up in my breast even the slightest signs of discontent; and all the resources of my mind were employed to create in me a factitious gaiety which might veil my profound sadness. This effort had on myself an unexpected effect. We are beings so mobile that the sentiments which we feign, we finish by experiencing. The regrets which I concealed, I in part forgot. My perpetual pleasantries dissipated my melancholy: and the assurances of tenderness which I addressed to Ellenor diffused in my heart a soft emotion which almost resembled love.

From time to time troublesome recollections beset me. I delivered myself up when alone to fits of uneasiness. I formed a thousand strange plans, to burst suddenly from the sphere in which I was unsuitably placed. But I repelled these impressions as distressing dreams. Ellenor seemed happy: could I disturb that happiness? Nearly five months passed in this manner.

One day, I saw Ellenor agitated and endeavouring to conceal a thought which occupied her. After long solicitations, she made me promise that I would not oppose the resolution which she had taken, and owned to me that M. de P —— had written to her. His suit was gained. He recollected, with gratitude, the services which she had rendered him, and their ten years of intimacy. He offered her a moiety of his fortune, not in order to be again united with her, that was no longer possible, but on condition that she would leave the ungrateful and perfidious man who had separated them. I have answered, said she, and you may well guess that I have refused. I guessed it but too well. I was affected, but it was with despair at the new sacrifice which Ellenor made to me. I dared not, however, object to any thing. My attempts in this way had always been so fruitless! I retired to reflect on the step I had to take. It was clear to me that our ties must break. They were grievous to me: they became hurtful to her. I was the sole obstacle to her finding again a comfortable condition and that consideration which, in the world, sooner or later follows opulence. I was the sole barrier between her and her children. I had no longer any excuse in my own eyes. To yield to her in this case was no more generosity, but culpable weakness. I had promised to my father to return free, as soon as I should be no longer necessary to Ellenor. It was time at last to enter upon some career, to begin an active life, to acquire some titles to the esteem of men, to make a noble use of my faculties. I returned to Ellenor, believing myself immovable in the design of compelling her not to reject the offers of Count de P——, and to declare to her, if necessary, that I no longer loved her. My dear friend, said I, we struggle sometimes against destiny, but we end always by yielding. The laws of society are more powerful than the will of men. Sentiments the most imperious are broken to pieces against the fatality of circumstances. In vain we obstinately resolve to consult only our heart: we are condemned sooner or later to listen to reason. I can no longer retain you in a situation equally unworthy of you and of me. I cannot do so—neither on your account nor on my own. In proportion as I spoke, without looking at Ellenor, I felt my ideas become more vague, and my resolution enfeebled. I wished to recover my energy, and I continued in a pre-cipitate voice:—I shall always be your friend. I shall always have for you affection the most profound. The two years of our intimacy will never be effaced from my memory; they will for ever be the most beautiful period of my life. But love, that transport of the senses, that involuntary ebriety, that forgetfulness of every interest and of every duty, Ellenor, I possess it no longer. I waited long her answer without raising my eyes. When at last I looked at her, she was immovable; she con-templated every object as if she recognized none. I took her hand: I found it cold. She pushed me from her. What want you of me? she said. Am I not alone, alone in the universe, alone without a being who understands me? What have you more to say to me? Have you not said all? Is not all ended, ended for ever? Leave me, quit me: is not that what you desire? She wished to retire, she faltered. I tried to detain her: she fell senseless at my feet. I raised her up, I embraced her, I re-called her senses. Ellenor, I exclaimed, return to yourself, return to me: I love you with love—with a love the most tender. I have deceived you that you might be the more free in your choice.—Credulities of the heart, you are inexplicable! These simple words, belied by so many preceding ones, restored Ellenor to life and to confidence.

She made me repeat them several times: she seemed to inhale them with avidity. She believed me; she intoxicated herself with her love which she mistook for ours; she confirmed her answer to Count de P——; and I saw myself more pledged to her than ever.

Three months after, a new possibility of change announced itself in the situation of Ellenor. One of those vicissitudes, common in republics which factions agitate, re-called her father to Poland, and re-established him in his property. Though he scarcely knew his daughter, whom her mother had carried to France at three years of age, he was anxious to settle her near to him. The report of the adventures of Ellenor had reached him but vaguely in Russia, where, during his exile, he had always resided. Ellenor was his only child: he dreaded the being left without connexions; he wished to be taken care of: he sought only to discover the abode of his daughter, and as soon as he learnt it, he earnestly desired her to come and join him. She could not have any real attachment for a father whom she did not remember to have seen. She felt, nevertheless, that it was her duty to obey. She ensured by that means, to her children, a considerable fortune, and re-ascended herself to the rank of which her misfortunes and her conduct had deprived her. But she declared to me positively that she would not go to Poland, unless I accompanied her. I am no longer, said she, at the age in which the mind opens to new impressions. My father is an unknown person to me. If I remain here, others will with avidity surround him. He will be equally happy with them. My children will have the fortune of M. de P——. I well know that I shall be generally blamed. I shall pass for an ungrateful daughter, and for a mother of little sensibility. But I have suffered too much. I am no longer young enough for the opinion of the world to have great power over me. If there is in my resolution something harsh, it is to yourself, Adolphe, that you ought to impute it. If I could subject myself to illusion respecting you, I should perhaps consent to an absence, of which the bitterness would be diminished by the perspective of a sweet and durable reunion. But you would not desire any thing better than to suppose me at the distance of two hundred leagues from you, contented and tranquil, in the bosom of my family and of opulence. You would accordingly write to me reasonable letters, as I easily foresee: they would rend my heart: I will not expose myself to them. I have not the consolation to reflect that, by the sacrifice of all my life, I have been able to inspire you with the sentiment which I merited. But yet you have accepted this sacrifice. I already suffer sufficiently by the dryness of your manners and the coldness of our relations: I undergo these sufferings which you inflict upon me; I will not voluntarily brave them.

There was in the voice and in the tone of Ellenor somewhat harsh and violent, which announced rather a firm determination, than a profound or affecting emotion. For some time past, she was irritated beforehand, when she asked of me any thing, as if I had already refused it. She disposed of my actions, but she knew that my judgment contradicted them. She would have wished to penetrate into the inmost sanctuary of my thoughts, to crush there a blind opposition which revolted her against me. I spoke to her of my situation, of the wish of my father, of my own desire: I entreated, I became angry. Ellenor was not to be shaken. I wished to awaken her generosity, as if love was not of all sentiments the most egotistical, and consequently, when wounded, the least generous. I endeavoured, by a singular effort, to excite her sympathy for the misfortune which I experienced in remaining near her. I succeeded only in exasperating her. I promised to go to see her in Poland: but she saw in my promises, without effusion of the heart and without unreserve, only an impatience to leave her.

The first year of our abode at Caden had just ended, without any change in our situation. When Ellenor found me dull or dejected, she was at first afflicted, was then wounded, and extorted from me, by her reproaches, an avowal of the weariness which I would have wished to disguise. On my side, when Ellenor appeared contented, I was vexed to see her enjoy a situation which cost me my happiness, and I disturbed her in that short enjoyment, by insinuations which informed her as to what I inwardly experienced. We then alternately attacked each other by indirect expressions, to withdraw afterwards in general protestations and vague justifications, and to regain silence: for we mutually knew so well all that we should say, that we were silent in order not to hear it. Sometimes one of us was ready to yield. But we lost the moment favorable for reconciliation. Our hearts, suspicious and wounded, did not meet again.

I asked myself often why I remained in a state so painful. I answered that, if I removed from Ellenor, she would follow me, and that I should have provoked a new sacrifice. I said to myself at last, that I must satisfy her a last time, and that she could not exact any thing more, when I should have replaced her in the midst of her family. I was about to propose to follow her to Poland, when she received the news that her father had suddenly died. He had constituted her his sole heir; but his will was contradicted by subsequent letters, which distant relations threatened to urge in their own right. Ellenor, notwithstanding the few relations which subsisted between her and her father, was grievously affected at his death. She reproached herself for having abandoned him. Soon she accused me for her fault. You have made me fail, said she, in a sacred duty. Now, the only question is as to my fortune. I shall sacrifice it to you more easily still. But assuredly I will not go alone into a country, where I have only enemies to meet. I have not been willing, I answered, to make you fail in any duty. I should have wished, I confess, that you would deign to reflect, that I also have felt hurt at failing in mine. I have not been able to obtain from you that justice. I yield, Ellenor: your interest prevails over all other considerations. We will depart together when you wish it.

We actually set out. The distractions of the journey, the novelty of objects, the efforts which we made over ourselves, from time to time, recalled between us some remains of intimacy. The long habitude which we had to each other, the varied circumstances in which we had together been, had attached to each word, almost to each gesture, remembrances which replaced us suddenly in the past, and filled us again with an involuntary soft emotion, as lightnings traverse the night without dissipating it. We lived, if I may say so, in a kind of memory of the heart, sufficiently powerful to render the idea of separation painful to us, too weak for us to find happiness in being united. I gave myself up to these emotions, in order to repose from my habitual constraint. I could have wished to give to Ellenor testimonies of tenderness which should content her. I resumed sometimes with her the language of love: but these emotions and this language resembled those pale and discoloured leaves, which, by a remnant of dying vegetation, grow droopingly on the branches of an up-rooted tree.

Chapter VII

Ellenor succeeded, as soon as she arrived, in being re-established in the enjoyment of the property which was disputed, by engaging not to dispose of it, unless her process was decided. She took up her residence on one of the estates of her father. Mine who never treated with me in his letters of any direct question, contented himself with filling them with insinuations against my journey. "You had informed me, he said, that you would not depart. You had unfolded to me, in detail, all the reasons which you had for not departing. I was, consequently, well convinced that you would depart. I cannot but pity you, that with your spirit of independence, you always do that which you do not wish. I do not judge, moreover, of a situation which is but impefectly known to me. Hitherto, you had appeared to me as the protector of Ellenor, and in that respect there was in your proceedings something noble, which elevated your character, whatever might be the object to which you attached yourself. At present, your relations are no longer the same. It is no longer you who protect her: it is she who protects you. You live with her, you are a stranger whom she introduces into her family. I do not pronounce on a position of which you make choice. But as it may have its inconveniences, I should wish to diminish them, as much as I am able. I write to Baron de T——, our minister in the country where you are, to recommend you to him. I know not whether it will suit you to make use of that recommendation. See in it, however, only a proof of my zeal, and by no means an attack on that independence which you have always known how to defend successfully against your father."

I stifled the reflections which this style of writing excited in me. The possession which I inhabited with Ellenor was situated at a little distance from Warsaw: I repaired, in that town, to the house of Baron de T——. He received me with friendship, asked me the causes of my abode in Poland, and questioned me as to my plans. I did not well know how to answer him. After some minutes of embarrassed conversation, I shall, said he, speak to you with frankness. I know the motives which have brought you into this country: your father has informed me of them. I will even say, I comprehend them. There is no man who may not, once in his life, find himself plagued by the desire to break an unsuitable intimacy, and by the fear of afflicting a woman whom he has loved. The inexperience of youth makes us greatly exaggerate the difficulties of such a position. We please ourselves in believing the truth of all those demonstrations of grief, which in a weak and passionate sex take the place of all the means of force and all those of reason. The heart suffers from it, but self-love flatters itself with it; and such a man, who really thinks he sacrifices himself to the despair which he has caused, sacrifices himself, in reality, only to the illusions of his own vanity. There is not one of these impassioned women, of which the world is full, who has not protested that she must die if abandoned. There is not one of them who is not still alive and who is not consoled. I wished to interrupt him. Pardon me, said he, my young friend, if I express myself with too little caution: but the good which has been told me of you, the talents which you announce, the career which you ought to follow, all make it a law for me to disguise nothing from you. I read in your mind in spite of you, and better than you. You are no longer enamoured of the woman who dominates over you, and who drags you after her. If you had loved her still, you would not have come to me. You knew that your father had written to me; and it was easy to foresee what I had to say to you. You have not been sorry to hear from my mouth reasonings which to yourself you repeat incessantly, and always uselessly. The reputation of Ellenor is far from being unblemished. . . . Let us terminate, I entreat you, replied I, a useless conversation. Unfortunate circumstances have been able to dispose of the early years of Ellenor. She may be judged unfavorably by deceitful appearances: but I have known her for three years, and there exists not on the earth a mind more elevated, a character more noble, a heart more pure and more generous. As you may wish, replied he, but these are shades which opinion does not distinguish. The facts are positive: they are public. In preventing my repeating them, do you think you destroy them? Hearken, continued he, we must, in this world, know what we wish. You will not marry Ellenor? —No, without doubt, said I, she herself has never desired it.—What mean you then to do? She is ten years older than you. You are twenty-six. You will attend her ten years longer. She will be old. You will have arrived at the middle of your life, without having commenced any thing, achieved any thing which might satisfy you. Weariness will take possession of you: fretfulness will take possession of her. She will every day be less agreeable to you: you will every day be more necessary to her: and the result of an illustrious birth, of a brilliant fortune, of a distinguished mind, will be to vegetate in a corner of Poland, forgot by your friends, lost to glory, and tormented by a woman who, whatever you may do, will never be contented with you. I add but one word and we will not again return to a subject which embarrasses you. Every career is open to you, letters, arms, administration; you may aspire to the most illustrious alliances; you are made to attain the highest station; but remember well that there is between you and all kinds of success an insurmountable obstacle, and that obstacle is Ellenor.— I conceived it to be my duty to you, Sir, I replied, to listen to you in silence, but I also owe it to myself to declare to you that you have not shaken me. No one but myself, I repeat, can judge of Ellenor. No one appreciates sufficiently the thrust of her sentiments, and the depth of her impressions. As long as she shall have need of me, I will remain with her. No success would console me for leaving her unhappy; and should it be my duty to restrict my career to the serving her as a support, to the sustaining her in her troubles, to the surrounding her with my affection, against the injustice of a opinion which does not recognize her, I should still believe that I had not uselessly employed my life.—I retired on uttering these words: but who shall explain to me, by what mobility the sentiment which dictated them was extinguished, before even I had finished their pronunciation! I wished, by returning on foot, to retard the moment of seeing that Ellenor whom I had just been defending. I precipitately traversed the town: I longed to find myself alone.

Arrived in the middle of the country, I slackened my pace, and a thousand thoughts assailed me. These fatal words: "between every kind of success and you, exists an insurmountable obstacle, and that obstacle is Ellenor" re-echoed around me. I cast a long and melancholy look over the time which had past away, never to return. I called to mind the hopes of my youth, the confidence with which I formerly believed I could command futurity, the eulogia, accorded to my first essays, the dawn of reputation which I had seen sparkle, and disappear. I repeated to myself the names of several of my fellow students, whom I had treated with proud disdain, and who, by the sole effect of persevering study and of a regular life, had left me far behind them in the road to fortune, to consideration, and to glory. I was overpowered by my own inaction. As misers represent to themselves, in the treasures which they accumulate, all the benefits which these treasures might purchase, I perceived in Ellenor the privation of all the success to which I might have pretended. It was not one single career which I regretted. As I had never tried any, I regretted them all. Never having employed my powers, I imagined them without limits, and I cursed them. I should have wished that nature had created me weak and of inferior capacity, to preserve me at least from the remorse of degrading myself voluntarily. All praise, all approbation of my mind or my knowledge, appeared to me an insupportable reproach. It seemed to me that I heard admired the vigorous arms of an athlete, loaded with irons at the bottom of a dungeon. If I wished to resume my courage, to say that the period of activity was not yet past, the image of Ellenor arose before me like a phantom, and repelled me into nothingness. I experienced against her fits of rage, and by an odd mixture, that rage did not in any way diminish the terror which the idea of afflicting her inspired me with.

My mind, fatigued by these bitter sentiments, suddenly sought refuge in opposite ones. Some words, spoken, perhaps, at hazard, by the Baron de T——, on the possibility of a mild and peaceful alliance, served me to create for myself the ideal picture of a female companion. I reflected on the repose, on the consideration, and even on the independence which such a lot would present to me; for the chains which I had dragged so long a time rendered me a thousand times more dependant than an acknowledged and attested union could have done. I imagined the joy of my father. I experienced an impatient desire to resume, in my country and in the society of my equals, the place which was due to me. I represented myself, opposing a mode of conduct austere and irreproachable, to all the opinions which a cold and frivolous malignity had pronounced against me, to all the reproaches with which Ellenor overwhelmed me.

She accuses me incessantly, said I, of being unfeeling, of being ungrateful, of being pityless. Ah! if heaven had granted me a woman whom the regulations of society might permit me to avow, whom my father blushed not to accept for a daughter, I should have been a thousand times happy in rendering her happy.

That sensibility which is forgot, because it is suffering and crushed, that sensibility of which are imperiously required testimonies, which my heart refuses to passion and to threats, how sweet would it be to resign myself to, with the cherished being, the companion of a life regular and respected! What have I not done for Ellenor! For her I have quitted my country and my family; I have for her afflicted the heart of an aged father who laments yet far from me; for her I inhabit these places, where my youth flies away in solitude, without glory, without honour, and without pleasure. Do not so many sacrifices, made without duty and without love, prove what love and duty would render me capable of performing! I fear so much the grief of a woman, who rules me only by her grief, with what care should I remove all affliction, all trouble, from her to whom I might openly devote myself without remorse and without reserve! How different should I then appear from what I am! How would that acerbity, which is deemed a crime in me, because its source is unknown, fly rapidly far from me! How grateful should I be to heaven, and benevolent to men!

I spoke thus, my eyes moistened with tears. A thousand recollections re-entered, as in torrents, into my mind. My relations with Ellenor had rendered all these recollections odious. All that recalled to me my infancy, the places where glided away my early years, the companions of my early years, the companions of my early pastimes, the aged parents who had lavished upon me the first marks of interest, hurt me and made me ill. I was under the necessity of repelling, as guilty thoughts, the images the most attractive, and and the desires the most natural. The companion whom my imagination had of a sudden created for me, allied herself on the contrary with all these images, and sanctioned all these desires. She associated herself with all my duties, with all my pleasures, with all my fancies. She re-united my present life to that period of my youth when hope opened before me so vast a futurity, a period from which Ellenor had separated me as by an abyss. The minutest details, the minutest objects retraced themselves in my memory. I saw again the ancient castle which I had inhabited with my father, the woods which surrounded it, the river which washed the foot of its walls, the mountains which bounded its horizon. All these things seemed to me so present, so full of life, that they caused in me a trembling which I could scarcely support. And my imagination placed beside them a creature innocent and young, who embellished them, who animated them by hope. I wandered, absorbed in this reverie, always without any fixed plan, not saying to myself, that I ought to break with Ellenor, having, of the reality, only a dark and confused idea, and in the state of a man oppressed by trouble, which sleep has soothed by a dream, and who is anxious this dream were ended. I discovered suddenly the mansion of Ellenor, which I had insensibly approached. I stopped. I took another road. I was happy to delay the moment when I should again hear her voice.

The day was declining: the sky was serene: the country became deserted. The labors of men had ceased: they abandoned nature to herself. My thoughts assumed gradually a tint more grave and more imposing. The shades of night, which thickened at each instant, the vast silence which surrounded me, and which was interrupted only by occasional and distant sounds, caused to succeed to my agitation a sentiment more calm and more solemn. I turned my eyes towards the greyish horizon of which I no longer distinguished the limits, and which consequently gave me, in some measure, the sensation of immensity. I had experienced nothing similar for a long time. Incessantly absorbed in reflections always personal, my mind always fixed on my situation, I had become a stranger to every general idea. I was occupied only about Ellenor and myself, about Ellenor who inspired me only with a pity mixed with fatigue, about myself for whom I had no longer any esteem. I had shrunk, if I may say so, into a new kind of egotism, into an egotism without courage, discontented and humbled. I rejoiced at the renewal of another train of thoughts, and to find again the faculty of forgetting myself, to give myself up to disinterested meditations. My mind seemed to elevate itself from a long and shameful degradation.

Almost the whole night passed thus away. I wandered at random: I ran over the fields, the woods, the hamlets where all was motionless. From time to time, I perceived in some distant habitation, a pale light which penetrated the obscurity. There, said I to myself, there perhaps some unfortunate being writhes under pain or struggles against death, against death that mystery inexplicable, of which daily experience appears not yet to have convinced men, that assured end which does not console us and does not appease us, that object of habitual carelessness and of transitory terror. And I also, continued I, deliver myself up to that senseless inconsistency! I revolt against life, as if life were not to end! I spread unhappiness around me, to recover some miserable years, which time will soon snatch from me! Ah! let us renounce these useless efforts: let us rejoice to see time glide away —our days precipitate themselves upon each other. Let us remain immovable, indifferent spectators of an existence half passed away. Let men seize upon it: let them scramble for it. They will not prolong its duration. Is it worth the trouble of dispute?

The idea of death has always had, over me, a powerful sway. In my most acute afflictions, it has always sufficed instantly to calm me. It produced on my mind its accustomed effect. My disposition towards Ellenor became less bitter. All my irritation disappeared. There remained to me of the impression of that night of delirium only a sentiment mild and almost tranquil. Perhaps the physical lassitude which I experienced contributed to that tranquillity.

The day was beginning to dawn. I already distinguished its objects. I knew that I was far from the abode of Ellenor. I depicted to myself her uneasiness, and, as much as fatigue would permit me, I hastened anxiously to arrive beside her, when I met a man on horseback, whom she had sent to look for me. He related to me that she had been, since midnight, in the greatest fear; that after having been at Warsaw, and having traversed the adjacent parts, she had returned home in a state of inexpressible anguish; and that from all parts the inhabitants of the village had spread themselves over the country to discover me. This recital filled me at first with an impatience considerably painful. I was irritated to see myself subjected by Ellenor to a troublesome superintendance. In vain I repeated to myself that her love alone was the cause of it. Was not that love also the cause of all my misfortune? I succeeded, however, in overcoming this sentiment with which I reproached myself. I knew her to be alarmed and suffering. I mounted on horse-back. I rapidly ran over the distance which separated us. She received me with transports of joy. I was affected at her emotion. Our conversation was short, because she soon conceived that I must stand in need of repose: and I left her, this time at least, without having said any thing which might afflict her heart.

Chapter VIII

The next day I rose, pursued by the same ideas which had agitated me the preceding day. My agitation redoubled on the following days. Ellenor in vain wished to penetrate the cause. Her impetuous questions, I answered by con-strained monosyllables. I became inflexible to her importunity, knowing too well, that to my frankness would succeed her grief, and that her grief would impose upon me new dissimulation.

Disquieted and surprised, she had recourse to one of her friends, to discover the secret which she accused me of concealing from her. Eager to deceive herself, she sought a circumstance where was only a sentiment. That friend spoke to me of my singular temper, of the care which I took to repel all idea of a durable connexion, of my inexplicable thirst for rupture and separation. I listened to her a long time in silence. I had never, until that moment, said to any one that I no longer loved Ellenor. My lips were repugnant to that avowal which seemed to me an act of perfidy. I wished, however, to justify myself: I related my history with circum-spection, giving many eulogia to Ellenor, granting the inconsistency of my con-duct, ascribing it to the difficulties of our situation, and this without permiting myself to use one word which might pronounce clearly, that the true difficulty was, on my part, the absence of love. The lady who listened to me was moved at my recital. She saw generosity in what I called weakness, misfortune in what I called cruelty. The same explanations which had thrown into a rage the passionate Ellenor, carried conviction to the mind of her impartial friend. We are so just when we are disinterested! Whoever you may be, never refer to another the interests of your heart. The heart alone is capable of pleading its cause: it alone probes its wounds. Every intermediate person becomes a judge. He analizes, he enters into particulars; he understands the difference; he admits it as possible, he recognizes it as inevitable; for the same reason he excuses it, and indifference finds itself thus, to its great surprise, legitimated in its own eyes. The reproaches of Ellenor had persuaded me, that I was culpable. I learnt from her who thought to defend her, that I was only unfortunate. I was dragged into a complete avowal of my sentiments. I granted that I had for Ellenor devotedness, sympathy, pity: but I added, that love entered as nothing into the duties which I imposed on myself. That truth, until then shut up in my own breast, and sometimes revealed to Ellenor, only in the midst of trouble and of anger, assumed in my own eyes more of reality and of force, by this circumstance alone that another had become its depository. It is a great step, it is an irreparable step when we unveil suddenly to the eyes of a third person the hidden folds of an intimate relationship. The day which penetrates into this sanctuary constitutes and achieves the destructions which the night enveloped in its shades: thus bodies inclosed in the tomb often preserve their first form, until the external air strikes them and reduces them to dust.

The friend of Ellenor left me. I know not what account she gave her of our conversation. But, on approaching the drawing-room, I heard Ellenor, who spoke in a very animated voice. On perceiving me, she was silent. Soon after, she re-produced, under various forms, general ideas, which were only particular attacks. Nothing is more singular, said she, than the zeal of certain friendships. There are people who are eager to charge themselves with your interests, the better to abandon your cause. They call this attachment: I should rather prefer hatred. I easily comprehended that the friend of Ellenor had taken my part against her, and had irritated her in not seeming to deem me sufficiently culpable. I thus perceived myself in intelligence with another against Ellenor: it was between our hearts one barrier more.

Some days after, Ellenor went further. She was incapable of all empire over herself. As soon as she believed she had a subject of complaint, she went straight to the explanation, without discretion and without calculation, and preferred the danger of breaking to the constraint of dissembling. The two friends separated forever embroiled.

Why mix strangers in our intimate discussions, said I to Ellenor? Have we need of a third person in order to understand each other? And if we no longer understand each other, what third person may remedy this? You are right, said she: but that is your fault. Formerly I addressed myself to no one, in order to reach to your heart.

Suddenly Ellenor announced the plan of changing her mode of life. I discovered by her discourse, that she attributed to the solitude in which we lived, the discontent which devoured me. She exhausted every false explication, before resigning herself to the true one. We passed together monotonous evenings in silence or in fretfulness. The source of long conversations was exhausted.

Ellenor resolved to attract to her house the noble families which resided in her neighbourhood, or at Warsaw. I easily saw the obstacles and the dangers of her attempts. The relations who disputed with her her inheritance had revealed her past errors, and propagated against her a thousand calumnious reports. I shuddered at the humiliations which she was about to brave, and I endeavoured to dissuade her from that enterprize. My representations were useless. I wounded her pride by my fears, even though I might express them only with caution! She supposed that I was embarrassed at our intimacy, because her situation was equivocal. She consequently was only the more eager to reacquire an honorable place in the world: her efforts obtained some success. The fortune which she enjoyed, her beauty which time had yet but slightly diminished, the report even of her adventures, every thing in her excited curiosity. She soon saw herself surrounded by a numerous society. But she was pursued by a secret sentiment of embarrassment and disquietude. I was discontented with my situation. She imagined that I was so with hers. She struggled to emerge from it. Her ardent desire permitted to her no calculation. Her false position threw inequality into her conduct, and precipitation into her measures. She had a mind accurate, but of little extent. The accuracy of her mind was perverted by the impetuosity of her character, and its limited extent hindered her from perceiving the most skilful line, and from seizing delicate shades. For the first time she had an object, and as she hurried towards that object, she failed in it. What disgusts did she suppress without communicating them to me! How often did I blush for her, without having the power to tell her of it! Such is, amongst men, the influence of reserve and discretion, that I had seen her more respected by the friends of Count de P——, as his mistress, than she was by her neighbours, as heiress of a great fortune, in the midst of her vassals. Alternately haughty and suppliant, one while officiously kind, another while irritable, there was in her actions and in her language some-what impetuous, destructive of consideration which is composed only of calmness.

In thus holding up the defects of Ellenor, it is myself whom I accuse and condemn. One word from me would have calmed her. Why have I not been able to pronounce that word?

We lived, however, more agreeably together. Distraction relieved us of our habitual thoughts. We were alone only at intervals, and as we had in each other a confidence without bounds, except as to our intimate sentiments, we substituted observations and facts for these sentiments, and our conversations had resumed some charm. But soon this new mode of life became to me the source of new perplexity. Lost in the crowd which surrounded Ellenor, I perceived that I was the object of surprise and of blame. The period approached, when her suit ought to be determined. Her adversaries pretended, that she had alienated the paternal heart by errors without number. My presence gave support to their assertions. Her friends reproached me with injuring her. They excused her passion for me: but they accused me of indelicacy. I abused, they said, a sentiment which I ought to have moderated. I alone knew, that in abandoning her, I should drag her in my footsteps, and that, to follow me she would neglect all care of her fortune, and all the calculations of prudence. I could not render the public the depository of this secret. I appeared, then, in the house of Ellenor, only as a stranger hurtful to the success even of the proceedings which were about to decide her fate, and by a strange subversion of truth, whilst I was the victim of her immovable resolves, it was she who was pitied, as the victim of my ascendancy.

A new circumstance added a further complication to this unhappy situation. All at once a singular transformation took place in Ellenor's behavior and manners: until this time she had appeared to be concerned solely with me; suddenly I saw her receiving and seeking the attentions of the men surrounding her. This woman, so reserved, so cold, so distrustful, seemed suddenly to change character. She was encouraging the sentiments and even the hopes of a crowd of young men, some of whom were attracted by her beauty, and others of whom, despite her past errors, were seriously aspiring to her hand in marriage. She granted them long *tête-à-têtes*; she adopted toward them those ambiguous but attractive attitudes which gently reject only to detain, because they betray indeci-sion rather than indifference, deferment rather than refusal. I learned from her later, and the facts prove the truth of her words, that she was acting in this way through a pitiful miscalculation. She thought she could revive my love by exciting my jealousy; but this only stirred ashes that nothing could rekindle. There may also have been in this attempt, without her realizing, something of feminine vanity. She was wounded by my coldness and wanted to prove to herself that she still had the power to please. Finally, perhaps she found in the waste in which I left her heart a sort of consolation in hearing words of love which I had long since stopped using.

Be that as it may, I was for some time deceived about her motives, I glimpsed the dawn of my liberty and rejoiced. Trembling lest I should interrupt by some false move this great crisis with which I thought my deliverance was bound up, I became gentler and appeared happier. Ellenor mistook my gentleness for tenderness, and my hope to see her at last happy without me for the desire to make her happy. She congratulated herself on her stratagem. Sometimes, however, she became alarmed at my freedom from uneasiness; she reproached me for putting no obstacles in the path of those affairs of hers which apparently threatened to make me lose her. I jokingly dismissed these accusations, but did not always manage to quiet her fears; her real character showed through the part she was forcing herself to play. The scenes began again, on other grounds, but no less stormy. Ellenor blamed me for her own faults, intimating that a single word would make her once again completely mine; then, offended by my silence, she once again plunged into flirtation with a kind of fury.

It is here, I feel, that I shall be accused of weakness. I wanted to be free and I could have been with general approbation; perhaps I should have, for Ellenor's conduct justified me and seemed to compel me to act. But did I not realize that this conduct of hers was my own work? Did I not realize that Ellenor, at the bottom of her heart, had not stopped loving me? Could I punish her for imprudences that I made her commit and, with cold hypocrisy, find a pretext in these imprudences for abandoning her without pity?

Certainly I do not wish to make excuses for myself. I condemn myself more severely than perhaps another would in my place; but I can at least solemnly testify that I have never acted with cold calculation and that I have always been guided by true and natural feelings. How is it that with these feelings I have for so long only caused my own unhappiness and that of others?

People in society, however, were observing me with surprise. My stay with Ellenor could only be explained by an extreme attachment to her, and yet my indifference concerning the liaisons in which she always seemed ready to involve herself belied this attachment. My inexplicable tolerance was attributed to a looseness of principles, to a heedlessness about morals which proclaimed, they said, a profoundly egotistical man whom the world has corrupted. These conjectures, which were the more likely to make an impression in that they were in keeping with the minds that conceived them, were generally accepted and repeated.

The report of this universal blame reached even me. I was indignant at the unexpected discovery. As a reward for my long services I was misjudged and calumniated. I had, for a woman, forgot all the interests, and rejected all the pleasures of life, and it was me whom opinion condemned.

I had a heated argument with Ellenor: one word from her dispelled this mob of admirers, whom she had summoned merely to make me fear I should lose her. She restricted her society to a few women and a small number of aged men. Everything about us resumed a regular appearance; but we were only the more unhappy. Ellenor believed herself to have new claims on me. I felt myself loaded with new chains.

I should be unable to paint what bitterness and what rage resulted from our relations thus complicated. Our life was no longer anything else than a perpetual storm. Intimacy lost all its charms, and love all its sweetness. There was no longer between us even those transitory returns, which seem to heal for a few moments incurable wounds. Truth burst out on all sides, and I borrowed, to make myself to be understood, expressions the most unfeeling and the most pitiless. I did not refrain until I saw Ellenor in tears; and even her tears were but a burning lava, which falling drop by drop on my heart, extorted from me cries, without the power of extorting from me a disavowal. It was then that, more than once, I saw her rise pale and prophetic. Adolphe, she exclaimed, you do not know the ill you do. You will learn it one day, you will learn it from me, when you shall have precipitated me into the tomb. Wretch that I was! when she spoke thus, why did I not throw myself at her feet?

Chapter IX

I had not returned to the Baron de T——'s since my first visit. One morning I received from him the following note.

"The counsels which I have given you did not deserve so long an absence. Whatever step you may take in what relates to yourself, you are no less the son of my dearest friend. I shall no less enjoy the pleasure of your society, and I shall have much of this in introducing you into a circle which I dare promise, it will be agreeable to you to join. Allow me to add, that the more your mode of life, which I do not wish to disapprove of, has in it somewhat singular, the more it behoves you to dissipate prejudices, ill founded without doubt, by shewing yourself in the world."

I was grateful for the kindness which an old man thus testified for me. I repaired to him: Ellenor was not mentioned. The Baron kept me to dinner. There were with him, that day, only some gentlemen of considerable wit and amiability. I was at first embarrassed: but I made an effort over myself. I assumed new life: I spoke. I displayed as much as I was able of wit and of knowledge. I perceived that I succeeded in gaining approbation. I again found in this species of success, an enjoyment of self-love of which I had been a long time deprived. That enjoyment rendered the society of the Baron de T—— more agreeable to me.

My visits to him became more frequent. He charged me with some labours relative to his mission, and which he believed he might confide to me without inconvenience. Ellenor was at first surprised at this revolution in my life: but I spoke to her of the friendship of the Baron for my father, and of the pleasure which I experienced in consoling the latter for my absence, by having the appearance of occupying myself usefully. The poor Ellenor, I say so at this moment with a sentiment of remorse, experienced some joy that I appeared more tranquil, and resigned herself without complaining much, to pass often the greater part of the day separated from me. The Baron, on his part, when a little confidence was established between us, spoke to me again of Ellenor: my positive intention was always to speak well of her: but, without perceiving it, I expressed myself respecting her in a tone less delicate and more careless. Sometimes I indicated, by general maxims, that I recognized the necessity of disengaging myself from her. Sometimes pleasantry came to my aid: I spoke, laughingly, of women, and of the difficulty of breaking with them. These discourses amused an old minister, whose mind was experienced, and who recollected vaguely that, in his youth, he also had been tormented by the intrigues of love. In this manner, by the circumstance alone that I had a sentiment concealed, I more or less deceived all the world. I deceived Ellenor; for I knew that the Baron wished to detach me from her, and to her I was silent respecting it. I deceived Mr. de T——; for I permitted him to hope that I was ready to break my ties. Such duplicity was very far from my natural character: but man becomes depraved, as soon as there is in his heart a single thought which he is constantly obliged to dissemble.

Hitherto, I had become acquainted at the Baron de T——'s only with the gentlemen who composed his particular society. One day, he proposed to me to remain at a great entertainment which he gave in celebration of the birth-day of his master. You will meet there, said he, the most beautiful women of Poland. You will not find there, it is true, her whom you love: I am sorry for it. But there are women who are seen only among them. I was painfully affected by that expression. I remained silent: but I inwardly reproached myself for not defending Ellenor, who, had I been attacked in her presence, would have so vigorously defended me.

The assembly was numerous. I was surveyed with attention. I heard, around me repeated in a low voice, the name of my father, that of Ellenor, that of the Count de P——. They were silent when I approached: they began again when I retired. It was evident to me, that they related my history, and each, without doubt, related it in his own way. My situation was insupportable: my forehead was covered with a cold sweat: I alternately blushed and grew pale.

The Baron perceived my embarrassment. He came to me; redoubled his attentions and his efforts to oblige; sought every occasion to eulogize me; and the ascendancy of his consideration soon forced the rest to testify for me the same regard.

When every one had retired, I wish, said M. de T——, to speak to you once more from the heart. Why will you remain in a situation from which you suffer? Whom do you benefit? Do you believe that what passes between you and Ellenor is unknown? The whole public is acquainted with your jarrings, and your reciprocal discontent. You injure yourself by your weakness: you do not injure yourself less by your firmness; for to complete the contradiction, you do not render happy the woman who renders you so wretched.

I was still crushed by the grief which I had experienced. The Baron showed me several letters from my father. They announced an affliction much more acute than I had supposed. I was shaken. The idea that I prolonged the agitations of Ellenor added to my irresolution. Finally, as if all had united against her, whilst I hesitated, she herself, by her vehemence, accomplished my decision. I had been absent the whole of the day. The Baron had detained me with him after the assembly. The night advanced. A letter from Ellenor was given me in the presence of Baron de T——. I saw, in his eyes, a sort of pity for my subjection. The letter of Ellenor was full of bitterness. What, said I to myself, I cannot pass one day free! I cannot respire one hour in peace! She follows me every where, like a slave who ought to be brought into subjection, and is so much the more violent as I find myself more feeble! Yes, cried I, I form the engagement to break with Ellenor: I will dare to declare it to her myself: you may inform my father beforehand.

On uttering these expressions, I rushed away from the Baron. I was oppressed by the words which I had just pronounced, and I scarcely believed as to the promise I had made.

Ellenor waited for me with impatience. By a strange accident, she had, during my absence, been, for the first time informed of the efforts of the Baron de T—— to detach me from her. They had reported to her the language which I had held, and the pleasantries in which I had indulged. Her suspicions being awake, she had collected in her mind several circumstances which appeared to her to confirm them. My sudden connection with a man whom I had never seen before, the intimacy which existed between that man and my father, seemed to her irrefragable proofs. Her inquietude had made such progress in a few hours, that I found her perfectly convinced of, what she called, my perfidy.

I had come to her, determined to tell her all. Accused by her, will it be believed? I occupied myself only in eluding all. I disavowed even, yes, I that day disavowed that which I was determined to declare to her on the following one.

It was late. I left her. I hastened to bed to terminate that long day, and when I was certain that it was ended, I felt myself, for the moment, delivered from an enormous weight.

I did not rise the day following till near the middle of the day, as if, by delaying the commencement of our interview, I had delayed the fatal instant.

Ellenor became re-assured during the night, both by her own reflections and by my discourse of the evening before. She spoke to me of her affairs with an air of confidence which but too well announced that she regarded our existences as indissolubly united. Where could I find words which might repel her into a state of insulation?

Time slipt away with frightful rapidity. Each moment added to the necessity of an explanation. Of the three days which I had fixed, the second was already near expiring. M. de T—— expected me, at the latest, on the third day. His letter to my father was gone, and I was about to break my promise without having made the slightest attempt to execute it. I went out; I came in again; I took the hand of Ellenor; I began a sentence which I immediately interrupted. I observed the course of the sun which inclined towards the horizon. Night returned. I delayed anew. One day remained for me. That was time enough.

That day passed like the preceding. I wrote to M. de T—— to request of him yet longer time: and, as it is natural for weak characters to do, I accumulated in my letter a thousand reasons to justify my delay; to show that it did not, in any way, change the resolution which I had taken, and that, even from that instant, my ties to Ellenor might be considered as broken for ever.

Chapter X and Last

I passed more tranquilly the following days. I had thrown again into uncertainty the necessity of acting. It no longer pursued me like a spectre. I believed I had time enough to prepare Ellenor. I wished to be more mild, more tender with her, to preserve at least the recollections of friendship. My distress was quite different from that which I had hitherto known. I had implored heaven, that it would suddenly elevate between Ellenor and me an obstacle which I might not be able to overcome. That obstacle had risen. I fixed my eyes on Ellenor as on a being whom I was about to lose. The exigence which so many times appeared to me insupportable, no longer frightened me. I felt myself freed from it by anticipation. I was more free in still yielding to her, and I no longer experienced that inward revolt which formerly excited me to rail at every thing. I was no longer impatient. I felt, on the contrary, a secret desire to delay the fatal moment.

Ellenor perceived this more affectionate and more feeling disposition: she herself became less bitter. I sought again the conversations which I had shunned: I enjoyed her expressions of love, but lately importunate, now precious to me, as likely each time to be the last.

One night, we had parted, after a conversation, more kind than usual. The secret which I shut up in my bosom made me sad: but my sadness had nothing of violence. The uncertainty as to the period of the separation which I had desired, enabled me to drive away the idea. During the night, I heard in the house, an unusual noise. That noise soon ceased, and I attached to it no importance. In the morning, however, the idea recurred to me: I wished to know the cause of it, and I directed my steps towards the chamber of Ellenor. What was my astonishment, when I was informed, that since midnight, she had had a burning fever; that a physician, whom her servants had called in, declared her life in danger; and that she had imperatively forbid that they should inform me of it, or that they should let me approach her.

I wished to insist upon this. The physician himself came out, to represent to me the necessity of not causing her any emotion. He ascribed her prohibition, of the motive of which he was ignorant, to the desire of not causing me any alarm. In anguish, I interrogated the servants of Ellenor, on what might have plunged her so suddenly into a state so dangerous. The evening before, after having left me, she had received, from Warsaw, a letter brought by a man on horseback; having opened and run it over, she had fainted; having recovered, she had thrown herself upon her bed, without speaking a word; one of her women, uneasy at the agitation which she saw in her, had, unknown to her, remained in her chamber; towards the middle of the night, this woman had observed her to be seized with a trembling which shook the bed on which she lay; she had wished to call me:

Ellenor had opposed it with a sort of terror so violent that they had not dared to disobey her; they had sent for a physician; Ellenor had refused and still refused to answer him; she had passed the night, uttering broken words which they had not been able to comprehend, and often holding her handkerchief to her mouth, as if to prevent herself from speaking.

Whilst they gave me these details, another woman, who had remained with Ellenor, ran out in alarm. Ellenor seemed to have lost the use of her senses. She distinguished nothing which surrounded her. She sometimes uttered shrieks; she repeated my name; then, in terror, she made a sign with her hand, as if they should remove from her some object which was odious to her.

I entered her chamber. I saw at the foot of her bed two letters. One was mine to Baron de T——: the other was from him to Ellenor. I then but too well imagined the solution of that frightful enigma. All my efforts to obtain the time which I wished still to consecrate to our last adieus, had in a manner turned against the unfortunate being whom I aimed at treating with gentleness. Ellenor had read, traced with my own hand, my promises to abandon her, promises which had been dictated only by the desire of remaining longer beside her, and which the earnestness of that very desire had induced me to repeat, to develop in a thousand ways. The unprejudiced eye of M. de T—— had easily discovered in these protestations reiterated in every line, the irresolution which I disguised, and the artifices of my own hesitation. But this cruel man had too well calculated that Ellenor would see in it an irrevocable decree. I approached her: she looked at me without knowing me. I spoke to her: she started. What noise is that, she cried? —it is that voice which has done me ill. The physician observed that my presence added to her delirium, and conjured me to retire. How depict what I experienced during three long hours? The physician came to me at last. Ellenor had fallen into a profound sleep. He did not despair of saving her, if on her awaking, the fever had abated.

Ellenor slept a long time. Informed of her being awake, I wrote requesting her to receive me. She desired that I might enter. I wished to speak. She interrupted me. Let me not hear from you, she said, one cruel word. I claim nothing, I oppose nothing; but let not that voice which I have loved so much, let not that voice, which resounds at the bottom of my heart, penetrate there to tear it. Adolphe, Adolphe, I have been violent, I may have offended you: but you know not what I have suffered. God grant that you may never know it.

Her agitation became extreme. She placed her forehead on my hand. It was burning. A terrible contraction disfigured her features. In the name of heaven, cried I, dear Ellenor, listen to me. Yes, I am guilty: that letter. . . . She trembled and wished to withdraw herself. I retained her. Weak, tormented, continued I, I have yielded an instant to a cruel persistance. But have you not yourself a thousand proofs that I am incapable of desiring that which should separate us? I have been discontented, wretched, unjust. Perhaps, by struggling with too much violence against a rebellious imagination, you have given strength to transitory wishes which I now condemn. But can you doubt my profound affection? Are not our souls bound to each other by a thousand ties which nothing can break? Is not all the past common to us both? Can we cast a look on the three years which have just elapsed, without retracing the impressions in which we have participated, the pleasures which we have tasted, and the troubles which we have endured together. Ellenor let us begin from this day a new period; let us call back the hours of happiness and of love. She looked at me for some time with an air of doubt. Your father, she replied at last, your duties, your family, that which is expected of you?... Without doubt, I replied, sometime, one day, perhaps...She observed that I hesitated. My God, she cried, why has he restored to me hope, to snatch it from me so soon! Adolphe, I thank you for your efforts. They have done me good, so much the more good that they will not cost you, I hope, any sacrifice. But I conjure you, let us talk no more of the future. Reproach yourself with nothing, whatever may happen. You have been good to me. I have desired that which was not possible. Love was all my life: it could not be yours. Watch over me now for yet a few days. Tears flowed abundantly from her eyes. Her respiration was less oppressed. She leaned her head on my shoulder. It is here, said she, that I have always desired to die. I clasped her to my heart. I again abjured my projects; I disavowed my cruel rage. No, resumed she, it is necessary that you should be free and content.—Can I be so if you are unhappy?—I shall not be long unhappy; you will not have long to complain of me.—I repelled far from me fears which I wished to think chimerical. No, no, dear Adolphe, said she; when we have long invoked death, Heaven sends us at last I know not what infallible presentiment, which informs us that our prayer is granted.—I swore never to leave her.—I have always hoped for that; now I am sure of it.

It was one of those days of winter, when the sun seems to enlighten faintly the greyish country, as if it looked with pity on the earth which it has ceased to warm. Ellenor proposed to me to walk out. It is very cold, I observed.—No matter, I should wish to walk with you. She took my arm: we walked a long time without saying any thing. She proceeded with difficulty, and supported herself almost entirely on me.—Let us pause an instant. No, she answered, I receive pleasure in feeling myself once more supported by you. We fell again into silence. The sky was serene: but the trees were leafless: not a breath agitated the air, no bird traversed it: all was motionless: and the only sound which was heard was that of the frozen grass which crackled under our feet. How calm is every thing said Ellenor: how nature resigns herself! The heart also—ought not it to learn resignation? She seated herself upon a stone. Suddenly she knelt down, and bowing her head, she supported it on both her hands. I heard some words pronounced in a low voice. I perceived that she prayed. Raising herself up at last, let us re-enter, she said; the cold has seized me. I fear I shall be ill. Say nothing to me. I am not in a condition to listen to you.

From that day I saw Ellenor grow weaker, and decay. I collected from all parts physicians around her. Some announced to me an illness without remedy. Others amused me with vain hopes. But nature sad and silent followed with an invisible arm her unpitying work. Now and then, Ellenor seemed to resume new life. One would have sometimes said that the iron hand which weighed so heavily upon her had been withdrawn. She raised her languid head. Her cheeks were suffused with colours a little more lively: her eyes were re-animated. But suddenly, by the cruel sport of an unknown power, that deceitful better disappeared, without art being able to divine the cause. I in a manner saw her by degrees advance to destruction. I saw engraven on that figure so noble and so expressive, the signs which are the precursors of death. I saw, sight humiliating and deplorable! that energetic and proud character, receive from physical suffering a thousand confused and incoherent impressions, as if, in these terrible moments, the mind, crushed by the body, metamorphosed itself in every way, to yield with less difficulty to the degradation of the organs.

One single sentiment never varied in the heart of Ellenor: that was her tenderness for me. Her weakness permitted her seldom to speak to me; but she fixed on me her eyes in silence, and it seemed to me then, that her look asked of me the life which I could no longer bestow on her. I feared to cause her any violent emotion: I invented pretexts to walk out: I wandered at random over all the places where I had been with her. I bathed with my tears the stones, the foot of the trees, all the objects which retraced to me recollections of her.

These were not the regrets of love: it was a sentiment more gloomy and more sad. Love identifies itself so perfectly with the object beloved, that even in its despair, there is some charm. It struggles against reality, against destiny: the ardor of its desire deceives it as to its powers, and exalts it in the midst of its grief. Mine was dull and solitary. I did not hope to die with Ellenor. I was about to live without her in that desert of a world, which I had desired so often to traverse independent. I had crushed the being who loved me: I had broken that heart, the companion of my own, which had persisted in devoting itself to me, in its unwearied tenderness. Already my insulation affected me: Ellenor still breathed; but I could no longer confide to her thoughts. I was already alone on the earth. I no longer lived in that atmosphere of love which she diffused around me. The air which I breathed seemed to me more harsh, the countenances of men whom I met more indifferent. All nature seemed to tell me that I was about to cease for ever to be loved.

The danger of Ellenor became suddenly more imminent. Symptoms which could not be mistaken announced her approaching end. A priest of her religion warned her of this. She begged of me to bring her a casket which contained many papers. She caused several of them to be burned before her: but she seemed to search for one which she did not find, and her uneasiness was extreme. I entreated her to cease that search which agitated her, and during which, she twice had fainted. I consent, she answered; but dear Adolphe, do not refuse me one request. You will find among my papers, I know not where, a letter which is addressed to you. Burn it without reading it, I conjure you, in the name of our love, in the name of these last moments, which you have soothed. I promised her this. She was more tranquil. Let me resign myself at present, said she, to the duties of my religion. I have many faults to expiate; my love for you was perhaps a fault: I should not however believe this, if that love had been able to render you happy.

I left her. I entered not again but with all her people to assist in the last and solemn prayers. Kneeling in a corner of her chamber, one while I was absorbed in thought, another while I contemplated, by an involuntary curiosity, all these men assembled; the terror of some, the distraction of others, and that singular effect of custom, which introduces indifference into all prescribed practices, and which makes ceremonies, the most august and the most terrible be looked upon as things of mere expedience and of pure form. I heard these men repeat mechanically the funeral words, as if they themselves were not also to be one day actors in a similar scene, as if they themselves were not also one day to die. I was far however from disdaining those customs. Is there even one of which man, in his ignorance, dare pronounce the inutility? They restored calmness to Ellenor: they aided her to pass that dreadful bourne, to which we are all advancing without any of us being able to foresee what he must then experience. My surprize is not that man has need of a system of religion: that which astonishes me, is that he ever believes himself sufficiently strong, sufficiently sheltered from affliction to dare to reject any one of them. He ought, it seems to me, to be induced, in his weakness to invoke all. In the obscure night which surrounds us, is there a glimmering which we can reject? in the midst of the torrent which drags us along, is there a branch to which we may dare refuse to attach ourselves?

The impression produced on Ellenor by a solemnity so mournful seemed to have fatigued her. She fell into a sleep sufficiently peaceful. She awoke less suffering. I was alone in her chamber. We spoke, from time to time at long intervals. The physician, who had shewn himself the most skilful in his conjectures, had predicted to me that she would not live twenty-four hours. I looked alternately at a clock which marked the hours, and the countenance of Ellenor, on which I perceived not any new change. Each minute which passed re-animated my hopes, and I called in question the presages of a deceitful art. All at once, Ellenor darted forward by a sudden movement. I held her in my arms. A convulsive trembling agitated all her body. Her eyes sought me; but in those eyes were depicted a vague fear, as if she had asked favour of some menacing object which was concealed from my view. She raised herself up; she fell down again; it was evident that she strove to escape. One would have said, that she struggled with an invisible physical power, which, weary of waiting for the fatal moment, had seized and retained her, to terminate her existence on that bed of death. She yielded at length to the rage of hostile nature. Her limbs sunk down. She seemed to regain some knowledge: she clasped my hand. She wished to cry; there were no tears to shed: she wished to speak; no voice remained. She let fall, as if in resignation, her head on the arm which supported it. Her respiration became more slow. Some instants after, she was no more.

I remained long immovable, near the lifeless Ellenor. The conviction of her death had not yet penetrated into my mind. My eyes contemplated, with stupid astonishment, that inanimate body. One of her women, having entered, spread through the house the fatal news. The noise which was made around me drew me from the lethargy in which I was plunged. I rose. It was then that I experienced the heart-rending anguish and all the horror of the eternal adieu. So much movement, that activity of common life, so many cares and agitations which no longer regarded her, dissipated that illusion which I prolonged, that illusion by which I believed myself yet to exist with Ellenor. I felt the last tie to break, and frightful reality to place itself for ever between her and me. How much was I now weighed down by that liberty which I had so greatly regretted! How much was wanting to my heart that dependance which had so often revolted me! But lately, all my actions had an aim. I was sure, by each of them, to save a pain or to cause a pleasure. I then complained. I was impatient that a friendly eye should observe my proceedings, that the happiness of another was attached to it. No one now observed them: they interested no one. No one disputed with me my time, nor my hours: no voice called me back when I went out: I was free indeed: I was no more beloved: I was a stranger to all the world.

All the papers of Ellenor were brought me, as she had directed. In each line, I met with new proofs of her love, new sacrifices which she had made for me, and which she had concealed from me. I found at last that letter which I had promised to burn. I did not at first recognize it. It was without address; it was open. Some words struck my eyes in spite of me. I attempted in vain to turn them away. I could not resist the desire to read it entirely. I have not the power to transcribe it. Ellenor had written it after one of the violent scenes which had preceded her illness. Adolphe, she said, why do you incense yourself against me? What is my crime?—To love you, not to be able to exist without you? By what strange pity is it that you do not dare to break a tie which weighs you down, and that you tear to pieces the wretched being beside whom your pity retains you? Why do you refuse me the sad pleasure of believing you at least to be generous? Why do you show yourself angry and weak? The idea of my grief follows you and the sight of that grief cannot arrest you! What do you require? that I leave you? Do you not see that I have not the power to do so? Ah! it is for you who do not love, it is for you to find such power in that heart tired of me, which so much love is unable to disarm. You will not communicate it to me; you will make me pine away in tears; you will make me die at your feet. Say one word, she wrote elsewhere. Is there a country whither I do not follow you, is there a retreat in which I do not hide myself, in order to live near you, without being a burthen in your life? But no; you do not wish it. All the plans which I propose, timid and trembling, for you have chilled me with fear, you repel with impatience. The best which I obtain is your silence. So much unfeelingness does not accord with your character. You are good: your actions are noble and devoted: but what actions could efface your words? Those keen words resound around me: I hear them at night: they follow me: they devour me: they tarnish all that you do. Must I then die, Adolphe? Well, you shall be satisfied. She will die, that poor creature whom you have protected, but whom you strike with redoubled blows. She will die, that troublesome Ellenor, whom you cannot bear to have near you, whom you consider as an obstacle, for whom you do not find on the earth one place which does not incommode you. She will die. You will walk alone in the midst of that crowd, in which you are impatient to mix. You will know those men whom you at present thank for being indifferent, and perhaps one day, hurt by these cold hearts, you will regret that heart of which you disposed, which lived in your affection, which would have braved a thousand perils in your defence, and which you no longer deign to recompense with a look.

Letter to the Editor

I return you, sir, the manuscript which you have had the goodness to intrust me with. I thank you for that act of complaisance, though it has awoke in me sad recollections, which time had effaced. I have known the greater number of those who have a part in that history: for it is but too true. I have often seen that strange and wretched Adolphe, who is at the same time its author and its hero. I have attempted to rescue, by my councils, that charming Ellenor, worthy of a milder fate and of a more faithful heart, from the mischievous being who, no less miserable than herself, ruled her by a species of magic, and tore her by his weakness. Alas! the last time I saw her, I thought I had given her some fortitude, had armed her reason against her heart.—After too long an absence, I have returned to the place where I had left her; and I have found only a tomb.

You ought, sir, to publish that anecdote. It cannot hereafter hurt any one, and could not be, in my opinion, without utility. The misfortune of Ellenor proves, that the most impassioned sentiment would be unable to struggle against the order of things. Society is too powerful: it reproduces itself under too many forms. It intermingles too much of bitterness with the love which it has not sanctioned. It favours that inclination for inconstancy, and that impatient fatigue, diseases of the mind, which seize it sometimes suddenly, in the bosom of intimacy. Indifferent persons have a wonderful eagerness to be slanderers in the name of morality and noxious through zeal for virtue. It might be said that the view of affection troubles them, because they are incapable of it; and when they can avail themselves of a pretext, they delight in attacking it, and in destroying it. Woe then to the woman who reposes on a sentiment which every thing combines to poison, and against which society, when it is not compelled to respect it as legitimate, arms itself with all that is bad in the heart of man, to discourage all that is good in it!

The example of Adolphe will not be less instructive, if you add, that after having repelled the being who loved him, he has not been less uneasy, less agitated, and less discontented; that he has not made any use of a liberty regained at the expense of so much grief and of so many tears; and that by rendering himself well deserving of blame, he has rendered himself also deserving of pity.

If you require proofs, Sir, read those letters which will inform you of the fate of Adolphe. You will see him, in many various circumstances, and always the victim of that mixture of egotism and of sensibility, which were combined in him for his misfortune and for that of others; foreseeing the ill before committing it, and drawing back, with despair, after having committed it; punished by his qualities still more than by his defects, because his qualities had their source in his emotions, and not in his principles; alternately the most devoted and the most unfeeling of men, but having always ended by unfeelingness, after commenced by devotedness, and never having thus left impressions but of injuries.

Answer

Yes, sir, I will publish the manuscript which you return me (not that I think like you as to the utility of which it may be: no one obtains instruction but at his own expense in this world; and the women who may read it will all imagine that they have met with better than Adolphe, or that they are more worthy than Ellenor:) but I will publish it, as a history sufficiently true of the misery of the human heart. If it contain an instructive lesson, it is to men that that lesson is addressed. It proves that that mind, of which we are so proud, serves neither to discover happiness, nor to bestow it: it proves that character, firmness, fidelity, benevolence, are gifts which must be asked of heaven; and I do not call benevolence that transitory pity, which does not subdue impatience, and does not hinder it from opening again the wounds which a moment of regret had closed. The great question in life is the grief which we cause; and the most ingenious metaphysics do not justify a man who has broken the heart which loved him. Moreover, I hate that fatuity of mind which thinks that it excuses what it explains; I hate that vanity which is only occupied with itself when recounting the evil it has done, which seeks to inspire pity in describing itself and which, hovering indestructible in the midst of ruins, analyzes itself instead of repenting. I hate that weakness which always blames others for its own impotence and does not see that the evil is not in its surroundings but in itself.

I should have guessed that Adolphe would be punished for his character *by* his character, that he would follow no fixed road, fill no useful post, waste his faculties with no other control than caprice, with no other force than irritation; I should have guessed all that, as I say, even if you had not sent me new details about his subsequent life. I cannot yet say whether I shall make use of them. Circumstances are of little importance, character is everything; it is of no use to break with objects and other beings; you cannot break with yourself. You can change your situation, but into each situation you carry the torment of which you had hoped to rid yourself, and, as you do not mend your ways by changing scenes, you discover that you have merely added remorse to regrets and sins to suffering.

The Region of Dead Calm

(1854)

Ivan Turgenev

Isabel F. Hapgood, translator

Ivan Sergeyevich Turgenev (1818–1883), Russian novelist and playwright, was born to an aristocratic family on an estate in the province of Orel. He studied at the universities of Moscow and St. Petersburg, and did graduate work at the University of Berlin in philosophy, literature, and history, receiving his degree in philosophy at St. Petersburg in 1842. He had already begun writing, and after filling a government post for two years he devoted himself completely to writing, living on his inheritance. After 1856 he spent much of his time traveling outside Russia. His first literary success was *A Sportsman's Sketches* (begun in 1847, published in 1852), which as a contribution to the abolition of serfdom deserves to be called the *Uncle Tom's Cabin* of Russia. These short pieces were followed by the novels *Rudin* (1856), *A Nest of Gentlefolk* (1858), *On the Eve* (1860), *Fathers and Sons* (1862), *Smoke* (1867), and *Virgin Soil* (1872); Turgenev also wrote a few plays, among them *A Month in the Country* (1849).

Turgenev was the first major Russian novelist to attract attention outside Russia. However, although he lived in France and died in Paris, his best work treats the Russian landowners and peasants much as Maria Edgeworth treated their Irish counterparts. (For evidence of a direct influence, see a letter signed "One who knew Turgenev" in *The London Daily News,* 7 September 1883.) The *novella* or novelette was his forte rather than the great sprawling novel we associate with his contemporaries Dostoyevsky and Tolstoy; even in his novels he thinks and constructs on the smaller scale with a greater economy and singleness of purpose. His novelettes include *The Diary of a Superfluous Man* (1850), *First Love* (1860), and *A King Lear of the Steppes* (1870).

The Region of Dead Calm, also known as *The Backwater* and *The Quiet Spot,* is typical of Turgenev's novelettes. The translation is by Isabel F. Hapgood (New York, 1903); notes are by the translator. For further reading, see Henry James, *French Poets and Novelists* (London, 1878) and *Partial Portraits* (London, 1888); E. Garnett, *Turgenev, a Study* (London, 1918); A. Yarmolinsky, *Turgenev* (New York, 1926); and D. Magarshack, *Turgenev, a Life* (New York, 1954).

196

I

In a fairly-large recently whitewashed chamber of a wing of the manor-house in the village of Sásovo, —— county, T—— Government, a young man in a paletot was sitting at a small, warped table, looking over accounts. Two stearine candles, in silver travelling-candlesticks, were burning in front of him; in one corner, on the wall-bench, stood an open bottle-case, in another a servant was setting up an iron bed. On the other side of a low partition a samovár was murmuring and hissing; a dog was nestling about on some hay which had just been brought in. In the doorway stood a peasant-man in a new overcoat girt with a red belt, with a large beard, and an intelligent face—the overseer, judging by all the tokens. He was gazing attentively at the seated young man.

Against one wall stood a very aged, tiny piano; beside it an equally ancient chest of drawers with holes in place of the locks; between the windows a small, dim mirror was visible; on the partition-wall hung an old portrait, which was almost completely peeled off, representing a woman with powdered hair, in a *robe ronde,* and with a black ribbon about her slender neck. Judging from the very perceptible sagging of the ceiling, and the slope of the floor, which was full of cracks, the little wing into which we have conducted the reader had existed for a very long time. No one lived in it permanently; it was put to use when the owners came. The young man who was sitting at the table was the owner of the village of Sásovo. He had arrived only on the previous day from his principal estate, situated a hundred versts[1] distant, and was preparing to depart on the morrow, after completing the inspection of the farming, listening to the demands of the peasants, and verifying all the documents.

"Well, that will do,"—he said, raising his head;—"I am tired. Thou mayest go now,"—he added, turning to the overseer;—"and come very early to-morrow morning, and notify the peasants at daybreak that they are to present themselves in assembly,—dost hear me?"

"I obey."

"And order the estate-clerk to present to me the report for the last month. But thou hast done well,"—the gentleman went on, casting a glance around him,—"in whitewashing the walls. Everything seems cleaner."

The overseer silently swept a glance around the walls also.

"Well, go now."

The overseer made his obeisance and left the room.

The gentleman stretched himself.

"Hey!"—he shouted.—"Give me some tea!. . .'T is time to go to bed."

His servant went to the other side of the partition, and speedily returned with a glass of tea, a bundle of town cracknels, and a cream-jug on an iron tray. The gentleman began to drink tea, but before he had had time to swallow two mouth-

---

[1] A verst is two-thirds of a mile.

fuls, the noise of persons entering resounded from an adjoining room, and some one's squeaking voice inquired:

"Is Vladímir Sergyéitch Astákhoff at home? Can he be seen?"

Vladímir Sergyéitch (that was the name of the young man in the paletot) cast a glance of surprise at his man, and said in a hurried whisper:

"Go, find out who it is."

The man withdrew, slamming behind him the door, which closed badly.

"Announce to Vladímir Sergyéitch,"—rang out the same squeaking voice as before,—"that his neighbour Ipátoff wishes to see him, if it will not incommode him; and another neighbour has come with me, Bodryakóff, Iván Ílitch, who also desires to pay his respects."

Vladímir Sergyéitch made an involuntary gesture of vexation. Nevertheless, when his man entered the room, he said to him:

"Ask them in." And he arose to receive his visitors.

The door opened, and the visitors made their appearance. One of them, a robust, grey-haired little old man, with a small, round head and bright little eyes, walked in advance; the other, a tall, thin man of three-and-thirty, with a long, swarthy face and dishevelled hair, walked behind, with a shambling gait. The old man wore a neat grey coat with large, mother-of-pearl buttons; a small, pink neckerchief, half concealed by the rolling collar of his white shirt, loosely encircled his neck; his feet shone resplendent in gaiters; the plaids of his Scotch trousers were agreeably gay in hue; and, altogether, he produced a pleasant impression. His companion, on the contrary, evoked in the spectator a less favourable sensation: he wore an old black dress-coat, buttoned up to the throat; his full trousers, of thick, winter tricot, matched his coat in colour; no linen was visible, either around his throat or around his wrists. The little old man was the first to approach Vladímir Sergyéitch, and, with an amiable inclination of the head, he began in the same shrill little voice:

"I have the honour to introduce myself,—your nearest neighbour, and even a relative, Ipátoff, Mikhaílo Nikoláitch. I have long wished to have the pleasure of making your acquaintance. I hope that I have not disturbed you."

Vladímir Sergyéitch replied that he was very glad to see him, and that he was not disturbed in the least, and would not he take a seat...and drink tea.

"And this nobleman,"—went on the little old man, after listening with a courteous smile to Vladímir Sergyéitch's unfinished phrases, and extending his hand in the direction of the gentleman in the dress-coat,—"also your neighbour... and my good acquaintance, Iván Ílitch, strongly desired to make your acquaintance."

The gentleman in the dress-coat, from whose countenance no one would have suspected that he was capable of desiring anything strongly in his life—so preoccupied and, at the same time, so sleepy was the expression of that countenance,— the gentleman in the dress-coat bowed clumsily and languidly. Vladímir Sergyéitch bowed to him in return, and again invited the visitors to be seated.

The visitors sat down.

"I am very glad,"—began the little old man, pleasantly throwing apart his hands, while his companion set to scrutinising the ceiling, with his mouth slightly open:—"I am very glad that I have, at last, the honour of seeing you personally. Although you have your permanent residence in a county which lies at a considerable distance from these localities, still, we regard you also as one of our own primordial landed proprietors, so to speak."

"That is very flattering to me,"—returned Vladímir Sergyéitch.

"Flattering or not, it is a fact. You must excuse us, Vladímir Sergyéitch; we people here in —— county are a straightforward folk; we live in our simplicity; we say what we think, without circumlocution. It is our custom, I must tell you, not to call upon each other on Name-days[2] otherwise than in our frock-coats. Truly! We have made that rule. On that account, we are called 'frock-coaters' in the adjoining counties, and we are even reproached for our bad style; but we pay no attention to that! Pray, what is the use of living in the country—and then standing on ceremony?"

"Of course, what can be better...in the country...than that naturalness of intercourse,"—remarked Vladímir Sergyéitch.

"And yet,"—replied the little old man,—"among us in our county dwell people of the cleverest sort,—one may say people of European culture, although they do not wear dress-suits. Take, for example, our historian Evsiukóff, Stepán Stepánitch: he is interesting himself in Russian history from the most ancient times, and is known in Petersburg—an extremely learned man! There is in our town an ancient Swedish cannon-ball...'t is placed yonder, in the centre of the public square...and 't was he who discovered it, you know! Certainly! Tzénteler, Antón Kárlitch...now he has studied natural history; but they say all Germans are successful in that line. When, ten years ago, a stray hyena was killed in our vicinity, it was this Antón Kárlitch who discovered that it really was a hyena, by cause of the peculiar construction of its tail. And then, we have a landed proprietor Kaburdín: he chiefly writes light articles; he wields a very dashing pen; his articles appear in 'Galatea.' Bodryakóff,...not Iván Ílitch; no, Iván Ílitch neglects that; but another Bodryakóff, Sergyéi...what the deuce was his father's baptismal name, Iván Ílitch...what the deuce was it?"

"Sergyéitch,"—prompted Iván Ílitch.

"Yes; Sergyéi Sergyéitch,—he busies himself with writing verses. Well, of course he's not a Púshkin, but sometimes he gets off things which would pass muster even in the capitals. Do you know his epigram on Agéi Fómitch?"

"What Agéi Fómitch?"

"Akh, pardon me; I keep forgetting that you are not a resident here, after all. He is our chief of police. The epigram is extremely amusing. Thou rememberest it, I believe, Iván Ílitch?"

"Agéi Fómitch,"—said Bodryakóff, indifferently—

"...not without cause is gloriously
    By the nobles' election honoured...."

---

2 The Name-day—that is, the day of the saint after whom a person is named—is observed with feasting and congratulation, instead of the birthday. For ceremonious calls, no matter at what hour of the day, a man who has no official uniform must wear his evening suit, on penalty of being considered ignorant or rude, or (in official circles) of being refused admittance.

"I must tell you,"—broke in Ipátoff,—"that he was elected almost exclusively by white balls, for he is a most worthy man."

"Agéi Fómitch,"—repeated Bodryakóff,

> "...not without cause is gloriously
> By the nobles' election honoured:
> He drinks and eats regularly...
> So why should not he be the regulator of order?"[3]

The little old man burst out laughing.

"Ha, ha, ha! that is n't bad, is it? Ever since then, if you 'll believe me, each one of us will say, for instances, to Agéi Fómitch: 'Good morning!'—and will invariably add: 'so why should not he be the regulator of order?' And does Agéi Fómitch get angry, think you? Not in the least. No—that's not our way. Just ask Iván Ílitch here if it is."

Iván Ílitch merely rolled up his eyes.

"Get angry at a jest—how is that possible? Now, take Iván Ílitch there; his nickname among us is 'The Folding Soul,' because he agrees to everything very promptly. What then? Does Iván Ílitch take offence at that? Never!"

Iván Ílitch, slowly blinking his eyes, looked first at the little old man, then at Vladímir Sergyéitch.

The epithet, "The Folding Soul," really did fit Iván Ílitch admirably. There was not a trace in him of what is called will or character. Any one who wished could lead him whithersoever he would; all that was necessary was to say to him: "Come on, Iván Ílitch!"—and he picked up his cap and went; but if another person turned up, and said to him: "Halt, Iván Ílitch!"—he laid down his cap and remained. He was of a peaceable, tranquil disposition, had lived a bachelor-life, did not play cards, but was fond of sitting beside the players and looking into each of their faces in turn. Without society he could not exist, and solitude he could not endure. At such times he became despondent; however, this happened very rarely with him. He had another peculiarity: rising from his bed betimes in the morning, he would sing in an undertone an old romance:

> "In the country once a Baron
> Dwelt in simplicity rural. ..."

In consequence of this peculiarity of Iván Ílitch's, he was also called "The Hawfinch," because, as is well known, the hawfinch when in captivity sings only once in the course of the day, early in the morning. Such was Iván Ílitch Bodryakóff.

The conversation between Ipátoff and Vladímir Sergyéitch lasted for quite a long time, but not in its original, so to speak, speculative direction. The little old man questioned Vladímir Sergyéitch about his estate, the condition of his forests and other sorts of land, the improvements which he had already introduced or

---

[3] A pun is intended: *isprávno*, regularly, in orderly manner; *ispravnik*, the chief of police in a rural district.

was only intending to introduce in his farming; he imparted to him several of his own observations; advised him, among other things, in order to get rid of hummocky pastures, to sprinkle them with oats, which, he said, would induce the pigs to plough them up with their snouts, and so forth. But, at last, perceiving that Vladímir Sergyéitch was so sleepy that he could hardly keep his eyes open, and that a certain deliberation and incoherence were making themselves evident in his speech, the little old man rose, and, with a courteous obeisance, declared that he would not incommode him any longer with his presence, but that he hoped to have the pleasure of seeing the valued guest at his own house not later than the following day, at dinner.

"And the first person you meet, not to mention any small child, but, so to speak, any hen or peasant-woman,"—he added,—"will point out to you the road to my village. All you have to do is to ask for Ipátoff. The horses will trot there of themselves."

Vladímir Sergyéitch replied with a little hesitation—which, however, was natural to him—that he would try...that if nothing prevented....

"Yes, we shall certainly expect you,"—the little old man interrupted him, cordially, shook his hand warmly, and briskly withdrew, exclaiming in the doorway, as he half turned round:—"Without ceremony!"

"Folding Soul" Bodryakóff bowed in silence and vanished in the wake of his companion, with a preliminary stumble on the threshold.

Having seen his unexpected guests off, Vladímir Sergyéitch immediately undressed, got into bed, and went to sleep.

Vladímir Sergyéitch Astákhoff belonged to the category of people who, after having cautiously tested their powers in two or three different careers, are wont to say of themselves that they have finally come to the conclusion to look at life from a practical point of view, and who devote their leisure to augmenting their revenues. He was not stupid, was rather penurious, and very sensible; was fond of reading, of society, of music—but all in moderation...and bore himself very decorously. He was twenty-seven years old. A great many young men of his sort have sprung up recently. He was of medium height, well built, and had agreeable though small features; their expression almost never varied; his eyes always gleamed with one and the same stern, bright glance; only now and then did this glance soften with a faint shade of something which was not precisely sadness, nor yet precisely boredom; a courteous smile rarely quitted his lips. He had very handsome, fair hair, silky, and falling in long ringlets. Vladímir Sergyéitch owned about six hundred souls[4] on a good estate, and he was thinking of marriage—a marriage of inclination, but which should, at the same time, be advantageous. He was particularly desirous of finding a wife with powerful connections. In a word, he merited the appellation of "gentleman" which had recently come into vogue.

When he rose on the following morning, very early, according to his wont, our gentleman occupied himself with business, and, we must do him the justice to say,

---

4 Male serfs. The women and children did not figure on the revision lists.

did so in a decidedly practical manner, which cannot always be said of practical young men among us in Russia. He patiently listened to the confused petitions and complaints of the peasants, gave them satisfaction so far as he was able, investigated the quarrels and dissensions which had arisen between relatives, exhorted some, scolded others, audited the clerk's accounts, brought to light two or three rascalities on the part of the overseer—in a word, handled matters in such wise that he was very well satisfied with himself, and the peasants, as they returned from the assembly to their homes, spoke well of him.

In spite of his promise given on the preceding evening to Ipátoff, Vladímir Sergyéitch had made up his mind to dine at home, and had even ordered his travelling-cook to prepare his favourite rice-soup with pluck; but all of a sudden, possibly in consequence of that feeling of satisfaction which had filled his soul ever since the early morning, he stopped short in the middle of the room, smote himself on the brow with his hand, and, not without some spirit, exclaimed aloud: "I believe I 'll go to that flowery old babbler!" No sooner said than done; half an hour later he was sitting in his new tarantás, drawn by four stout peasant-horses, and driving to Ipátoff's house, which was reckoned to be not more than twenty-five versts distant by a capital road.

II

Mikhaílo Nikoláevitch Ipátoff's manor consisted of two separate small mansions, built opposite each other on the two sides of a huge pond through which ran a river. A long dam, planted with silver poplars, shut off the pond; almost on a level with it the red roof of a small hand-mill was visible. Built exactly alike, and painted with the same lilac hue, the tiny houses seemed to be exchanging glances across the broad, watery expanse, with the glittering panes of their small, clean windows. From the middle of each little house a circular terrace projected, and a sharp-peaked pediment rose aloft, supported by four white pillars set close together. The ancient park ran all the way round the pond; lindens stretched out in alleys, and stood in dense clumps; aged pine-trees, with pale yellow boles, dark oaks, magnificent maples here and there reared high in air their solitary crests; the dense verdure of the thickly spreading lilacs and acacias advanced close up to the very sides of the two little houses, leaving revealed only their fronts, from which winding paths paved with brick ran down the slope. Motley-hued ducks, white and grey geese were swimming in separate flocks on the clear water of the pond; it never became covered with scum, thanks to abundant springs which welled into its "head" from the base of the steep, rocky ravine. The situation of the manor was good, pleasant, isolated, and beautiful.

In one of the two little houses dwelt Mikhaíl Nikoláevitch himself; in the other lived his mother, a decrepit old woman of seventy years. When he drove on to the dam, Vladímir Sergyéitch did not know to which house to betake himself. He glanced about him: a small urchin of the house-serfs was fishing, as he stood barefooted on a half-rotten tree-stump. Vladímir Sergyéitch hailed him.

"But to whom are you going—to the old lady or to the young master?"—replied the urchin, without taking his eyes from his float.

"What lady?"—replied Vladímir Sergyéitch.—"I want to find Mikhaílo Nikoláitch."

"Ah! the young master? Well, then, turn to the right."

And the lad gave his line a jerk, and drew from the motionless water a small, silvery carp. Vladímir Sergyéitch drove to the right.

Mikhaíl Nikoláitch was playing at draughts with The Folding Soul when the arrival of Vladímir Sergyéitch was announced to him. He was delighted, sprang from his arm-chair, ran out into the anteroom and there kissed the visitor three times.

"You find me with my invariable friend, Vladímir Sergyéitch,"—began the loquacious little old man:—"with Iván Ílitch, who, I will remark in passing, is completely enchanted with your affability." (Iván Ílitch darted a silent glance at the corner.) "He was so kind as to remain to play draughts with me, while all my household went for a stroll in the park; but I will send for them at once...."

"But why disturb them?"—Vladímir Sergyéitch tried to expostulate....

"Not the least inconvenience, I assure you. Hey, there, Vánka, run for the young ladies as fast as thou canst...tell them that a guest has favoured us with a visit. And how does this locality please you? It's not bad, is it? Kaburdin has composed some verses about it. 'Ipátovka, refuge lovely'—that's the way they begin,—and the rest of it is just as good, only I don't remember all of it. The park is large, that's the trouble; beyond my means. And these two houses, which are so much alike, as you have, perhaps, deigned to observe, were erected by two brothers—my father Nikolái, and my uncle Sergyéi; they also laid out the park; they were exemplary friends.... Damon and...there now! I've forgotten the other man's name...."

"Python,"—remarked Iván Ílitch.

"Not really? Well, never mind." (At home the old man talked in a much more unconventional manner than when he was paying calls.)—"You are, probably, not ignorant of the fact, Vladímir Sergyéitch, that I am a widower, that I have lost my wife; my elder children are in government educational institutions,[5] and I have with me only the youngest two, and my sister-in-law lives with me—my wife's sister; you will see her directly. But why don't I offer you some refreshment? Iván Ílitch, my dear fellow, see to a little luncheon...what sort of vodka are you pleased to prefer?"

"I drink nothing until dinner."

"Goodness, how is that possible! However, as you please. The truest hospitality is to let the guest do as he likes. We are very simple-mannered folk here, you see. Here with us, if I may venture so to express myself, we live not so much in a lonely as in a dead-calm place, a remote nook—that's what! But why don't you sit down?"

---

[5] Of different grades (civil and military), for the children of the nobility or gentry. They are not charities.

Vladímir Sergyéitch seated himself, without letting go of his hat.

"Permit me to relieve you,"—said Ipátoff, and delicately taking his hat from him, he carried it off to a corner, then returned, looked his visitor in the eye with a cordial smile, and, not knowing just what agreeable thing to say to him, inquired, in the most hearty manner,—whether he was fond of playing draughts.

"I play all games badly,"—replied Vladímir Sergyéitch.

"And that's a very fine thing in you,"—returned Ipátoff:—"but draughts is not a game, but rather a diversion—a way of passing leisure time; is n't that so, Iván Ílitch?"

Iván Ílitch cast an indifferent glance at Ipátoff, as though he were thinking to himself, "The devil only knows whether it is a game or a diversion," but, after waiting a while, he said:

"Yes; draughts don't count."

"Chess is quite another matter, they say,"—pursued Ipátoff;—"'t is a very difficult game, I'm told. But, in my opinion...but yonder come my people!"—he interrupted himself, glancing through the half-open glass door, which gave upon the park.

Vladímir Sergyéitch rose, turned round, and beheld first two little girls, about ten years of age, in pink cotton frocks and broad-brimmed hats, who were running alertly up the steps of the terrace; not far behind them a tall, plump, well-built young girl of twenty, in a dark gown, made her appearance. They all entered the house, and the little girls courtesied sedately to the visitor.

"Here, sir, let me present you,"—said the host;—"my daughters, sir. This one here is named Kátya, and this one is Nástya, and this is my sister-in-law, Márya Pávlovna, whom I have already had the pleasure of mentioning to you. I beg that you will love and favour them."

Vladímir Sergyéitch made his bow to Márya Pávlovna; she replied to him with a barely perceptible inclination of the head.

Márya Pávlovna held in her hand a large, open knife; her thick, ruddy-blond hair was slightly dishevelled,—a small green leaf had got entangled in it, her braids had escaped from the comb,—her dark-skinned face was flushed, and her red lips were parted; her gown looked crumpled. She was breathing fast; her eyes were sparkling; it was evident that she had been working in the garden. She immediately left the room; the little girls ran out after her.

"She's going to rearrange her toilet a bit,"—remarked the old man, turning to Vladímir Sergyéitch;—"they can't get along without that, sir!"

Vladímir Sergyéitch grinned at him in response, and became somewhat pensive. Márya Pávlovna had made an impression on him. It was long since he had seen such a purely Russian beauty of the steppes. She speedily returned, sat down on the divan, and remained motionless. She had smoothed her hair, but had not changed her gown,—had not even put on cuffs. Her features expressed not precisely pride, but rather austerity, almost harshness; her brow was broad and low, her nose short and straight; a slow, lazy smile curled her lips from time to time; her straight eyebrows contracted scornfully. She kept her large, dark eyes almost constantly lowered. "I know," her unfriendly young face seemed to be saying; "I know that you are all looking at me; well, then, look; you bore me." But when she raised her eyes, there was something wild, beautiful, and stolid about them, which was suggestive of the eyes of a doe. She had a magnificent figure. A classical poet would have compared her to Ceres or Juno.

"What have you been doing in the garden?"—Ipátoff asked her, being desirous of bringing her into the conversation.

"I have been cutting off dead branches, and digging up the flower-beds," she replied, in a voice which was rather low, but agreeable and resonant.

"And are you tired?"

"The children are; I am not."

"I know,"—interposed the old man, with a smile;—"thou art a regular Bobélina! And have you been to grandmamma's?"

"Yes; she is asleep."

"Are you fond of flowers?"—Vladímir Sergyéitch asked her.

"Yes."

"Why dost thou not put on thy hat when thou goest out of doors?"—Ipátoff remarked to her.—"Just see how red and sunburned thou art."

She silently passed her hand over her face. Her hands were not large, but rather broad, and decidedly red. She did not wear gloves.

"And are you fond of gardening?"—Vladímir Sergyéitch put another question to her.

"Yes."

Vladímir Sergyéitch began to narrate what a fine garden there was in his neighbourhood, belonging to a wealthy landed proprietor named N——. —The head gardener, a German, received in wages alone two thousand rubles, silver[6]—he said, among other things.

"And what is the name of that gardener?"—inquired Iván Ílitch, suddenly.

"I don't remember,—Meyer or Müller, I think. But why do you ask?"

"For no reason in particular, sir,"—replied Iván Ílitch.—"To find out his name."

Vladímir Sergyéitch continued his narration. The little girls, Mikhaíl Nikoláitch's daughters, entered, sat down quietly, and quietly began to listen. . . .

A servant made his appearance at the door, had announced that Egór Kapítonitch had arrived.

"Ah! Ask him in, ask him in!"—exclaimed Ipátoff.

There entered a short, fat little old man, one of the sort of people who are called squat or dumpy, with a puffy and, at the same time, a wrinkled little face, after the fashion of a baked apple. He wore a grey hussar jacket with black braiding and a standing collar; his full coffee-coloured velveteen trousers ended far above his ankles.

"Good morning, my most respected Egór Kapítonitch,"—exclaimed Ipátoff, advancing to meet him.—"We have n't seen each other for a long time."

"Could n't be helped,"—returned Egór Kapítonitch in a lisping and whining

---

6 In those days there was a great difference in the value of silver and paper money; hence the kind is usually specified.

voice, after having preliminarily exchanged salutations with all present;—"surely you know, Mikhaíl Nikoláitch, whether I am a free man or not?"

"And how are you not a free man, Egór Kapítonitch?"

"Why, of course I'm not, Mikhaíl Nikoláitch; there's my family, my affairs. . . . And there's Matryóna Márkovna to boot," and he waved his hand in despair.

"But what about Matryóna Márkovna?"

And Ipátoff launched a slight wink at Vladímir Sergyéitch, as though desirous of exciting his interest in advance.

"Why, everybody knows,"—returned Egór Kapítonitch, as he took a seat;— "she's always discontented with me, don't you know that? Whatever I say, it's wrong, not delicate, not decorous. And why it is n't decorous, the Lord God alone knows. And the young ladies, my daughters that is to say, do the same, taking pattern by their mother. I don't say but what Matryóna Márkovna is a very fine woman, but she's awfully severe on the score of manners."

"But, good gracious! in what way are your manners bad, Egór Kapítonitch?"

"That's exactly what I'd like to know myself; but, evidently, she's hard to suit. Yesterday, for instance, I said at table: 'Matryóna Márkovna,'" (and Egór Kapítonitch imparted to his voice an insinuating inflection,—" 'Matryóna Már-kovna," says I, 'what's the meaning of this,—that Aldóshka is n't careful with the horses, does n't know how to drive?' says I; 'there's the black stallion quite foundered.'—I'iikh! how Matryóna Márkovna did flare up, and set to crying shame on me: 'Thou dost not know how to express thyself decently in the society of ladies,' says she; and the young ladies instantly galloped away from the table, and on the next day, the Biriúloff young ladies, my wife's nieces, had heard all about it. And how had I expressed myself badly? And no matter what I say—and sometimes I really am incautious,—no matter to whom I say it, especially at home,—those Biriúloff girls know all about it the next day. A fellow simply does n't know what to do. Sometimes I'm just sitting so, thinking after my fashion,—I breathe hard, as perhaps you know,—and Matryóna Márkovna sets to berating me again: 'Don't snore,' says she; 'nobody snores nowadays!'—'What art thou scolding about, Matryóna Márkovna?' says I. 'Good mercy, thou shouldst have compassion, but thou scoldest.' So I don't meditate at home any more. I sit and look down— so—all the time. By Heaven, I do. And then, again, not long ago, we got into bed; 'Matryóna Márkovna,' says I, 'what makes thee spoil thy page-boy, mátushka?[7] Why, he's a regular little pig,' says I, 'and he might wash his face of a Sunday, at least.' And what happened? It strikes me that I said it distantly, tenderly, but I didn't hit the mark even then; Matryóna Márkovna began to cry shame on me again: 'Thou dost not understand how to behave in the society of ladies,' says she; and the next day the Biriúloff girls knew all about it. What time have I to think of visits under such circumstances, Mikhaíl Nikoláitch?"

"I'm amazed at what you tell me,"—replied Ipátoff;—"I did not expect that from Matryóna Márkovna. Apparently, she is. . . ."

"An extremely fine woman,"—put in Egór Kapítonitch;—"a model wife and

---

[7] Literally, "dear little mother."

mother, so to speak, only strict on the score of manners. She says that *ensemble* is necessary in everything, and that I haven't got it. I don't speak French, as you are aware, I only understand it. But what's that *ensemble* that I haven't got?"

Ipátoff, who was not very strong in French himself, only shrugged his shoulders.

"And how are your children—your sons, that is to say?"—he asked Egór Kapítonitch after a brief pause.

Egór Kapítonitch darted an oblique glance at him.

"My sons are all right. I'm satisfied with them. The girls have got out of hand, but I'm satisfied with my sons. Lyólya discharges his service well, his superior officers approve of him; that Lyólya of mine is a clever fellow. Well, Míkhetz— he's not like that; he has turned out some sort of a philanthropist."

"Why a philanthropist?"

"The Lord knows; he speaks to nobody, he shuns folks. Matryóna Márkovna mostly abashes him. 'Why dost thou take pattern by thy father?' she says to him. 'Do thou respect him, but copy thy mother as to manners.' He'll get straightened out, he'll turn out all right also."

Vladímir Sergyéitch asked Ipátoff to introduce him to Egór Kapítonitch. They entered into conversation. Márya Pávlovna did not take part in it; Iván Ílitch seated himself beside her, and said two words, in all, to her; the little girls came up to him, and began to narrate something to him in a whisper. . . . The house-keeper entered, a gaunt old woman, with her head bound up in a dark kerchief, and announced that dinner was ready. All wended their way to the dining-room.

The dinner lasted for quite a long time. Ipátoff kept a good cook, and ordered pretty good wines, not from Moscow, but from the capital of the government. Ipátoff lived at his ease, as the saying goes. He did not own more than three hundred souls, but he was not in debt to any one, and had brought his estate into order. At table, the host himself did the greater part of the talking; Egór Kapítonitch chimed in, but did not forget himself, at the same time; he ate and drank gloriously. Márya Pávlovna preserved unbroken silence, only now and then replying with half-smiles to the hurried remarks of the two little girls, who sat one on each side of her. They were, evidently, very fond of her. Vladímir Sergyéitch made several attempts to enter into conversation with her, but without particular success. Folding Soul Bodryakóff even ate indolently and languidly. After dinner all went out on the terrace to drink coffee. The weather was magnificent; from the garden was wafted the sweet perfume of the lindens, which were then in full flower; the summer air, slightly cooled by the thick shade of the trees, and the humidity of the adjacent pond, breathed forth a sort of caressing warmth. Suddenly, from behind the poplars of the dam, the trampling of a horse's hoofs became audible, and a moment later, a horsewoman made her appearance in a long riding-habit and a grey hat, mounted on a bay horse; she was riding at a gallop; a page was galloping behind her, on a small, white cob.

"Ah!"—exclaimed Ipátoff,—"Nadézhda Alexyéevna is coming. What a pleasant surprise!"

"Alone?"—asked Márya Pávlovna, who up to that moment had been standing motionless in the doorway.

"Alone. . . . Evidently, something has detained Piótr Alexyéevitch."

Márya Pávlovna darted a sidelong glance from beneath her brows, a flush overspread her face, and she turned away.

In the meantime, the horsewoman had ridden through the wicket-gate into the garden, galloped up to the terrace, and sprang lightly to the ground, without waiting either for her groom or for Ipátoff, who had started to meet her. Briskly gathering up the train of her riding-habit, she ran up the steps, and springing upon the terrace, exclaimed blithely:

"Here I am!"

"Welcome!"—said Ipátoff.—"How unexpected, how charming this is! Allow me to kiss your hand. . . ."

"Certainly,"—returned the visitor; "only, you must pull off the glove yourself. —I cannot." And, extending her hand to him, she nodded to Márya Pávlovna.— "Just fancy, Másha, my brother will not be here to-day,"—she said, with a little sigh.

"I see for myself that he is not here,"—replied Márya Pávlovna in an undertone.

"He bade me say to thee that he is busy. Thou must not be angry. Good morning, Egór Kapítonitch; good morning, Iván Ílitch; good morning, children. . . . Vásya,"—added the guest, turning to her small groom,—"order them to walk Little Beauty up and down well, dost hear? Másha, please give me a pin, to fasten up my train. . . . Come here, Mikhaíl Nikoláitch."

Ipátoff went closer to her.

"Who is that new person?"—she asked, quite loudly.

"That is a neighbour, Astákhoff, Vladímir Sergyévitch, you know, the owner of Sásovo. I'll introduce him if you like, shall I?"

"Very well. . . afterward. Akh, what splendid weather!"—she went on.— "Egór Kapítonitch, tell me—can it be possible that Matryóna Márkovna growls even in such weather as this?"

"Matryóna Márkovna never grumbles in any sort of weather, madam; and she is merely strict on the score of manners. . . ."

"And what are the Biriúloff girls doing? They know all about it the next day, don't they?. . ." And she burst into a ringing, silvery laugh.

"You are pleased to laugh constantly,"—returned Egór Kapítonitch.—"However, when should a person laugh, if not at your age?"

"Egór Kapítonitch, don't get angry, my dear man! Akh, I'm tired; allow me to sit down. . . ."

Nadézhda Alexyéevna dropped into an armchair, and playfully pulled her hat down over her very eyes.

Ipátoff led Vladímir Sergyéitch up to her.

"Permit me, Nadézhda Alexyéevna, to present to you our neighbour, Mr. Astákhoff, of whom you have, probably, heard a great deal."

Vladímir Sergyéitch made his bow, while Nadézhda Alexyéevna looked up at him from under the brim of her round hat.

"Nadézhda Alexyéevna Véretyeff, our neighbour,"—went on Ipátoff, turning to

Vladímir Sergyéitch.—"She lives here with her brother, Piótr Alexyéitch, a retired lieutenant of the Guards. She is a great friend of my sister-in-law, and bears good will to our household in general."

"A whole formal inventory,"—said Nadézhda Alexyéevna, laughing, and, as before, scanning Vladímir Sergyéitch from under her hat.

But, in the meantime, Vladímir Sergyéitch was thinking to himself: "Why, this is a very pretty woman also." And, in fact, Nadézhda Alexyéevna was a very charming young girl. Slender and graceful, she appeared much younger than she really was. She was already in her twenty-eighth year. She had a round face, a small head, fluffy fair hair, a sharp, almost audaciously upturned little nose, and merry, almost crafty little eyes. Mockery fairly glittered in them, and kindled in them in sparks. Her features, extremely vivacious and mobile, sometimes assumed an almost amusing expression; humour peered forth from them. Now and then, for the most part suddenly, a shade of pensiveness flitted across her face,—and at such times it became gentle and kindly; but she could not surrender herself long to meditation. She easily seized upon the ridiculous sides of people, and drew very respectable caricatures. Everybody had petted her ever since she was born, and that is something which is immediately perceptible; people who have been spoiled in childhood preserve a certain stamp to the end of their lives. Her brother loved her, although he asserted that she stung, not like a bee, but like a wasp; because a bee stings and then dies, whereas it signifies nothing for a wasp to sting. This comparison enraged her.

"Have you come here for long?"—she asked Vladímir Sergyéitch, dropping her eyes, and twisting her riding-whip in her hands.

"No; I intend to go away from here to-morrow."

"Whither?"

"Home."

"Home? Why, may I venture to ask?"

"What do you mean by 'why'? I have affairs at home which do not brook delay."

Nadézhda Alexyéevna looked at him.

"Are you such a . . . punctual man?"

"I try to be a punctual man,"—replied Vladímir Sergyéitch.—"In our sedate era, every honourable man *must* be sedate and punctual."

"That is perfectly just,"—remarked Ipátoff.—"Is n't that true Iván Ílitch?"

Iván Ílitch merely glanced at Ipátoff; but Egór Kapítonitch remarked: "Yes, that's so."

"'T is a pity,"—said Nadézhda Alexyéevna;—"precisely what we lack is a *jeune premier*. You know how to act comedy, I suppose?"

"I have never put my powers in that line to the test."

"I am convinced that you would act well. You have that sort of bearing . . . a stately mien, which is indispensable in a *jeune premier*. My brother and I are preparing to set up a theatre here. However, we shall not act comedies only: we shall act all sorts of things—dramas, ballets, and even tragedies. Why would n't Másha do for Cleopatra or Phèdre? Just look at her!"

Vladímir Sergyéitch turned round. . . . Márya Pávlovna was gazing thoughtfully into the distance, as she stood leaning her head against the door, with folded arms. . . . At that moment, her regular features really did suggest the faces of ancient statues. She did not catch Nadézhda Alexyéevna's last words; but, perceiving that the glances of all present were suddenly directed to her, she immediately divined what was going on, blushed, and was about to retreat into the drawing-room. . . . Nadézhda Alexyéevna briskly grasped her by the hand and, with the coquettish caressing action of a kitten, drew her toward her, and kissed that almost masculine hand. Márya Pávlovna flushed more vividly than before.

"Thou art always playing pranks, Nádya,"—she said.

"Did n't I speak the truth about thee? I am ready to appeal to all. . . . Well, enough, enough, I won't do it again. But I will say again,"—went on Nadézhda Alexyéevna, addressing Vladímir Sergyéitch,—"that it is a pity you are going away. We have a *jeune premier,* it is true; he calls himself so, but he is very bad."

"Who is he? permit me to inquire."

"Bodryakóff the poet. How can a poet be a *jeune premier?* In the first place, he dresses in the most frightful way; in the second place, he writes epigrams, and gets shy in the presence of every woman, even in mine. He lisps, one of his hands is always higher than his head, and I don't know what besides. Tell me, please, M'sieu Astákhoff, are all poets like that?"

Vladímir Sergyéitch drew himself up slightly.

"I have never known a single one of them, personally; but I must confess that I have never sought acquaintance with them."

"Yes, you certainly are a positive man. We shall have to take Bodryakóff; there's nothing else to be done. Other *jeunes premiers* are even worse. That one, at all events, will learn his part by heart. Másha, in addition to tragic rôles, will fill the post of prima donna. . . . You have n't heard her sing, have you, M'sieu Astákhoff?"

"No,"—replied Vladímir Sergyéitch, displaying his teeth in a smile; "and I did not know. . . ."

"What is the matter with thee to-day, Nádya?"—said Márya Pávlovna, with a look of displeasure.

Nadézhda Alexyéevna sprang to her feet.

"For Heaven's sake, Másha, do sing us something, please. . . . I won't let thee alone until thou singest us something, Másha dearest. I would sing myself, to entertain the visitors, but thou knowest what a bad voice I have. But, on the other hand, thou shalt see how splendidly I will accompany thee."

Márya Pávlovna made no reply.

"There's no getting rid of thee,"—she said at last.—"Like a spoiled child, thou art accustomed to have all thy caprices humoured. I will sing, if you like."

"Bravo, bravo!"—exclaimed Nadézhda Alexyéevna, clapping her hands.—"Let us go into the drawing-room, gentlemen.—And as for caprices,"—she added, laughing,—"I'll pay you off for that! Is it permissible to expose my weaknesses in the presence of strangers? Egór Kapítonitch, does Matryóna Márkovna shame you *thus* before people?"

"Matryóna Márkovna,"—muttered Egór Kapítonitch,—"is a very worthy lady; only, on the score of manners. . . ."

"Well, come along, come along!"—Nadézhda Alexyéevna interrupted him, and entered the drawing-room.

All followed her. She tossed off her hat and seated herself at the piano. Márya Pávlovna stood near the wall, a good way from Nadézhda Alexyéevna.

"Másha,"—said the latter, after reflecting a little,—"sing us 'The farm-hand is sowing the grain.' "[8]

Márya Pávlovna began to sing. Her voice was pure and powerful, and she sang well—simply, and without affectation. All listened to her with great attention, while Vladímir Sergyéitch could not conceal his amazement. When Márya Pávlovna had finished, he stepped up to her, and began to assure her that he had not in the least expected. . . .

"Wait, there's something more coming!"—Nadézhda Alexyéevna interrupted him.—"Másha, I will soothe thy Topknot[9] soul:—Now sing us 'Humming, humming in the trees.' "

"Are you a Little Russian?"—Vladímir Sergyéitch asked her.

"I am a native of Little Russia," she replied, and began to sing "Humming, humming."

At first she uttered the words in an indifferent manner; but the mournfully passionate lay of her fatherland gradually began to stir her, her cheeks flushed scarlet, her glance flashed, her voice rang out fervently. She finished.

"Good heavens! How well thou hast sung that!"—said Nadézhda Alexyéevna, bending over the keys.—"What a pity that my brother was not here!"

"Márya Pávlovna instantly dropped her eyes, and laughed with her customary bitter little laugh.

"You must give us something more,"—remarked Ipátoff.

"Yes, if you will be so good,"—added Vladímir Sergyéitch.

"Excuse me, I will not sing any more to-day,"—said Márya Pávlovna, and left the room.

Nadézhda Alexyéevna gazed after her, first reflected, then smiled, began to pick out "The farm-hand is sowing the grain" with one finger, then suddenly began to play a brilliant polka, and without finishing it, struck a loud chord, clapped to the lid of the piano, and rose.

" 'T is a pity that there is no one to dance with!"—she exclaimed.—"It would be just the thing!"

Vladímir Sergyéitch approached her.

"What a magnificent voice Márya Pávlovna has,"—he remarked;—"and with how much feeling she sings!"

"And are you fond of music?"

"Yes. . .very."

"Such a learned man, and you are fond of music!"

"But what makes you think that I am learned?"

"Akh, yes; excuse me, I am always forgetting that you are a positive man. But where has Márya Pávlovna gone? Wait, I'll go after her."

And Nadézhda Alexyéevna fluttered out of the drawing-room.

---

[8] A little Russian song.

[9] The popular nickname among Great Russians for the Little Russians.

"A giddy-pate, as you see,"—said Ipátoff, coming up to Vladímir Sergyéitch;—"but the kindest heart. And what an education she received you cannot imagine; she can express herself in all languages. Well, they are wealthy people, so that is comprehensible."

"Yes,"—articulated Vladímir Sergyéitch, abstractedly,—"she is a very charming girl. But permit me to inquire, Was your wife also a native of Little Russia?"

"Yes, she was, sir. My late wife was a Little Russian, as her sister Márya Pávlovna is. My wife, to tell the truth, did not even have a perfectly pure pronunciation; although she was a perfect mistress of the Russian language, still she did not express herself quite correctly; they pronounce *i, ui,* there, and their *kha* and *zhe* are peculiar also, you know; well, Márya Pávlovna left her native land in early childhood. But the Little Russian blood is still perceptible, is n't it?"

"Márya Pávlovna sings wonderfully,"—remarked Vladímir Sergyéitch.

"Really, it is not bad. But why don't they bring us some tea? And where have the young ladies gone? 'T is time to drink tea."

The young ladies did not return very speedily. In the meantime, the samovár was brought, the table was laid for tea. Ipátoff sent for them. Both came in together. Márya Pávlovna seated herself at the table to pour the tea, while Nadézhda Alexyéevna walked to the door opening on the terrace, and began to gaze out into the garden. The brilliant summer day had been succeeded by a clear, calm evening; the sunset was flaming; the broad pond, half flooded with its crimson, stood a motionless mirror, grandly reflecting in its deep bosom all the airy depths of the sky, and the house, and the trees turned upside down, and had grown black, as it were. Everything was silent round about. There was no noise anywhere.

"Look, how beautiful!"—said Nadézhda Alexyéevna to Vladímir Sergyéitch, as he approached her;—"down below there, in the pond, a star has kindled its fire by the side of the light in the house; the house-light is red, the other is golden. And yonder comes grandmamma,"—she added in a loud voice.

From behind a clump of lilac-bushes a small calash made its appearance. Two men were drawing it. In it sat an old lady, all wrapped up, all doubled over, with her head resting on her breast. The ruffle of her white cap almost completely concealed her withered and contracted little face. The tiny calash halted in front of the terrace. Ipátoff emerged from the drawing-room, and his little daughters ran out after him. They had been constantly slipping from room to room all the evening, like little mice.

"I wish you good evening, dear mother,"—said Ipátoff, stepping up close to the old woman, and elevating his voice.—"How do you feel?"

"I have come to take a look at you,"—said the old woman in a dull voice, and with an effort.—"What a glorious evening it is. I have been asleep all day, and now my feet have begun to ache. Okh, those feet of mine! They don't serve me, but they ache."

"Permit me, dear mother, to present to you our neighbour, Astákhoff, Vladímir Sergyéitch."

"I am very glad to meet you,"—returned the old woman, scanning him with her large, black, but dim-sighted eyes.—"I beg that you will love my son. He is a fine man; I gave him what education I could; of course, I did the best a woman could. He is still somewhat flighty, but, God willing, he will grow steady, and 't is high time he did; 't is time for me to surrender matters to him. Is that you, Nádya?"—added the old woman, glancing at Nadézhda Alexyéevna.

"Yes, grandmamma."

"And is Másha pouring tea?"

"Yes, grandmamma, she is pouring tea."

"And who else is there?"

"Iván Ilitch, and Egór Kapítonitch."

"The husband of Matryóna Márkovna?"

"Yes, dear mother."

The old woman mumbled with her lips.

"Well, good. But why is it, Mìkhaíl, that I can't manage to get hold of the overseer? Order him to come to me very early to-morrow morning; I shall have a great deal of business to arrange with him. I see that nothing goes as it should with you, without me. Come, that will do, I am tired; take me away.... Farewell, bátiushka;[10] I don't remember your name and patronymic,"—she added, addressing Vladímir Sergyéitch. "Pardon an old woman. But don't come with me, grandchildren, it is n't necessary. All you care for is to run all the time. Másha spoils you. Well, start on."

The old woman's head, which she had raised with difficulty, fell back again on her breast....

The tiny calash started, and rolled softly away.

"How old is your mother?"—inquired Vladímir Sergyéitch.

"Only in her seventy-third year; but it is twenty-six years since her legs failed her; that happened soon after the demise of my late father. But she used to be a beauty."

All remained silent for a while.

Suddenly, Nadézhda Alexyéevna gave a start.

"Was that—a bat flying past? Aï, what a fright!"

And she hastily returned to the drawing-room.

"It is time for me to go home, Mikhaíl Nikoláitch; order my horse to be saddled."

"And it is time for me to be going, too,"—remarked Vladímir Sergyéitch.

"Where are you going?"—said Ipátoff.—"Spend the night here. Nadézhda Alexyéevna has only two versts to ride, while you have fully twelve. And what's your hurry, too, Nadézhda Alexyéevna? Wait for the moon; it will soon be up now. It will be lighter to ride."

"Very well,"—said Nadézhda Alexyéevna.—"It is a long time since I had a moonlight ride."

"And will you spend the night?"—Ipátoff asked Vladímir Sergyéitch.

"Really, I don't know.... However, if I do not incommode you...."

---

10 Literally, "dear little father": the genuinely Russian mode of address to a man of any class, as *mátushka* ("dear little mother") is for women of all classes.

"Not in the least, I assure you; I will immediately order a chamber to be prepared for you."

"But it is nice to ride by moonlight,"—began Nadézhda Alexyéevna, as soon as candles were brought, tea was served, and Ipátoff and Egór Kapítonitch had sat down to play preference together, while The Folding Soul seated himself silently beside them:—"especially through the forest, between the walnut-trees. It is both terrifying and agreeable, and what a strange play of light and shade there is—it always seems as though some one were stealing up behind you, or in front of you. . . ."

Vladímir Sergyéitch smirked condescendingly.

"And here's another thing,"—she went on;—"have you ever happened to sit beside the forest on a warm, dark, tranquil night? At such times it always seems to me as though two persons were hotly disputing in an almost inaudible whisper, behind me, close at my very ear."

"That is the blood beating,"—said Ipátoff.

"You describe in a very poetical way,"—remarked Vladímir Sergyéitch. Nadézhda Alexyéevna glanced at him.

"Do you think so? . . . In that case, my description would not please Másha."

"Why?" Is not Márya Pávlovna fond of poetry?"

"No; she thinks all that sort of thing is made up—is all false; and she does not like that."

"A strange reproach!"—exclaimed Vladímir Sergyéitch. "Made up! How could it be otherwise? But, after all, what are composers for?"

"Well, there, that's exactly the point; but I am sure you cannot be fond of poetry."

"On the contrary, I love good verses, when they really are good and melodious, and—how shall I say it?—when they present ideas, thoughts. . . ."

Márya Pávlovna rose.

Nadézhda Alexyéevna turned swiftly toward her.

"Whither art thou going, Másha?"

"To put the children to bed. It is almost nine o'clock."

"But cannot they go to bed without thee?"

But Márya Pávlovna took the children by the hand and went away with them.

"She is out of sorts to-day,"—remarked Nadézhda Alexyéevna;—"and I know why,"—she added in an undertone.—"But it will pass off."

"Allow me to inquire,"—began Vladímir Sergyéitch,—"where you intend to spend the winter?"

"Perhaps here, perhaps in Petersburg. It seems to me that I shall be bored in Petersburg."

"In Petersburg! Good gracious! How is that possible?"

And Vladímir Sergyéitch began to describe all the comforts, advantages, and charm of life in our capital. Nadézhda Alexyéevna listened to him with attention, never taking her eyes from him. She seemed to be committing his features to memory, and laughed to herself from time to time.

"I see that you are very eloquent,"—she said at last.—"I shall be obliged to spend the winter in Petersburg."

"You will not repent of it,"—remarked Vladímir Sergyéitch.

"I never repent of anything; it is not worth the bother. If you have perpetrated a blunder, try to forget it as speedily as possible—that's all."

"Allow me to ask,"—began Vladímir Sergyéitch, after a brief pause, and in the French language;—"have you known Márya Pávlovna long?"

"Allow me to ask,"—retorted Nadézhda Alexyéevna, with a swift laugh;—"why you have put precisely that question to me in French?"

"Because...for no particular reason. ..."

Again Nadézhda Alexyéevna laughed.

"No; I have not known her very long. But she is a remarkable girl, is n't she?"

"She is very original,"—said Vladímir Sergyéitch, through his teeth.

"And in your mouth—in the mouth of positive persons—does that constitute praise? I do not think so. Perhaps I seem original to you, also? But,"—she added, rising from her seat and casting a glance through the window,—"the moon must have risen; that is its light on the poplars. It is time to depart. ...I will go and give order that Little Beauty shall be saddled."

"He is already saddled, ma'am,"—said Nadézhda Alexyéevna's groom, stepping out from the shadow in the garden into a band of light which fell on the terrace.

"Ah! Well, that 's very good, indeed! Másha, where art thou? Come and bid me good-bye."

Márya Pávlovna made her appearance from the adjoining room. The men rose from the card-table.

"So you are going already?"—inquired Ipátoff.

"I am; it is high time."

She approached the door leading into the garden.

"What a night!"—she exclaimed.—"Come here; hold out your face to it; do you feel how it seems to breathe upon you? And what fragrance! all the flowers have waked up now. They have waked up—and we are preparing to go to sleep. ...Ah, by the way, Másha,"—she added:—"I have told Vladímir Sergyéitch, you know, that thou art not fond of poetry. And now, farewell...yonder comes my horse. ..."

And she ran briskly down the steps of the terrace, swung herself lightly into the saddle, said, "Good-bye until to-morrow!"—and lashing her horse on the neck with her riding-switch, she galloped off in the direction of the dam. ...The groom set off at a trot after her.

All gazed after her. ...

"Until to-morrow!"—her voice rang out once more from behind the poplars.

The hoof-beats were still audible for a long time in the silence of the summer night. At last, Ipátoff proposed that they should go into the house again.

"It really is very nice out of doors,"—he said;—"but we must finish our game."

All obeyed him. Vladímir Sergyéitch began to question Márya Pávlovna as to why she did not like poetry.

"Verses do not please me,"—she returned, with apparent reluctance.

"But perhaps you have not read many verses?"

"I have not read them myself, but I have had them read to me."

"And is it possible that they did not please you?"

"No; none of them."

"Not even Púshkin's verses?"

"Not even Púshkin's."

"Why?"

Márya Pávlovna made no answer; but Ipátoff, twisting round across the back of his chair, remarked, with a good-natured laugh, that she not only did not like verses, but sugar also, and, in general, could not endure anything sweet.

"But, surely, there are verses which are not sweet,"—retorted Vladímir Sergyéitch.

"For example?"—Márya Pávlovna asked him.

Vladímir Sergyéitch scratched behind his ear. . . . He himself knew very few verses by heart, especially of the sort which were not sweet.

"Why, here now,"—he exclaimed at last;—"do you know Púshkin's 'The Upas-Tree'?[11] No? That poem cannot possibly be called sweet."

"Recite it,"—said Márya Pávlovna, dropping her eyes.

Vladímir Sergyéitch first stared at the ceiling, frowned, mumbled something to himself, and at last recited "The Upas-Tree."

After the first four lines, Márya Pávlovna slowly raised her eyes, and when Vladímir Sergyéitch ended, she said, with equal slowness:

"Please recite it again."

"So these verses do please you?"—asked Vladímir Sergyéitch.

"Recite it again."

Vladímir Sergyéitch repeated "The Upas-Tree." Márya Pávlovna rose, went out into the next room, and returned with a sheet of paper, an inkstand and a pen.

"Please write that down for me,"—she said to Vladímir Sergyéitch.

"Certainly; with pleasure,"—he replied, beginning to write.—"But I must confess that I am puzzled to know why these verses have pleased you so. I recited them simply to prove to you that not all verses are sweet."

"So am I!"—exclaimed Ipátoff.—"What do you think of those verses, Iván Ílitch?"

Iván Ílitch, according to his wont, merely glanced at Ipátoff, but did not utter a word.

"Here, ma'am,—I have finished,"—said Vladímir Sergyéitch, as he placed an interrogation-point at the end of the last line.

Márya Pávlovna thanked him, and carried the written sheet off to her own room.

Half an hour later supper was served, and an hour later all the guests dispersed to their rooms. Vladímir Sergyéitch had repeatedly addressed Márya Pávlovna; but it was difficult to conduct a conversation with her, and his anecdotes did not seem to interest her greatly. He probably would have fallen asleep as soon as he got into bed had he not been hindered by his neighbour, Egór Kapítonitch. Matryóna Márkovna's husband, after he was fully undressed and had got into

---

11 The poem, after describing the deadly qualities of the upas-tree, narrates how a potentate sent one of his slaves to bring him flowers from it. The slave, thoroughly aware of his danger, fulfilled his sovereign's behest, returned with branches of the tree, and dropped dead.

bed, talked for a very long time with his servant, and kept bestowing reprimands on him. Every word he uttered was perfectly audible to Vladímir Sergyéitch: only a thin partition separated them.

"Hold the candle in front of thy breast,"—said Egór Kapítonitch, in a querulous voice;—"hold it so that I can see thy face. Thou hast aged me, aged me, thou conscienceless man—hast aged me completely."

"But, for mercy's sake, Egór Kapítonitch, how have I aged you?"—the servant's dull and sleepy voice made itself heard.

"How? I'll tell thee how. How many times have I said to thee: 'Mítka,' I have said to thee, 'when thou goest a-visiting with me, always take two garments of each sort, especially'. . .hold the candle in front of thy breast. . .'especially underwear.' And what hast thou done to me to-day?"

"What, sir?"

" 'What, sir?' What am I to put on to-morrow?"

"Why, the same things you wore to-day, sir."

"Thou hast aged me, malefactor, aged me. I was almost beside myself with the heat to-day, as it was. Hold the candle in front of thy breast, I tell thee, and don't sleep when thy master is talking to thee."

"Well, but Matryóna Márkovna said, sir, 'That 's enough. Why do you always take such a mass of things with you? They only get worn out for nothing. ' "

"Matryóna Márkovna. . . .Is it a woman's business, pray, to enter into that? You have aged me. Okh, you have made me old before my time!"

"Yes; and Yakhím said the same thing, sir."

"What 's that thou saidst?"

"I say, Yakhím said the same thing, sir."

"Yakhím! Yakhím!"—repeated Egór Kapítonitch, reproachfully.—"Ekh, you have aged me, ye accursed, and don't even know how to speak Russian intelligibly. Yakhím! Who 's Yakhím! Efrím,—well, that might be allowed to pass, it is permissible to say that; because the genuine Greek name is Evthímius, dost understand me?. . .Hold the candle in front of thy breast. . . .So, for the sake of brevity, thou mayest say Efrím, if thou wilt, but not Yakhím by any manner of means. Yákhim!"[12] Egór Kapítonitch, emphasising the syllable *Ya*.—"You have aged me, ye malefactors. Hold the candle in front of thy breast!"

And for a long time, Egór Kapítonitch continued to berate his servant, in spite of sighs, coughs, and other tokens of impatience on the part of Vladímir Sergyéitch. . . .

At last he dismissed his Mítka, and fell asleep; but Vladímir Sergyéitch was no better off for that: Egór Kapítonitch snored so mightily and in so deep a voice, with such playful transitions from high tones to the very lowest, with such accompanying whistlings, and even snappings, that it seemed as though the very partition were shaking in response to him; poor Vladímir Sergyéitch almost wept. It was very stifling in the chamber which had been allotted to him, and the feather-bed whereon he was lying embraced his whole body in a sort of crawling heat.

12 It should be Akím, popular for Iakínthos, Hyacinth.

At last, in despair, Vladímir Sergyéitch rose, opened the window, and began with avidity to inhale the nocturnal freshness. The window looked out on the park. It was light overhead, the round face of the full moon was now clearly reflected in the pond, and stretched itself out in a long, golden sheaf of slowly transfused spangles. On one of the paths Vladímir Sergyéitch espied a figure in woman's garb; he looked more intently; it was Márya Pávlovna; in the moonlight her face seemed pale. She stood motionless, and suddenly began to speak. . . . Vladímir Sergyéitch cautiously put out his head. . . .

> "But a man—with glance imperious—
> Sent a man to the Upas-tree. . . ."

reached his ear. . . .

"Come,"—he thought,—"the verses must have taken effect. . . ."

And he began to listen with redoubled attention. . . . But Márya Pávlovna speedily fell silent, and turned her face more directly toward him; he could distinguish her large, dark eyes, her severe brows and lips. . . .

Suddenly, she started, wheeled round, entered the shadow cast by a dense wall of lofty acacias, and disappeared. Vladímir Sergyéitch stood for a considerable time at the window, then got into bed again, but did not fall asleep very soon.

"A strange being,"—he thought, as he tossed from side to side;—"and yet they say that there is nothing particular in the provinces. . . . The idea! A strange being! I shall ask her to-morrow what she was doing in the park."

And Egór Kapítonitch continued to snore as before.

III

On the following morning Vladímir Sergyéitch awoke quite late, and immediately after the general tea and breakfast in the dining-room, drove off home to finish his business on his estate, in spite of all old Ipátoff's attempts to detain him. Márya Pávlovna also was present at the tea; but Vladímir Sergyéitch did not consider it necessary to question her concerning her late stroll of the night before; he was one of the people who find it difficult to surrender themselves for two days in succession to any unusual thoughts and assumptions whatsoever. He would have been obliged to discuss verses, and the so-called "poetical" mood wearied him very quickly. He spent the whole day until dinner in the fields, ate with great appetite, dozed off, and when he woke up, tried to take up the clerk's accounts; but before he had finished the first page, he ordered his tarantás to be harnessed, and set off for Ipátoff's. Evidently, even positive people do not bear about in their breasts hearts of stone, and they are no more fond of being bored than other plain mortals.

As he drove upon the dam he heard voices and the sound of music. They were singing Russian ballads in chorus in Ipátoff's house. He found the whole company which he had left in the morning on the terrace; all, Nadézhda Alexyéevna among the rest, were sitting in a circle around a man of two-and-thirty—a swarthy-skinned, black-eyed, black-haired man in a velvet jacket, with a scarlet kerchief carelessly knotted about his neck, and a guitar in his hands. This was Piótr Alexyéevitch Véretyeff, brother of Nadézhda Alexyéevna. On catching sight of Vladímir Sergyéitch, old Ipátoff advanced to meet him with a joyful cry, led him up to Véretyeff, and introduced them to each other. After exchanging the customary greetings with his new acquaintance, Astákhoff made a respectful bow to the latter's sister.

"We 're singing songs in country fashion, Vladímir Sergyéitch,"—began Ipátoff, and pointing to Véretyeff he added:—"Piótr Alexyéitch is our leader,—and what a leader! Just you listen to him!"

"This is very pleasant,"—replied Vladímir Sergyéitch.

"Will not you join the choir?"—Nadézhda Alexyéevna asked him.

"I should be heartily glad to do so, but I have no voice."

"That does n't matter! See, Egór Kapítonitch is singing, and I 'm singing. All you have to do is to chime in. Pray, sit down; and do thou strike up, my dear fellow!"

"What song shall we sing now?"—said Véretyeff, thrumming the guitar; and suddenly stopping short, he looked at Márya Pávlovna, who was sitting by his side.—"I think it is your turn now,"—he said to her.

"No; do you sing,"—replied Márya Pávlovna.

"Here 's a song now: 'Adown dear Mother Volga' "—said Vladímir Sergyéitch, with importance.

"No, we will save that up for the last,"—replied Véretyeff, and tinkling the strings of the guitar, he struck up, in slow measure, "The sun is setting."

He sang splendidly, dashingly, and blithely. His manly face, already expressive, became still more animated when he sang; now and then he shrugged his shoulders, suddenly pressed the strings with his palm, raised his arm, shook his curls, and darted a falcon-like look around him. More than once in Moscow he had seen the famous Ilyá, and he imitated him. The chorus chimed in lustily. Márya Pávlovna's voice separated itself in a melodious flood from the other voices; it seemed to drag them after it; but she would not sing alone, and Véretyeff remained the leader to the end.

They sang a great many other songs. . . .

In the meantime, along with the evening shadows, a thunder-storm drew on. From noonday it had been steaming hot, and thunder had kept rumbling in the distance; but now a broad thunder-cloud, which had long lain like a leaden pall on the very rim of the horizon, began to increase and show itself above the crests of the trees, the stifling air began to quiver more distinctly, shaken more and more violently by the approaching storm; the wind rose, rustled the foliage abruptly, died into silence, again made a prolonged clamour, and began to roar; a surly gloom flitted over the earth, swiftly dispelling the last reflection of the sunset glow; dense clouds suddenly floated up, as though rending themselves free, and sailed across the sky; a fine rain began to patter down, the lightning flashed in a red flame, and the thunder rumbled heavily and angrily.

"Let us go,"—said old Ipátoff,—"or we shall be drenched."

All rose.

"Directly!"—exclaimed Piótr Alexyéitch.—"One more song, the last. Listen:

"Akh, thou house, thou house of mine,
Thou new house of mine. . . ."

he struck up in a loud voice, briskly striking the strings of the guitar with his whole hand. "My new house of maple-wood," joined in the chorus, as though reluctantly carried away. Almost at the same moment, the rain began to beat down in streams; but Véretyeff sang "My house" to the end. From time to time, drowned by the claps of thunder, the dashing ballad seemed more dashing than ever beneath the noisy rattle and gurgling of the rain. At last the final detonation of the chorus rang out—and the whole company ran, laughing, into the drawing-room. Loudest of all laughed the little girls, Ipátoff's daughters, as they shook the rain-drops from their frocks. But, by way of precaution, Ipátoff closed the window, and locked the door; and Egór Kapítonitch lauded him, remarking that Matryóna Márkovna also always gave orders to shut up whenever there was a thunder-storm, because electricity is more capable of acting in an empty space. Bodryakóff looked him straight in the face, stepped aside, and overturned a chair. Such trifling mishaps were constantly happening to him.

The thunder-storm passed over very soon. The doors and windows were opened again, and the rooms were filled with moist fragrance. Tea was brought. After tea the old men sat down to cards again. Iván Ílitch joined them, as usual. Vladímir Sergyéitch was about to go to Márya Pávlovna, who was sitting at the window with Véretyeff; but Nadézhda Alexyéevna called him to her, and immediately entered into a fervent discussion with him about Petersburg and Petersburg life. She attacked it; Vladímir Sergyéitch began to defend it. Nadézhda Alexyéevna appeared to be trying to keep him by her side.

"What are you wrangling about?"—inquired Véretyeff, rising and approaching them.

He swayed lazily from side to side as he walked; in all his movements there was perceptible something which was not exactly carelessness, nor yet exactly fatigue.

"Still about Petersburg,"—replied Nadézhda Alexyéevna.—"Vladímir Sergyéitch cannot sufficiently praise it."

"'T is a fine town,"—remarked Véretyeff;—"but, in my opinion, it is nice everywhere. By Heaven, it is. If one only has two or three women, and—pardon my frankness—wine, a man really has nothing left to wish for."

"You surprise me,"—retorted Vladímir Sergyéitch. "Can it be possible that you are really of one opinion, that there does not exist for the cultured man. . . ."

"Perhaps. . .in fact. . .I agree with you,"—interrupted Véretyeff, who, notwithstanding all his courtesy, had a habit of not listening to the end of retorts;—"but that 's not in my line; I 'm not a philosopher."

"Neither am I a philosopher,"—replied Vladímir Sergyéitch;—"and I have not the slightest desire to be one; but here it is a question of something entirely different."

Véretyeff cast an abstracted glance at his sister, and she, with a faint laugh, bent toward him, and whispered in a low voice:

"Petrúsha, my dear, imitate Egór Kapítonitch for us, please."

Véretyeff's face instantly changed, and, Heaven knows by what miracle, became remarkably like the face of Egór Kapítonitch, although the features of the two faces had absolutely nothing in common, and Véretyeff himself barely wrinkled up his nose and pulled down the corners of his lips.

"Of course,"—he began to whisper, in a voice which was the exact counterpart of Egór Kapítonitch's,—"Matryóna Márkovna is a severe lady on the score of manners; but, on the other hand, she is a model wife. It is true that no matter what I may have said. . . ."

"The Biriúloff girls know it all,"—put in Nadézhda Alexyéevna, hardly restraining her laughter.

"Everything is known on the following day,"—replied Véretyeff, with such a comical grimace, with such a perturbed sidelong glance, that even Vladímir Sergyéitch burst out laughing.

"I see that you possess great talent for mimicry,"—he remarked.

Véretyeff passed his hand over his face, his features resumed their ordinary expression, while Nadézhda Alexyéevna exclaimed:

"Oh, yet! he can mimic any one whom he wishes. . . . He 's a master hand at that."

"And would you be able to imitate me, for example?"—inquired Vladímir Sergyéitch.

"I should think so!"—returned Nadézhda Alexyéevna:—"of course."

"Akh, pray do me the favour to represent me,"—said Astákhoff, turning to Véretyeff.—"I beg that you will not stand on ceremony."

"And so you too have believed her?"—replied Véretyeff, slightly screwing up one eye, and imparting to his voice the sound of Astákhoff's voice, but so cautiously and slightly that only Nadézhda Alexyéevna noticed it, and bit her lips.—"Please do not believe her; she will tell you other untrue things about me."

"And if you only knew what an actor he is!"—pursued Nadézhda Alexyéevna:—"he plays every conceivable sort of a part. And so splendidly! He is our stage-manager, and our prompter, and everything you like. It 's a pity that you are going away so soon."

"Sister, thy partiality blinds thee,"—remarked Véretyeff, in a pompous tone, but still with the same touch of Astákhoff.—"What will Mr. Astákhoff think of thee?—He will regard thee as a rustic."

"No, indeed,"—Vladímir Sergyéitch was beginning. . . .

"See here, Petrúsha,"—interposed Nadézhda Alexyéevna;—"please show us how a drunken man is utterly unable to get his handkerchief out of his pocket; or no: show us, rather, how a boy catches a fly on the window, and how it buzzes under his fingers."

"Thou art a regular child,"—replied Véretyeff.

Nevertheless he rose, and stepping to the window, beside which Márya Pávlovna was sitting, he began to pass his hand across the panes, and represent how a small boy catches a fly.

The accuracy with which he imitated its pitiful squeak was really amazing. It seemed as though a live fly were actually struggling under his fingers. Nadézhda Alexyéevna burst out laughing, and gradually every one in the room got to laughing. Márya Pávlovna's face alone underwent no change, not even her lips quivered. She sat with downcast eyes, but raised them at last, and casting a serious glance at Véretyeff, she muttered through her set teeth:

"What possesses you to make a clown of yourself?"

Véretyeff instantly turned away from the window, and, after standing still for a moment in the middle of the room, he went out on the terrace, and thence into the garden, which had already grown perfectly dark.

"How amusing that Piótr Alexyéitch is!"—exclaimed Egór Kapítonitch, slapping down the seven of trumps with a flourish on some one else's ace.— "Really, he's very amusing!"

Nadézhda Alexyéevna rose, and hastily approaching Márya Pávlovna, asked her in an undertone:

"What didst thou say to my brother?"

"Nothing,"—replied the other.

"What dost thou mean by 'nothing'? Impossible."

And after waiting a little, Nadézhda Alexyéevna said: "Come!"—took Márya Pávlovna by the hand, forced her to rise, and went off with her into the garden.

Vladímir Sergyéitch gazed after the two young girls not without perplexity. But they were not absent long; a quarter of an hour later they returned, and Piótr Alexyéitch entered the room with them.

"What a splendid night!" exclaimed Nadézhda Alexyéevna, as she entered.— "How beautiful it is in the garden!"

"Akh, yes. By the way,"—said Vladímir Sergyéitch;—"allow me to inquire, Márya Pávlovna, whether it was you whom I saw in the garden last night?"

Márya Pávlovna gave him a swift look straight in the eyes.

"Moreover, so far as I could make out, you were declaiming Púshkin's 'The Upas-Tree.'"

Véretyeff frowned slightly, and he also began to stare at Astákhoff.

"It really was I,"—said Márya Pávlovna;—"only, I was not declaiming anything; I never declaim."

"Perhaps it seemed so to me,"—began Vladímir Sergyéitch;—"but. . . ."

"It did seem so to you?"—remarked Márya Pávlovna, coldly.

"What's 'The Upas-Tree'?"—inquired Nadézhda Alexyéevna.

"Why, don't you knew?—retorted Astákhoff.—"Do you mean to say you don't remember Púshkin's verses: 'On the unhealthy, meagre soil'?"

"Somehow I don't remember. . . . That upas-tree is a poisonous tree, is n't it?" "Yes."

"Like the datura. . . . Dost remember, Másha, how beautiful the datura were on our balcony, in the moonlight, with their long, white blossoms? Dost remember what fragrance poured from them,—so sweet, insinuating, and insidious?"

"An insidious fragrance!"—exclaimed Vladímir Sergyéitch.

"Yes; insidious. What are you surprised at? They say it is dangerous, but it is attractive. Why can evil attract? Evil should not be beautiful."

"Oh, what theories!"—remarked Piótr Alexyéitch;—"how far away we have got from verses!"

"I recited those verses yesterday evening to Márya Pávlovna," interposed Vladímir Sergyéitch;—"and they pleased her greatly."

"Akh, please recite them,"—said Nadézhda Alexyéevna.

"Certainly, madam."

And Astákhoff recited "The Upas-Tree.'

"Too bombastic,"—ejaculated Véretyeff, as though against his will, as soon as Vladímir Sergyéitch had finished.

"The poem is too bombastic?"

"No, not the poem. . . . Excuse me, it seems to me that you do not recite with sufficient simplicity. The thing speaks for itself; however, I may be mistaken."

"No, thou art not mistaken,"—said Nadézhda Alexyéevna, pausing between her words.

"Oh, yes; that is a matter of course! In thy eyes I am a genius, an extremely gifted man, who knows everything, can do everything; unfortunately, he is overcome with laziness; is n't that so?"

Nadézhda Alexyéevna merely shook her head.

"I shall not quarrel with you; you must know best about that,"—remarked Vladímir Sergyéitch, somewhat sulkily.—"That 's not in my line."

"I made a mistake, pardon me,"—ejaculated Véretyeff, hastily.

In the meantime, the game of cards had come to an end.

"Akh, by the way,"—said Ipátoff, as he rose;—"Vladímir Sergyéitch, one of the local landed proprietors, a neighbour, a very fine and worthy man, Akílin, Gavríla Stepánitch, has commissioned me to ask you whether you will not do him the honour to be present at his ball,—that is, I just put it so, for beauty of style, and said 'ball,' but it is only an evening party with dancing, quite informal. He would have called upon you himself without fail, only he was afraid of disturbing you."

"I am much obliged to the gentleman,"—returned Vladímir Sergyéitch;—"but it is imperatively necessary that I should return home. . . ."

"Why—but when do you suppose the ball takes place? 'T is to-morrow. To-morrow is Gavríla Stepánitch's Name-day. One day more won't matter, and how much pleasure you will give him! And it 's only ten versts from here. If you will allow, we will take you thither."

"Really, I don't know,"—began Vladímir Sergyéitch.—"And are you going?"

"The whole family! And Nadézhda Alexyéevna and Piótr Alexyéitch,—everybody is going!"

"You may invite me on the spot for the fifth quadrille, if you like,"—remarked Nadézhda Alexyéevna.—"The first four are already bespoken."

"You are very kind; and are you already engaged for the mazurka?"

"I? Let me think . . . no, I think I am not."

"In that case, if you will be so kind, I should like to have the honour. ...."

"That means that you will go? Very good. Certainly."

"Bravo!"—exclaimed Ipátoff.—"Well, Vladímir Sergyéitch, you have put us under an obligation. Gavrílo Stepánitch will simply go into raptures. Is n't that so, Iván Ílitch?"

Iván Ílitch would have preferred to hold his peace, according to his wont, but thought it better to utter a sound of approval.

"What possessed thee,"—said Piótr Alexyéitch an hour later to his sister, as he sat with her in a light two-wheeled cart, which he was driving himself,—"what possessed thee to saddle thyself with that sour-visaged fellow for the mazurka?"

"I have reasons of my own for that,"—replied Nadézhda Alexyéevna.

"What reasons?—permit me to inquire."

"That 's my secret."

"Oho!"

And with his whip he lightly flicked the horse, which was beginning to prick up its ears, snort, and shy. It was frightened by the shadow of a huge willow bush which fell across the road, dimly illuminated by the moon.

"And shalt thou dance with Másha?"—Nadézhda Alexyéevna, in her turn, questioned her brother.

"Yes," he said indifferently.

"Yes! yes!"—repeated Nadézhda Alexyéevna, reproachfully.—"You men,"— she added, after a brief pause,—"positively do not deserve to be loved by nice women."

"Dost think so? Well, and that sour-visaged Petersburger—does he deserve it?"

"Sooner than thou."

"Really!"

And Piótr Alexyéitch recited, with a sigh:

> "What a mission, O Creator,
> To be...the brother of a grown-up sister!"

Nadézhda Alexyéevna burst out laughing.

"I cause thee a great deal of trouble, there 's no denying that. I have a commission to thee."

"Really?—I had n't the slightest suspicion of that."

"I 'm speaking of Másha."

"On what score?"

Nadézhda Alexyéevna's face assumed a slight expression of pain.

"Thou knowest thyself,"—she said softly.

"Ah, I understand!—What 's to be done, Nadézhda Alexyéevna, ma'am? I love to drink with a good friend, ma'am sinful man that I am; I love it' ma'am."

"Stop, brother, please don't talk like that!...This is no jesting matter."

"Tram-tram-tam-poom!"—muttered Piótr Alexyéitch through his teeth.

"It is thy perdition, and thou jestest. ...."

> "The farm-hand is sowing the grain, his wife does not agree. ...."

struck up Piótr Alexyéitch loudly, slapped the horse with the reins, and it dashed onward at a brisk trot.

IV

On reaching home Véretyeff did not undress, and a couple of hours later, when the flush of dawn was just colouring the sky, he was no longer in the house.

Half-way between his estate and Ipátoff's on the very brink of a broad ravine, stood a small birch grove. The young trees grew very close together, and no axe had yet touched their graceful trunks; a shadow which was not dense, but continuous, spread from the tiny leaves on the soft, thin grass, all mottled with the golden heads of buttercups,[13] the white dots of wood-campanula, and the tiny deep-crimson crosses of wild pinks. The recently risen sun flooded the whole grove with a powerful though not brilliant light; dewdrops glittered everywhere, while here and there large drops kindled and glowed red; everything exhaled freshness, life, and that innocent triumph of the first moments of the morning, when everything is still so bright and still so silent. The only thing audible was the carolling voices of the larks above the distant fields, and in the grove itself two or three small birds were executing, in a leisurely manner, their brief songs, and then, apparently, listening to see how their performance had turned out. From the damp earth arose a strong, healthy scent; a pure, light breeze fluttered all about in cool gusts. Morning, glorious morning, breathed forth from everything—everything looked and smiled of the morning, like the rosy, freshly washed face of a baby who has just waked up.

Not far from the ravine, in the middle of a small glade, on an outspread cloak, sat Véretyeff. Márya Pávlovna was standing beside him, leaning against a birch-tree, with her hands clasped behind her.

Both were silent. Márya Pávlovna was gazing fixedly into the far distance; a white scarf had slipped from her head to her shoulders, the errant breeze was stirring and lifting the ends of her hastily-knotted hair. Véretyeff sat bent over, tapping the grass with a small branch.

"Well,"—he began at last,—'are you angry with me?"

Márya Pávlovna made no reply.

Véretyeff darted a glance at her.

"Másha, are you angry?"—he repeated.

Márya Pávlovna scanned him with a swift glance from head to foot, turned slightly away, and said:

"Yes."

"What for?"—asked Véretyeff, and flung away his branch.

Again Márya Pávlovna made no reply.

"But, as a matter of fact, you have a right to be angry with me,"—began Véretyeff, after a brief pause.—"You must regard me as a man who is not only frivolous, but even. . . ."

---

13 The unpoetical Russian name is "chicken-blindness" (night-blindness).

"You do not understand me,"—interrupted Márya Pávlovna.—"I am not in the least angry with you on my own account."

"On whose account, then?"

"On your own."

Véretyeff raised his head and laughed.

"Ah! I understand!"—he said.—"Again! again the thought is beginning to agitate you: 'Why don't I make something of myself?' Do you know what, Másha, you are a wonderful being; by Heaven, you are! You worry so much about other people and so little about yourself. There is not a bit of egoism in you; really, really there is n't. There 's no other girl in the world like you. It's a pity about one thing: I decidedly am not worthy of your affection; I say that without jesting."

"So much the worse for you. You feel and do nothing."—Again Véretyeff laughed.

"Másha, take your hand from behind your back, and give it to me,"—he said, with insinuating affection in his voice.

Márya Pávlovna merely shrugged her shoulders.

"Give me your beautiful, honest hand; I want to kiss it respectfully and tenderly. Thus does a giddy-pated scholar kiss the hand of his condescending tutor."

And Véretyeff reached out toward Márya Pávlovna.

"Enough of that!"—said she. "You are always laughing and jesting, and you will jest away your life like that."

"H'm! jest away my life! A new expression! But I hope, Márya Pávlovna, that you used the verb 'to jest' in the active sense?"

Márya Pávlovna contracted her brows.

"Enough of that, Véretyeff,—she repeated.

"To jest away life,"—went on Véretyeff, half rising;—"but you are imagining me as worse than I am; you are wasting your life in seriousness. Do you know, Másha, you remind me of a scene from Púshkin's 'Don Juan.' You have not read Púshkin's 'Don Juan'?"

"No."

"Yes, I had forgotten, you see, that you do not read verses.—In that poem guests come to a certain Laura; she drives them all away and remains alone with Carlos. The two go out on the balcony; the night is wonderful. Laura admires, and Carlos suddenly begins to demonstrate to her that she will grow old in course of time.—'Well,' replies Laura, 'it may be cold and rainy in Paris now, but here, with us, "the night is redolent of orange and of laurel." Why make guesses at the future?' Look around you, Másha; is it not beautiful here? See how everything is enjoying life, how young everything is. And are n't we young ourselves?"

Véretyeff approached Márya Pávlovna; she did not move away from him, but she did not turn her head toward him.

"Smile, Másha,"—he went on;—"only with your kind smile, not with your usual grin. I love your kind smile. Raise your proud, stern eyes.—What ails you? You turn away. Stretch out your hand to me, at least."

"Akh, Véretyeff,"—began Másha;—"you know that I do not understand how to express myself. You have told me about that Laura. But she was a woman, you see. . . . A woman may be pardoned for not thinking of the future."

"When you speak, Másha,"—returned Véretyeff,—"you blush incessantly with self-love and modesty: the blood fairly flows in a crimson flood into your cheeks. I 'm awfully fond of that in you."

Márya Pávlovna looked Véretyeff straight in the eye.

"Farewell,"—she said, and threw her scarf over her head.

Véretyeff held her back. "Enough, enough. Stay!"—he cried.—"Come, why are you going? Issue your commands! Do you want me to enter the service, to become an agriculturist? Do you want me to publish romances with accompaniment for the guitar; to print a collection of poems, or of drawings; to busy myself with painting, sculpture, dancing on the rope? I 'll do anything, anything, anything you command, if only you will be satisfied with me! Come, really now, Másha, believe me."

Again Márya Pávlovna looked at him.

"You will do all that in words only, not in deeds. You declare that you will obey me. . . ."

"Of course I do."

"You obey, but how many times have I begged you. . . ."

"What about?"

Márya Pávlovna hesitated.

"Not to drink liquor,"—she said at last.

Véretyeff laughed.

"Ekh, Másha! And you are at it, too! My sister is worrying herself to death over that also. But, in the first place, I 'm not a drunkard at all; and in the second place, do you know why I drink? Look yonder, at that swallow. . . . Do you see how boldly it manages its tiny body,—and hurls it wherever it wishes? Now it has soared aloft, now it has darted downward. It has even piped with joy: do you hear? So that is why I drink, Másha, in order to feel those same sensations which that swallow experiences. . . . Hurl yourself whithersoever you will, soar wheresoever you take a fancy. . . ."

"But to what end?"—interrupted Másha.

"What do you mean by that? What is one to live on then?"

"But is n't it possible to get along without liquor?"

"No, it is not; we are all damaged, rumpled. There 's passion. . . it produces the same effect. That 's why I love you."

"Like wine. . . . I 'm much obliged to you."

"No, Másha, I do not love you like wine. Stay, I 'll prove it to you sometime,—when we are married, say, and go abroad together. Do you know, I am planning in advance how I shall lead you in front of the Venus of Milo. At this point it will be appropriate to say:

> "And when she stands with serious eyes
> Before the Chyprian of Milos—
> Twain are they, and the marble in comparison
> Suffers, it would seem, affront. . . ."

"What makes me talk constantly in poetry to-day? It must be that this morning is affecting me. What air! 'T is exactly as though one were quaffing wine."

"Wine again,"—remarked Márya Pávlovna.

"What of that! A morning like this, and you with me, and not feel intoxicated! 'With serious eyes. . . .' Yes,"—pursued Véretyeff, gazing intently at Márya Pávlovna,—"that is so. . . . For I remember, I have beheld, rarely, but yet I have beheld these dark, magnificent eyes, I have beheld them tender! And how beautiful they are then! Come, don't turn away, Másha; pray, smile at least. . . show me your eyes merry, at all events, if they will not vouchsafe me a tender glance."

"Stop, Véretyeff,"—said Márya Pávlovna.—"Release me! It is time for me to go home."

"But I'm going to make you laugh,"—interposed Véretyeff; "by Heaven, I will make you laugh, Eh, by the way, yonder runs a hare. . . ."

"Where?"—asked Márya Pávlovna.

"Yonder, beyond the ravine, across the field of oats. Some one must have startled it; they don't run in the morning. I 'll stop it on the instant, if you like."

And Véretyeff whistled loudly. The hare immediately squatted, twitched its ears, drew up its fore paws, straightened itself up, munched, sniffed the air, and again began to munch with its lips. Véretyeff promptly squatted down on his heels, like the hare, and began to twitch his sniff, and munch like it. The hare passed its paws twice across its muzzle and shook itself,—they must have been wet with dew,—stiffened its ears, and bounded onward. Véretyeff rubbed his hands over his cheeks and shook himself also. . . . Márya Pávlovna could not hold out, and burst into a laugh.

"Bravo!"—cried Véretyeff, springing up. "Bravo! That 's exactly the point— you are not a coquette. Do you know, if any fashionable young lady had such teeth as you have she would laugh incessantly. But that 's precisely why I love you, Másha, because you are not a fashionable young lady, don't laugh without cause, and don't wear gloves on your hands, which it is a joy to kiss, because they are sunburned, and one feels their strength. . . . I love you, because you don't argue, because you are proud, taciturn, don't read books, don't love poetry. . . ."

"I 'll recite some verses to you, shall I?"—Márya Pávlovna interrupted him, with a certain peculiar expression on her face.

"Verses?"—inquired Véretyeff, in amazement.

"Yes, verses; the very ones which that Petersburg gentleman recited last night."

" 'The Upas-Tree' again?. . . So you really were declaiming in the garden, by night? That 's just like you. . . . But does it really please you so much?"

"Yes, it does."

"Recite it."

Márya Pávlovna was seized with shyness. . . .

"Recite it, recite it,"—repeated Véretyeff.

Márya Pávlovna began to recite; Véretyeff stood in front of her, with his arms folded on his breast, and bent himself to listen. At the first line Márya Pávlovna raised her eyes heavenward; she did not wish to encounter Véretyeff's gaze. She recited in her even, soft voice, which reminded one of the sound of a violincello; but when she reached the lines:

"And the poor slave expired at the feet
Of his invincible sovereign. ...."

her voice began to quiver, her impassive, haughty brows rose ingenuously, like those of a little girl, and her eyes, with involuntary devotion, fixed themselves on Véretyeff. ...

He suddenly threw himself at her feet and embraced her knees.

"I am thy slave"—he cried.—"I am at thy feet, thou art my sovereign, my goddess, my ox-eyed Hera, my Medea. ...."

Márya Pávlovna attempted to repulse him, but her hands sank helplessly in his thick curls, and, with a smile of confusion, she dropped her head on her breast. ...

V

Gavríla Stepánitch Akílin, at whose house the ball was appointed, belonged to the category of landed proprietors who evoked the admiration of the neighbours by their ingenuity in living well on very insignificant means. Although he did not own more than four hundred serfs, he was in the habit of entertaining the whole government in a huge stone mansion, with a tower and a flag on the tower, erected by himself. The property had descended to him from his father, and had never been distinguished for being well ordered; Gavríla Stepánitch had been an absentee for a long time—had been in the service in Petersburg. At last, twenty-five years before the date of our story, he returned to his native place, with the rank of Collegiate Assessor,[14] and, with a wife and three daughters, had simultaneously undertaken reorganisation and building operations, had gradually set up an orchestra, and had begun to give dinners. At first everybody had prophesied for him speedy and inevitable ruin; more than once rumours had become current to the effect that Gavríla Stepánitch's estate was to be sold under the hammer; but the years passed, dinners, balls, banquets, concerts, followed each other in their customary order, new buildings sprang out of the earth like mushrooms, and still Gavríla Stepánitch's estate was not sold under the hammer, and he himself continued to live as before, and had even grown stout of late.

Then the neighbours' gossip took another direction; they began to hint at certain vast sums which were said to be concealed; they talked of a treasure. ...

"And if he were only a good farmer, ..." so argued the nobles among themselves; "but that 's just what he is n't, you know! Not at all! So it is deserving of surprise, and incomprehensible." However that may have been, every one went very gladly to Gavríla Stepánitch's house. He received his guests cordially, and played cards for any stake they liked. He was a grey-haired little man, with a small, pointed head, a yellow face, and yellow eyes, always carefully shaven and perfumed with eau-de-cologne; both on ordinary days and on holidays he wore a roomy blue

14 The eighth (out of fourteen) in Peter the Great's Table of Ranks.

dress-coat, buttoned to the chin, a large stock, in which he had a habit of hiding his chin, and he was foppishly fastidious about his linen; he screwed up his eyes and thrust out his lips when he took snuff, and spoke very politely and softly, incessantly employing the letter *s*.[15]

In appearance, Gavríla Stepánitch was not distinguished by vivacity, and, in general, his exterior was not prepossessing, and he did not look like a clever man, although, at times, craft gleamed in his eye. He had settled his two elder daughters advantageously; the youngest was still at home, and of marriageable age. Gavríla Stepánitch also had a wife, an insignificant and wordless being.

At seven o'clock in the evening, Vladímir Sergyéitch presented himself at the Ipátoffs' in dress-suit and white gloves. He found them all entirely dressed; the little girls were sitting sedately, afraid of mussing their starched white frocks; old Ipátoff, on catching sight of Vladímir Sergyéitch in his dress-suit, affectionately upbraided him, and pointed to his own frock-coat; Márya Pávlovna wore a muslin gown of a deep rose colour, which was extremely becoming to her. Vladímir Sergyéitch paid her several compliments. Márya Pávlovna's beauty attracted him, although she was evidently shy of him; he also liked Nadézhda Alexyéevna, but her free-and-easy manners somewhat disconcerted him. Moreover, in her remarks, her looks, her very smiles, mockery frequently peeped forth, and this disturbed his citified and well-bred soul. He would not have been averse to making fun of others with her, but it was unpleasant to him to think that she was probably capable of jeering at himself.

The ball had already begun; a good many guests had assembled, and the home-bred orchestra was crashing and booming and screeching in the gallery, when the Ipátoff family, accompanied by Vladímir Sergyéitch, entered the hall of the Akílin house. The host met them at the very door, thanked Vladímir Sergyéitch for his tender procuration of an agreeable surprise,—that was the way he expressed himself,—and, taking Ipátoff's arm, he led him to the drawing-room, to the card-tables. Gavríla Stepánitch had received a bad education, and everything in his house, both the music and the furniture and the food and the wines, not only could not be called first-class, but were not even fit to be ranked as second-class. On the other hand, there was plenty of everything, and he himself did not put on airs, was not arrogant. . . the nobles demanded nothing more from him, and were entirely satisfied with his entertainment. At supper, for instance, the caviar was served cut up in chunks and heavily salted; but no one objected to your taking it in your fingers, and there was plenty wherewith to wash it down; wines which were cheap, it is true, but were made from grapes, nevertheless, and not some other concoction. The springs in Gavríla Stepánitch's furniture were rather uncomfortable, owing to their stiffness and inflexibility; but, not to mention the fact that there were no springs whatever in many of the couches and easy-chairs, any one could place under him a worsted cushion, and there was a great number of such cushions lying about, embroidered by the hands of Gavríla Stepánitch's spouse herself—and then there was nothing left to desire.

---

[15] "S," a polite addition to sentences, equivalent to a contraction of the words for "sir" or "madam."

In a word, Gavríla Stepánitch's house could not possibly have been better adapted to the sociable and unceremonious style of ideas of the inhabitants of —— county, and it was solely owing to Mr. Akílin's modesty that at the assemblies of the nobility he was not elected Marshal, but a retired Major Podpékin, a greatly respected and worthy man, despite the fact that he brushed his hair over to the right temple from the left ear, dyed his moustache a lilac hue, and as he suffered from asthma, had of late fallen into melancholy.

So, then, the ball had already begun. They were dancing a quadrille of ten pairs. The cavaliers were the officers of a regiment stationed close by, and divers not very youthful squires, and two or three officials from the town. Everything was as it should be, everything was proceeding in due order. The Marshal of the Nobility was playing cards with a retired Actual Councillor of State[16] and a wealthy gentleman, the owner of three thousand souls. The actual state councillor wore on his forefinger a ring with a diamond, talked very softly, kept the heels of his boots closely united, and did not move them from the position used by dancers of former days, and did not turn his head, which was half concealed by a capital velvet collar. The wealthy gentleman, on the contrary, was constantly laughing at something or other, elevating his eyebrows, and flashing the whites of his eyes. The poet Bodryakóff, a man of shy and clumsy aspect, was chatting in a corner with the learned historian Evsiukóff: each had clutched the other by the button. Beside them, one noble, with a remarkably long waist, was expounding certain audacious opinions to another noble who was timidly staring at his forehead. Along the wall sat the mammas in gay-hued caps; around the doors pressed the men of simple cut, young fellows with perturbed faces, and elderly fellows with peaceable ones; but one cannot describe everything. We repeat: everything was as it should be.

Nadézhda Alexyéevna had arrived even earlier than the Ipátoffs; Vladímir Sergyéitch saw her dancing with a young man of handsome appearance in a dandified dress-suit, with expressive eyes, thin black moustache, and gleaming teeth; a gold chain hung in a semicircle on his stomach. Nadézhda Alexyéevna wore a light-blue gown with white flowers; a small garland of the same flowers encircled her curly head; she was smiling, fluttering her fan, and gaily gazing about her; she felt that she was the queen of the ball. Vladímir Sergyéitch approached her, made his obeisance, and looking her pleasantly in the face, he asked her whether she remembered her promise of the day before.

"What promise?"

"Why, that you would dance the mazurka with me."

"Yes, of course I will dance it with you."

The young man who stood alongside Nadézhda Alexyéevna suddenly flushed crimson.

"You have probably forgotten, mademoiselle,"—he began,—"that you had already previously promised to-day's mazurka to me."

Nadézhda Alexyéevna became confused.

---

16 The fourth from the top in the Table of Ranks.

"Akh! good heavens, what am I to do?"—she said: "excuse me, pray, M'sieu Steltchínsky, I am so absent-minded; I really am ashamed. . . ."

M'sieu Steltchínsky made no reply, and merely dropped his eyes; Vladímir Sergyéitch assumed a slight air of dignity.

"Be so good, M'sieu Steltchínsky,"—went on Nadézhda Alexyéevna; "you and I are old acquaintances, but M'sieu Astákhoff is a stranger among us; do not place me in an awkward position: permit me to dance with him."

"As you please,"—returned the young man.—"But you must begin."

"Thanks,"—said Nadézhda Alexyeevna, and fluttered off to meet her vis-à-vis.

Steltchínsky followed her with his eyes, then looked at Vladímir Sergyéitch. Vladímir Sergyéitch, in his turn, looked at him, then stepped aside.

The quadrille soon came to an end. Vladímir Sergyéitch strolled about the hall a little, then he betook himself to the drawing-room and paused at one of the card-tables. Suddenly he felt some one touch his hand from behind; he turned round—before him stood Steltchínsky.

"I must have a couple of words with you in the next room, if you will permit," —said the latter, in French, very courteously, and with an accent which was not Russian.

Vladímir Sergyéitch followed him.

Steltchínsky halted at a window.

"In the presence of ladies,"—he began, in the same language as before,—"I could not say anything else than what I did say; but I hope you do not think that I really intend to surrender to you my right to the mazurka with M-lle. Véretyeff."

Vladímir Sergyéitch was astounded.

"Why so?"—he asked.

"Because, sir,"—replied Steltchínsky, quietly, laying his hand on his breast and inflating his nostrils,—"I don't intend to,—that 's all."

Vladímir Sergyéitch also laid his hand on his breast, but did not inflate his nostrils.

"Permit me to remark to you, my dear sir,"—he began,—"that by this course you may drag M-lle. Véretyeff into unpleasantness, and I assume. . . ."

"That would be extremely unpleasant to me, but no one can prevent your declining, declaring that you are ill, or going away. . . ."

"I shall not do it. For whom do you take me?"

"In that case, I shall be compelled to demand satisfaction from you."

"In what sense do you mean . . . satisfaction?"

"The sense is evident."

"You will challenge me to a duel?"

"Precisely so, sir, if you do not renounce the mazurka."

Steltchínsky endeavoured to utter these words as negligently as possible. Vladímir Sergyéitch's heart set to beating violently. He looked his wholly unexpected antagonist in the face. "Phew, O Lord, what stupidity!" he thought.

"You are not jesting?"—he articulated aloud.

"I am not in the habit of jesting in general,"—replied Steltchínsky, pompously;—"and particularly with people whom I do not know. You will not renounce the mazurka?"—he added, after a brief pause.

"I will not,"—retorted Vladímir Sergyéitch, as though deliberating.

"Very good! We will fight to-morrow."

"Very well."

"To-morrow morning my second will call upon you."

And with a courteous inclination, Steltchínsky withdrew, evidently well pleased with himself.

Vladímir Sergyéitch remained a few minutes longer by the window.

"Just look at that, now!"—he thought.—"This is the result of thy new acquaintances! What possessed me to come? Good! Splendid"

But at last he recovered himself, and went out into the hall.

In the hall they were already dancing the polka. Before Vladímir Sergyéitch's eyes Màrya Pávlovna flitted past with Piótr Alexyéitch, whom he had not noticed up to that moment; she seemed pale, and even sad; then Nadézhda Alexyéevna darted past, all beaming and joyous, with some youthful, bow-legged, but fiery artillery officer; on the second round, she was dancing with Steltchínsky. Steltchínsky shook his hair violently when he danced.

"Well, my dear fellow,"—suddenly rang out Ipátoff's voice behind Vladímir Sergyéitch's back;—"you 're only looking on, but not dancing yourself? Come, confess that, in spite of the fact that we live in a dead-calm region, so to speak, we are n't badly off, are we, hey?"

"Good! damn the dead-calm region!" thought Vladímir Sergyéitch, and mumbling something in reply to Ipátoff, he went off to another corner of the hall.

"I must hunt up a second,"—he pursued his meditations;—"but where the devil am I to find one? I can't take Véretyeff; I know no others; the devil only knows what a stupid affair this is!"

Vladímir Sergyéitch, when he got angry, was fond of mentioning the devil.

At this moment, Vladímir Sergyéitch's eyes fell upon The Folding Soul, Iván Ílitch, standing idly by the window.

"Would n't he do?"—he thought, and shrugging his shoulders, he added almost aloud:—"I shall have to take him."

Vladímir Sergyéitch stepped up to him.

"A very strange thing has just happened to me,"—began our hero with a forced smile:—"just imagine some young man or other, a stranger to me, has challenged me to a duel; it is utterly impossible for me to refuse; I am in indispensable need of a second: will not you act?"

Although Iván Ílitch was characterised, as we know, by imperturbable indifference, yet such an unexpected proposition startled even him. Thoroughly perplexed, he riveted his eyes on Vladímir Sergyéitch.

"Yes,"—repeated Vladímir Sergyéitch;—"I should be greatly indebted to you. I am not acquainted with any one here. You alone...."

"I can't,"—said Iván Ílitch, as though just waking up;—"I absolutely can't."

"Why not? You are afraid of unpleasantness; but all this will, I hope, remain a secret. . . ."

As he spoke these words, Vladímir Sergyéitch felt himself blushing and growing confused.

"Excuse me, I can't possibly,"—repeated Iván Ílitch, shaking his head and drawing back, in which operation he again overturned a chair.

For the first time in his life it was his lot to reply to a request by a refusal; but then, the request was such a queer one!

"At any rate,"—pursued Vladímir Sergyéitch, in an agitated voice, as he grasped his hand,—"do me the favour not to speak to any one concerning what I have said to you. "I earnestly entreat this of you."

"I can do that, I can do that,"—hastily replied Iván Ílitch;—"but the other thing I cannot do, say what you will; I positively am unable to do it."

"Well, very good, very good,"—said Vladímir Sergyéitch;—"but do not forget that I rely on your discretion. . . . I shall announce to-morrow to that gentleman," he muttered to himself with vexation,—"that I could not find a second, so let him make what arrangements he sees fit, for I am a stranger here. And the devil prompted me to apply to that gentleman! But what else was there for me to do?"

Vladímir Sergyéitch was very, very unlike his usual self.

In the meantime, the ball went on. Vladímir Sergyéitch would have greatly liked to depart at once, but departure was not to be thought of until the end of the mazurka. How was he to give up to his delighted antagonist? Unhappily for Vladímir Sergyéitch, the dances were in charge of a free-and-easy young gentleman with long hair and a sunken chest, over which, in semblance of a miniature waterfall, meandered a black satin neckcloth, transfixed with a huge gold pin. This young gentleman had the reputation, throughout the entire government, of being a man who had assimilated, in their most delicate details, all the customs and rules of highest society, although he had lived in Petersburg only six months altogether, and had not succeeded in penetrating any loftier heights than the houses of Collegiate Assessor Sandaráki and his brother-in-law, State Councillor Kostandaráki. He superintended the dances at all balls, gave the signal to the musicians by clapping his hands, and in the midst of the roar of the trumpets and the squeaking of the violins shouted: *"En avant deux!"* or *"Grande chaîne!"* or *"A vous, mademoiselle!"* and was incessantly flying, all pale and perspiring, through the hall, slipping head-long, and bowing and scraping. He never began the mazurka before midnight. "And that is a concession,"—he was wont to say;—"in Petersburg I would keep you in torment until two o'clock."

This ball seemed very long to Vladímir Sergyéitch. He prowled about like a shadow from hall to drawing-room, now and again exchanging cold glances with his antagonist, who never missed a single dance, and undertook to invite Márya Pávlovna for a quadrille, but she was already engaged—and a couple of times he bandied words with the anxious host, who appeared to be harassed by the tedium which was written on the countenance of the new guest. At last, the music of the longed-for mazurka thundered out. Vladímir Sergyéitch hunted up his lady, brought two chairs, and seated himself with her, near the end of the circle almost opposite Steltchínsky.

The young man who managed affairs was in the first pair, as might have been expected. With what a face he began the mazurka, how he dragged his lady after him, how he beat the floor with his foot, and twitched his head the while,—all this is almost beyond the power of human pen to describe.

"But it seems to me, M'sieu Astákhoff, that you are bored,"—began Nadézhda Alexyéevna, suddenly turning to Vladímir Sergyéitch.

"I? Not in the least. What makes you think so?"

"Why, because I do from the expression of your face. . . . You have never smiled a single time since you arrived. I had not expected that of you. It is not becoming to you positive gentlemen to be misanthropical and to frown à la Byron. Leave that to the authors."

"I notice, Nadézhda Alexyéevna, that you frequently call me a positive man, as though mockingly. It must be that you regard me as the coldest and most sensible of beings, incapable of anything which. . . . But do you know, I will tell you something; a positive man is often very sad at heart, but he does not consider it necessary to display to others what is going on there inside of him; he prefers to hold his peace."

"What do you mean by that?"—inquired Nadézhda Alexyéevna, surveying him with a glance.

"Nothing, ma'am,"—replied Vladímir Sergyéitch, with feigned indifference, assuming an air of mystery.

"Really?"

"Really, nothing. . . . You shall know some day, later on."

Nadézhda Alexyéevna wanted to pursue her questions, but at that moment a young girl, the host's daughter, led up to her Steltchínsky and another cavalier in blue spectacles.

"Life or death?"—she asked in French.

"Life,"—exclaimed Nadézhda Alexyéevna; "I don't want death just yet."

Steltchínsky bowed; she went off with him.[17]

The cavalier in the blue glasses, who was called Death, started off with the host's daughter. Steltchínsky had invented the two designations.

"Tell me, please, who is that Mr. Steltchínsky?"—inquired Vladímir Sergyéitch of Nadézhda Alexyéevna, as soon as the latter returned to her place.

"He is attached to the Governor's service, and is a very agreeable man. He does not belong in these parts. He is somewhat of a coxcomb, but that runs in the blood of all of them. I hope you have not had any explanations with him on account of the mazurka?"

"None whatever, I assure you,"—replied Vladímir Sergyéitch, with a little hesitation.

"I 'm such a forgetful creature! You can't imagine!"

---

[17] The figures in the mazurka are like those in the cotillion (which is often danced the same evening), but the step is very animated and original.

"I am bound to be delighted with your forgetfulness: it has afforded me the pleasure of dancing with you to-night."

Nadézhda Alexyéevna gazed at him, with her eyes slightly narrowed.

"Really? You find it agreeable to dance with me?"

Vladímir Sergyéitch answered her with a compliment. Little by little he got to talking freely. Nadézhda Alexyéevna was always charming, and particularly so that evening; Vladímir Sergyéitch thought her enchanting. The thought of the duel on the morrow, while it fretted his nerves, imparted brilliancy and vivacity to his remarks; under its influence he permitted himself slight exaggerations in the expression of his feelings. . . . "I don't care!" he thought. Something mysterious, involuntarily sad, something elegantly hopeless peeped forth in all his words, in his suppressed sighs, in his glances which suddenly darkened. At last, he got to chattering to such a degree that he began to discuss love, women, his future, the manner in which he conceived of happiness, what he demanded of Fate. . . . He explained himself allegorically, by hints. On the eve of his possible death, Vladímir Sergyéitch flirted with Nadézhda Alexyéevna.

She listened to him attentively, laughed, shook her head, now disputed with him, again pretended to be incredulous. . . . The conversation, frequently interrupted by the approach of ladies and cavaliers, took a rather strange turn toward the end. . . . Vladímir Sergyéitch had already begun to interrogate Nadézhda Alexyéevna about herself, her character, her sympathies. At first she parried the questions with a jest, then, suddenly, and quite unexpectedly to Vladímir Sergyéitch, she asked him when he was going away.

"Whither,"—he said, in surprise.

"To your own home."

"To Sásovo?"

"No, home, to your village, a hundred versts from here."

Vladímir Sergyéitch cast down his eyes.

"I should like to go as promptly as possible,"—he said with a preoccupied look on his face.—"To-morrow, I think. . . if I am alive. For I have business on hand. But why have you suddenly taken it into your head to ask me about that?"

"Because I have!"—retorted Nadézhda Alexyéevna.

"But what is the reason?"

"Because I have!"—she repeated.—"I am surprised at the curiosity of a man who is going away to-morrow, and to-day wants to find out about my character. . . ."

"But, pardon me. . ." began Vladímir Sergyéitch. . . .

"Ah, here, by the way. . .read this,"—Nadézhda Alexyéevna interrupted him with a laugh, as she handed him a motto-slip of paper from bonbons which she had just taken from a small table that stood near by, as she rose to meet Márya Pávlovna, who had stopped in front of her with another lady.

Márya Pávlovna was dancing with Piótr Alexyéitch. Her face was covered with a flush, and was flaming, but not cheerful.

Vladímir Sergyéitch glanced at the slip of paper; thereon, in wretched French letters, was printed:

"Qui me néglige me perd."

He raised his eyes, and encountered Steltchínsky's gaze bent upon him. Vladímir Sergyéitch smiled constrainedly, threw his elbow over the back of the chair, and crossed his legs—as much as to say: "I don't care for thee!"

The fiery artillery officer brought Nadézhda Alexyéevna up to her chair with a dash, pirouetted gently in front of her, bowed, clicked his spurs, and departed. She sat down.

"Allow me to inquire,"—began Vladímir Sergyéitch, with pauses between his words,—"in what sense I am to understand this billet?. . . ."

"But what in the world does it say?"—said Nadézhda Alexyéevna.—"Ah, yes! '*Qui me néglige me perd.*' Well! that 's an admirable rule of life, which may be of service at every step. In order to make a success of anything, no matter what, one must not neglect anything whatsoever. . . . One must endeavour to obtain everything; perhaps one will obtain something. But I am ridiculous. I. . . I am talking to you, a practical man, about rules of life. . . ."

Nadézhda Alexyéevna burst into a laugh, and Vladímir Sergyéitch strove, in vain, to the very end of the mazurka, to renew their previous conversation. Nadézhda Alexyéevna avoided it with the perversity of a capricious child. Vladímir Sergyéitch talked to her about his sentiments, and she either did not reply to him at all, or else she called his attention to the gowns of the ladies, to the ridiculous faces of some of the men, to the skill with which her brother danced, to the beauty of Márya Pávlovna; she began to talk about music, about the day before, about Egór Kapítonitch and his wife, Matryóna Márkovna. . . and only at the very close of the mazurka, when Vladímir Sergyéitch was beginning to make her his farewell bow, did she say, with an ironical smile on her lips and in her eyes:

"So you are positively going to-morrow?"

"Yes; and very far away, perhaps,"—said Vladímir Sergyéitch, significantly.

"I wish you a happy journey."

And Nadézhda Alexyéevna swiftly approached her brother, merrily whispered something in his ear, then asked aloud:

"Grateful to me? Yes? art thou not? otherwise he would have asked *her* for the mazurka."

He shrugged his shoulders, and said:

"Nevertheless, nothing will come of it. . . ."

She led him off into the drawing-room.

"The flirt!"—thought Vladímir Sergyéitch, and taking his hat in his hand, he slipped unnoticed from the hall, hunted up his footman, to whom he had previously given orders to hold himself in readiness, and was already donning his overcoat, when suddenly, to his intense surprise, the lackey informed him that it was impossible to depart, as the coachman, in some unknown manner, had drunk to intoxication, and that it was utterly impossible to arouse him. After cursing the coachman in a remarkably brief but extremely powerful manner (this took place in the anteroom, outside witnesses were present), and informing his footman that if the coachman was not in proper condition by day-light to-morrow, then no one in the world would be capable of picturing to himself what the result would be, Vladímir Sergyéitch returned to the hall, and requested the major-domo to allot him a chamber, without waiting for supper, which was already prepared in the drawing-room. The master of the house suddenly popped up, as it were, out of the floor, at Vladímir Sergyéitch's very elbow (Gavríla Stepánitch wore boots without heels, and therefore moved about without the slightest sound), and began to hold him back, assuring him that there would be caviar of the very best quality for supper; but Vladímir Sergyéitch excused himself on the plea of a headache. Half an hour later he was lying in a small bed, under a short coverlet, and trying to get to sleep.

But he could not get to sleep. Toss as he would from side to side, strive as he would to think of something else, the figure of Steltchínsky importunately towered up before him. . . . Now he is taking aim . . . now he has fired. . . . "Astákhoff is killed," says some one. Vladímir Sergyéitch could not be called a brave man, yet he was no coward; but even the thought of a duel, no matter with whom, had never once entered his head. . . . Fight! with his good sense, peaceable disposition, respect for the conventions, dreams of future prosperity, and an advantageous marriage! If it had not been a question of his own person, he would have laughed heartily, so stupid and ridiculous did this affair seem to him. Fight! with whom, and about what?!

"Phew! damn it! what nonsense!"—he exclaimed involuntarily aloud.—"Well, and what if he really does kill me?"—he continued his meditations;—"I must take measures, make arrangements. . . . Who will mourn for me?"

And in vexation he closed his eyes, which were staringly-wide open, drew the coverlet up around his neck . . . but could not get to sleep, nevertheless. . . .

Dawn was already breaking, and exhausted with the fever of insomnia, Vladímir Sergyéitch was beginning to fall into a doze, when suddenly be felt some weight or other on his feet. He opened his eyes. . . . On his bed sat Véretyeff.

Vladímir Sergyéitch was greatly amazed, especially when he noticed that Véretyeff had no coat on, that beneath his unbuttoned shirt his bare breast was visible, that his hair was tumbling over his forehead, and that his very face appeared changed. Vladímir Sergyéitch got half-way out of bed. . . .

"Allow me to ask . . ." he began, throwing his hands apart. . . .

"I have come to you,"—said Véretyeff, in a hoarse voice;—"excuse me for coming in such a guise. . . . We have been drinking a bit yonder. I wanted to put you at ease. I said to myself: 'Yonder lies a gentleman who, in all probability, cannot get to sleep.—Let's help him.'—Understand; you are not going to fight to-morrow, and can go to sleep. . . ."

Vladímir Sergyéitch was still more amazed than before.

"What was that you said?"—he muttered.

"Yes; that has all been adjusted,"—went on Véretyeff;—"that gentleman from the banks of the Visla . . . Steltchínsky . . . makes his apologies to you . . . to-morrow you will receive a letter. . . . I repeat to you:—all is settled. . . . Snore away."

So saying, Véretyeff rose, and directed his course, with unsteady steps, toward the door.

"But permit me, permit me,"—began Vladímir Sergyéitch.—"How could you have found out, and how can I believe. . . ."

"Akh! you think that I . . . you know . . ." (and he reeled forward slightly). . . .

"I tell you...he will send a letter to you to-morrow. . . . You do not arouse any particular sympathy in me, but magnanimity is my weak side. But what 's the use of talking. . . . It 's all nonsense anyway. . . . But confess,"—he added, with a wink;—"you were pretty well scared, were n't you, hey?"

Vladímir Sergyéitch flew into a rage.

"Permit me, in conclusion, my dear sir,"—said he. . . .

"Well, good, good,"—Véretyeff interrupted him with a good-natured smile.— "Don't fly into a passion. Evidently you are not aware that no ball ever takes place without that sort of thing. That 's the established rule. It never amounts to anything. Who feels like exposing his brow? Well, and why not bluster, hey? at newcomers, for instance? *In vino veritas.* However, neither you nor I know Latin. But I see by your face that you are sleepy. I wish you good night, Mr. Positive Man, well-intentioned mortal. Accept this wish from another mortal who is n't worth a brass farthing himself. *Addio, mio caro!*"

And Véretyeff left the room.

"The devil knows what this means!"—exclaimed Vladímir Sergyéitch, after a brief pause, banging his fist into the pillow;—"no one ever heard the like!...this must be cleared up! I won't tolerate this!"

Nevertheless, five minutes later he was already sleeping softly and profoundly. . . . Danger escaped fills the soul of man with sweetness, and softens it.

This is what had taken place before that unanticipated nocturnal interview between Véretyeff and Vladímir Sergyéitch.

In Gavríla Stepánitch's house lived his grand-nephew, who occupied bachelor quarters in the lower story. When there were balls on hand, the young men dropped in at his rooms between the dances, to smoke a hasty pipe, and after supper they assembled there for a friendly drinking-bout. A good many of the guests had dropped in on him that night. Steltchínsky and Véretyeff were among the number; Iván Ílitch, The Folding Soul, also wandered in there in the wake of the others. They brewed a punch. Although Iván Ílitch had promised Astákhoff that he would not mention the impending duel to any one whomsoever, yet, when Véretyeff accidentally asked him what he had been talking about with that glum fellow (Véretyeff never alluded to Astákhoff otherwise), The Folding Soul could not contain himself, and repeated his entire conversation with Vladímir Sergyéitch, word for word.

Véretyeff burst out laughing, then lapsed into meditation.

"But with whom is he going to fight?"—he asked.

"That 's what I cannot say,"—returned Iván Ílitch.

"At all events, with whom has he been talking?"

"With different people. . . . With Egór Kapítonitch. It cannot be that he is going to fight with him?"

Véretyeff went away from Iván Ílitch.

So, then, they made a punch, and began to drink. Véretyeff was sitting in the most conspicuous place. Jolly and profligate, he held the pre-eminence in gatherings of young men. He threw off his waistcoat and neckcloth. He was asked to sing; he took a guitar and sang several songs. Heads began to wax rather hot; the young men began to propose toasts. Suddenly Steltchínsky, all red in the face, sprang upon the table, and elevating his glass high above his head, exclaimed loudly:

"To the health...of I know whom,"—he hastily caught himself up, drank off his liquor, and smashed his glass on the floor, adding:—"May my foe be shivered into just such pieces to-morrow!"

Véretyeff, who had long had his eye on him, swiftly raised his head....

"Steltchínsky,"—said he,—"in the first place, get off the table; that 's indecorous, and you have very bad boots into the bargain; and, in the second place, come hither, I will tell thee something."

He led him aside.

"Hearken, brother; I know that thou art going to fight to-morrow with that gentleman from Petersburg."

Steltchínsky started.

"How...who told thee?"

"I tell thee it is so. And I also know on whose account thou art going to fight."

"Who is it? I am curious to know."

"Akh, get out with thee, thou Talleyrand! My sister's, of course. Come, come, don't pretend to be surprised. It gives you a goose-like expression. I can't imagine how this has come about, but it is a fact. That will do, my good fellow,"—pursued Véretyeff.—"What 's the use of shamming? I know, you see, that you have been paying court to her this long time."

"But, nevertheless, that does not prove...."

"Stop, if you please. But hearken to what I am about to say to you. I won't permit that duel under any circumstances whatsoever. Dost understand? All this folly will descend upon my sister. Excuse me: so long as I am alive...that shall not be. As for thou and I, we shall perish—we 're on the road to it; but she must live a long time yet, and live happily. Yes, I swear,"—he added, with sudden heat,—"that I will betray all others, even those who might be ready to sacrifice everything for me, but I will not permit any one to touch a single hair of her head."

Steltchínsky emitted a forced laugh.

"Thou art drunk, my dear fellow, and art raving...that's all."

"And art not thou, I 'd like to know? But whether I am drunk or not, is a matter of not the slightest consequence. But I 'm talking business. Thou shalt not fight with that gentleman, I guarantee that. And what in the world possessed thee to have anything to do with him? Hast grown jealous, pray? Well, those speak the truth who say that men in love are stupid! Why she danced with him simply in order to prevent his inviting.... Well, but that 's not the point. But this duel shall not take place."

"H'm! I should like to see how thou wilt prevent me?"

"Well, then, this way: if thou dost not instantly give me thy word to renounce this duel, I will fight with thee myself."

"Really?"

"My dear fellow, entertain no doubt on that score. I will insult thee on the spot, my little friend, in the presence of every one, in the most fantastic manner, and then fight thee across a handkerchief, if thou wilt. But I think that will be disagreeable to thee, for many reasons, hey?"

Steltchínsky flared up, began to say that this was *intimidation*,[18] that he would not permit any one to meddle with his affairs, that he would not stick at anything...and wound up by submitting, and renouncing all attempts on the life of Vladímir Sergyéitch. Véretyeff embraced him, and half an hour had not elapsed, before the two had already drunk Brüderschaft for the tenth time,—that is to say, they drank with arms interlocked.... The young man who had acted as floor-manager of the ball also drank Brüderschaft with them, and at first clung close to them, but finally fell asleep in the most innocent manner, and lay for a long time on his back in a condition of complete insensibility.... The expression of his tiny, pale face was both amusing and pitiful.... Good heavens! what would those fashionable ladies, his acquaintances, have said, if they had beheld him in that condition! But, luckily for him, he was not acquainted with a single fashionable lady.

Iván Ílitch also distinguished himself on that night. First he amazed the guests by suddenly striking up: "In the country a Baron once dwelt."

"The hawfinch! The hawfinch has begun to sing!"—shouted all. "When has it ever happened that a hawfinch has sung by night?"

"As though I knew only one song,"—retorted Iván Ílitch, who was heated with liquor;—"I know some more, too."

"Come, come, come, show us your art."

Iván Ílitch maintained silence for a while, and suddenly struck up in a bass voice: "Krambambuli,[19] bequest of our fathers!" but so incoherently and strangely, that a general outburst of laughter immediately drowned his voice, and he fell silent. When all had dispersed, Véretyeff betook himself to Vladímir Sergyéitch, and the brief conversation already reported, ensued between them.

On the following day, Vladímir Sergyéitch drove off to his own Sásovo very early. He passed the whole morning in a state of excitement, came near mistaking a passing merchant for a second, and breathed freely only when his lackey brought him a letter from Steltchínsky. Vladímir Sergyéitch perused that letter several times,—it was very adroitly worded.... Steltchínsky began with the words: *"La nuit porte conseil, Monsieur,"*—made no excuses whatever, because, in his opinion, he had not insulted his antagonist in any way; but admitted that he had been somewhat irritated on the preceding evening, and wound up with the statement that he held himself entirely at the disposition of Mr. Astákhoff (*"de M-r Astákhoff"*), but no longer demanded satisfaction himself. After having composed and despatched a reply, which was filled, simultaneously with courtesy which bordered on playfulness, and a sense of dignity, in which, however, no trace of braggadocio was perceptible, Vladímir Sergyéitch sat down to dinner, rubbing his hands, ate with great satisfaction, and immediately afterward set off, without having even

---

18 He uses an impromptu Russification of a foreign word: *intimidátziya.*
19 A mixed drink.

sent relays on in advance. The road along which he drove passed at a distance of four versts from Ipátoff's manor. . . . Vladímir Sergyéitch looked at it.

"Farewell, region of dead calm!"—he said with a smile.

The images of Nadézhda Alexyéevna and Márya Pávlovna presented themselves for a moment to his imagination; he dismissed them with a wave of his hand, and sank into a doze.

VI

More than three months had passed. Autumn had long since set in; the yellow forests had grown bare, the tomtits had arrived, and—unfailing sign of the near approach of winter—the wind had begun to howl and wail. But there had been no heavy rains, as yet, and mud had not succeeded in spreading itself over the roads. Taking advantage of this circumstance, Vladímir Sergyéitch set out for the government capital, for the purpose of winding up several matters of business. He spent the morning in driving about, and in the evening went to the club. In the vast, gloomy hall of the club he encountered several acquaintances, and, among others, the old retired captain of cavalry Flitch, a busybody, wit, gambler, and gossip, well known to every one. Vladímir Sergyéitch entered into conversation with him.

"Ah, by the way!"—suddenly exclaimed the retired cavalry-captain; "an acquaintance of yours passed through here the other day, and left her compliments for you."

"Who was she?"

"Madame Steltchínsky."

"I don't know any Madame Steltchínsky."

"You knew her as a girl. . . . She was born Véretyeff. . . . Nadézhda Alexyéevna. Her husband served our Governor. You must have seen him also. . . . A lively man, with a moustache. . . . He's hooked a splendid woman, with money to boot."

"You don't say so,"—said Vladímir Sergyéitch.—"So she has married him. . . . H'm! And where have they gone?"

"To Petersburg. She also bade me remind you of a certain bonbon motto. . . . What sort of a motto was it, allow me to inquire?"

And the old gossip thrust forward his sharp nose.

"I don't remember, really; some jest or other,"—returned Vladímir Sergyéitch.—"But permit me to ask, where is her brother now?"

"Piótr? Well, he's in a bad way."

Mr. Flitch rolled up his small, foxy eyes, and heaved a sigh.

"Why, what's the matter?"—asked Vladímir Sergyéitch.

"He has taken to dissipation! He's a ruined man."

"But where is he now?"

"It is absolutely unknown where he is. He went off somewhere or other after a gipsy girl; that's the most certain thing of all. He's not in this government, I'll guarantee that."

"And does old Ipátoff still live there?"

"Mikhaíl Nikoláitch? That eccentric old fellow? Yes, he still lives there."

"And is everything in his household...as it used to be?"

"Certainly, certainly. Here now, why don't you marry his sister-in-law? She 's not a woman, you know, she 's simply a monument, really. Ha, ha! People have already been talking among us...'why,' say they...."

"You don't say so, sir,"—articulated Vladímir Sergyéitch, narrowing his eyes.

At that moment, Flitch was invited to a card-game, and the conversation terminated.

Vladímir Sergyéitch had intended to return home promptly; but suddenly he received by special messenger a report from the overseer, that six of the peasants' homesteads had burned down in Sásovo, and he decided to go thither himself. The distance from the government capital to Sásovo was reckoned at sixty versts. Vladímir Sergyéitch arrived toward evening at the wing with which the reader is already acquainted, immediately gave orders that the overseer and clerk should be summoned, scolded them both in proper fashion, inspected the scene of the conflagration next morning, took the necessary measures, and after dinner, after some wavering, set off to visit Ipátoff. Vladímir Sergyéitch would have remained at home, had he not heard from Flitch of Nadézhda Alexyéevna's departure; he did not wish to meet her; but he was not averse to taking another look at Márya Pávlovna.

Vladímir Sergyéitch, as on the occasion of his first visit, found Ipátoff busy at draughts with The Folding Soul. The old man was delighted to see him; yet it seemed to Vladímir Sergyéitch as though his face were troubled, and his speech did not flow freely and readily as of old.

Vladímir Sergyéitch exchanged a silent glance with Iván Ílitch. Both winced a little; but they speedily recovered their serenity.

"Are all your family well?"—inquired Vladímir Sergyéitch.

"Yes, thank God, I thank you sincerely,"—replied Ipátoff.—"Only Márya Pávlovna is n't quite...you know, she stays in her room most of the time."

"Has she caught cold?"

"No...she just likes to. She will make her appearance at tea."

"And Egór Kapítonitch? What is he doing?"

"Akh! Egór Kapítonitch is a dead man. His wife has died."

"It cannot be!"

"She died in twenty-four hours, of cholera. You would n't know him now, he has become simply unrecognisable. 'Without Matryóna Márkovna,' he says, 'life is a burden to me. I shall die,' he says, 'and God be thanked,' he says; 'I don't wish to live,' says he. Yes, he 's done for, poor fellow."

"Akh! good heavens, how unpleasant that is!"—exclaimed Vladímir Sergyéitch.— "Poor Egór Kapítonitch!"

All were silent for a time.

"I hear that your pretty neighbour has married,"—remarked Vladímir Sergyéitch, flushing faintly.

"Nadézhda Alexyéevna? Yes, she has."

Ipátoff darted a sidelong glance at Vladímir Sergyéitch.

"Certainly. . .certainly, she has married and gone away."

"To Petersburg?"

"To St. Petersburg."

"Márya Pávlovna must miss her, I think. I believe they were great friends."

"Of course she misses her. That cannot be avoided. But as for friendship, I 'll just tell you, that the friendship of girls is even worse than the friendship of men. So long as they are face to face, it 's all right; but, otherwise, it vanishes."

"Do you think so?"

"Yes, by Heaven, 't is so! Take Nadézhda Alexyéevna, for example. She has n't written to us since she went away; but how she promised, even vowed that she would! In truth, she 's in no mood for that now."

"And has she been gone long?"

"Yes; it must be fully six weeks. She hurried off on the very day after the wedding, foreign fashion."

"I hear that her brother is no longer here, either?"—said Vladímir Sergyéitch, after a brief pause.

"No; he is not. They are city folk, you see; as though they would live long in the country!"

"And does no one know where he has gone?"

"No."

"He just went into a rage, and—slap-bang on the ear," remarked Iván Ílitch.

"He just went into a rage, and—slap-bang on the ear," repeated Ipátoff. "Well, and how about yourself, Vladímir Sergyéitch,—what nice things have you been doing?"—he added, wheeling round on his chair.

Vladímir Sergyéitch began to tell about himself; Ipátoff listened and listened to him, and at last exclaimed:

"But why does n't Márya Pávlovna come? Thou hadst better go for her, Iván Ílitch."

Iván Ílitch left the room, and returning, reported that Márya Pávlovna would be there directly.

"What 's the matter? Has she got a headache?"—inquired Ipátoff, in an undertone.

"Yes," replied Iván Ílitch.

The door opened, and Márya Pávlovna entered. Vladímir Sergyéitch rose, bowed, and could not utter a word, so great was his amazement: so changed was Márya Pávlovna since he had seen her the last time! The rosy bloom had vanished from her emaciated cheeks; a broad black ring encircled her eyes; her lips were bitterly compressed; her whole face, impassive and dark, seemed to have become petrified.

She raised her eyes, and there was no spark in them.

"How do you feel now?" Ipátoff asked her.

"I am well,"—she replied; and sat down at the table, on which the samovár was already bubbling.

Vladímir Sergyéitch was pretty thoroughly bored that evening. But no one was in good spirits. The conversation persisted in taking a cheerless turn.

"Just listen,"—said Ipátoff, among other things, as he lent an ear to the howling of the wind;—"what notes it emits! The summer is long since past; and here is autumn passing, too, and winter is at the door. Again we shall be buried in snow-drifts. I hope the snow will fall very soon. Otherwise, when you go out into the garden, melancholy descends upon you. . . . Just as though there were some sort of a ruin there. The branches of the trees clash together. . . . Yes, the fine days are over!"

"They are over,"—repeated Iván Ílitch.

Márya Pávlovna stared silently out of the window.

"God willing, they will return,"—remarked Ipátoff.

No one answered him.

"Do you remember how finely they sang songs here that time?"—said Vladímir Sergyéitch.

"I should think they did,"—replied the old man, with a sigh.

"But you might sing to us,"—went on Vladímir Sergyéitch, turning to Márya Pávlovna;—"you have such a fine voice."

She did not answer him.

"And how is your mother?"—Vladímir Sergyéitch inquired of Ipátoff, not knowing what to talk about.

"Thank God! she gets on nicely, considering her ailments. She came over in her little carriage to-day. She 's a broken tree, I must tell you—creak, creak, and the first you know, some young, strong sapling falls over; but she goes on standing and standing. Ekh, ha, ha!"

Márya Pávlovna dropped her hands in her lap, and bowed her head.

"And, nevertheless, her existence is hard,"—began Ipátoff again;—"rightly is it said: 'old age is no joy.' "

"And there 's no joy in being young,"—said Márya Pávlovna, as though to herself.

Vladímir Sergyéitch would have liked to return home that night, but it was so dark out of doors that he could not make up his mind to set out. He was assigned to the same chamber, up-stairs, in which, three months previously, he had passed a troubled night, thanks to Egór Kapítonitch. . . .

"Does he snore now?"—thought Vladímir Sergyéitch, as he recalled his drilling of his servant, and the sudden appearance of Márya Pávlovna in the garden. . . .

Vladímir Sergyéitch walked to the window, and laid his brow against the cold glass. His own face gazed dimly at him from out of doors, as though his eyes were riveted upon a black curtain, and it was only after a considerable time that he was able to make out against the starless sky the branches of the trees, writhing wildly in the gloom. They were harassed by a turbulent wind.

Suddenly it seemed to Vladímir Sergyéitch as though something white had flashed along the ground. . . . He gazed more intently, laughed, shrugged his shoulders, and exclaiming in an undertone: "That 's what imagination will do!" got into bed.

He fell asleep very soon; but he was not fated to pass a quiet night on this occasion either. He was awakened by a running to and fro, which arose in the house.

...He raised his head from the pillow.... Agitated voices, exclamations, hurried footsteps were audible, doors were banging; now the sound of women weeping rang out, shouts were set up in the garden, other cries farther off responded.... The uproar in the house increased, and became more noisy with every moment.... "Fire!" flashed through Vladímir Sergyéitch's mind. In alarm he sprang from his bed, and rushed to the window; but there was no redness in the sky; only, in the garden, points of flame were moving briskly along the paths,—caused by people running about with lanterns. Vladímir Sergyéitch went quickly to the door, opened it, and ran directly into Iván Ílitch. Pale, dishevelled, half-clothed, the latter was dashing onward, without himself knowing whither.

"What is it? What has happened?"—inquired Vladímir Sergyéitch, excitedly, seizing him by the arm.

"She has disappeared; she has thrown herself into the water,"—replied Iván Ílitch, in a choking voice.

"Who has thrown herself into the water? Who has disappeared?"

"Márya Pávlovna! Who else could it be but Márya Pávlovna? She has perished, the darling! Help! Good heavens, let us run as fast as we can! Be quick, my dear people!"

And Iván Ílitch rushed down the stairs.

Vladímir Sergyéitch put on his shoes somehow, threw his cloak over his shoulders, and ran after him.

In the house he no longer encountered any one, all had hastened out into the garden; only the little girls, Ipátoff's daughters, met him in the corridor, near the anteroom; deadly pale with terror, they stood there in their little white petticoats, with clasped hands and bare feet, beside a night-lamp set on the floor. Through the drawing-room, past an overturned table, flew Vladímir Sergyéitch to the terrace. Through the grove, in the direction of the dam, light and shadows were flashing....

"Go for boat-hooks! Go for boat-hooks as quickly as possible!"—Ipátoff's voice could be heard shouting.

"A net, a net, a boat!"—shouted other voices.

Vladímir Sergyéitch ran in the direction of the shouts. He found Ipátoff on the shore of the pond; a lantern hung on a bough brilliantly illuminated the old man's grey head. He was wringing his hands, and reeling like a drunken man; by his side, a woman lay writhing and sobbing on the grass; round about men were bustling. Iván Ílitch had already advanced into the water up to his knees, and was feeling the bottom with a pole; a coachman was undressing, trembling all over as he did so; two men were dragging a boat along the shore; a sharp trampling of hoofs was audible along the village street.... The wind swept past with a shriek, as though endeavouring to quench the lantern, while the pond plashed noisily, darkling in a menacing way....

"What do I hear?"—exclaimed Vladímir Sergyéitch, rushing up to Ipátoff.— "Is it possible?"

"The boat-hooks—fetch the boat-hooks!"—moaned the old man by way of reply to him....

"But good gracious, perhaps you are mistaken, Mikháíl Nikoláitch. . . ."

"No, mistaken indeed!"—said the woman who was lying on the grass, Márya Pávlovna's maid, in a tearful voice. "Unlucky creature that I am, I heard her myself, the darling, throw herself into the water, and struggling in the water, and screaming: 'Save me!' and then, once more: 'Save me!' "

"Why did n't you prevent her, pray?"

"But how was I to prevent her, dear little father, my lord? Why, when I discovered it, she was no longer in her room, but my heart had a foreboding, you know; these last days she has been so sad all the time, and has said nothing; so I knew how it was, and rushed straight into the garden, just as though some one had made me do it; and suddenly I heard something go splash! into the water: 'Save me!' I heard the cry: 'Save me!'. . . . Okh, my darling, light of my eyes!"

"But perhaps it only seemed so to thee!"

"Seemed so, forsooth! But where is she? what has become of her?"

"So that is what looked white to me in the gloom," thought Vladímir Sergyéitch. . . .

In the meanwhile, men had run up with boat-hooks, dragged thither a net, and begun to spread it out on the grass, a great throng of people had assembled, a commotion had arisen, and a jostling. . . the coachman seized one boat-hook, the village elder seized another, both sprang into the boat, put off, and set to searching the water with the hooks; the people on the shore lighted them. Strange and dreadful did their movements seem, and their shadows in the gloom, above the agitated pond, in the dim and uncertain light of the lanterns.

"He. . . here, the hook has caught!"—suddenly cried the coachman.

All stood stock-still where they were.

The coachman pulled the hook toward him, and bent over. . . . Something horned and black slowly came to the surface. . . .

"A tree-stump,"—said the coachman, pulling away the hook.

"But come back, come back!"—they shouted to him from the shore.—"Thou wilt accomplish nothing with the hooks; thou must use the net."

"Yes, yes, the net!"—chimed in others.

"Stop,"—said the elder;—"I 've got hold of something also. . . something soft, apparently,"—he added, after a brief pause.

A white spot made its appearance alongside the boat. . . .

"The young lady!"—suddenly shouted the elder.—" 'T is she!"

He was not mistaken. . . . The hook had caught Márya Pávlovna by the sleeve of her gown. The coachman immediately seized her, dragged her out of the water. . . in a couple of powerful strokes the boat was at the shore. . . . Ipátoff, Iván Ílitch, Vladímir Sergyéitch, all rushed to Márya Pávlovna, raised her up, bore her home in their arms, immediately undressed her, and began to roll her, and warm her. . . . But all their efforts, their exertions, proved vain. . . . Márya Pávlovna did not come to herself. . . . Life had already left her.

Early on the following morning, Vladímir Sergyéitch left Ipátovka; before his departure, he went to bid farewell to the dead woman. She was lying on the table in the drawing-room in a white gown. . . . Her thick hair was not yet entirely dry, a sort of mournful surprise was expressed on her pale face, which had not had time to grow distorted; her parted lips seemed to be trying to speak, and ask something;...her hands, convulsively clasped, as though with grief, were pressed tight to her breast.... But with whatever sorrowful thought the poor drowned girl had perished, death had laid upon her the seal of its eternal silence and peace...and who understands what a dead face expresses during those few moments when, for the last time, it meets the glance of the living before it vanishes forever and is destroyed in the grave?

Vladímir Sergyéitch stood for a while in decorous meditation before the body of Márya Pávlovna, crossed himself thrice, and left the room, without having noticed Iván Ílitch who was weeping softly in one corner.... And he was not the only one who wept that day: all the servants in the house wept bitterly: Márya Pávlovna had left a good memory behind her.

The following is what old Ipátoff wrote, a week later, in reply to a letter which had come, at last, from Nadézhda Alexyéevna:

"One week ago, dear Madam, Nadézhda Alexyéevna, my unhappy sister-in-law, your acquaintance, Márya Pávlovna, wilfully ended her own life, by throwing herself by night into the pond, and we have already committed her body to the earth. She decided upon this sad and terrible deed, without having bidden me farewell, without leaving even a letter or so much as a note, to declare her last will. ... But you know better than any one else, Nadézhda Alexyéevna, on whose soul this great and deadly sin must fall! May the Lord God judge your brother, for my sister-in-law could not cease to love him, nor survive the separation. ..."

Nadézhda Alexyéevna received this letter in Italy, whither she had gone with her husband, Count de Steltchínsky, as he was called in all the hotels. He did not visit hotels alone, however; he was frequently seen in gambling-houses, in the Kur-Saal at the baths.... At first he lost a great deal of money, then he ceased to lose, and his face assumed a peculiar expression, not precisely suspicious, nor yet precisely insolent, like that which a man has who unexpectedly gets involved in scandals.... He saw his wife rarely. But Nadézhda Alexyéevna did not languish in his absence. She developed a passion for painting and the fine arts. She associated chiefly with artists, and was fond of discussing the beautiful with young men. Ipátoff's letter grieved her greatly, but did not prevent her going that same day to "the Dogs' Cave," to see how the poor animals suffocated when immersed in sulphur fumes.

She did not go alone. She was escorted by divers cavaliers. Among their number, a certain Mr. Popelin, an artist—a Frenchman, who had not finished his course—with a small beard, and dressed in a checked sack-coat, was the most agreeable. He sang the newest romances in a thin tenor voice, made very free-and-easy jokes, and although he was gaunt of form, yet he ate a very great deal.

VII

It was a sunny, cold January day; a multitude of people were strolling on the Névsky Prospékt. The clock on the tower of the city hall marked three o'clock. Along the broad stone slabs, strewn with yellow sand, was walking, among others, our acquaintance Vladímir Sergyéitch Astákhoff. He has grown very virile since we parted from him; his face is framed in whiskers, and he has grown plump all over, but he has not aged. He was moving after the crowd at a leisurely pace, and now and then casting a glance about him; he was expecting his wife; she had preferred to drive up in the carriage with her mother. Vladímir Sergyéitch married five years ago, precisely in the manner which he had always desired: his wife was wealthy, and with the best of connections. Courteously lifting his splendidly brushed hat when he met his numerous acquaintances, Vladímir Sergyéitch was still stepping out with the free stride of a man who is satisfied with his lot, when suddenly, just at the Passage,[20] he came near colliding with a gentleman in a Spanish cloak and foraging-cap, with a decidedly worn face, a dyed moustache, and large, swollen eyes. Vladímir Sergyéitch drew aside with dignity, but the gentleman in the foraging-cap glanced at him, and suddenly exclaimed:

"Ah! Mr. Astákhoff, how do you do?"

Vladímir Sergyéitch made no reply, and stopped short in surprise. He could not comprehend how a gentleman who could bring himself to walk on the Névsky in a foraging-cap could be acquainted with his name.

"You do not recognise me,"—pursued the gentleman in the cap:—"I saw you eight years ago, in the country, in the T—— Government, at the Ipátoffs'. My name is Véretyeff."

"Akh! Good heavens! excuse me!"—exclaimed Vladímir Sergyéitch.—"But how you have changed since then!..."

"Yes, I have grown old,"—returned Piótr Alexyéitch, passing his hand, which was devoid of a glove, over his face.—"But you have not changed."

Véretyeff had not so much aged as fallen away and sunk down. Small, delicate wrinkles covered his face; and when he spoke, his lips and cheeks twitched slightly. From all this it was perceptible that the man had been living hard.

"Where have you disappeared to all this time, that you have not been visible?" —Vladímir Sergyéitch asked him.

"I have been wandering about here and there. And you have been in Petersburg all the while?"

"Yes, most of the time."

"Are you married?"

"Yes."

And Vladímir Sergyéitch assumed a rather severe mien, as though with the object of saying to Véretyeff: "My good fellow, don't take it into thy head to ask me to present thee to my wife."

Véretyeff understood him, apparently. An indifferent sneer barely flitted across his lips.

"And how is your sister?"—inquired Vladímir Sergyéitch.—"Where is she?"

"I cannot tell you for certain. She must be in Moscow. I have not received any letters from her this long time!"

"Is her husband alive?"

"Yes."

---

20 A large collection of shops, under one roof, extending from the Névsky Prospékt to the Bolsháya Italyánskaya ("Great Italian Street"), in St. Petersburg.

"And Mr. Ipátoff?"

"I don't know; probably he is alive also; but he may be dead."

"And that gentleman—what the deuce was his name?—Bodryakóff,—what of him?"

"The one you invited to be your second—you remember, when you were so scared? Why, the devil knows!"

Vladímir Sergyéitch maintained silence for a while, with dignity written on his face.

"I always recall with pleasure those evenings,"—he went on,—"when I had the opportunity" (he had nearly said, "the honour") "of making the acquaintance of your sister and yourself. She was a very amiable person. And do you sing as agreeably as ever?"

"No; I have lost my voice.... But that was a good time!"

"I visited Ipátovka once afterward,"—added Vladímir Sergyéitch, elevating his eyebrows mournfully. "I think that was the name of that village—on the very day of a terrible event...."

"Yes, yes, that was frightful, frightful,"—Véretyeff hastily interrupted him.— "Yes, yes. And do you remember how you came near fighting with my present brother-in-law?"

"H'm! I remember!"—replied Vladímir Sergyéitch, slowly.—"However, I must confess to you that so much time has elapsed since then, that all that sometimes seems to me like a dream...."

"Like a dream,"—repeated Véretyeff, and his pale cheeks flushed;—"like a dream...no, it was not a dream, for me at all events. It was the time of youth, of mirth and happiness, the time of unlimited hopes, and invincible powers; and if it was a dream, then it was a very beautiful dream. And now, you and I have grown old and stupid, we dye our moustaches, and saunter on the Névsky, and have become good for nothing; like broken-winded nags, we have become utterly vapid and worn out; it cannot be said that we are pompous and put on airs, nor that we spend our time in idleness; but I fear we drown our grief in drink,—that is more like a dream, and a hideous dream. Life has been lived, and lived in vain, clumsily, vulgarly—that's what is bitter! That's what one would like to shake off like a dream, that 's what one would like to recover one's self from!...And then ...everywhere, there is one frightful memory, one ghost.... But farewell!"

Véretyeff walked hastily away; but on coming opposite the door of one of the principal confections on the Névsky, he halted, entered, and after drinking a glass of orange vodka at the buffet, he wended his way through the billiard-room, all dark and dim with tobacco-smoke, to the rear room. There he found several acquaintances, his former comrades—Pétya Lazúrin, Kóstya Kovróvsky, and Prince Serdiukóff, and two other gentlemen who were called simply Vasiúk, and Filát. All of them were men no longer young, though unmarried; some of them had lost their hair, others were growing grey; their faces were covered with wrinkles, their chins had grown double; in a word, these gentlemen had all long since passed their prime, as the saying is. Yet all of them continued to regard Véretyeff as a remarkable man, destined to astonish the universe; and he was wiser than they only because he was very well aware of his utter and radical uselessness. And even outside of his circle, there were people who thought concerning him, that if he had not ruined himself, the deuce only knows what he would have made of himself. . . . These people were mistaken. Nothing ever comes of Véretyeffs.

Piótr Alexyéitch's friends welcomed him with the customary greetings. At first he dumbfounded them with his gloomy aspect and his splenetic speeches; but he speedily calmed down, cheered up, and affairs went on in their wonted rut.

But Vladímir Sergyéitch, as soon as Véretyeff left him, contracted his brows in a frown and straightened himself up. Piótr Alexyéitch's unexpected sally had astounded, even offended him extremely.

" 'We have grown stupid, we drink liquor, we dye our moustaches'. . . *parlez pour vous, mon cher,*"—he said at last, almost aloud, and emitting a couple of snorts caused by an access of involuntary indignation, he was preparing to continue his stroll.

"Who was that talking with you?"—rang out a loud and self-confident voice behind him.

Vladímir Sergyéitch turned round and beheld one of his best friends, a certain Mr. Pompónsky. This Mr. Pompónsky, a man of lofty stature, and stout, occupied a decidedly important post, and never once, from his very earliest youth, had he doubted himself.

"Why, a sort of eccentric,"—said Vladímir Sergyéitch, linking his arm in Mr. Pompónsky's.

"Good gracious, Vladímir Sergyéitch, is it permissible for a respectable man to chat on the street with an individual who wears a foraging-cap on his head? 'T is indecent! I 'm amazed! Where could you have made acquaintance with such a person?"

"In the country."

"In the country. . . . One does not bow to one's country neighbours in town. . . *ce n'est pas comme il faut.* A gentleman should always bear himself like a gentleman if he wishes that. . . ."

"Here is my wife,"—Vladímir Sergyéitch hastily interrupted him.—"Let us go to her."

And the two gentlemen directed their steps to a low-hung, elegant carriage, from whose window there peered forth the pale, weary, and irritatingly arrogant little face of a woman who was still young, but already faded.

Behind her another lady, also apparently in a bad humour,—her mother,—was visible. Vladímir Sergyéitch opened the door of the carriage, and offered his arm to his wife. Pompónsky gave his to the mother-in-law, and the two couples made their way along the Névsky Prospékt, accompanied by a short, black-haired footman in yellowish-grey gaiters, and with a big cockade on his hat.

A Simple Soul

(1877)

Gustave Flaubert

Anonymous Translation

Gustave Flaubert (1821–1880) was the son of the resident physician at the Rouen hospital; he was educated in Rouen and went to Paris in 1840 to study law. He had already begun to write, cared nothing for his law studies, and at length, after attacks of a disease that may have been epilepsy, returned to Rouen. After the death of his father and sister in 1846, he settled with his mother near Rouen, overlooking the Seine, and remained there for the rest of his life except for occasional trips. His masterpiece, the novel *Madame Bovary* (1857), was a landmark in the development of French naturalism and a model of the novel wrought as carefully as a poem. This was followed by his historical romance, *Salammbô* (1862), his spiritual autobiography, *The Sentimental Education* (1869), and *The Temptation of St. Anthony* (1874). In his last years, after his mother's death, near a mental and physical breakdown, Flaubert worked on *Bouvard and Pécuchet,* an unwieldy satire on modern bourgeois society. In 1875, on the advice of his old friend George Sand, he undertook some shorter fiction, beginning with *The Legend of St. Julien the Hospitaler* and followed by a modern equivalent of a saint's life, the *nouvelle, A Simple Soul (Un Coeur simple)*. A third tale, *Hérodias,* was added, and the group was published in 1877 as *Three Tales (Trois Contes).* As Harry Levin has noted, Félicité in *A Simple Soul* grew, in a sense, out of the servant woman, Cathérine Leroux, in *Madame Bovary,* who was awarded a prize at the agricultural show for half a century's domestic service: "a single heroic figure in a crowd of *mufles"* (Introduction, *Three Tales,* Norfolk, Connecticut, 1947, p. 3). See also Philip Spencer, *Flaubert, a Biography* (New York, 1952).

The anonymous translator (Robert Arnot's edition, New York, and London: M. Walter Dunne, 1904) renders the title, usually called *A Simple Heart,* as *A Simple Soul;* this, an English idiom, seems to me more expressive of Flaubert's intention than the literal translation.

I

For half a century the housewives of Pont-l'Evêque had envied Madame Aubain her servant Félicité.

252

For a hundred francs a year, she cooked and did the housework, washed, ironed, mended, harnessed the horse, fattened the poultry, made the butter and remained faithful to her mistress—although the latter was by no means an agreeable person.

Madame Aubain had married a comely youth without any money, who died in the beginning of 1809, leaving her with two young children and a number of debts. She sold all her property excepting the farm of Toucques and the farm of Geffosses, the income of which barely amounted to 5,000 francs; then she left her house in Saint-Melaine, and moved into a less pretentious one which had belonged to her ancestors and stood back of the market-place. This house, with its slate-covered roof, was built between a passage-way and a narrow street that led to the river. The interior was so unevenly graded that it caused people to stumble. A narrow hall separated the kitchen from the parlour, where Madame Aubain sat all day in a straw armchair near the window. Eight mahogany chairs stood in a row against the white wainscoting. An old piano, standing beneath a barometer, was covered with a pyramid of old books and boxes. On either side of the yellow marble mantelpiece, in Louis XV style, stood a tapestry armchair. The clock represented a temple of Vesta; and the whole room smelled musty, as it was on a lower level than the garden.

On the first floor was Madame's bed-chamber, a large room papered in a flowered design and containing the portrait of Monsieur dressed in the costume of a dandy. It communicated with a smaller room, in which there were two little cribs, without any mattresses. Next, came the parlour (always closed), filled with furniture covered with sheets. Then a hall, which led to the study, where books and papers were piled on the shelves of a book-case that enclosed three quarters of the big black desk. Two panels were entirely hidden under pen-and-ink sketches, Gouache landscapes and Audran engravings, relics of better times and vanished luxury. On the second floor, a garret-window lighted Félicité's room, which looked out upon the meadows.

She arose at daybreak, in order to attend mass, and she worked without interruption until night; then, when dinner was over, the dishes cleared away and the door securely locked, she would bury the log under the ashes and fall asleep in front of the hearth with a rosary in her hand. Nobody could bargain with greater obstinacy, and as for cleanliness, the lustre on her brass sauce-pans was the envy and despair of other servants. She was most economical, and when she ate she would gather up crumbs with the tip of her finger, so that nothing should be wasted of the loaf of bread weighing twelve pounds which was baked especially for her and lasted three weeks.

Summer and winter she wore a dimity kerchief fastened in the back with a pin, a cap which concealed her hair, a red skirt, grey stockings, and an apron with a bib like those worn by hospital nurses.

Her face was thin and her voice shrill. When she was twenty-five, she looked forty. After she had passed fifty, nobody could tell her age; erect and silent always, she resembled a wooden figure working automatically.

II

Like every other woman, she had had an affair of the heart. Her father, who was a mason, was killed by falling from a scaffolding. Then her mother died and her sisters went their different ways; a farmer took her in, and while she was quite small, let her keep cows in the fields. She was clad in miserable rags, beaten for the slightest offence and finally dismissed for a theft of thirty sous which she did not commit. She took service on another farm where she tended the poultry; and as she was well thought of by her master, her fellow-workers soon grew jealous.

One evening in August (she was then eighteen years old), they persuaded her to accompany them to the fair at Colleville. She was immediately dazzled by the noise, the lights in the trees, the brightness of the dresses, the laces and gold crosses, and the crowd of people all hopping at the same time. She was standing modestly at a distance, when presently a young man of well-to-do apearance, who had been leaning on the pole of a wagon and smoking his pipe, approached her, and asked her for a dance. He treated her to cider and cake, bought her a silk shawl, and then, thinking she had guessed his purpose, offered to see her home. When they came to the end of a field he threw her down brutally. But she grew frightened and screamed, and he walked off.

One evening, on the road leading to Beaumont, she came upon a wagon loaded with hay, and when she overtook it, she recognised Théodore. He greeted her calmly, and asked her to forget what had happened between them, as it "was all the fault of the drink."

She did not know what to reply and wished to run away.

Presently he began to speak of the harvest and of the notables of the village; his father had left Colleville and bought the farm of Les Écots, so that now they would be neighbors. "Ah!" she exclaimed. He then added that his parents were looking around for a wife for him, but that he, himself, was not so anxious and preferred to wait for a girl who suited him. She hung her head. He then asked her whether she had ever thought of marrying. She replied, smilingly, that it was wrong of him to make fun of her. "Oh! no, I am in earnest," he said, and put his left arm around her waist while they sauntered along. The air was soft, the stars were bright, and the huge load of hay oscillated in front of them, drawn by four horses whose ponderous hoofs raised clouds of dust. Without a word from their driver they turned to the right. He kissed her again and she went home. The following week, Théodore obtained meetings.

They met in yards, behind walls or under isolated trees. She was not ignorant, as girls of well-to-do families are—for the animals had instructed her—but her reason and her instinct of honour kept her from falling. Her resistance exasperated Théodore's love and so in order to satisfy it (or perchance ingenuously), he offered to marry her. She would not believe him at first, so he made solemn promises. But, in a short time he mentioned a difficulty; the previous year, his parents had purchased a substitute for him; but any day he might be drafted and the prospect of serving in the army alarmed him greatly. To Félicité his cowardice appeared a proof of his love for her, and her devotion to him grew stronger. When she met him, he would torture her with his fears and his entreaties. At last, he announced that he was going to the prefect himself for information, and would let her know everything on the following Sunday, between eleven o'clock and midnight.

When the time drew near, she ran to meet her lover.

But instead of Théodore, one of his friends was at the meeting-place.

He informed her that she would never see her sweetheart again; for, in order to escape the conscription, he had married a rich old woman, Madame Lehoussais, of Toucques.

The poor girl's sorrow was frightful. She threw herself on the ground, she cried and called on the Lord, and wandered around desolately until sunrise. Then she went back to the farm, declared her intention of leaving, and at the end of the month, after she had received her wages, she packed all her belongings in a handkerchief and started for Pont-l'Evêque.

In front of the inn, she met a woman wearing widow's weeds, and upon questioning her, learned that she was looking for a cook. The girl did not know very much, but appeared so willing and so modest in her requirements, that Madame Aubain finally said:

"Very well, I will give you a trial."

And half an hour later Félicité was installed in her house.

At first she lived in a constant anxiety that was caused by "the style of the household" and the memory of "Monsieur" that hovered over everything. Paul and Virginia, the one aged seven, and the other barely four, seemed made of some precious material; she carried them pig-a-back, and was greatly mortified when Madame Aubain forbade her to kiss them every other minute.

But in spite of all this, she was happy. The comfort of her new surroundings had obliterated her sadness.

Every Thursday, friends of Madame Aubain dropped in for a game of cards, and it was Félicité's duty to prepare the table and heat the foot-warmers. They arrived at exactly eight o'clock and departed before eleven.

Every Monday morning, the dealer in second-hand goods, who lived under the alley-way, spread out his wares on the sidewalk. Then the city would be filled with a buzzing of voices in which the neighing of horses, the bleating of lambs, the grunting of pigs, could be distinguished, mingled with the sharp sound of wheels on the cobble-stones. About twelve o'clock, when the market was in full swing, there appeared at the front door a tall, middle-aged peasant, with a hooked nose and a cap on the back of his head; it was Robelin, the farmer of Geffosses. Shortly afterwards came Liébard, the farmer of Toucques, short, rotund and ruddy, wearing a grey jacket and spurred boots.

Both men brought their landlady either chickens or cheese. Félicité would invariably thwart their ruses and they held her in great respect.

At various times, Madame Aubain received a visit from the Marquis de Grémanville, one of her uncles, who was ruined and lived at Falaise on the remainder of his estates. He always came at dinner-time and brought an ugly poodle with him, whose paws soiled the furniture. In spite of his efforts to appear a man of breeding (he even went so far as to raise his hat every time he said "My deceased father"), his habits got the better of him, and he would fill his glass a little too often and relate broad stories. Félicité would show him out very politely and say: "You have had enough for this time, Monsieur de Grémanville! Hoping to see you again!" and would close the door.

She opened it gladly for Monsieur Bourais, a retired lawyer. His bald head and white cravat, the ruffling of his shirt, his flowing brown coat, the manner in which he took snuff, his whole person, in fact, produced in her the kind of awe which we feel when we see extraordinary persons. As he managed Madame's estates, he spent hours with her in Monsieur's study; he was in constant fear of being compromised, had a great regard for the magistracy and some pretensions to learning.

In order to facilitate the children's studies, he presented them with an engraved geography which represented various scenes of the world: cannibals with feather head-dresses, a gorilla kidnapping a young girl, Arabs in the desert, a whale being harpooned, etc.

Paul explained the pictures to Félicité. And, in fact, this was her only literary education.

The children's studies were under the direction of a poor devil employed at the town-hall, who sharpened his pocket-knife on his boots and was famous for his penmanship.

When the weather was fine, they went to Geffosses. The house was built in the centre of the sloping yard; and the sea looked like a grey spot in the distance. Félicité would take slices of cold meat from the lunch basket and they would sit down and eat in a room next to the dairy. This room was all that remained of a cottage that had been torn down. The dilapidated wall-paper trembled in the drafts. Madame Aubain, overwhelmed by recollections, would hang her head, while the children were afraid to open their mouths. Then, "Why don't you go and play?" their mother would say; and they would scamper off.

Paul would go to the old barn, catch birds, throw stones into the pond, or pound the trunks of the trees with a stick till they resounded like drums. Virginia would feed the rabbits and run to pick the wild flowers in the fields, and her flying legs would disclose her little embroidered pantalettes. One autumn evening, they struck out for home through the meadows. The new moon illumined part of the sky and a mist hovered like a veil over the sinuosities of the river. Oxen, lying in the pastures, gazed mildly at the passing persons. In the third field, however, several of them got up and surrounded them. "Don't be afraid," cried Félicité; and murmuring a sort of lament she passed her hand over the back of the nearest ox; he turned away and the others followed. But when they came to the next pasture, they heard frightful bellowing.

It was a bull which was hidden from them by the fog. He advanced towards the two women, and Madame Aubain prepared to flee for her life. "No, no! not so fast," warned Félicité. Still they hurried on, for they could hear the noisy breathing of the bull close behind them. His hoofs pounded the grass like hammers, and presently he began to gallop! Félicité turned around and threw patches of grass in his eyes. He hung his head, shook his horns and bellowed with fury. Madame Aubain and the children, huddled at the end of the field, were trying to jump over the ditch. Félicité continued to back before the bull, blinding him with dirt, while she shouted to them to make haste.

Madame Aubain finally slid into the ditch, after shoving first Virginia and then Paul into it, and though she stumbled several times she managed, by dint of courage, to climb the other side of it.

The bull had driven Félicité up against a fence; the foam from his muzzle flew in her face and in another minute he would have disembowelled her. She had just time to slip between two bars and the huge animal, thwarted, paused.

For years, this occurrence was a topic of conversation in Pont-l'Evéque. But Félicité took no credit to herself, and probably never knew that she had been heroic.

Virginia occupied her thoughts solely, for the shock she had sustained gave her a nervous affection, and the physician, M. Poupart, prescribed the saltwater bathing at Trouville. In those days, Trouville was not greatly patronised. Madame Aubain gathered information, consulted Bourais, and made preparations as if they were going on an extended trip.

The baggage was sent the day before on Liébard's cart. On the following morning, he brought around two horses, one of which had a woman's saddle with a velveteen back to it, while on the crupper of the other was a rolled shawl that was to be used for a seat. Madame Aubain mounted the second horse, behind Liébard. Félicité took change of the little girl, and Paul rode M. Lechaptois' donkey, which had been lent for the occasion on the condition that they should be careful of it.

The road was so bad that it took two hours to cover the eight miles. The two horses sank knee-deep into the mud and stumbled into ditches; sometimes they had to jump over them. In certain places, Liébard's mare stopped abruptly. He waited patiently till she started again, and talked of the people whose estates bordered the road, adding his own moral reflections to the outline of their histories. Thus, when they were passing through Toucques, and came to some windows draped with nasturtiums, he shrugged his shoulders and said: "There's a woman, Madame Lehoussais, who, instead of taking a young man——" Félicité could not catch what followed; the horses began to trot, the donkey to gallop, and they turned into a lane; then a gate swung open, two farm-hands appeared and they all dismounted at the very threshold of the farm-house.

Mother Liébard, when she caught sight of her mistress, was lavish with joyful demonstrations. She got up a lunch which comprised a leg of mutton, tripe, sausages, a chicken fricassée, sweet cider, a fruit tart and some preserved prunes; then to all this the good woman added polite remarks about Madame, who appeared to be in better health, Mademoiselle, who had grown to be "superb," and Paul, who had become singularly sturdy; she spoke also of their deceased grandparents, whom the Liébards had known, for they had been in the service of the family for several generations.

Like its owners, the farm had an ancient appearance. The beams of the ceiling were mouldy, the walls black with smoke and the windows grey with dust. The oak sideboard was filled with all sorts of utensils, plates, pitchers, tin bowls, wolf-traps. The children laughed when they saw a huge syringe. There was not a tree in the yard that did not have mushrooms growing around its foot, or a bunch of mistletoe hanging in its branches. Several of the trees had been blown down, but they had started to grow in the middle and all were laden with quantities of apples. The thatched roofs, which were of unequal thickness, looked like brown velvet and could resist the fiercest gales. But the wagon-shed was fast crumbling to ruins. Madame Aubain said that she would attend to it, and then gave orders to have the horses saddled.

It took another thirty minutes to reach Trouville. The little caravan dismounted in order to pass Les Ecores, a cliff that overhangs the bay, and a few minutes later, at the end of the dock, they entered the yard of the Golden Lamb, an inn kept by Mother David.

During the first few days, Virginia felt stronger, owing to the change of air and the action of the seabaths. She took them in her little chemise, as she had no bathing suit, and afterwards her nurse dressed her in the cabin of a customs officer, which was used for that purpose by other bathers.

In the afternoon, they would take the donkey and go to the Roches-Noires, near Hennequeville. The path led at first through undulating grounds, and thence to a plateau, where pastures and tilled fields alternated. At the edge of the road, mingling with the brambles, grew holly bushes, and here and there stood large dead trees whose branches traced zigzags upon the blue sky.

Ordinarily, they rested in a field facing the ocean, with Deauville on their left, and Havre on their right. The sea glittered brightly in the sun and was as smooth as a mirror, and so calm that they could scarcely distinguish its murmur; sparrows chirped joyfully and the immense canopy of heaven spread over it all. Madame Aubain brought out her sewing, and Virginia amused herself by braiding reeds; Félicité wove lavender blossoms, while Paul was bored and wished to go home.

Sometimes they crossed the Toucques in a boat, and started to hunt for sea-shells. The outgoing tide exposed star-fish and sea-urchins, and the children tried to catch the flakes of foam which the wind blew away. The sleepy waves lapping the sand unfurled themselves along the shore that extended as far as the eye could see, but where land began, it was limited by the downs which separated it from the "Swamp," a large meadow shaped like a hippodrome. When they went home that way, Trouville, on the slope of a hill below, grew larger and larger as they advanced, and, with all its houses of unequal height, seemed to spread out before them in a sort of giddy confusion.

When the heat was too oppressive, they remained in their rooms. The dazzling sunlight cast bars of light between the shutters. Not a sound in the village, not a soul on the sidewalk. This silence intensified the tranquillity of everything. In the distance, the hammers of some calkers pounded the hull of a ship, and the sultry breeze brought them an odour of tar.

The principal diversion consisted in watching the return of the fishing-smacks.

As soon as they passed the beacons, they began to ply to windward. The sails were lowered to one third of the masts, and with their fore-sails swelled up like balloons they glided over the waves and anchored in the middle of the harbour. Then they crept up alongside of the dock and the sailors threw the quivering fish over the side of the boat; a line of carts was waiting for them, and women with white caps sprang forward to receive the baskets and embrace their men-folk.

One day, one of them spoke to Félicité, who, after a little while, returned to the house gleefully. She had found one of her sisters, and presently Nastasie Barette, wife of Léroux, made her appearance, holding an infant in her arms, another child by the hand, while on her left was a little cabin-boy with his hands in his pockets and his cap on his ear.

At the end of fifteen minutes, Madame Aubain bade her go.

They always hung around the kitchen, or approached Félicité when she and the children were out walking. The husband, however, did not show himself.

Félicité developed a great fondness for them; she bought them a stove, some shirts and a blanket; it was evident that they exploited her. Her foolishness annoyed Madame Aubain, who, moreover did not like the nephew's familiarity, for he called her son "thou";—and, as Virginia began to cough and the season was over, she decided to return to Pont-l'Evêque.

Monsieur Bourais assisted her in the choise of a college. The one at Caen was considered the best. So Paul was sent away and bravely said good-bye to them all, for he was glad to go to live in a house where he would have boy companions.

Madame Aubain resigned herself to the separation from her son because it was unavoidable. Virginia brooded less and less over it. Félicité regretted the noise he made, but soon a new occupation diverted her mind; beginning from Christmas, she accompanied the little girl to her catechism lesson every day.

III

After she had made a curtsey at the threshold, she would walk up the aisle between the double lines of chairs, open Madame Aubain's pew, sit down and look around.

Girls and boys, the former on the right, the latter on the left-hand side of the church, filled the stalls of the choir; the priest stood beside the reading-desk; on one stained window of the side-aisle the Holy Ghost hovered over the Virgin; on another one, Mary knelt before the Child Jesus, and behind the altar, a wooden group represented Saint Michael felling the dragon.

The priest first read a condensed lesson of sacred history. Félicité evoked Paradise, the Flood, the Tower of Babel, the blazing cities, the dying nations, the shattered idols; and out of this she developed a great respect for the Almighty and a great fear of His wrath. Then, when she listened to the Passion, she wept. Why had they crucified Him who loved little children, nourished the people, made the blind see, and who, out of humility, had wished to be born among the poor, in a stable? The sowings, the harvests, the wine-presses, all those familiar things which the Scriptures mention, formed a part of her life; the word of God sanctified them; and she loved the lambs with increased tenderness for the sake of the Lamb, and the doves because of the Holy Ghost.

She found it hard, however, to think of the latter as a person, for was it not a bird, a flame, and sometimes only a breath? Perhaps it is its light that at night hovers over swamps, its breath that propels the clouds, its voice that renders church-bells harmonious. And Félicité worshipped devoutly, while enjoying the coolness and the stillness of the church.

As for the dogma, she could not understand it and did not even try. The priest discoursed, the children recited, and she went to sleep, only to awaken with a start when they were leaving the church and their wooden shoes clattered on the stone pavement.

In this way, she learned her catechism, her religious education having been neglected in her youth; and thenceforth she imitated all Virginia's religious practices, fasted when she did, and went to confession with her. At the Corpus-Christi Day they both decorated an altar.

She worried in advance over Virginia's first communion. She fussed about the shoes, the rosary, the book and the gloves. With what nervousness she helped the mother dress the child!

During the entire ceremony, she felt anguished. Monsieur Bourais hid part of the choir from view, but directly in front of her, the flock of maidens, wearing white wreaths over their lowered veils, formed a snow-white field, and she recognised her darling by the slenderness of her neck and her devout attitude. The bell tinkled. All the heads bent and there was a silence. Then, at the peals of the organ the singers and the worshippers struck up the Agnus Dei; the boys' procession began; behind them came the girls. With clasped hands, they advanced step by step to the lighted altar, knelt at the first step, received one by one the Host, and returned to their seats in the same order. When Virginia's turn came, Félicité leaned forward to watch her, and through that imagination which springs from true affection, she at once became the child, whose face and dress became hers, whose heart beat in her bosom, and when Virginia opened her mouth and closed her lids, she did likewise and came very near fainting.

The following day, she presented herself early at the church so as to receive communion from the curé. She took it with the proper feeling, but did not experience the same delight as on the previous day.

Madame Aubain wished to make an accomplished girl of her daughter; and as Guyot could not teach English nor music, she decided to send her to the Ursulines at Honfleur.

The child made no objection, but Félicité sighed and thought Madame was heartless. Then, she thought that perhaps her mistress was right, as these things were beyond her sphere. Finally, one day, an old *fiacre* stopped in front of the door and a nun stepped out. Félicité put Virginia's luggage on top of the carriage, gave the coachman some instructions, and smuggled six jars of jam, a dozen pears and a bunch of violets under the seat.

At the last minute, Virginia had a fit of sobbing; she embraced her mother again and again, while the latter kissed her on her forehead, and said: "Now, be brave, be brave!" The step was pulled up and the *fiacre* rumbled off.

Then Madame Aubain had a fainting spell, and that evening all her friends, including the two Lormeaus, Madame Lechaptois, the ladies Rochefeuille, Messieurs de Houppeville and Bourais, called on her and tendered their sympathy.

At first the separation proved very painful to her. But her daughter wrote her three times a week and the other days she, herself, wrote to Virginia. Then she walked in the garden, read a little, and in this way managed to fill out the emptiness of the hours.

Each morning, out of habit, Félicité entered Virginia's room and gazed at the walls. She missed combing her hair, lacing her shoes, tucking her in her bed, and the bright face and little hand when they used to go out for a walk. In order to occupy herself she tried to make lace. But her clumsy fingers broke the threads; she had no heart for anything, lost her sleep and "wasted away," as she put it.

In order to have some distraction, she asked leave to receive the visits of her nephew Victor.

He would come on Sunday, after church, with ruddy cheeks and bared chest, bringing with him the scent of the country. She would set the table and they would sit down opposite each other, and eat their dinner; she ate as little as possible, herself, to avoid any extra expense, but would stuff him so with food that he would finally go to sleep. At the first stroke of vespers, she would wake him up, brush his trousers, tie his cravat and walk to church with him, leaning on his arm with maternal pride.

His parents always told him to get something out of her, either a package of brown sugar, or soap, or brandy, and sometimes even money. He brought her his clothes to mend, and she accepted the task gladly, because it meant another visit from him.

In August, his father took him on a coasting-vessel.

It was vacation time and the arrival of the children consoled Félicité. But Paul was capricious, and Virginia was growing too old to be thee-and-thou'd, a fact which seemed to produce a sort of embarrassment in their relations.

Victor went successively to Morlaix, to Dunkirk, and to Brighton; whenever he returned from a trip he would bring her a present. The first time it was a box of shells; the second, a coffee-cup; the third, a big doll of ginger-bread. He was growing handsome, had a good figure, a tiny moustache, kind eyes, and a little leather cap that sat jauntily on the back of his head. He amused his aunt by telling her stories mingled with nautical expressions.

One Monday, the 14th of July, 1819 (she never forgot the date), Victor announced that he had been engaged on a merchant-vessel and that in two days he would take the steamer at Honfleur and join his sailer, which was going to start from Havre very soon. Perhaps he might be away two years.

The prospect of his departure filled Félicité with despair, and in order to bid him farewell, on Wednesday night, after Madame's dinner, she put on her pattens and trudged the four miles that separated Pont-l'Evêque from Honfleur.

When she reached the Calvary, instead of turning to the right, she turned to the left and lost herself in coal-yards; she had to retrace her steps; some people she spoke to advised her to hasten. She walked helplessly around the harbour filled with vessels, and knocked against hawsers. Presently the ground sloped abruptly, lights fitted to and fro, and she thought all at once that she had gone mad when she saw some horses in the sky.

Others, on the edge of the dock, neighed at the sight of the ocean. A derrick pulled them up in the air and dumped them into a boat, where passengers were bustling about among barrels of cider, baskets of cheese and bags of meal; chickens cackled, the captain swore and a cabin-boy rested on the railing, apparently indifferent to his surroundings. Félicité, who did not recognise him, kept shouting: "Victor!" He suddenly raised his eyes, but while she was preparing to rush up to him, they withdrew the gangplank.

The packet, towed by singing women, glided out of the harbour. Her hull squeaked and the heavy waves beat up against her sides. The sail had turned and nobody was visible;—and on the ocean, silvered by the light of the moon, the vessel formed a black spot that grew dimmer and dimmer, and finally disappeared.

When Félicité passed the Calvary again, she felt as if she must entrust that which was dearest to her to the Lord; and for a long while she prayed, with uplifted eyes and a face wet with tears. The city was sleeping; some customs officials were taking the air; and the water kept pouring through the holes of the dam with a deafening roar. The town clock struck two.

The parlour of the convent would not open until morning, and surely a delay would annoy Madame; so, in spite of her desire to see the other child, she went home. The maids of the inn were just arising when she reached Pont-l'Evêque.

So the poor boy would be on the ocean for months! His previous trips had not alarmed her. One can come back from England and Brittany; but America, the colonies, the islands, were all lost in an uncertain region at the very end of the world.

From that time on, Félicité thought solely of her nephew. On warm days she feared he would suffer from thirst, and when it stormed, she was afraid he would be struck by lightning. When she harkened to the wind that rattled in the chimney and dislodged the tiles on the roof, she imagined that he was being buffeted by the same storm, perched on top of a shattered mast, with his whole body bent backward and covered with sea-foam; or,—these were recollections of the engraved geography—he was being devoured by savages, or captured in a forest by apes, or dying on some lonely coast. She never mentioned her anxieties, however.

Madame Aubain worried about her daughter.

The sisters thought that Virgina was affectionate but delicate. The slightest emotion enervated her. She had to give up her piano lessons. Her mother insisted upon regular letters from the convent. One morning, when the postman failed to come, she grew impatient and began to pace to and fro, from her chair to the window. It was really extraordinary! No news since four days!

In order to console her mistress by her own example, Félicité said:

"Why, Madame, I haven't had any news since six months!"—

"From whom?"—

The servant replied gently:

"Why—from my nephew."

"Oh, yes, your nephew!" And shrugging her shoulders, Madame Aubain continued to pace the floor as if to say: "I did not think of it.—Besides, I do not care, a cabin-boy, a pauper!—but my daughter—what a difference! just think of it!—"

Félicité, although she had been reared roughly, was very indignant. Then she forgot about it.

It appeared quite natural to her that one should lose one's head about Virginia.

The two children were of equal importance; they were united in her heart and their fate was to be the same.

The chemist informed her that Victor's vessel had reached Havana. He had read the information in a newspaper.

Félicité imagined that Havana was a place where people did nothing but smoke, and that Victor walked around among negroes in a cloud of tobacco. Could a person, in case of need, return by land? How far was it from Pont-l'Evêque? In order to learn these things, she questioned Monsieur Bourais. He reached for his map and began some explanations concerning longitudes, and smiled with superiority at Félicité's bewilderment. At last, he took his pencil and pointed out an imperceptible black point in the scallops of an oval blotch, adding: "There it is." She bent over the map; the maze of coloured lines hurt her eyes without enlightening her; and when Bourais asked her what puzzled her, she requested him to show her the house Victor lived in. Bourais threw up his hands, sneezed, and then laughed uproariously; such ignorance delighted his soul; but Félicité failed to understand the cause of his mirth, she whose intelligence was so limited that she perhaps expected to see even the picture of her nephew!

It was two weeks later that Liébard came into the kitchen at market-time, and handed her a letter from her brother-in-law. As neither of them could read, she called upon her mistress.

Madame Aubain, who was counting the stitches of her knitting, laid her work down beside her, opened the letter, started, and in a low tone and with a searching look said: "They tell you of a——misfortune. Your nephew——."

He had died. The letter told nothing more.

Félicité dropped on a chair, leaned her head against the back and closed her lids; presently they grew pink. Then, with drooping head, inert hands and staring eyes she repeated at intervals:

"Poor little chap! poor little chap!"

Liébard watched her and sighed. Madame Aubain was trembling.

She proposed to the girl to go to see her sister in Trouville.

With a single motion, Félicité replied that it was not necessary.

There was a silence. Old Liébard thought it about time for him to take leave. Then Félicité uttered:

"They have no sympathy, they do not care!"

Her head fell forward again, and from time to time, mechanically, she toyed with the long knitting-needles on the work-table.

Some women passed through the yard with a basket of wet clothes.

When she saw them through the window, she suddenly remembered her own wash; as she had soaked it the day before, she must go and rinse it now. So she arose and left the room.

Her tub and her board were on the bank of the Toucques. She threw a heap of clothes on the ground, rolled up her sleevs and grasped her bat; and her loud pounding could be heard in the neighbouring gardens. The meadows were empty, the breeze wrinkled the stream, at the bottom of which were long grasses that looked like the hair of corpses floating in the water. She restrained her sorrow and was very brave until night; but, when she had gone to her own room, she gave way to it, burying her face in the pillow and pressing her two fists against her temples.

A long while afterward, she learned through Victor's captain, the circumstances which surrounded his death. At the hospital they had bled him too much, treating him for yellow fever. Four doctors held him at one time. He died almost instantly, and the chief surgeon had said:

"Here goes another one!"

His parents had always treated him barbarously; she preferred not to see them again, and they made no advances, either from forgetfulness or out of innate hardness.

Virginia was growing weaker.

A cough, continual fever, oppressive breathing and spots on her cheeks indicated some serious trouble. Monsieur Poupart had advised a sojourn in Provence. Madame Aubain decided that they would go, and she would have had her daughter come home at once, had it not been for the climate of Pont-l'Evêque.

She made an arrangement with a livery-stable man who drove her over to the convent every Tuesday. In the garden there was a terrace, from which the view extends to the Seine. Virginia walked in it, leaning on her mother's arm and treading the dead vine leaves. Sometimes the sun, shining through the clouds, made her blink her lids, when she gazed at the sails in the distance, and let her eyes roam over the horizon from the chateau of Tancarville to the lighthouses of Havre. Then they rested in the arbour. Her mother had bought a little cask of fine Malaga wine, and Virginia, laughing at the idea of becoming intoxicated, would drink a few drops of it, but never more.

Her strength returned. Autumn passed. Félicité began to reassure Madame Aubain. But, one evening, when she returned home after an errand, she met M. Boupart's coach in front of the door; M. Boupart himself was standing in the vestibule and Madame Aubain was tying the strings of her bonnet. "Give me my foot-warmer, my purse and my gloves; and be quick about it," she said.

Virginia had congestion of the lungs; perhaps it was desperate.

"Not yet," said the physician, and both got into the carriage, while the snow fell in thick flakes. It was almost night and very cold.

Félicité rushed to the church to light a candle. Then she ran after the coach which she overtook after an hour's chase, sprang up behind and held on to the straps. But suddenly a thought crossed her mind: "The yard had been left open; supposing that burglars got in!" And down she jumped.

The next morning, at daybreak, she called at the doctor's. He had been home, but had left again. Then she waited at the inn, thinking that strangers might bring her a letter. At last, at daylight she took the diligence for Lisieux.

The convent was at the end of a steep and narrow street. When she arrived about at the middle of it, she heard strange noises, a funeral knell. "It must be for some one else," thought she; and she pulled the knocker violently.

After several minutes had elapsed, she heard footsteps, the door was half opened and a nun appeared. The good sister, with an air of compunction, told her that "she had just passed away." And at the same time the tolling of Saint-Léonard's increased.

Félicité reached the second floor. Already at the threshold, she caught sight of Virginia lying on her back, with clasped hands, her mouth open and her head thrown back, beneath a black crucifix inclined toward her, and stiff curtains which were less white than her face. Madame Aubain lay at the foot of the couch, clasping it with her arms and uttering groans of agony. The Mother Superior was standing on the right side of the bed. The three candles on the bureau made red blurs, and the windows were dimmed by the fog outside. The nuns carried Madame Aubain from the room.

For two nights, Félicité never left the corpse. She would repeat the same prayers, sprinkle holy water over the sheets, get up, come back to the bed and contemplate the body. At the end of the first vigil, she noticed that the face had taken on a yellow tinge, the lips grew blue, the nose grew pinched, the eyes were sunken. She kissed them several times and would not have been greatly astonished had Virginia opened them; to souls like these the supernatural is always quite simple. She washed her, wrapped her in a shroud, put her into the casket, laid a wreath of flowers on her head and arranged her curls. They were blond and of an extraordinary length for her age. Félicité cut off a big lock and put half of it into her bosom, resolving never to part with it.

The body was taken to Pont-l'Evéque, according to Madame Aubain's wishes; she followed the hearse in a closed carriage.

After the ceremony it took three quarters of an hour to reach the cemetery. Paul, sobbing, headed the procession; Monsieur Bourais followed, and then came the principal inhabitants of the town, the women covered with black capes, and Félicité. The memory of her nephew, and the thought that she had not been able to render him these honors, made her doubly unhappy, and she felt as if he were being buried with Virginia.

Madame Aubain's grief was uncontrollable. At first she rebelled against God, thinking that he was unjust to have taken away her child—she who had never done anything wrong, and whose conscience was so pure! But no! she ought to have taken her South. Other doctors would have saved her. She accused herself, prayed to be able to join her child, and cried in the midst of her dreams. Of the latter, one more especially haunted her. Her husband, dressed like a sailor, had come back from a long voyage, and with tears in his eyes told her that he had received the order to take Virginia away. Then they both consulted about a hiding-place.

Once she came in from the garden, all upset. A moment before (and she showed the place), the father and daughter had appeared to her, one after the other; they did nothing but look at her.

During several months she remained inert in her room. Félicité scolded her gently; she must keep up for her son and also for the other one, for "her memory."

"Her memory!" replied Madame Aubain, as if she were just awakening, "Oh! yes, yes, you do not forget her!" This was an allusion to the cemetery where she had been expressly forbidden to go.

But Félicité went there every day. At four o'clock exactly, she would go through the town, climb the hill, open the gate and arrive at Virginia's tomb. It was a small column of pink marble with a flat stone at its base, and it was surrounded by a little plot enclosed by chains. The flower-beds were bright with blossoms. Félicité watered their leaves, renewed the gravel, and knelt on the ground in order to till the earth properly. When Madame Aubain was able to visit the cemetery she felt very much relieved and consoled.

Years passed, all alike and marked by no other events than the return of the great church holidays: Easter, Assumption, All Saints' Day. Household happenings constituted the only data to which in later years they often referred. Thus, in 1825, workmen painted the vestibule; in 1827, a portion of the roof almost killed a man by falling into the yard. In the summer of 1828, it was Madame's turn to offer the hallowed bread; at that time, Bourais disappeared mysteriously; and the old acquaintances, Guyot, Liébard, Madame Lechaptois, Robelin, old Grémanville, paralysed a long time, since passed away one by one. One night, the driver of the mail in Pont-l'Evêque announced the Revolution of July. A few days afterward a new sub-prefect was nominated, the Baron de Larsonnière, ex-consul in America, who, besides his wife, had his sister-in-law and her three grown daughters with him. They were often seen on their lawn, dressed in loose blouses, and they had a parrot and a negro servant. Madame Aubain received a call, which she returned promptly. As soon as she caught sight of them, Félicité would run and notify her mistress. But only one thing was capable of arousing her: a letter from her son.

He could not follow any profession as he was absorbed in drinking. His mother paid his debts and he made fresh ones; and the sighs that she heaved while she knitted at the window reached the ears of Félicité who was spinning in the kitchen.

They walked in the garden together, always speaking of Virginia, and asking each other if such and such a thing would have pleased her, and what she would probably have said on this or that occasion.

All her little belongings were put away in a closet of the room which held the two little beds. But Madame Aubain looked them over as little as possible. One summer day, however, she resigned herself to the task and when she opened the closet the moths flew out.

Virginia's frocks were hung under a shelf where there were three dolls, some hoops, a doll-house, and a basin which she had used. Félicité and Madame Aubain also took out the skirts, the handkerchiefs, and the stockings and spread them on the beds, before putting them away again. The sun fell on the piteous things, disclosing their spots and the creases formed by the motions of the body. The atmosphere was warm and blue, and a blackbird trilled in the garden; everything seemed to live in happiness. They found a little hat of soft brown plush, but it was entirely moth-eaten. Félicité asked for it. Their eyes met and filled with tears; at last the mistress opened her arms and the servant threw herself against her breast and they hugged each other, giving vent to their grief in a kiss which equalized them for a moment.

It was the first time that this had ever happened, for Madam Aubain was not of an expansive nature. Félicité was as grateful for it as if it had been some favour, and thenceforth loved her with animal-like devotion and a religious veneration.

Her kind-heartedness developed. When she heard the drums of a marching regiment passing through the street, she would stand in the doorway with a jug of cider and give the soldiers a drink. She nursed cholera victims. She protected Polish refugees, and one of them even declared that he wished to marry her. But they quarrelled, for one morning when she returned from the Angelus she found him in the kitchen coolly eating a dish which he had prepared for himself during her absence.

After the Polish refugees came Colmiche, an old man who was credited with having committed frightful misdeeds in '93. He lived near the river in the ruins of a pig-sty. The urchins peeped at him through the cracks in the walls and threw stones that fell on his miserable bed, where he lay gasping with catarrh, with long hair, inflamed eyelids, and a tumor as big as his head on one arm.

She got him some linen, tried to clean his hovel and dreamed of installing him in the bake-house without his being in Madame's way. When the cancer broke, she dressed it every day; sometimes she brought him some cake and placed him in the sun on a bundle of hay; and the poor old creature, trembling and drooling, would thank her in his broken voice, and put out his hands whenever she left him. Finally he died; and she had a mass said for the repose of his soul.

That day a great joy came to her; at dinner-time, Madame de Larsonnière's servant called with the parrot, the cage, and the perch and chain and lock. A note from the baroness told Madame Aubain that, as her husband had been promoted to a prefecture, they were leaving that night, and she begged her to accept the bird as a remembrance and a token of her esteem.

For a long time the parrot had been on Félicité's mind, because he came from America, which reminded her of Victor, and she had approached the negro on the subject.

Once even, she had said:

"How glad Madame would be to have him!"

The man had repeated this remark to his mistress who, not being able to keep the bird, took this means of getting rid of it.

IV

He was called Loulou. His body was green, his head blue, the tips of his wings were pink and his breast was golden.

But he had the tiresome tricks of biting his perch, pulling his feathers out, scattering refuse and spilling the water of his bath. Madame Aubain grew tired of him and gave him to Félicité for good.

She undertook his education, and soon he was able to repeat: "Pretty boy! Your servant, sir! I salute you, Marie!" His perch was placed near the door and several persons were astonished that he did not answer to the name of "Jacquot," for every parrot is called Jacquot. They called him a goose and a log, and these taunts were like so many dagger thrusts to Félicité. Strange stubbornness of the bird which would not talk when people watched him!

Nevertheless, he sought society; for on Sunday, when the ladies Rochefeuille, Monsieur de Houppeville and the new habitués, Onfroy, the chemist, Monsieur Varin and Captain Mathieu, dropped in for their game of cards, he struck the window-panes with his wings and made such a racket that it was impossible to talk.

Bourais' face must have appeared very funny to Loulou. As soon as he saw him he would begin to roar. His voice re-echoed in the yard, and the neighbors would come to the windows and begin to laugh, too; and in order that the parrot might not see him, Monsieur Bourais edged along the wall, pushed his hat over his eyes to hide his profile, and entered by the garden door, and the looks he gave the bird lacked affection. Loulou having thrust his head into the butcher-boy's basket, received a slap, and from that time he always tried to nip his enemy. Fabu threatened to wring his neck, although he was not cruelly inclined, notwithstanding his big whiskers and tattooings. On the contrary, he rather liked the bird and, out of deviltry, tried to teach him oaths. Félicité, whom his manner alarmed, put Loulou in the kitchen, took off his chain and let him walk all over the house.

When he went downstairs, he rested his beak on the steps, lifted his right foot and then his left one; but his mistress feared that such feats would give him vertigo. He became ill and was unable to eat. There was a small growth under his tongue like those chickens are sometimes afflicted with. Félicité pulled it off with her nails and cured him. One day, Paul was imprudent enough to blow the smoke of his cigar in his face; another time, Madame Lormeau was teasing him with the tip of her umbrella and he swallowed the tip. Finally he got lost.

She had put him on the grass to cool him and went away only for a second; when she returned, she found no parrot! She hunted among the bushes, on the bank of the river, and on the roofs, without paying any attention to Madame Aubain who screamed at her: "Take care! you must be insane!" Then she searched every garden in Pont-l'Evêque and stopped the passers-by to inquire of them: "Haven't you perhaps seen my parrot?" To those who had never seen the parrot, she described him minutely. Suddenly she thought she saw something green fluttering behind the mills at the foot of the hill. But when she was at the top of the hill she could not see it. A hod-carrier told her that he had just seen the bird in Saint-Melaine, in Mother Simon's store. She rushed to the place. The people did not know what she was talking about. At last she came home, exhausted, with her slippers worn to shreds, and despair in her heart. She sat down on the bench near Madame and was telling of her search when presently a light weight dropped on her shoulder—Loulou! What the deuce had he been doing? Perhaps he had just taken a little walk around the town!

She did not easily forget her scare; in fact, she never got over it. In consequence of a cold, she caught a sore throat; and some time afterward she had an earache. Three years later she was stone deaf, and spoke in a very loud voice even in church. Although her sins might have been proclaimed throughout the diocese without any shame to herself, or ill effects to the community, the curé thought it advisable to receive her confession in the vestry-room.

Imaginary buzzings also added to her bewilderment. Her mistress often said to her: "My goodness, how stupid you are!" and she would answer: "Yes, Madame," and look for something.

The narrow circle of her ideas grew more restricted than it already was; the bellowing of the oxen, the chime of the bells no longer reached her intelligence. All things moved silently, like ghosts. Only one noise penetrated her ears; the parrot's voice.

As if to divert her mind, he reproduced for her the tick-tack of the spit in the kitchen, the shrill cry of the fish-vendors, the saw of the carpenter who had a shop opposite, and when the door-bell rang, he would imitate Madame Aubain: "Félicité! go to the front door."

They held conversations together, Loulou repeating the three phrases of his repertory over and over, Félicité replying by words that had no greater meaning, but in which she poured out her feelings. In her isolation, the parrot was almost a son, a lover. He climbed upon her fingers, pecked at her lips, clung to her shawl, and when she rocked her head to and fro like a nurse, the big wings of her cap and the wings of the bird flapped in unison. When clouds gathered on the horizon and the thunder rumbled, Loulou would scream, perhaps because he remembered the storms in his native forests. The dripping of the rain would excite him to frenzy; he flapped around, struck the ceiling with his wings, upset everything, and would finally fly into the garden to play. Then he would come back into the room, light on one of the andirons, and hop around in order to get dry.

One morning during the terrible winter of 1837, when she had put him in front of the fire-place on account of the cold, she found him dead in his cage, hanging to the wire bars with his head down. He had probably died of congestion. But she believed that he had been poisoned, and although she had no proofs whatever, her suspicion rested on Fabu.

She wept so sorely that her mistress said: "Why don't you have him stuffed?"

She asked the advice of the chemist, who had always been kind to the bird.

He wrote to Havre for her. A certain man named Fellacher consented to do the work. But, as the diligence driver often lost parcels entrusted to him, Félicité resolved to take her pet to Honfleur herself.

Leafless apple-trees lined the edges of the road. The ditches were covered with ice. The dogs on the neighboring farms barked; and Félicité, with her hands beneath her cape, her little black sabots and her basket, trotted along nimbly in the middle of the roadway. She crossed the forest, passed by the Haut-Chêne and reached Saint-Gatien.

Behind her, in a cloud of dust and impelled by the steep incline, a mail-coach drawn by galloping horses advanced like a whirlwind. When he saw a woman in the middle of the road, who did not get out of the way, the driver stood up in his seat and shouted to her and so did the postilion, while the four horses, which he could not hold back, accelerated their pace; the two leaders were almost upon her; with a jerk of the reins he threw them to one side, but, furious at the incident, he lifted his big whip and lashed her from her head to her feet with such violence that she fell to the ground unconscious.

Her first thought, when she recovered her senses, was to open the basket. Loulou was unharmed. She felt a sting on her right cheek; when she took her hand away it was red, for the blood was flowing.

She sat down on a pile of stones, and sopped her cheek with her handkerchief; then she ate a crust of bread she had put in her basket, and consoled herself by looking at the bird.

Arriving at the top of Ecquemanville, she saw the lights of Honfleur shining in the distance like so many stars; further on, the ocean spread out in a confused mass. Then a weakness came over her; the misery of her childhood, the disappointment of her first love, the departure of her nephew, the death of Virginia; all these things came back to her at once, and, rising like a swelling tide in her throat, almost choked her.

Then she wished to speak to the captain of the vessel, and without stating what she was sending, she gave him some instructions.

Fellacher kept the parrot a long time. He always promised that it would be ready for the following week; after six months he announced the shipment of a case, and that was the end of it. Really, it seemed as if Loulou would never come back to his home. "They have stolen him," thought Félicité.

Finally he arrived, sitting bolt upright on a branch which could be screwed into a mahogany pedestal, with his foot in the air, his head on one side, and in his beak a nut which the naturalist, from love of the sumptuous, had gilded. She put him in her room.

This place, to which only a chosen few were admitted, looked like a chapel and a second-hand shop, so filled was it with devotional and heterogeneous things. The door could not be opened easily on account of the presence of a large wardrobe. Opposite the window that looked out into the garden, a bull's-eye opened on the yard; a table was placed by the cot and held a wash-basin, two combs, and a piece of blue soap in a broken saucer. On the walls were rosaries, medals, a number of Holy Virgins, and a holy-water basin made out of a cocoanut; on the bureau, which was covered with a napkin like an altar, stood the box of shells that Victor had given her; also a watering-can and a balloon, writing-books, the engraved geography and a pair of shoes; on the nail which held the mirror, hung Virginia's little plush hat! Félicité carried this sort of respect so far that she even kept one of Monsieur's old coats. All the things which Madame Aubain discarded, Félicité begged for her own room. Thus, she had artificial flowers on the edge of the bureau, and the picture of the Comte d'Artois in the recess of the window. By means of a board, Loulou was set on a portion of the chimney which advanced into the room. Every morning when she awoke, she saw him in the dim light of dawn and recalled bygone days and the smallest details of insignificant actions, without any sense of bitterness or grief.

As she was unable to communicate with people, she lived in a sort of somnambulistic torpor. The processions of Corpus-Christi Day seemed to wake her up. She visited the neighbors to beg for candlesticks and mats so as to adorn the temporary altars in the street.

In church, she always gazed at the Holy Ghost, and noticed that there was something about it that resembled a parrot. The likeness appeared even more striking on a colored picture by Espinal, representing the baptism of our Saviour. With his scarlet wings and emerald body, it was really the image of Loulou. Having bought the picture, she hung it near the one of the Comte d'Artois so that she could take them in at one glance.

They associated in her mind, the parrot becoming sanctified through the neighbourhood of the Holy Ghost, and the latter becoming more lifelike in her eyes, and more comprehensible. In all probability the Father had never chosen as messenger a dove, as the latter has no voice, but rather one of Loulou's ancestors. And Félicité said her prayers in front of the colored picture, though from time to time she turned slightly toward the bird.

She desired very much to enter in the ranks of the "Daughters of the Virgin." But Madame Aubain dissuaded her from it.

A most important event occurred: Paul's marriage.

After being first a notary's clerk, then in business, then in the customs, and a tax collector, and having even applied for a position in the administration of woods and forests, he had at last, when he was thirty-six years old, by a divine inspiration, found his vocation: registrature! and he displayed such a high ability that an inspector had offered him his daughter and his influence.

Paul, who had become quite settled, brought his bride to visit his mother.

But she looked down upon the customs of Pont-l'Evêque, put on airs, and hurt Félicité's feelings. Madame Aubain felt relieved when she left.

The following week they learned of Monsieur Bourais' death in an inn.

There were rumours of suicide, which were confirmed; doubts concerning his integrity arose. Madame Aubain looked over her accounts and soon discovered his numerous embezzlements; sales of wood which had been concealed from her, false receipts, etc. Furthermore, he had an illegitimate child, and entertained a friendship for "a person in Dozulé."

These base actions affected her very much. In March, 1853, she developed a pain in her chest; her tongue looked as if it were coated with smoke, and the leeches they applied did not relieve her oppression; and on the ninth evening she died, being just seventy-two years old.

People thought that she was younger, because her hair, which she wore in bands framing her pale face, was brown. Few friends regretted her loss, for her manner was so haughty that she did not attract them. Félicité mourned for her as servants seldom mourn for their masters. The fact that Madame should die before herself perplexed her mind and seemed contrary to the order of things, and absolutely monstrous and inadmissible. Ten days later (the time to journey from Besançon), the heirs arrived. Her daughter-in-law ransacked the drawers, kept some of the furniture, and sold the rest; then they went back to their own home.

Madame's armchair, foot-warmer, work-table, the eight chairs, everything was gone! The places occupied by the pictures formed yellow squares on the walls. They had taken the two little beds, and the wardrobe had been emptied of Virginia's belongings! Félicité went upstairs, overcome with grief.

The following day a sign was posted on the door; the chemist screamed in her ear that the house was for sale.

For a moment she tottered, and had to sit down.

What hurt her most was to give up her room,—so nice for poor Loulou! She looked at him in despair and implored the Holy Ghost, and it was this way that she contracted the idolatrous habit of saying her prayers kneeling in front of the bird. Sometimes the sun fell through the window on his glass eye, and lighted a great spark in it which sent Félicité into ecstasy.

Her mistress had left her an income of three hundred and eighty francs. The garden supplied her with vegetables. As for clothes, she had enough to last her till the end of her days, and she economised on the light by going to bed at dusk.

She rarely went out, in order to avoid passing in front of the second-hand dealer's shop where there was some of the old furniture. Since her fainting spell, she dragged her leg, and as her strength was failing rapidly, old Mother Simon, who had lost her money in the grocery business, came every morning to chop the wood and pump the water.

Her eyesight grew dim. She did not open the shutters after that. Many years passed. But the house did not sell or rent. Fearing that she would be put out, Félicité did not ask for repairs. The laths of the roof were rotting away, and during one whole winter her bolster was wet. After Easter she spit blood.

Then Mother Simon went for a doctor. Félicité wished to know what her complaint was. But, being too deaf to hear, she caught only one word: "Pneumonia." She was familiar with it and gently answered:—"Ah! like Madame," thinking it quite natural that she should follow her mistress.

The time for the altars in the street drew near.

The first one was always erected at the foot of the hill, the second in front of the post-office, and the third in the middle of the street. This position occasioned some rivalry among the women and they finally decided upon Madame Aubain's yard.

Félicité's fever grew worse. She was sorry that she could not do anything for the altar. If she could, at least, have contributed something toward it! Then she thought of the parrot. Her neighbors objected that it would not be proper. But the curé gave his consent and she was so grateful for it that she begged him to accept after her death, her only treasure, Loulou. From Tuesday until Saturday, the day before the event, she coughed more frequently. In the evening her face was contracted, her lips stuck to her gums and she began to vomit; and on the following day, she felt so low that she called for a priest.

Three neighbors surrounded her when the dominie administered the Extreme Unction. Afterwards she said that she wished to speak to Fabu.

He arrived in his Sunday clothes, very ill at ease among the funereal surroundings.

"Forgive me," she said, making an effort to extend her arm, "I believed it was you who killed him!"

What did such accusations mean? Suspect a man like him of murder! And Fabu became excited and was about to make trouble.

"Don't you see she is not in her right mind?"

From time to time Félicité spoke to shadows. The women left her and Mother Simon sat down to breakfast.

A little later, she took Loulou and holding him up to Félicité:

"Say good-bye to him, now!" she commanded.

Although he was not a corpse, he was eaten up by worms; one of his wings was broken and the wadding was coming out of his body. But Félicité was blind now, and she took him and laid him against her cheek. Then Mother Simon removed him in order to set him on the altar.

V

The grass exhaled an odour of summer; flies buzzed in the air, the sun shone on the river and warmed the slated roof. Old Mother Simon had returned to Félicité and was peacefully falling asleep.

The ringing of bells woke her; the people were coming out of church. Félicité's delirium subsided. By thinking of the procession, she was able to see it as if she had taken part in it. All the school-children, the singers and the firemen walked on the sidewalks, while in the middle of the street came first the custodian of the church with his halberd, then the beadle with a large cross, the teacher in charge of the boys and a sister escorting the little girls; three of the smallest ones, with curly heads, threw rose leaves into the air; the deacon with out-stretched arms conducted the music; and two incense-bearers turned with each step they took toward the Holy Sacrament, which was carried by M. le Curé, attired in his handsome chasuble and walking under a canopy of red velvet supported by four men. A crowd of people followed, jammed between the walls of the houses hung with white sheets; at last the procession arrived at the foot of the hill.

A cold sweat broke out on Félicité's forehead. Mother Simon wiped it away with a cloth, saying inwardly that some day she would have to go through the same thing herself.

The murmur of the crowd grew louder, was very distinct for a moment and then died away. A volley of musketry shook the window-panes. It was the postilions saluting the Sacrament. Félicité rolled her eyes and said as loudly as she could:

"Is he all right?" meaning the parrot.

Her death agony began. A rattle that grew more and more rapid shook her body. Froth appeared at the corners of her mouth, and her whole frame trembled. In a little while could be heard the music of the bass horns, the clear voices of the children and the men's deeper notes. At intervals all was still, and their shoes sounded like a herd of cattle passing over the grass.

The clergy appeared in the yard. Mother Simon climbed on a chair to reach the bull's-eye, and in this manner could see the altar. It was covered with a lace cloth and draped with green wreaths. In the middle stood a little frame containing relics; at the corners were two little orange-trees, and all along the edge were silver candlesticks, porcelain vases containing sun-flowers, lilies, peonies, and tufts of hydrangeas. This mound of bright colors descended diagonally from the first floor to the carpet that covered the sidewalk. Rare objects arrested one's eye. A golden sugar-bowl was crowned with violets, earrings set with Alençon stones were displayed on green moss, and two Chinese screens with their bright landscapes were near by. Loulou, hidden beneath roses, showed nothing but his blue head which looked like a piece of lapis-lazuli.

The singers, the canopy-bearers and the children lined up against the sides of the yard. Slowly the priest ascended the steps and placed his shining sun on the lace cloth. Everybody knelt. There was deep silence; and the censers slipping on their chains were swung high in the air. A blue vapor rose in Félicité's room. She opened her nostrils and inhaled it with a mystic sensuousness; then she closed her lids. Her lips smiled. The beats of her heart grew fainter and fainter, and vaguer, like a fountain giving out, like an echo dying away;—and when she exhaled her last breath, she thought she saw in the half-opened heavens a gigantic parrot hovering above her head.

Daisy Miller

A Study (1878)

Henry James

Henry James (1843–1916) was born in New York City but spent his boyhood shuttling back and forth between Europe and America, attending schools in Switzerland, France, England, and Germany. After briefly taking up painting and studying law, he published his first article in 1864 and his first story in 1865. By 1876, when he published his first novel, *Roderick Hudson,* he had established himself in London, where he remained for twenty years, until he moved to Rye, in Sussex. He became a British subject a year before his death, but was buried in Cambridge, Massachusetts. He was himself, he confessed to Hamlin Garland, "a man who is neither American nor European." His characteristic theme is the relationship between the old world and the new: one impinges upon the other; an American goes to France or Italy, perhaps marries a European, or vice versa (e.g., *The American,* 1877; *Daisy Miller,* 1879; *The Portrait of a Lady,* 1881; *The Ambassadors,* 1903; *The Golden Bowl,* 1904). He achieved popular success with *Daisy Miller* and *The Portrait of a Lady;* his later work, as it grew in subtlety and complexity, spread his influence among writers (who gave him the title of "the Master") but considerably diminished the size of his reading public.

Although the author of plays, literary and travel essays, biographical and auto-biographical studies, and, above all, novels, James insisted that his favorite form was the nouvelle—what he called "our ideal, the beautiful and blest *nouvelle,*" or "the shapely *nouvelle,*" which possessed the great advantage of having "a length proper to itself." He discusses the form in the prefaces to volumes XV, XVI, XVII, and XVIII of the New York edition of his works (1907ff.); these are reprinted in R. P. Blackmur's *The Art of the Novel* (New York, 1948, pp. 217–87). Leon Edel has edited James' "tales" (1961ff.)—a term James sometimes used inter-changeably with *nouvelle,* but which also includes his short stories; Edel's definitive biography of James is in process of publication, and he has also edited a collection of critical essays on James (Prentice-Hall, Twentieth-Century Views, 1963) which contains a selective list of the innumerable studies of James.

Daisy Miller first appeared in the June-July issues of *Cornhill Magazine* in 1878 and was published by Harper and Brothers of New York in the next year. James made extensive revisions of his works for the New York edition of 1907, but in the case of *Daisy Miller,* at any rate, the first version remains superior and is here reprinted. The preface to volume XVIII of the New York edition, however, may be consulted for James' account of the story's genesis.

Part I

At the little town of Vevey, in Switzerland, there is a particularly comfortable hotel. There are, indeed, many hotels; for the entertainment of tourists is the business of the place, which, as many travellers will remember, is seated upon the edge of a remarkably blue lake—a lake that it behoves every tourist to visit. The shore of the lake presents an unbroken array of establishments of this order, of every category, from the "grand hotel" of the newest fashion, with a chalk-white front, a hundred balconies, and a dozen flags flying from its roof, to the little Swiss *pension* of an elder day, with its name inscribed in German-looking lettering upon a pink or yellow wall, and an awkward summer-house in the angle of the garden. One of the hotels at Vevey, however, is famous, even classical, being distinguished from many of its upstart neighbours by an air both of luxury and of maturity. In this region, in the month of June, American travellers are extremely numerous; it may be said, indeed, that Vevey assumes at this period some of the characteristics of an American watering-place. There are sights and sounds which evoke a vision, an echo, of Newport and Saratoga. There is a flitting hither and thither of "stylish" young girls, a rustling of muslin flounces, a rattle of dance-music in the morning hours, a sound of high-pitched voices at all times. You receive an impression of these things at the excellent inn of the "Trois Couronnes," and are transported in fancy to the Ocean House or to Congress Hall. But at the "Trois Couronnes," it must be added, there are other features that are much a variance with these suggestions: neat German waiters, who look like secretaries of legation; Russian princesses sitting in the garden; little Polish boys walking about, held by the hand, with their governors; a view of the snowy crest of the Dent du Midi and the picturesque towers of the Castle of Chillon.

I hardly know whether it was the analogies or the differences that were uppermost in the mind of a young American, who, two or three years ago, sat in the garden of the "Trois Couronnes," looking about him, rather idly, at some of the graceful objects I have mentioned. It was a beautiful summer morning, and in whatever fashion the young American looked at things, they must have seemed to him charming. He had come from Geneva the day before, by the little steamer, to see his aunt, who was staying at the hotel—Geneva having been for a long time his place of residence. But his aunt had a headache—his aunt had almost always a headache—and now she was shut up in her room, smelling camphor, so that he was at liberty to wander about. He was some seven-and-twenty years of age; when his friends spoke of him, they usually said that he was at Geneva, "studying." When his enemies spoke of him they said—but, after all, he had no enemies; he was an extremely amiable fellow, and universally liked. What I should say is, simply, that when certain persons spoke of him they affirmed that the reason of his spending so much time at Geneva was that he was extremely devoted to a lady who lived there—a foreign lady—a person older than himself. Very few Americans—indeed I think none—had ever seen this lady, about whom there were some singular stories. But Winterbourne had an old attachment for the little metropolis of Calvinism; he had been put to school there as a boy, and he had afterwards gone to college there—circumstances which had led to his forming a great many youthful friendships. Many of these he had kept, and they were a source of great satisfaction to him.

After knocking at his aunt's door and learning that she was indisposed, he had taken a walk about the town, and then he had come in to his breakfast. He had now finished his breakfast; but he was drinking a small cup of coffee, which had been served to him on a little table in the garden by one of the waiters who looked like an *attaché*. At last he finished his coffee and lit a cigarette. Presently a small boy came walking along the path—an urchin of nine or ten. The child, who was diminutive for his years, had an aged expression of countenance, a pale complexion, and sharp little features. He was dressed in knickerbockers, with red stockings, which displayed his poor little spindleshanks; he also wore a brilliant red cravat. He carried in his hand a long alpenstock, the sharp point of which he thrust into everything that he approached—the flower-beds, the garden-benches, the trains of the ladies' dresses. In front of Winterbourne he paused, looking at him with a pair of bright, penetrating little eyes.

"Will you give me a lump of sugar?" he asked, in a sharp, hard little voice— a voice immature, and yet, somehow, not young.

Winterbourne glanced at the small table near him, on which his coffee-service rested, and saw that several morsels of sugar remained. "Yes, you may take one," he answered; "but I don't think sugar is good for little boys."

This little boy stepped forward and carefully selected three of the coveted fragments, two of which he buried in the pocket of his knickerbockers, depositing the other as promptly in another place. He poked his alpenstock, lance-fashion, into Winterbourne's bench, and tried to crack the lump of sugar with his teeth.

"Oh, blazes; it's har-r-d!" he exclaimed, pronouncing the adjective in a peculiar manner.

Winterbourne had immediately perceived that he might have the honour of claiming him as a fellow-countryman. "Take care you don't hurt your teeth," he said, paternally.

"I haven't got any teeth to hurt. They have all come out. I have only got seven teeth. My mother counted them last night, and one came out right after-wards. She said she'd slap me if any more came out. I can't help it. It's this old Europe. It's the climate that makes them come out. In America they didn't come out. It's these hotels."

Winterbourne was much amused. "If you eat three lumps of sugar, your mother will certainly slap you," he said.

"She's got to give me some candy, then," rejoined his young interlocutor. "I can't get any candy here—any American candy. American candy's the best candy."

"And are American little boys the best little boys?" asked Winterbourne.

"I don't know. I'm an American boy," said the child.

"I see you are one of the best!" laughed Winterbourne.

"Are you an American man?" pursued this vivacious infant. And then, on Winterbourne's affirmative reply—"American men are the best," he declared.

His companion thanked him for the compliment; and the child, who had now got astride of his alpenstock, stood looking about him, while he attacked a second lump of sugar. Winterbourne wondered if he himself had been like this in his infancy, for he had been brought to Europe at about this age.

"Here comes my sister!" cried the child, in a moment. "She's an American girl."

Winterbourne looked along the path and saw a beautiful young lady advancing. "American girls are the best girls," he said, cheerfully, to his young companion.

"My sister ain't the best!" the child declared. "She's always blowing at me."

"I imagine that is your fault, not hers," said Winterbourne. The young lady meanwhile had drawn near. She was dressed in white muslin, with a hundred frills and flounces, and knots of pale-coloured ribbon. She was bare-headed; but she balanced in her hand a large parasol, with a deep border of embroidery; and she was strikingly, admirably pretty. "How pretty they are!" thought Winterbourne, straightening himself in his seat, as if he were prepared to rise.

The young lady paused in front of his bench, near the parapet of the garden, which overlooked the lake. The little boy had now converted his alpenstock into a vaulting-pole, by the aid of which he was springing about in the gravel, and kicking it up not a little.

"Randolph," said the young lady, "what *are* you doing?"

"I'm going up the Alps," replied Randolph. "This is the way!" And he gave another little jump, scattering the pebbles about Winterbourne's ears.

"That's the way they come down," said Winterbourne.

"He's an American man!" cried Randolph, in his little hard voice.

The young lady gave no heed to this announcement, but looked straight at her brother. "Well, I guess you had better be quiet," she simply observed.

It seemed to Winterbourne that he had been in a manner presented. He got up and stepped slowly towards the young girl, throwing away his cigarette. "This little boy and I have made acquaintance," he said, with great civility. In Geneva, as he had been perfectly aware, a young man was not at liberty to speak to a young unmarried lady except under certain rarely occurring conditions; but here at Vevey, what conditions could be better than these?—a pretty American girl coming and standing in front of you in a garden. This pretty American girl, however, on hearing Winterbourne's observation, simply glanced at him; she then turned her head and looked over the parapet, at the lake and the opposite mountains. He wondered whether he had gone too far; but he decided that he must advance farther, rather than retreat. While he was thinking of something else to say, the young lady turned to the little boy again.

"I should like to know where you got that pole," she said.

"I bought it!" responded Randolph.

"You don't mean to say you're going to take it to Italy."

"Yes, I am going to take it to Italy!" the child declared.

The young girl glanced over the front of her dress, and smoothed out a knot or two of ribbon. Then she rested her eyes upon the prospect again. "Well, I guess you had better leave it somewhere," she said, after a moment.

"Are you going to Italy?" Winterbourne inquired, in a tone of great respect.

The young lady glanced at him again. "Yes, sir," she replied. And she said nothing more.

"Are you—a—going over the Simplon?" Winterbourne pursued, a little embarrassed.

"I don't know," she said. "I suppose it's some mountain. Randolph, what mountain are we going over?"

"Going where?" the child demanded.

"To Italy," Winterbourne explained.

"I don't know," said Randolph. "I don't want to go to Italy. I want to go to America."

"Oh, Italy is a beautiful place!" rejoined the young man.

"Can you get candy there?" Randolph loudly inquired.

"I hope not," said his sister. "I guess you have had enough candy, and mother thinks so too."

"I haven't had any for ever so long—for a hundred weeks!" cried the boy, still jumping about.

The young lady inspected her flounces and smoothed her ribbons again; and Winterbourne presently risked an observation upon the beauty of the view. He was ceasing to be embarrassed, for he had begun to perceive that she was not in the least embarrassed herself. There had not been the slightest alteration in her charming complexion; she was evidently neither offended nor fluttered. If she looked another way when he spoke to her, and seemed not particularly to hear him, this was simply her habit, her manner. Yet, as he talked a little more, and pointed out some of the objects of interest in the view, with which she appeared quite unacquainted, she gradually gave him more of the benefit of her glance; and then he saw that this glance was perfectly direct and unshrinking. It was not, however, what would have been called an immodest glance, for the young girl's eyes were singularly honest and fresh. They were wonderfully pretty eyes; and, indeed, Winterbourne had not seen for a long time anything prettier than his fair countrywoman's various features—her complexion, her nose, her ears, her teeth. He had a great relish for feminine beauty; he was addicted to observing and analysing it; and as regards this young lady's face he made several observations. It was not at all insipid, but it was not exactly expressive; and though it was eminently delicate Winterbourne mentally accused it—very forgivingly—of a want of finish. He thought it very possible that Master Randolph's sister was a coquette; he was sure she had a spirit of her own; but in her bright, sweet, superficial little visage there was no mockery, no irony. Before long it became obvious that she was much disposed towards conversation. She told him that they were going to Rome for the winter—she and her mother and Randolph. She asked him if he was a "real American;" she wouldn't have taken him for one; he seemed more like a German—this was said after a little hesitation, especially when he spoke. Winterbourne, laughing, answered that he had met Germans who spoke like Americans; but that he had not, so far as he remembered, met an American who spoke like a German. Then he asked her if she would not be more comfortable in sitting upon the bench which he had just quitted. She answered that she liked standing up and walking about; but she presently sat down. She told him she was from New York State—"if you know where that is." Winterbourne learned more about her by catching hold of her small, slippery brother and making him stand a few minutes by his side.

"Tell me your name, my boy," he said.

"Randolph C. Miller," said the boy, sharply. "And I'll tell you her name," and he levelled his alpenstock at his sister.

"You had better wait till you are asked!" said this young lady, calmly.

"I should like very much to know your name," said Winterbourne.

"Her name is Daisy Miller!" cried the child. "But that isn't her real name; that isn't her name on her cards."

"It's a pity you haven't got one of my cards!" said Miss Miller.

"Her real name is Annie P. Miller," the boy went on.

"Ask him *his* name," said his sister, indicating Winterbourne.

But on this point Randolph seemed perfectly indifferent; he continued to supply information with regard to his own family. "My father's name is Ezra B. Miller," he announced. "My father ain't in Europe; my father's in a better place than Europe."

Winterbourne imagined for a moment that this was the manner in which the child had been taught to intimate that Mr Miller had been removed to the sphere of celestial rewards. But Randolph immediately added, "My father's in Schenectady. He's got a big business. My father's rich, you bet."

"Well!" ejaculated Miss Miller, lowering her parasol and looking at the embroidered border. Winterbourne presently released the child, who departed, dragging his alpenstock along the path. "He doesn't like Europe," said the young girl. "He wants to go back."

"To Schenectady, you mean?"

"Yes; he wants to go right home. He hasn't got any boys here. There is one boy here, but he always goes round with a teacher; they won't let him play."

"And your brother hasn't any teacher?" Winterbourne inquired.

"Mother thought of getting him one, to travel round with us. There was a lady told her of a very good teacher; an American lady—perhaps you know her —Mrs Sanders. I think she came from Boston. She told her of this teacher, and we thought of getting him to travel round with us. But Randolph said he didn't want a teacher travelling round with us. He said he wouldn't have lessons when he was in the cars. And we *are* in the cars about half the time. There was an English lady we met in the cars—I think her name was Miss Featherstone; perhaps you know her. She wanted to know why I didn't give Randolph lessons —give him 'instruction,' she called it. I guess he could give me more instruction than I could give him. He's very smart."

"Yes," said Winterbourne; "he seems very smart."

"Mother's going to get a teacher for him as soon as we get to Italy. Can you get good teachers in Italy?"

"Very good, I should think," said Winterbourne.

"Or else she's going to find some school. He ought to learn some more. He's only nine. He's going to college." And in this way Miss Miller continued to converse upon the affairs of her family, and upon other topics. She sat there with her extremely pretty hands, ornamented with very brilliant rings, folded in her lap, and with her pretty eyes now resting upon those of Winterbourne, now wandering over the garden, the people who passed by, and the beautiful view. She talked to Winterbourne as if she had known him a long time. He found it very pleasant. It was many years since he had heard a young girl talk so much. It might have been said of this unknown young lady, who had come and sat down beside him upon a bench, that she chattered. She was very quiet, she sat in a charming tranquil attitude; but her lips and her eyes were constantly moving. She had a soft, slender, agreeable voice, and her tone was decidedly sociable. She gave Winterbourne a history of her movements and intentions, and those of her mother and brother, in Europe, and enumerated, in particular, the various hotels at which they had stopped. "That English lady in the cars," she said—"Miss Featherstone—asked me if we didn't all live in hotels in America. I told her I had never been in so many hotels in my life as since I came to Europe. I have never seen so many—it's nothing but hotels." But Miss Miller did not make this remark with a querulous accent; she appeared to be in the best humour with everything. She declared that the hotels were very good, when once you got used to their ways, and that Europe was perfectly sweet. She was not disappointed—not a bit. Perhaps it was because she had heard so much about it before. She had ever so many intimate friends that had been there ever so many times. And then she had had ever so many dresses and things from Paris. Whenever she put on a Paris dress she felt as if she were in Europe.

"It was a kind of a wishing-cap," said Winterbourne.

"Yes," said Miss Miller, without examining this analogy; "it always made me wish I was here. But I needn't have done that for dresses. I am sure they send all the pretty ones to America; you see the most frightful things here. The only thing I don't like," she proceeded, "is the society. There isn't any society; or, if there is, I don't know where it keeps itself. Do you? I suppose there is some society somewhere, but I haven't seen anything of it. I'm very fond of society, and I have always had a great deal of it. I don't mean only in Schenectady, but in New York. I used to go to New York every winter. In New York I had lots of society. Last winter I had seventeen dinners given me; and three of them were by gentlemen," added Daisy Miller. "I have more friends in New York than in Schenectady—more gentlemen friends; and more young lady friends too," she resumed in a moment. She paused again for an instant; she was looking at Winterbourne with all her prettiness in her lively eyes and in her light, slightly monotonous smile. "I have always had," she said, "a great deal of gentlemen's society."

Poor Winterbourne was amused, perplexed, and decidedly charmed. He had never yet heard a young girl express herself in just this fashion; never, at least, save in cases where to say such things seemed a kind of demonstrative evidence of a certain laxity of deportment. And yet was he to accuse Miss Daisy Miller of actual or potential *inconduite,* as they said at Geneva? He felt that he had lived at Geneva so long that he had lost a good deal; he had become dishabituated to the American tone. Never, indeed, since he had grown old enough to appreciate things, had he encountered a young American girl of so pronounced a type as this. Certainly she was very charming; but how deucedly sociable! Was she simply a pretty girl from New York State—were they all like that, the pretty girls who had a good deal of gentlemen's society? Or was she also a designing, an audacious, an unscrupulous young person? Winterbourne had lost his instinct in this matter, and his reason could not help him. Miss Daisy Miller looked extremely innocent. Some people had told him that, after all, American girls were exceedingly innocent; and others had told him that, after all, they were not. He was inclined to think Miss Daisy Miller was a flirt—a pretty American flirt. He had never, as yet, had any relations with young ladies of this category. He had known, here in Europe, two or three women—persons older than Miss Daisy Miller, and provided, for respectability's sake, with husbands—who were great coquettes—dangerous, terrible women, with whom one's relations were liable to take a serious turn. But this young girl was not a coquette in that sense; she was very unsophisticated; she was only a pretty American flirt. Winterbourne was almost grateful for having found the formula that applied to Miss Daisy Miller. He leaned back in his seat; he remarked to himself that she had the most charming nose he had ever seen; he wondered what were the regular conditions and limitations of one's intercourse with a pretty American flirt. It presently became apparent that he was on the way to learn.

"Have you been to that old castle?" asked the young girl, pointing with her parasol to the far-gleaming walls of the Château de Chillon.

"Yes, formerly, more than once," said Winterbourne. "You too, I suppose, have seen it?"

"No; we haven't been there. I want to go there dreadfully. Of course I mean to go there. I wouldn't go away from here without having seen that old castle."

"It's a very pretty excursion," said Winterbourne, "and very easy to make. You can drive, you know, or you can go by the little steamer."

"You can go in the cars," said Miss Miller.

"Yes; you can go in the cars," Winterbourne assented.

"Our courier says they take you right up to the castle," the young girl continued. "We were going last week; but my mother gave out. She suffers dreadfully from dyspepsia. She said she couldn't go. Randolph wouldn't go either; he says he doesn't think much of old castles. But I guess we'll go this week, if we can get Randolph."

"Your brother is not interested in ancient monuments?" Winterbourne inquired, smiling.

"He says he don't care much about old castles. He's only nine. He wants to stay at the hotel. Mother's afraid to leave him alone, and the courier won't stay with him; so we haven't been to many places. But it will be too bad if we don't go up there." And Miss Miller pointed again at the Château de Chillon.

"I should think it might be arranged," said Winterbourne. "Couldn't you get some one to stay—for the afternoon—with Randolph?"

Miss Miller looked at him a moment; and then, very placidly—"I wish *you* would stay with him!" she said.

Winterbourne hesitated a moment. "I would much rather go to Chillon with you."

"With me?" asked the young girl, with the same placidity.

She didn't rise, blushing, as a young girl at Geneva would have done; and yet Winterbourne, conscious that he had been very bold, thought it possible she was offended. "With your mother," he answered very respectfully.

But it seemed that both his audacity and his respect were lost upon Miss Daisy Miller. "I guess my mother won't go, after all," she said. "She don't like to ride round in the afternoon. But did you really mean what you said just now; that you would like to go up there?"

"Most earnestly," Winterbourne declared.

"Then we may arrange it. If mother will stay with Randolph, I guess Eugenio will."

"Eugenio?" the young man inquired.

"Eugenio's our courier. He doesn't like to stay with Randolph; he's the most fastidious man I ever saw. But he's a splendid courier. I guess he'll stay at home with Randolph if mother does, and then we can go to the castle."

Winterbourne reflected for an instant as lucidly as possible—"we" could only mean Miss Daisy Miller and himself. This programme seemed almost too agreeable for credence; he felt as if he ought to kiss the young lady's hand. Possibly he would have done so—and quite spoiled the project; but at this moment another person—presumably Eugenio—appeared. A tall, handsome man, with superb whiskers, wearing a velvet morning-coat and a brilliant watch-chain, approached Miss Miller, looking sharply at her companion. "Oh, Eugenio!" said Miss Miller, with the friendliest accent.

Eugenio had looked at Winterbourne from head to foot; he now bowed gravely to the young lady. "I have the honour to inform mademoiselle that luncheon is upon the table."

Miss Miller slowly rose. "See here, Eugenio," she said. "I'm going to that old castle, any way."

"To the Château de Chillon, mademoiselle?" the courier inquired. "Mademoiselle has made arrangements?" he added, in a tone which struck Winterbourne as very impertinent.

Eugenio's tone apparently threw, even to Miss Miller's own apprehension, a slightly ironical light upon the young girl's situation. She turned to Winterbourne, blushing a little—a very little. "You won't back out?" she said.

"I shall not be happy till we go!" he protested.

"And you are staying in this hotel?" she went on. "And you are really an American?"

The courier stood looking at Winterbourne, offensively. The young man, at least, thought his manner of looking an offence to Miss Miller; it conveyed an imputation that she "picked up" acquaintances. "I shall have the honour of presenting to you a person who will tell you all about me," he said smiling, and referring to his aunt.

"Oh, well, we'll go some day," said Miss Miller. And she gave him a smile and turned away. She put up her parasol and walked back to the inn beside Eugenio. Winterbourne stood looking after her; and as she moved away, drawing her muslin furbelows over the gravel, said to himself that she had the *tournure* of a princess.

He had, however, engaged to do more than proved feasible, in promising to present his aunt, Mrs Costello, to Miss Daisy Miller. As soon as the former lady had got better of her headache he waited upon her in her apartment; and, after the proper inquiries in regard to her health, he asked her if she had observed, in the hotel, an American family—a mamma, a daughter, and a little boy.

"And a courier?" said Mrs Costello. "Oh, yes, I have observed them. Seen them—heard them—and kept out of their way." Mrs Costello was a widow with a fortune; a person of much distinction, who frequently intimated that, if she were not so dreadfully liable to sick-headaches, she would probably have left a deeper impress upon her time. She had a long pale face, a high nose, and a great deal of very striking white hair, which she wore in large puffs and *rouleaux* over the top of her head. She had two sons married in New York, and another who was now in Europe. This young man was amusing himself at Hamburg, and, though he was on his travels, was rarely perceived to visit any particular city at the moment selected by his mother for her own appearance there. Her nephew, who had come up to Vevey expressly to see her, was therefore more attentive than those who, as she said, were nearer to her. He had imbibed at Geneva the idea that one must always be attentive to one's aunt. Mrs Costello had not seen him for many years, and she was greatly pleased with him, manifesting her approbation by initiating him into many of the secrets of that social sway which, as she gave him to understand, she exerted in the American capital. She admitted that she was very exclusive; but, if he were acquainted with New York, he would see that one had to be. And her picture of the minutely hierarchical constitution of the society of that city, which she presented to him in many different lights, was, to Winterbourne's imagination, almost oppressively striking.

He immediately perceived, from her tone, that Miss Daisy Miller's place in the social scale was low. "I am afraid you don't approve of them," he said.

"They are very common," Mrs Costello declared. "They are the sort of Americans that one does one's duty by not—not accepting."

"Ah, you don't accept them?" said the young man.

"I can't, my dear Frederick. I would if I could, but I can't."

"The young girl is very pretty," said Winterbourne, in a moment.

"Of course she's pretty. But she is very common."

"I see what you mean, of course," said Winterbourne, after another pause.

"She has that charming look that they all have," his aunt resumed. "I can't think where they pick it up; and she dresses in perfection—no, you don't know how well she dresses. I can't think where they get their taste."

"But, my dear aunt, she is not, after all, a Comanche savage."

"She is a young lady," said Mrs. Costello, "who has an intimacy with her mamma's courier."

"An intimacy with the courier?" the young man demanded.

"Oh, the mother is just as bad! They treat the courier like a familiar friend—like a gentleman. I shouldn't wonder if he dines with them. Very likely they have never seen a man with such good manners, such fine clothes, so like a gentleman. He probably corresponds to the young lady's idea of a Count. He sits with them in the garden, in the evening. I think he smokes."

Winterbourne listened with interest to these disclosures; they helped him to make up his mind about Miss Daisy. Evidently she was rather wild. "Well," he said, "I am not a courier, and yet she was very charming to me."

"You had better have said at first," said Mrs Costello, with dignity, "that you had made her acquaintance."

"We simply met in the garden, and we talked a bit."

"*Tout bonnement!* And pray what did you say?"

"I said I should take the liberty of introducing her to my admirable aunt."

"I am much obliged to you."

"It was to guarantee my respectability," said Winterbourne.

"And pray who is to guarantee hers?"

"Ah, you are cruel!" said the young man. "She's a very nice girl."

"You don't say that as if you believed it," Mrs Costello observed.

"She is completely uncultivated," Winterbourne went on. "But she is wonderfully pretty, and, in short, she is very nice. To prove that I believe it, I am going to take her to the Château de Chillon."

"You two are going off there together? I should say it proved just the contrary. How long had you known her, may I ask, when this interesting project was formed? You haven't been twenty-four hours in the house."

"I had known her half-an-hour!" said Winterbourne, smiling.

"Dear me!" cried Mrs Costello. "What a dreadful girl!"

Her nephew was silent for some moments. "You really think, then," he began, earnestly, and with a desire for trust-worthy information—"you really think that——" But he paused again.

"Think what, sir?" said his aunt.

"That she is the sort of young lady who expects a man—sooner or later—to carry her off?"

"I haven't the least idea what such young ladies expect a man to do. But I really think that you had better not meddle with little American girls that are uncultivated, as you call them. You have lived too long out of the country. You will be sure to make some great mistake. You are too innocent."

"My dear aunt, I am not so innocent," said Winterbourne, smiling and curling his moustache.

"You are too guilty, then!"

Winterbourne continued to curl his moustache, meditatively. "You won't let the poor girl know you then?" he asked at last.

"Is it literally true that she is going to the Château de Chillon with you?"

"I think that she fully intends it."

"Then, my dear Frederick," said Mrs Costello, "I must decline the honour of her acquaintance. I am an old woman, but I am not too old—thank Heaven— to be shocked!"

"But don't they all do these things—the young girls in America?" Winterbourne inquired.

Mrs Costello stared a moment. "I should like to see my granddaughters do them!" she declared, grimly.

This seemed to throw some light upon the matter, for Winterbourne remembered to have heard that his pretty cousins in New York were "tremendous flirts." If, therefore, Miss Daisy Miller exceeded the liberal license allowed to these young ladies, it was probable that anything might be expected of her. Winterbourne was impatient to see her again, and he was vexed with himself that, by instinct, he should not appreciate her justly.

Though he was impatient to see her, he hardly knew what he should say to her about his aunt's refusal to become acquainted with her; but he discovered, promptly enough, that with Miss Daisy Miller there was no great need of walking on tiptoe. He found her that evening in the garden, wandering about in the warm starlight, like an indolent sylph, and swinging to and fro the largest fan he had ever beheld. It was ten o'clock. He had dined with his aunt, had been sitting with her since dinner, and had just taken leave of her till the morrow. Miss Daisy Miller seemed very glad to see him; she declared it was the longest evening she had ever passed.

"Have you been all alone?" he asked.

"I have been walking round with mother. But mother gets tired walking round," she answered.

"Has she gone to bed?"

"No; she doesn't like to go to bed," said the young girl. "She doesn't sleep— not three hours. She says she doesn't know how she lives. She's dreadfully nervous. I guess she sleeps more than she thinks. She's gone somewhere after Randolph; she wants to try to get him to go to bed. He doesn't like to go to bed."

"Let us hope she will persuade him," observed Winterbourne.

"She will talk to him all she can; but he doesn't like her to talk to him," said Miss Daisy, opening her fan. "She's going to try to get Eugenio to talk to him. But he isn't afraid of Eugenio. Eugenio's a splendid courier, but he can't make much impression on Randolph! I don't believe he'll go to bed before eleven." It appeared that Randolph's vigil was in fact triumphantly prolonged, for Winterbourne strolled about with the young girl for some time without meeting her mother. "I have been looking round for that lady you want to introduce me to," his companion resumed. "She's your aunt." Then, on Winterbourne's admitting the fact, and expressing some curiosity as to how she had learned it, she said she had heard all about Mrs Costello from the chambermaid. She was very quiet and very *comme il faut;* she wore white puffs; she spoke to no one, and she never dined at the *table d'hôte*. Every two days she had a headache. "I think that's a lovely description, headache and all!" said Miss Daisy, chattering along in her thin, gay voice. "I want to know her ever so much. I know just what *your* aunt would be; I know I should like her. She would be very exclusive. I like a lady to be exclusive; I'm dying to be exclusive myself. Well, we *are* exclusive, mother and I. We don't speak to every one—or they don't speak to us. I suppose it's about the same thing. Any way, I shall be ever so glad to know your aunt."

Winterbourne was embarrassed. "She would be most happy," he said; "but I am afraid those headaches will interfere."

The young girl looked at him through the dusk. "But I suppose she doesn't have a headache every day," she said, sympathetically.

Winterbourne was silent a moment. "She tells me she does," he answered at last—not knowing what to say.

Miss Daisy Miller stopped and stood looking at him. Her prettiness was still visible in the darkness; she was opening and closing her enormous fan. "She doesn't want to know me!" she said, suddenly. "Why don't you say so? You needn't be afraid. I'm not afraid!" And she gave a little laugh.

Winterbourne fancied there was a tremor in her voice; he was touched, shocked, mortified by it. "My dear young lady," he protested, "she knows no one. It's her wretched health."

The young girl walked on a few steps, laughing still. "You needn't be afraid," she repeated. "Why should she want to know me?" Then she paused again; she was close to the parapet of the garden, and in front of her was the starlit lake. There was a vague sheen upon its surface, and in the distance were dimly seen mountain forms. Daisy Miller looked out upon the mysterious prospect, and then she gave another little laugh. "Gracious! she *is* exclusive!" she said. Winterbourne wondered whether she was seriously wounded, and for a moment almost wished that her sense of injury might be such as to make it becoming in him to attempt to reassure and comfort her. He had a pleasant sense that she would be very approachable for consolatory purposes. He felt then, for the instant, quite ready to sacrifice his aunt, conversationally; to admit that she was a proud, rude woman, and to declare that they needn't mind her. But before he had time to commit himself to this perilous mixture of gallantry and impiety, the young lady, resuming her walk, gave an exclamation in quite another tone. "Well; here's mother! I guess she hasn't got Randolph to go to bed." The figure of a lady appeared, at a distance, very indistinct in the darkness, and advancing with a slow and wavering movement. Suddenly it seemed to pause.

"Are you sure it is your mother? Can you distinguish her in this thick dusk?" Winterbourne asked.

"Well!" cried Miss Daisy Miller, with a laugh, "I guess I know my own mother. And when she has got on my shawl, too! She is always wearing my things."

The lady in question, ceasing to advance, hovered vaguely about the spot at which she had checked her steps.

"I am afraid your mother doesn't see you," said Winterbourne. "Or perhaps," he added—thinking, with Miss Miller, the joke permissible—"perhaps she feels guilty about your shawl."

"Oh, it's a fearful old thing!" the young girl replied, serenely. "I told her she could wear it. She won't come here, because she sees you."

"Ah, then," said Winterbourne, "I had better leave you."

"Oh no; come on!" urged Miss Daisy Miller.

"I'm afraid your mother doesn't approve of my walking with you."

Miss Miller gave him a serious glance. "It isn't for me; it's for you—that is, it's for *her*. Well; I don't know who it's for! But mother doesn't like any of my gentlemen friends. She's right down timid. She always makes a fuss if I introduce a gentleman. But I *do* introduce them—almost always. If I didn't introduce my gentlemen friends to mother," the young girl added, in her little soft, flat monotone, "I shouldn't think I was natural."

"To introduce me," said Winterbourne, "you must know my name." And he proceeded to pronounce it.

"Oh, dear; I can't say all that!" said his companion, with a laugh. But by this time they had come up to Mrs Miller, who, as they drew near, walked to the parapet of the garden and leaned upon it, looking intently at the lake and turning her back upon them. "Mother!" said the young girl, in a tone of decision. Upon this the elder lady turned round. "Mr Winterbourne," said Miss Daisy Miller, introducing the young man very frankly and prettily. "Common," she was, as Mrs Costello had pronounced her; yet it was a wonder to Winterbourne that, with her commonness, she had a singularly delicate grace.

Her mother was a small, spare, light person, with a wandering eye, a very exiguous nose, and a large forehead, decorated with a certain amount of thin, much-frizzled hair. Like her daughter, Mrs Miller was dressed with extreme elegance; she had enormous diamonds in her ears. So far as Winterbourne could observe, she gave him no greeting—she certainly was not looking at him. Daisy was near her, pulling her shawl straight. "What are you doing, poking round here?" this young lady inquired; but by no means with that harshness of accent which her choice of words may imply.

"I don't know," said her mother, turning towards the lake again.

"I shouldn't think you'd want that shawl!" Daisy exclaimed.

"Well—I do!" her mother answered, with a little laugh.

"Did you get Randolph to go to bed?" asked the young girl.

"No; I couldn't induce him," said Mrs Miller, very gently. "He wants to talk to the waiter. He likes to talk to that waiter."

"I was telling Mr Winterbourne," the young girl went on; and to the young man's ear her tone might have indicated that she had been uttering his name all her life.

"Oh, yes!" said Winterbourne; "I have the pleasure of knowing your son."

Randolph's mamma was silent; she turned her attention to the lake. But at last she spoke. "Well, I don't see how he lives!"

"Anyhow, it isn't so bad as it was at Dover," said Daisy Miller.

"And what occurred at Dover?" Winterbourne asked.

"He wouldn't go to bed at all. I guess he sat up all night—in the public parlour. He wasn't in bed at twelve o'clock: I know that."

"It was half-past twelve," declared Mrs Miller, with mild emphasis.

"Does he sleep much during the day?" Winterbourne demanded.

"I guess he doesn't sleep much," Daisy rejoined.

"I wish he would!" said her mother. "It seems as if he couldn't."

"I think he's real tiresome," Daisy pursued.

Then, for some moments, there was silence. "Well, Daisy Miller," said the elder lady, presently, "I shouldn't think you'd want to talk against your own brother!"

"Well, he *is* tiresome, mother," said Daisy, quite without the asperity of a retort.

"He's only nine," urged Mrs Miller.

"Well, he wouldn't go to that castle," said the young girl. "I'm going there with Mr Winterbourne."

To this announcement, very placidly made, Daisy's mamma offered no response. Winterbourne took for granted that she deeply disapproved of the projected excursion; but he said to himself that she was a simple, easily managed person, and that a few deferential protestations would take the edge from her displeasure. "Yes," he began; "your daughter has kindly allowed me the honour of being her guide."

Mrs Miller's wandering eyes attached themselves, with a sort of appealing air, to Daisy, who, however, strolled a few steps farther, gently humming to herself. "I presume you will go in the cars," said her mother.

"Yes; or in the boat," said Winterbourne.

"Well, of course, I don't know," Mrs Miller rejoined. "I have never been to that castle."

"It is a pity you shouldn't go," said Winterbourne, beginning to feel reassured as to her opposition. And yet he was quite prepared to find that, as a matter of course, she meant to accompany her daughter.

"We've been thinking ever so much about going," she pursued; "but it seems as if we couldn't. Of course Daisy—she wants to go round. But there's a lady here —I don't know her name—she says she shouldn't think we'd want to go to see castles *here;* she should think we'd want to wait till we got to Italy. It seems as if there would be so many there," continued Mrs Miller, with an air of increasing confidence. "Of course, we only want to see the principal ones. We visited several in England," she presently added.

"Ah, yes! in England there are beautiful castles," said Winterbourne. "But Chillon, here, is very well worth seeing."

"Well, if Daisy feels up to it——," said Mrs Miller, in a tone impregnated with a sense of the magnitude of the enterprise. "It seems as if there was nothing she wouldn't undertake."

"Oh, I think she'll enjoy it!" Winterbourne declared. And he desired more and more to make it a certainty that he was to have the privilege of a *tête-à-tête* with the young lady, who was still strolling along in front of them, softly vocalising. "You are not disposed, madam," he inquired, "to undertake it yourself?"

Daisy's mother looked at him, an instant, askance, and then walked forward in silence. Then—"I guess she had better go alone," she said, simply.

Winterbourne observed to himself that this was a very different type of maternity from that of the vigilant matrons who massed themselves in the forefront of social intercourse in the dark old city at the other end of the lake. But his meditations were interrupted by hearing his name very distinctly pronounced by Mrs Miller's unprotected daughter.

"Mr Winterbourne!" murmured Daisy.

"Mademoiselle!" said the young man.

"Don't you want to take me out in a boat?"

"At present?" he asked.

"Of course!" said Daisy.

"Well, Annie Miller!" exclaimed her mother.

"I beg you, madam, to let her go," said Winterbourne, ardently; for he had never yet enjoyed the sensation of guiding through the summer starlight a skiff freighted with a fresh and beautiful young girl.

"I shouldn't think she'd want to," said her mother. "I should think she'd rather go indoors."

"I'm sure Mr Winterbourne wants to take me," Daisy declared. "He's so awfully devoted!"

"I will row you over to Chillon, in the starlight."

"I don't believe it!" said Daisy.

"Well!" ejaculated the elder lady again.

"You haven't spoken to me for half-an-hour," her daughter went on.

"I have been having some very pleasant conversation with your mother," said Winterbourne.

"Well; I want you to take me out in a boat!" Daisy repeated. They had all stopped, and she had turned round and was looking at Winterbourne. Her face wore a charming smile, her pretty eyes were gleaming, she was swinging her great fan about. No; it's impossible to be prettier than that, thought Winterbourne.

"There are half-a-dozen boats moored at that landing-place," he said, pointing to certain steps which descended from the garden to the lake. "If you will do me the honour to accept my arm, we will go and select one of them."

Daisy stood there smiling; she threw back her head and gave a little light laugh. "I like a gentleman to be formal!" she declared.

"I assure you it's a formal offer."

"I was bound I would make you say something," Daisy went on.

"You see it's not very difficult," said Winterbourne. "But I am afraid you are chaffing me."

"I think not, sir," remarked Mrs Miller, very gently.

"Do, then, let me give you a row," he said to the young girl.

"It's quite lovely, the way you say that!" cried Daisy.

"It will be still more lovely to do it."

"Yes, it would be lovely!" said Daisy. But she made no movement to accompany him; she only stood there laughing.

"I should think you had better find out what time it is," interposed her mother.

"It is eleven o'clock, madam," said a voice, with a foreign accent, out of the neighbouring darkness; and Winterbourne, turning, perceived the florid personage who was in attendance upon the two ladies. He had apparently just approached.

"Oh, Eugenio," said Daisy, "I am going out in a boat!"

Eugenio bowed. "At eleven o'clock, mademoiselle?"

"I am going with Mr Winterbourne. This very minute."

"Do tell her she can't," said Mrs Miller to the courier.

"I think you had better not go out in a boat, mademoiselle," Eugenio declared.

Winterbourne wished to Heaven this pretty girl were not so familiar with her courier; but he said nothing.

"I suppose you don't think it's proper!" Daisy exclaimed. "Eugenio doesn't think anything's proper."

"I am at your service," said Winterbourne.

"Does mademoiselle propose to go alone?" asked Eugenio of Mrs Miller.

"Oh, no; with this gentleman!" answered Daisy's mamma.

The courier looked for a moment at Winterbourne—the latter thought he was smiling—and then, solemnly, with a bow, "As mademoiselle pleases!" he said.

"Oh, I hoped you would make a fuss!" said Daisy. "I don't care to go now."

"I myself shall make a fuss if you don't go," said Winterbourne.

"That's all I want—a little fuss!" And the young girl began to laugh again.

"Mr Randolph has gone to bed!" the courier announced, frigidly.

"Oh, Daisy; now we can go!" said Mrs Miller.

Daisy turned away from Winterbourne, looking at him, smiling and fanning herself. "Good night," she said; "I hope you are disappointed, or disgusted, or something!"

He looked at her, taking the hand she offered him. "I am puzzled," he answered.

"Well; I hope it won't keep you awake!" she said, very smartly; and, under the escort of the privileged Eugenio, the two ladies passed towards the house.

Winterbourne stood looking after them; he was indeed puzzled. He lingered beside the lake for a quarter of an hour, turning over the mystery of the young girl's sudden familiarities and caprices. But the only very definite conclusion he came to was that he should enjoy deucedly "going off" with her somewhere.

Two days afterwards he went off with her to the Castle of Chillon. He waited for her in the large hall of the hotel, where the couriers, the servants, the foreign tourists were lounging about and staring. It was not the place he would have chosen, but she had appointed it. She came tripping downstairs, buttoning her long gloves, squeezing her folded parasol against her pretty figure, dressed in the perfection of a soberly elegant travelling-costume. Winterbourne was a man of imagination and, as our ancestors used to say, of sensibility; as he looked at her dress and, on the great staircase, her little rapid, confiding step, he felt as if there were something romantic going forward. He could have believed he was going to elope with her. He passed out with her among all the idle people that were assembled there; they were all looking at her very hard; she had begun to chatter as soon as she joined him. Winterbourne's preference had been that they should be conveyed to Chillon in a carriage; but she expressed a lively wish to go in the little steamer; she declared that she had a passion for steamboats. There was always such a lovely breeze upon the water, and you saw such lots of people. The sail was not long, but Winterbourne's companion found time to say a great many things. To the young man himself their little excursion was so much of an escapade —an adventure—that, even allowing for her habitual sense of freedom, he had some expectation of seeing her regard it in the same way. But it must be confessed that, in this particular, he was disappointed. Daisy Miller was extremely animated, she was in charming spirits; but she was apparently not at all excited; she was not fluttered; she avoided neither his eyes nor those of any one else; she blushed neither when she looked at him nor when she saw that people were looking at her. People continued to look at her a great deal, and Winterbourne took much satisfaction in his pretty companion's distinguished air. He had been a little afraid that she would talk loud, laugh overmuch, and even, perhaps, desire to move about the boat a good deal. But he quite forgot his fears; he sat smiling, with his eyes upon her face, while, without moving from her place, she delivered herself of a great number of original reflections. It was the most charming garrulity he had ever heard. He had assented to the idea that she was "common," but was she so, after all, or was he simply getting used to her commonness? Her conversation was chiefly of what metaphysicians term the objective cast; but every now and then it took a subjective turn.

"What on *earth* are you so grave about?" she suddenly demanded, fixing her agreeable eyes upon Winterbourne's.

"Am I grave?" he asked. "I had an idea I was grinning from ear to ear."

"You look as if you were taking me to a funeral. If that's a grin, your ears are very near together."

"Should you like me to dance a hornpipe on the deck?"

"Pray do, and I'll carry round your hat. It will pay the expenses of our journey."

"I never was better pleased in my life," murmured Winterbourne.

She looked at him a moment, and then burst into a little laugh. "I like to make you say those things! You're a queer mixture!"

In the castle, after they had landed, the subjective element decidedly prevailed. Daisy tripped about the vaulted chambers, rustled her skirts in the corkscrew staircases, flirted back with a pretty little cry and a shudder from the edge of the *oubliettes,* and turned a singularly well-shaped ear to everything that Winterbourne told her about the place. But he saw that she cared very little for feudal antiquities, and that the dusky traditions of Chillon made but a slight impression upon her. They had the good fortune to have been able to walk about without other companionship than that of the custodian; and Winterbourne arranged with this functionary that they should not be hurried—that they should linger and pause wherever they chose. The custodian interpreted the bargain generously— Winterbourne, on his side, had been generous—and ended by leaving them quite to themselves. Miss Miller's observations were not remarkable for logical consistency; for anything she wanted to say she was sure to find a pretext. She found a great many pretexts in the rugged embrasures of Chillon for asking Winterbourne sudden questions about himself—his family, his previous history, his tastes, his habits, his intentions—and for supplying information upon corresponding points in her own personality. Of her own tastes, habits and intentions Miss Miller was prepared to give the most definite, and indeed the most favourable, account.

"Well; I hope you know enough!" she said to her companion, after he had told her the history of the unhappy Bonivard. "I never saw a man that knew so much!" The history of Bonivard had evidently, as they say, gone into one ear and out of the other. But Daisy went on to say that she wished Winterbourne would travel with them and "go round" with them; they might know something, in that case. "Don't you want to come and teach Randolph?" she asked. Winterbourne said that nothing could possibly please him so much; but that he had unfortunately other occupations. "Other occupations? I don't believe it!" said Miss Daisy. "What do you mean? You are not in business." The young man admitted that he was not in business; but he had engagements which, even within a day or two, would force him to go back to Geneva. "Oh, bother!" she said, "I don't believe it!" and she began to talk about something else. But a few moments later, when he was pointing out to her the pretty design of an antique fireplace, she broke out irrelevantly, "You don't mean to say you are going back to Geneva?"

"It is a melancholy fact that I shall have to return to Geneva to-morrow."

"Well, Mr Winterbourne," said Daisy; "I think you're horrid!"

"Oh, don't say such dreadful things!" said Winterbourne—"just at the last."

"The last!" cried the young girl; "I call it the first. I have half a mind to leave you here and go straight back to the hotel alone." And for the next ten minutes she did nothing but call him horrid. Poor Winterbourne was fairly bewildered; no young lady had as yet done him the honour to be so agitated by the announcement of his movements. His companion, after this, ceased to pay any attention to the curiosities of Chillon or the beauties of the lake; she opened fire upon the mysterious charmer in Geneva, whom she appeared to have instantly taken it for granted that he was hurrying back to see. How did Miss Daisy Miller know that there was a charmer in Geneva? Winterbourne, who denied the existence of such a person, was quite unable to discover; and he was divided between amazement at the rapidity of her induction and amusement at the frankness of her *persiflage*. She seemed to him, in all this, an extraordinary mixture of innocence and crudity. "Does she never allow you more than three days at a time?" asked Daisy, ironically. "Doesn't she give you a vacation in summer? There's no one so hard worked but they can get leave to go off somewhere at this season. I suppose, if you stay another day, she'll come after you in the boat. Do wait over till Friday, and I will go down to the landing to see her arrive!" Winterbourne began to think he had been wrong to feel disappointed in the temper in which the young lady had embarked. If he had missed the personal accent, the personal accent was now making its appearance. It sounded very distinctly, at last, in her telling him she would stop "teasing" him if he would promise her solemnly to come down to Rome in the winter.

"That's not a difficult promise to make," said Winterbourne. "My aunt has taken an apartment in Rome for the winter, and has already asked me to come and see her."

"I don't want you to come for your aunt," said Daisy; "I want you to come for me." And this was the only allusion that the young man was ever to hear her make to his invidious kinswoman. He declared that, at any rate, he would certainly come. After this Daisy stopped teasing. Winterbourne took a carriage, and they drove back to Vevey in the dusk; the young girl was very quiet.

In the evening Winterbourne mentioned to Mrs Costello that he had spent the afternoon at Chillon, with Miss Daisy Miller.

"The Americans—of the courier?" asked this lady.

"Ah, happily," said Winterbourne, "the courier stayed at home."

"She went with you all alone?"

"All alone."

Mrs Costello sniffed a little at her smelling-bottle. "And that," she exclaimed, "is the young person you wanted me to know!"

Part II : Rome

Winterbourne, who had returned to Geneva the day after his excursion to Chillon, went to Rome towards the end of January. His aunt had been established there for several weeks, and he had received a couple of letters from her. "Those people you were so devoted to last summer at Vevey have turned up here, courier and all," she wrote. "They seem to have made several acquaintances, but the courier continues to be the most *intime*. The young lady, however, is also very intimate with some third-rate Italians, with whom she rackets about in a way that makes much talk. Bring me that pretty novel of Cherbuliez's—'Paule Méré'— and don't come later than the 23rd."

In the natural course of events, Winterbourne, on arriving in Rome, would presently have ascertained Mrs Miller's address at the American banker's and have gone to pay his compliments to Miss Daisy. "After what happened at Vevey I certainly think I may call upon them," he said to Mrs Costello.

"If, after what happens—at Vevey and everywhere—you desire to keep up the acquaintance, you are very welcome. Of course a man may know every one. Men are welcome to the privilege!"

"Pray what is it that happens—here, for instance?" Winterbourne demanded.

"The girl goes about alone with her foreigners. As to what happens farther, you must apply elsewhere for information. She has picked up half-a-dozen of the regular Roman fortune-hunters, and she takes them about to people's houses. When she comes to a party she brings with her a gentleman with a good deal of manner and a wonderful moustache."

"And where is the mother?"

"I haven't the least idea. They are very dreadful people."

Winterbourne meditated a moment. "They are very ignorant—very innocent only. Depend upon it they are not bad."

"They are hopelessly vulgar," said Mrs Costello. "Whether or no being hope- lessly vulgar is being 'bad' is a question for the metaphysicians. They are bad enough to dislike, at any rate; and for this short life that is quite enough."

The news that Daisy Miller was surrounded by half-a-dozen wonderful moustaches checked Winterbourne's impulse to go straightway to see her. He had perhaps not definitely flattered himself that he had made an ineffaceable impression upon her heart, but he was annoyed at hearing of a state of affairs so little in harmony with an image that had lately flitted in and out of his own meditations; the image of a very pretty girl looking out of an old Roman window and asking herself urgently when Mr Winterbourne would arrive. If, however, he determined to wait a little before reminding Miss Miller of his claims to her consideration, he went very soon to call upon two or three other friends. One of these friends was an American lady who had spent several winters at Geneva, where she had placed her children at school. She was a very accomplished woman and she lived in the Via Gregoriana. Winterbourne found her in a little crimson drawing-room, on a third floor; the room was filled with southern sunshine. He had not been there ten minutes when the servant came in, announcing "Madame Mila!" This announcement was presently followed by the entrance of little Randolph Miller, who stopped in the middle of the room and stood staring at Winterbourne. An instant later his pretty sister crossed the threshold; and then, after a considerable interval, Mrs Miller slowly advanced.

"I know you!" said Randolph.

"I'm sure you know a great many things," exclaimed Winterbourne, taking him by the hand. "How is your education coming on?"

Daisy was exchanging greetings very prettily with her hostess; but when she heard Winterbourne's voice she quickly turned her head. "Well, I declare!" she said.

"I told you I should come, you know," Winterbourne rejoined, smiling.

"Well—I didn't believe it," said Miss Daisy.

"I am much obliged to you," laughed the young man.

"You might have come to see me!" said Daisy.

"I arrived only yesterday."

"I don't believe that!" the young girl declared.

Winterbourne turned with a protesting smile to her mother; but this lady evaded his glance, and seating herself, fixed her eyes upon her son. "We've got a bigger place than this," said Randolph. "It's all gold on the walls."

Mrs Miller turned uneasily in her chair. "I told you if I were to bring you, you would say something!" she murmured.

"I told *you!*" Randolph exclaimed. "I tell *you,* sir!" he added jocosely, giving Winterbourne a thump on the knee. "It *is* bigger, too!"

Daisy had entered upon a lively conversation with her hostess; Winterbourne judged it becoming to address a few words to her mother. "I hope you have been well since we parted at Vevey," he said.

Mrs Miller now certainly looked at him—at his chin. "Not very well, sir," she answered.

"She's got the dyspepsia," said Randolph. "I've got it too. Father's got it. I've got it worst!"

This announcement, instead of embarrassing Mrs Miller, seemed to relieve her.

"I suffer from the liver," she said. "I think it's this climate; it's less bracing than Schenectady, especially in the winter season. I don't know whether you know we reside at Schenectady. I was saying to Daisy that I certainly hadn't found any one like Dr Davis, and I didn't believe I should. Oh, at Schenectady, he stands first; they think everything of him. He has so much to do, and yet there was nothing he wouldn't do for me. He said he never saw anything like my dyspepsia, but he was bound to cure it. I'm sure there was nothing he wouldn't try. He was just going to try something new when we came off. Mr Miller wanted Daisy to see Europe for herself. But I wrote to Mr Miller that it seems as if I couldn't get on without Dr Davis. At Schenectady he stands at the very top; and there's a great deal of sickness there, too. It affects my sleep."

Winterbourne had a good deal of pathological gossip with Dr Davis's patient, during which Daisy chattered unremittingly to her own companion. The young man asked Mrs Miller how she was pleased with Rome. "Well, I must say I am disappointed," she answered. "We had heard so much about it; I suppose we had heard too much. But we couldn't help that. We had been led to expect something different."

"Ah, wait a little, and you will become very fond of it," said Winterbourne.

"I hate it worse and worse every day!" cried Randolph.

"You are like the infant Hannibal," said Winterbourne.

"No, I ain't!" Randolph declared, at a venture.

"You are not much like an infant," said his mother. "But we have seen places," she resumed, "that I should put a long way before Rome." And in reply to Winterbourne's interrogation, "There's Zurich," she observed; "I think Zurich is lovely; and we hadn't heard half so much about it."

"The best place we've seen is the City of Richmond!" said Randolph.

"He means the ship," his mother explained. "We crossed in that ship. Randolph had a good time on the City of Richmond."

"It's the best place I've seen," the child repeated. "Only it was turned the wrong way."

"Well, we've got to turn the right way some time," said Mrs Miller, with a little laugh. Winterbourne expressed the hope that her daughter at least found some gratification in Rome, and she declared that Daisy was quite carried away. "It's on account of the society—the society's splendid. She goes round everywhere; she has made a great number of acquaintances. Of course she goes round more than I do. I must say they have been very sociable; they have taken her right in. And then she knows a great many gentlemen. Oh, she thinks there's nothing like Rome. Of course, it's a great deal pleasanter for a young lady if she knows plenty of gentlemen."

By this time Daisy had turned her attention again to Winterbourne. "I've been telling Mrs Walker how mean you were!" the young girl announced.

"And what is the evidence you have offered?" asked Winterbourne, rather annoyed at Miss Miller's want of appreciation of the zeal of an admirer who on his way down to Rome had stopped neither at Bologna nor at Florence, simply because of a certain sentimental impatience. He remembered that a cynical compatriot had once told him that American women—the pretty ones, and this gave a largeness to the axiom—were at once the most exacting in the world and the least endowed with a sense of indebtedness.

"Why, you were awfully mean at Vevey," said Daisy. "You wouldn't do anything. You wouldn't stay there when I asked you."

"My dearest young lady," cried Winterbourne, with eloquence, "have I come all the way to Rome to encounter your reproaches?"

"Just hear him say that!" said Daisy to her hostess, giving a twist to a bow on this lady's dress. "Did you ever hear anything so quaint?"

"So quaint, my dear?" murmured Mrs Walker, in the tone of a partisan of Winterbourne.

"Well, I don't know," said Daisy, fingering Mrs Walker's ribbons. "Mrs Walker, I want to tell you something."

"Mother," interposed Randolph, with his rough ends to his words, "I tell you you've got to go. Eugenio'll raise something!"

"I'm not afraid of Eugenio," said Daisy, with a toss of her head. "Look here, Mrs Walker," she went on, "you know I'm coming to your party."

"I am delighted to hear it."

"I've got a lovely dress."

"I am very sure of that."

"But I want to ask a favour—permission to bring a friend."

"I shall be happy to see any of your friends," said Mrs Walker, turning with a smile to Mrs Miller.

"Oh, they are not my friends," answered Daisy's mamma, smiling shyly, in her own fashion. "I never spoke to them!"

"It's an intimate friend of mine—Mr Giovanelli," said Daisy, without a tremor in her clear little voice or a shadow on her brilliant little face.

Mrs Walker was silent a moment, she gave a rapid glance at Winterbourne. "I shall be glad to see Mr Giovanelli," she then said.

"He's an Italian," Daisy pursued, with the prettiest serenity. "He's a great friend of mine—he's the handsomest man in the world—except Mr Winterbourne! He knows plenty of Italians, but he wants to know some Americans. He thinks ever so much of Americans. He's tremendously clever. He's perfectly lovely!"

It was settled that this brilliant personage should be brought to Mrs Walker's party, and then Mrs Miller prepared to take her leave. "I guess we'll go back to the hotel," she said.

"You may go back to the hotel, mother, but I'm going to take a walk," said Daisy.

"She's going to walk with Mr Giovanelli," Randolph proclaimed.

"I am going to the Pincio," said Daisy, smiling.

"Alone, my dear—at this hour?" Mrs Walker asked. The afternoon was drawing to a close—it was the hour for the throng of carriages and of contemplative pedestrians. "I don't think it's safe, my dear," said Mrs Walker.

"Neither do I," subjoined Mrs Miller. "You'll get the fever as sure as you live. Remember what Dr Davis told you!"

"Give her some medicine before she goes," said Randolph.

The company had risen to its feet; Daisy, still showing her pretty teeth, bent over and kissed her hostess. "Mrs Walker, you are too perfect," she said. "I'm not going alone; I am going to meet a friend."

"Your friend won't keep you from getting the fever," Mrs Miller observed.

"Is it Mr Giovanelli?" asked the hostess.

Winterbourne was watching the young girl; at this question his attention quickened. She stood there smiling and smoothing her bonnet-ribbons; she glanced at Winterbourne. Then, while she glanced and smiled, she answered without a shade of hesitation, "Mr Giovanelli—the beautiful Giovanelli."

"My dear young friend," said Mrs Walker, taking her hand, pleadingly, "don't walk off to the Pincio at this hour to meet a beautiful Italian."

"Well, he speaks English," said Mrs Miller.

"Gracious me!" Daisy exclaimed, "I don't want to do anything improper. There's an easy way to settle it." She continued to glance at Winterbourne. "The Pincio is only a hundred yards distant, and if Mr Winterbourne were as polite as he pretends he would offer to walk with me!"

Winterbourne's politeness hastened to affirm itself, and the young girl gave him gracious leave to accompany her. They passed down-stairs before her mother, and at the door Winterbourne perceived Mrs Miller's carriage drawn up, with the ornamental courier whose acquaintance he had made at Vevey seated within. "Good-bye, Eugenio!" cried Daisy, "I'm going to take a walk." The distance from the Via Gregoriana to the beautiful garden at the other end of the Pincian Hill is, in fact, rapidly traversed. As the day was splendid, however, and the concourse of vehicles, walkers, and loungers numerous, the young Americans found their progress much delayed. This fact was highly agreeable to Winterbourne, in spite of his consciousness of his singular situation. The slow-moving, idly-gazing Roman crowd bestowed much attention upon the extremely pretty young foreign lady who was passing through it upon his arm; and he wondered what on earth had been in Daisy's mind when she proposed to expose herself, unattended, to its appreciation. His own mission, to her sense, apparently, was to consign her to the hands of Mr Giovanelli; but Winterbourne, at once annoyed and gratified, resolved that he would do no such thing.

"Why haven't you been to see me?" asked Daisy. "You can't get out of that."

"I have had the honour of telling you that I have only just stepped out of the train."

"You must have stayed in the train a good while after it stopped!" cried the young girl, with her little laugh. "I suppose you were asleep. You have had time to go to see Mrs Walker."

"I knew Mrs Walker—" Winterbourne began to explain.

"I knew where you knew her. You knew her at Geneva. She told me so. Well, you knew me at Vevey. That's just as good. So you ought to have come." She asked him no other question than this; she began to prattle about her own affairs. "We've got splendid rooms at the hotel; Eugenio says they're the best rooms in Rome. We are going to stay all winter—if we don't die of the fever; and I guess we'll stay then. It's a great deal nicer than I thought; I thought it would be fearfully quiet; I was sure it would be awfully poky. I was sure we should be going round all the time with one of those dreadful old men that explain about the pictures and things. But we only had about a week of that, and now I'm enjoying myself. I know ever so many people, and they are all so charming. The society's extremely select. There are all kinds—English, and Germans, and Italians. I think I like the English best. I like their style of conversation. But there are some lovely Americans. I never saw anything so hospitable. There's something or other every day. There's not much dancing; but I must say I never thought dancing was everything. I was always fond of conversation. I guess I shall have plenty at Mrs Walker's—her rooms are so small." When they had passed the gate of the Pincian Gardens, Miss Miller began to wonder where Mr Giovanelli might be. "We had better go straight to that place in front," she said, "where you look at the view."

"I certainly shall not help you to find him," Winterbourne declared.

"Then I shall find him without you," said Miss Daisy.

"You certainly won't leave me!" cried Winterbourne.

She burst into her little laugh. "Are you afraid you'll get lost—or run over? But there's Giovanelli, leaning against that tree. He's staring at the women in the carriages: did you ever see anything so cool?"

Winterbourne perceived at some distance a little man standing with folded arms, nursing his cane. He had a handsome face, an artfully poised hat, a glass in one eye and a nosegay in his button-hole. Winterbourne looked at him a moment and then said, "Do you mean to speak to that man?"

"Do I mean to speak to him? Why, you don't suppose I mean to communicate by signs?"

"Pray understand, then," said Winterbourne, "that I intend to remain with you."

Daisy stopped and looked at him, without a sign of troubled consciousness in her face; with nothing but the presence of her charming eyes and her happy dimples. "Well, she's a cool one!" thought the young man.

"I don't like the way you say that," said Daisy. "It's too imperious."

"I beg your pardon if I say it wrong. The main point is to give you an idea of my meaning."

The young girl looked at him more gravely, but with eyes that were prettier than ever. "I have never allowed a gentleman to dictate to me, or to interfere with anything I do."

"I think you have made a mistake," said Winterbourne. "You should sometimes listen to a gentleman—the right one?"

Daisy began to laugh again. "I do nothing but listen to gentlemen!" she exclaimed. "Tell me if Mr Giovanelli is the right one."

The gentleman with the nosegay in his bosom had now perceived our two friends, and was approaching the young girl with obsequious rapidity. He bowed to Winterbourne as well as to the latter's companion; he had a brilliant smile, an intelligent eye; Winterbourne thought him not a bad-looking fellow. But he nevertheless said to Daisy—"No, he's not the right one."

Daisy evidently had a natural talent for performing introductions; she mentioned the name of each of her companions to the other. She strolled along with one of them on each side of her; Mr Giovanelli, who spoke English very cleverly— Winterbourne afterwards learned that he had practised the idiom upon a great many American heiresses—addressed her a great deal of very polite nonsense; he was extremely urbane, and the young American, who said nothing, reflected upon that profundity of Italian cleverness which enables people to appear more gracious in proportion as they are more acutely disappointed. Giovanelli, of course, had counted upon something more intimate; he had not bargained for a party of three. But he kept his temper in a manner which suggested far-stretching intentions. Winterbourne flattered himself that he had taken his measure. "He is not a gentleman," said the young American; "he is only a clever imitation of one. He is a music-master, or a penny-a-liner, or a third-rate artist. Damn his good looks!" Mr Giovanelli had certainly a very pretty face; but Winterbourne felt a superior indignation at his own lovely fellow-countrywoman's not knowing the difference between a spurious gentleman and a real one. Giovanelli chattered and jested and made himself wonderfully agreeable. It was true that if he was an imitation the imitation was very skilful. "Nevertheless," Winterbourne said to himself, "a nice girl ought to know!" And then he came back to the question whether this was in fact a nice girl. Would a nice girl—even allowing for her being a little American flirt—make a rendezvous with a presumably low-lived foreigner? The rendezvous in this case, indeed, had been in broad daylight, and in the most crowded corner of Rome; but was it not impossible to regard the choice of these circumstances as a proof of extreme cynicism? Singular though it may seem, Winterbourne was vexed that the young girl, in joining her *amoroso,* should not appear more impatient of his own company, and he was vexed because of his inclination. It was impossible to regard her as a perfectly well-conducted young lady; she was wanting in a certain indispensable delicacy. It would therefore simplify matters greatly to be able to treat her as the object of one of those sentiments which are called by romancers "lawless passions." That she should seem to wish to get rid of him would help him to think more lightly of her, and to be able to think more lightly of her would make her much less perplexing. But Daisy, on this occasion, continued to present herself as an inscrutable combination of audacity and innocence.

She had been walking some quarter of an hour, attended by her two cavaliers, and responding in a tone of very childish gaiety, as it seemed to Winterbourne, to the pretty speeches of Mr Giovanelli, when a carriage that had detached itself from the revolving train drew up beside the path. At the same moment Winterbourne perceived that his friend Mrs Walker—the lady whose house he had lately left—was seated in the vehicle and was beckoning to him. Leaving Miss Miller's side, he hastened to obey her summons. Mrs Walker was flushed; she wore an excited air. "It is really too dreadful," she said. "That girl must not do this sort of thing. She must not walk here with you two men. Fifty people have noticed her."

Winterbourne raised his eyebrows. "I think it's a pity to make too much fuss about it."

"It's a pity to let the girl ruin herself!"

"She is very innocent," said Winterbourne.

"She's very crazy!" cried Mrs Walker. "Did you ever see anything so imbecile as her mother? After you had all left me, just now, I could not sit still for thinking of it. It seemed too pitiful, not even to attempt to save her. I ordered the carriage and put on my bonnet, and came here as quickly as possible. Thank heaven I have found you!"

"What do you propose to do with us?" asked Winterbourne, smiling.

"To ask her to get in, to drive her about here for half-an-hour, so that the world may see she is not running absolutely wild, and then to take her safely home."

"I don't think it's a very happy thought," said Winterbourne; "but you can try."

Mrs Walker tried. The young man went in pursuit of Miss Miller, who had simply nodded and smiled at his interlocutrix in the carriage and had gone her way with her own companion. Daisy, on learning that Mrs Walker wished to speak to her, retraced her steps with a perfect good grace and with Mr Giovanelli at her side. She declared that she was delighted to have a chance to present this gentleman to Mrs Walker. She immediately achieved the introduction, and declared that she had never in her life seen anything so lovely as Mrs Walker's carriage-rug.

"I am glad you admire it," said this lady, smiling sweetly. "Will you get in and let me put it over you?"

"Oh, no, thank you," said Daisy. "I shall admire it much more as I see you driving round with it."

"Do get in and drive with me," said Mrs Walker.

"That would be charming, but it's so enchanting just as I am!" and Daisy gave a brilliant glance at the gentlemen on either side of her."

"It may be enchanting, dear child, but it is not the custom here," urged Mrs Walker, leaning forward in her victoria with her hands devoutly clasped.

"Well, it ought to be, then!" said Daisy. "If I didn't walk I should expire."

"You should walk with your mother, dear," cried the lady from Geneva, losing patience.

"With my mother dear!" exclaimed the young girl. Winterbourne saw that she scented interference. "My mother never walked ten steps in her life. And then, you know," she added with a laugh, "I am more than five years old."

"You are old enough to be more reasonable. You are old enough, dear Miss Miller, to be talked about."

Daisy looked at Mrs Walker, smiling intensely. "Talked about? What do you mean?"

"Come into my carriage and I will tell you."

Daisy turned her quickened glance again from one of the gentlemen beside her to the other. Mr Giovanelli was bowing to and fro, rubbing down his gloves and laughing very agreeably; Winterbourne thought it a most unpleasant scene. "I don't think I want to know what you mean," said Daisy presently. "I don't think I should like it."

Winterbourne wished that Mrs Walker would tuck in her carriage-rug and drive away; but this lady did not enjoy being defied, as she afterwards told him. "Should you prefer being thought a very reckless girl?" she demanded.

"Gracious me!" exclaimed Daisy. She looked again at Mr Giovanelli, then she turned to Winterbourne. There was a little pink flush in her cheek; she was tremendously pretty. "Does Mr Winterbourne think," she asked slowly, smiling, throwing back her head and glancing at him from head to foot, "that—to save my reputation—I ought to get into the carriage?"

Winterbourne coloured; for an instant he hesitated greatly. It seemed so strange to hear her speak that way of her "reputation." But he himself, in fact, must speak in accordance with gallantry. The finest gallantry, here, was simply to tell her the truth; and the truth, for Winterbourne, as the few indications I have been able to give have made him known to the reader, was that Daisy Miller should take Mrs Walker's advice. He looked at her exquisite prettiness; and then he said very gently, "I think you should get into the carriage."

Daisy gave a violent laugh. "I never heard anything so stiff! If this is improper, Mrs Walker," she pursued, "then I am all improper, and you must give me up. Good-bye; I hope you'll have a lovely ride!" and, with Mr Giovanelli, who made a triumphantly obsequious salute, she turned away.

Mrs Walker sat looking after her, and there were tears in Mrs Walker's eyes. "Get in here, sir," she said to Winterbourne, indicating the place beside her. The young man answered that he felt bound to accompany Miss Miller; whereupon Mrs Walker declared that if he refused her this favour she would never speak to him again. She was evidently in earnest. Winterbourne overtook Daisy and her companion, and, offering the young girl his hand, told her that Mrs Walker had made an imperious claim upon his society. He expected that in answer she would say something rather free, something to commit herself still farther to that "recklessness" from which Mrs Walker had so charitably endeavoured to dissuade her. But she only shook his hand, hardly looking at him, while Mr Giovanelli bade him farewell with a too emphatic flourish of the hat.

Winterbourne was not in the best possible humour as he took his seat in Mrs Walker's victoria. "That was not clever of you," he said candidly, while the vehicle mingled again with the throng of carriages.

"In such a case," his companion answered, "I don't wish to be clever, I wish to be *earnest!*"

"Well, your earnestness has only offended her and put her off."

"It has happened very well," said Mrs Walker. "If she is so perfectly determined to compromise herself, the sooner one knows it the better; one can act accordingly."

"I suspect she meant no harm," Winterbourne rejoined.

"So I thought a month ago. But she has been going too far."

"What has she been doing?"

"Everything that is not done here. Flirting with any man she could pick up; sitting in corners with mysterious Italians; dancing all the evening with the same partners; receiving visits at eleven o'clock at night. Her mother goes away when visitors come."

"But her brother," said Winterbourne, laughing, "sits up till midnight."

"He must be edified by what he sees. I'm told that at their hotel every one is talking about her, and that a smile goes round among the servants when a gentleman comes and asks for Miss Miller."

"The servants be hanged!" said Winterbourne angrily. "The poor girl's only fault," he presently added, "is that she is very uncultivated."

"She is naturally indelicate," Mrs Walker declared. "Take that example this morning. How long had you known her at Vevey?"

"A couple of days."

"Fancy, then, her making it a personal matter that you should have left the place!"

Winterbourne was silent for some moments; then he said, "I suspect, Mrs Walker, that you and I have lived too long at Geneva!" And he added a request that she should inform him with what particular design she had made him enter her carriage.

"I wished to beg you to cease your relations with Miss Miller—not to flirt with her—to give her no farther opportunity to expose herself—to let her alone, in short."

"I'm afraid I can't do that," said Winterbourne. "I like her extremely."

"All the more reason that you shouldn't help her to make a scandal."

"There shall be nothing scandalous in my attentions to her."

"There certainly will be in the way she takes them. But I have said what I had on my conscience," Mrs Walker pursued. "If you wish to rejoin the young lady I will put you down. Here, by-the-way, you have a chance."

The carriage was traversing that part of the Pincian Garden which overhangs the wall of Rome and overlooks the beautiful Villa Borghese. It is bordered by a large parapet, near which there are several seats. One of the seats, at a distance, was occupied by a gentleman and a lady, towards whom Mrs Walker gave a toss of her head. At the same moment these persons rose and walked towards the parapet. Winterbourne had asked the coachman to stop; he now descended from the carriage. His companion looked at him a moment in silence; then, while he raised his hat, she drove majestically away. Winterbourne stood there; he had turned his eyes towards Daisy and her cavalier. They evidently saw no one; they were too deeply occupied with each other. When they reached the low garden-wall they stood a moment looking off at the great flat-topped pine-clusters of the Villa Borghese; then Giovanelli seated himself familiarly upon the broad ledge of the wall. The western sun in the opposite sky sent out a brilliant shaft through a couple of cloud-bars; whereupon Daisy's companion took her parasol out of her hands and opened it. She came a little nearer and he held the parasol over her; then, still holding it, he let it rest upon her shoulder, so that both of their heads were hidden from Winterbourne. This young man lingered a moment, then he began to walk. But he walked—not towards the couple with the parasol; towards the residence of his aunt, Mrs Costello.

He flattered himself on the following day that there was no smiling among the servants when he, at least, asked for Mrs Miller at her hotel. This lady and her daughter, however, were not at home; and on the next day after, repeating his visit, Winterbourne again had the misfortune not to find them. Mrs Walker's party took place on the evening of the third day, and in spite of the frigidity of his last interview with the hostess Winterbourne was among the guests. Mrs Walker was one of those American ladies who, while residing abroad, make a point, in their own phrase, of studying European society; and she had on this occasion collected several specimens of her diversely born fellow-mortals to serve, as it were, as text-books. When Winterbourne arrived Daisy Miller was not there; but in a few moments he saw her mother come in alone, very shyly and ruefully. Mrs Miller's hair, above her exposed-looking temples, was more frizzled than ever. As she approached Mrs Walker, Winterbourne also drew near.

"You see I've come all alone," said poor Mrs Miller. "I'm so frightened; I don't know what to do; it's the first time I've ever been to a party alone—especially in this country. I wanted to bring Randolph or Eugenio, or some one, but Daisy just pushed me off by myself. I ain't used to going round alone."

"And does not your daughter intend to favour us with her society?" demanded Mrs Walker, impressively.

"Well, Daisy's all dressed," said Mrs Miller, with that accent of the dispassionate, if not of the philosophic, historian with which she always recorded the current incidents of her daughter's career. "She got dressed on purpose before dinner. But she's got a friend of hers there; that gentleman—the Italian—that she wanted to bring. They've got going at the piano; it seems as if they couldn't leave off. Mr Giovanelli sings splendidly. But I guess they'll come before very long," concluded Mrs Miller hopefully.

"I'm sorry she should come—in that way," said Mrs Walker.

"Well, I told her that there was no use in her getting dressed before dinner if she was going to wait three hours," responded Daisy's mamma. "I didn't see the use of her putting on such a dress as that to sit round with Mr Giovanelli."

"This is most horrible!" said Mrs Walker, turning away and addressing herself to Winterbourne. "*Elle s'affiche.* It's her revenge for my having ventured to remonstrate with her. When she comes I shall not speak to her."

Daisy came after eleven o'clock, but she was not, on such an occasion, a young lady to wait to be spoken to. She rustled forward in radiant loveliness, smiling and chattering, carrying a large bouquet and attended by Mr Giovanelli. Every one stopped talking, and turned and looked at her. She came straight to Mrs Walker. "I'm afraid you thought I never was coming, so I sent mother off to tell you. I wanted to make Mr Giovanelli practise some things before he came; you know he sings beautifully, and I want you to ask him to sing. This is Mr Giovanelli; you know I introduced him to you; he's got the most lovely voice and he knows the most charming set of songs. I made him go over them this evening, on purpose; we had the greatest time at the hotel." Of all this Daisy delivered herself with the sweetest, brightest audibleness, looking now at her hostess and now round the room, while she gave a series of little pats, round her shoulders, to the edges of her dress. "Is there any one I know?" she asked.

"I think every one knows you!" said Mrs Walker pregnantly, and she gave a very cursory greeting to Mr Giovanelli. This gentleman bore himself gallantly. He smiled and bowed and showed his white teeth, he curled his moustaches and rolled his eyes, and performed all the proper functions of a handsome Italian at an evening party. He sang, very prettily, half-a-dozen songs, though Mrs Walker afterwards declared that she had been quite unable to find out who asked him. It was apparently not Daisy who had given him his orders. Daisy sat at a distance from the piano, and though she had publicly, as it were, professed a high admiration for his singing, talked, not inaudibly, while it was going on.

"It's a pity these rooms are so small; we can't dance," she said to Winterbourne, as if she had seen him five minutes before.

"I am not sorry we can't dance," Winterbourne answered; "I don't dance."

"Of course you don't dance; you're too stiff," said Miss Daisy. "I hope you enjoyed your drive with Mrs Walker."

"No, I didn't enjoy it; I preferred walking with you."

"We paired off, that was much better," said Daisy. "But did you ever hear anything so cool as Mrs Walker's wanting me to get into her carriage and drop poor Mr Giovanelli; and under the pretext that it was proper? People have different ideas! It would have been most unkind; he had been talking about that walk for ten days."

"He should not have talked about it at all," said Winterbourne; "he would never have proposed to a young lady of this country to walk about the streets with him."

"About the streets?" cried Daisy, with her pretty stare. "Where then would he have proposed to her to walk? The Pincio is not the streets, either; and I, thank goodness, am not a young lady of this country. The young ladies of this country have a dreadfully poky time of it, so far as I can learn; I don't see why I should change my habits for *them*."

"I am afraid your habits are those of a flirt," said Winterbourne gravely.

"Of course they are," she cried, giving him her little smiling stare again. "I'm a fearful, frightful flirt! Did you ever hear of a nice girl that was not? But I suppose you will tell me now that I am not a nice girl."

"You're a very nice girl, but I wish you would flirt with me, and me only," said Winterbourne.

"Ah! thank you, thank you very much; you are the last man I should think of flirting with. As I have had the pleasure of informing you, you are too stiff."

"You say that too often," said Winterbourne.

Daisy gave a delighted laugh. "If I could have the sweet hope of making you angry, I would say it again."

"Don't do that; when I am angry I'm stiffer than ever. But if you won't flirt with me, do cease at least to flirt with your friend at the piano; they don't understand that sort of thing here."

"I thought they understood nothing else!" exclaimed Daisy.

"Not in young unmarried women."

"It seems to me much more proper in young unmarried women than in old married ones," Daisy declared.

"Well," said Winterbourne, "when you deal with natives you must go by the custom of the place. Flirting is a purely American custom; it doesn't exist here. So when you show yourself in public with Mr Giovanelli and without your mother——"

"Gracious! poor mother!" interposed Daisy.

"Though you may be flirting, Mr Giovanelli is not; he means something else."

"He isn't preaching, at any rate," said Daisy with vivacity. "And if you want very much to know, we are neither of us flirting; we are too good friends for that; we are very intimate friends."

"Ah!" rejoined Winterbourne, "if you are in love with each other it is another affair."

She had allowed him up to this point to talk so frankly that he had no expectation of shocking her by this ejaculation; but she immediately got up, blushing visibly, and leaving him to exclaim mentally that little American flirts were the queerest creatures in the world. "Mr Giovanelli, at least," she said, giving her interlocutor a single glance, "never says such very disagreeable things to me."

Winterbourne was bewildered; he stood staring. Mr Giovanelli had finished singing; he left the piano and came over to Daisy. "Won't you come into the other room and have some tea?" he asked, bending before her with his decorative smile.

Daisy turned to Winterbourne, beginning to smile again. He was still more perplexed, for this inconsequent smile made nothing clear, though it seemed to prove, indeed, that she had a sweetness and softness that reverted instinctively to the pardon of offences. "It has never occurred to Mr Winterbourne to offer me any tea," she said, with her little tormenting manner.

"I have offered you advice," Winterbourne rejoined.

"I prefer weak tea!" cried Daisy, and she went off with the brilliant Giovanelli. She sat with him in the adjoining room, in the embrasure of the window, for the rest of the evening. There was an interesting performance at the piano, but neither of these young people gave heed to it. When Daisy came to take leave of Mrs Walker, this lady conscientiously repaired the weakness of which she had been guilty at the moment of the young girl's arrival. She turned her back straight upon Miss Miller and left her to depart with what grace she might. Winterbourne was standing near the door; he saw it all. Daisy turned very pale and looked at her mother, but Mrs Miller was humbly unconscious of any violation of the usual social forms. She appeared, indeed, to have felt an incongruous impulse to draw attention to her own striking observance of them. "Good night, Mrs Walker," she said; "we've had a beautiful evening. You see if I let Daisy come to parties without me, I don't want her to go away without me." Daisy turned away, looking with a pale, grave face at the circle near the door; Winterbourne saw that, for the first moment, she was too much shocked and puzzled even for indignation. He on his side was greatly touched.

"That was very cruel," he said to Mrs Walker.

"She never enters my drawing-room again," replied his hostess.

Since Winterbourne was not to meet her in Mrs Walker's drawing-room, he went as often as possible to Mrs Miller's hotel. The ladies were rarely at home, but when he found them the devoted Giovanelli was always present. Very often the polished little Roman was in the drawing-room with Daisy alone, Mrs Miller being apparently constantly of the opinion that discretion is the better part of surveillance. Winterbourne noted, at first with surprise, that Daisy on these occasions was never embarrassed or annoyed by his own entrance; but he very presently began to feel that she had no more surprises for him; the unexpected in her behaviour was the only thing to expect. She showed no displeasure at her *tête-à-tête* with Giovanelli being interrupted; she could chatter as freshly and freely with two gentlemen as with one; there was always in her conversation, the same odd mixture of audacity and puerility. Winterbourne remarked to himself that if she was seriously interested in Giovanelli it was very singular that she should not take more trouble to preserve the sanctity of their interviews, and he liked her the more for her innocent-looking indifference and her apparently inexhaustible good humour. He could hardly have said why, but she seemed to him a girl who would never be jealous. At the risk of exciting a somewhat derisive smile on the reader's part, I may affirm that with regard to the women who had hitherto interested him it very often seemed to Winterbourne among the possibilities that, given certain contingencies, he should be afraid—literally afraid—of these ladies. He had a pleasant sense that he should never be afraid of Daisy Miller. It must be added that this sentiment was not altogether flattering to Daisy; it was part of his conviction, or rather of his apprehension, that she would prove a very light young person.

But she was evidently very much interested in Giovanelli. She looked at him whenever he spoke; she was perpetually telling him to do this and to do that; she was constantly "chaffing" and abusing him. She appeared completely to have forgotten that Winterbourne had said anything to displease her at Mrs Walker's little party. One Sunday afternoon, having gone to St Peter's with his aunt, Winterbourne perceived Daisy strolling about the great church in company with the inevitable Giovanelli. Presently he pointed out the young girl and her cavalier to Mrs Costello. This lady looked at them a moment through her eyeglass, and then she said:

"That's what makes you so pensive in these days, eh?"

"I had not the least idea I was pensive," said the young man.

"You are very much pre-occupied, you are thinking of something."

"And what is it," he asked, "that you accuse me of thinking of?"

"Of that young lady's—Miss Baker's, Miss Chandler's—what's her name?—Miss Miller's intrigue with that little barber's block."

"Do you call it an intrigue," Winterbourne asked—"an affair that goes on with such peculiar publicity?"

"That's their folly," said Mrs Costello, "it's not their merit."

"No," rejoined Winterbourne, with something of that pensiveness to which his aunt had alluded. "I don't believe that there is anything to be called an intrigue."

"I have heard a dozen people speak of it; they say she is quite carried away by him."

"They are certainly very intimate," said Winterbourne.

Mrs Costello inspected the young couple again with her optical instrument. "He is very handsome. One easily sees how it is. She thinks him the most elegant man in the world, the finest gentleman. She has never seen anything like him; he is better even than the courier. It was the courier probably who introduced him, and if he succeeds in marrying the young lady, the courier will come in for a magnificent commission."

"I don't believe she thinks of marrying him," said Winterbourne, "and I don't believe he hopes to marry her."

"You may be very sure she thinks of nothing. She goes on from day to day, from hour to hour, as they did in the Golden Age. I can imagine nothing more vulgar. And at the same time," added Mrs Costello, "depend upon it that she may tell you any moment that she is 'engaged.' "

"I think that is more than Giovanelli expects," said Winterbourne.

"Who is Giovanelli?"

"The little Italian. I have asked questions about him and learned something. He is apparently a perfectly respectable little man. I believe he is in a small way a *cavaliere avvocato*. But he doesn't move in what are called the first circles. I think it is really not absolutely impossible that the courier introduced him. He is evidently immensely charmed with Miss Miller. If she thinks him the finest gentleman in the world, he, on his side, has never found himself in personal contact with such splendour, such opulence, such expensiveness, as this young lady's. And then she must seem to him wonderfully pretty and interesting. I rather doubt whether he dreams of marrying her. That must appear to him too impossible a piece of luck. He has nothing but his handsome face to offer, and there is a substantial Mr Miller in that mysterious land of dollars. Giovanelli knows that he hasn't a title to offer. If he were only a count or a *marchese!* He must wonder at his luck at the way they have taken him up."

"He accounts for it by his handsome face, and thinks Miss Miller a young lady *qui se passe ses fantaisies!*" said Mrs Costello.

"It is very true," Winterbourne pursued, "that Daisy and her mamma have not yet risen to that stage of—what shall I call it?—of culture, at which the idea of catching a count or a *marchese* begins. I believe that they are intellectually incapable of that conception."

"Ah! but the *cavaliere* can't believe it," said Mrs Costello.

Of the observation excited by Daisy's "intrigue," Winterbourne gathered that day at St Peter's sufficient evidence. A dozen of the American colonists in Rome came to talk with Mrs Costello, who sat on a little portable stool at the base of one of the great pilasters. The vesper-service was going forward in splendid chants and organ-tones in the adjacent choir, and meanwhile, between Mrs Costello and her friends, there was a great deal said about poor little Miss Miller's going really "too far." Winterbourne was not pleased with what he heard; but when, coming out upon the great steps of the church, he saw Daisy, who had emerged before him, get into an open cab with her accomplice and roll away through the cynical streets of Rome, he could not deny to himself that she was going very far indeed. He felt very sorry for her—not exactly that he believed that she had completely lost her head, but because it was painful to hear so much that was pretty and undefended and natural assigned to a vulgar place among the categories of disorder. He made an attempt after this to give a hint to Mrs Miller. He met one day in the Corso a friend—a tourist like himself—who had just come out of the Doria Palace, where he had been walking through the beautiful gallery. His friend talked for a moment about the superb portrait of Innocent X by Velasquez, which hangs in one of the cabinets of the palace, and then said, "And in the same cabinet, by-the-way, I had the pleasure of contemplating a picture of a different kind—that pretty American girl whom you pointed out to me last week." In answer to Winterbourne's inquiries, his friend narrated that the pretty American girl—prettier than ever—was seated with a companion in the secluded nook in which the great papal portrait is enshrined.

"Who was her companion?" asked Winterbourne.

"A little Italian with a bouquet in his button-hole. The girl is delightfully pretty, but I thought I understood from you the other day that she was a young lady *du meilleur monde*."

"So she is!" answered Winterbourne; and having assured himself that his informant had seen Daisy and her companion but five minutes before, he jumped into a cab and went to call on Mrs Miller. She was at home; but she apologised to him for receiving him in Daisy's absence.

"She's gone out somewhere with Mr Giovanelli," said Mrs Miller. "She's always going round with Mr Giovanelli."

"I have noticed that they are very intimate," Winterbourne observed.

"Oh! it seems as if they couldn't live without each other!" said Mrs Miller. "Well, he's a real gentleman, anyhow. I keep telling Daisy she's engaged!"

"And what does Daisy say?"

"Oh, she says she isn't engaged. But she might as well be!" this impartial parent resumed. "She goes on as if she was. But I've made Mr Giovanelli promise to tell me, if *she* doesn't. I should want to write to Mr Miller about it—shouldn't you?"

Winterbourne replied that he certainly should; and the state of mind of Daisy's mamma struck him as so unprecedented in the annals of parental vigilance that he gave up as utterly irrelevant the attempt to place her upon her guard.

After this Daisy was never at home, and Winterbourne ceased to meet her at the houses of their common acquaintance, because, as he perceived, these shrewd people had quite made up their minds that she was going too far. They ceased to invite her, and they intimated that they desired to express to observant Europeans the great truth that, though Miss Daisy Miller was a young American lady, her behaviour was not representative—was regarded by her compatriots as abnormal. Winterbourne wondered how she felt about all the cold shoulders that were turned towards her, and sometimes it annoyed him to suspect that she did not feel at all. He said to himself that she was too light and childish, too uncultivated and unreasoning, too provincial, to have reflected upon her ostracism or even to have perceived it. Then at other moments he believed that she carried about in her elegant and irresponsible little organism a defiant, passionate, perfectly observant consciousness of the impression she produced. He asked himself whether Daisy's defiance came from the consciousness of innocence or from her being, essentially, a young person of the reckless class. It must be admitted that holding oneself to a belief in Daisy's "innocence" came to seem to Winterbourne more and more a matter of fine-spun gallantry. As I have already had occasion to relate, he was angry at finding himself reduced to chopping logic about this young lady; he was vexed at his want of instinctive certitude as to how far her eccentricities were generic, national, and how far they were personal. From either view of them he had somehow missed her, and now it was too late. She was "carried away" by Mr Giovanelli.

A few days after his brief interview with her mother, he encountered her in that beautiful abode of flowering desolation known as the Palace of the Cæsars. The early Roman spring had filled the air with bloom and perfume, and the rugged surface of the Palatine was muffled with tender verdure. Daisy was strolling along the top of one of those great mounds of ruin that are embanked with mossy marble and paved with monumental inscriptions. It seemed to him that Rome had never been so lovely as just then. He stood looking off at the enchanting harmony of line and colour that remotely encircles the city, inhaling the softly humid odours and feeling the freshness of the year and the antiquity of the place reaffirm themselves in mysterious interfusion. It seemed to him also that Daisy had never looked so pretty; but this had been an observation of his whenever he met her. Giovanelli was at her side, and Giovanelli, too, wore an aspect of even unwonted brilliancy.

"Well," said Daisy, "I should think you would be lonesome!"

"Lonesome?" asked Winterbourne.

"You are always going round by yourself. Can't you get any one to walk with you?"

"I am not so fortunate," said Winterbourne, "as your companion."

Giovanelli, from the first, had treated Winterbourne with distinguished politeness; he listened with a deferential air to his remarks; he laughed, punctiliously, at his pleasantries; he seemed disposed to testify to his belief that Winterbourne was a superior young man. He carried himself in no degree like a jealous wooer; he had obviously a great deal of tact; he had no objection to your expecting a little humility of him. It even seemed to Winterbourne at times that Giovanelli would find a certain mental relief in being able to have a private understanding with him—to say to him, as an intelligent man, that, bless you, *he* knew how extraordinary was this young lady, and didn't flatter himself with delusive—or at least *too* delusive—hopes of matrimony and dollars. On this occasion he strolled away from his companion to pluck a sprig of almond blossom, which he carefully arranged in his button-hole.

"I know why you say that," said Daisy, watching Giovanelli. "Because you think I go round too much with *him!*" And she nodded at her attendant.

"Every one thinks so—if you care to know," said Winterbourne.

"Of course I care to know!" Daisy exclaimed seriously. "But I don't believe it. They are only pretending to be shocked. They don't really care a straw what I do. Besides, I don't go round so much."

"I think you will find they do care. They will show it—disagreeably."

Daisy looked at him a moment. "How—disagreeably?"

"Haven't you noticed anything?" Winterbourne asked.

"I have noticed you. But I noticed you were as stiff as an umbrella the first time I saw you."

"You will find I am not so stiff as several others," said Winterbourne, smiling.

"How shall I find it?"

"By going to see the others."

"What will they do to me?"

"They will give you the cold shoulder. Do you know what that means?"

Daisy was looking at him intently; she began to colour. "Do you mean as Mrs Walker did the other night?"

"Exactly!" said Winterbourne.

She looked away at Giovanelli, who was decorating himself with his almond-blossom. Then looking back at Winterbourne—"I shouldn't think you would let people be so unkind!" she said.

"How can I help it?" he asked.

"I should think you would say something."

"I do say something;" and he paused a moment. "I say that your mother tells me that she believes you are engaged."

"Well, she does," said Daisy very simply.

Winterbourne began to laugh. "And does Randolph believe it?" he asked.

"I guess Randolph doesn't believe anything," said Daisy. Randolph's scepticism excited Winterbourne to farther hilarity, and he observed that Giovanelli was coming back to them. Daisy, observing it too, addressed herself again to her countryman. "Since you have mentioned it," she said, "I *am* engaged."...Winterbourne looked at her; he had stopped laughing. "You don't believe it!" she added.

He was silent a moment; and then, "Yes, I believe it!" he said.

"Oh, no, you don't," she answered. "Well, then—I am not!"

The young girl and her cicerone were on their way to the gate of the enclosure, so that Winterbourne, who had but lately entered, presently took leave of them. A week afterwards he went to dine at a beautiful villa on the Cælian Hill, and, on arriving, dismissed his hired vehicle. The evening was charming, and he promised himself the satisfaction of walking home beneath the Arch of Constantine and past the vaguely lighted monuments of the Forum. There was a waning moon in the sky, and her radiance was not brilliant, but she was veiled in a thin cloud-curtain which seemed to diffuse and equalise it. When, on his return from the villa (it was eleven o'clock), Winterbourne approached the dusky circle of the Colosseum, it occurred to him, as a lover of the picturesque, that the interior, in the pale moonshine, would be well worth a glance. He turned aside and walked to one of the empty arches, near which, as he observed, an open carriage—one of the little Roman street-cabs—was stationed. Then he passed in among the cavernous shadows of the great structure, and emerged upon the clear and silent arena. The place had never seemed to him more impressive. One-half of the gigantic circus was in deep shade; the other was sleeping in the luminous dusk. As he stood there he began to murmur Byron's famous lines, out of "Manfred;" but before he had finished his quotation he remembered that if nocturnal meditations in the Colosseum are recommended by the poets, they are deprecated by the doctors. The historic atmosphere was there, certainly; but the historic atmosphere, scientifically considered, was no better than a villanous miasma. Winterbourne walked to the middle of the arena, to take a more general glance, intending thereafter to make a hasty retreat. The great cross in the centre was covered with shadow; it was only as he drew near it that he made it out distinctly. Then he saw that two persons were stationed upon the low steps which formed its base. One of these was a woman, seated; her companion was standing in front of her.

Presently the sound of the woman's voice came to him distinctly in the warm night-air. "Well, he looks at us as one of the old lions or tigers may have looked at the Christian martyrs!" These were the words he heard, in the familiar accent of Miss Daisy Miller.

"Let us hope he is not very hungry," responded the ingenious Giovanelli. "He will have to take me first; you will serve for dessert!"

Winterbourne stopped, with a sort of horror; and, it must be added, with a sort of relief. It was as if a sudden illumination had been flashed upon the ambiguity of Daisy's behaviour and the riddle had become easy to read. She was a young lady whom a gentleman need no longer be at pains to respect. He stood there looking at her—looking at her companion, and not reflecting that though he saw them vaguely, he himself must have been more brightly visible. He felt angry with himself that he had bothered so much about the right way of regarding Miss Daisy Miller. Then, as he was going to advance again, he checked himself; not from the fear that he was doing her injustice, but from a sense of the danger of appearing unbecomingly exhilarated by this sudden revulsion from cautious criticism. He turned away towards the entrance of the place; but as he did so he heard Daisy speak again.

"Why, it was Mr Winterbourne! He saw me—and he cuts me!"

What a clever little reprobate she was, and how smartly she played an injured innocence! But he wouldn't cut her. Winterbourne came forward again, and went towards the great cross. Daisy had got up; Giovanelli lifted his hat. Winterbourne had now begun to think simply of the craziness, from a sanitary point of view, of a delicate young girl lounging away the evening in this nest of malaria. What if she *were* a clever little reprobate? that was no reason for her dying of the *perniciosa*. "How long have you been here?" he asked, almost brutally.

Daisy, lovely in the flattering moonlight, looked at him a moment. Then—"All the evening," she answered gently. . . . "I never saw anything so pretty."

"I am afraid," said Winterbourne, "that you will not think Roman fever very pretty. This is the way people catch it. I wonder," he added, turning to Giovanelli, "that you, a native Roman, should countenance such a terrible indiscretion."

"Ah," said the handsome native, "for myself, I am not afraid."

"Neither am I—for you! I am speaking for this young lady."

Giovanelli lifted his well-shaped eyebrows and showed his brilliant teeth. But he took Winterbourne's rebuke with docility. "I told the Signorina it was a grave indiscretion; but when was the Signorina ever prudent?"

"I never was sick, and I don't mean to be!" the Signorina declared. "I don't look like much, but I'm healthy! I was bound to see the Colosseum by moonlight;

I shouldn't have wanted to go home without that; and we have had the most beautiful time, haven't we, Mr Giovanelli? If there has been any danger, Eugenio can give me some pills. He has got some splendid pills."

"I should advise you," said Winterbourne, "to drive home as fast as possible and take one!"

"What you say is very wise," Giovanelli rejoined. "I will go and make sure the carriage is at hand." And he went forward rapidly.

Daisy followed with Winterbourne. He kept looking at her; she seemed not in the least embarrassed. Winterbourne said nothing; Daisy chattered about the beauty of the place. "Well, I *have* seen the Colosseum by moonlight!" she exclaimed. "That's one good thing." Then, noticing Winterbourne's silence, she asked him why he didn't speak. He made no answer; he only began to laugh. They passed under one of the dark archways; Giovanelli was in front with the carriage. Here Daisy stopped a moment, looking at the young American. "*Did* you believe I was engaged the other day?" she asked.

"It doesn't matter what I believed the other day," said Winterbourne, still laughing.

"Well, what do you believe now?"

"I believe that it makes very little difference whether you are engaged or not!"

He felt the young girl's pretty eyes fixed upon him through the thick gloom of the archway; she was apparently going to answer. But Giovanelli hurried her forward. "Quick, quick," he said; "if we get in by midnight we are quite safe."

Daisy took her seat in the carriage, and the fortunate Italian placed himself beside her. "Don't forget Eugenio's pills!" said Winterbourne, as he lifted his hat.

"I don't care," said Daisy, in a little strange tone, "whether I have Roman fever or not!" Upon this the cab-driver cracked his whip, and they rolled away over the desultory patches of the antique pavement.

Winterbourne—to do him justice, as it were—mentioned to no one that he had encountered Miss Miller, at midnight, in the Colosseum with a gentleman; but nevertheless, a couple of days later, the fact of her having been there under these circumstances was known to every member of the little American circle, and commented accordingly. Winterbourne reflected that they had of course known it at the hotel, and that, after Daisy's return, there had been an exchange of jokes between the porter and the cab-driver. But the young man was conscious at the same moment that it had ceased to be a matter of serious regret to him that the little American flirt should be "talked about" by low-minded menials. These people, a day or two later, had serious information to give: the little American flirt was alarmingly ill. Winterbourne, when the rumour came to him, immediately went to the hotel for more news. He found that two or three charitable friends had preceded him, and that they were being entertained in Mrs Miller's salon by Randolph.

"It's going round at night," said Randolph—"that's what made her sick. She's always going round at night. I shouldn't think she'd want to—it's so plaguey dark. You can't see anything here at night, except when there's a moon. In America there's always a moon!" Mrs Miller was invisible; she was now, at least, giving her daughter the advantage of her society. It was evident that Daisy was dangerously ill.

Winterbourne went often to ask for news of her, and once he saw Mrs Miller, who, though deeply alarmed, was—rather to his surprise—perfectly composed, and, as it appeared, a most efficient and judicious nurse. She talked a good deal about Dr Davis, but Winterbourne paid her the compliment of saying to himself that she was not, after all, such a monstrous goose. "Daisy spoke of you the other day," she said to him. "Half the time she doesn't know what she's saying, but that time I think she did. She gave me a message; she told me to tell you. She told me to tell you that she never was engaged to that handsome Italian. I am sure I am very glad; Mr Giovanelli hasn't been near us since she was taken ill. I thought he was so much of a gentleman; but I don't call that very polite! A lady told me that he was afraid I was angry with him for taking Daisy round at night. Well, so I am; but I suppose he knows I'm a lady. I would scorn to scold him. Any way, she says she's not engaged. I don't know why she wanted you to know; but she said to me three times—'Mind you tell Mr Winterbourne.' And then she told me to ask if you remembered the time you went to that castle, in Switzerland. But I said I wouldn't give any such messages as that. Only, if she is not engaged, I'm sure I'm glad to know it."

But, as Winterbourne had said, it mattered very little. A week after this the poor girl died; it had been a terrible case of the fever. Daisy's grave was in the little Protestant cemetery, in an angle of the wall of imperial Rome, beneath the cypresses and the thick spring-flowers. Winterbourne stood there beside it, with a number of other mourners; a number larger than the scandal excited by the young lady's career would have led you to expect. Near him stood Giovanelli, who came nearer still before Winterbourne turned away. Giovanelli was very pale; on this occasion he had no flower in his button-hole; he seemed to wish to say something. At last he said, "She was the most beautiful young lady I ever saw, and the most amiable." And then he added in a moment, "And she was the most innocent."

Winterbourne looked at him and presently repeated his words, "And the most innocent?"

"The most innocent!"

Winterbourne felt sore and angry. "Why the devil," he asked, "did you take her to that fatal place?"

Mr Giovanelli's urbanity was apparently imperturbable. He looked on the ground a moment, and then he said, "For myself, I had no fear; and she wanted to go."

"That was no reason!" Winterbourne declared.

The subtle Roman again dropped his eyes. "If she had lived, I should have got nothing. She would never have married me, I am sure."

"She would never have married you?"

"For a moment I hoped so. But no. I am sure."

Winterbourne listened to him; he stood staring at the raw protuberance among the April daisies. When he turned away again Mr Giovanelli, with his light slow step, had retired.

Winterbourne almost immediately left Rome; but the following summer he again met his aunt, Mrs Costello, at Vevey. Mrs Costello was fond of Vevey. In the interval Winterbourne had often thought of Daisy Miller and her mystifying manners. One day he spoke of her to his aunt—said it was on his conscience that he had done her injustice.

"I am sure I don't know," said Mrs Costello. "How did your injustice affect her?"

"She sent me a message before her death which I didn't understand at the time. But I have understood it since. She would have appreciated one's esteem."

"Is that a modest way," asked Mrs Costello, "of saying that she would have reciprocated one's affection?"

Winterbourne offered no answer to this question; but he presently said, "You were right in that remark that you made last summer. I was booked to make a mistake. I have lived too long in foreign parts."

Nevertheless, he went back to live at Geneva, whence there continue to come the most contradictory accounts of his motives of sojourn: a report that he is "studying" hard—an intimation that he is much interested in a very clever foreign lady.

Black Bread

(1883)

Giovanni Verga

D. H. Lawrence, translator

The Italian novelist Giovanni Verga (1840–1922) was born in Sicily, and though he spent much of his life in Italy, he wrote his best books about the Sicilian peasantry. His early works were romantic (*Eve* and *Storia di una capinera,* 1869), but his best tales are naturalistic, closest (among the other pieces in this volume) to *Castle Rackrent* in employing the language of the peasants as a medium. These include the novels *I Malavoglia* (*The House by the Medlar Tree*) of 1881 and *Maestro Don Gesualdo* of 1889; and the books of *novelle* (actually short stories and sketches as well as what we would call *novelle*), *Medda* (1874) and *Vita dei campi* (1880). The latter includes Verga's most popular story, *Cavalleria Rusticana,* used by Pietro Mascagni for the libretto of his opera. *Black Bread* appeared in *Novelle Rusticane* (1883), which D. H. Lawrence translated as *Little Novels of Sicily* in 1925. See also T. G. Bergin, *Giovanni Verga* (New Haven, Conn., 1931).

Black Bread from *Little Novels of Sicily* is reprinted by permission of William Heinemann Limited, Laurence Pollinger Limited, and the Estate of the Late Mrs. Frieda Lawrence.

Neighbour Nanni had hardly taken his last breath, and the priest in his stole was still there, when the quarrel broke out between the children as to who should pay the costs of the burial, and they went at it till the priest with the aspersorium under his arm was driven away.

For neighbour Nanni's illness had been a long one, the sort that eats away the flesh off your bones and your things out of your house. Every time the doctor spread his piece of paper on his knee to write out the prescription, neighbour Nanni watched his hands with beseeching eyes, and numbled, "Write it short, your honour, anyhow write it short, for mercy's sake."

The doctor carried out his own job. Everybody in the world carries out his own job. In carrying out his, Farmer Nanni had caught that fever down there at Lamia, land blessed by God, producing corn as high as a man. In vain the neighbours said to him, "Neighbour Nanni, you'll leave your bones on that half-profits farm!"

"As if I was a baron," he replied, "to do what I like and choose!"

The brothers, who were like the fingers on the same hand as long as their father lived, had now each one to think for himself. Santo had a wife and children on his back; Lucia was left without any dowry, as good as turned on the street; and Carmenio, if he wanted to have bread to eat, would have to go away from home and find himself a master. Then the mother, who was old and ailing, didn't know whose business it was to keep her, for none of the three of the children had anything at all.

The oxen, the sheep, the store in the granary had all gone with their owner. There remained the dark house, with the empty bed, and the equally dark faces of the orphans. Santo carried his things across, with Red-head, his wife, and said he'd take his mamma to live with him. "Then he won't have to pay house-rent," said the others. Carmenio made up his own bundle and went as shepherd to herdsman Vito, who had a piece of grazing land at Camemi; and Lucia threatened to go into service rather than live with her sister-in-law.

"No!" said Santo. "It shan't be said that my sister had to be servant to other folks."

"He wants me to be servant to Red-head," grumbled Lucia.

The great question was this sister-in-law, who had driven herself into the family like a nail. "What is there to be done, now I've got her?" sighed Santo, shrugging his shoulders. "I should have listened in time to that good soul, my father."

That good soul had preached to him: "Leave that Nena alone, for she's got never a bit of dowry, nor house, nor land."

But Nena was always at his side, at the Castelluccio farm; whether he was hoeing or mowing, she was there gathering the corn into sheaves, or removing the stones from under his feet with her hands; and when they rested, at the door of the great farm-place, they sat together with their backs to the wall, at the hour when the sun was dying over the fields, and everything was going still.

"Neighbour Santo, if God is good, you won't have lost your labours this year."

"Neighbour Santo, if the harvest turns out well you ought to take the big field, down on the plain; because the sheep have been on it, and it's rested for two years."

"Neighbour Santo, this winter, if I've time, I want to make you a pair of thick gaiters to keep you warm."

Santo had got to know Nena while he was working at Castelluccio, a girl with red hair, daughter of the keeper, whom nobody wanted. So for that reason, poor thing, she made a fuss of every dog that passed, and she denied herself the bread from her mouth in order to make neighbour Santo a present of a black silk stocking-cap every year at Saint Agrippina's day, and to have a flask of wine for him, or a piece of cheese, when he arrived at Castelluccio. "Take this, for my sake, neighbour Santo. It's the same as the master drinks." Or else: "I've been thinking, you never had a bit of something to eat with your bread not all last week."

He didn't say no, but took everything. The most he ever did was to say out of politeness: "This won't do, neighbour Nena, you deny your own self to give to me."

"I like it better for you to have it."

And then, every Saturday night when Santo went home, that dear departed soul used to tell him again: Leave that Nena alone, for she hasn't got this; leave that Nena alone, for she hasn't got the other.

"I know I've got nothing," said Nena as she sat on the low wall facing the setting sun. "I've neither land nor houses; and to get together that bit of linen I've had to go without bread to eat. My father is a poor keeper, who lives at his master's charge, and nobody wants to saddle himself with a wife without a dowry."

Nevertheless the nape of her neck was fair, as it usually is with red-haired people; and as she sat with her head bowed, all those thoughts heavy inside it, the sun glowed among the golden-coloured hairs behind her ears, and lit on her cheeks that had a fine down like a peach; and Santo looked at her flaxblue eyes, and at her breast which filled her stays and swayed like the corn-field.

"Don't you worry, neighbour Nena," he said. "You won't go short of husbands."

She shook her head, saying no; and her red earrings that were almost like coral caressed her cheeks. "No, no, neighbour Santo. I know I'm not beautiful, and nobody wants me."

"Look though!" said he all at once, as the idea came to him. "Look how opinions vary! They say red hair is ugly, and yet now you've got it it doesn't strike me as bad."

The good departed soul, his father, when he had seen that Santo was altogether smitten with Nena and wanted to marry her, had said to him one Sunday: "You want her whether or not, that Red-head? Say the truth, you want her whether or not?"

Santo, with his back to the wall and his hands behind him, didn't dare to raise his head; but he nodded yes, yes, that he didn't know what to do with himself without the Red-head, and it was the will of God it should be so.

"And have you given it a thought as to how you're going to keep a wife? You know I can give you nothing. But I've one thing to tell you, and your mother here will say the same: think it over before you go and get married, for bread is scarce, and children come quick."

His mother, crouching on the stool, pulled him by the jacket and said to him sotto voce, with a long face: "Try and fall in love with the widow of Farmer Mariano; she's rich, and she won't ask a great deal of you, being part paralysed."

"Oh yes!" grumbled Santo. "You may bet Farmer Mariano's widow would take up with a beggar like me!"

Neighbour Nanni also agreed that Farmer Mariano's widow was looking for a husband as rich as herself, hip-lame though she was. And then there'd have been that other misery to look forward to, seeing your grandchildren born lame as well.

"Well, it's for you to think about it," he repeated to his son. "Remember that bread is scarce, and children come quick."

Then towards evening on St. Bridget's Day Santo had met the Red-head by chance, as she was gathering wild asparagus beside the path, and she blushed at seeing him as if she didn't know quite well that he had to pass that way going back to the village, and she dropped down the hem of her skirt that she had turned up round her waist for going on all-fours among the cactus plants. The young man

looked at her, he also went red in the face, and could say nothing. At last he began
to stammer that the week was over and he was going home. "You've no messages
to send to the village, neighbour Nena? Tell me if I can do anything."

"If I'm going to sell the asparagus, I'll come along with you, and we'll go the
same way," said Red-head. And he, as if stupefied, nodded yes, yes; she added,
with her chin on her heaving bosom: "But you don't want me, women are a
nuisance to you."

"I'd like to carry you in my arms, neighbour Nena, carry you in my arms."

Then neighbour Nena began to chew the corner of the red handkerchief she
wore round her head. And neighbour Santo again had nothing to say; but he
looked at her, and looked at her, and changed his saddle-bag from one shoulder
to the other, as if he couldn't find words to begin. The mint and the marjoram
were making the air merry, and the side of the mountain, above the cactuses, was
all red with sunset. "You go now," Nena said to him. "You go now; it's late."
Then she stood listening to the night crickets rattling away. But Santo didn't move.
"You go now, somebody might see us here by ourselves."

Neighbour Santo, who was really going at last, came out again to his old assertion, with another shake of the shoulder to settle his double sack, that he'd have
carried her in his arms, he would, he'd have carried her if they'd been going the
same road. And he looked neighbour Nena in the eyes, and she avoided his looks
and kept on seeking for the wild asparagus among the stones, and he watched her
face that was as red as if the sunset were beating upon it.

"No, neighbour Santo, you go on by yourself; you know I'm a poor girl with no
dowry."

"Let us do as Providence wishes, let us——"

She kept on saying no, that she was not for him, and now her face was dark and
frowning. Then neighbour Santo, downcast, settled his bag on his shoulder and
moved away, with bent head. But Red-head wanted at least to give him the
asparagus that she had gathered for him. They'd make a nice little dish for him,
if he would eat them for her sake. And she held out to him the two corners of the
full apron. Santo put his arm round her waist and kissed her on the cheek, his
heart melting inside him.

At that moment her father appeared, and the girl ran away in a fright. The
keeper had his gun on his arm, and didn't see at all what should prevent him from
laying neighbour Santo out for practising this treachery on him.

"No! I'm not like that!" replied Santo, with his hands crossed on his breast. "I
want to marry your daughter, I do. Not for fear of the gun; but I'm the son of a
good man, and Providence will help us because we do no wrong."

So the wedding took place on a Sunday, with the bride in her holiday dress, and
her father the keeper in new boots in which he waddled like a tame duck. Wine
and baked beans made even neighbour Nanni merry, though he had the malaria
on him bad; and the mother took out of the chest a pound or two of worsted yarn
which she had put aside toward a dowry for Lucia, who was already eighteen, and
who combed and arranged her hair for half an hour every Sunday morning before
going to mass, looking at herself in the water of the wash-bowl, for a mirror.

Santo, with the tips of his ten fingers stuck in the pockets of his coat, exulted as he looked at the red hair of his bride, at the yarn, and at all the celebration which there was for him that Sunday. The keeper, with a red nose, hobbled inside his shoes and wanted to kiss them all round one after the other.

"Not me!" said Lucia, sulky because of the yarn they were taking from her. "This isn't water for my mouth."

She stayed in a corner pulling a sulky face, as if she already knew what her lot would be the moment her parents were gone.

And now sure enough she had to cook the bread and sweep the house for her sister-in-law, who as soon as God sent daylight set off for the field with her husband, although she was again with child, for she was worse than a cat for filling the house with little ones. There was more needed now than presents at Christmas and at St. Agrippina's Day, or than the pretty talk she used to have with neighbour Santo at Castelluccio. That swindler of a keeper had done well for himself marrying off his daughter without a dowry, and now neighbour Santo had to see about maintaining her. Since he'd got Nena he saw that there wasn't bread enough for the two of them, and that they'd got to wring it out of the earth at Licciardo, in the sweat of their brow.

As they went to Licciardo with the double bag over their shoulder, wiping the sweat from their foreheads on their shirt-sleeves, they had the young corn always in their mind and in front of their eyes, they saw nothing else but that between the stones of the path. It was to them like the thought of one who is sick and whom you have always heavy on your heart, that corn; first yellow, swamped in mud with all the rain; and then, when it did begin to get a bit of hold, the weeds, so that Nena had made pitiful work of both her hands, pulling them out one by one, bending down over all that load of her belly, drawing her skirt above her knees so as not to hurt the corn. And she didn't feel the weight of her child, nor the pains of her back, as if every green blade which she freed from the weeds was a child she had borne. And when at last she squatted on the little bank, panting, pushing her hair behind her ears with both her hands, she seemed to see before her the tall ears of June, bending over one above the other as the breeze touched them; and they would reckon up—she and her husband, as he was untying his soaking gaiters, and cleaning his hoe on the grass of the bank. So much seed they had taken, and therefore they'd have so much corn if the ear came to twelvefold or to tenfold or even to sevenfold; the stalk wasn't very stout, but the growth was thick. If only March was not too dry, and if only it didn't rain except when rain was needed! Blessed Saint Agrippina must remember them. The sky was clear and the sun lingered in gold on the green meadows, from the fiery west, whence the larks fell singing on to the clods, like black dots. Spring was really beginning everywhere, in the cactus hedges, in the bushes of the little road, between the stones, on the roofs of the hamlet, green with hope; and Santo, walking heavily behind his companion, who was bent beneath the sack of straw for the animals, with all that belly on her, felt his heart swell with tenderness for the poor thing, and went along talking to her, his voice broken by the steep climb, about what he'd do if the Lord blessed the corn up to the last. Now they didn't have to talk any more about red hair, whether it was beautiful or ugly, or any such nonsense. And when treacherous May came with its mists to rob them of all their labours and their hopes of harvest, the husband and wife, seated once more on the bank watching the field going yellow under their eyes, like a sick man departing to the other world, said not a word, their elbows on their knees and their eyes stony in their pale faces.

"This is God's punishment!" muttered Santo. "That sainted soul my father told me how it would be."

And into the hovel of the poor penetrated the ill-humour of the black, muddy little road outside. Husband and wife turned their backs on one another stupefied, and they quarrelled every time Red-head asked for money to buy necessaries, or whenever the husband came home late, or when there wasn't enough wood for the winter, or when the wife became slow and idle with her child-bearing; long faces, ugly words, and even blows. Santo seized Nena by her red hair, and she set her nails in his face; the neighbours came running up, and Red-head squealed that that villain wanted to make her have a miscarriage, and that he didn't care if he sent a soul to limbo. Then, when Nena had her baby, they made peace again, and neighbour Santo went carrying the infant girl in his arms, as if he had fathered a princess, and ran to show her to his relations and his friends, he was so pleased. And for his wife, as long as she was in bed he made her broth, he swept the house, he cleaned the rice, he stood there in front of her to see that she wanted for nothing. Then he went to the door with the baby at his shoulder, like a wet-nurse; and to anybody who asked him, as they were passing, he replied: "It's a girl, neighbour! Bad luck follows me even here, and I've got a girl born to me. My wife couldn't do any better than that."

And when Red-head got knocks from her husband, she turned round on her sister-in-law, who never did a hand's turn to help in the house, and Lucia flew back at her saying that without having any husband of her own she'd got all the burden of other folk's children foisted on her. The mother-in-law, poor thing, tried to make peace in these quarrels, repeating: "It's my fault, I'm no good for anything now. I eat idle bread, I do."

She was no good for anything but to hear all those miseries, and to brood over them inside herself: Santo's difficulties, his wife's crying, the thought of her other son far away, a thought that stuck in her heart like a nail; Lucia's bad temper, because she hadn't got a rag of a Sunday frock and never saw so much as a dog pass under her window. On Sundays, if they called her to join the group of gossips who were chattering in the shadow, she replied with a shrug of the shoulders: "What do you want me to come for? To show you the silk frock I haven't got?"

Sometimes, however, Pino the Tome, him of the frogs, would join the group of neighbour women, though he never opened his mouth, but stood with his back to the wall and his hands in his pockets listening, and spitting all over the place. Nobody knew what he came for; but when neighbour Lucia appeared in the doorway, Pino looked at her from under his eyes, pretending to be turning to spit. And at evening, when all the street-doors were shut, he went so far as to sing her little songs outside the door, making his own bass for himself—huum! huum! huum! Sometimes the young fellows of the village going home late, recognising his voice, would strike up the frog tune, to mock him.

Meanwhile Lucia pretended to be busying herself about the house, as far as possible from the light, her head sunk, so that they shouldn't see her face. But if her sister-in-law grumbled, "There goes the music!" she turned round like a viper to retort: "Even the music is a trouble to you, is it? In this galley-hole there mustn't be anything for eyes to see nor ears to hear, my word!"

The mother, who noticed everything, and who was also listening, watching her daughter, said that as far as she was concerned that music made her feel happy inside herself. Lucia pretended not to understand anything. Yet every day, at the time when the frog fellow was due to be passing, she did not fail to be standing in the doorway with her distaff in her hand. The Tome, as soon as he got back from the river, went round and round the village, always returning to that particular quarter, with the remains of his frogs in his hand, crying, "Song-fish! song-fish!" as if the poor folks of those mean streets could afford to buy song-fish.

"But they must be good for sick people!" said Lucia, who was dying to get started bargaining with the Tome. But the mother wouldn't let them spend money on her.

The Tome, seeing Lucia watching him from under her eyes, her chin on her breast, slackened his pace before the door, and on Sunday he summoned up enough courage to draw a little nearer, till he came so far as to sit on the steps of the next terrace, with his hands hanging between his thighs; and he told all the women in the group about how you caught frogs, how it needed the devil's own cunning. He was more cunning than a red-haired ass, was Pino the Tome, and he waited till the goodwives had gone away to say to neighbour Lucia, "We want rain badly for the corn, don't we!" Or else, "Olives will be scarce this year!"

"What does that matter to you? You live by your frogs," Lucia said to him.

"You hark here, my dear friend; we are all like the fingers on one hand; or like the tiles on the roof of the house, one sending water to the other. If there's no crop of corn or of olives, there'll be no money coming into the village, and nobody will buy my frogs. You follow what I mean?"

That "my dear friend" went sweet as honey to the heart of the girl, and she thought about it all evening long as she was spinning silently beside the lamp; and she turned it round and round in her mind, like her spool that spun from her fingers.

The mother seemed as if she read into the secrets of the distaff, and when for a few weeks no more songs had been heard in the evening, and the frog-seller had not been seen going past, she said to her daughter-in-law: "How miserable the winter is! We don't hear a living soul in the neighbourhood."

Now they had to keep the door shut, for the cold, and through the little opening they never saw a thing except the window of the house across the road, black with rain, or some neighbour going home in his soaking wet cloak. But Pino the Tome never showed his face, so that if a poor sick person wanted a drop of frog broth, said Lucia, there was no telling how you were going to get it her.

"He'll have gone to earn his bread some other road," said the sister-in-law. "It's a poor trade, that is, and nobody would follow it who could do anything else."

Santo, who had heard the chatter one Saturday evening, made his sister the following speech, out of love for her: "I don't like this talk about the Tome. He'd be a fancy match for my sister! A man who lives on frog-catching, and stands with his legs in the wet all day long! You ought to get a man who works on the land, so that even if he owned nothing, at least he'd be drawn from the same class as yourself."

Lucia was silent, her head lowered and her brows knit, biting her lips from time to time so as not to blurt out: "And where am I going to find a man who works on the land?" How indeed was she to find him, all by herself? The only one she had managed to find now never showed his face any more, probably because Red-head had played her some nasty trick, envious, tattling creature that she was. There was Santo, who never said anything but what his wife said, and she, the Red-head, had gone round repeating that the frog man was a good-for-naught, which bit of news, of course, had come to the ears of neighbour Pino.

Therefore squabbles broke out every moment between the two sisters-in-law.

"The mistress here isn't me, that it isn't," grumbled Lucia. "The mistress in this house is the one who was clever enough to wheedle round my brother and snap him up for a husband."

"If I'd only known what was coming I'd never have wheedled round him, I wouldn't, brother or no brother; because if I needed one loaf of bread before, now I need five."

"What does it matter to you whether the frog-catcher has got a proper trade or not? If he was my husband, it would be his business to look after keeping me."

The mother, poor thing, came between them to soothe them down; but she was a woman of few words, and she didn't know what to do but run from one to the other, clutching her hair with her hands, stammering: "For pity's sake! for pity's sake!"

But the women took not the slightest notice of her, setting their nails in each other's faces after Red-head had called Lucia that bad word, "Nasty-cat!"

"Nasty-cat yourself! You stole my brother from me!"

Then arrived Santo, and gave both of them knocks to quiet them, so that Red-head, weeping, grumbled: "I say it for her own good! because if a woman marries a man who's got nothing, troubles come fast enough."

And to his sister, who was screaming and tearing her hair, Santo said, to quiet her: "Well, what do you expect of her, now that she is my wife? But I'm fond of you and I speak for your own sake. You see what a lot of good we've done ourselves by getting married, us two!"

Lucia lamented to her mother: "I want to do as much good for myself as they've done for themselves! I'd rather go out to service! If a mortal man does show his face round here, they drive him away." And she thought about the frog-catcher of whom there was never a sign nowadays.

Afterwards they got to know that he had gone to live with the widow of Farmer Massaro; even that he was thinking of getting married to her; because though it was true he hadn't got a proper trade, he was none the less a fine piece of a young fellow, built without any sparing of material, and as handsome as San Vito in flesh and blood, that he was; and the lame woman had property enough to be able to take what husband she liked and chose.

"Look at this, neighbour Pino," she said. "This is all white things, linen and everything; these are all gold ear-rings and necklaces; in this jar there are twelve gallons of oil; and that section is full of beans. If you like you can live with your hands in your pockets, and you needn't stand up to your knees in the bog catching frogs."

"I should like it all right," said the Tome. But he thought of Lucia's black eyes looking for him under the cotton panes of the window, and then of the hips of the lame woman, which woggled like a frog's as she went about the house showing him all her stuff. However, one day, when he hadn't been able to get a scrap of anything for three days and had had to stay in the widow's house, eating and drinking and watching the rain fall outside the door, he persuaded himself to say yes, out of love for daily bread.

"It was for the sake of my daily bread, I swear to you," he said, with his hands crossed on his breast, when he came back to look for neighbour Lucia outside her door. "If it hadn't been for the hard times, I wouldn't have married the lame woman, I wouldn't, neighbour Lucia!"

"Go and tell that to the lame woman herself," replied the girl, green with bile. "I've only got this to say to you: you don't set foot here any more."

And the lame woman also told him that he wasn't to set foot there any more, for if he did she'd turn him out of her house, naked and hungry as when she had taken him in. "Don't you know that, even more than to God, you're obliged to me for the bread you eat?"

But as her husband he went short of nothing: well clad, well fed, with shoes on his feet and nothing else to do but lounge in the market-place all day, at the greengrocer's, at the butcher's, at the fish-monger's, with his hands behind his back and his belly full, watching them buy and sell.

"That's his real trade, being a vagabond!" said Red-head. And Lucia gave it her again, saying that if he did nothing it was because he'd got a rich wife who kept him. "If he'd married me he'd have worked to keep his wife." Santo, with his head in his hands, was thinking how his mother had told him to take the lame woman himself, and how it was his own fault if he'd let the bread slip from his mouth.

"When we're young," he preached to his sister, "we have these notions in our heads, like you have now, and we only think of pleasing ourselves, without counting what comes after. Ask Red-head now if she thinks folks ought to do as we have done."

Red-head, squatting on the threshold, shook her head in agreement with him, while her brats squealed round her, pulling her by the dress and the hair.

"At least the Lord God shouldn't send the plague of children," she said fretfully.

As many children as she could she took with her to the field, every morning, like a mare with her foals; the least one inside the bag over her shoulder, and the one a bit bigger she led by the hand. But she was forced to leave the other three at home, to drive her sister-in-law crazy. The one in the sack and the one that trotted limping behind her screamed in concert the length of the rough road, in the cold of the white dawn, and the mother had to stop from time to time scratching her head and sighing: "Oh my Lord!" And she breathed on the tiny blue hands of the little girl to warm them, or she took the baby out of the sack to put it to her breast as she walked. Her husband went in front, bent under his load, and if he turned half round, waiting to give her time to overtake him, all out of breath as she was, dragging the little girl by the hand, and with her breast bare, it wasn't to look at the hair of Red-head, or at her breast which heaved inside her stays, like at Castelluccio. Now Red-head tipped out her breast in sun and frost, as if it served for nothing now except to give out milk, exactly like a mare. A real beast of burden, though as far as that went her husband could not complain of her: hoeing, mowing, sowing, better than a man, when she pulled up her skirts, and was black half-way up her legs, on the corn-land. She was twenty-seven years old now, with something else to do besides think of thin shoes and blue stockings. "We are old," said her husband, "and we've got the children to think of." But anyhow they helped one another like two oxen yoked to the same plough, which was what their marriage amounted to now.

"I know only too well," grumbled Lucia, "that I've got all the trouble of children, without ever having a husband. When that poor old woman shuts her eyes at last, if they want to give me my bit of bread they'll give it, and if they don't they'll turn me out on to the streets."

The mother, poor thing, didn't know what to answer, and sat there listening to her, seated beside the bed with the kerchief round her head and her face yellow with illness. During the day she sat in the doorway, in the sun, keeping still and quiet till the sunset paled upon the blackish roofs opposite, and the goodwives called the fowls to roost.

Only, when the doctor came to see her, and her daughter put the candle near her face, she asked him, with a timid smile: "For mercy's sake, your honour, is it a long job?"

Santo, who had a heart of gold, replied: "I don't mind spending money on medicine, so long as we can keep the poor old mother here with us, and I can know I shall find her in her corner when I come home. Then she's worked her share, in her own day, and when we are old our children will do as much for us."

And then it happened that Carmenio had caught the fever at Camemi. If the master had been rich he'd have bought him medicine; but herdsman Vito was a poor devil who lived on that bit of a flock, and he kept the boy really out of charity, for he could have looked after that handful of sheep himself, if it hadn't been for fear of the malaria. And then he wanted to do the good work of giving bread to neighbour Nanni's orphan, hoping by that means to win over Providence to his help, as it ought to help him, if there was justice in heaven. How was it his fault if he owned nothing but that bit of grazing land at Camemi, where the malaria curdled like snow, and Carmenio had caught the tertian fever? One day when the boy felt his bones broken by the fever, he let himself sink asleep behind a rock which printed a black shadow on the dusty little road, while heavy flies were buzzing in the sultry air of May, and in a minute the sheep broke into the neighbour's corn, a poor little field as big as a pocket-handkerchief, already half eaten up by the hot draught. Nevertheless Uncle Cheli, who was curled up under a little roof of boughs, cherished it like the apple of his eye, that corn-patch that had cost him so much sweat and was the hope of the year for him. Seeing the sheep devouring him, he cried: "Ah! You Christians don't eat bread, don't you?"

And Carmenio woke up under the blows and kicks of Uncle Cheli, and began to run like a madman after the scattered sheep, weeping and yelling. Carmenio, who had his bones already broken by the tertian fever, stood badly in need of that cudgelling! But he thought, did he, that he could pay in squeals and laments for the damage done to his neighbour?

"A year's work lost, and my children without bread this winter! Look at the damage you've done, you assassin! If I skin you alive it won't be as much as you deserve."

Uncle Cheli went round getting witnesses to go to law with the sheep of herdsman Vito. The latter, when he was served with the summons, felt as if he was struck with paralysis, and his wife as well. "Ah, that villain of a Carmenio has ruined us all! You do somebody a good turn, and this is how they pay you back! Did he expect me to stop there in all the malaria and watch the sheep? Now Uncle Cheli will finish us off into poverty, making us pay costs." The poor devil ran to Camemi at midday, blinded by despair, because of all the misfortunes which were raining down on him, and with every kick and every punch on the jaw he fetched Carmenio he stammered, panting: "You've brought us down to nothing! You've landed us in ruin, you brigand!"

"Don't you see how sick I am?" Carmenio tried to answer, parrying the blows. "How is it my fault, if I couldn't stand on my feet with fever? It got me unawares, there, under the rock."

None the less he had to make up his bundle there and then, and say good-bye to the two half-guineas which were due to him from herdsman Vito, and leave the flock. And herdsman Vito was downright glad to catch the fever again, he was so overwhelmed by his troubles.

Carmenio said nothing at home, when he came back empty-handed and empty-bellied, with his bundle on a stick over his shoulder. Only his mother grieved at seeing him so pale and wasted, and didn't know what to think. She learned everything later from Don Venerando, who lived just near and had also land at Camemi, next the field of Uncle Cheli.

"Don't you tell anybody why Uncle Vito sent you away," said the mother to her boy. "If you do, nobody will take you on as a hired lad." And Santo added as well: "Don't say anything about having tertian fever, because if you do nobody will want you, knowing that you're ill."

However, Don Venerando took him for his flock at Santa Margherita, where the shepherd was robbing him right and left, and doing him more hurt even than the sheep in the corn. "I'll give you medicine myself, and so you'll have no excuse for going to sleep and letting the sheep rove where they like."

Don Venerando had developed a kindly feeling towards all the family, out of love for Lucia, whom he used to see from his little terrace when he was taking the air after dinner. "If you like to give me the girl as well I'll give her half a crown a month." And he said moreover that Carmenio could go to Santa Margherita with his mother, because the old woman was losing ground from day to day, and with the flock she would at any rate not lack for eggs, and milk, and a bit of mutton broth, when a sheep died. Red-head stripped herself of the best of anything she had worth taking, to get together a little bundle of white washing to the old woman. It was now sowing time, and they couldn't come and go every day from Licciardo, and winter, the season of scarcity of everything, would be on them again. So now Lucia said she absolutely would go as servant in the house of Don Venerando.

They put the old woman on the ass, Santo on one side and Carmenio on the other, and the bundle behind; and the mother, while she let them have their way with her, said to her daughter, looking at her with heavy eyes from her blanched face: "Who knows if we shall ever see one another again? Who knows if we shall ever see one another again? They say I shall come back in April. You live in the fear of the Lord, in your master's house. Anyhow you'll want for nothing there."

Lucia sobbed in her apron, and Red-head did the same, poor thing. At that moment they had made peace, and held their arms round one another, weeping together.

"Red-head has got a good heart," said her husband. "The trouble is we aren't rich enough to be always fond of one another. When hens have got nothing else to peck at in the fowl-house, they peck at one another."

Lucia was now well settled in Don Venerando's house, and she said she never wanted to leave it till she died, as folks always say, to show their gratitude to the master. She had as much bread and soup as she wanted, a glass of wine every day, and her own plate of meat on Sundays and holidays. So that her month's wages lay in her pocket untouched, and at evening she had also time to spin herself linen for her dowry on her own account. She had already got the man ready to hand, there in the selfsame house: Brasi, the kitchen-man, who did the cooking and also helped in the fields when necessary. The master had got rich in the same way, in service at the baron's, and now he was a Don, and had farm-land and cattle in abundance. Because Lucia came from a respectable family that had fallen on evil days, and they knew she was honest, they had given her the lighter jobs to do, to wash the dishes, and go down into the cellar, and look after the fowls; with a cupboard under the stairs to sleep in, quite like a little bedroom, with a bed and a chest of drawers and everything; so that Lucia never wanted to leave till she died. Meanwhile she turned her eyes on Brasi, and confided to him that in two or three years' time she'd have a bit of savings of her own and would be able to "go out into the world," if the Lord called her.

Brasi was deaf in that ear. But Lucia pleased him, with her eyes as black as coals, and the good flesh she had on her bones; and for her part she liked Brasi too, a little, curly-headed fellow with the delicate cunning face of a little fox-dog. While they were washing dishes or putting wood under the boiler he invented every kind of roguery to make her laugh, as if he was trying to rouse her up. He squirted water on to the back of her neck, and stuck endive leaves in her hair. Lucia squealed subduedly, so that the master shouldn't hear; she took refuge in the corner by the oven, her face as red as fire, and she threw dish-rags and twigs in his face, whilst the water trickled down her back like a thrill.

"With meat you make rissoles—I've made mine, you make yours."

"I won't," replied Lucia. "I don't like these jokes."

Brasi pretended to be mortified. He picked up the leaf of endive which she had thrown at him, and stuck it in his bosom, inside his shirt, grumbling: "This belongs to me. I don't touch you. It belongs to me and is going to stop here. Don't you want something from me, to put in the same place, you?" And he pretended to pull out a handful of his hair to offer her, sticking out the length of his tongue as he did so.

She punched him with the solid punches of a peasant woman, which made him hunch up his back, and gave him bad dreams at night, he said. She seized him like a little dog by the hair, and found a certain pleasure in thrusting her fingers in that soft, curly wool.

"Keep it up! Keep it up! I'm not touchy like you, and I'd let myself be pounded to sausage-meat by your hands."

One day Don Venerando caught them at these games, and made the devil of a row. He wasn't going to have carrying-on in his house; he'd kick them both out if there was any more of it. And yet when he found the girl alone in the kitchen he took her by the chin and wanted to caress her with two fingers.

"No! no!" replied Lucia, "I don't like these tricks. If you don't leave me alone I'll get my things and go."

"You like them from him all right, you like them from him. And yet not from me who are your master! What do you mean by it? Don't you know I can give you gold rings and gold ear-rings with pendants, and make you up your dowry if I like."

Certainly he could, Brasi assured her, for the master had any amount of money, and his wife wore a silk mantle like a lady, now that she was old and thin as a mummy, for which reason her husband came down to the kitchen to have his little joke with the maids. And he came as well to watch his own interests, how much wood they burnt, and how much meat they were putting down to roast. He was rich, yes, but he knew what it cost to get property together, and he quarrelled all day long with his wife, who had no end of vanities in her head, now that she played the lady, and had taken to complaining of the smoke from the kindly and the nasty smell of onions.

"I want to gather my dowry together with my own hands," retorted Lucia. "My mother's daughter wants to remain an honest girl, in case any Christian should ask her to be his wife."

"Remain it then!" replied her master. "You'll see what a grand dowry it will be, and how many men will come after your honesty!"

If the macaroni was a little over-cooked, if Lucia brought to table a couple of eggs fried in the casserole that smelled a bit singed, Don Venerando abused her thoroughly, quite another man in his wife's presence, with his stomach stuck out and his voice loud. Did they think they were making swill for the pigs? With two servants in the kitchen sending everything to rack and ruin! Another time he'd throw the dish in her face! The mistress, blessed dear, didn't want all that racket, because of the neighbours, and she sent away the servant, squealing in falsetto: "Be off into the kitchen; get out of here, you jackanapes! you wastrel!"

Lucia went to cry her eyes out in the corner by the oven, but Brasi consoled her, with that tricky face of his.

"What does it matter? Let them rattle! If we took any notice of the masters it would be poor us! The eggs smelt burnt? All the worse for them! I can't split the wood in the yard and turn the eggs at the same time. They make me do the cooking and the outside work as well, and then they expect to be waited on like the king. I should think they've forgotten the days when he used to eat bread and onion under an olive tree, and she used to go gleaning corn."

Then servant-maid and cook discussed their "misfortunes," born as they were of "respectable people," and their parents were richer than the master, once upon a time. Brasi's father was a cart-builder, no less, and it was the son's own fault if he hadn't wanted to follow the same trade, but had taken it into his head to go wandering round the fairs, following the cart of the travelling draper, and it was then he had learnt to cook and look after a horse and cattle.

Lucia recommenced the litany of her woes—her father, the cattle, Red-head, the bad harvest—both of them alike, she and Brasi, in that kitchen; they seemed made for one another.

"What, another case of your brother and Red-head?" replied Brasi. "Much obliged!" However, he did not want to insult her with it, straight to her face. He didn't care a rap that she was a peasant. He didn't reject her out of pride. But they were both of them poor, and it would have been better to throw themselves down the well with a stone round their necks.

Lucia swallowed that bitter pill without saying a word, and if she wanted to cry she went and hid in the stair-cupboard, or in the oven corner, when Brasi wasn't there. For she was now very fond of that Christian, what with being with him in front of the fire all day long. The reprimands and abuse of the master she took upon herself, and kept the best plate of food for him, and the fullest glass of wine, and went into the yard to chop wood for him, and had learned to turn the eggs and dish up the macaroni to a nicety. Brasi, as he saw her crossing herself, with her bowl on her knees, before she began to eat, said to her: "Have you never seen food in your life before?"

He grumbled at everything all the time; that it was a galley-slave's life, and that he had only three hours an evening to go for a walk or to go to the inn. Lucia sometimes went so far as to ask him, with her head bent and her face growing red: "Why do you go to the inn? Leave the inn alone, it's not the place for you."

"Anybody can see you're a peasant," he replied. "You folks think there's the devil in the public-house. I was born of shop-workers, masters of their trade, my dear. I am not a clod-hopper!"

"I say it for your good. You spend all your money, and besides there's always a chance of you starting a quarrel with somebody."

Brasi felt himself soften at these words, and at those eyes which avoided looking at him. And he allowed himself the gratification of asking: "Well, does it matter to you, anyhow?"

"No, it doesn't matter to me. I speak for your own sake."

"Well, doesn't it get on your nerves, stopping here in the house all day long?"

"No, I thank the Lord I am so well off, and I wish all my own people were like me, and lacked for nothing."

She was just drawing the wine, squatting with the jug between her knees, and Brasi had come down into the cellar with her to show her a light. As the cellar was big and dark as a church, and not even a fly was to be heard in that subterranean place, only they two alone, Brasi and Lucia, he put his arm around her neck and kissed her on her coral-red mouth.

The poor lass remained overcome, as she crouched with her eyes on the jug, and they were both silent, she hearing his heavy breathing, and the gurgling of the wine. But then she gave a stifled cry, drawing back all trembling, so that a little of the red froth was spilled on the floor.

"Why, what's amiss?" exclaimed Brasi. "As if I'd given you a slap on the face! It isn't true, then, that you like me?"

She dared not look him in the face, though she was dying to. She stared at the spilled wine, embarrassed, stammering:

"Oh poor me! oh poor me! What have I done? The master's wine!"

"Eh! let it go; he's got plenty, the master has! Listen to me rather. Don't you care for me? Say it, yes or no!"

This time she let him take her hand, without replying, and when Brasi asked her to give him the kiss back again, she gave it him, red with something that was not altogether shame.

"Have you never had one before?" asked Brasi, laughing. "What a joke! You are all trembling, as if I'd said I was going to kill you."

"Yes, I do like you," she replied, "but I could hardly tell you. Don't take any notice if I'm trembling. It's because I was frightened about the——"

"There now, think of that! You do, eh? Since when? Why didn't you tell me?"

"Since that saying we were made for one another."

"Ah!" said Brasi, scratching his head. "Let's go up, the master might come."

Lucia was all happiness since that kiss, it seemed to her as if Brasi had sealed on her mouth his promise to marry her. But he never spoke of it, and if the girl tried him on that score, he replied: "What are you bothering about? Besides, what's the good putting our necks in the yoke, when we can be together just as if we were married."

"No, it's not the same. Now you fend for yourself and I fend for myself, but when we are married we shall be all one."

"And a lovely thing that will be, an' all! Besides, we don't belong to the same walk of life. It would be different if you had a bit of dowry."

"Ah! what a black heart you've got! No! You've never cared for me!"

"Yes I have! And I'm ready for you for whatever you want of me; but without talking about that there——"

"No! I don't want any of that sort of thing! Leave me alone, and don't look at me any more!"

Now she knew what men were like. All liars and traitors. She didn't want to hear of it any more. She'd rather throw herself head first down the well; she wanted to become a Daughter of Mary; she wanted to take her good name and throw it out of the window! What good was it to her, without a dowry? She wanted to break her neck with that old creature her master, and get her dowry out of her shame. Now that—! Now that—! Don Venerando was always hanging round her, first saying nice things and then nasty, looking after his own interests, seeing if they put too much wood on the fire, how much oil they used for the frying, sending Brasi to buy a ha'porth of snuff, and trying to take Lucia by the chin, running round after her in the kitchen, on tip-toe so his wife shouldn't hear, scolding the girl for her lack of respect for him, making him run in that fashion! "No! No!" She was like a mad cat. She'd rather take her things and go! "And where shall you find anything to eat? And how shall you find a husband, without a dowry? Look at these ear-rings! Then I'll give you ten guineas for your dowry. Brasi would have both his eyes pulled out for ten guineas."

Ah, that black-hearted Brasi! He left her in the wicked hands of her master, which trembled as they pawed at her. Left her with the thought of her mother, who hadn't long to live; and of the bare house empty of everything except trouble, and of Pino the Tome who had thrown her over to go and eat the bread of the widow! He left her with the temptation of the ear-rings and the ten guineas in her head!

And one day she came into the kitchen with her face all dismayed, and the gold pendants dangling against her cheeks. Brasi opened his eyes, and said to her: "How fine you look now, neighbour Lucia!"

"Ah! You like me in them? All right, all right!"

Brasi, now that he saw the ear-rings and all the rest, strove so hard to show himself helpful and useful to her, that you might have thought she had become another mistress in the house. He left her the fuller plate, and the best seat at the fire. And he opened his heart wide to her, that they were two poor things both of them, and it did your soul good to tell your troubles to somebody you were fond of. And as soon as he could scrape ten pounds together he'd set up a little public-house and take a wife. He in the kitchen, she behind the counter. And then you weren't at anybody's bidding. If the master liked to do them a good turn, he could do it without hurting himself, because ten pounds was a pinch of snuff to him. And Brasi wouldn't look down his nose, not he! One hand washes the other in this world. And it wasn't his fault if he tried to earn his living as best he could. Poverty wasn't a sin.

But Lucia went red and white, her eyes swelled with tears, or she hid her face in her apron. After some time she didn't show herself outside the house, neither for mass, nor for confession, nor at Easter, nor at Christmas. In the kitchen she hid herself in the darkest corner, with her face dropped, huddled in the new dress her master had given her, wide around the waist.

Brasi consoled her with kind words. He put his arm round her neck, felt the fine stuff of her frock, and praised it. Those gold ear-rings were made for her. Anybody who is well dressed and has money in their pocket has no need to feel ashamed and walk with their eyes down; above all when the eyes are as lovely as neighbour Lucia's. The poor thing took courage by looking into his face with those same eyes, still overcome, and she stammered: "Do you mean it, Master Brasi? Do you still care for me?"

"Yes, yes, I do really!" replied Brasi, with his hand on his conscience. "But is it my fault if I'm not rich enough to marry you? If you'd got ten pounds, I'd marry you with my eyes shut."

Don Venerando had now taken to liking him also, and gave him his left-off clothes and his broken boots. When he went down into the cellar he gave him a good pot of wine, saying to him:

"Here, drink my health!"

And his fat belly shook with laughing, seeing the grimaces which Brasi made, and hearing him stuttering to Lucia, pale as a dead man: "The master is a gentleman, neighbour Lucia! Let the neighbours cackle, they're all jealous, because they're dying with hunger, and they'd like to be in your shoes."

Santo, the brother, heard the gossip in the square some month or so later. He ran to his wife, staggered. Poor they had always been, but honoured. Red-head was also overwhelmed, and she ran in dismay to her sister-in-law, who couldn't utter a word. But when she came back home, she was quite different, serene and with roses in her cheeks.

"If you saw her! A chest as high as this, full of white goods! and rings, and pendant-ear-rings, and necklaces of fine gold. Then there are ten guineas for the dowry. A real God's provision!"

"It doesn't matter," the brother kept saying from time to time, unable to take it all in. "At least she might have waited till our mother had closed her eyes!"

All this took place in the year of the snow, when a good many roofs fell in, and there was a great mortality among the cattle of the district, God preserve us!

At Lamia and on the Mount of Santa Margherita, as folks saw that livid evening declining, heavy with ill-omened cloud, so that the oxen looked suspiciously behind them, and mooed, all the people stood outside their huts to gaze far off towards the sea, with one hand over their eyes, not speaking. The bell of the Old Monastery, at the top of the village, was ringing to drive away the bad night, and on the Castle hill-crest there was a great swarming of goodwives, seen black against the pale horizon, watching the Dragon's Tail in the sky, a pitch-black stripe that smelled of sulphur, they said, and which meant it was going to be a bad night. The women made signs with their fingers to conjure him away, the dragon, and they showed him the little medal of the Madonna on their bare breast, and spat in his face, making the sign of the cross upon themselves right down to their navel, and praying God and the souls in purgatory, and Santa Lucia, whose eve it was, to protect their fields, their cattle, and also their men, all live creatures that were outside the village. At the beginning of winter Carmenio had gone with the flock to Santa Margherita. His mother wasn't well that evening, and tossed in her bed, with her dilated eyes, and wouldn't keep quiet like she used to, but wanted this and wanted that, and wanted to get up, and wanted them to turn her over on to the other side. Carmenio had run round for a while, attending to her, trying to do something. Then he had posted himself by the bed, stupefied, with his hands clutching his hair.

The hut was across the stream, in the bed of the valley, between two great rocks which leaned over the roof. Opposite, the coast, seeming to stand on end, was beginning to fade in the darkness which was rising from the valley, naked and black with stones, and between the stones the white stripe of the road-track lost itself. When the sun was setting the neighbours had come from the flock in the cactus grove, to see if the sick woman wanted anything; but she was lying quite still in her bit of a bed, with her face upwards and her nose going black, as if dusted with soot.

"A bad sign!" herdsman Decu had said. "If I hadn't got the sheep up above, and the bad weather that's coming on, I wouldn't leave you alone to-night. Call me, if there's anything!"

Carmenio said yes, with his head leaning against the doorpost; but seeing him going away step by step, to be lost in the night, he had a great desire to run after him, to begin to shout, and tear his hair—to do he knew not what.

"If there's anything," shouted herdsman Decu from the distance, "run up to the flock in the cactus thicket, up there; there's people there."

The flock was still to be seen on the rocky height, skywards, in that bit of twilight which still gathered on the tops of the mountains, and penetrated the thickets of the cactus. Far, far away, towards Lamia and the plain, was heard the howling of dogs—waow! waow! waow!—the sound coming right up to there and making your bones turn cold.

Then the sheep suddenly were possessed and began to rush about in a mass in the enclosure, driven by a mad terror, as if they heard the wolf in the neighbourhood; and at that frantic clanging of sheep-bells, it seemed as if the shadows had become lit up with so many fiery eyes, all going round. Then the sheep stopped still, huddled close together, with their noses down to the ground, and the dog, with one long and lamentable howl, left off barking, seated there on his tail.

"If I'd known," thought Carmenio, "it would have been better to tell herdsman Decu not to leave me alone."

Outside, in the darkness, the bells of the flock were heard shuddering from time to time. Through the window-hole you could see the square of the black doorway, black as the mouth of an oven; nothing else. And the coast away opposite and the deep valley and the plain of Lamia, all was plunged in that bottomless blackness so that it seemed as if you, what you saw was nothing but the noise of the torrent, away below, mounting up towards the hut, swollen and threatening.

If he had known this too, he'd have run to the village before it got dark, to fetch his brother; and then of course by this time he'd have been there with him, and Lucia as well, and the sister-in-law.

Then the mother began to speak, but you couldn't make out what she said, and she kept grasping the bedclothes with her wasted hands.

"Mamma! Mamma! What do you want?" asked Carmenio. "Tell me what it is, I'm here with you!"

But the mother did not answer. She shook her head instead, as if to say no! no!

she didn't want to. The boy put the candle under her nose and burst out crying with fear.

"Oh, mamma! oh, mamma!" whimpered Carmenio. "Oh, I'm all alone and I can't help you!"

He opened the door to call the folks from the flock among the cactus. But nobody heard him.

Everywhere there was a dense glimmer; on the coast, in the valley, and down on the plain—like a silence made of cotton-wool. All at once came the sound of a muffled bell from far off—'nton! 'nton! 'nton!—and it seemed to curdle in the snow.

"Oh, holiest Madonna! sobbed Carmenio. "Whatever bell is that? Oh, you with the cactus sheep, help! Help Holy Christians!" he began to shout.

At last, above there, at the top of the cactus hill, was heard a far-off voice, like the bell of Francofonte.

"Ooooh!—what's a-maaatter? What's a-maaatter?"

"Help, good Christians! help, here at shepherd Decu-u-u's."

"Ooooh—follow the shee-eeep!—fo-o-ollow!"

"No! no! it isn't the sheep—it *isn't*!"

Just then the screech-owl flew past and began to screech over the hut.

"There!" murmured Carmenio, crossing himself. "Now the screech-owl has smelt the smell of dead people. Now my mamma is going to die!"

Having to stay alone in the cabin with his mother, who no longer spoke, made him want to cry. "Mamma, what's a-matter? Mamma, tell me! Mamma, are you cold?" She did not breathe, her face was dark. He lit the fire between the two stones of the hearth, and sat watching how the boughs burned, how they made a flame and then breathed out as if they were saying something about it.

When he had been with the flocks at Resecone, the Francofonte man, as they sat up at night, had told tales of witches who ride on broomsticks, and do witchcraft over the flames of the hearth. Carmenio remembered even now how the farm-people had gathered to listen, with all their eyes open, in front of the little light hung to the pillar of the great dark mill-stone, and that not one of them had had the courage afterwards to go and sleep in his own corner that evening.

Against these things he had the medal of the Madonna under his shirt, and the ribbon of Santa Agrippina tied round his wrist, till it had become black with wear. And in his pocket he had the reed whistle, which reminded him of summer evenings—yoo! yoo!—when they let the sheep into the stubble that is yellow as gold, and the grass-hoppers explode in sound at the hour of noon, and the larks fall whistling to nestle behind the sods at sunset, when the scent of wild mint and marjoram wakes up. Yoo! Yoo! Infant Jesu! At Christmas, when he had gone to the village, that was how they had played for the novena in front of the little altar that was lit up and adorned with boughs of orange tree; and in front of the doors of all the houses the children had been playing chuck-stone, the fine December sun shining on their backs. Then they had all set off for the midnight mass, in a crowd with the neighbours, colliding and laughing through the dark streets. Ah, why had he got this thorn in his heart now! And why didn't his mother say anything! It still wanted a long time to midnight. Between the stones of the unplastered walls it seemed as if there were eyes watching from every hole, looking into the hut, at the hearth, eyes black and frozen.

On a straw-stack in a corner a jacket was thrown down, spread out long, and it seemed as if the sleeves were swelling out; and the devil with the Archangel Michael, in the image-card stuck on to the bed-head, gnashed his white teeth, with his hands in his hair, among the red zigzags of hell.

Next day, pale as so many corpses, arrived Santo, and Red-head with the children trailing after her, and Lucia, who had no thought for concealing her condition, in that hour of anguish. Around the bed of the dead woman they tore their hair and beat their heads, and thought of nothing else. Then as Santo noticed his sister with so much stomach on her that it was shameful, he began saying in the midst of all the blubbering: "You might at least have let that poor old woman close her eyes first, you might——"

And Lucia on her side: "If I'd only known, if I'd only known! She shouldn't have gone short of doctor or druggist, now I've got ten guineas of my own."

"She is in Paradise praying to God for us sinners," concluded Red-head. "She knows you've got your dowry, and she's at peace, poor thing. Now Master Brasi will marry you without fail."

The Death of Iván Ilych

(1884)

Leo Tolstoy

Aylmer Maude, translator

Count Leo Tolstoy (1828–1910) was a descendant of noble families famous in Russian history, on whose records he drew for his research into the Napoleonic period. His first writing, *Sevastopol* (1856), was a report of the Crimean War, in which he served as a soldier after leaving Kazan University. He married in 1861 and, living as a prosperous country gentleman, he wrote *War and Peace* (1865–1869) and *Anna Karenina* (1875–1877), two of the world's great novels. Around 1878 Tolstoy suffered a conversion and renounced contemporary society and art, including his own earlier fiction. His conversion was also reflected in his turning to shorter, more oracular works, beginning with *My Confession* (1879, published in 1884), and culminating in his attack on Shakespeare and others, *What is Art?* (1898). At the same time, however, he produced a brilliant series of short fictions —parables and novelettes, sometimes mixed. These include, besides *The Death of Iván Ilych* (1884), *Memoir of a Madman* (1884), *The Kreutzer Sonata* (1889), *The Devil* (1889, published in 1911), *Master and Man* (1895), and *Hadji Murád* (1904). Finally, in 1910 Tolstoy signed over his property to his wife and set out on a religious pilgrimage, dying a few days later at a railway station.

The translation of *The Death of Iván Ilych* by Aylmer Maude (Oxford, 1935) is reprinted by permission of the Oxford University Press. See also Maude's *Leo Tolstoy* (London, 1918).

During an interval in the Melvínski trial in the large building of the Law Courts the members and public prosecutor met in Iván Egórovich Shébek's private room, where the conversation turned on the celebrated Krasóvski case. Fëdor Vasílievich warmly maintained that it was not subject to their jurisdiction, Iván Egórovich maintained the contrary, while Peter Ivánovich, not having entered into the discussion at the start, took no part in it but looked through the *Gazette* which had just been handed in.

"Gentlemen," he said, "Iván Ilych has died!"

"You don't say!"

"Here, read it yourself," replied Peter Ivánovich, handing Fëdor Vasílievich the paper still damp from the press. Surrounded by a black border were the words: "Praskóvya Fëdorovna Golviná, with profound sorrow, informs relatives and friends of the demise of her beloved husband Iván Ilych Golovín, Member of the Court of Justice, which occurred on February the 4th of this year 1882. The funeral will take place on Friday at one o'clock in the afternoon."

Iván Ilych had been a colleague of the gentlemen present and was liked by them all. He had been ill for some weeks with an illness said to be incurable. His post had been kept open for him, but there had been conjectures that in case of his death Alexéev might receive his appointment, and that either Vínnikov or Shtábel would succeed Alexéev. So on receiving the news of Iván Ilych's death the first thought of each of the gentlemen in that private room was of the changes and promotions it might occasion among themselves or their acquaintances.

"I shall be sure to get Shtábel's place or Vínnikov's," thought Fëdor Vasílievich. "I was promised that long ago, and the promotion means an extra eight hundred rubles a year for me besides the allowance."

"Now I must apply for my brother-in-law's transfer from Kalúga," thought Peter Ivánovich. "My wife will be very glad, and then she won't be able to say that I never do anything for her relations."

"I thought he would never leave his bed again," said Peter Ivánovich aloud. "It's very sad."

"But what really was the matter with him?"

"The doctors couldn't say—at least they could, but each of them said something different. When last I saw him I thought he was getting better."

"And I haven't been to see him since the holidays. I always meant to go."

"Had he any property?"

"I think his wife had a little—but something quite trifling."

"We shall have to go to see her, but they live so terribly far away."

"Far away from you, you mean. Everything's far away from your place."

"You see, he never can forgive my living on the other side of the river," said Peter Ivánovich, smiling at Shébek. Then, still talking of the distances between different parts of the city, they returned to the Court.

Besides considerations as to the possible transfers and promotions likely to result from Iván Ilych's death, the mere fact of the death of a near acquaintance aroused, as usual, in all who heard of it the complacent feeling that, "it is he who is dead and not I."

Each one thought or felt, "Well, he's dead but I'm alive!" But the more intimate of Iván Ilych's acquaintances, his so-called friends, could not help thinking also that they would now have to fulfil the very tiresome demands of propriety by attending the funeral service and paying a visit of condolence to the widow.

Fëdor Vasílievich and Peter Ivánovich had been his nearest acquaintances. Peter Ivánovich had studied law with Iván Ilych and had considered himself to be under obligations to him.

Having told his wife at dinner-time of Iván Ilych's death, and of his conjecture that it might be possible to get her brother transferred to their circuit, Peter Ivánovich sacrificed his usual nap, put on his evening clothes, and drove to Iván Ilych's house.

At the entrance stood a carriage and two cabs. Leaning against the wall in the hall downstairs near the cloak-stand was a coffin-lid covered with cloth of gold, ornamented with gold cord and tassels, that had been polished up with metal powder. Two ladies in black were taking off their fur cloaks. Peter Ivánovich recognized one of them as Iván Ilych's sister, but the other was a stranger to him. His colleague Schwartz was just coming downstairs, but on seeing Peter Ivánovich enter he stopped and winked at him, as if to say: "Iván Ilych has made a mess of things—not like you and me."

Schwartz's face with his Piccadilly whiskers, and his slim figure in evening dress, had as usual an air of elegant solemnity which contrasted with the playfulness of his character and had a special piquancy here, or so it seemed to Peter Ivánovich.

Peter Ivánovich allowed the ladies to precede him and slowly followed them upstairs. Schwartz did not come down but remained where he was, and Peter Ivánovich understood that he wanted to arrange where they should play bridge that evening. The ladies went upstairs to the widow's room, and Schwartz with seriously compressed lips but a playful look in his eyes, indicated by a twist of his eyebrows the room to the right where the body lay.

Peter Ivánovich, like everyone else on such occasions, entered feeling uncertain what he would have to do. All he knew was that as such times it is always safe to cross oneself. But he was not quite sure whether one should make obeisances while doing so. He therefore adopted a middle course. On entering the room he began crossing himself and made a slight movement resembling a bow. At the same time, as far as the motion of his head and arm allowed, he surveyed the room. Two young men—apparently nephews, one of whom was a high-school pupil—were leaving the room, crossing themselves as they did so. An old woman was standing motionless, and a lady with strangely arched eyebrows was saying something to her in a whisper. A vigorous, resolute Church Reader, in a frock-coat, was reading something in a loud voice with an expression that precluded any contradiction. The butler's assistant, Gerásim, stepping lightly in front of Peter Ivánovich, was strewing something on the floor. Noticing this, Peter Ivánovich was immediately aware of a faint odour of a decomposing body.

The last time he had called on Iván Ilych, Peter Ivánovich had seen Gerásim in the study. Iván Ilych had been particularly fond of him and he was performing the duty of a sick nurse.

Peter Ivánovich continued to make the sign of the cross slightly inclining his head in an intermediate direction between the coffin, the Reader, and the icons on the table in a corner of the room. Afterwards, when it seemed to him that this movement of his arm in crossing himself had gone on too long, he stopped and began to look at the corpse.

The dead man lay, as dead men always lie, in a specially heavy way, his rigid limbs sunk in the soft cushions of the coffin, with the head forever bowed on the pillow. His yellow waxen brow with bald patches over his sunken temples was thrust up in the way peculiar to the dead, the protruding nose seeming to press on the upper lip. He was much changed and had grown even thinner since Peter Ivánovich had last seen him, but, as is always the case with the dead, his face was handsomer and above all more dignified than when he was alive. The expression on the face said that what was necessary had been accomplished, and accomplished rightly. Besides this there was in that expression a reproach and a warning to the living. This warning seemed to Peter Ivánovich out of place, or at least not applicable to him. He felt a certain discomfort and so he hurriedly crossed himself once more and turned and went out of the door—too hurriedly and too regardless of propriety, as he himself was aware.

Schwartz was waiting for him in the adjoining room with legs spread wide apart and both hands toying with his top-hat behind his back. The mere sight of that playful, well-groomed, and elegant figure refreshed Peter Ivánovich. He felt that Schwartz was above all these happenings and would not surrender to any depressing influences. His very look said that this incident of a church service for Iván Ilych could not be a sufficient reason for infringing the order of the session—in other words, that it would certainly not prevent his unwrapping a new pack of cards and shuffling them that evening while a footman placed four fresh candles on the table: in fact, that there was no reason for supposing that this incident would hinder their spending the evening agreeably. Indeed he said this in a whisper as Peter Ivánovich passed him, proposing that they should meet for a game at Fëdor Vasílievich's. But apparently Peter Ivánovich was not destined to play bridge that evening. Praskóvya Fëdorovna (a short, fat woman who despite all efforts to the contrary had continued to broaden steadily from her shoulders downwards and who had the same extraordinary arched eyebrows as the lady who had been standing by the coffin), dressed all in black, her head covered with lace, came out of her own room with some other ladies, conducted them to the room where the dead body lay, and said: "The service will begin immediately. Please go in."

Schwartz, making an indefinite bow, stood still, evidently neither accepting nor declining this invitation. Praskóvya Fëdorovna recognizing Peter Ivánovich, sighed, went close up to him, took his hand, and said: "I know you were a true friend to Iván Ilych..." and looked at him awaiting some suitable response. And Peter Ivánovich knew that, just as it had been the right thing to cross himself in that room, so what he had to do here was to press her hand, sigh, and say, "Believe me...." So he did all this and as he did it felt that the desired result had been achieved: that both he and she were touched.

"Come with me. I want to speak to you before it begins," said the widow. "Give me your arm."

Peter Ivánovich gave her his arm and they went to the inner rooms, passing Schwartz who winked at Peter Ivánovich compassionately.

"That does for our bridge! Don't object if we find another player. Perhaps you can cut in when you do escape," said his playful look.

Peter Ivánovich sighed still more deeply and despondently, and Praskóvya Fëdorovna pressed his arm gratefully. When they reached the drawing-room, upholstered in pink cretonne and lighted by a dim lamp, they sat down at the table—she on a sofa and Peter Ivánovich on a low pouffe, the springs of which yielded spasmodically under his weight. Praskóvya Fëdorovna had been on the point of warning him to take another seat, but felt that such a warning was out of keeping with her present condition and so changed her mind. As he sat down on the pouffe Peter Ivánovich recalled how Iván Ilych had arranged this room and had consulted him regarding this pink cretonne with green leaves. The whole room was full of furniture and knick-knacks, and on her way to the sofa the lace of the widow's black shawl caught on the carved edge of the table. Peter Ivánovich rose to detach it, and the springs of the pouffe, relieved of his weight, rose also and gave him a push. The widow began detaching her shawl herself, and Peter Ivánovich again sat down, suppressing the rebellious springs of the pouffe under him. But the widow had not quite freed herself and Peter Ivánovich got up again, and again the pouffe rebelled and even creaked. When this was all over she took out a clean cambric handkerchief and began to weep. The episode with the shawl and the struggle with the pouffe had cooled Peter Ivánovich's emotions and he sat there with a sullen look on his face. This awkward situation was interrupted by Sokolóv, Iván Ilych's butler, who came to report that the plot in the cemetery that Praskóvya Fëdorovna had chosen would cost two hundred rubles. She stopped weeping and, looking at Peter Ivánovich with the air of a victim, remarked in French that it was very hard for her. Peter Ivánovich made a silent gesture signifying his full conviction that it must indeed be so.

"Please smoke," she said in a magnanimous yet crushed voice, and turned to discuss with Sokolóv the price of the plot for the grave.

Peter Ivánovich while lighting his cigarette heard her inquiring very circumstantially into the prices of different plots in the cemetery and finally decide which she would take. When that was done she gave instructions about engaging the choir. Sokolóv then left the room.

"I look after everything myself," she told Peter Ivánovich, shifting the albums that lay on the table; and noticing that the table was endangered by his cigarette-ash, she immediately passed him an ash-tray, saying as she did so: "I consider it an affectation to say that my grief prevents my attending to practical affairs. On the contrary, if anything can—I won't say console me, but—distract me, it is seeing to everything concerning him." She again took out her handkerchief as if preparing to cry, but suddenly, as if mastering her feeling, she shook herself and began to speak calmly. "But there is something I want to talk to you about."

Peter Ivánovich bowed, keeping control of the springs of the pouffe, which immediately began quivering under him.

"He suffered terribly the last few days."

"Did he?" said Peter Ivánovich.

"Oh, terribly! He screamed unceasingly, not for minutes but for hours. For the last three days he screamed incessantly. It was unendurable. I cannot understand how I bore it; you could hear him three rooms off. Oh, what I have suffered!"

"Is it possible that he was conscious all that time?" asked Peter Ivánovich.

"Yes," she whispered. "To the last moment. He took leave of us a quarter of an hour before he died, and asked us to take Volódya away."

The thought of the sufferings of this man he had known so intimately, first as a merry little boy, then as a school-mate, and later as a grown-up colleague, suddenly struck Peter Ivánovich with horror, despite an unpleasant consciousness of his own and this woman's dissimulation. He again saw that brow, and that nose pressing down on the lip, and felt afraid for himself.

"Three days of frightful suffering and then death! Why, that might suddenly, at any time, happen to me," he thought, and for a moment felt terrified. But—he did not himself know how—the customary reflection at once occurred to him that this had happened to Iván Ilych and not to him, and that it should not and could not happen to him, and that to think that it could would be yielding to depression which he ought not to do, as Schwartz's expression plainly showed. After which reflection Peter Ivánovich felt reassured, and began to ask with interest about the details of Iván Ilych's death, as though death was an accident natural to Iván Ilych but certainly not to himself.

After many details of the really dreadful physical sufferings Iván Ilych had endured (which details he learnt only from the effect those sufferings had produced on Praskóvya Fëdorovna's nerves) the widow apparently found it necessary to get to business.

"Oh, Peter Ivánovich, how hard it is! How terribly, terribly hard!" and she again began to weep.

Peter Ivánovich sighed and waited for her to finish blowing her nose. When she had done so he said, "Believe me..." and she again began talking and brought out what was evidently her chief concern with him—namely, to question him as to how she could obtain a grant of money from the government on the occasion of her husband's death. She made it appear that she was asking Peter Ivánovich's advice about her pension, but he soon saw that she already knew about that to the minutest detail, more even than he did himself. She knew how much could be got out of the government in consequence of her husband's death, but wanted to find out whether she could not possibly extract something more. Peter Ivánovich tried to think of some means of doing so, but after reflecting for a while and, out of propriety, condemning the government for its niggardliness, he said he thought that nothing more could be got. Then she sighed and evidently began to devise means of getting rid of her visitor. Noticing this, he put out his cigarette, rose, pressed her hand, and went out into the anteroom.

In the dining-room where the clock stood that Iván Ilych had liked so much and had bought at an antique shop, Peter Ivánovich met a priest and a few acquaintances who had come to attend the service, and he recognized Iván Ilych's daughter, a handsome young woman. She was in black and her slim figure appeared slimmer than ever. She had a gloomy, determined, almost angry expression, and bowed to Peter Ivánovich as though he were in some way to blame. Behind her, with the same offended look, stood a wealthy young man, an examining magistrate, whom Peter Ivánovich also knew and who was her fiancé, as he had heard. He bowed mournfully to them and was about to pass into the death-chamber, when from under the stairs appeared the figure of Iván Ilych's schoolboy son, who was extremely like his father. He seemed a little Iván Ilych, such as Peter Ivánovich remembered when they studied law together. His tear-stained eyes had in them the look that is seen in the eyes of boys of thirteen or fourteen who are not pure-minded. When he saw Peter Ivánovich he scowled morosely and shame-facedly. Peter Ivánovich nodded to him and entered the death-chamber. The service began: candles, groans, incense, tears, and sobs. Peter Ivánovich stood looking gloomily down at his feet. He did not look once at the dead man, did not yield to any depressing influence, and was one of the first to leave the room. There was no one in the anteroom, but Gerásim darted out of the dead man's room, rummaged with his strong hands among the fur coats to find Peter Ivánovich's and helped him on with it.

"Well, friend Gerásim," said Peter Ivánovich, so as to say something. "It's a sad affair, isn't it?"

"It's God's will. We shall all come to it some day," said Gerásim, displaying his teeth—the even, white teeth of a healthy peasant—and, like a man in the thick of urgent work, he briskly opened the front door, called the coachman, helped Peter Ivánovich into the sledge, and sprang back to the porch as if in readiness for what he had to do next.

Peter Ivánovich found the fresh air particularly pleasant after the smell of incense, the dead body, and carbolic acid.

"Where to, sir?" asked the coachman.

"It's not too late even now. . . . I'll call round on Fëdor Vasílievich."

He accordingly drove there and found them just finishing the first rubber, so that it was quite convenient for him to cut in.

Iván Ilych's life had been most simple and most ordinary and therefore most terrible.

He had been a member of the Court of Justice, and died at the age of forty-five. His father had been an official who after serving in various ministries and depart-ments in Petersburg had made the sort of career which brings men to positions from which by reason of their long service they cannot be dismissed, though they are obviously unfit to hold any responsible position, and for whom therefore posts are specially created, which though fictitious carry salaries of from six to ten thousand rubles that are not fictitious, and in receipt of which they live on to a great age.

Such was the Privy Councillor and superfluous member of various superfluous institutions, Ilya Epímovich Golovín.

He had three sons, of whom Iván Ilych was the second. The eldest son was following in his father's footsteps only in another department, and was already approaching that stage in the service at which a similar sinecure would be reached. The third son was a failure. He had ruined his prospects in a number of positions and was now serving in the railway department. His father and brothers, and still more their wives, not merely disliked meeting him, but avoided remembering his existence unless compelled to do so. His sister had married Baron Greff, a Petersburg official of her father's type. Iván Ilych was *le phénix de la famille* as people said. He was neither as cold and formal as his elder brother nor as wild as the younger, but was a happy mean between them—an intelligent, polished, lively, and agreeable man. He had studied with his younger brother at the School of Law, but the latter had failed to complete the course and was expelled when he was in the fifth class. Iván Ilych finished the course well. Even when he was at the School of Law he was just what he remained for the rest of his life: a capable, cheerful, good-natured, and sociable man, though strict in the fulfilment of what he considered to be his duty: and he considered his duty to be what was so considered by those in authority. Neither as a boy nor as a man was he a toady, but from early youth was by nature attracted to people of high station as a fly is drawn to the light, assimilating their ways and views of life and establishing friendly relations with them. All the enthusiasms of childhood and youth passed without leaving much trace on him; he succumbed to sensuality, to vanity, and latterly among the highest classes to liberalism, but always within limits which his instinct unfailingly indicated to him as correct.

At school he had done things which had formerly seemed to him very horrid and made him feel disgusted with himself when he did them; but when later on he saw that such actions were done by people of good position and that they did not regard them as wrong, he was able not exactly to regard them as right, but to forget about them entirely or not be at all troubled at remembering them.

Having graduated from the School of Law and qualified for the tenth rank of the civil service, and having received money from his father for his equipment, Iván Ilych ordered himself clothes at Scharmer's, the fashionable tailor, hung a medallion inscribed *respice finem* on his watch-chain, took leave of his professor and the prince who was patron of the school, had a farewell dinner with his comrades at Donon's first-class restaurant, and with his new and fashionable portmanteau, linen, clothes, shaving and other toilet appliances, and a travelling rug, all purchased at the best shops, he set off for one of the provinces where, through his father's influence, he had been attached to the governor as an official for special service.

In the province Iván Ilych soon arranged as easy and agreeable a position for himself as he had had at the School of Law. He performed his official tasks, made his career, and at the same time amused himself pleasantly and decorously. Occasionally he paid official visits to country districts, where he behaved with dignity both to his superiors and inferiors, and performed the duties entrusted to him, which related chiefly to the sectarians, with an exactness and incorruptible honesty of which he could not but feel proud.

In official matters, despite his youth and taste for frivolous gaiety, he was exceedingly reserved, punctilious, and even severe; but in society he was often amusing and witty, and always good-natured, correct in his manner, and *bon enfant,* as the governor and his wife—with whom he was like one of the family— used to say of him.

In the province he had an affair with a lady who made advances to the elegant young lawyer, and there was also a milliner; and there were carousals with aides-de-camp who visited the district, and after-supper visits to a certain outlying street of doubtful reputation; and there was too some obsequiousness to his chief and even to his chief's wife, but all this was done with such a tone of good breeding that no hard names could be applied to it. It all came under the heading of the French saying: *"Il faut que jeunesse se passe."*[1] It was all done with clean hands, in clean linen, with French phrases, and above all among people of the best society and consequently with the approval of people of rank.

So Iván Ilych served for five years and then came a change in his official life. The new and reformed judicial institutions were introduced, and new men were needed. Iván Ilych became such a new man. He was offered the post of Examining Magistrate, and he accepted it though the post was in another province and obliged him to give up the connexions he had formed and to make new ones. His friends met to give him a send-off; they had a group-photograph taken and presented him with a silver cigarette-case, and he set off to his new post.

As examining magistrate Iván Ilych was just as *comme il faut* and decorous a man, inspiring general respect and capable of separating his official duties from his private life, as he had been when acting as an official on special service. His duties now as examining magistrate were far more interesting and attractive than before. In his former position it had been pleasant to wear an undress uniform made by Scharmer, and to pass through the crowd of petitioners and officials who were timorously awaiting an audience with the governor, and who envied him as with free and easy gait he went straight into his chief's private room to have a cup of tea and a cigarette with him. But not many people had then been directly dependent on him—only police officials and the sectarians when he went on special missions—and he liked to treat them politely, almost as comrades, as if he were letting them feel that he who had the power to crush them was treating them in this simple, friendly way. There were then but few such people. But now, as an examining magistrate, Iván Ilych felt that everyone without exception, even the most important and self-satisfied, was in his power, and that he need only write a few words on a sheet of paper with a certain heading, and this or that important, self-satisfied person would be brought before him in the role of an accused person or a witness, and if he did not choose to allow him to sit down, would have to stand before him and answer his questions. Iván Ilych never abused his power; he tried on the contrary to soften its expression, but the consciousness of it and of the possibility of softening its effect, supplied the chief interest and attraction of his office. In his work itself, especially in his examinations, he very soon acquired a method of eliminating all considerations irrelevant to the legal aspect of the case, and reducing even the most complicated case to a form in which it would be presented on paper only in its externals, completely excluding his personal opinion of the matter, while above all observing every prescribed formality. The work was new and Iván Ilych was one of the first men to apply the new Code of 1864.[2]

On taking up the post of examining magistrate in a new town, he made new acquaintances and connexions, placed himself on a new footing, and assumed a somewhat different tone. He took up an attitude of rather dignified aloofness towards the provincial authorities, but picked out the best circle of legal gentlemen

---

[1] Youth must have its fling.

[2] The emancipation of the serfs in 1861 was followed by a thorough all-round reform of judicial proceedings.

and wealthy gentry living in the town and assumed a tone of slight dissatisfaction with the government, of moderate liberalism, and of enlightened citizenship. At the same time, without at all altering the elegance of his toilet, he ceased shaving his chin and allowed his beard to grow as it pleased.

Iván Ilych settled down very pleasantly in this new town. The society there, which inclined towards opposition to the governor, was friendly, his salary was larger, and he began to play *vint* [a form of bridge], which he found added not a little to the pleasure of life, for he had a capacity for cards, played good-humouredly, and calculated rapidly and astutely, so that he usually won.

After living there for two years he met his future wife, Praskóvya Fëdorovna Míkhel, who was the most attractive, clever, and brilliant girl of the set in which he moved, and among other amusements and relaxations from his labours as examining magistrate, Iván Ilych established light and playful relations with her.

While he had been an official on special service he had been accustomed to dance, but now as an examining magistrate it was exceptional for him to do so. If he danced now, he did it as if to show that though he served under the reformed order of things, and had reached the fifth official rank, yet when it came to dancing he could do it better than most people. So at the end of an evening he sometimes danced with Praskóvya Fëdorovna, and it was chiefly during these dances that he captivated her. She fell in love with him. Iván Ilych had at first no definite intention of marrying, but when the girl fell in love with him he said to himself: "Really, why shouldn't I marry?"

Praskóvya Fëdorovna came of a good family, was not bad looking, and had some little property. Iván Ilych might have aspired to a more brilliant match, but even this was good. He had his salary, and she, he hoped, would have an equal income. She was well connected, and was a sweet, pretty, and thoroughly correct young woman. To say that Iván Ilych married because he fell in love with Praskóvya Fëdorovna and found that she sympathized with his views of life would be as incorrect as to say that he married because his social circle approved of the match. He was swayed by both these considerations: the marriage gave him personal satisfaction, and at the same time it was considered the right thing by the most highly placed of his associates.

So Iván Ilych got married.

The preparations for marriage and the beginning of married life, with its conjugal caresses, the new furniture, new crockery, and new linen, were very pleasant until his wife became pregnant—so that Iván Ilych had begun to think that marriage would not impair the easy, agreeable, gay, and always decorous character of his life, approved of by society and regarded by himself as natural, but would even improve it. But from the first months of his wife's pregnancy, something new, unpleasant, depressing, and unseemly, and from which there was no way of escape, unexpectedly showed itself.

His wife, without any reason—*de gaieté de coeur* as Iván Ilych expressed it to himself—began to disturb the pleasure and propriety of their life. She began to be jealous without any cause, expected him to devote his whole attention to her, found fault with everything, and made coarse and ill-mannered scenes.

At first Iván Ilych hoped to escape from the unpleasantness of this state of affairs by the same easy and decorous relation to life that had served him heretofore: he tried to ignore his wife's disagreeable moods, continued to live in his usual easy and pleasant way, invited friends to his house for a game of cards, and also tried going out to his club or spending his evenings with friends. But one day his wife began upbraiding him so vigorously, using such coarse words, and continued to abuse him every time he did not fulfil her demands, so resolutely and with such evident determination not to give way till he submitted—that is, till he stayed at home and was bored just as she was—that he became alarmed. He now realized that matrimony—at any rate with Praskóvya Fëdorovna—was not always conducive to the pleasures and amenities of life, but on the contrary often infringed both comfort and propriety, and that he must therefore entrench himself against such infringement. And Iván Ilych began to seek for means of doing so. His official duties were the one thing that imposed upon Praskóvya Fëdorovna, and by means of his official work and the duties attached to it he began struggling with his wife to secure his own independence.

With the birth of their child, the attempts to feed it and the various failures in doing so, and with the real and imaginary illnesses of mother and child, in which Iván Ilych's sympathy was demanded but about which he understood nothing, the need of securing for himself an existence outside his family life became still more imperative.

As his wife grew more irritable and exacting and Iván Ilych transferred the centre of gravity of his life more and more to his official work, so did he grow to like his work better and became more ambitious than before.

Very soon, within a year of his wedding, Iván Ilych had realized that marriage, though it may add some comforts to life, is in fact a very intricate and difficult affair towards which in order to perform one's duty, that is, to lead a decorous life approved of by society, one must adopt a definite attitude just as towards one's official duties.

And Iván Ilych evolved such an attitude towards married life. He only required of it those conveniences—dinner at home, housewife, and bed—which it could give him, and above all that propriety of external forms required by public opinion. For the rest he looked for light-hearted pleasure and propriety, and was very thankful when he found them, but if he met with antagonism and querulousness he at once retired into his separate fenced-off world of official duties, where he found satisfaction.

Iván Ilych was esteemed a good official, and after three years was made Assistant Public Prosecutor. His new duties, their importance, the possibility of indicting and imprisoning anyone he chose, the publicity his speeches received, and the success he had in all these things, made his work still more attractive.

More children came. His wife became more and more querulous and ill-tempered, but the attitude Iván Ilych had adopted towards his home life rendered him almost impervious to her grumbling.

After seven years' service in that town he was transferred to another province as Public Prosecutor. They moved, but were short of money and his wife did not like the place they moved to. Though the salary was higher the cost of living was greater, besides which two of their children died and family life became still more unpleasant for him.

Praskóvya Fëdorovna blamed her husband for every inconvenience they encountered in their new home. Most of the conversations between husband and wife, especially as to the children's education, led to topics which recalled former disputes, and those disputes were apt to flare up again at any moment. There remained only those rare periods of amorousness which still came to them at times but did not last long. These were islets at which they anchored for a while and then again set out upon that ocean of veiled hostility which showed itself in their aloofness from one another. This aloofness might have grieved Iván Ilych had he considered that it ought not to exist, but he now regarded the position as normal, and even made it the goal at which he aimed in family life. His aim was to free himself more and more from those unpleasantnesses and to give them a semblance of harmlessness and propriety. He attained this by spending less and less time with his family, and when obliged to be at home he tried to safeguard his position by the presence of outsiders. The chief thing however was that he had his official duties. The whole interest of his life now centered in the official world and that interest absorbed him. The consciousness of his power, being able to ruin anybody he wished to ruin, the importance, even the external dignity of his entry into court, or meetings with his subordinates, his success with superiors and inferiors, and above all his masterly handling of cases, of which he was conscious—all this gave him pleasure and filled his life, together with chats with his colleagues, dinners, and bridge. So that on the whole Iván Ilych's life continued to flow as he considered it should do—pleasantly and properly.

So things continued for another seven years. His eldest daughter was already sixteen, another child had died, and only one son was left, a schoolboy and a subject of dissensions. Iván Ilych wanted to put him in the School of Law, but to spite him Praskóvya Fëdorovna entered him at the High School. The daughter had been educated at home and had turned out well: the boy did not learn badly either.

So Iván Ilych lived for seventeen years after his marriage. He was already a Public Prosecutor of long standing, and had declined several proposed transfers while awaiting a more desirable post, when an unanticipated and unpleasant occurrence quite upset the peaceful course of his life. He was expecting to be offered the post of presiding judge in a University town, but Happe somehow came to the front and obtained the appointment instead. Iván Ilych became irritable, reproached Happe, and quarrelled both with him and with his immediate superiors—who became colder to him and again passed him over when other appointments were made.

This was in 1880, the hardest year of Iván Ilych's life. It was then that it became evident on the one hand that his salary was insufficient for them to live on, and on the other that he had been forgotten, and not only this, but that what was for him the greatest and most cruel injustice appeared to others a quite ordinary occurrence. Even his father did not consider it his duty to help him. Iván Ilych felt himself abandoned by everyone, and that they regarded his position with a salary of 3,500 rubles as quite normal and even fortunate. He alone knew that with the consciousness of the injustices done him, with his wife's incessant nagging, and with the debts he had contracted by living beyond his means, his position was far from normal.

In order to save money that summer he obtained leave of absence and went with his wife to live in the country at her brother's place.

In the country, without his work, he experienced *ennui* for the first time in his life, and not only *ennui* but intolerable depression, and he decided that it was impossible to go on living like that, and that it was necessary to take energetic measures.

Having passed a sleepless night pacing up and down the veranda, he decided to go to Petersburg and bestir himself, in order to punish those who had failed to appreciate him and to get transferred to another ministry.

Next day, despite many protests from his wife and her brother, he started for Petersburg with the sole object of obtaining a post with a salary of five thousand rubles a year. He was no longer bent on any particular department, or tendency, or kind of activity. All he now wanted was an appointment to another post with a salary of five thousand rubles, either in the administration, in the banks, with the railways, in one of the Empress Márya's Institutions, or even in the customs— but it had to carry with it a salary of five thousand rubles and be in a ministry other than that in which they had failed to appreciate him.

And this quest of Iván Ilych's was crowned with remarkable and unexpected success. At Kursk an acquaintance of his, F. I. Ilyín, got into the first-class carriage, sat down beside Iván Ilych, and told him of a telegram just received by the governor of Kursk announcing that a change was about to take place in the ministry: Peter Ivánovich was to be superseded by Iván Semënovich.

The proposed change, apart from its significance for Russia, had a special significance for Iván Ilych, because by bringing forward a new man, Peter Petróvich, and consequently his friend Zachár Ivánovich, it was highly favourable for Iván Ilych, since Zachár Ivánovich was a friend and colleague of his.

In Moscow this news was confirmed, and on reaching Petersburg Iván Ilych found Zachár Ivánovich and received a definite promise of an appointment in his former department of Justice.

A week later he telegraphed to his wife: "Zachár in Miller's place. I shall receive appointment on presentation of report."

Thanks to this change of personnel, Iván Ilych had unexpectedly obtained an appointment in his former ministry which placed him two stages above his former colleagues besides giving him five thousand rubles salary and three thousand five hundred rubles for expenses connected with his removal. All his ill humour towards his former enemies and the whole department vanished, and Iván Ilych was completely happy.

He returned to the country more cheerful and contented than he had been for a long time. Praskóvya Fëdorovna also cheered up and a truce was arranged between them. Iván Ilych told of how he had been fêted by everybody in Petersburg, how all those who had been his enemies were put to shame and now fawned on him, how envious they were of his appointment, and how much everybody in Petersburg had liked him.

Praskóvya Fëdorovna listened to all this and appeared to believe it. She did not contradict anything, but only made plans for their life in the town to which they were going. Iván Ilych saw with delight that these plans were his plans, that he and his wife agreed, and that, after a stumble, his life was regaining its due and natural character of pleasant lightheartedness and decorum.

Iván Ilych had come back for a short time only, for he had to take up his new duties on the 10th of September. Moreover, he needed time to settle into the new place, to move all his belongings from the province, and to buy and order many additional things: in a word, to make such arrangements as he had resolved on, which were almost exactly what Praskóvya Fëdorovna too had decided on.

Now that everything had happened so fortunately, and that he and his wife were at one in their aims and moreover saw so little of one another, they got on together better than they had done since the first years of marriage. Iván Ilych had thought of taking his family away with him at once, but the insistence of his wife's brother and her sister-in-law, who had suddenly become particularly amiable and friendly to him and his family, induced him to depart alone.

So he departed, and the cheerful state of mind induced by his success and by the harmony between his wife and himself, the one intensifying the other, did not leave him. He found a delightful house, just the thing both he and his wife had dreamt of. Spacious, lofty reception rooms in the old style, a convenient and dignified study, rooms for his wife and daughter, a study for his son—it might have been specially built for them. Iván Ilych himself superintended the arrangements, chose the wallpapers, supplemented the furniture (preferably with antiques which he considered particularly *comme il faut*), and supervised the upholstering. Everything progressed and progressed and approached the ideal he had set himself: even when things were only half completed they exceeded his expectations. He saw what a refined and elegant character, free from vulgarity, it would all have when it was ready. On falling asleep he pictured to himself how the reception-room would look. Looking at the yet unfinished drawing-room he could see the fireplace, the screen, the what-not, the little chairs dotted here and there, the dishes and plates on the walls, and the bronzes, as they would be when everything was in place. He was pleased by the thought of how his wife and daughter, who shared his taste in this matter, would be impressed by it. They were certainly not expecting as much. He had been particularly successful in finding, and buying cheaply, antiques which gave a particularly aristocratic character to the whole place. But in his letters he intentionally understated everything in order to be able to surprise them. All this so absorbed him that his new duties—though he liked his official work—interested him less than he had expected. Sometimes he even had moments of absent-mindedness during the Court Sessions, and would consider whether he should have straight or curved cornices for his curtains. He was so interested in it all that he often did things himself, rearranging the furniture, or rehanging the curtains. Once when mounting a step-ladder to show the upholsterer, who did not understand, how he wanted the hangings draped, he made a false step and slipped, but being a strong and agile man he clung on and only knocked his side against the knob of the window frame. The bruised place was painful but the pain soon passed, and he felt particularly bright and well just then. He wrote: "I feel fifteen years younger." He thought he would have everything ready by September, but it dragged on till mid-October. But the result was charming not only in his eyes but to everyone who saw it.

In reality it was just what is usually seen in the houses of people of moderate means who want to appear rich, and therefore succeed only in resembling others like themselves: there were damasks, dark wood, plants, rugs, and dull and polished bronzes—all the things people of a certain class have in order to resemble other people of that class. His house was so like the others that it would never have been noticed, but to him it all seemed to be quite exceptional. He was very happy when he met his family at the station and brought them to the newly furnished house all lit up, where a footman in a white tie opened the door into the hall decorated with plants, and when they went on into the drawing-room and the study uttering exclamations of delight. He conducted them everywhere, drank in their praises eagerly, and beamed with pleasure. At tea that evening, when Praskóvya Fëdorovna among other things asked him about his fall, he laughed, and showed them how he had gone flying and had frightened the upholsterer.

"It's a good thing I'm a bit of an athlete. Another man might have been killed, but I merely knocked myself, just here; it hurts when it's touched, but it's passing off already—it's only a bruise."

So they began living in their new home—in which, as always happens, when they got thoroughly settled in they found they were just one room short—and with the increased income, which as always was just a little (some five hundred rubles) too little, but it was all very nice.

Things went particularly well at first, before everything was finally arranged and while something had still to be done: this thing bought, that thing ordered, another thing moved, and something else adjusted. Though there were some disputes between husband and wife, they were both so well satisfied and had so much to do that it all passed off without any serious quarrels. When nothing was left to arrange it became rather dull and something seemed to be lacking, but they were then making acquaintances, forming habits, and life was growing fuller.

Iván Ilych spent his mornings at the law court and came home to dinner, and at first he was generally in a good humour, though he occasionally became irritable just on account of his house. (Every spot on the tablecloth or the upholstery, and every broken window-blind string, irritated him. He had devoted so much trouble to arranging it all that every disturbance of it distressed him.) But on the whole his life ran its course as he believed life should do: easily, pleasantly, and decorously.

He got up at nine, drank his coffee, read the paper, and then put on his undress uniform and went to the law courts. There the harness in which he worked had already been stretched to fit him and he donned it without a hitch: petitioners, inquiries at the chancery, the chancery itself, and the sittings public and administrative. In all this the thing was to exclude everything fresh and vital, which always disturbs the regular course of official business, and to admit only official relations with people, and then only on official grounds. A man would come, for instance, wanting some information. Iván Ilych, as one in whose sphere the matter did not lie, would have nothing to do with him: but if the man had some business with him in his official capacity, something that could be expressed on officially stamped paper, he would do everything, positively everything he could within the limits of such relations, and in doing so would maintain the semblance of friendly human relations, that is, would observe the courtesies of life. As soon as the official relations ended, so did everything else. Iván Ilych possessed this capacity to separate his real life from the official side of affairs and not mix the two, in the highest degree, and by long practice and natural aptitude had brought it to such a pitch that sometimes, in the manner of a virtuoso, he would even allow himself to let the human and official relations mingle. He let himself do this just because he felt that he could at any time he chose resume the strictly official attitude again and drop the human relation. And he did it all easily, pleasantly, correctly, and even artistically. In the intervals between the sessions he smoked, drank tea, chatted a little about politics, a little about general topics, a little about cards, but most of all about official appointments. Tired, but with the feelings of a virtuoso—one of the first violins who has played his part in an orchestra with precision—he would return home to find that his wife and daughter had been out paying calls, or had a visitor, and that his son had been to school, had done his homework with his tutor, and was duly learning what is taught at High Schools. Everything was as it should be. After dinner, if they had no visitors, Iván Ilych sometimes read a book that was being much discussed at the time, and in the evening settled down to work, that is, read official papers, compared the depositions of witnesses, and noted paragraphs of the Code applying to them. This was neither dull nor amusing. It was dull when he might have been playing bridge, but if no bridge was available it was at any rate better than doing nothing or sitting with his wife. Iván Ilych's chief pleasure was giving little dinners to which he invited men and women of good social position, and just as his drawing-room resembled all other drawing-rooms so did his enjoyable little parties resemble all other such parties.

Once they even gave a dance. Iván Ilych enjoyed it and everything went off well, except that it led to a violent quarrel with his wife about the cakes and sweets. Praskóvya Fëdorovna had made her own plans, but Iván Ilych insisted on getting everything from an expensive confectioner and ordered too many cakes, and the quarrel occurred because some of those cakes were left over and the confectioner's bill came to forty-five rubles. It was a great and disagreeable quarrel. Praskóvya Fëdorovna called him "a fool and an imbecile," and he clutched at his head and made angry allusions to divorce.

But the dance itself had been enjoyable. The best people were there, and Iván Ilych had danced with Princess Trúfonova, a sister of the distinguished founder of the Society "Bear my Burden."

The pleasures connected with his work were pleasures of ambition; his social pleasures were those of vanity; but Iván Ilych's greatest pleasure was playing bridge. He acknowledged that whatever disagreeable incident happened in his life, the pleasure that beamed like a ray of light above everything else was to sit down to bridge with good players, not noisy partners, and of course to four-handed bridge (with five players it was annoying to have to stand out, though one pretended not to mind), to play a clever and serious game (when the cards allowed it) and then to have supper and drink a glass of wine. After a game of bridge, especially if he had won a little (to win a large sum was unpleasant), Iván Ilych went to bed in specially good humour.

So they lived. They formed a circle of acquaintances among the best people and were visited by people of importance and by young folk. In their views as to their acquaintances, husband, wife, and daughter were entirely agreed, and tacitly and unanimously kept at arm's length and shook off the various shabby friends and relations who, with much show of affection, gushed into the drawing-room with its Japanese plates on the walls. Soon these shabby friends ceased to obtrude themselves and only the best people remained in the Golovíns' set.

Young men made up to Lisa, and Petríshchev, an examining magistrate and Dmítri Ivánovich Petríshchev's son and sole heir, began to be so attentive to her that Iván Ilych had already spoken to Praskóvya Fëdorovna about it, and considered whether they should not arrange a party for them, or get up some private theatricals.

So they lived, and all went well, without change, and life flowed pleasantly.

They were all in good health. It could not be called ill health if Iván Ilych sometimes said that he had a queer taste in his mouth and felt some discomfort in his left side.

But this discomfort increased and, though not exactly painful, grew into a sense of pressure in his side accompanied by ill humour. And his irritability became worse and worse and began to mar the agreeable, easy, and correct life that had established itself in the Golovín family. Quarrels between husband and wife became more and more frequent, and soon the ease and amenity disappeared and even the decorum was barely maintained. Scenes again became frequent, and very few of those islets remained on which husband and wife could meet without an explosion. Praskóvya Fëdorovna now had good reason to say that her husband's temper was trying. With characteristic exaggeration she said he had always had a dreadful temper, and that it had needed all her good nature to put up with it for twenty years. It was true that now the quarrels were started by him. His bursts of temper always came just before dinner, often just as he began to eat his soup. Sometimes he noticed that a plate or dish was chipped, or the food was not right, or his son put his elbow on the table, or his daughter's hair was not done as he liked it, and for all this he blamed Praskóvya Fëdorovna. At first she retorted and said disagreeable things to him, but once or twice he fell into such a rage at the beginning of dinner that she realized it was due to some physical derangement brought on by taking food, and so she restrained herself and did not answer, but only hurried to get the dinner over. She regarded this self-restraint as highly praiseworthy. Having come to the conclusion that her husband had a dreadful temper and made her life miserable, she began to feel sorry for herself, and the more she pitied herself the more she hated her husband. She began to wish he would die; yet she did not want him to die because then his salary would cease. And this irritated her against him still more. She considered herself dreadfully unhappy just because not even his death could save her, and though she concealed her exasperation, that hidden exasperation of hers increased his irritation also.

After one scene in which Iván Ilych had been particularly unfair and after which he had said in explanation that he certainly was irritable but that it was due to his not being well, she said that if he was ill it should be attended to, and insisted on his going to see a celebrated doctor.

He went. Everything took place as he had expected and as it always does. There was the usual waiting and the important air assumed by the doctor, with which he was so familiar (resembling that which he himself assumed in court), and the sounding and listening, and the questions which called for answers that were foregone conclusions and were evidently unnecessary, and the look of importance which implied that "if only you put yourself in our hands we will arrange every-thing—we know indubitably how it has to be done, always in the same way for everybody alike." It was all just as it was in the law courts. The doctor put on just the same air towards him as he himself put on towards an accused person.

The doctor said that so-and-so indicated that there was so-and-so inside the patient, but if the investigation of so-and-so did not confirm this, then he must assume that and that. If he assumed that and that, then...and so on. To Iván Ilych only one question was important: was his case serious or not? But the doctor ignored that inappropriate question. From his point of view it was not the one under consideration, the real question was to decide between a floating kidney, chronic catarrh, or appendicitis. It was not a question of Iván Ilych's life or death, but one between a floating kidney and appendicitis. And that question the doctor solved brilliantly, as it seemed to Iván Ilych, in favour of the appendix, with the reservation that should an examination of the urine give fresh indications the matter would be reconsidered. All this was just what Iván Ilych had himself brilliantly accomplished a thousand times in dealing with men on trial. The doctor summed up just as brilliantly, looking over his spectacles triumphantly and even gaily at the accused. From the doctor's summing up Iván Ilych concluded that things were bad, but that for the doctor, and perhaps for everybody else, it was a matter of indifference, though for him it was bad. And this conclusion struck him painfully, arousing in him a great feeling of pity for himself and of bitterness towards the doctor's indifference to a matter of such importance.

He said nothing of this, but rose, placed the doctor's fee on the table, and remarked with a sigh: "We sick people probably often put inappropriate questions. But tell me, in general, is this complaint dangerous, or not?..."

The doctor looked at him sternly over his spectacles with one eye, as if to say: "Prisoner, if you will not keep to the questions put to you, I shall be obliged to have you removed from the court."

"I have already told you what I consider necessary and proper. The analysis may show something more." And the doctor bowed.

Iván Ilych went out slowly, seated himself disconsolately in his sledge, and drove home. All the way home he was going over what the doctor had said, trying to translate those complicated, obscure, scientific phrases into plain language and find in them an answer to the question: "Is my condition bad? Is it very bad? Or is there as yet nothing much wrong?" And it seemed to him that the meaning of what the doctor had said was that it was very bad. Everything in the streets seemed depressing. The cabmen, the houses, the passers-by, and the shops, were dismal. His ache, this dull gnawing ache that never ceased for a moment, seemed to have acquired a new and more serious significance from the doctor's dubious remarks. Iván Ilych now watched it with a new and oppressive feeling.

He reached home and began to tell his wife about it. She listened, but in the middle of his account his daughter came in with her hat on, ready to go out with her mother. She sat down reluctantly to listen to this tedious story, but could not stand it long, and her mother too did not hear him to the end.

"Well, I am very glad," she said. "Mind now to take your medicine regularly. Give me the prescription and I'll send Gerásim to the chemist's." And she went to get ready to go out.

While she was in the room Iván Ilych had hardly taken time to breathe, but he sighed deeply when she left it.

"Well," he thought, "perhaps it isn't so bad after all."

He began taking his medicine and following the doctor's directions, which had been altered after the examination of the urine. But then it happened that there was a contradiction between the indications drawn from the examination of the urine and the symptoms that showed themselves. It turned out that what was happening differed from what the doctor had told him, and that he had either forgotten, or blundered, or hidden something from him. He could not, however, be blamed for that, and Iván Ilych still obeyed his orders implicitly and at first derived some comfort from doing so.

From the time of his visit to the doctor, Iván Ilych's chief occupation was the exact fulfilment of the doctor's instructions regarding hygiene and the taking of medicine, and the observation of his pain and his excretions. His chief interests came to be people's ailments and people's health. When sickness, deaths, or recoveries were mentioned in his presence, especially when the illness resembled his own, he listened with agitation which he tried to hide, asked questions, and applied what he heard to his own case.

The pain did not grow less, but Iván Ilych made efforts to force himself to think that he was better. And he could do this so long as nothing agitated him. But as soon as he had any unpleasantness with his wife, any lack of success in his official work, or held bad cards at bridge, he was at once acutely sensible of his disease. He had formerly borne such mischances, hoping soon to adjust what was wrong, to master it and attain success, or make a grand slam. But now every mischance upset him and plunged him into despair. He would say to himself: "There now, just as I was beginning to get better and the medicine had begun to take effect, comes this accursed misfortune, or unpleasantness...." And he was furious with the mishap, or with the people who were causing the unpleasantness and killing him, for he felt that this fury was killing him but could not restrain it.

One would have thought that it should have been clear to him that this exasperation with circumstances and people aggravated his illness, and that he ought therefore to ignore unpleasant occurrences. But he drew the very opposite conclusion: he said that he needed peace, and he watched for everything that might disturb it and became irritable at the slightest infringement of it. His condition was rendered worse by the fact that he read medical books and consulted doctors. The progress of his disease was so gradual that he could deceive himself when comparing one day with another—the difference was so slight. But when he consulted the doctors it seemed to him that he was getting worse, and even very rapidly. Yet despite this he was continually consulting them.

That month he went to see another celebrity, who told him almost the same as the first had done but put his questions rather differently, and the interview with this celebrity only increased Iván Ilych's doubts and fears. A friend of a friend of his, a very good doctor, diagnosed his illness again quite differently from the others, and though he predicted recovery, his questions and suppositions bewildered Iván Ilych still more and increased his doubts. A homoeopathist diagnosed the disease in yet another way, and prescribed medicine which Iván Ilych took secretly for a week. But after a week, not feeling any improvement and having lost confidence both in the former doctor's treatment and in this one's, he became still more despondent. One day a lady acquaintance mentioned a cure effected by a wonder-working icon. Iván Ilych caught himself listening attentively and beginning to believe that it had occurred. This incident alarmed him. "Has my mind really weakened to such an extent?" he asked himself. "Nonsense! It's all rubbish. I mustn't give way to nervous fears but having chosen a doctor must keep strictly to his treatment. That is what I will do. Now it's all settled. I won't think about it, but will follow the treatment seriously till summer, and then we shall see. From now there must be no more of this wavering!" This was easy to say but impossible to carry out. The pain in his side oppressed him and seemed to grow worse and more incessant, while the taste in his mouth grew stranger and stranger. It seemed to him that his breath had a disgusting smell, and he was conscious of a loss of appetite and strength. There was no deceiving himself: something terrible, new, and more important than anything before in his life, was taking place within him of which he alone was aware. Those about him did not understand or would not understand it, but thought everything in the world was going on as usual. That tormented Iván Ilych more than anything. He saw that his household, especially his wife and daughter who were in a perfect whirl of visiting, did not understand anything of it and were annoyed that he was so depressed and so exacting, as if he were to blame for it. Though they tried to disguise it he saw that he was an obstacle in their path, and that his wife had adopted a definite line in regard to his illness and kept to it regardless of anything he said or did. Her attitude was this: "You know," she would say to her friends, "Iván Ilych can't do as other people do, and keep to the treatment prescribed for him. One day he'll take his drops and keep strictly to his diet and go to bed in good time, but the next day unless I watch him he'll suddenly forget his medicine, eat sturgeon—which is forbidden—and sit up playing cards till one o'clock in the morning."

"Oh, come, when was that?" Iván Ilych would ask in vexation. "Only once at Peter Ivánovich's."

"And yesterday with Shébek."

"Well, even if I hadn't stayed up, this pain would have kept me awake."

"Be that as it may you'll never get well like that, but will always make us wretched."

Praskóvya Fëdorovna's attitude to Iván Ilych's illness, as she expressed it both to others and to him, was that it was his own fault and was another of the annoyances he caused her. Iván Ilych felt that this opinion escaped her involuntarily—but that did not make it easier for him.

At the law courts too, Iván Ilych noticed, or thought he noticed, a strange attitude towards himself. It sometimes seemed to him that people were watching him inquisitively as a man whose place might soon be vacant. Then again, his friends would suddenly begin to chaff him in a friendly way about his low spirits, as if the awful, horrible, and unheard-of thing that was going on within him, incessantly gnawing at him and irresistibly drawing him away, was a very agreeable subject for jests. Schwartz in particular irritated him by his jocularity, vivacity, and *savoir-faire*, which reminded him of what he himself had been ten years ago.

Friends came to make up a set and they sat down to cards. They dealt, bending the new cards to soften them, and he sorted the diamonds in his hand and found he had seven. His partner said "No trumps" and supported him with two diamonds. What more could be wished for? It ought to be jolly and lively. They would make a grand slam. But suddenly Iván Ilych was conscious of that gnawing pain, that taste in his mouth, and it seemed ridiculous that in such circumstances he should be pleased to make a grand slam.

He looked at his partner Mikháil Mikháylovich, who rapped the table with his strong hand and instead of snatching up the tricks pushed the cards courteously and indulgently towards Iván Ilych that he might have the pleasure of gathering them up without the trouble of stretching out his hand for them. "Does he think I am too weak to stretch out my arm?" thought Iván Ilych, and forgetting what he was doing he over-trumped his partner, missing the grand slam by three tricks. And what was most awful of all was that he saw how upset Mikháil Mikháylovich was about it but did not himself care. And it was dreadful to realize why he did not care.

They all saw that he was suffering, and said: "We can stop if you are tired. Take a rest." Lie down? No, he was not at all tired, and he finished the rubber. All were gloomy and silent. Iván Ilych felt that he had diffused this gloom over them and could not dispel it. They had supper and went away, and Iván Ilych was left alone with the consciousness that his life was poisoned and was poisoning the lives of others, and that this poison did not weaken but penetrated more and more deeply into his whole being.

With this consciousness, and with physical pain besides the terror, he must go to bed, often to lie awake the greater part of the night. Next morning he had to get up again, dress, go to the law courts, speak, and write; or if he did not go out, spend at home those twenty-four hours a day each of which was a torture. And he had to live thus all alone on the brink of an abyss, with no one who understood or pitied him.

So one month passed and then another. Just before the New Year his brother-in-law came to town and stayed at their house. Iván Ilych was at the law courts and Praskóvya Fëdorovna had gone shopping. When Iván Ilych came home and entered his study he found his brother-in-law there—a healthy, florid man—unpacking his portmanteau himself. He raised his head on hearing Iván Ilych's footsteps and looked up at him for a moment without a word. That stare told Iván Ilych everything. His brother-in-law opened his mouth to utter an exclamation of surprise but checked himself, and that action confirmed it all.

"I have changed, eh?"

"Yes, there is a change."

And after that, try as he would to get his brother-in-law to return to the subject of his looks, the latter would say nothing about it. Praskóvya Fëdorovna came home and her brother went out to her. Iván Ilych locked the door and began to examine himself in the glass, first full face, then in profile. He took up a portrait of himself taken with his wife, and compared it with what he saw in the glass. The change in him was immense. Then he bared his arms to the elbow, looked at them, drew the sleeves down again, sat down on an ottoman, and grew blacker than night.

"No, no, this won't do!" he said to himself, and jumped up, went to the table, took up some law papers and began to read them, but could not continue. He unlocked the door and went into the reception-room. The door leading to the drawing-room was shut. He approached it on tiptoe and listened.

"No, you are exaggerating!" Praskóvya Fëdorovna was saying.

"Exaggerating! Don't you see it? Why, he's a dead man! Look at his eyes—there's no light in them. But what is it that is wrong with him?"

"No one knows. Nikoláevich [that was another doctor] said something, but I don't know what. And Leshchetítsky [this was the celebrated specialist] said quite the contrary. . . ."

Iván Ilych walked away, went to his own room, lay down, and began musing: "The kidney, a floating kidney." He recalled all the doctors had told him of how it detached itself and swayed about. And by an effort of imagination he tried to catch that kidney and arrest it and support it. So little was needed for this, it seemed to him. "No, I'll go to see Peter Ivánovich again." [That was the friend whose friend was a doctor.] He rang, ordered the carriage, and got ready to go.

"Where are you going, Jean?" asked his wife, with a specially sad and exceptionally kind look.

This exceptionally kind look irritated him. He looked morosely at her.

"I must go to see Peter Ivánovich."

He went to see Peter Ivánovich, and together they went to see his friend, the doctor. He was in, and Iván Ilych had a long talk with him.

Reviewing the anatomical and physiological details of what in the doctor's opinion was going on inside him, he understood it all.

There was something, a small thing, in the vermiform appendix. It might all come right. Only stimulate the energy of one organ and check the activity of another, then absorption would take place and everything would come right. He got home rather late for dinner, ate his dinner, and conversed cheerfully, but could not for a long time bring himself to go back to work in his room. At last, however, he went to his study and did what was necessary, but the consciousness that he had put something aside—an important, intimate matter which he would revert to when his work was done—never left him. When he had finished his work he remembered that this intimate matter was the thought of his vermiform appendix. But he did not give himself up to it, and went to the drawing-room for tea. There were callers there, including the examining magistrate who was a desirable match for his daughter, and they were conversing, playing the piano, and singing. Iván Ilych, as Praskóvya Fëdorovna remarked, spent that evening more cheerfully than usual, but he never for a moment forgot that he had postponed the important matter of the appendix. At eleven o'clock he said good-night and went to his bedroom. Since his illness he had slept alone in a small room next to his study. He undressed and took up a novel by Zola, but instead of reading it he fell into thought, and in his imagination that desired improvement in the vermiform appendix occurred. There was the absorption and evacuation and the re-establishment of normal activity. "Yes, that's it!" he said to himself. "One need only assist nature, that's all." He remembered his medicine, rose, took it, and lay down on his back watching for the beneficent action of the medicine and for it to lessen the pain. "I need only take it regularly and avoid all injurious influences. I am already feeling better, much better." He began touching his side: it was not painful to the touch. "There, I really don't feel it. It's much better already." He put out the light and turned on his side.... "The appendix is getting better, absorption is occurring." Suddenly he felt the old, familiar, dull, gnawing pain, stubborn and serious. There was the same familiar loathsome taste in his mouth. His heart sank and he felt dazed. "My God! My God!" he muttered. "Again, again! And it will never cease." And suddenly the matter presented itself in a quite different aspect. "Vermiform appendix! Kidney!" he said to himself. "It's not a question of appendix or kidney, but of life and...death. Yes, life was there and now it is going, going and I cannot stop it. Yes. Why deceive myself? Isn't it obvious to everyone but me that I'm dying, and that it's only a question of weeks, days...it may happen this moment. There was light and now there is darkness. I was here and now I'm going there! Where?" A chill came over him, his breathing ceased, and he felt only the throbbing of his heart.

"When I am not, what will there be? There will be nothing. Then where shall I be when I am no more? Can this be dying? No, I don't want to!" He jumped up and tried to light the candle, felt for it with trembling hands, dropped candle and candlestick on the floor, and fell back on his pillow.

"What's the use? It makes no difference," he said to himself, staring with wide-open eyes into the darkness. "Death. Yes, death. And none of them know or wish to know it, and they have no pity for me. Now they are playing." (He heard through the door the distant sound of a song and its accompaniment.) "It's all the same to them, but they will die too! Fools! I first, and they later, but it will be the same for them. And now they are merry...the beasts!"

Anger choked him and he was agonizingly, unbearably miserable. "It is impossible that all men have been doomed to suffer this awful horror!" He raised himself.

"Something must be wrong. I must calm myself—must think it all over from the beginning." And he again began thinking. "Yes, the beginning of my illness: I knocked my side, but I was still quite well that day and the next. It hurt a little, then rather more. I saw the doctors, then followed despondency and anguish, more doctors, and I drew nearer to the abyss. My strength grew less and I kept coming nearer and nearer, and now I have wasted away and there is no light in my eyes. I think of the appendix—but this is death! I think of mending the appendix, and all the while here is death! Can it really be death?" Again terror seized him and he gasped for breath. He leant down and began feeling for the matches, pressing with his elbow on the stand beside the bed. It was in his way and hurt him, he grew furious with it, pressed on it still harder, and upset it. Breathless and in despair he fell on his back, expecting death to come immediately.

Meanwhile the visitors were leaving. Praskóvya Fëdorovna was seeing them off. She heard something fall and came in.

"What has happened?"

"Nothing. I knocked it over accidentally."

She went out and returned with a candle. He lay there panting heavily, like a man who has run a thousand yards, and stared upwards at her with a fixed look.

"What is it, Jean?"

"No...o...thing. I upset it." ("Why speak of it? She won't understand," he thought.)

And in truth she did not understand. She picked up the stand, lit his candle, and hurried away to see another visitor off. When she came back he still lay on his back, looking upwards.

"What is it? Do you feel worse?"

"Yes."

She shook her head and sat down.

"Do you know, Jean, I think we must ask Leshchetítsky to come and see you here."

This meant calling in the famous specialist, regardless of expense. He smiled malignantly and said "No." She remained a little longer and then went up to him and kissed his forehead.

While she was kissing him he hated her from the bottom of his soul and with difficulty refrained from pushing her away.

"Good-night. Please God you'll sleep."

"Yes."

Iván Ilych saw that he was dying, and he was in continual despair.

In the depth of his heart he knew he was dying, but not only was he not accustomed to the thought, he simply did not and could not grasp it.

The syllogism he had learned from Kiezewetter's Logic: "Caius is a man, men are mortal, therefore Caius is mortal," had always seemed to him correct as applied to Caius, but certainly not as applied to himself. That Caius—man in the abstract—was mortal, was perfectly correct, but he was not Caius, not an abstract man, but a creature quite, quite separate from all others. He had been little Ványa, with a mamma and a papa, with Mítya and Volódya, with the toys, a coachman and a nurse, afterwards with Kátenka and with all the joys, griefs, and delights of childhood, boyhood, and youth. What did Caius know of the smell of that striped leather ball Ványa had been so fond of? Had Caius kissed his mother's hand like that, and did the silk of her dress rustle so for Caius? Had he rioted like that at school when the pastry was bad? Had Caius been in love like that? Could Caius preside at a session as he did? "Caius really was mortal, and it was right for him to die; but for me, little Ványa, Iván Ilych, with all my thoughts and emotions, it's altogether a different matter. It cannot be that I ought to die. That would be too terrible."

Such was his feeling.

"If I had to die like Caius I should have known it was so. An inner voice would have told me so, but there was nothing of the sort in me and I and all my friends felt that our case was quite different from that of Caius. And now here it is!" he said to himself. "It can't be. It's impossible! But here it is. How is this? How is one to understand it?"

He could not understand it, and tried to drive this false, incorrect, morbid thought away and to replace it by other proper and healthy thoughts. But that thought, and not the thought only but the reality itself, seemed to come and confront him.

And to replace that thought he called up a succession of others, hoping to find in them some support. He tried to get back into the former current of thoughts that had once screened the thought of death from him. But strange to say, all that had formerly shut off, hidden, and destroyed, his consciousness of death, no longer had that effect. Iván Ilych now spent most of his time in attempting to re-establish that old current. He would say to himself: "I will take up my duties again—after all I used to live by them." And banishing all doubts he would go to the law courts, enter into conversation with his colleagues, and sit carelessly as was his wont, scanning the crowd with a thoughtful look and leaning both his emaciated arms on the arms of his oak chair; bending over as usual to a colleague and drawing his papers nearer he would interchange whispers with him, and then suddenly raising his eyes and sitting erect would pronounce certain words and open the proceedings. But suddenly in the midst of those proceedings the pain in his side, regardless of the stage the proceedings had reached, would begin its own gnawing work. Iván Ilych would turn his attention to it and try to drive the thought of it away, but without success. *It* would come and stand before him and look at him, and he would be petrified and the light would die out of his eyes, and he would again begin asking himself whether *It* alone was true. And his colleagues and subordinates would see with surprise and distress that he, the brilliant and subtle judge, was becoming confused and making mistakes. He would shake himself, try to pull himself together, manage somehow to bring the sitting to a close, and return home with the sorrowful consciousness that his judicial labours could not as formerly hide from him what he wanted them to hide, and could not deliver him from *It*. And what was worst of all was that *It* drew his attention to itself not in order to make him take some action but only that he should look at *It,* look it straight in the face: look at it without doing anything, suffer inexpressibly.

And to save himself from this condition Iván Ilych looked for consolations—new screens—and new screens were found and for a while seemed to save him, but then they immediately fell to pieces or rather became transparent, as if *It* penetrated them and nothing could veil *It*.

In these latter days he would go into the drawing-room he had arranged—that drawing-room where he had fallen and for the sake of which (how bitterly ridiculous it seemed) he had sacrificed his life—for he knew that his illness originated with that knock. He would enter and see that something had scratched the polished table. He would look for the cause of this and find that it was the bronze ornamentation of an album, that had got bent. He would take up the expensive album which he had lovingly arranged, and feel vexed with his daughter and her friends for their untidiness—for the album was torn here and there and some of the photographs turned upside down. He would put it carefully in order and bend the ornamentation back into position. Then it would occur to him to place all those things in another corner of the room, near the plants. He would call the footman, but his daughter or wife would come to help him. They would not agree, and his wife would contradict him, and he would dispute and grow angry. But that was all right, for then he did not think about *It*. *It* was invisible.

But then, when he was moving something himself, his wife would say: "Let the servants do it. You will hurt yourself again." And suddenly *It* would flash through the screen and he would see it. It was just a flash, and he hoped it would disappear, but he would involuntarily pay attention to his side. "It sits there as before, gnawing just the same!" And he could no longer forget *It,* but could distinctly see it looking at him from behind the flowers. "What is it all for?"

"It really is so! I lost my life over that curtain as I might have done when storming a fort. Is that possible? How terrible and how stupid. It can't be true! It can't, but it is."

He would go to his study, lie down, and again be alone with *It*: face to face with *It*. And nothing could be done with *It* except to look at it and shudder.

How it happened it is impossible to say because it came about step by step, unnoticed, but in the third month of Iván Ilych's illness, his wife, his daughter, his son, his acquaintances, the doctors, the servants, and above all he himself, were aware that the whole interest he had for other people was whether he would soon vacate his place, and at last release the living from the discomfort caused by his presence and be himself released from his sufferings.

He slept less and less. He was given opium and hypodermic injections of morphine, but this did not relieve him. The dull depression he experienced in a somnolent condition at first gave him a little relief, but only as something new, afterwards it became as distressing as the pain itself or even more so.

Special foods were prepared for him by the doctors' orders, but all those foods became increasingly distasteful and disgusting to him.

For his excretions also special arrangements had to be made, and this was a torment to him every time—a torment from the uncleanliness, the unseemliness, and the smell, and from knowing that another person had to take part in it.

But just through this most unpleasant matter, Iván Ilych obtained comfort. Gerásim, the butler's young assistant, always came in to carry the things out. Gerásim was a clean, fresh peasant lad, grown stout on town food and always cheerful and bright. At first the sight of him, in his clean Russian peasant costume, engaged on that disgusting task embarrassed Iván Ilych.

Once when he got up from the commode too weak to draw up his trousers, he dropped into a soft armchair and looked with horror at his bare, enfeebled thighs with the muscles so sharply marked on them.

Gerásim with a firm light tread, his heavy boots emitting a pleasant smell of tar and fresh winter air, came in wearing a clean Hessian apron, the sleeves of his print shirt tucked up over his strong bare young arms; and refraining from looking at his sick master out of consideration for his feelings, and restraining the joy of life that beamed from his face, he went up to the commode.

"Gerásim!" said Iván Ilych in a weak voice.

Gerásim started, evidently afraid he might have committed some blunder, and with a rapid movement turned his fresh, kind, simple young face which just showed the first downy signs of a beard.

"Yes, sir?"

"That must be very unpleasant for you. You must forgive me. I am helpless."

"Oh, why, sir," and Gerásim's eyes beamed and he showed his glistening white teeth, "what's a little trouble? It's a case of illness with you, sir."

And his deft strong hands did their accustomed task, and he went out of the room stepping lightly. Five minutes later he as lightly returned.

Iván Ilych was still sitting in the same position in the armchair.

"Gerásim," he said when the latter had replaced the freshly washed utensil. "Please come here and help me." Gerásim went up to him. "Lift me up. It is hard for me to get up, and I have sent Dmítri away."

Gerásim went up to him, grasped his master with his strong arms deftly but gently, in the same way that he stepped—lifted him, supported him with one hand, and with the other drew up his trousers and would have set him down again, but Iván Ilych asked to be led to the sofa. Gerásim, without an effort and without apparent pressure, led him, almost lifting him, to the sofa and placed him on it.

"Thank you. How easily and well you do it all!"

Gerásim smiled again and turned to leave the room. But Iván Ilych felt his presence such a comfort that he did not want to let him go.

"One thing more, please move up that chair. No, the other one—under my feet. It is easier for me when my feet are raised."

Gerásim brought the chair, set it down gently in place, and raised Iván Ilych's legs on to it. It seemed to Iván Ilych that he felt better while Gerásim was holding up his legs.

"It's better when my legs are higher," he said. "Place that cushion under them."

Gerásim did so. He again lifted the legs and placed them, and again Iván Ilych

felt better while Gerásim held his legs. When he set them down Iván Ilych fancied
he felt worse.

"Gerásim," he said. "Are you busy now?"

"Not at all, sir," said Gerásim, who had learnt from the townsfolk how to speak
to gentlefolk.

"What have you still to do?"

"What have I to do? I've done everything except chopping the logs for
to-morrow."

"Then hold my legs up a bit higher, can you?"

"Of course I can. Why not?" And Gerásim raised his master's legs higher and
Iván Ilych thought that in that position he did not feel any pain at all.

"And how about the logs?"

"Don't trouble about that, sir. There's plenty of time."

Iván Ilych told Gerásim to sit down and hold his legs, and began to talk to him.
And strange to say it seemed to him that he felt better while Gerásim held his legs
up.

After that Iván Ilych would sometimes call Gerásim and get him to hold his
legs on his shoulders, and he liked talking to him. Gerásim did it all easily, willingly,
simply, and with a good nature that touched Iván Ilych. Health, strength, and
vitality in other people were offensive to him, but Gerásim's strength and vitality
did not mortify but soothed him.

What tormented Iván Ilych most was the deception, the lie, which for some
reason they all accepted, that he was not dying but was simply ill, and that he only
need keep quiet and undergo a treatment and then something very good would
result. He however knew that do what they would nothing would come of it, only
still more agonizing suffering and death. This deception tortured him—their not
wishing to admit what they all knew and what he knew, but wanting to lie to him
concerning his terrible condition, and wishing and forcing him to participate in
that lie. Those lies—lies enacted over him on the eve of his death and destined to
degrade this awful, solemn act to the level of their visitings, their curtains, their
sturgeon for dinner—were a terrible agony for Iván Ilych. And strangely enough,
many times when they were going through their antics over him he had been
within a hairbreadth of calling out to them: "Stop lying! You know and I know
that I am dying. Then at least stop lying about it!" But he had never had the
spirit to do it. The awful, terrible act of his dying was, he could see, reduced by
those about him to the level of a casual, unpleasant, and almost indecorous incident
(as if someone entered a drawing-room diffusing an unpleasant odour) and this
was done by that very decorum which he had served all his life long. He saw that
no one felt for him, because no one even wished to grasp his position. Only
Gerásim recognized and pitied him. And so Iván Ilych felt at ease only with him.
He felt comforted when Gerásim supported his legs (sometimes all night long)
and refused to go to bed, saying: "Don't you worry, Iván Ilych. I'll get sleep
enough later on," or when he suddenly became familiar and exclaimed: "If you
weren't sick it would be another matter, but as it is, why should I grudge a little
trouble?" Gerásim alone did not lie; everything showed that he alone understood

the facts of the case and did not consider it necessary to disguise them, but simply felt sorry for his emaciated and enfeebled master. Once when Iván Ilych was sending him away he even said straight out: 'We shall all of us die, so why should I grudge a little trouble?"—expressing the fact that he did not think his work burdensome, because he was doing it for a dying man and hoped someone would do the same for him when his time came.

Apart from this lying, or because of it, what most tormented Iván Ilych was that no one pitied him as he wished to be pitied. At certain moments after prolonged suffering he wished most of all (though he would have been ashamed to confess it) for someone to pity him as a sick child is pitied. He longed to be petted and comforted. He knew he was an important functionary, that he had a beard turning grey, and that therefore what he longed for was impossible, but still he longed for it. And in Gerásim's attitude towards him there was something akin to what he wished for, and so that attitude comforted him. Iván Ilych wanted to weep, wanted to be petted and cried over, and then his colleague Shébek would come, and instead of weeping and being petted, Iván Ilych would assume a serious, severe, and profound air, and by force of habit would express his opinion on a decision of the Court of Cassation and would stubbornly insist on that view. This falsity around him and within him did more than anything else to poison his last days.

It was morning. He knew it was morning because Gerásim had gone, and Peter the footman had come and put out the candles, drawn back one of the curtains, and begun quietly to tidy up. Whether it was morning or evening, Friday or Sunday, made no difference, it was all just the same: the gnawing, unmitigated, agonizing pain, never ceasing for an instant, the consciousness of life inexorably waning but not yet extinguished, the approach of that ever dreaded and hateful Death which was the only reality, and always the same falsity. What were days, weeks, hours, in such a case?

"Will you have some tea, sir?"

"He wants things to be regular, and wishes the gentlefolk to drink tea in the morning," thought Iván Ilych, and only said "No."

"Wouldn't you like to move onto the sofa, sir?"

"He wants to tidy up the room, and I'm in the way. I am uncleanliness and disorder," he thought, and said only:

"No, leave me alone."

The man went on bustling about. Iván Ilych stretched out his hand. Peter came up, ready to help.

"What is it, sir?"

"My watch."

Peter took the watch which was close at hand and gave it to his master.

"Half-past eight. Are they up?"

"No sir, except Vladímir Ivánich" (the son) "who has gone to school. Praskóvya Fëdorovna ordered me to wake her if you asked for her. Shall I do so?"

"No, there's no need to." "Perhaps I'd better have some tea," he thought, and added aloud: "Yes, bring me some tea."

Peter went to the door, but Iván Ilych dreaded being left alone. "How can I keep him here? Oh yes, my medicine." "Peter, give me my medicine." "Why not? Perhaps it may still do me some good." He took a spoonful and swallowed it. "No, it won't help. It's all tomfoolery, all deception," he decided as soon as he became aware of the familiar, sickly, hopeless taste. "No, I can't believe in it any longer. But the pain, why this pain? If it would only cease just for a moment!" And he moaned. Peter turned towards him. "It's all right. Go and fetch me some tea."

Peter went out. Left alone Iván Ilych groaned not so much with pain, terrible though that was, as from mental anguish. Always and forever the same, always these endless days and nights. If only it would come quicker! If only *what* would come quicker? Death, darkness?...No, no! Anything rather than death!

When Peter returned with the tea on a tray, Iván Ilych stared at him for a time in perplexity, not realizing who and what he was. Peter was disconcerted by that look and his embarrassment brought Iván Ilych to himself.

"Oh, tea! All right, put it down. Only help me to wash and put on a clean shirt."

And Iván Ilych began to wash. With pauses for rest, he washed his hands and then his face, cleaned his teeth, brushed his hair, and looked in the glass. He was terrified by what he saw, especially by the limp way in which his hair clung to his pallid forehead.

While his shirt was being changed he knew that he would be still more frightened at the sight of his body, so he avoided looking at it. Finally he was ready. He drew on a dressing-gown, wrapped himself in a plaid, and sat down in the armchair to take his tea. For a moment he felt refreshed, but as soon as he began to drink the tea he was again aware of the same taste, and the pain also returned. He finished it with an effort, and then lay down stretching out his legs, and dismissed Peter.

Always the same. Now a spark of hope flashes up, then a sea of despair rages, and always pain; always pain, always despair, and always the same. When alone he had a dreadful and distressing desire to call someone, but he knew beforehand that with others present it would be still worse. "Another dose of morphine—to lose consciousness. I will tell him, the doctor, that he must think of something else. It's impossible, impossible, to go on like this."

An hour and another pass like that. But now there is a ring at the door bell. Perhaps it's the doctor? It is. He comes in fresh, hearty, plump, and cheerful, with that look on his face that seems to say: "There now, you're in a panic about something, but we'll arrange it all for you directly!" The doctor knows this expression is out of place here, but he has put it on once for all and can't take it off—like a man who has put on a frock-coat in the morning to pay a round of calls.

The doctor rubs his hands vigorously and reassuringly.

"Brr! How cold it is! There's such a sharp frost; just let me warm myself!" he says, as if it were only a matter of waiting till he was warm, and then he would put everything right.

"Well now, how are you?"

Iván Ilych feels that the doctor would like to say: "Well, how are our affairs?" but that even he feels that this would not do, and says instead: "What sort of a night have you had?"

Iván Ilych looks at him as much as to say: "Are you really never ashamed of lying?" But the doctor does not wish to understand this question, and Iván Ilych says: "Just as terrible as ever. The pain never leaves me and never subsides. If only something. . . ."

"Yes, you sick people are always like that. . . . There, now I think I'm warm enough. Even Praskóvya Fëdorovna, who is so particular, could find no fault with my temperature. Well, now I can say good-morning," and the doctor presses his patient's hand.

Then, dropping his former playfulness, he begins with a most serious face to examine the patient, feeling his pulse and taking his temperature, and then begins the sounding and auscultation.

Iván Ilych knows quite well and definitely that all this is nonsense and pure deception, but when the doctor, getting down on his knee, leans over him, putting his ear first higher then lower, and performs various gymnastic movements over him with a significant expression on his face, Iván Ilych submits to it all as he used to submit to the speeches of the lawyers, though he knew very well that they were all lying and why they were lying.

The doctor, kneeling on the sofa, is still sounding him when Praskóvya Fëdorovna's silk dress rustles at the door and she is heard scolding Peter for not having let her know of the doctor's arrival.

She comes in, kisses her husband, and at once proceeds to prove that she has been up a long time already, and only owing to a misunderstanding failed to be there when the doctor arrived.

Iván Ilych looks at her, scans her all over, sets against her the whiteness and plumpness and cleanness of her hands and neck, the gloss of her hair, and the sparkle of her vivacious eyes. He hates her with his whole soul. And the thrill of hatred he feels for her makes him suffer from her touch.

Her attitude towards him and his disease is still the same. Just as the doctor had adopted a certain relation to his patient which he could not abandon, so had she formed one towards him—that he was not doing something he ought to do and was himself to blame, and that she reproached him lovingly for this—and she could not now change that attitude.

"You see he doesn't listen to me and doesn't take his medicine at the proper time. And above all he lies in a position that is no doubt bad for him—with his legs up."

She described how he made Gerásim hold his legs up.

The doctor smiled with a contemptuous affability that said: "What's to be done? These sick people do have foolish fancies of that kind, but we must forgive them."

When the examination was over the doctor looked at his watch, and then Praskóvya Fëdorovna announced to Iván Ilych that it was of course as he pleased, but she had sent to-day for a celebrated specialist who would examine him and have a consultation with Michael Danílovich (their regular doctor).

"Please don't raise any objections. I am doing this for my own sake," she said ironically, letting it be felt that she was doing it all for his sake and only said this to leave him no right to refuse. He remained silent, knitting his brows. He felt that he was so surrounded and involved in a mesh of falsity that it was hard to unravel anything.

Everything she did for him was entirely for her own sake, and she told him she was doing for herself what she actually was doing for herself, as if that was so incredible that he must understand the opposite.

At half-past eleven the celebrated specialist arrived. Again the sounding began and the significant conversations in his presence and in another room, about the kidneys and the appendix, and the questions and answers, with such an air of importance that again, instead of the real question of life and death which now alone confronted him, the question arose of the kidney and the appendix which were not behaving as they ought to and would now be attacked by Michael Danílovich and the specialist and forced to amend their ways.

The celebrated specialist took leave of him with a serious though not hopeless look, and in reply to the timid question Iván Ilych, with eyes glistening with fear and hope, put to him as to whether there was a chance of recovery, said that he could not vouch for it but there was a possibility. The look of hope with which Iván Ilych watched the doctor out was so pathetic that Praskóvya Fëdorovna, seeing it, even wept as she left the room to hand the doctor his fee.

The gleam of hope kindled by the doctor's encouragement did not last long. The same room, the same pictures, curtains, wall-paper, medicine bottles, were all there, and the same aching suffering body, and Iván Ilych began to moan. They gave him a subcutaneous injection and he sank into oblivion.

It was twilight when he came to. They brought him his dinner and he swallowed some beef tea with difficulty, and then everything was the same again and night was coming on.

After dinner, at seven o'clock, Praskóvya Fëdorovna came into the room in evening dress, her full bosom pushed up by her corset, and with traces of powder on her face. She had reminded him in the morning that they were going to the theatre. Sarah Bernhardt was visiting the town and they had a box, which he had insisted on their taking. Now he had forgotten about it and her toilet offended him, but he concealed his vexation when he remembered that he had himself insisted on their securing a box and going because it would be an instructive and aesthetic pleasure for the children.

Praskóvya Fëdorovna came in, self-satisfied but yet with a rather guilty air. She sat down and asked how he was, but, as he saw, only for the sake of asking and not in order to learn about it, knowing that there was nothing to learn—and then went on to what she really wanted to say: that she would not on any account have gone but that the box had been taken and Helen and their daughter were going, as well as Petríshchev (the examining magistrate, their daughter's fiancé) and that it was out of the question to let them go alone; but that she would have much preferred to sit with him for a while; and he must be sure to follow the doctor's orders while she was away.

"Oh, and Fëdor Petróvich" (the fiancé) "would like to come in. May he? And Lisa?"

"All right."

Their daughter came in full evening dress, her fresh young flesh exposed (making a show of that very flesh which in his own case caused so much suffering), strong, healthy, evidently in love, and impatient with illness, suffering, and death, because they interfered with her happiness.

Fëdor Petróvich came in too, in evening dress, his hair curled *à la Capoul,* a tight stiff collar round his long sinewy neck, an enormous white shirt-front and narrow black trousers tightly stretched over his strong thighs. He had one white glove tightly drawn on, and was holding his opera hat in his hand.

Following him the schoolboy crept in unnoticed, in a new uniform, poor little fellow, and wearing gloves. Terribly dark shadows showed under his eyes, the meaning of which Iván Ilych knew well.

His son had always seemed pathetic to him, and now it was dreadful to see the boy's frightened look of pity. It seemed to Iván Ilych that Vásya was the only one besides Gerásim who understood and pitied him.

They all sat down and again asked how he was. A silence followed. Lisa asked her mother about the opera-glasses, and there was an altercation between mother and daughter as to who had taken them and where they had been put. This occasioned some unpleasantness.

Fëdor Petróvich inquired of Iván Ilych whether he had ever seen Sarah Bernhardt. Iván Ilych did not at first catch the question, but then replied: "No, have you seen her before?"

"Yes, in *Adrienne Lecouvreur.*"

Praskóvya Fëdorovna mentioned some rôles in which Sarah Bernhardt was particularly good. Her daughter disagreed. Conversation sprang up as to the elegance and realism of her acting—the sort of conversation that is always repeated and is always the same.

In the midst of the conversation Fëdor Petróvich glanced at Iván Ilych and became silent. The others also looked at him and grew silent. Iván Ilych was staring with glittering eyes straight before him, evidently indignant with them. This had to be rectified, but it was impossible to do so. The silence had to be broken, but for a time no one dared to break it and they all became afraid that the conventional deception would suddenly become obvious and the truth become plain to all. Lisa was the first to pluck up courage and break that silence, but by trying to hide what everybody was feeling, she betrayed it.

"Well, if we are going it's time to start," she said, looking at her watch, a present from her father, and with a faint and significant smile at Fëdor Petróvich relating to something known only to them. She got up with a rustle of her dress.

They all rose, said good-night, and went away.

When they had gone it seemed to Iván Ilych that he felt better; the falsity had gone with them. But the pain remained—that same pain and that same fear that made everything monotonously alike, nothing harder and nothing easier. Everything was worse.

Again minute followed minute and hour followed hour. Everything remained the same and there was no cessation. And the inevitable end of it all became more and more terrible.

"Yes, send Gerásim here," he replied to a question Peter asked.

His wife returned late at night. She came in on tiptoe, but he heard her, opened his eyes, and made haste to close them again. She wished to send Gerásim away and to sit with him herself, but he opened his eyes and said: "No, go away."

"Are you in great pain?"

"Always the same."

"Take some opium."

He agreed and took some. She went away.

Till about three in the morning he was in a state of stupefied misery. It seemed to him that he and his pain were being thrust into a narrow, deep black sack, but though they were pushed further and further in they could not be pushed to the bottom. And this, terrible enough in itself, was accompanied by suffering. He was frightened yet wanted to fall through the sack, he struggled but yet co-operated. And suddenly he broke though, fell, and regained consciousness. Gerásim was sitting at the foot of the bed dozing quietly and patiently, while he himself lay with his emaciated stockinged legs resting on Gerásim's shoulders; the same shaded candle was there and the same unceasing pain.

"Go away, Gerásim," he whispered.

"It's all right, sir. I'll stay a while."

"No. Go away."

He removed his legs from Gerásim's shoulders, turned sideways onto his arm, and felt sorry for himself. He only waited till Gerásim had gone into the next room and then restrained himself no longer but wept like a child. He wept on account of his helplessness, his terrible loneliness, the cruelty of man, the cruelty of God, and the absence of God.

"Why hast Thou done all this? Why hast Thou brought me here? Why dost Thou torment me so terribly?"

He did not expect an answer and yet wept because there was no answer and could be none. The pain again grew more acute, but he did not stir and did not call. He said to himself: "Go on! Strike me! But what is it for? What have I done to Thee? What is it for?"

Then he grew quiet and not only ceased weeping but even held his breath and became all attention. It was as though he were listening not to an audible voice but to a voice of his soul, to the current of thoughts arising within him.

"What is it you want?" was the first clear conception capable of expression in words, that he heard.

"What do you want? What do you want?" he repeated to himself.

"What do I want? To live and not to suffer," he answered.

And again he listened with such concentrated attention that even his pain did not distract him.

"To live? How?" asked his inner voice.

"Why, to live as I used to—well and pleasantly."

"As you lived before, well and pleasantly?" the voice repeated.

And in imagination he began to recall the best moments of his pleasant life. But strange to say none of those best moments of his pleasant life now seemed at all what they had then seemed—none of them except the first recollections of childhood. There, in childhood, there had been something really pleasant with which it would be possible to live if it could return. But the child who had experienced that happiness existed no longer, it was like a reminiscence of somebody else.

As soon as the period began which had produced the present Iván Ilych, all that had then seemed joys now melted before his sight and turned into something trivial and often nasty.

And the further he departed from childhood and the nearer he came to the present the more worthless and doubtful were the joys. This began with the School of Law. A little that was really good was still found there—there was light-heartedness, friendship, and hope. But in the upper classes there had already been fewer of such good moments. Then during the first years of his official career, when he was in the service of the Governor, some pleasant moments again occurred: they were the memories of love for a woman. Then all became confused and there was still less of what was good; later on again there was still less that was good, and the further he went the less there was. His marriage, a mere accident, then the disenchantment that followed it, his wife's bad breath and the sensuality and hypocrisy: then that deadly official life and those preoccupations about money, a year of it, and two, and ten, and twenty, and always the same thing. And the longer it lasted the more deadly it became. "It is as if I had been going downhill while I imagined I was going up. And that is really what it was. I was going up in public opinion, but to the same extent life was ebbing away from me. And now it is all done and there is only death."

"Then what does it mean? Why? It can't be that life is so senseless and horrible. But if it really has been so horrible and senseless, why must I die in agony? There is something wrong!"

"May be I did not live as I ought to have done," it suddenly occurred to him. "But how could that be, when I did everything properly?" he replied, and immediately dismissed from his mind this, the sole solution of all the riddles of life and death, as something quite impossible.

"Then what do you want now? To live? Live how? Live as you lived in the law courts when the usher proclaimed 'The judge is coming!' The judge is coming, the judge!" he repeated to himself. "Here he is, the judge. But I am not guilty!" he exclaimed angrily. "What is it for?" And he ceased crying, but turning his face to the wall continued to ponder on the same question: Why, and for what purpose, is there all this horror? But however much he pondered he found no answer. And whenever the thought occurred to him, as it often did, that it all resulted from his not having lived as he ought to have done, he at once recalled the correctness of his whole life, and dismissed so strange an idea.

Another fortnight passed. Iván Ilych now no longer left his sofa. He would not lie in bed but lay on the sofa, facing the wall nearly all the time. He suffered ever the same unceasing agonies and in his loneliness pondered always on the same insoluble question: "What is this? Can it be that it is Death?" And the inner voice answered: "Yes, it is Death."

"Why these sufferings?" And the voice answered, "For no reason—they just are so." Beyond and besides this there was nothing.

From the very beginning of his illness, ever since he had first been to see the doctor, Iván Ilych's life had been divided between two contrary and alternating moods: now it was despair and the expectation of this uncomprehended and terrible death, and now hope and an intently interested observation of the functioning of his organs. Now before his eyes there was only a kidney or an intestine that temporarily evaded its duty, and now only that incomprehensible and dreadful death from which it was impossible to escape.

These two states of mind had alternated from the very beginning of his illness, but the further it progressed the more doubtful and fantastic became the conception of the kidney, and the more real the sense of impending death.

He had but to call to mind what he had been three months before and what he was now, to call to mind with what regularity he had been going downhill, for every possibility of hope to be shattered.

Latterly during that loneliness in which he found himself as he lay facing the back of the sofa, a loneliness in the midst of a populous town and surrounded by numerous acquaintances and relations but that yet could not have been more complete anywhere—either at the bottom of the sea or under the earth—during that terrible loneliness Iván Ilych had lived only in memories of the past. Pictures of his past rose before him one after another. They always began with what was nearest in time and then went back to what was most remote—to his childhood—and rested there. If he thought of the stewed prunes that had been offered him that day, his mind went back to the raw shrivelled French plums of his childhood, their peculiar flavour and the flow of saliva when he sucked their stones, and along with the memory of that taste came a whole series of memories of those days: his nurse, his brother, and their toys. "No, I mustn't think of that.... It is too painful," Iván Ilych said to himself, and brought himself back to the present —to the button on the back of the sofa and the creases in its morocco. "Morocco is expensive, but it does not wear well: there had been a quarrel about it. It was a different kind of quarrel and a different kind of morocco that time when we tore father's portfolio and were punished, and mamma brought us some tarts...." And again his thoughts dwelt on his childhood, and again it was painful and he tried to banish them and fix his mind on something else.

Then again together with that chain of memories another series passed through his mind—of how his illness had progressed and grown worse. There also the further back he looked the more life there had been. There had been more of what was good in life and more of life itself. The two merged together. "Just as the pain went on getting worse and worse, so my life grew worse and worse," he thought. "There is one bright spot there at the back, at the beginning of life, and afterwards all becomes blacker and blacker and proceeds more and more rapidly —in inverse ratio to the square of the distance from death," thought Iván Ilych. And the example of a stone falling downwards with increasing velocity entered his mind. Life, a series of increasing sufferings, flies further and further towards its end—the most terrible suffering. "I am flying. . . ." He shuddered, shifted himself, and tried to resist, but was already aware that resistance was impossible, and again with eyes weary of gazing but unable to cease seeing what was before them, he stared at the back of the sofa and waited—awaiting that dreadful fall and shock and destruction.

"Resistance is impossible!" he said to himself. "If I could only understand what it is all for! But that too is impossible. An explanation would be possible if it could be said that I have not lived as I ought to. But it is impossible to say that," and he remembered all the legality, correctitude, and propriety of his life. "That at any rate can certainly not be admitted," he thought, and his lips smiled ironically as if someone could see that smile and be taken in by it. "There is no explanation! Agony, death. . . . What for?"

Another two weeks went by in this way and during that fortnight an event occurred that Iván Ilych and his wife had desired. Petríshchev formally proposed. It happened in the evening. The next day Praskóvya Fëdorovna came into her husband's room considering how best to inform him of it, but that very night there had been a fresh change for the worse in his condition. She found him still lying on the sofa but in a different position. He lay on his back, groaning and staring fixedly straight in front of him.

She began to remind him of his medicines, but he turned his eyes towards her with such a look that she did not finish what she was saying; so great an animosity, to her in particular, did that look express.

"For Christ's sake let me die in peace!" he said.

She would have gone away, but just then their daughter came in and went up to say good morning. He looked at her as he had done at his wife, and in reply to her inquiry about his health said dryly that he would soon free them all of himself. They were both silent and after sitting with him for a while went away.

"Is it our fault?" Lisa said to her mother. "It's as if we were to blame! I am sorry for papa, but why should we be tortured?"

The doctor came at his usual time. Iván Ilych answered "Yes" and "No," never taking his angry eyes from him, and at last said: "You know you can do nothing for me, so leave me alone."

"We can ease your sufferings."

"You can't even do that. Let me be."

The doctor went into the drawing-room and told Praskóvya Fëdorovna that the case was very serious and that the only resource left was opium to allay her husband's sufferings, which must be terrible.

It was true, as the doctor said, that Iván Ilych's physical sufferings were terrible, but worse than the physical sufferings were his mental sufferings which were his chief torture.

His mental sufferings were due to the fact that that night, as he looked at Gerásim's sleepy, good-natured face with its prominent cheek-bones, the question suddenly occurred to him: "What if my whole life has really been wrong?"

It occurred to him that what had appeared perfectly impossible before, namely that he had not spent his life as he should have done, might after all be true. It occurred to him that his scarcely perceptible attempts to struggle against what was considered good by the most highly placed people, those scarcely noticeable impulses which he had immediately suppressed, might have been the real thing, and all the rest false. And his professional duties and the whole arrangement of his life and of his family, and all his social and official interests, might all have been false. He tried to defend all those things to himself and suddenly felt the weakness of what he was defending. There was nothing to defend.

"But if that is so," he said to himself, "and I am leaving this life with the consciousness that I have lost all that was given me and it is impossible to rectify it—what then?"

He lay on his back and began to pass his life in review in quite a new way. In the morning when he saw first his footman, then his wife, then his daughter, and then the doctor, their every word and movement confirmed to him the awful truth that had been revealed to him during the night. In them he saw himself—all that for which he had lived—and saw clearly that it was not real at all, but a terrible and huge deception which had hidden both life and death. This consciousness intensified his physical suffering tenfold. He groaned and tossed about, and pulled at his clothing which choked and stifled him. And he hated them on that account.

He was given a large dose of opium and became unconscious, but at noon his sufferings began again. He drove everybody away and tossed from side to side.

His wife came to him and said:

"Jean, my dear, do this for me. It can't do any harm and often helps. Healthy people often do it."

He opened his eyes wide.

"What? Take communion? Why? It's unnecessary! However. . . ."

She began to cry.

"Yes, do, my dear. I'll send for our priest. He is such a nice man."

"All right. Very well," he muttered.

When the priest came and heard his confession, Iván Ilych was softened and seemed to feel a relief from his doubts and consequently from his sufferings, and for a moment there came a ray of hope. He again began to think of the vermiform appendix and the possibility of correcting it. He received the sacrament with tears in his eyes.

When they laid him down again afterwards he felt a moment's ease, and the hope that he might live awoke in him again. He began to think of the operation that had been suggested to him. "To live! I want to live!" he said to himself.

His wife came in to congratulate him after his communion, and when uttering the usual conventional words she added:

"You feel better, don't you?"

Without looking at her he said "Yes."

Her dress, her figure, the expression of her face, the tone of her voice, all revealed the same thing. "This is wrong, it is not as it should be. All you have lived for and still live for is falsehood and deception, hiding life and death from you." And as soon as he admitted that thought, his hatred and his agonizing physical suffering again sprang up, and with that suffering a consciousness of the unavoidable, approaching end. And to this was added a new sensation of grinding shooting pain and a feeling of suffocation.

The expression of his face when he uttered that "yes" was dreadful. Having uttered it, he looked her straight in the eyes, turned on his face with a rapidity extraordinary in his weak state and shouted:

"Go away! Go away and leave me alone!"

From that moment the screaming began that continued for three days, and was so terrible that one could not hear it through two closed doors without horror. At the moment he answered his wife he realized that he was lost, that there was no return, that the end had come, the very end, and his doubts were still unsolved and remained doubts.

"Oh! Oh! Oh!" he cried in various intonations. He had begun by screaming "I won't!" and continued screaming on the letter "o."

For three whole days, during which time did not exist for him, he struggled in that black sack into which he was being thrust by an invisible, resistless force. He struggled as a man condemned to death struggles in the hands of the executioner, knowing that he cannot save himself. And every moment he felt that despite all his efforts he was drawing nearer and nearer to what terrified him. He felt that his agony was due to his being thrust into that black hole and still more to his not being able to get right into it. He was hindered from getting into it by his conviction that his life had been a good one. That very justification of his life held him fast and prevented his moving forward, and it caused him most torment of all.

Suddenly some force struck him in the chest and side, making it still harder to breathe, and he fell through the hole and there at the bottom was a light. What had happened to him was like the sensation one sometimes experiences in a railway carriage when one thinks one is going backwards while one is really going forwards and suddenly becomes aware of the real direction.

"Yes, it was all not the right thing," he said to himself, "but that's no matter. It can be done. But what *is* the right thing?" he asked himself, and suddenly grew quiet.

This occurred at the end of the third day, two hours before his death. Just then his schoolboy son had crept softly in and gone up to the bedside. The dying man was still screaming desperately and waving his arms. His hand fell on the boy's head, the boy caught it, pressed it to his lips, and began to cry.

At that very moment Iván Ilych fell through and caught sight of the light, and it was revealed to him that though his life had not been what it should have been, this could still be rectified. He asked himself, "What *is* the right thing?"

and grew still, listening. Then he felt that someone was kissing his hand. He opened his eyes, looked at his son, and felt sorry for him. His wife came up to him and he glanced at her. She was gazing at him open-mouthed, with undried tears on her nose and cheek and a despairing look on her face. He felt sorry for her too.

"Yes, I am making them wretched," he thought. "They are sorry, but it will be better for them when I die." He wished to say this but had not the strength to utter it. "Besides, why speak? I must act," he thought. With a look at his wife he indicated his son and said: "Take him away...sorry for him...sorry for you too...." He tried to add, "forgive me," but said "forego" and waved his hand, knowing that He whose understanding mattered would understand.

And suddenly it grew clear to him that what had been oppressing him and would not leave him was all dropping away at once from two sides, from ten sides, and from all sides. He was sorry for them, he must act so as not to hurt them: release them and free himself from these sufferings. "How good and how simple!" he thought. "And the pain?" he asked himself. "What has become of it? Where are you, pain?"

He turned his attention to it.

"Yes, here it is. Well, what of it? Let the pain be."

"And death...where is it?"

He sought his former accustomed fear of death and did not find it. "Where is it? What death?" There was no fear because there was no death.

In place of death there was light.

"So that's what it is!" he suddenly exclaimed aloud. "What joy!"

To him all this happened in a single instant, and the meaning of that instant did not change. For those present his agony continued for another two hours. Something rattled in his throat, his emaciated body twitched, then the gasping and rattle became less and less frequent.

"It is finished!" said someone near him.

He heard these words and repeated them in his soul.

"Death is finished," he said to himself. "It is no more!"

He drew in a breath, stopped in the midst of a sigh, stretched out, and died.

34073

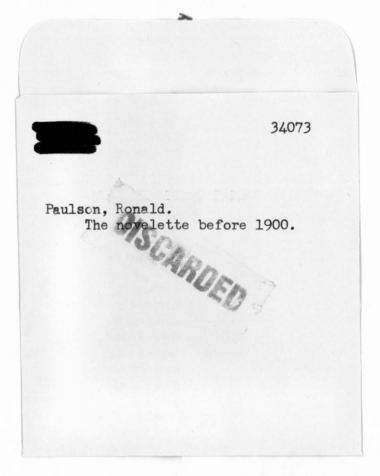